STALKING
THE APOCALYPSE

J. E. Bruce

BooksForABuck.com
2014

This is a work of fiction. All characters, events, and locations are fictitious or used fictitiously. Any resemblance to actual events or people is coincidental.

This novel is dedicated to the memory of my beloved Robert

What we do for ourselves dies with us.
What we do for others and the world remains and is immortal.

~ Albert Pine

PART I

Chapter 1

Ensign Sirin Corsali peered through her grit-hazed goggles at the bleak, wind-rippled vastness of Rasal Ghul Seven's equatorial desert and made a face. Not a happy face. In fact a sweaty, tired and *very* frustrated face. For five long, tedious hours she'd been slowly roasting inside a protective softsuit with absolutely nothing to show for her misery, and worse, no end in sight for it, either—

And I volunteered for this! She shook her head as she made yet another slitted-eye scan of the scattered remains of the craft whose automated distress call had drawn the patrol ship *Baidarka* to this desiccated corpse of a planet.

It was obvious almost from the moment they'd made planet-fall that the wreck was not the hoped-for lifeboat of the missing passenger liner, *Herrick*. Too small, far too old; all that remained was the tiresome but—now they were here—requisite duty of determining, if possible, who had been piloting the craft, what it was doing so far off the beaten path… and why it had crashed.

Hate as she did to admit it, if only to herself, she was beginning to suspect the *Baidarka*'s acting second in command, Edwin Teague, had been right all along. *Smugglers—gotta be.*

As for why it had crashed, she only needed to look into the dazzle that was the binary of Rasal Ghul. Through the planet's thick atmosphere the sinuous contact ribbon that shackled the two stars together was clearly visible. So were the massive flares that spurted unpredictably from the cauldron-like surfaces of the mismatched suns.

She looked to her left, to the looming hulk of the wreck itself.

Split open by the force of the impact and coated in ocher dust, it suddenly reminded her of an overripe melon that had been carelessly dropped.

Helluva place to die.

She suppressed a shudder at what she'd seen inside, then turned and squinted into the late morning's glare, straining the limits of her goggles' ability to react and darken accordingly. To the east, row upon row of low dunes formed up like so many schooling eels, and beyond them rose the weathered spine of an ancient escarpment. To the west, more desert; desert for as far as the eye could see.

Helluva place, period.

Orbital scans suggested that this area had once been a massive lagoon—but that was before the system's unstable suns began their slow deaths, before the Rasal Ghul Seven's vast and life-giving oceans shrank under the binary's relentless cannonade—oceans that were now no more than shallow, salt-soupy seas.

With a weary sigh, she trudged over to a shoulder-high, wind-smoothed outcrop then used her boot to irritably kick at a fluttering scrap of insulation the wind had trapped against its ink-black, shadowy base. *Nothing. Not a goddamned thing—*

She smiled and nodded as two of the landing party's marines, Lundgren and Gislasen, and the medtech, Jarvis ambled towards her. All were breathing hard.

"Anything?" Jarvis asked as she stopped in front of her, arms akimbo.

"Nope," she exhaled.

"Us neither," Gislasen grumbled. "How long do ya think the commander's gonna to make us search? It's pointless. And I'm damned hot."

"Me too, and I don't know," Corsali replied.

Jarvis pointed to a nearby swale between dunes. "We haven't looked over there."

"Yes, we have," Lundgren muttered wearily as he dusted off a rock with his gloved hand, clearly intending on sitting down.

"No, we haven't," she said, and started off, tossing over her shoulder: "Sooner we finish, the sooner we get flicked back aboard and the sooner I can buy you two whingers a round of cold beers."

The two marines clearly took heart in that—the cold beer part, not the whinger part.

Lundgren said, "You heard the lady, Neil," and with a tired wave of his hand, began plodding after the medtech. "All the ice cold beer you can drink's on Julie."

"I never said that," came Jarvis's quick rejoinder.

"Make sure you stay in sight of us or the wreck," Gislasen said to Corsali.

"Of course." She smiled.

With a shake of his head, he reluctantly followed the other two.

Corsali braced her back against the rock then turned her attention back to the debris field, this time making only a token effort at searching for any clues not blown away on the ceaseless wind or covered by drifts of the loose, talc-like sand. Her eyes were tired, *she* was tired. And hot. And really thirsty—the mention of cold beer had only made it worse. And there was a spot at the base of her back that itched almost to the point of distraction. She carefully wriggled against the rock, hoping for a little relief, at least from the sweat-itch, but the softsuit's padding was just too effective. If anything, her actions made the spot itch even more.

She exhaled, slowly. *All for nothing. All this effort for a worthless bunch of smugg—*

A faint, metallic twinkle caught her distracted gaze. It hadn't been there a moment before, she was sure of that. Well, almost.

Just another scrap of insulation. She shook her head and shifted her narrowed gaze, then looked back at it as it dawned on her that unlike the other bits and pieces of metallic foil, this *wasn't* fluttering in the wind.

Huh.

She took a step, and another as she kept her eyes fixed on the spot as the wind-blown sand quickly re-covered whatever it was. Then she knelt and brushed away the sand to reveal the tip and, despite its gritty coating of blackened sand, the razor edge of what was clearly a dagger. And a damned big dagger at that. The blade alone was over half the length of her forearm. *What the…?* Another anxious flick of her gloved hand sent fine grit swirling in the stiff, bone-dry breeze and exposed more of the blade and part of an intricately carved and inlaid handle.

She no sooner reached for it when an impatient voice crackled from her tac-pac: *"Corsali!"*

She flinched, startled, jerked her head up and glared at the wreck as she slipped the tac-pac from her belt. She pressed it to her filter mask and replied, "Yessir?"

"Where are you?" Aquila's disembodied voice demanded.

"Just outside, sir. And sir? I've found—"

"We need you and your data reader in here—pronto!"

"Coming, sir." Corsali looked back at her find. *Maybe this is the clue we need. A clue, anyway...*

With a shrug she snatched it up, lurched to her feet... and froze.

Was it her imagination, or did she really feel the faintest of icy tingles running from the dagger's handle into her gloved hand and up her arm? Despite the almost unbearable heat, the elaborate grip felt uncomfortably cold to the touch, even though the thick gloves.

She dropped the blade, jumped back and grimaced. *Oh... ICK!*

"On the double, Ensign...!"

"Yessir." She shoved the tac-pac in its holster then yanked a collection bag from her belt. Biting her lip and after a moment's hesitation, she gingerly snatched up the dagger and stuffed it in the bag. *Just your imagination, Sirin, that's all.* Nevertheless, she wiped her gloved palm on her softsuit, and rather than reattaching the collection bag to her belt, she held the bag at arm's length as she started towards a largest hole in the wreck.

As she reached the ruined craft, she reluctantly attached the bag to her belt—the last thing she wanted was for one of the marines to notice and make a remark about her letting the situation getting the better of her—then she glanced over her shoulder at the desolate landscape and was relieved to find that the nearby marines in question had their backs to her and were clearly fully engaged in a heated, albeit private discussion, going by the hand gestures.

Truth be told this place'd give anyone the creeps. She hugged herself against a sudden chill, hurriedly clambered into the wreckage through the exploded remains of the airlock, then fought her way through dangling insulation and wiring to reach the pilot pod.

"Sir?"

Aquila, hunched over the ruined nav console, peered over his shoulder at her then jerked his chin towards the small craft's largely intact computer interface. "Niebuhr's got some juice flowing. See if you can access the data."

She nodded and pushed her way over to the interface. "Might take a while."

He replied with a preoccupied grunt as she mated the data reader with the computer's data port. She wasn't particularly surprised when nothing happened. She jiggled the connection, waited a moment then jiggled it again, this time with more vigor. *Come on, damn you!*

Finally a green telltale flashed, signaling the start of a download. She exhaled. *'Bout time.*

Satisfied the connection was solid—at least for now—and with morbid curiosity getting the better of her, she risked a look around. The planet's fine sand powdered everything in a dull ocher mantle: the surrounding desolate landscape, the wreck, even the interior of the relatively intact pilot pod. Inside it was thick enough to camouflage the pools of dried blood on the impact-twisted decking—until a misplaced footstep sluiced it away.

It even clung to the blood spatter on the walls and on the ceiling where it formed grotesque miniature stalactites…

There had been a good reason she'd been so relieved when Aquila had ordered her to assist the others outside. *A damned good reason.* Even the desert's sweltering air, thickly populated by eerie, shimmering apparitions, was better than this claustrophobic tomb.

Curiosity more than satisfied, she again fixed her gaze on something familiar, something safe: her portable data reader.

It didn't help. Her filter mask, able to scrub the stifling air free of the fine grit, was unable to completely remove the faint, sickly sweet stench of burnt electrical wiring and flesh.

"What's taking so long?"

She glanced sidelong at Aquila. "The craft's data packs were damaged on impact—"

"Holy shit!"

The startled oath from under the pod's nav-console drew Aquila's attention as well as Corsali's anxious stare.

A moment later and as Aquila stepped aside, Owen Niebuhr's lanky, soft-suited frame wriggled from under the tangled mass of crushed and burned composite. "Sir, you won't believe what I just found."

Oh, yes I would, Corsali thought with anticipatory dread as a host of extremely unpleasant surprises instantly came to mind. *Damned straight I would.*

He held up a soot-blackened object.

Aquila snatched it from his gloved hand and hissed, *"A goddamned Hahtooshan maser pistol!"*

Corsali, her nerves already frayed, repeated unsteadily, "Ha-Hahtooshan?" as her mind swiveled on its hinges. She'd been expecting a body part, something yuckily recognizable. A hand maybe... or the burnt-to-a-crisp head of one of the smugglers.

A Hahtooshan *anything* had not been on her exhaustive list of unhappy finds. Maybe because a Hahtooshan anything was far, far more than an unhappy find. It qualified as a stupendously alarming find.

She gave the very alien-looking weapon a wary look and swallowed, hard. *Hahtooshan!* More the stuff of rumor than reality, it was nevertheless a name rarely spoken aloud, as if by doing so the speaker risked conjuring up one of the dreaded mercenaries in the flesh, shadowy creatures alleged to be shape-shifters or from a different dimension entirely, able to appear and disappear at will—

Suddenly the tiny pilot pod seemed very crowded indeed, filled with ghosts of all descriptions. "Are you sure?"

"Yup." Aquila's intense gaze never wavered from the *very* alien appearing pistol. "If you'll excuse the expression, Ensign, *dead* sure."

Niebuhr scrambled to his feet. "And sir, didya notice?"

Corsali braced herself as she looked first at the engineer, then Aquila, only to find the officer running his fingers over the weapon's smoothly curved surfaces while nodding in grudging admiration. A sidelong glance at Niebuhr confirmed he too seemed enthralled by the pistol, seemingly oblivious to its potential ramifications.

"Notice?" Aquila asked, briefly looking up.

Niebuhr tapped the heavy weapon's power pack with a soot-blackened gloved finger. "Drained. *Completely.*"

Corsali leaned forward for a closer look. "So?"

Niebuhr answered, "Not like mercs to drain a weapon, Ensign, not like 'em at all."

"Maybe they were desperate." She looked around again. It hadn't taken a scanner to confirm that something horrific had happened within the cramped confines of the pod—something that had happened *after* the crash. In many places the blood spatter had been smeared before it had dried, as if *licked*. And most obvious of all: no bodies.

After spending an entire morning searching a twenty-kilometer square area, not even a scrap of clothing had turned up. Debris from the crash, yes—any signs of her ill-fated crew? No. Not a trace—

The dagger! Corsali pulled the collection bag from her belt. "Sir?"

"Mercs are never *that* desperate," Aquila muttered as he reluctantly returned the pistol to its finder.

"Besides," Niebuhr said, "their weapons, or at least what someone's claiming are genuine Hahtooshan weapons, have been known to turn up on the black market on rare occasions, huge demand for 'em, as you can well imagine—" Corsali's impatient squint prompted his quick rejoinder, "—or so I've been told."

"*Sir.*" Corsali held up the transparent bag, "I found—"

"Where'd you get this?" Aquila took it from her hand.

"Just outside, not ten meters—"

The loud *chirp* from her data reader drew her attention. *Perfect timing.* She picked it up and scowled at its small display. What she saw was not what she'd been expecting, not that she'd been at all sure what to expect. An archaic version of the Coalition standard, followed by lines of encrypted data would not have made the list. Like the Hahtooshan pistol, this was a completely unexpected—not to mention unwelcome and potentially ominous—find. What were smugglers doing with encrypted Coalition data—and outdated data too—close to seventy-five years out of date, she figured.

She tapped a series of commands into her reader, sending it off to search for a corresponding cypher within its own databanks. Then, overhearing hushed voices, she turned to find Aquila and Niebuhr standing huddled together not far away. Niebuhr still held the alien pistol while Aquila pointed to and speculated on various functions. Both were clearly transfixed by the exotic weapon.

She pursed her lips, then, hearing another beep, turned her attention back to her reader. The small machine had finally deciphered a few fragmentary pieces of information recovered from the tiny ship's stores and as she absorbed the data, her throat muscles tightened. *"Sir...."*

Aquila looked up from the pistol, alerted by her tone.

"You'd better see this." She handed him the reader and he swept his suddenly apprehensive eyes down its tiny screen.

Niebuhr leaned close and gave the readouts a quick study as Aquila whispered, *"Gods!"*

"But biological weapons research was outlawed after Tindari!" Niebuhr gasped.

"Guess someone wasn't told," Aquila replied, "or more likely wasn't listening." He smacked his gloved fist against the console, knocking loose a shower of fine ocher dust. "Damn it to hell!"

Corsali found herself staring at the maser pistol Niebuhr clutched, temporarily forgotten, in one gloved hand, the bagged dagger in the other. "Sir, you don't think the Hahtooshans—"

"Are involved in this?" Aquila interrupted heatedly. "Let's hope to hell not!" He paused, took a deep, steadying breath, then added, "As Niebuhr said, merc pistols like this have been known to crop up on the black market—and of course there's no guarantee, no way to prove they really *are* merc weapons—which tells me we won't have to look any further than one of the non-aligned worlds and this certainly isn't a merc boat—looks to be Gorm, maybe Thalamian." He glanced sidelong at Niebuhr, who eagerly nodded his agreement, then he tapped the data reader with his gloved forefinger. "The instant this damned interference abates, I want this information transmitted to the *Baidarka*."

Corsali started to acknowledge the order, but was cut off by a faint, throbbing, *pop... pop... poppoppoppopop.*

Niebuhr wheeled towards the pod's open hatch. "Sounds like—"

"Weapons fire!" Aquila finished for him. Shocker in one hand, tac-pac in the other, he used his elbows and forearms to fight his way through dangling insulation and loops of scorched wiring to reach the open hatch. Niebuhr followed.

Corsali hesitated just long enough to unholster her own shocker before she too stepped through the hatch.

"Gianakis! Arctoi! Report!"

The two marines had kept themselves out of Aquila's sight and mind, as well as out of the harsh sunlight by making an unhurried search of the craft's small staging bay. Now they crouched on either side of another gaping wound in the hull, weapons at the ready.

Gianakis motioned with his shocker to the sliver of desert visible beyond. "Came from that dir—"

He was interrupted by a high-pitched staccato, *POPPOPPOPPOP!* and he tucked himself into an even tighter ball as the rest took cover behind a bulkhead.

"There," Corsali pointed as she spotted a flicker of red among the heat ripples.

Aquila and Niebuhr followed her finger and squinted into the glare beyond the gash in the hull.

"Jarvis!" Niebuhr gasped. "It's Jarvis, sir!"

And it was. The medtech was running full out towards the wreck but as a rolling curtain of dust caught up with her, she vanished from sight; an instant later, they heard a distant, muffled scream.

"Jarvis…? *Jarvis!*" Aquila snarled into his tac-pac. "Jarvis, answer—"

"Listen!" Corsali grabbed his hand. *"Do you hear that?"*

The others glanced around the ruined bay, their ears now drawn to the same faint thrumming sound Corsali had heard; at first it was barely noticeable over the faint rasp of wind-blown sand across the hull, but it was getting louder with each passing second.

Aquila looked back at her. "Recall Gislasen and Lundgren; tell 'em to get back here on the doub—"

Another scream rang out from somewhere outside and behind them and as one they turned to face whatever new menace was headed their way. Through the ragged hole that had once been the exterior airlock, they saw the two blue-clad marines running pell-mell towards them, a curtain of dust following. One was clutching his shoulder while the other, following closely behind, was firing wildly back the way they'd come, into another wall of dust.

POP-POPPOPPOP-POP!

Arctoi, Niebuhr and Gianakis sidled closer to the airlock, then raised their shockers and took aim—at a dust cloud.

"Hold your fire!" Aquila barked as he too took up a defensive position. *"They're outta range."* He squinted into the glare. "Just a little closer…" he whispered, his finger on his shocker's trigger as

his eyes and those of the marines desperately searched for something to shoot at. "Come on! *Come on!*"

The two marines never made it. Less than twenty meters from the wreck they abruptly disappeared as the ground beneath their feet suddenly opened, swallowing them whole, and just as suddenly closed again. The roiling wall of dust continued barreling towards the wreck as if it had a mind of its own.

For a moment no one moved, no one breathed. The deep thrumming grew louder, stronger, enough to loosen the caked dust on the ceiling of the wrecked craft.

Aquila turned to Corsali. "Pilot pod, *go!*"

She scrambled to her feet as the staging bay filled with the thick, swirling ocher grit. It poured from above and spilled in through the rents, leaving her nearly blind. She activated her emergency locator then felt her way across the buckled deck, but she'd no sooner wrapped her fingers around the hatch's lock-seal when the ship shuddered, almost knocking her to her knees.

A blood-curdling chorus of high-pitched screeching followed.

"Gianakis, Arctoi, Niebuhr!" she overheard Aquila bellow, "In the pod!"

She stumbled through the hatch, through the tangle of twisted composite and wiring and over to the nav-console. Bracing herself against it, she brought her tac-pac to her breather mask and over the cacophony of screeching, over the near-deafening *POP-POP-POP-POP!* of weapons fire, shouted, "*Baidarka*, we're under attack! *Baidarka*, respond!" She tried again, louder, her voice bordering on a scream: *"BAIDARKA!"*

The ship rocked again, violently. A moment later Aquila, gripping his side, stumbled through the hatch. Gianakis was right behind him, covering their clumsy retreat with wild sweeps of his shocker's targeting beam. Once inside, the trooper smacked the airlock release with his gloved fist.

For an instant nothing happened, then, with a protesting groan the lock closed, muffling the enraged squeals.

"That," Gianakis gasped as he sagged against the lock frame, *"...that'll... hold 'em."*

"But not for long," Aquila forced out through clenched teeth as Corsali helped him to the pilot's chair.

He slumped onto it, looked down at himself and grimaced: his quilted softsuit was in tatters and his flank was soaked in blood. "Well... *crap.*"

Corsali knelt beside him and checked to make sure his locator was activated before she began rummaging around in Jarvis' field triage kit, left by the medic once it was clear that there were no survivors.

"Niebuhr?" Aquila asked thickly. "Arctoi?"

Corsali glanced at up Gianakis; the marine corporal, still gulping hungrily for breath, managed a sharp shake of his head.

"Bugs... fuckin' bugs...." Aquila shivered involuntarily as Corsali pressed a dressing pack against his side. "The *Baidarka...*were you able—"

Another violent shudder ran through the wreck.

From every direction they heard frantic scraping and scratching noises, and then, abruptly, silence. Even the thrumming sound stopped.

Corsali looked at Aquila, then up Gianakis. The corporal clutched his shocker in both hands as his nervous gaze darted around the cramped pilot pod, the glitter of his wide eyes visible through his grit-hazed goggles and the suspended dust.

Seconds stretched into minutes.

"I think they've given up." Gianakis leaned heavily against the wall, steadied his breathing.

No sooner had he smiled a relieved smile when a faint metallic *clink* drew their startled stares to a buckled deck plate not far from the hatch.

A flurry of scratching was followed by high-pitched squealing and even more determined scraping.

He backed up an unsteady step as the plate bulged, ever so slightly. "They're trying to break through! Get behind that," he motioned to the ruined nav-console with his chin as he pointed his shocker at the deck plate, "I'll cover you!"

Corsali slipped her arm around Aquila's waist, helped him back to his feet and together they stumbled over to the console.

No sooner had the two hunkered down behind it than a deep, concussive *THAWHUMP-THAWHUMP-THAWHUMP!* vibrated through the pod, shaking loose more dust.

She flicked Gianakis a hopeful look.

He replied with a confirming grin and, "About time the damned cav—"

The hatch exploded and he was hurled against a nearby bulkhead by the force of the blast.

Chapter 2

"What?" Doctor William Amalfitano gasped.

Teague fastened his uniform collar, snatched back the data disc the flickerstage tech held out for him, stuffed it into his breast pocket then strode out of the flickerstage chamber, tossing over his shoulder, "You heard me, Doctor."

The Coalition patrol ship *Baidarka*'s CMO looked around. The seven marines and their sergeant, Delatorre, the remaining members of the second landing party still in varying stages of getting out of their armor—no soft suits this time, this time it was full battle kit—stared back at him, equally stunned.

Amalfitano muttered, "Doctor Fleming's waiting for you in sickbay." Then he hurried after Teague, up the gently rising corridor towards the control room. "I heard you, Edwin, I just didn't believe my ears."

Teague stopped just short of the control room's blue-framed airlock and wheeled around to face him, eyes flashing. "Then I'll repeat what I just said. I see no point to yet *another* search."

"But those are our people down there!"

"Where? Where, *exactly?* Need I remind you I just flicked back from the surface? That I just spent over *three* hours personally directing the search, a search that turned up absolutely nothing in that time, not *one* clue as to the fate of our missing, and which was called off only because the conditions on the surface had so deteriorated that you yourself considered it unsafe to remain—"

"But you saw Niebuhr and Arctoi—or should I say what's left of them!"

"Which is why I won't risk sending another search party to the surface until this current phase of stellar activity dies down and—"

"But that could take hours—*days!*"

"Or until those rescued recover sufficiently to tell us what happened."

"You're assuming they're going to survive, much less regain consciousness."

"I'm depending upon your skills for both, Doctor. Meanwhile, I won't risk any more lives, something I thought you, of all people, would understand."

"Normally I'd agree with you but in this case time is of the essence!"

"Then the sooner the injured regain consciousness, the better. True?"

Amalfitano started to open his mouth then thought better of it. Much as he hated to admit it, Teague was right—

"Now, perhaps you should go tend to them?" He tapped the airlock activator.

Amalfitano ran his fingers through his thick, graying hair and in a suddenly weary voice said, "I've done all I can for them."

"Then I suggest you try harder." Teague stepped through the now open airlock, into the ship's control room, leaving Amalfitano to stare, incredulously, after him.

"Why you fu—"

"Stoker," Teague asked, "any break in the interference?"

"No, sir," the com-op replied. "Still unable to send your message to HQ."

Teague seated himself at his console then looked up to find Amalfitano standing beside him. "Aren't you supposed to be somewhere else?"

Amalfitano, as a reply, held a small, hand-held scanner close to Teague's left wrist and its bio-band then gave the device's readouts a quick study.

"I asked you a question."

"I'm picking up some unexpected fluctuations in your basal metabolism." Amalfitano looked up from the scanner, smiled sweetly and whispered, "Maybe being an autocratic bastard doesn't suit you. Perhaps you should stick with just being a bureaucratic bastard and not try to rise above your level of incompetence?"

Teague's glare turned frigid.

"If *you* remember, *you* agreed to my stipulation that immediately upon *your* return—"

"I'm well aware of what I agreed to, Doctor, and I'll present myself as soon as I deem it convenient."

"Well that's *not* what I agreed to. We don't know what the hell we're dealing with—"

"I just underwent full de-con in the flickerstage. You were there, supervising."

"Yes, yes," Amalfitano angrily waved off the remark, "but—"

"And as the acting captain, I have the privilege of changing the rules if the situation warrants it."

"And how does the situation warrant it, *Lieutenant?*"

Teague blinked in feigned astonishment. "Do I need to remind you that our commanding officer is missing? As are five crewmembers? That we're out of contact with HQ and in orbit around a planet whose binary is dangerously unpredictable? If any situation warranted changing the rules, this would be it."

Amalfitano stared back, arms crossed and unimpressed.

"In your medical opinion, do you believe I'm truly incompetent, unfit for command? You do have the power to remove me, you know."

Amalfitano's eyes opened wide as his arms fell to his sides, genuinely shocked Teague had actually called his bluff. "I said nothing about being unfit for command—"

"Yes, you *did.*"

He wet his lips and tapped the scanner. "It's just these readings—"

"Your concerns and wishes have been noted and unless you plan on exercising your right as CMO and declare me unfit for command, your duty's been done. Now let me do mine. Besides, as Captain, I don't have to discuss the reasons for any of my actions with you, unless, as I just said, you can medically declare me unfit for the job, in which case my replacement would tell you exactly the same thing."

Amalfitano pursed his lips and began slowly counting to ten as his narrowed gaze made a slow circuit of the ominously silent control room; the crew were trying to look like they weren't listening, but the absence of any talking gave ample evidence that all ears had been tuned into their heated, albeit softly-worded conversation.

"Perhaps I didn't make myself clear," Teague continued, drawing Amalfitano's sidelong stare. "Your presence here is neither needed nor wanted. If that's not clear enough, I'll have no choice but to have you escorted to sickbay."

"Don't be such an ass—"

"Do I have to call security?" Teague rested a finger on a toggle on his console.

"Of course not—"

"Then leave, and do not return unless I specifically order it."

Amalfitano swallowed the obscenity that had formed on his tongue, spun on his heel and stalked through the airlock.

— ii —

Corsali opened her eyes, awakened by an odd, faintly pungent and totally unfamiliar smell—*No, not unfamiliar. Out of place.*

For a moment, she wasn't sure if she was indeed awake or dreaming—but it was just a moment, until she tried to move only to find that her hands and feet were tightly bound. She fought down a surge of panic as she glanced around; at first she was only able to make out dim shapes in the surrounding gloom then ever-so-slowly details began to emerge.

The rough, wood plank floor on which she lay was crisscrossed with dusty slivers of faint purplish light. Above was a crudely thatched roof and suspended from it soft, loosely woven walls swayed in cadence with the floor's gentle rocking. Beyond the walls something glittered.

The air too was odd. It was cool and damp.

She took another cautious sniff and her nose immediately identified the sour smell as that of brine. *What the—*

A muffled moan drew her startled gaze and her full attention to a shadowy mound nearby.

—hell. She hesitated, then with a mental shrug wriggled closer and, gently bumping it with her feet, hissed, *"Hey you, wake up!"*

The mound stirred and slowly turned a bruise-mottled face towards her.

"Commander?"

Aquila stared blankly at her for a moment before mumbling groggily, "Corsali…?"

"Yessir." A glance confirmed her worst fears: his shocker and tac-pac holsters were empty. The emergency locator too was gone, ripped from the shoulder of his softsuit. She didn't have to look to know that the same was true of hers.

Aquila lifted his head. "What—" His eyes cleared as he too realized he was tied up. "Where… where the hell are we?"

"Not sure, sir."

"Last thing I remember—*the wreck!*"

"Yeah," she replied uneasily as his startled comment instantly evoked her own last cogent memory. "And Niebuhr—"

"Niebuhr..." Aquila swept their dimly lit surroundings with narrowed eyes. "Where is he? Where the hell's the rest of 'em?"

"Don't know," she replied. "Just woke up, saw you—"

"First things first, let's get out of these bindings." He began working his arms down his back. Half way down, he suddenly grimaced and grunted softly.

"Sir—you all right?"

Instead of answering, he drew his legs tight against his body and wriggled his arms down to his ankles.

As he did so, Corsali gave him a quick once over with her eyes. In the shifting light, it was impossible to tell if the dark stains on his face and clothing were blood or just a combination of grime and shadow. "Sir...?"

"Yeah, yeah, I'm all right!"

Corsali wiggled closer. Now she was sure. It *was* blood. "But—"

"How 'bout you worry about that bump on your head, and I'll worry 'bout my side, *'kay?'*"

She bit back an equally snippy retort then watched in silent frustration and growing worry as he resumed his now frantic struggle against the bindings.

Finally, and with an explosive release of breath he slipped his arms from under his feet then fixed her with a triumphant look and between heaving breaths, managed, "Didn't... th-think I c-c-could d-d-do it, d-d-did ya?"

She replied with a skeptical arch of a brow. "No. Sir."

He steadied his breathing, managed a half-hearted chuckle and said, "Captain Vildur always said, if really you want an honest answer, go to Ensign Corsali." He motioned to her with his bloodied and bruised chin. "Come on, let's get those off you."

She wiggled closer and he began tugging at the ropes. His off-the-cuff remark, clearly meant as a compliment, had had the opposite effect and she found her vision blurring.

Gildun Vildur... mentor, friend... surrogate mother. Dead—killed in the Matarran ambush that had cost the Baidarka twenty eight of her crew. She tried to blink away the hot, angry tears. *And now this, whatever the hell this is—*

"Ensign."

She squinted over her shoulder.

"Don't you start falling apart on me."

She stiffened. "I'm *not* falling apart, sir."

"Good." He gave the ropes another sharp tug. "Have these off you in a sec."

While he pulled and yanked and cursed to himself, she made another uneasy sweep of the small room's interior, confirming they were indeed alone and as she did so, all of the pieces—the gentle rocking motion, the out-of-place smell, the oddly familiar sparkle beyond the slat-work—abruptly fell into place.

"Commander, we're on a boat."

Aquila stopped his tugging. *"A boat?"*

"That's water out there, and the air, it's salt air."

He took a test sniff, and as he too recognized their surroundings for what they were, replied charily, "Yeah… you're right—but wasn't the closest body of water a good twenty kilometers from the crash site?"

"Forty at least. *And sir?* The Blatto didn't possess the technology to build anything like this when this planet was last surveyed."

"The *what?*"

"The Blatto, the sentient insectoids native to this—"

"Right. *Bugs.*" He made a face as he worked on a knot. "Don't like bugs, 'specially *bright* bugs." He suddenly stopped what he was doing and gave her a sharp look. "So?"

"They were very low on the technological ladder when this system was surveyed one hundred and forty six years ago—"

"There," he interrupted. "See if you can pull your hands free."

After a moment's struggle she managed to slip one bony hand from the loosened ropes then the other.

"That's a long time." He held out his hands as she rolled over to face him. "Your turn."

She peered at the bindings then began working the unfamiliar knot.

"Things can happen," he added.

"Agreed, but it's doubtful they could've made this sort of progress within that amount of time without outside help—it'd be like making the technological leap from the paleolithic to the bronze age in the same period of time—*there.*"

"I'll take your word on that." He jerked his hands free of the now loosened ropes, tossed them aside and together they started on their leg bindings.

"Well," he said a moment later as he kicked his feet from of the tangle of rope, "I think the first order of business is... *to...*"

Hearing Aquila's voice trail off, Corsali looked at him, then, following his wide-eyed and now slack-jawed stare, glanced over her shoulder. A burly humanoid stood in the doorway, the limp body of the equally bulky Gianakis in its thickset arms as if the man weighed no more than a vac-bag of hot air.

The alien's swarthy face was covered in a complex and grotesque pattern of black swirls, barbs and dots, all framed by a lank black mane that fell almost to its waist. The rest, from neck to feet, was an all-over dull black—and she couldn't tell if it was a trick of the shifting light, but what she could see of its attire appeared to be... *writhing*, as if covered in tiny snakes. *What the...*

Its thick lips drew back into a gap-toothed grin, clearly pleased by her and Aquila's stunned reaction. *"Tah. Badathsu tanhah."* With that, the alien unceremoniously released its burden and Gianakis hit the deck with a substantial *thud.* *"Hehtak tooq."*

Far from hot air, she winced as she risked a quick glance at Gianakis, then she looked up as the humanoid stepped over him.

"Edu hai-ti, uuman?" It reached for a small knife strapped to its forearm, but before it unsheathed it Aquila launched himself at the creature.

The startled alien stumbled back, tripped over Gianakis and tore through the fabric walls only to land spread-eagle on the deck with a meaty *THWUMP!*

Aquila followed, throwing himself on top of the creature before it could recover and scramble to its feet; the two grappled, then together they rolled across the deck, punching and kicking at each other.

Corsali pulled her horrified stare off them long enough to look for something, anything she could use as a weapon, then a flash of movement drew her darting, panicky gaze: more of the creatures had clambered up from below-decks, drawn by the sounds of the struggle—five in all and from all sides, seemingly in the blink of an eye. *Oh... gods!*

They quickly spread out to form a loose ring, then grunted and hooted in apparent delight as a punch sent Aquila sprawling. But their glee abruptly changed to surprise when he quickly recovered, tripped his attacker and using the combined force of his upward swinging fists and the falling alien, delivered a blow squarely against the creature's exposed throat.

It crumpled with a strangled gurgle.

Aquila sank to his knees beside the now loudly wheezing humanoid and laboring for breath, stared up at his audience of stunned faces.

With a chuckle and gesture from one, the five began to close in.

Corsali shook herself free of the terror that had frozen her in place, snatched up a splintered, meter-length piece of what a few minutes before had been a wall support then stumbling out onto the deck, screamed, *"GET AWAY FROM HIM!"*

The aliens' shaggy heads swiveled towards her and the two closest, seeing her take a defensive stance, immediately positioned themselves between her and Aquila.

Corsali looked at one, then the other as she tightened her grip on the length of wood while sizing up her chances of getting past them. They glanced at each other and grinned in reply, as if sharing a private joke.

Then, hearing a soft cough behind her, she wheeled around and found herself face to chest with a seventh alien, the biggest of the lot. *Oh... fuck.* She looked up... and up, until she reached its truly bizarre face.

The creature drew back its lips in a grotesque parody of a human smile then backed up a step and beckoned with its gauntleted hands, urging her to make her move. She suddenly wanted nothing more than to wipe that challenging smirk off its horrific face and took a swing at it just as Aquila yelled a hoarse, *"NO!"* but too late.

It kicked out, knocking the makeshift weapon from her hands with enough force to send it flying overboard and her sprawling on the deck at its feet. Then, before she was able to scramble away, it seized her by her uniform, lifted her bodily and pulled her tightly against its chest.

Corsali squirmed; the creature easily pinned her arms painfully against her back and burst into a strange, barking laughter. The others quickly joined in.

"*Jekat!*"

The aliens' laughter instantly died on their lips and Corsali, following her captor's now surly gaze, looked to her left to find that two more of the creatures had climbed up from below decks. *Oh... Gods!*

The taller and heavier of the two remained at the ladder and turned its piercing stare on the now grim-faced troopers as its companion strode across the deck towards Aquila. As it passed Corsali, it flicked her captor a sidelong, icy glance and hissed, "*Hoi-tu.*"

The alien gently lowered her to the deck and let go; it even tried to smooth her hair with its gauntleted fingers.

Glaring fiercely at it, she slapped at its gauntleted hand while backing well out of easy reach.

The latest arrival stopped in front of Aquila and looked down at his still wheezing opponent. "*Jaipuu ta-ar quuf.*" It pointed to the ladder. "*D'juuk!*"

The creature grabbed the nearby railing, pulled itself to a rubbery-legged stand, flicked Aquila a murderous glance, then clutching its throat backed—stumbled—away.

The alien scowled at the rest and motioned to the ruined cabin. "*Ta'ak. Lehsuh!*"

They immediately scattered, snatching up bits and pieces of wood as the creature's silent companion strode over to the cabin to assess the damage.

Satisfied, the alien turned to Aquila and offered him its gauntleted hand, but Aquila pointedly ignored the gesture and staggered, unassisted, to his feet.

It dropped its outstretched hand with a shrug of its shoulders, gestured to the cabin, and pivoting on its heel, started for it, clearly expecting them to follow.

Aquila remained where he was, as did Corsali.

Realizing they were not following, the alien stopped and turned back to them. "Come."

"Go to hell," Aquila grumbled as he wiped his profusely bleeding nose on the tattered sleeve of his softsuit.

The humanoid looked around, then again fixing its gaze on Aquila and in perfectly accented trade-use Standard said, "We're already there. Now, do as I tell you—or, if you insist, I can force the issue."

Aquila glanced around. The other aliens, having overheard the remark, had stopped what they'd been doing to stare menacingly at him. With a shake of his head and a resigned albeit angry sigh, he began to limp after the creature, blotting his nose.

Corsali wasted no time in following. Once they were past the gauntlet of sullen-faced creatures and back inside the cabin, Aquila leaned close to her. *"You okay?"*

"Yessir, just a little shaken up, that's all." Corsali hugged herself as she gave the nearby alien a sidelong glance. *Okay, okay,* she admitted as she realized she couldn't stop trembling, *a lot shaken up.* "Sir, are you—"

"As for your crewman," the humanoid began, "my medical officer has stabilized his injuries."

Aquila gave the unconscious Gianakis a quick glance before meeting the creature's gaze. "What the hell've you done with the rest of my crew?"

"We found only two others... and they were beyond our limited ability to help."

"So you just left them to those bugs?" Aquila snarled.

"*We* were under attack at the time, Commander. By those same... *bugs.* I was not about to lose any more of my—"

"You goddamned..." his voice trailed off as his face contorted in a wince. He visibly wobbled.

"Sir?" Corsali grabbed his arm to steady him as she eyed his bruise-swollen and now blood-smeared face. Then she dropped her gaze to his flank and her eyes widened. More fresh blood darkened the already blood-caked fabric of his tattered softsuit. "Sir—"

"Leave it." He favored her with a warning look.

Undeterred, she gently pressed her hand against his side. To her surprise, she felt not only the warm, sticky wetness of blood, but also the bulk of a bandage. "But—"

"I said leave it," Aquila hissed as he roughly pushed her hand away, placing his own over the area in preference to staunching the blood trickling from his nose.

Corsali mumbled, "Yessir," then steeled herself and looked at the alien to find the creature watching the interaction with what on a human's face would pass for an amused smile. But this wasn't a human's face, and the expression was far more sinister than friendly, surrounded as it was by what she now realized was a complex combination of elaborate scarification overlaid with black tattoos, tattoos that appeared, in the filtered light of the cabin, to float eerily just above the surface of the alien's olive-brown skin. And its eyes... the pupils were surrounded by bluish-gray irises, made all the more startling by the creature's swarthy complexion.

It extended its gauntleted hands, palms up. It was a near universal gesture of salutation among the diverse cultures that made up the Rim as it was one that could be easily adapted to almost all shapes of appendages. "I am *Chercjengh'khusaaq Abhijit'tischinjgra*, Signals and Sensors Specialist of the A'tuu'shahn Orthodoxy."

A'tuu'shahn...? Now it was Corsali's knees' turn to wobble. *As in... Hahtooshan?*

Aquila stared back, mouth agape, his hand falling from his side, his injuries instantly forgotten.

"You're both staring at me like you've seen a wraith," the creature said, clearly delighting in their stunned, bordering on horrified, reaction. "Then again, it's not every day you Rimmers come face to face with a... what do you call us? Oh, yes, *mercs?* Among other things."

Hahtooshan. Corsali tried to get her still reeling mind around the heart-thumping fact that she was staring at a living, breathing Hahtooshan—assuming the creature wasn't just claiming to be one. An easy enough deception after all, but that begged the question: why would anyone want to claim to be a Hahtooshan? If the aim was to terrify, the Rim was chock full of fearsome creatures, many of whom were known only by name, or rumor. Assuming it was being truthful, what was even more unsettling was that behind the hideous mask of tattoos and scarification was a face, and not just any face. A human *looking* face.

But, she quickly reminded herself, Hahtooshans were shape-shifters, yet another terror weapon in their truly astonishing repertoire when it came to wreaking havoc, and what better way to keep an enemy unbalanced than to take that enemy's form... but with a decidedly alien twist? *Sneaky fucking bastard.*

Thus bolstered, she met its gaze squarely and with as much defiance as she could muster, which in truth wasn't a lot, desperately supporting her rapidly crumbling bravado with, *Don't believe what you see, Sirin—it's all just an act.* But that begged the question, what did it *really* look like under that bizarre smokescreen of scarification and tattooing? She suppressed a shudder at the shape-shifting possibilities—and shivered again at the sudden, horrifying realization that this being might, in fact, *not* be the first Hahtooshan she'd met.

As if reading her thoughts, the alien's amused smile turned into a pleased, bordering on leering grin, which made the disconcerting situation even more intensely uncomfortable—and frightening.

She'd long ago accepted what she looked like: despite being in her mid-twenties, her body had never filled out the way her mother had repeatedly promised her it would, given time—to which her elder brother had jokingly disagreed, suggesting she would be perpetually mistaken for a gangly, prepubescent boy. The painful comparison had then been tempered with the hasty addition of the dreaded adjective, "cute". And then, the most damning of all: "really smart". Her unruly white blond hair, deathly pale skin and watery blue eyes had not helped, not one damned bit.

Okay, so a cute, really smart albino prepubescent boy.

She had also long ago stopped envying women who stopped men in their tracks just by breathing. Now she had a Hahtooshan—of all creatures—looking at her like she was about to be served up as the main course. *Maybe this is something akin to a sailor looking at a manatee and seeing a mermaid?*

Before her mind could take that analogy and run with it, the Hahtooshan shifted its unsettling gaze to Aquila and she breathed a silent sigh of relief.

"And now... I apologize, but in all the excitement, I never caught your name?"

Aquila, recovered from his initial shock, forced out through a grimace, "My name's none of your goddamned business."

"Indeed? Well," it looked down at the unconscious Gianakis and nudged him, none-too-gently, with the toe of its heavy campaign boot, "Commander None-Of-Your-Goddamned-Business..."

Aquila's scowl crumbled into a frigid glower as he dabbed his oozing nose with his fingers.

"…as I was saying, my medical officer has tended to his injuries and has assured me that none are immediately life-threatening."

"How… fortunate," Aquila growled.

The alien lifted its gaze, said, "A human philosopher once said 'attack is a reaction. If one hits hard, one must expect it to rebound'." It prodded Gianakis again, lightly. "We wouldn't have found it necessary to sedate him so heavily had he not tried to strangle one of my escort while my medical officer was treating his injuries. You really *must* train your people in restraint—"

"The same could be said for yours," Aquila replied.

"Gienah was only following orders—"

"And you expected me to do nothing, just let it kill us?"

"Kill you?" the Hahtooshan gasped with mock horror. "Why would I order Gienah to kill you?"

"You need a reason? You're a goddamned mer—"

"A'tuu'shahn. And we kill for the pleasure of killing, yes?"

"You said it, *merc*, not me," Aquila glared at the alien as Corsali rubbed her rope-raw wrists.

The Hahtooshan's strange eyes flicked to her hands before returning to Aquila. "I regret having you bound, but I was concerned you might—"

"Try to escape?" Aquila finished for it.

"Yes. And in the process, further injure yourselves."

"So you sent one of your thugs—"

"I sent one of my most trusted soldiers to cut your bindings, after returning your crewman to you."

Corsali looked down at Gianakis and noticed for the first time that he wasn't bound. Her startled eyes cut to Aquila.

"And I'm supposed to believe that?" He gave the soldier's rank insignia a quick glance and after an instant of uncertainty, sneered, *"Ruk... tak?"*

The mercenary looked down at its dusty, medallion-encrusted panoply, then lifted its gaze and grinned. "I had *am* impressed, Commander—"

"That makes one of us."

"—I was unaware that you Rimmers are, to some extent, knowledgeable of our rank insignia. But in fact I am not a *Ruh'ta'aq*, but rather a *Sha'ashahn*."

Aquila couldn't fully conceal his surprise. "A battle commander."

"Yes." It again extended its gauntleted hands, palms up. "You may call me Khusaaq..."

Aquila made no move to reciprocate, physically or otherwise, instead he kept one hand firmly pressed against his side, the other occupied dabbing at his nose.

"...currently assigned to the research ship, *Makhaira*."

Aquila growled, "You mean *warship.*"

"I'm fluent in your language, Commander," the alien replied, undaunted and in the same maddeningly affable tone. "I *meant* research ship. Despite what you've been told, not all of our energies are directed towards warfare. We too indulge in scientific research."

Aquila snorted, "But only as a means to an end, and that end being further aggression," but the contemptuous effect was somewhat diminished when his nose, which had just stopped oozing, started bleeding again. He blotted it angrily, scowling at the merc over his sleeve.

"Science has always been the tool of aggression, Commander." With that it unclipped a small device from its belt and turned its back to them, a subtle but at the same time blatant signal as to who was in control despite its outwardly friendly demeanor.

As the creature stared intently at the device it held, seemingly utterly absorbed, Corsali was struck again with the obvious yet utterly astounding fact that she was standing less than two meters from a living, breathing Hahtooshan—yes, she believed it now—*not a facsimile of a Hahtooshan in full panoply put forth by a Looper claiming to be an expert on the matter and based on very sketchy reports several centuries old, but which truthfully,* she grudgingly admitted to herself, *wasn't all that far off the mark. Not a training sim based on that infamous, yet obviously heavily doctored vid of the one and only known time humans and Hahtooshans had come face-to-face, so to speak, and where humans lived to tell about it, but the real thing—well, okay, maybe what I'm seeing isn't the* real *thing, but rather what this creature wants us to see. Something familiar, something marginally less threatening—something we can relate to on some level—but why? That in itself might be the key as to why it took us prisoner...*

And the alien indeed appeared—at least superficially—to be human, not just humanoid under the guise of its truly alien-appearing attire. Now that her eyes had fully readjusted to the patterned and shifting gloom of the cabin she noted that all of the visible parts were in the correct place, of the correct proportion and the correct number for a human. And though the distracting mask of scarification and tattoos made it difficult to accurately judge its face, it clearly had a mouth, lips, teeth and nose, with high cheekbones, browridge capped with thick brows, intense, deep-set eyes, and a head crowned by a mane of black hair that had been gathered at the base of its skull and elaborately plaited, the long, thick braid falling almost to the hem of its mid-thigh length hauberk. And while strapping by human standards, this one wasn't quite as brawny and broad-shouldered as its companions—*likely integral to the illusion it wants to create, so focus on the illusion and maybe what's underneath will reveal itself.*

She ran her own narrowed gaze across the creature's broad back then down, following the diagonal sash of its wide bandoleer to an equally wide belt—a belt that sported a now all-too-familiar looking pistol, along with a host of other, even more malevolent-looking items, the functions of which she could only guess.

Not that I care to, she thought as she went about firmly affixing each and every detail of the creature and its uniform, no matter how seemingly mundane or insignificant, in her mind—*'cuz eventually you'll slip up, all shapers do, forget some minor element in a moment of distraction—my memory against yours, merc—may the real human win.*

As she continued to keenly study it, study its panoply, she realized that what she was attempting was no easy task: almost every square centimeter of its hauberk, bandoleer, belt, trousers and knee-high campaign boots bore some ominous-looking appendage—*just what one would expect from a merc, just what you expect us to expect: a veritable walking arsenal.* Then with a wry, private smile: *Gods help you if you ever trip...*

Worse, it was no trick of the cabin's shifting light: the surface of the underlying uniform indeed kept shifting, changing texture and appearance, from utterly smooth and iridescent black, to matt black and suddenly covered with tiny bumps and peaks only to flatten out again, all within the space of a few blinks of the eye. The ultimate ghillie suit... or conjurer's clothing. This instantly reminded her of another epithet often attributed to mercs, especially by newly settled colonists who were by nature exceedingly jumpy and willing to credit Hahtooshans with any unexpected disappearance, any lurking shadow caught out of the tail of the eye: *yowies*.

Her brother had frightened her, frightened her friends during sleepovers by telling tales of yowies snatching silly girls from their beds, never to be seen again—and she'd believed him.

"I had no idea scientific research paid so well," Aquila commented testily as he wiped his oozing nose on his sleeve.

The remark broke her train of thought, her intense scrutiny and painstaking cataloguing of the alien's remarkable uniform and she flicked the man a sidelong, exasperated look. *Thanks! Now I'll have to start all over—*

The merc slowly turned around to face them and she dearly hoped she looked innocent of gawking, but its interest wasn't with her, it was with Aquila. Its unblinking gaze was fixed on him to the exclusion of all else, instantly reminding her of a snake preparing to strike; clearly the alien was becoming exasperated with Aquila's dogged, albeit clearly pain-induced impudence—not that she could really blame it, Hahtooshan or no. While Aquila had a lot of admirable traits—Vildur wouldn't have hand-selected him for her second in command if he wasn't an extraordinarily capable officer—and he was very popular with the crew, he also had a peculiar knack for pissing off people he didn't like and in amazingly quick order; not that he was the first person she'd dealt with who possessed this particular skill.

Her own father had been known to tweak people just for the sake of tweaking them and the more powerful or pompous the person the better. *But a Hahtooshan?* Even her father wouldn't have had the audacity to pick a quarrel with one.

Aquila, as far too many within the Coalition, had lost loved ones to acts credited to Hahtooshans. If that wasn't enough, he had audacity in spades and she briefly speculated that if one looked up the word "audacity" on a data reader in the very near future, one would see an image of the man standing next her, along with a terse, wholly unsympathetic obituary. Add to the mix that he was clearly in a lot of pain and scared and, well... he wasn't thinking all that rationally. She could only hope he wouldn't push his luck too far, or that this particular merc had more patience than a proverbial saint—a concept that was difficult if not impossible to square with its very malevolent appearance and its species' truly fearsome reputation.

"Pure research always has its rewards," the Hahtooshan replied evenly as it reclipped the device to its belt, drawing her attention and her gaze back to the matter at hand. "Even *you* should know that."

"So what rewards would've brought an Orthodoxy warship to this backwater system, and a merc battle commander to this planet?" Aquila persisted as he tried to adjust his hold on his flank without wincing.

The merc slowly arched a brow. "I would like to ask the same question of you, Commander None-Of-Your—"

"Aquila, all right?"

"*Aquila?*" This time both brows went up in a perfect parody of human bafflement and Corsali had to hand it to the merc; it had made a truly sincere effort at getting human facial expressions just right. "I don't understand—"

"My name. It's *Aquila.*" He angrily wiped a fresh trickle of blood from his nose. "Robert Eugene Aquila, commanding officer of the Coalition Expeditionary Forces Patrol Ship *Baidarka.*"

The merc stared at him for a moment then let loose a sharp, startled bark of laughter. "*Commanding officer?*" it repeated incredulously. "Of an entire vessel *and* her crew?"

Corsali inwardly cringed at the alien's tone of amused disbelief—another dead-on mockery of a response Aquila, whose features teetered perilously close to the baby-faced, had become inured to; even Vildur had indulged in some friendly teasing of her at times headstrong second-in-command. But in this instance, it was painfully obvious to her that Aquila found the predictable reaction particularly galling—

"*Yes,*" he hissed through clenched teeth.

"Well then, *Commander* Aquila, as I was about to say, I would like to ask what a Rim patrol vessel was doing here. Perhaps you were curious as to what we A'tuu'shahn'i were up to, yes? What we found so interesting in this... backwater system?"

"*We* diverted here in response to a distress call—"

"Indeed? I didn't think Rimmers performed missions of mercy when it involved A'tuu'shahn'i."

Corsali blinked. *What?*

Aquila's lips parted in surprise then he quickly recovered and replied a little too vehemently, "Despite what you've been told, *merc*, we don't differentiate when it comes to calls for help. As far as we're concerned, a distress call is a distress call—"

"You didn't realize the distress call was from one of our craft, *did you?*"

Aquila stared back at the creature but said nothing. He didn't need to.

"Ah, yes. Truth always has a way of slipping out at the most inconvenient of times, doesn't it? Lies, on the other hand are so much better behaved—"

"So what's your warship doing here in the first place?" Aquila interrupted. "This isn't disputed territory."

"Neither is it Coalition. As for what our *research* ship is doing here, consider yourselves very fortunate that we were not only on this planet, but very close to the crash site when you were attacked. You and your companions would have been dead within minutes had we not driven off those creatures—at the cost of the lives of two of *my* soldiers I might add."

"What?"

"We also picked up a distress call. *Yours.*" The merc chuckled at Aquila's poorly concealed shock. "Yes, Commander, *we* saved *you.* Ironic, yes? So be grateful that we—to use your term, *'mercs'*—aren't the cold-blooded monsters your Coalition propaganda would have you believe."

Aquila replied with a loud, derisive snort and a sneered, *"Yeah, right.* You're just a bunch of damned boy scouts. Try telling that to the victims of the Torthah-Gaal massacre," he added with more than a little heat, "or how 'bout Raumalle or—"

"Cotopaxi?" The Hahtooshan, catching Aquila's flustered blink, smiled coldly. It also briefly, slipped its hand under its bandoleer, drawing Corsali's curious gaze to the wide strap. But it wasn't whatever it was fingering—hidden from her view—that drew her attention. It was what the bandoleer sported: a sheathed dagger. Only the grip was visible, but its elaborately carved and inlaid haft suddenly brought to mind the dagger she'd found near the wreck. In

fact the more she looked at it, the more it looked if not identical, then at least very similar. *So that's—*

"As you no doubt know," the alien continued, and, for the first time, its voice held a decidedly sharp edge and the sudden change in tone drew her preoccupied gaze to its no longer friendly face, "had it not been for *our* timely intervention, *our* unquestioned bravery and *our* enormous sacrifice, *your* precious colony on Cotopaxi would now be in the hands of the Matarii—"

"Fat lot of good it does anyone—the entire planet's now a damned radioactive wasteland no one wants!"

"That was not *our* doing, and you—"

"Sha'ashahn..."

All three wheeled towards the new voice, Aquila and the merc in visible anger at the untimely interruption, Corsali in relief.

Another humanoid was now standing, silhouetted, in the hastily repaired doorway. "...I heard a commotion—"

"Ah, Suhjai," the officer purred, its voice once again easygoing. "I was just about to send for you. Commander, Ensign, this is Mihr-Suhjai'baldah, junior medical officer of *Makhaira.*"

The alien responded to the introduction with a contemptuous nod as it stepped out of the doorway's glare and as it did so, Corsali suddenly found herself the sole object of the creature's mica-cold gaze.

She ignored its unblinking stare in preference for taking in the alien as a whole only to find it, like its more substantial companion, cloaked neck to toe in identical panoply—minus only the bandoleer—its skull crowned in an unruly, shoulder-length mop of black hair that in this alien's case was also adorned with a scattering of silvery beads, and its face was likewise covered in a grotesque pattern of tattoos and scars—

"Do not be fooled by Suhjai's... um, *fragile* appearance," the soldier continued amiably. "She could break your neck before you even knew she was within striking distance."

So, so, so. An unintentional slip that appearances are deceiving. Or maybe not unintentional, maybe you suspect I'm on to you and are trying to throw me off? And—she? That's a she? A female? Corsali gave the alien another sidelong look just in time to catch Suhjai flicking its—her?—companion a venomous glance as it—she?—knelt beside Gianakis.

She, not it—that was going to take some getting used to. Corsali had never wondered if Hahtooshans had genders. In fact she'd always tried really, *really* hard not to think of Hahtooshans at all. *But... since we're on the subject...* She risked a furtive glance at the taller, heavier officer. *I assume this means you're male—a classic case of sexual dimorphism? Or is this just another ruse? Is this all for appearance? But if it is a ruse, then it's a ruse for a reason, and I'd be smart to start thinking of you two as male and female to better understand what makes you tick. And if it isn't....*

Suddenly her private joke about manatees seemed a tad bit *too* apropos.

She suppressed a shiver then turned to find Suhjai examining Gianakis' crudely splinted leg while shaking *her* shaggy head and clicking *her* tongue. "I see my ministrations have been given the proper respect by one of your *most trusted* men, Sha'ashahn. I do hope you'll bear this in mind?"

The merc shrugged, but said nothing as its—*his, dammit, Sirin, his!*—fingers toyed with the haft of the dagger that protruded from *his* bandoleer.

A nervous tic? Corsali wondered. *Gods, I hope so.*

Suhjai rose and unshouldered a satchel, then turned to Aquila and motioned to his softsuit. "Remove your clothing."

He looked sidelong and wide-eyed at Corsali as if expecting an explanation—or protection—and despite the situation Corsali struggled not to laugh.

"I cannot examine your injuries with you fully dressed," Suhjai added impatiently. "Strip to the waist—*no* further," she added, as if just as uncomfortable about the matter as Aquila.

He scowled warily at her then slowly, carefully and with a minimum of wincing, managed to pull one arm free of the tattered softsuit, then the other.

Suhjai impatiently finished the job by roughly jerking the top of the suit down around his hips and for a moment he stood there, the center of attention, bare-chested and clearly very unhappy about it.

Corsali was shocked by what she saw, from the livid bruising that darkened his entire torso, to fresh bruises on his arms and throat and the bulky and blood-soaked dressing on his flank.

He followed her startled stare and what he saw was clearly worse than even he'd imagined, then he tensed but stood his ground as Suhjai ran her bare, elaborately tattooed fingers over his badly mottled but otherwise utterly unadorned skin with a blatant mixture of curiosity and revulsion.

"You'll live." She didn't need to add "unfortunately". It was obvious in her voice as she opened the satchel.

Corsali's eyes widened in instant recognition: *Jarvis's field triage kit—*

"Where'd you get that?" Aquila snapped, clearly grasping at anything to get the attention off of him and his battered body.

Suhjai flicked her companion another sharp, sidelong look.

"I found it beside you," the merc answered evenly. "I thought, considering your injuries—"

"Your wound needs to be repacked and redressed," Suhjai interrupted, motioning to Aquila's flank.

He reluctantly looked down at himself and replied, almost pleadingly, "But the bleeding's stopped."

Suhjai ignored the remark and ripped the blood-stiffened dressing from his side.

Aquila visibly paled and Corsali reached out to steady him, but he waved her off as Suhjai immediately slapped a clean dressing over the now oozing wound. She sealed it then stepped back and Aquila gingerly touched the freshly applied bandage as if it were a bomb strapped to his side.

"The evening meal should be ready," the merc said pleasantly, drawing Corsali's distracted gaze. "I know I speak for Suhjai when I say that we would both welcome your company."

Suhjai expression's left little doubt what her true feelings were on that subject.

Aquila glared at him as he angrily shoved one arm into a sleeve, followed by the other, clearly startled and, just as clearly, greatly annoyed that at least this particular merc was not acting as he thought a merc should.

"You'd prefer bread and water?" The Hahtooshan chuckled, *"Come,* Commander! We're all civilized beings here."

Suhjai muttered something unintelligible under her breath as she again knelt beside Gianakis, her back to the others.

Aquila eyed her as he hastily ran his finger up his softsuit's seal seam. He even fastened the collar tight under his chin for good measure.

"Sir," Corsali said, "I think getting some food into you would be a really good idea."

Aquila stared sidelong at her for what seemed like an eternity then finally muttered very grudgingly, "I suppose you're right."

"Excellent." The mercenary smiled. "I'll inform our hosts." He strode from the cabin.

Corsali gave Suhjai another quick glance to find her still tending to Gianakis then turned to Aquila. His face had still not regained its color under its false blush of smeared blood and fresh bruising and he was noticeably swaying.

"Perhaps you should sit down, sir."

"Yeah," Aquila nodded and with her help, eased himself down onto the rough planking. Corsali had no sooner seated herself beside him than the officer returned with one of the planet's natives in tow.

So, that's what you *really look like,* she noted with some relief, while out of the corner of her eye, she noticed Aquila watching the newest arrival with a look of poorly concealed disgust. In a world where outward appearances were no longer trustworthy, where everything was suspect, it was almost comforting to be confronted by something concrete, even if that reassuring solidity came guised in a rather off-putting form: records from the only known Coalition survey of the planet contained a few very sketchy verbal descriptions and a handful of blurry images of the reclusive insectoids.

The creatures had never displayed any hostility towards that survey team—quite the contrary. They always fled into their soft-walled and steeply angled burrows at the approach of a survey party—burrows that were deemed far too unstable for the surveyors to enter, burrows that scanners determined turned into a maze of tunnels that stretched for kilometers in every direction and reached depths of well over two hundred meters. But those records and what she now saw closely matched what one surveyor had jokingly described as something akin to acromegalic cockroaches—hence the name the surveyors gave them, Blattos, short for *Blattodea*.

This particular Blatto had brought a small lantern, four mugs, a small platter mounded with food and lastly, a pitcher that looked like it weighed more than the multi-armed creature carrying it.

"Commander," the Hahtooshan said as he took the pitcher and a mug, "might I interest you in something hot to drink?" He filled the cup and offered it to him but Aquila only stared at it.

"It's perfectly safe to drink. I wouldn't have gone to all the trouble of rescuing you only to poison you, now would I?" To prove his point, he took a large gulp from the mug. He swallowed, wiped the froth from his lips with the back of his gauntleted hand, then picked up another mug and filled it, but this time offered it to Corsali.

She took it awkwardly, wanting to avoid his gauntleted fingers then she looked to Aquila as he reluctantly accepted another from the alien.

The Hahtooshan sat, crossed legged and facing them then held up his cup. "I believe the proper Rimmer expression is...'*prosit*'?" With that he emptied his mug in several loud gulps.

When he failed to clutch his throat and keel over dead, Corsali decided to risk a sip of the thick, foamy liquid.

It was warm and bitter and had a distinctive musty aftertaste, but it wasn't unpleasant, in fact it produced an almost instantaneous warm glow in her stomach. She took another small sip as she watched him drain his mug in a series of loud, wincing gulps. *But keep that up and you just might keel over dead drunk—*

"This ale," the merc said, noticing Corsali's cautious stare, "is one of the few small pleasures this forgettable world has to offer."

"Even small pleasures can be overdone, Sha'ashahn," Suhjai muttered as she gathered up her supplies.

He grabbed the pitcher and ignoring the remaining mug, poured himself another. "Perhaps." He took a more measured sip as he favored Corsali with another inquisitive look, gray eyes glittering from within the elaborate swirl of tattoos.

She willed herself to meet his intense stare with one of her own and was surprised when he immediately turned his gaze to the gathering darkness beyond the open doorway.

Interesting reaction. Realizing that perhaps mercs considered it the height of bad manners to stare, or at least to be stared *at*—a very reasonable reaction for a shape-shifter, whose outward appearance might not stand up to prolonged scrutiny—and that it wouldn't be a good idea to offend a merc, even accidentally, she followed suit and fixed her eyes on the mug she held in her hands.

After a thorough examination of its contents, she found her curiosity getting the better of her and resumed her sidelong study of the distracted alien. The fact that no one had ever been this up close and personal with a Hahtooshan, at least no one who *knew* they were this up close and personal with a Hahtooshan—if you discounted those at the award ceremony and as far as she was concerned, that really didn't count—and had lived to tell the tale was not lost on her at that particular moment.

But here she was, up to her figurative eyeballs in them—a claim to fame she would have preferred to have avoided altogether—yet she, Aquila and Gianakis were still alive and as a direct result of merc intervention—*if* one believed his claims, and she wasn't entirely sure she did; he was a shape-shifter after all, a creature whose physical appearance was often as not a lie.

Yet... if he *was* telling the truth, the perversity of the situation was almost laughable. *Almost*—there was something very sobering about having a creature of the Hahtooshans' horrifically thuggish reputation seated within striking distance, even if at that moment said merc appeared to be far more interested in dispatching the contents of his mug.

So, yet again, she used his distraction to her cautious, curious advantage while praying Aquila would keep his mouth shut for a few precious minutes: first, a quick, discreet look-see to see if some minor detail in the merc's disguise had gone missing.... *nope*. If one ignored the skin-crawling, ever-changing texture of the underlying uniform, its multitude of extremely lethal-looking trappings were exactly where she remembered them to be.

And now that he was even closer, with his features illuminated by the steady glow of the nearby lamp even more details immerged: the elaborate tattoos on his face perfectly matched the scarification patterns, giving the bizarre ornamentation an unsettling three-dimensional effect. While the scarification appeared to be limited to his face, the tattoos disappeared into his hair and down his neck, to the collar of his uniform, suggesting they went even further. Suhjai's hands were tattooed after all, so likely his were, too.

Before her mind could follow that train of thought to its likely and not particularly appealing destination, she realized something else, possibly something critical: his uniform wasn't dusty, it was *filthy*, as was his long, thick black mane. It clung to his skull in thick, greasy strands and along with the pungent odor of the merc himself, she also smelled the strong reek of the native alcohol. While he wasn't blatantly drunk, he was far from sober and she wondered how much of the potent liquor he'd already consumed, assuming this wasn't yet another deliberate contrivance on his part, to appear disheveled and intoxicated and therefore—

An impatient clacking drew everyone's startled attention to the native.

"Of course," the merc murmured and the Blatto promptly stepped forward, into the flickering lamplight, and thrust out the tray.

Corsali grimaced; whatever it was offering her looked like withered lumps of meat. At her hesitation, it fluttered its iridescent wings and stepped even closer to hold the tray directly under her nose and she felt her stomach lurch in protest. *And it smells just like—*

"You don't find it appetizing?" the Hahtooshan asked with just a hint of deliberate innocence.

Corsali managed a quick, sharp shake of her head.

The merc waved his hand and much to her relief the tray was immediately withdrawn, but not without a decidedly offended wing rustling from the Blatto.

"It's a native delicacy—or so they tell us." He leaned forward, glanced first at Aquila, then Corsali and added in a conspiratorial whisper. "*I suspect it's actually their dung.*" He chuckled at her horrified blink. "But," he shrugged as he flicked the Blatto a sidelong, slightly wicked smile, "it's *only* a suspicion and they do *so* enjoy preparing it for us." He untied a small pouch from his belt, said, "Here," and tossed it onto the deck between Corsali and Aquila.

"What's this?" Aquila said, not touching it.

"Field rations. *Ours.* They may not be up to your *refined* Rimmer tastes, but—"

"For some reason, I've lost my appetite," Aquila grumbled.

"Perhaps?" The merc looked hopefully at Corsali; she shook her head. "As you wish." He rose in one fluid movement, catlike, utterly and eerily silent, and with a challenging glance at Suhjai, picked up the pitcher and wandered over to the doorway. Bracing his shoulder against the frame and squinting into the stiff breeze, he brought the pitcher to his lips and began gulping down its contents.

Corsali squinted at him. *Damn, you can sure pack it away, can't you?* She gave Suhjai a glance to see her staring sidelong at her companion with a look of utter revulsion. *Clearly no love lost between the two of you.* That bit of potentially useful information was filed away as well—along with the possibility that this too was an act for their benefit—*make us think the two of you are at odds.*

She absently rubbed the side of her head—all this guessing what was real, what was ruse was giving her a serious headache—or maybe that was due to the liquor. *Or maybe it's not liquor... maybe,* she thought with a private grimace, *it's their pee... Oh, ick!* She looked down at her own barely touched mug and quickly set it down, then, noticing that Aquila had brought his mug to his lips, she gave hers a slight nudge, pushing it towards him, hoping he'd get the hint. *Here, sir... all yours, sir.*

The native scuttled over to the door with the untouched tray, but as it tried to slip, unnoticed, around the merc, he suddenly thrust out the pitcher, briefly pinning the hapless Blatto against the doorframe. It reacted by dropping the tray then wriggling all of its appendages wildly and chittering pleadingly.

The Hahtooshan leaned close and muttered something to it in its strange, clicking tongue then released it and the startled Blatto took the pitcher and scuttled across the deck to the ladder, leaving the tray and its scattered contents behind.

When the creature reappeared a few minutes later with the replenished pitcher, the merc snatched it without so much as a nod then sent the Blatto away with a preoccupied flick of his hand—*not that it looked like it needed much encouragement,* Corsali observed as it half-scurried, half-flew back to the ladder.

Then, as he sauntered back to them Suhjai squinted up at him. "You've decided to rejoin us?" She dropped her gaze to the pitcher as he squatted beside her. "Ah. I see you come well-armed."

"So, Commander," the merc began as he refilled his mug, and then, almost as an afterthought, sloshed some into Suhjai's as if to shut her up, "you're the captain of a patrol vessel."

Aquila hesitated an uncomfortably long time before answering, "Yes."

"That's quite a responsibility, and at such a young age?" When it became apparent that Aquila was not going to reply at all this time, he prodded, "You must be very ambitious—or very lucky?"

Aquila's uneasy stare darkened into a scowl.

"Not much of a conversationalist, are you, Commander?" He turned to Corsali and his expression instantly brightened. "What about you, Ensign?"

"What about her?" Aquila grumbled as he shifted around in search of a more comfortable position.

This time the Hahtooshan's unsettling pale eyes never wavered from Corsali's. "I'm curious as to what role you fill aboard your vessel."

"She's the captain's adjutant," Aquila said before Corsali could even open her mouth and Suhjai snorted derisively.

Aquila glared at her then turned to the soldier. "How 'bout you answer some of my questions?"

"Of course." He sat on the deck facing them and shrugged. "I for one have nothing to hide."

"Why take us captive? That's not exactly standard merc doctrine."

"Ah. That's quite a long story. Perhaps one best told once we—"

"You do have a captive audience," Aquila said sourly.

The Hahtooshan smiled, leaned back against a roof support and, cradling his replenished mug in his lap, stretched out his long legs as he nodded, "True…"

Corsali glanced down at the booted foot that ended up right next to her and swallowed, hard, as her imagination replaced a human-shaped foot with all sorts of hideous, alien appendages—it didn't help that the surface of the knee-high boot, just like the mercs' uniform, seemed to have a mind of its own. While she wasn't exactly a xenophobe—she wouldn't have been accepted in the forces if she had—she still harbored the usual human unease of aliens who looked, well… *alien*. But even worse, she now realized, were, paradoxically, aliens who *looked* human.

"…and I shall start by telling you that I disobeyed a direct order by rescuing you," the Hahtooshan continued, drawing her uneasy gaze back to his equally unsettling face.

Undaunted by Aquila's suspicious squint or Suhjai's muffled oath, he said, "Why, you ask? A'tuu'shahn'i aren't known for their mercy, and for good reason. We're mercenaries and mercenaries cannot afford to be merciful—"

"Unless you're *paid* to be," Aquila interrupted, the mounting discomfort of sitting on the hard deck tainting his already tetchy voice.

"Or we deem it to be in our best, long term interest, yes," the alien replied, unoffended.

"I assume our capture..."

"Rescue," he interjected politely.

"...falls into the latter category, since I'm unaware of any bounty—"

"The latter, Commander, *definitely* the latter, although my commanding officer wouldn't see it that way. You see—"

"You've said *enough*, Sha'ashahn," Suhjai growled. "The alcohol's affecting your tongue."

He smiled at her, picked up the pitcher and topped off his mug.

Her eyes widened to bulging proportions and she scrambled to her feet.

"Leaving so soon?" he asked sweetly.

She hissed, *"Your excesses are your problem, I won't have you make them mine!"* With a snort of disgust, she stalked out of the cabin.

Corsali followed her with her eyes until Suhjai vanished down the ladder, then she turned back to the merc to find him staring after her as well.

He chuckled softly then promptly sank into what seemed a vast and vacant pause as his body sagged heavily against the roof support.

After a moment Aquila impatiently cleared his throat.

The Hahtooshan slowly shifted his gaze back to them and Corsali wondered if Suhjai had been right, that the alcohol had finally caught up with him as his strange eyes had taken on a dull, exhausted and decidedly bleak look.

"You were saying...?" Aquila prompted irritably.

"I was?" The merc squinted at him then wincing straightened himself up. "Yes... yes, I was." He fixed his bleary-eyed stare on his mug and for a moment Corsali thought he'd drifted off again, lost in his own drunken distraction, then: "We found something," he began, his voice barely above a whisper, his gaze never wavering from the mug he clutched in his hand, "something in this system. If it were to fall into the wrong hands…"

"Some might say that's already happened," Aquila grumbled and before she could stop herself Corsali shot him an 'I don't care if you're in pain, just shut the fuck up!' glance. For once he took the hint and clamped his mouth shut—not that it mattered as the merc appeared oblivious to his testy remark or the silent and silencing exchange.

"…it would mean the end of us all. I rescued you because…" He hesitated, took a deep, unsteady breath then squarely meeting Aquila's suspicious gaze added, "I… I need your help."

"Our… *help?*"

"Yes."

"Assuming you're telling us the truth."

The Hahtooshan studied Aquila's taut face for a moment before replying, "I'm not so naïve as to expect you to believe me, Commander. I have proof, proof even you—"

"What proof?" Aquila grunted as he clutched his side.

"This backwater system—as you called it—has much to offer. Not just to us, surely not, but at least at one time to your Coalition."

"I don't follow."

"You're unaware of the Coalition base on the fourth planet?"

Aquila turned a perplexed stare on Corsali; she shook her head.

The merc also briefly shifted his gaze to her then back to Aquila before adding, "Perhaps it's not so surprising. You are, after all, only the captain of a patrol vessel. And this base was—what do you Rimmers call such things? A deep, dark secret? *A very dark secret indeed.*"

"For what purpose?" Aquila waved his free arm about as he forced a laugh, a laugh cut short by an involuntary grimace before he added tightly, "There's nothing in this god-forsaken system anyone wants!"

"It had one thing: its isolation—and isolation was vital."

"For what?" Aquila countered.

"To create a weapon, Commander, a weapon the likes of which this part of the Rim has not seen in thousands of years. That was the base's sole purpose, and why it was located in what you so aptly called a backwater system, where no one would come snooping and your Coalition could work its mischief completely safe from detection."

Gods! Corsali's stomach muscles tightened into a knot and she turned to Aquila, but he had no quick denial on the tip of his tongue.

After a moment to gather his thoughts, Aquila said, "You said there *was* a base on the fourth planet—meaning it no longer exists?"

"It was abandoned one hundred and thirty Standard years ago. As for what we're doing here, on *this* planet, we uncovered more evidence of the Coalition's hidden agenda *here*, specifically on an island—"

"And that's where you're taking us?"

"Yes. And it is there you'll see the proof of my claims."

"Proof or no proof, I don't see..." Aquila's voice trailed off as he found himself in the path of the Hahtooshan's suddenly fierce gaze.

Still holding Aquila's stare, he crushed the heavy mug with his armored fingers.

Corsali swallowed convulsively. *Point made*—

"Didn't you hear me?" he hissed as he hurled the ruined mug aside. "I've uncovered the ultimate weapon! If you don't help me stop this madness, here and now, it will be the end of us all!"

Corsali shrank back as the soldier lurched unsteadily to his feet, then he spun on his heel and stalked out of the cabin, over to the ladder and quickly descended, leaving his human captives to stare after him in stunned silence.

Corsali finally let out the breath she didn't realize she'd been holding in one spasmodic rush of air, gave herself a hug and turned to Aquila.

He tried and failed to look unruffled as he cleared his throat and gave his softsuit's collar a tug.

"Sir, this weapon must be the same one mentioned in the data stores in the wreck."

"My thoughts as well..." Aquila's suddenly suspicious eyes cut to the ladder. "But then again, this all might be some sort of elaborate ruse."

"To what end?"

He grabbed his mug and downed what remained before replying, "Hell if I know, but I'll be damned if I'm going to take anything one of those fuckin' butchers says, if you'll excuse the pun, at *face* value—goddamned shapers, hiding behind this human-like façade of theirs—makes me wonder what else are they hiding? My guess—the truth."

"But—"

"I do know that right now I'm freezing cold and bone-tired." Aquila gave his upper arms a vigorous rub for emphasis.

And in a whole lot of pain I'd wager, Corsali added to herself as she watched him ease himself down onto the deck, grimacing as he did so.

"If I were a betting man," he said, cupping the back of his head in his hands, "I'd say those mercs *liberated* that craft from some smugglers, brought it here and deliberately crashed it into the desert, then activated the distress call, luring us here to investigate in order to get us off the scent of that missing liner." He nodded to himself, added wearily, "Yeah. Bet that's it." He closed his eyes, exhaled slowly, clearly trying to force his battered body to relax. "Needed a diversion, a way of keeping us occupied. Gotta be it."

"But... but what about the data, the maser pistol, the dagger?"

"All part of an elaborate cock and bull story, Ensign."

"But—"

"And we—correction—*I* walked right into it."

She raised a startled brow at his admission, exhaustion, pain and ale-induced it might be.

Oblivious to her reaction, he shook his head and muttered, *"Shit."*

She crawled on hands and knees over to Gianakis, pressed her finger to his throat and relieved to find a strong pulse, she looked back at Aquila. "But sir, why rescue us? Why not—"

"What better way to keep the *Baidarka* here, in orbit, instead of out there, looking for the *Herrick?*"

"But—"

"Get some sleep."

"But sir, I—"

"Enough, Ensign." With that he rolled onto his side, away from her.

With a clipped, "Yessir," she scooted back against the cabin wall, next to Gianakis.

She leaned her shoulder against the wall and peered through its loose weave to the starlit ocean beyond as her frustration at the man, at their situation, abruptly drained away, leaving her feeling exhausted, not to mention rather stupid. What he'd suggested made sense. Damned if it didn't.

She hugged herself against a shiver, her skin suddenly turning to gooseflesh despite the softsuit as the salt-laden breeze picked up, cutting through the porous walls and bringing with it a hint of a much, much chillier night ahead. A quick glance around turned up nothing she could use as makeshift covers, not even a scrap of torn reed matting as the soldiers, she realized to her great annoyance, had been very efficient in tidying up. She forced a smile—*who knew yowies were neat-freaks?*

Her private attempt at humor fell flat.

Another shiver left her teeth chattering and she vigorously rubbed her upper arms. *Damn, it's gonna be cold—wait a minute.* Her eyes darted to the doorway and to the open, star-lit deck beyond. *Maybe they just left it outside—definitely worth a look-see.* "Be right back, sir." She snatched up the now sputtering lamp, lurched to her feet, turned back to the doorway and started violently.

A merc now stood in the hastily repaired opening, his bulk blotting out most of the night sky. He hadn't been there a heartbeat before—at least she hadn't heard him approach—for all she knew, he could have been standing there for some time, undetectable, watching her and she grabbed onto that, tried to use indignation to trump her fright. *Fucking cowardly shaper!*

Didn't work. Truth was she was alone with a merc and scared to death. "Wh-wha-what d-d-do you w-w-want?" she stammered an instant before she realized she really might not want to know.

In reply he stepped into the cabin, visible only by his movement, of the odd glimmer of starlight on his ghillie suit and in absolute silence, specter-like in his advance. And as the faint lamplight washed over his exposed face, it created an even more bizarre appearance of a negative image, where only the underlying skin was visible, the inky black markings not. If she thought the tattoos were disturbing, this cutwork effect was doubly so as it completely obscured his features.

She backed up, promptly bumped up against a roof support pole and unable to retreat any further, swallowed hard as he stopped less than a meter away.

"What do you want?" she managed this time without stammering; she even managed to sound angry—at least to her own ears.

In response he shoved something against her with enough force to knock her back into the pole. She fearfully glanced down, to her shock realized by feel alone that she was now clutching several rolled up blankets. Then she looked up at the shadowy alien who loomed over her and this close, and with the faint glow of the dying lamplight alone she was able to just make out the baleful set of his mouth, the intricate patterns carved into his face, the glitter of his pale eyes, and a thick mane of coarse long hair, every bit as long as the officer's. Loose—caught by the night breeze, it eeled around him to brush against her cheeks, her throat, its light tickle leaving her with a severe case of gooseflesh.

"Gift from Sha'ashahn," he grumbled, breaking the awkward silence.

Taken aback by his fetid breath and truly rank body odor, she couldn't immediately find her voice and tried to hide her reaction by fumbling, one-handed, with the blankets, unwilling to free her other hand of the lamp, worthless as it was as a steady source of useable light.

He grunted in matched disgust then walked back to the doorway where he abruptly stopped and glanced over his shoulder.

She tightened her hold on the lamp. It might not be much when it came to a weapon, but it was slightly better than nothing, certainly better than trying to pummel him into submission with the rolled up blankets.

"Remain on *this* deck. *Understood?*"

She managed a quick nod then watched as he strode across the deck and over to the ladder, his uniform glimmering in the starlight, in absolute and eerie silence despite his bulk. With belated bravado she whispered, "Don't you mercs ever knock?" She wrinkled her nose. "Or bathe? *Peewhewww!*"

She gave herself a shake then knelt and setting the sputtering lamp aside, quickly untied the rolled up blankets—three in all. *How... convenient—*

She glanced back at the doorway, suddenly fearful the soldier might have returned but the doorway again appeared empty, the starlit deck beyond seemingly deserted. But, as she reminded herself, he could have just as easily slipped back into the cabin. He could be standing right next to her. He could be—*STOP IT!*

Realizing she could drive herself crazy if not into a total panic with such thoughts, she decided she was going to believe he really had left. *Still...* As far as she knew shape-shifters weren't smell-shifters too, and the alien's overpowering body odor definitely trumped the salt-sour smell of the surrounding sea, at least up close. So she sniffed the cold air, just to be on the safe side, tentatively at first—just in case he was nearby and took umbrage at her tactic—then emboldened, a little more vigorously. *Nothing.* Finally satisfied she was in fact alone, she grumbled, "Damn, shapers give me the creeps."

She turned to Aquila, murmured, "Here, sir, this should help," and drew one of the blankets over him. When he didn't answer, she touched his shoulder. *"Sir?"* Realizing he had lapsed into an exhausted, ale-assisted sleep, she grabbed another roll and covered Gianakis.

She snatched up her mug, picked up the remaining blanket then resuming her seat next to Gianakis, drew the blanket around her chilled shoulders. She stared down at the mug she held, tempted to follow Aquila's example and down it in a few gulps and then get some much needed sleep—but more she stared at it, the less the thought appealed. Someone needed to keep her wits about her—and there was still the nagging worry that it really was Blatto urine, or some other body fluid.

She set it aside with the less than convincing thought, *Maybe later,* then tugged the blanket tighter around her as she looked down at Gianakis. Unlike the always affable Lundgren, or the overly somber Gislasen, she only knew the bombastic Gianakis in passing but the young marine had always shown her deference, mindful of her position as the captain's adjutant and as irrational as it was, she found some small comfort in his nearness—*as if you could protect me—*

The lamp, starved of fuel, suddenly sputtered and went out, plunging the cabin into total darkness... until her eyes adjusted to the faint starlight that filtered in through the gaps in the walls and through the doorway.

Within the darkness and without warning she began to shake uncontrollably; tears welled up in her eyes. She hugged herself tightly then flicked Aquila a sidelong glare. *I'm not falling apart!*

Really? An inner voice asked. *Certainly looks like you are.*

I'm just tired! She wiped her eyes and nose on her grubby sleeve. *But so what if I am?*

The commander needs you. He's depending on you.

What about me? She angrily wiped her nose again. *Who the hell can I depend on?*

When no answer beyond the obvious was forthcoming, she took a deep, steadying breath. *I need to get ahold of myself.*

She leaned back into the cabin wall then concentrated on putting some order to her chaotic thoughts by asking herself the same question she'd asked herself countless times in the past two weeks, since the Matarran ambush: *What would Captain Vildur say?* It was a question that, just by its asking, evoked the woman's reassuring, calming presence. *Tell me what to do!*

This time the answer was immediate: *Survive. Do what you have to to survive—*

How? Tell me how! There are at least ten mercs out there, any one of 'em would happily slit my throat just for breathing their air—

If that were the case, wouldn't they have done it already?

But what if the commander's right? What if this is all an elaborate ruse?

And what if it isn't?

A chill gathered around her shoulders that had nothing to do with the dropping temperature, goose-pimpling her flesh anew as she recalled the disturbing look in the alien's strange eyes and the noticeable inflections in his voice. *Fear. Desperation. Despair.*

Not the sort of thing one would expect in a Hahtooshan—*a merc.*

Don't believe everything you think—that had been one of Vildur's favorite comebacks.

She burrowed down into the blanket as another shiver ran up her spine then whispered, *"Yeah..."*

Chapter 3

"You believe I was wrong."

Suhjai kept her gaze fixed on the stern cabin's fire pot, aware that her companion had stopped his agitated pacing and was now standing directly behind her. "I believe many things, Sha'ashahn. And you have committed *so many* wrongs—"

"You think it was a mistake to bring the Rimmers into our confidence—"

"Our confidence? You mean *your* confidence. I would've thought of anyone, you would not have forgotten the lessons of Cotopaxi." She twisted around and looked up, satisfied by the look in his eyes. It was almost too easy. Cotopaxi hung around his neck like a practice target; its mere mention never failed to elicit the desired response.

"I haven't forgotten. I've just learned to put it in its proper place."

Have you? she smirked. *The Hero of Cotopaxi. My, how far you've fallen from those glory days.*

He squatted beside her. "As you've told me more times than I can remember, one must not live in the past."

"Now you choose to listen to me."

"Better once than never, yes?"

"And as you've told me more times than I can count, my opinions, the opinions of a *lowly* Shar'ataan, are of no importance—"

"I never referred to Shar'ataan'i as lowly."

"You didn't need to. The sneer of your voice was enough, always enough to remind me, remind *all* Shar'ataan'i of our humble position relative to high-born Elkanaghalli'i, and who are we to question, or suggest another course of action—"

"It never stopped Tu'indai, and I can honestly say I never remember you *ever* being the least bit reticent about speaking your mind to anyone, even to Tarqk."

"—but dare to question the motives of the Hero of Cotopaxi?"

He clamped his mouth shut; another direct hit and she couldn't help but grin.

"If my 'motives' as you put it," he continued stiffly, "were never questioned, then I—*we*—wouldn't be here."

She shrugged, more a slight twitch of the shoulders, then, "Well, since you asked... I told you what I thought when you first took the humans captive. You chose to disregard my warnings, just as you chose to disobey Tarqk's direct orders. If you didn't have the stomach to pull the trigger, you should've just left them to those... those *creatures*. No one would have been the wiser—"

"Rest assured, I didn't tell them of Tarqk's plan to test the weapon before turning it over—"

She snorted loudly.

"That is if he plans on turning it over."

She met his sidelong gaze squarely, suddenly suspicious, of him... and, she realized to her surprise, Tarqk.

As his bond-mate, she'd accompanied Tarqk when he was transferred, promoted unexpectedly to Nahru'tzhri of *Makhaira* upon the death of her previous captain and over the obvious—and anticipated—choice of the ship's popular and highly-decorated Elkanaghalli second in command, Qharubi.

Unlike Qharubi or Khusaaq, both of whom came from storied linages, Tarqk was a relative unknown Khighalli from one of the less notable houses, someone usually doomed to spend his or her career accepting contracts everyone else had refused as too belittling or where the reward in no way matched the risk. He'd eagerly sought out those contracts and made something of them and of himself in the process, and along the line had cultivated a few friends who were in turn friends of friends in high places. Very high places.

As a Shar'ataan, she had few opportunities that would lead to the chance of participating in one of those infrequent, highly sought-after and very lucrative contracts that would make the successful recipient and his or her crew a small fortune, not to mention open doors to more choice assignments. So, she did as many of her caste did: she attached herself to someone with potential, someone who wasn't a Shar'ataan, someone who, with a little help, a judicious push here, a careful word there might, just might end up being offered one of those plum contracts. But as a

Shar'ataan, she wasn't exactly spoiled for choice—the obvious eligibles were all snapped up almost from birth.

Tarqk had not been her first choice, or her second, or even her tenth. He was known as a risk taker, often as not without due diligence as to what he was truly risking. The more unsavory the contract, the more he was drawn to it as if it had become a game to him: take a hire no one else would touch—least of all a high-born Elkanaghalli or Kri'taaka—and somehow turn it into a better ship, a better crew. And with each surprising success, he enhanced his burgeoning reputation. But he was also dogged by rumors—all unsubstantiated of course—that he wasn't adverse to free-lancing, hiring himself out without the consent or even the knowledge of the Q'shaathrah.

He was also prone to public and quite violent fits of pique when he didn't get what he felt was his due—a character flaw by any measure. Most of the time such displays of temper were limited to the savage dressing down of a subordinate for what was a minor infraction worthy of nothing more than a sharp look. But there were times his bad humor turned physical, towards crew he disliked for no reason other than their superior caste affiliation, or when Suhjai in some way failed to satisfy his baser needs. And it was a well-known fact that he'd ordered the killing of a dozen Thalamian hostages rather than hand them over for far less than the demanded ransom. When his crew refused without direct orders from the Q'shaathrah or the Loopers who'd ordered the kidnappings in the first place, he became so enraged he carried out the act himself. It was a minor blot on his career, but a blot none the less, and one that made his surprising elevation to Nahru'tzhri of *Makhaira* so soon afterwards even more suspect.

She remembered with a slight smile that Tarqk had reacted with dumbfounded silence to the news, then, with her well-practiced and prompting flattery, he quickly recovered, agreeing that his change of fortunes—and hers, he'd added belatedly—was all due to the Q'shaathrah finally recognizing his talent, his genius, his sheer audacity. That he'd been right to execute the Thalamians—teaching both the Loopers and Thalamians never to try to cheat an A'tuu'shahn when it came to an already agreed upon price.

He'd promised her that this promotion was just the start of bigger and better things, much, *much* bigger and better things, for both of them, and she'd believed him. She had to believe him because she'd staked everything—her career, her reputation, her family's honor, even her own life—on him making something of himself and of course it went without saying that he would always share that something, whatever it was, with her.

And if what Khusaaq was suggesting was true, well, what bigger risk could one take than to default on a contract such as this? That wasn't just audacious. It was unheard of—worse, knowing Tarqk as she did, it wasn't entirely unthinkable for him, especially if he was repeatedly assured it was a simply brilliant idea, one that would reap untold glory, not to mention personal vindication for all the real and perceived slights, the mistreatment he and his close kin had endured through the years. And she knew just who would be whispering those ideas into his ear, or not even bothering to whisper, now that she was conveniently planetside.

He'd promised her he wouldn't leave her behind, that this was all a ruse, to gain Khusaaq's trust and get him to not only admit he and Qharubi had been plotting a mutiny, but to reveal who else was in on the scheme. The longer she stayed, the more she was left to wonder... and worry.

She flicked Khusaaq a sidelong look, measuring her tone and her words carefully: "You think he plans on keeping it for himself? What proof do you have?"

Khusaaq selected a stick from the remaining kindling and used it to prod the dying fire back to life. "His unreserved ambitions are proof enough for me."

"Don't you mean *Tu'indai's* ambitions?" she replied coolly, demonstrating yet again those subtle tricks of malice that made all the difference. Khusaaq's bond-mate might be from the same caste as she was, but she definitely wasn't close kin, and the moment Tu'indai sensed Tarqk was targeting Khusaaq, she didn't waste any time switching allegiances. In fact Suhjai wouldn't have been the least bit surprised to learn that Tu'indai had been behind her being included in the landing party—or that Tu'indai had concocted the whole mutiny idea just to rid herself of her suddenly inconvenient bond-mate, not to mention her chief rival.

He snapped the stick in half, tossed the pieces into the fire, then rose and fixed his slitted eyes on the doorway. Fingering the enameled gorget that hung suspended from his collar he whispered, *"The Elkanasu never meant us for this—"*

"The Elkanasu! Is that all you Elkanaghalli'i think about?"

His hand fell away from the gorget as he turned towards her.

"They're *gone,"* she continued harshly, her anger, her fears getting the better of her, "have been gone for *thousands* of generations, abandoning us—"

"Silence!"

She stared back, unfazed and spat, *"Tah!* Tu'indai's right! You listen to voices not of reason, but of that dagger—voices only *you* can hear!"

He looked away, jaw muscles bunching.

Emboldened, embittered, she continued, "Does your precious knife mutter to you in your low tongue, Sha'ashahn? Do its voices tell you that you are not a traitor to the Q'shaathrah? Do your long dead ancestors speak to you, whispering of past glories, past honor? Do their lies soothe your—"

"Siah'ushu does not speak to me," he interrupted as he touched the dagger, briefly. "I've yet to prove myself worthy to hear its voice."

"Perhaps it's because you too often seek it in the bottle."

He flicked her a hateful glance, muttered, *"Sleep,"* and started for the door. "I'll wake you if the Rimmers require your attention."

You do that, she scowled at his retreating back then she slowly turned back to the fire pot. Baiting him had long been her hobby; with his archaic Elkanaghalli dialect and rigid, anachronistic code of personal conduct, he was just too tempting a target. He'd always been an active, albeit involuntary participant, but the pastime was rapidly losing its allure, just as his physical appearance was rapidly losing its attractiveness.

Sober, you were a challenge, not to mention very easy on the eye. Drunk, you're anything but. And in the past few days, he'd been drunk more than sober. *Game over.* He might not have provided any proof of the suspected mutiny or names of potential mutineers, a scheme even she doubted, but what she did have was even better, good enough, she hoped, to buy her passage back to *Makhaira* and into Tarqk's favors. *Oh, yes. Much, much better.*

She glanced over her shoulder at the doorway and took a cautious sniff of the air, filtering out all the noxious and at times overpowering odors this planet had on offer, looking for one particular spoor among the multitude. After a moment, and satisfied only his scent lingered, that he was indeed beyond eavesdropping distance, she withdrew her tac-net from its holster and brought the small device close to her lips. *"Makhaira..."*

— ii —

Qharubi, rousted from a very sound and well-deserved sleep by the com-op's urgent page, gave his hastily donned duty uniform one last check then took a deep, steadying breath as he pressed the airlock release.

It irised open and he stepped onto the bridge of *Makhaira*.

Tarqk was waiting for him. "What took you so long?"

"Ta'ahn, I—"

"There!" Tarqk pointed an accusing finger at the communications console. "A message from the planet!"

Startled, Qharubi replied with a curt nod and hurried over to the console.

He stopped behind the nervous com-op, slowly ran his eyes down the display and as he absorbed the brusque communiqué, his chest muscles tightened in mounting dread. *In the names of our ancestors, Khusaaq, what are you thinking?*

He re-read the message, said a silent prayer, for himself, for his kinsman, straightened up, turned—and to his surprise found Tarqk's scowl had been replaced by a smile. On this particular A'tuu'shahn the expression bore little resemblance to anything amicable, even to another A'tuu'shahn. It was a cold, fleeting smile, like the icy glint of light on a knife's honed edge. And surrounding that smile was a coarse-featured, hollow-cheeked face, capped by eagerly malevolent eyes, eyes that at that very moment were fixed on someone else: Tu'indai had just stepped onto the bridge.

Out of the tail of his eye, Qharubi watched her too. He felt a fresh stab of murderous rage at Khusaaq's bond-mate for her betrayal, but it was a reaction he dared not show. He was a loyal friend and kinsman, but—despite Tarqk's repeated assertions—he was no fool.

As Tu'indai slipped into her station, Tarqk reluctantly turned his attention back to Qharubi, his smile instantly replaced by a surly glare. He crooked a finger at his second and Qharubi dutifully stepped close.

"Well?"

"Most interesting, ta'ahn."

"Is that the best you can do, Sha'ashahn?" He feigned astonishment, then added, "Were the Q'shaathrah grossly misled when it came to your abilities? Based on all I've seen, I would certainly say so."

"I'll endeavor to be more precise—"

"Then do so!"

Qharubi hesitated—just an instant too long—and Tarqk added with a suspicious sneer, "Perhaps the shock of learning that the Hero of Cotopaxi is in fact a traitor has left you speechless?"

That comment drew an over-the-shoulder, decidedly pleased glance from Tu'indai before she quickly concealed her reaction.

"I'm understandably stunned, ta'ahn. Khusaaq Sha'ashahn has always impressed me as an officer of unquestionable honor and fidelity. Perhaps Mihr-Suhjai misunderstood his intentions?"

"*MISUNDERSTOOD?*" Tarqk bellowed, startling the bridge crew into a flurry of feigned activity. "He took prisoners and now he's taking them to the island! Well," he snorted, "he can show them anything he wants. No one's getting off that planet alive!"

"But—"

"But what?"

"Perhaps, if what Mihr-Suhjai reports is true..." Qharubi gave him a sidelong look. He knew he needed to tread lightly. Tu'indai had replaced Suhjai in Tarqk's affections, but it was remotely possible Suhjai could regain that favored position. "Then we must also consider the likelihood that Sha'ashahn took the Rimmers captive for some reason which Mihr-Suhjai, being only a *junior* medical officer, would not immediately grasp, and for which Sha'ashahn felt no obligation to explain—"

Tarqk crossed his arms. "Such as?"

"She reports that one of the prisoners claims to be the captain of the Coalition patrol ship."

Tarqk brushed aside the comment with a dismissive flick of his hand. "A typically feeble Rimmer ploy—a distraction!"

"Perhaps, ta'ahn. But what if this Rimmer is indeed who he claims to be? Perhaps Khusaaq Sha'ashahn was given convincing evidence and felt the risk of taking him prisoner was outweighed by his potential worth as a source of information on the abandoned base—"

"And as a bargaining chip?" Tarqk said.

The same thought had occurred to Qharubi and he kept his eyes fixed on the tactical display as he continued, "Why else would a Coalition vessel be patrolling this area but to keep watch on the base? And by taking his prisoners to the island—"

"It makes it that much more unlikely that their own vessel will be able to locate them once under its diffusion screen." Tarqk tugged at his lower lip. Finally and very grudgingly he admitted, "It might work."

Qharubi kept his relief to himself and his eyes staring straight ahead. "To our added advantage, ta'ahn," he said for good measure. *Not to mention Khusaaq's.*

Tarqk looked past him, asked, "Has *Acholilah* attained orbit yet?"

The com-op replied, "Not as yet, ta'ahn."

"The moment she does, contact her. Extend my warmest greetings and an invitation to Ru'asooli Kshira'tzrhi to honor us again with his presence aboard *Makhaira*. Tell him I wish to inform him of new developments."

The com-op's gaze darted to Qharubi but Qharubi knew better than to make eye contact with him. Tarqk frowned on such silent conversations among his crew and had, of late, the tendency to make the silence permanent.

"But ta'ahn—"

"But *what?*" Tarqk fixed his stare on the com-op.

"We risk revealing ourselves to the Coalition vessel."

"So? Unlike the Coalition, *we* have nothing to hide." Tarqk briefly fixed each member of the bridge crew with his chilling smile before adding in voice for all to hear, "The sooner they learn of our presence, the more time they'll have to prepare, making them a more sporting target, yes?"

There was the requisite murmur of agreement and forced, barking chuckles from the crew and Tarqk's smile broadened into a smug grin. "Yes. Things are turning out better than even I could have planned."

— iii —

Amalfitano, sensing he was being watched, looked up to find the *Baidarka*'s intelligence officer, Zarijan Izraad, leaning against the doorframe of his office.

"Am I interrupting anything?"

He dropped his gaze back to the stack of report flimsies. Unless invited or ordered to do so, Izraad rarely violated the protective mental barriers of others. But there were times when she surreptitiously eavesdropped, augmenting her genetically enhanced ability to 'smell' emotional states with her telepathic skill to sift through the stray images and thoughts that constantly flowed around her.

And this, Amalfitano felt, was just one of those times. "Just going over the labs on Niebuhr and Arctoi."

"And?"

"Nothing definitive."

"Then maybe you should take a break? Jenna tells me you haven't eaten all day."

"Been busy."

"Too busy to have dinner with me?" She pushed herself away from the doorframe and sauntered very suggestively towards him.

He couldn't help but chuckle.

Zarijan Izraad was not beautiful. In fact she was quite ordinary looking, bordering on plain. With her shy smile and soft-spoken approach that immediately put people at ease, she was anything but intimidating. On her tiny frame her Intelligence grays acted more like protective coloration, helping her blend into the background, unnoticed. But cloaked in that unpretentious uniform and modest demeanor was one of those extremely rare individuals who was not only a telepath, but also a true chempath: her body could generate chemical compounds at will that could break down any mental barrier, and that meant that Zarijan Izraad was, simply put, the most formidable person he'd ever met.

It certainly keeps our love life interesting... Then, realizing by her expression that she'd 'overheard' the thought, he added quickly, "I suppose I could take a break."

"And maybe after dinner..." She sat on the edge of his desk and fingered the collar of his medreds. "We could revisit that love life? It's been a tad neglected of late."

"I know, and it's not like I haven't wanted to," he protested, "it's just—"

"You know what they say, all work and no pleasure makes William a very dull boy." She leaned close, nibbled his earlobe then caressing his chin whispered, "We can't have that now, can we?"

"No, we most certainly cannot," he replied and started to push himself out of his chair. "In fact, I'm not that hungry, so how 'bout we wait on dinner and—"

"Doctor Amalfitano?" the com-op's voice crackled from the desk speaker.

He sighed, slumped back into his chair, grumbled, "Now what?" and thumbed the switch. "Amalfitano here."

"Sir, you're to report to Lieutenant Teague's cabin, immediately."

He raised his brows, replied, "Tell him I'm on my way," and looked at the equally baffled Izraad. "No break for the horny, as they say."

— iv —

Amalfitano gave the gray-framed door a sharp rap with his knuckles, then, as the door opened, he stepped in. "You wanted to see me, Edwin?"

"Take a seat. Be with you shortly."

"Look, can this wait? I'm—"

"I *said* I'd be with you shortly."

Amalfitano sat then squinted at Teague, who never once looked up from the flimsy he held. While he couldn't prove it, he swore Teague was just making him wait... and wait, for no other reason than to make him wait.

Just as he was about to make his suspicions known, Teague set the flimsy aside and cleared his throat and Amalfitano straightened up in his chair.

"Now," Teague began, "we need to talk. To be more precise, *I* need to talk and *you* need to listen for once."

"Okay, I'm lis—"

"You will never, I repeat *never* undermine my authority in front of the crew again."

Amalfitano couldn't help but snort. "You don't need me, Edwin. You're doing a helluva job all on—"

"Like it or not, until we recover Commander Aquila, or make contact with HQ, I'm in command."

"Of course, *Lieutenant*. Is that all? Because if it is—"

"It isn't."

"Look, Edwin, the lecture can wait—"

"I'm done with my 'lecture'." He fixed his stare on the stack of flimsies as if they were his primary interest.

Amalfitano pushed himself out the chair. "Good, 'cuz—"

"Sit down. That's an order."

Amalfitano hesitated, just long enough to draw Teague's narrowed gaze then he threw himself back into the chair with a loud huff of breath.

Seemingly satisfied, Teague thumbed the log recorder toggle on his desk. He took a deep, steadying breath then began speaking in the clipped, asthmatic monotone Amalfitano was convinced he saved for those times when he wanted to bore or anger. In this case, Amalfitano realized, he was probably aiming for both.

"Ship's log, Lieutenant Teague reporting in the absence of Commander Robert Aquila..."

He then began a detailed retelling of events leading up to the present situation, starting with the Matarran ambush that had left twenty eight crewmembers dead—over a tenth of the crew—including the captain. Then he moved on to the wholly unexpected orders to divert from the *Baidarka*'s intended destination of Mirfak Prime and its desperately needed repair bays to search for the missing passenger liner, *Herrick*, the automated distress call that had drawn them to this isolated system, and lastly to the disastrous first landing. All the while, Amalfitano impatiently fidgeted in his chair.

"...two and half hours after the recovery of Private Arctoi and Crewman Niebuhr," Teague concluded, "I, as acting captain..."

"The blind leading the blind," Amalfitano grumbled.

"...decided to risk another flick-down, taking advantage of this phase of stellar quiescence in order to attempt a ground search for the missing. After three hours of fruitless search, we succeeded only in downloading some very fragmentary data from the wreck's severely damaged comp—" He stopped and patted his breast pocket, drawing Amalfitano's arched stare, then pulled out the disc and with a sidelong glance at Amalfitano stuffed it in the slot of his desktop computer. "With surface conditions rapidly deteriorating, I decided to abandon the on-planet search. The data recovered from the wreck is currently being deciphered," he added, to which Amalfitano pointedly coughed, "but I doubt it'll be of much help in explaining the fate of her crew or our missing.

"Once the newest phase in activity decreases, which computer extrapolation states will occur in a little over twenty five hours, I'll order a full sweep of the planet, using both the onboard scanners and the array of sensors we left behind on the planet. End log." He switched off the recorder and met Amalfitano's annoyed squint. "I asked you here to listen to my official entry into the captain's log. In your opinion, does that accurately cover—"

"I thought you didn't want my opinion," he replied irritably.

"I said you were not to undermine my authority—"

"Then I'd like my official request for a physical on you to be logged, along with the reasons for your refusal. As you yourself just stated in the log, we don't know what the hell we're dealing with."

"Doctor, the subject of my physical is closed. I've already explained the reasons for my decision. I don't intend on repeating them."

"There's no need to repeat them, *dammit*, I heard you the first time—"

"That's refreshing to hear because I, unlike Captain Vildur, have no intention of repeating orders—"

Amalfitano felt a flush of anger and before he could stop himself, he lurched forward in his chair, startling Teague into pushing back into his. "What the hell's eating at you? You've been acting like you've got a thorn in your side ever since you got back from the planet!"

Teague, recovered from his initial surprise, fired back with equal heat: "I'm acting in a manner consistent with Expeditionary Forces regulations, Doctor. And you're judging proper behavior of a commanding officer by the standards set by Captain Vildur, and she, in my opinion, always showed far too much leniency towards the crew and you—*especially* you!"

Amalfitano fell back into the chair and stared at him in open mouthed disbelief, then snarled, "Why you... *you cold-blooded bastard!* Gildun Vildur was the best battle commander in the fleet and for some god knows reason considered you not only a competent officer but a close friend! Now she's dead you take the opportunity to stab her in the back?"

"The operative word is *was*. As you yourself just pointed out, Doctor, Captain Vildur is dead. And now that Commander Aquila's been lost, I'm in command and I will not tolerate your meddling or your incessant demands—"

"That's it, isn't it? That's why you insisted you flick down, even though it went against all those damned regs you hold so near and dear—"

"I elected to lead the search party because I won't ask a member of the crew to volunteer for a mission that I myself wouldn't, just as Commander—"

"And that's why you won't send another search party down!" he blurted out, "You're worried they might *find* Robert!"

Teague stared at him in genuine shock. "Are you seriously accusing me—"

"Well, we'll see what HQ says about all this!" Amalfitano lurched to his feet.

Teague replied with a clipped, "You haven't been dismissed."

Amalfitano opened his mouth but Teague held up his hand—a shaky hand, Amalfitano noticed. "Your behavior is bordering on insubordination. I strongly suggest that from here on out, you carefully weigh your actions and words."

Amalfitano wisely snapped his mouth shut.

"Good. Now, I'm ordering you to return to sickbay, and there you're to remain. *Understood?"*

Amalfitano replied with a curt nod.

"Now you're dismissed." Teague thumbed the door release and Amalfitano spun on his heel and stalked out.

Chapter 4

Aquila started awake, eyes snapping open. *"Huh!"*

"It's just me, sir," replied a calm, female voice.

He peered at the shadowy figure kneeling beside him and croaked angrily, "Who the hell is 'me'?"

"Corsali, sir. Ensign Corsali?"

Corsali? He squinted into the gloom, expecting to find the familiar contours of his cabin as he growled, "What're you doing here…" His voice trailed off as he realized that wherever he was, it wasn't his cabin. He turned his perplexed stare back on her. "Where…?"

"I can hear movement below, sir. Must be getting close to dawn and I thought—"

"Yes, yes of course," he muttered, still unsure of exactly where he was as he cautiously levered himself onto his elbows; the movement re-ignited the throbbing ache in his flank and his head began to pound in sickening cadence. But on the upside, the pain also sharpened his thoughts. *Now I remember—*

"How do you feel?"

"Sore as hell—" He jerked his head up, looked around again. *"Gianakis?"*

"Whatever their medic gave him last night helped—*sir,"* she glanced worriedly over her shoulder then turned back to him and whispered, *"someone's coming."*

"Hope to hell it's room service." He tossed the blanket aside and lurched to his knees.

"Here, sir, let me help you."

He gratefully took her offered hands, said, "Thanks, wasn't sure I could manage," and staggered to his feet, then continued to hold onto her as his vision blurred and his knees wobbled. "Don't know 'bout you," he said with half a smile, "but I'm dying for a cuppa coffee."

Corsali glanced to her left and he followed her now frightened gaze to find a shadowy figure in the doorway.

"What do you want?" he grumbled as he let go of her only to press his hand against his side.

"Ah, so you are awake. Excellent!"

He instantly recognized the mercenary officer's irritatingly cheerful voice and was mildly surprised to find himself relaxing just a little as the merc stepped into the cabin.

"I did not wish to awaken you, but—"

"Rather difficult to sleep under the circumstances," Aquila grumbled, tugging his torn and blood-stained softsuit into some semblance of order as the Hahtooshan walked past him, over to the cabin's small table and set something on it.

He heard a muffled *click*, then a bright flare of light dazzled his eyes and he instinctively shielded them with his hand. A moment later the cabin was bathed in soft green lamplight.

"Much better." The merc turned back to them and smiled.

To Aquila's annoyance, the creature looked to be no worse for his excesses of the night before. Nor did he appear to be harboring any grudges. In fact, he looked almost... smug. *Gods only know what you've got up your sleeve—*

"Suhjai'll be up shortly—says it's time for a booster and a dressing change."

"Oh, joy," Aquila whispered under his breath as the merc shifted his gaze to the doorway.

"Ah, here she is, as well as something hot to eat and drink if I'm not mistaken."

Suhjai entered the cabin, followed by a Blatto carrying a bottle and tray piled high with small, steaming spheres.

Without looking at or speaking to anyone, Suhjai knelt beside Gianakis, roughly jerking the blanket off him in the process, while the Blatto placed the tray on the table, cautiously handed the bottle to the officer and hastily withdrew.

"Commander," the merc began, "I cannot offer you... *coffee*, but I hope this will suffice?" He held out the bottle and motioned to the tray and the mound of mottled greenish-brown globes. "And something hot to eat, yes?"

Aquila glanced at the tray. Despite the food's unappetizing color and the throbbing pain that left him slightly queasy—not to mention the mercenary's warning of the night before—he found his mouth watering at the spheres' warm, bread-like aroma.

"This is the standard fare of the natives while at sea and quite edible." To prove his point, the alien took a sphere, tore off a bite-sized piece and stuffed it in his mouth. As he chewed, tattooed and scarified cheeks bulging, he smiled at Aquila and again offered him the bottle.

What the hell. Aquila accepted the bottle, hoping whatever it was would dull the pain as he seriously doubted he'd be offered anything to ease the constant throbbing—and he was damned if he was going to *ask* a merc for something, anything, least of all a painkiller. *They might just take me literally.*

Frowning at the officer, as if the withholding of anything for the pain was a done deal, he took a small, tentative sip from the bottle. It wasn't the ale, rather it was something sweet and it was piping hot. He swallowed his mouthful, took another, deeper gulp and another then offered the bottle to Corsali.

She shook her head.

The merc, not to be outdone in the courtesy department, picked up another of the spheres, tore it in two and offered the steaming halves to her.

This time, and to Aquila's chagrin, she reluctantly took one of the pieces and murmured, "Ah, thank you, Sha'ashahn."

In reply the merc's smile broke into a broad and decidedly disarming grin. "You're most welcome, Ensign." He then flicked Suhjai a cold stare as they all overheard her muffled grunt of contempt.

Suhjai scowled back at him, then looked at Aquila and held up a ject-it. "This is from your own emergency packs. It's a mild stimulant and broad-spectrum antibiotic. Do I have your permission to give it to him?"

"I… suppose so," Aquila replied uneasily as Corsali knelt and carefully rolled up Gianakis' sleeve, clearly wanting to spare the corporal more of Suhjai's rough treatment.

True to form, Suhjai wasted no time or gentleness as she shoved the ject-it against the man's exposed forearm; she then gathered up the medical kit and got back to her feet. "Now you." She motioned to Aquila as she loaded the ject-it with another vial. "This is a booster to the injection I gave you yesterday—and something for the pain, yes?"

Unwilling to admit his relief and yes, his surprise, he simply unbuckled his collar and shrugged off his softsuit to expose his shoulder, wanting to get this ordeal over with, suspecting Suhjai would make it as unpleasant as possible.

She didn't waste any time and pressed the ject-it against his skin. The metal cylinder was ice-cold and he reacted with a sharp, involuntary intake of breath.

"Rimmer," she snorted, "I haven't even given you the injection yet!"

He felt is face flush, but before he could reply, he gasped again as she pressed the ject-it's activator and the medicine was delivered with an eye-watering, bee-like sting. *Damn!*

She slipped the tool back into the kit, then, to his astonishment, began to massage his bare shoulder with surprising gentleness. "I'm truly amazed how *soft* you Rimmers are," she purred as she continued to knead the cold-stiff muscle with very warm fingers—hate as he did to admit it, it actually felt good. Really, *really* good. So much so he briefly wished she'd move on to his equally sore neck and shoulders, in the process not fully grasping what she'd said until she added, "And you a Coalition officer. I would've thought that of anyone, you'd be in top physical condition."

Aquila stared at her, not sure what to say, but the instant she let go he hurriedly pulled up his sleeve as her companion chuckled, "I believe you've insulted our guest, Suhjai."

"I spoke the truth. Rimmers *are* soft. Any A'tuu'shahn worth his family glyph would never allow himself to fall into such a pathetic physical state."

Aquila opened his mouth, too late realizing he had no suitably withering come-back and was saved by a soft moan from Gianakis, which drew everyone's attention.

Corsali leaned close and lightly touched the man's arm. "Nico?"

The corporal opened his eyes and looked at her for a moment, blinked, looked some more and managed a very confused and raspy, "Ensign?"

She smiled and nodded.

Aquila squatted beside her, in the process drawing the man's muzzy gaze. "You had us worried there for a while."

"Sir... what happ—" Gianakis' eyes widened and he hissed, *"Aliens, sir! I—"*

"We know," Corsali interrupted, placing her hand on his arm. "Just don't..."

The marine started to sit up, groaned and squeezed his eyes shut against a grimace.

"...move," she ended lamely as Aquila turned his anxious stare on Suhjai.

She knelt across from Aquila and clicking her tongue, ran her hand over the corporal's bandaged and splinted thigh.

Gianakis reopened his eyes and stared blankly at her for a moment then his body stiffened. *"YOU!"* he snarled and made a grab for his non-existent weapon.

Aquila grasped his wrist with one hand and planted his other hand squarely on the corporal's chest. "It's all right—"

"But—"

"This is Suhjai." Aquila jerked his chin towards her as he got a firmer grip on the man's wrist. "She *saved* your life, Corporal."

Gianakis' bewildered eyes flicked to her and then back to Aquila. *"Sir?"*

"And this," Aquila looked up as the officer stepped closer, "is Sha'ashahn—"

"Chercjengh'qhusaaq Abhijit'tischinjgra," the imposing merc interrupted as his left hand came to rest on the grip of his holstered pistol. "Of the A'tuu'shahn Orthodoxy..."

Gianakis mouthed, *Hahtooshan?* and shot Aquila a horrified glance, to which Aquila nodded unhappily.

"...you and your companions are my *guests*, Corporal. I strongly urge that you behave accordingly."

"Just relax," Aquila said as he loosened his grip, just a little. "Everything's under control."

"But sir—"

"I'll explain everything later." *If I can*, he added to himself. "You're to cooperate with our... *hosts*—understood?"

Gianakis gave him a look that said he clearly didn't understand, more importantly didn't even want to understand.

"That's an *order*," Aquila added, the throbbing pain edging his voice. *"Got it?"*

Gianakis replied grudgingly, "Yessir," then looked away, fixing his narrowed eyes on the nearby slat-work wall.

Leaving him to Corsali, hoping she might talk some sense into him, Aquila lurched to his feet, snatched up the bottle and quickly took another swig of the hot liquid to conceal his own grimace of pain.

"Commander." The Hahtooshan also stepped away from Gianakis, clearly hoping by doing so he'd defuse the situation, "perhaps you'd like to see where we're headed?"

Aquila choked on his mouthful, startled; he quickly swallowed, wiped his mouth on the back of his hand and answered huskily, "What? I mean, yes, of course."

He unclipped a small device from his belt then held it out for Aquila who, after a moment's hesitation, plucked it from his open hand.

The mercenary stepped close, to stand next to him and as Aquila tried to ignore their difference in height not to mention their decidedly uncomfortable proximity. The Hahtooshan tapped his gauntleted fingertip on a flashing telltale on the tiny display. "We're *here*, relative to the mainland. Yes?"

At Aquila's uncertain nod, he slid his finger across the screen to a cluster of other markers. "We're headed for this archipelago, specifically this island." He again tapped the screen. "It's there you'll see for yourself the irrefutable proof of my claims."

Aquila kept his slitted eyes fixed on the display. *Sure. And there really is an Easter Bunny.* After an awkward pause, he said, "How long will it take to reach this island?"

The merc cocked his head to one side and studied his bruise-swollen face for a moment, then said, "Not quite ready to trust me, are you, Commander?"

Aquila looked up. Confronted yet again by the alien's doggedly friendly smile, all of the frustration, fear and unremitting pain that whatever Suhjai had given him hadn't even touched, not to mention his long-held hatreds suddenly came to a head and he snapped, "Why the hell should I? For all I know this could be just a hoax to keep us here, away from what you mercs are really up to—like maybe using some defenseless passenger liner as target practice?"

What followed was a very long, very tense pause. Long enough for Aquila to swallow convulsively despite trying desperately not to;

long enough for him to realize that somewhere along the line he'd forgotten whom he was dealing with; long enough for him to wonder how he was about to die: would the Hahtooshan yield to his visible anger and make it quick and relatively painless or would he choose prolonged and agonizing, finding that method far more satisfying—

The merc snatched the device back from his hand then without saying a word turned and stalked out of the cabin.

Aquila, realizing he was not about to die, blinked and let loose the breath he didn't realize he'd been holding then, overhearing a soft, derisive chuckle, he glanced over his shoulder.

Suhjai favored him with a dangerously pleased smile, then she too left... with decidedly triumphant swagger.

As he stared after her, it dawned on him that he'd played right into those deceptively delicate hands of hers. He clenched his teeth and balled his fists. *Dammit! Dammit all to hell!*

Suddenly remembering Corsali and Gianakis, he turned to them only to find Corsali staring back at him with an expression of surprise and, he realized, utter exasperation. Gianakis just looked mightily confused.

He clenched his teeth and squeezed his eyes shut. *You certainly blew that, didn't you, you fucking idiot! What the hell were you thinking? What's to stop him now from throwing us overboard?*

"Sir?" Corsali asked, "Maybe you should lie down, give what Suhjai gave you a chance to work?"

"I'm fine. Leave it."

"Sir?" Gianakis asked hoarsely as he managed to leaver himself up onto one elbow. "Why are we cooperating with these... these *butchers?* If we—"

"Corporal," Corsali interrupted, stepping between the two, clearly assuming the worst from both and not without good reason Aquila was forced to admit to himself, "what would you have us do? Overpower them? The three of us? Against," she waved her hand about, "who knows exactly how many? At least ten, maybe more—"

"But... but sir," Gianakis looked past her to Aquila, effectively dismissing her, "we can't just do nothing! If we were to grab the female—"

"That's enough, dammit!" Aquila snarled, startling both Gianakis and Corsali. He quickly turned away and gripping his side

with one hand, the cabin's center pole with the other, squeezed his eyes shut and clenched his teeth against the sudden urge to vomit.

"Sir," Corsali touched his arm and drew his wary, decidedly pinched stare as he visibly gulped down the nausea, "you really need to lie down—you look like you're about to collapse."

He almost nodded—*almost,* as she was giving him a face-saving way out of the unholy mess he'd just created. He knew she knew what she was doing, and worse, she knew he knew she knew it and *that* made him even angrier. He *was* tired, damned tired and his side and head hurt to the point it was hard to push past it, much less to stay angry, even at himself. He glanced back to where he'd left the blanket and suddenly wasn't sure if he could make it that far. He could sit down right where he was, but close to the doorway, it wasn't as sheltered. *Just a few meters—you can make it.*

As if reading his thoughts, she wrapped her fingers around his elbow. "I'll help you, sir, come on."

"But what about the officer, he—"

"I doubt he'll be back for a while."

He replied with a sickly smile, nodded, "Yeah," and this time, using her proffered arm for support, he walked slowly and unsteadily back to his sleeping spot, painfully aware that Gianakis was watching him the entire way, watching him noticeably wobble with each step, taking in his blood-stained softsuit, his badly bruised face. He worried what thoughts might be racing through the young corporal's mind. Heroic thoughts, no doubt, even if it meant disobeying a direct order.

The last thing he wanted to do was to trip, or worse, fall—not out of male pride, he assured himself. No. Not even out of fear it might encourage Gianakis into some well-meaning but reckless act that would indeed get them all killed. It was because any sudden jolt would only make the pain that much worse and make escape into sleep impossible—at least not without calling for Suhjai and he wasn't sure he could face that.

He reached their sleeping spot, a corner of the cabin out of the draft without incident despite the rolling deck and his rubbery legs and with a sigh of relief he slipped from Corsali's embrace and carefully eased himself back down onto the deck.

He stretched out and as she covered him with the blanket, he met her gaze.

"I'll keep first watch," she said, and he knew who she'd be watching. "Try to get some sleep. I'll wake you in a few hours."

He nodded and closed his eyes, then exhaling, suddenly exhausted... and, he realized, in less pain and no longer nauseous. He allowed his battered body to relax, in the process letting the drug to finally take full hold.

— ii —

"William...?"

Amalfitano opened his eyes and squinted at the familiar figure silhouetted in the open doorway of his private cabin. "Yeah, Jenna, what is it?" He rolled over and hit the bedside light activator.

The expression on the doctor's face was like a punch to the stomach. The words were worse. "Arctoi's dead."

He sat up. "Why didn't you come get me?"

Jenna Fleming started to reply, but he waved it off with a muttered, "Never mind," then rose from his bunk as he gave his gritty eyes a brisk rub. "Tell me everything that happened."

"Better yet, I'll show you."

He followed Fleming as she walked out of his darkened cabin, into his adjoining sickbay office and over to the report strewn desk. With the press of a button, she activated the desktop terminal's screen.

Amalfitano sat as she requested chronological readings from Private Arctoi's medical file.

As the computer began displaying the data, she leaned over his shoulder and pointed. "There, at oh-one twenty six, that's when the arachnoid hemorrhaging began, see?"

"Yeah."

"At oh-one twenty nine there was a discrete change in cardiac output. By now renal shutdown was complete. Platelet levels had dropped to less than ten thousand. I initiated a total blood exchange at oh-one thirty."

Amalfitano looked up. "That would have made a total of what, four...?"

"Five."

"...on him in the past eight hours alone."

"Yeah, but what else could we do?"

Amalfitano nodded then watched the screen as it replayed the last minutes of the young marine's life functions.

"There, see?" she said as her fingertip touched the screen. "That's when it became obvious that the exchange wasn't working."

He saw a dramatic change in cardiac output and central venous pressure. Platelet and fibrinogen counts were non-existent, despite the transfusions.

"He died at oh-one thirty five."

"Nine minutes!" He pushed himself to his feet. *"Nine god-damned minutes!"* He began to pace his office, unaware that a handful of his equally haggard staff—two medtechs, an optech and a nurse—now stood in the doorway that opened onto sprawling sickbay, watching him.

After several circuits, he stopped beside Fleming and looked her in the eye—a very blood-shot eye he noticed. "Sorry, Jenna. I know you," he motioned to the techs and nurse, "and you did everything you could, too."

"Yeah," Fleming replied; the others merely shrugged.

He looked at the screen. "There's gotta be an answer. There's just gotta be!"

"But can we find it soon enough?" she replied.

"And what about the others?" one of the medtechs countered. "If they—"

"There's no point in speculating." Amalfitano turned to Fleming. "Have those path' reports come back yet?"

"Not yet."

"What the hell's taking so long?" He punched the com-toggle. "Lab!"

After a moment, a weary voice answered, *"Lab, Tasende here—"*

"Anything?"

"So far all the cultures are negative, Chief. Nothing seems to touch these bugs. One thing though, their growth rate's slowed somewhat, but I suspect that's a result of the lack of growing space within the cultures rather than a drug induced alteration in reproductive activity. We might have a co-factor at work here."

"My thoughts too."

There was a moment of silence then Tasende asked, *"Something's happened, hasn't it?"*

"Just lost Arctoi."

"Ay chingado," the pathologist swore softly, then, *"I'll try to speed things up,"* and cut the connection.

Amalfitano looked at Fleming. "Are the levels of bishydroxycoumarin showing any change?"

"Nothing conclusive, at least not yet."

He rubbed the back of his neck. "Has Teague been notified?"

"No, I thought—"

"I'll do it. Go get some coffee or something—all of you." He waved them off and as Fleming and the others shuffled out of the office, he glanced at the chronometer. *Oh-one fifty.* He thumbed the desk-com activator. "Control."

"C and C," came the disembodied reply from the com-op, Masursky.

"Amalfitano here. I need to speak with Lieutenant Teague."

"But sir, it's—"

"Now."

"Yessir."

There was a long pause, then Teague's sleep-raspy voice crackled from the speaker, *"Yes, Doc—"*

"Arctoi's dead."

There was another pause, then: *"Be right there."*

A few minutes later, Amalfitano heard a knock at his office door.

"Come." He looked up as Teague stepped into his office and raised a brow at the man's uncharacteristically rumpled appearance. He'd always suspected Teague of being the sort who starched his underwear. *You look like you were sleeping in your command blues—*

"When?"

"A coupla minutes ago."

"How, I mean, exactly what—"

"Massive hemorrhage."

"Any idea what we're dealing with?"

"Basically, yes." Amalfitano motioned to a nearby chair, waited until Teague sat down then began, "The culprit's a gram negative bacterium. Hemorrhaging's due to an endotoxin produced when the alien bacteria invades the circulatory system." He stopped as Teague blinked back a yawn and felt a twinge at waking the man rather than waiting a few hours. Arctoi certainly wouldn't have cared either way.

He tapped an order into the desk's servo-panel. "What we're dealing with, in essence, is a form of disseminated intravascular coagulation or defibrinogenation syndrome—"

"DIC," Teague interrupted with tired impatience as he ran both hands over his balding head. "Heard of it."

Undeterred, Amalfitano continued, "The bacterium was introduced into Arctoi and Niebuhr's blood stream through puncture wounds, which led to sepsis. An endotoxin was produced and a rapid decrease in platelet formation occurred. The bacterium also weakens the vascular wall, causing capillaries to rupture. Combined with few or no platelets and a dysfunctional fibrinogen production, they developed numerous small hemorrhages and—" He was interrupted by a soft chime.

He turned to the servo-door behind his desk and withdrew two steaming cups of coffee. "Here."

Teague fought back another yawn as he accepted one. "Can you give me something to keep me on my feet for, say, the next twenty four hours?"

"Wouldn't recommend it."

"I'm not asking you to recommend it," he snapped.

Amalfitano stared at him, lips pursed.

"Okay, make you a deal," Teague replied in a marginally more conciliatory tone. "Keep me on my feet and thinking clearly for the next twenty four hours, long enough for the interference to lessen, long enough for us to scan the surface for the missing and, with any luck, recover them, and then get the hell out this blasted system and I'll—"

"Present yourself for a full physical?"

Teague eyed him then nodded in weary capitulation.

"Stay put." Amalfitano strode out of his office and over to the main sickbay's central console. As he opened a drug cart, he found himself briefly tempted to give the man a short-acting sedative, just enough to give him a few hours of much needed sleep. Instead he grabbed a vial of stimulant and a ject-it and walked back into the office. "In Niebuhr's case we've been able to control the localize hemorrhages—"

"Huh?" Teague flinched, almost spilling his coffee. "Oh, uh, yes, yes of course."

"Roll up your damned sleeve."

Teague did as he was told and Amalfitano pressed the ject-it against his forearm. "This'll keep you... well not exactly bright-eyed and bushy-tailed, but awake and functional for twenty four hours, give or take an hour, but after that, you'd best find a bunk and find it *fast*. Understood?"

Teague nodded as he tried his best to smooth out his wrinkled sleeve. "Twenty four hours. Bunk. Got it."

Amalfitano sat down on the corner of his desk and stared at the expended ject-it. "Now, as I was saying, at least in Niebuhr's case, we've been able to control the hemorrhages with massive infusions of coagulation factors, aggressive hormone therapy and vitamin K infusions.

"Unfortunately, as we suspected, and later confirmed with Arctoi, this is just an early stage. The disease soon progresses to massive disruption in blood flow and hemorrhages in major organs and the brain. Renal shutdown is usually the first sign of this stage—"

"And you believe the creatures that attacked the landing party are the vectors?"

"No doubt about it—right now we're managing to keep Niebuhr stable with platelet and plasma concentrates, blood expanders, coag factors and continuous protamine sulfate and phytonadione infusions. If he shows any signs of further bleeding, we'll have no option but to initiate total blood transfers, not that it was very successful when we did it on Arctoi. Besides, there's always a risk of DIC occurring strictly due to the transfusions, unassociated with the DIC produced by the endotoxin and—" He was interrupted again, this time by the bleat of the intercom; he thumbed the toggle and said irritably, "Yes?"

"Sir," Masursky began, *"is Lieutenant Teague with you?"*

Teague leaned forward. "Teague here."

"Sir," came a new voice, Ensign Ife Lesedi's voice, *"would you please come to Control?"*

Teague and Amalfitano exchanged uneasy glances. The woman's distinctive, clipped voice was audibly tainted with a note of urgency. "Is there a problem?"

"Very possibly, sir."

"On my way." Teague pushed himself out of his chair and strode from the office.

Amalfitano looked down at the stack of report flimsies on his desk, then at Arctoi's data still active on his desktop's screen and finally back to the open doorway. With a shrug, he hurried after Teague, catching up to him just as Teague stepped into the control room and was mildly surprised when Teague didn't immediately order him back to sickbay. *Maybe he's forgotten?*

"Sir," Lesedi rose from her weapons console, "scanners just picked up a brief, intense surge—"

"From the binary?"

"Nossir, it appears to have originated from deep space, but was deflected by the planet's upper atmosphere."

Teague turned to the woman manning the scanner console. "Can you pin-point point of origin?"

Cyllo gave her monitor another quick study before replying, "Computer enhancement suggests it was actually a tight beam transmission, but too garbled, and brief, and the EM interference too disruptive to determine its contents or precise point of origin."

Amalfitano felt a cold knot form in his belly. "What the hell—"

Teague's eyes cut to him.

So. Not forgotten. He pressed his lips tightly together. *I'm allowed as long as I stay quiet. Deal.*

"But it was definitely not emanating from the planet," Teague offered.

"Definitely not, sir." Cyllo knit her brows as she gave the readings another look. "That's... odd."

"What's odd?" Teague asked sharply.

"Further analysis suggests a double bounce-back, sir, most likely caused by the mirroring of the original reflection on the ion curtain."

"Most likely?"

Cyllo twisted around in her chair to face him, said, "Positive, sir—" and turned back to her display as it chirped loudly. "Sir! Hahtooshan ship off the port bow!"

"What?" Teague gasped.

"Caravel-class—"

"She's just beyond flatspace weapons range," Lesedi added matter-of-factly.

Amalfitano glanced around, realized everyone was staring at Teague, then he too turned to the man to find him frozen in place, staring blankly at Cyllo and the cold knot in his belly jerked tight. *For god sakes, Edwin, now's not the time—*

"Sir?" Lesedi prompted uneasily. "Sir, what are your orders?"

"Ah..." Teague licked his lips as his eyes flicked to her.

"Go to yellow alert, sir?" Lesedi offered.

He nodded a little too vigorously, "Yes, yes—yellow alert."

"Sir." Cyllo looked up briefly. "They're trying to maintain their distance, just out of range. They seem unaware of the residual ionic effect on their ship's hull, making it more reflective to scanner sweep. I don't think they realize we've spotted them—"

"Maybe they haven't spotted us, either," the tac-op, Zayyad, offered with little conviction.

Lesedi responded to him with a sickly smile. "Oh, yeah."

Amalfitano, overhearing the echo of rapidly approaching footsteps, turned towards the airlock just as Izraad stepped into the cramped control room. He felt a brief flush of relief at the sight of the woman. *Salvation! Thank the gods—*

"I was notified we have a situation?" Izraad asked.

Amalfitano wanted to kiss the com-op. Instead he flicked Masursky a tight smile and a nod of thanks; the comp-op replied with an ever so slight tip of the head.

"We have uninvited company," the navigator, Pardix, growled.

"Goddamned mercs," Lesedi said, "can you believe it?"

"This isn't a disputed system," Teague said. Then he looked at Izraad and his eyes widened. *"The wreck!"*

"And the missing liner?" Amalfitano added as his imagination, fueled by mounting dread and long simmering hatreds, jumped from one possibility to another, each one more horrific than the last. "And what about Robert and the—"

"Let's not get ahead of ourselves," Izraad interrupted in a firm, composed tone, and turned to the scanner operator. "Any improvement in surface readings?"

Cyllo shifted her intense stare from one active screen to another. "Improving slightly. Still impossible to locate the missing landing party—*sir!* The Hahtooshan ship's changed course—"

"Tactical display," Teague ordered.

"Aye," Zayyad replied as his fingers raced over his weapons console.

Amalfitano, following Izraad's lead, fixed his apprehensive gaze on a three-dimensional, holographic grid that formed, suspended half way between deck and overhead. It was immediately speckled with numerous telltales and one bright red, oscillating blip.

As everyone watched in uneasy silence, the blip changed to a solid, quickly enlarging dot and Cyllo twisted around to face Teague. "Sir, she's definitely spotted us—"

"Sir," Lesedi said, glancing over her shoulder, "she's altering course to bring her within weapons range."

This time Teague needed no prompting and blurted out, *"Go to red alert!"*

Chapter 5

"Sir, incoming message from the Hahtooshan ship."

Teague took a deep breath, clasped his clammy hands behind his back and drawing upon the officious persona that was his stock and trade, his private body armor, answered with a steadiness of voice that belied his true, knee-knocking reaction, "Put it through."

"Aye, sir," Masursky replied, adding, "Audio only, no visual," as the harsh crackle of interstellar static instantly filled the deathly quiet control room.

Teague turned to Izraad, eyebrows raised.

"Standard Hahtooshan practice, sir."

Pardix muttered, *"Cowardly bast—"*

"Who are you?" a harsh, metallic voice boomed from the com station speaker, startling everyone and causing Pardix to visibly flinch, *"and what are you doing in this system?"*

Teague cleared his throat then began with a steadiness of voice that belied his inner panic, "This is the CEFS *Baidarka*. Our presence here is not a provocative one, Hahtooshan vessel. We diverted here in response to a distress call."

Several seconds passed; the only response was the wavering hiss and snap of static, then a new voice, only slightly less gruff than the first, said, *"This is Tarqk Nahru'tzrhi of the A'tuu'shahn Orthodoxy vessel* Makhaira. *To whom am I speaking?"*

"This is Lieutenant Teague—"

"I'll speak only with your vessel's captain, Lieutenant."

Teague squinted at the blip and did his best to sound indignant. "You *are* speaking with him, Nahru'tzrhi."

There was a short, sharp bark of what he assumed passed for Hahtooshan laughter, then the alien, said, *"Oh yes? Well then, Captain Teague, to the business at hand. As you may have surmised, the wrecked vessel on the planet below is one of ours…"*

Teague's eyes again flicked to Izraad; this time she stared back with equal surprise.

"...and now that we're here, there's absolutely no need for you to remain. In fact the quicker you depart the better as this system is highly unstable and I wouldn't wish the fate that befell our scout craft to befall your poorly shielded patrol ship as well."

Teague couldn't help but scowl at the suspended tactical display. As the first line of defense against any Matarran invasion, the *Baidarka* was highly maneuverable and exceedingly swift, but she was also armed to the teeth, outfitted with more firepower, not to mention more shielding than most cruisers twice her size. *Just ask the Matarrans,* he added with a private, very grim smile, *who picked on the wrong goddamned—*

"Tell that f'ing merc to go to stuff itself, Edwin!" Amalfitano whispered.

Teague motioned the com-op to cut the audio as he glared at the doctor.

"The doc's right, sir," Lesedi cut in. "We only have that merc's 'word', if you can call it that," she jabbed a finger at the suspended display, "that that wrecked ship down there is theirs—"

"For all we know," Amalfitano added, "they might have chased it here, forcing it into a crash landing, and now they want us out of the way so they can cover their tracks! Hell, knowing them and their track record, I bet this is all connected, in some way, to the *Herrick.*"

Teague saw heads nodding in uneasy agreement.

"Sir," Masursky said, "the Hahtooshan ship is hailing us, asking us to repeat our last transmission—"

"And what about the commander and the others?" Pardix interrupted. "What if—"

"Enough!" Teague snapped and turned to the com-op. "Open a responding channel."

Masursky nodded, "Go ahead, sir."

"Nahru'tzrhi," Teague began, "I apologize for the brief interruption in communications. As for your request that we leave you to your rescue efforts, I regret I cannot comply. We dispatched a rescue party to the surface upon our arrival, and presently cannot contact or recall them due to the EM interference. We should be able to re-establish contact in…?" He turned to Cyllo.

"Seventeen hours, fifteen—"

"Approximately seventeen Standard hours." He turned back to the suspended tactical display. "Until that time we'll remain where we are. And since we'll not leave until we've retrieved our rescue party, might I suggest we collaborate in a search for your missing and ours?" Out of the corner of his eye, he saw Amalfitano turn to stare, open-mouthed, at him.

Before Amalfitano blurted out something damning, the alien officer replied, *"Your offer is most generous, Captain."*

"Then you accept?"

"It is tempting, and, I admit, startling. As you are well aware, A'tuu'shahn'i rely solely on our own abilities. We do not ask or expect help from others—"

"And you fucking well wouldn't get it even if you did ask," Pardix grumbled.

Teague flicked the navigator a sidelong, silencing glower. *Good gods, would you all just shut the hell up—*

"—I will have to discuss this… novel proposition with my senior officers before I could accept—"

"Whether you accept or not, Nahru'tzrhi, we will not break orbit until we've recovered our landing party. *Baidarka* out." Teague glanced at the com-op and ran his finger across his throat; Masursky responded, but not quite quickly enough and the control room was treated to a brief explosion of what Teague assumed were Hahtooshan obscenities.

He took a deep breath, made a vain attempt at tugging the sweat-wrinkles out of his uniform as he marshaled what remained of his composure and finally turned to Amalfitano and Pardix. "Doctor. Ensign. I'm well aware of your shared hatred of Hahtooshans, and I do sympathize with your losses. However, if you really want to recover the commander and the others, I strongly suggest you keep your feelings to yourselves from now on." His narrowed gaze flicked to Lesedi, and then to each remaining member of the command crew. "Same goes for the rest of you. *Understood?"*

There were the compulsory, if half-hearted murmurs of, "Yessir."

"And one more thing, something I shouldn't think I'd need to point out, but obviously I do. *That*", he gestured towards the tactical grid, "is no Matarran border raider. Yes, we survived the ambush, and destroyed the two Matarran ships, which clearly has left some of you a wee bit cocky, but at what cost? And need I remind you that the *Baidarka* suffered major damage in that skirmish, damage that has yet to be repaired.

"So, if the Hahtooshans were to attack, I think it unlikely we'd survive this time, and speaking for myself and yes, the rest of the crew, we'd all greatly appreciate it if you'd do your best to avoid goading them into doing just that? *Yes?*" His angry gaze again swept the small chamber and the faces that stared back at him. "We're all agreed? Excellent!" He sat down and twisted around to face the suspended tactical grid before anyone noticed that he was shaking.

— ii —

Qharubi squeezed his eyes shut and clenched his teeth as Tarqk continued to hurl abuses at the main tactical display. Then as suddenly as it started, the verbal salvo stopped and Qharubi cautiously reopened his eyes as Tarqk, to everyone's surprise, began to chuckle.

It started out as a deep, spasmodic rumble, but the laughter rapidly escalated into an almost hysterical giggle before Tarqk managed to get himself back under control. He slapped the arms of his chair with his balled fists. "Rimmers are even more gullible than even I thought possible! They've taken the bait!"

"Indeed, ta'ahn," Qharubi replied and turned his attention to the tactical display. His eyes took in the blips that marked the relative positions of the alien patrol ship and his own, as well as the ghost-like dot that marked the position of Ru'asooli's light destroyer, *Acholilah*.

Acholilah was keeping station just beyond the scanner range of the Coalition vessel, its sensor shroud, like *Makhaira*'s, useless in the intense electromagnetic bombardment. But the fierce barrage was a boon along with a hindrance. It hid the radiative transfer that might have given away *Acholilah*'s presence, making the EM interference almost as effective a screen to the patrol vessel's probes as the shroud—

With none of the shroud's disturbing side effects, Qharubi added to himself as he shifted uneasily in his seat. He'd never been fond of the device, undeniably useful as it was as a terror weapon; it always left him with a seriously upset stomach and throbbing headache—

"Are you certain the Coalition ship knows nothing of *Acholilah*'s presence?" Tarqk asked no one in particular, breaking the ominous silence that had settled over the bridge.

The crew, to a man, looked at Qharubi.

Thanks. He swiveled his chair around to face to Tarqk. "Their attempts at flatspace have been limited to attempts to contact their landing party—"

"Did you expect them to advertise their knowledge by sending out a greeting," Tarqk sneered, "inviting Ru'asooli to afternoon tea?"

Qharubi overheard Tu'indai's stifled snort of laughter. If Tarqk heard it, he had chosen to ignore it. "I asked *you* a question, Sha'ashahn."

Qharubi, his eyes never wavering from Tarqk's, answered flatly, "No, ta'ahn."

"Good," Tarqk murmured triumphantly as he slumped back in his chair. "Speaking of invitations, has the *Acholilah* responded to my encoded message?"

"Not yet, ta'ahn. Perhaps the interference…"

Tarqk grunted his annoyance, rose from his chair and flicking Tu'indai a pointed look, announced, "I'll be in my quarters. Notify me immediately of any response to my message."

"Of course, ta'ahn," Qharubi replied as he too rose and started for the command chair as Tarqk strode towards the airlock.

"And Qharubi?"

Oh, now what? He wiped the reflexive response from his face and even more importantly, his voice. "Ta'ahn?"

"I thought I ordered a complete check of environmental control systems," Tarqk said as he pointedly wiped his forehead.

"I oversaw the systems check myself, and all checked out—"

"Then do it again! This ship is no better than a sweat box!"

He dipped his head. "Yes, ta'ahn."

Muttering furiously about incompetent Elkanaghalli'i, Tarqk spun on his heel and stepped through the double ruby rings of airlock, into the corridor beyond.

The hatch snapped closed and Qharubi eased himself down into the command chair then gave each station and its operator a visual once-over to assure himself all was in readiness for any eventuality.

As his eyes finally came to the science station, he found Tu'indai staring at him, her full lips pulled back in a sly smile.

He jerked his chair around to face the tactical display, scowled at its readouts as he angrily wiped a rivulet of sweat from his cheek, then he smacked of his fist to the chair's com panel and tersely relayed the order to do another complete environmental systems check, adding ominously, "And get it *right* this time, or it will be *you* answering to Nahru'tzhri... and me." Satisfied by the chief engineer's stammering reply, he cut the connection then risked a sidelong look at her station; it was unoccupied.

Tu'indai had indeed left the bridge.

— iii —

"Does Tarqk think me an old fool?" Ru'asooli grumbled to no one in particular, interrupting his second in command's terse recitation of Tarqk's equally terse invitation.

When no answer was forthcoming, Ru'asooli slowly turned, suddenly feeling the urge to engage in his favorite amusement of late, and fixed his now suspicious glare on his youthful second. "Do *you* think me an old fool, Lura'jaii?"

Lura'jaii looked aghast. "*Of course not, ta'ahn!* You are the Hero of Beycesültan, Raumalle and Ladjah-Höyük—"

"All of which took place long before you were born," he interrupted dryly. Granted, he'd had many successes since those grueling campaigns, but those engagements were still classified and therefore unknown to the up-and-comer.

"But... but the Q'shaathrah selected you to command this mission. You were their first choice. They certainly wouldn't have given such an important contract to, as you say and apologies, 'an old fool', ta'ahn."

Ru'asooli studied her for a moment. What she'd said was true—about being the Q'shaathrah's first choice, news he'd found flattering and at the same time quite perplexing. He had had a storied career, no one would deny it, but even he readily admitted those glory days were long gone. Finally: "Is that all the idiot had to say?"

"No, ta'ahn. Nahru'tzrhi also reports that the landing force is now on its way back to the island—"

"With prisoners!"

"Indeed, ta'ahn," Lura'jaii agreed. "A most regrettable—"

"Tarqk's penchant for unbridled thought has become contagious!" Ru'asooli snarled then gave his throbbing temples a vigorous, two-handed massage with gnarled fingers that ached. In fact all of his joints ached and his head ached to the point he had been finding it hard to sleep. Just symptoms of fatigue from taking on such a demanding mission, the medical officer had said, rather than the more obvious, but far less complimentary diagnosis of advanced age. Truth was he *was* getting too old for this; he'd done his time, he'd had a very successful career, he'd heaped more honors on his house than any other member of his generation.

But the enticement of one last mission, not to mention one last very high-paying contract was just too good to pass up. Or so he thought. Now, between his achy, age-battered body and having to deal the upstart Tarqk on a daily, if not hourly basis, constantly reminding the infuriatingly ambitious officer who was in command of the overall mission, he was beginning to think he should have listened to his bond-mate and taken a pass.

Then again, how could he have possibly anticipated two capable officers making such an unbelievable hash out of what should have been a relatively simple task when success was so close at hand?

Had Tarqk not taken it upon himself to order the scout back to the base in the first place, they wouldn't now be dealing with an overly inquisitive Coalition patrol ship. The whole plan of slipping into the isolated system unnoticed to retrieve data on a weapon that wasn't supposed to exist, from a secret base that had been abandoned over one hundred standard years before and also wasn't supposed to exist and was therefore not being guarded—an imprudent but not unexpected response from the rather, in his educated opinion, *careless* Coalition—then leave without anyone being the wiser was rapidly going up in flames, flames that would draw even more unwanted attention to forgotten system and a mission that paid as exceedingly well as it did *because* of the clearly stipulated, not to mention *guaranteed* discretion.

And then there was Khusaaq, the last person anyone would have suspected of what by any standard was subversive behavior. Ru'asooli's eyes crinkled into a very unhappy glower. It was a maddening puzzle as to why he would choose now to act in such a shockingly rebellious way. *Perhaps... perhaps he's just snapped.*

Yes. The pressures of his position, and then add Tarqk to the mix... if I had to deal with that upstart Khighalli on a minute-by-minute basis I might snap too.

He nodded to himself, almost but not quite satisfied he had it right. *That must be it. Nothing nefarious. Just someone who'd finally reached his breaking point.* There had been those troubling rumors that had dogged Khusaaq ever since Cotopaxi, ugly whispers—all lies of course, spread by the Khighalli fearful of an Elkanaghalli resurgence. But Khusaaq hadn't helped himself one bit when he'd adamantly refused further accolades, refused even the command of his own ship. Perhaps Khusaaq himself knew he couldn't handle the unremitting expectations of a people who longed to return to the glory days, with Khusaaq the living, breathing embodiment of those aspirations—it would certainly explain his surprising requests for routine assignments, assignments that also always had him accompanied by close kinsmen. And the Q'shaathrah had quietly granted him his wish. Perhaps they all knew, perhaps they all feared that their desperately needed hero would crumble if pushed too hard.

He snorted softly. *Didn't work out as planned though, did it? What appeared as self-effacement endeared you even more to those who prized what you personified, and deepened the bitter resentments of those who hated you for the same reason.*

Ru'asooli rubbed his eyes with his fingertips. *Be that as it may... I have to deal with the result of your ill-timed foolishness and that of Tarqk. Did either of you ever once realize this crisis could, and probably will bring ruin on us all? No?*

He shook his head then grumbled, "Status."

"All data has been transferred and Science Officer is now in the process of interpretation. We remain in *Makhaira*'s shadow. To the Coalition vessel, we're nothing more than a spectral artifact—"

"Spectral artifact indeed!" he replied peevishly.

"Agreed ta'ahn, but non-existence is to our advantage."

Ru'asooli replied with a half-hearted grunt then asked, "Have you subverted Tarqk's communications officer yet?"

Lura'jaii smiled unpleasantly. "He was *most* willing to cooperate."

Ru'asooli grunted. *I bet; I bet Tarqk's entire crew would happily toss him out the nearest airlock if they thought they could get away with it. Whoever pulled strings for him to get this contract is going to answer to me when we return—*

"All transmissions between the Coalition vessel and *Makhaira* will be patched directly here," Lura'jaii continued, oblivious to his private musings.

"Without Tarqk's knowledge."

"Yes, ta'ahn," she nodded eagerly. "We can override communications between the two ships at any time."

"And it will be impossible for the Coalition vessel to determine that the transmission originated from a different source?"

"All evidence points to that, ta'ahn—"

"But?" He eyed her; Lura'jaii had a tendency towards obsequiousness, a trait he blamed on the officer's inexperience and youthful zeal. Most of the time it didn't aggravate him, at least not too much, but he was in a *mood* now, furious at Tarqk—furious that Khusaaq, who of anyone should have appreciated the delicacy of the mission yet had taken this opportunity of all opportunities to go renegade, and furious most of all at himself for allowing his vanity to lead him by the nose into this unholy mess. Tarqk was safely out of reach—at least for now—as was Khusaaq, but Lura'jaii wasn't.

"There are eddies of stellar wind that might—"

"Might...?" he growled.

"We have attempted to verify, ta'ahn, but the particle flow is too erratic. But I believe this may work in our favor."

Ru'asooli squinted at her. *Think, Lura'jaii—stop trying to impress me and think!* If there was one thing, one small success he could salvage from this now otherwise botched mission, it was to bring back a smarter, far more capable second-in-command, just as he'd done with so many others over his career, and one who could, given some time, overcome the taint of this now almost certain and utterly unavoidable disaster. "In what way?"

"It will make it impossible for the Coalition vessel to pin-point the true location of the transmission. If we maintain our position within *Makhaira*'s shadow, the Rimmers will just assume that the outpouring of radiation is responsible for the minor overlap, rather than the presence of a second ship."

There you are. Ru'asooli almost smiled—almost. "Very well. Now, as for Tarqk..." He laced his gnarled, throbbing fingers together, leaned back in his chair and began framing a suitably humiliating response to the upstart and hopefully salvage something of the mission.

After a moment, realizing Lura'jaii—always the stickler for protocol—hadn't moved, he added irritably, "Station!"

— iv —

Qharubi kept his eyes fixed on the main tactical display, uncomfortably aware that Tu'indai had returned to the bridge and was now standing behind him.

His ultra-sensitive nose couldn't help but pick up the pungent blending of sweat and semen—and he knew she was keenly aware of *his* tightly controlled response and delighted in it. He found the heady mixture both intensely arousing and revolting—a brazen advertisement of her new status, as well as a flagrant disregard of A'tuu norms. In a society that based interpersonal interaction as much on scent as sight and sound, to be unwashed—*to stink*—was as offensive as a verbal insult or physical threat.

And Tu'indai was not alone in her lapse of... decorum. There had been a number of fights reported—serious enough to land the combatants in sickbay, others in the brig.

Tarqk's capriciousness is spreading, Qharubi thought as he plucked at the sweat damp collar of his tunic and wished for the hundredth time he could retreat to his cabin for a shower and fresh duty uniform. *Yes,* he thought with a twist of his lip, *I stink too.*

He pointedly ignored Tu'indai—hoping to wait her out—and flinched as a slim hand slipped down his chest to his bandoleer.

"Tarqk's losing his patience with your bumbling, Qharubi," she whispered in his ear. This close, her musky scent was blatant: an open invitation—or a slap in the face. "I can intervene only so much. *Think* before you speak. But do not think too long. That was Khusaaq's failing."

She entwined her fingers around the grip of his dagger and began stroking it, and, despite himself, he found his gaze drawn to the suggestive movement. "Do you find me so... *unattractive?*"

"You're Nahru'tzrhi's consort, ta'ashan," he replied tightly. "My opinion is of no importance."

"Interesting. By your blundering earlier, I didn't think you capable of such careful words." She moved to his side and wrapped her other arm around his neck, making it impossible to turn his head away. She leaned closer and lipped his earlobe, then lightly ran the tip of her tongue down his cheek to the corner of his taut mouth.

He replied with an involuntary gasp; she tightened her near stranglehold and forced the tip of her tongue between his lips and against his clenched teeth. Satisfied, she slowly slid her tongue back up his tattooed and scarified cheek, the tip following one channel that ran from chin to temple, then she nuzzled his earlobe again and whispered in his ear, "Qharubi, you and I—"

The hiss of the airlock started her; she released her hold and jumped back, wide-eyed as Qharubi spun the command chair around, fully expecting to find a shocked, rapidly turning to enraged Tarqk standing in the open lock.

Instead it was relief navigator. He replied with an equally startled nod before he hurried to his station.

"Ta'ahn!"

Qharubi turned to the communications console and its operator.

"Encoded message from Ru'asooli Kshira'tzrhi."

He jammed his hips back into the chair and as he turned his gaze back to the tactical display, he tried to remember what he'd been doing before Tu'indai had distracted him. "Pipe it through to Nahru'tzrhi immediately," he muttered hoarsely as he gave the now occupied science station a sidelong glance. Tu'indai had her back to him and appeared to be fully engrossed in her monitor's readouts.

He no sooner turned back to his own duties when he overheard the metallic ring of approaching footsteps and steeled himself. *Tarqk.* He didn't need to know the gist of Ru'asooli's encoded message. The angry cadence of the captain's footfalls in the passageway left no doubt Ru'asooli had refused to be a party to Tarqk's plans—

"Qharubi!"

He slowly swiveled the chair around to find Tarqk now standing in the airlock.

—And you blame me.

"My quarters. *Now!*"

"Yes, ta'ahn." He exhaled and rose slowly, aware that every eye on the bridge followed him, some with sympathy, others, like Tu'indai, with glee. He gave his bandoleer a tug then strode through the lock and into the corridor where Tarqk waited for him.

With a curt nod to his second, Tarqk started down the narrow passageway; Qharubi trailed a respectful, two paces behind him. Tarqk could have paged him, but no. This was far more humiliating, far more frightening. When Tarqk came for you personally, everyone knew you were in deep, deep trouble.

Several approaching crewmen saw the look on their captain's face and wisely melted into the hollows between the bulkheads. Tarqk marched past their hiding places, through the open doorway of his cabin and over to his desk.

Qharubi entered a moment later and placed himself directly in front of the captain, his eyes fixed on the featureless wall just above Tarqk's head. It was a spot with which he'd become far too familiar. In the short time Tarqk had been in command of *Makhaira*, Qharubi had come to know the wall behind the officer's desk better than the ceiling above his own bunk.

At first the visits were nothing more than routine: Tarqk wanting information on the workings of the unfamiliar ship he now commanded, or reports on crew efficiency. But everything changed once they arrived in this accursed system; the routine status meetings between commander and his first officer turned into Tarqk reciting a litany of utterly unfounded complaints against Qharubi, and each time the grievances were of an increasingly serious nature.

At first he wasn't sure the cause—beyond the obvious: like Khusaaq he was the wrong caste, and again, like Khusaaq he was a highly decorated Cotopaxi survivor with the accompanying acclaim. But unlike Khusaaq, he'd done everything Tarqk had asked of him and then some. And, more importantly to him—and, he assumed Tarqk—he'd never shown any resentment, publicly or privately, of Tarqk's usurpation of what was by all rights his option on commanding the *Makhaira*.

But then came Khusaaq's ominous selection to lead the landing shortly after rumors began to circulate that Qharubi was planning to lead a mutiny, assisted by Khusaaq and the ship's senior medical officer, Ouda'yai. If Qharubi had heard them, then Tarqk had heard them too. At first he, like Khusaaq, had dismissed the whispers as nothing more than wishful thinking on the part of the crew, or perhaps a clumsy attempt on the part of one of Tarqk's supporters—there were more than a few aboard, all Khighalli—to test the crew's loyalties.

Ouda'yai, when he'd heard about the rumors had said, privately and clearly in jest, that any move against Tarqk wouldn't be a mutiny because Tarqk had appropriated the ship and her crew for his own purposes.

To Qharubi it didn't matter if the rumors were true or not; he knew if Tarqk felt threatened he would react accordingly. The officer had not failed him in that respect and proof of that was obvious. Of the three, now only he remained. Tarqk, after all, had no sense of humor or sense of proportion.

It was a matter that had been simmering just under the surface, never addressed by Tarqk, never raised by him, and now, Qharubi feared, it had come to a boil. Perhaps Tarqk was fearful that Qharubi would see no reason in delaying putting Khusaaq's plan into action, in fact there was every reason to put into action as soon as possible, while there was still time to rescue his kinsman.

What Tarqk or whomever had started the rumor failed to grasp was that Elkanaghalli'i did not lead mutinies, no matter the cause, and he certainly entertained no desire the break that mold—no matter the justification. The Q'shaathrah, once fully informed of the facts, would order a ship to come collect Khusaaq and his escort, he was confident of that, and Khusaaq was undoubtedly resourceful enough to keep everyone alive until that happened.

Tarqk had also succeeded spectacularly in getting onto Ru'asooli's really bad side. Qharubi harbored no doubts the aging officer would, at the first opportunity, happily tear Tarqk and his bourgeoning career to shreds—with the Q'shaathrah's blessing in light of the thoroughly botched mission. But in order for him to savor that thought, to in fact actually witness it, he would have to survive the next few days—something that, at this moment, seemed rather improbable.

Tarqk had come to the *Makhaira* with a well-earned reputation for unpredictability. In their line of work, it was a trait that had its advantages. However nothing in his records had suggested irrational volatility. But since entering the system the officer had gone from impulsive to incendiary, with a scorched earth policy for anyone who dared cross him.

Khusaaq had crossed him one too many times. The ship's senior medical officer, too, and both had paid dearly for those transgressions. Now Ru'asooli had crossed Tarqk, upsetting his carefully laid plans. *But Ru'asooli isn't here.* He tried not to lick his lips in fearful anticipation. *I am.*

Tarqk slipped his pistol out of its holster and placed it on the desk before seating himself. "You are aware of Ru'asooli's refusal to come here and discuss my plan," he began, not as a question, but as a statement of fact. "Khusaaq must've contacted him before I did and convinced him the risks of my plan were too great." He stared up at Qharubi in open disgust. "All you Elkanaghalli are cowards—too hidebound, too trapped by your outmoded, rigid beliefs to see the possibilities all around you!"

Like leading a mutiny? Aloud he replied calmly, "It is highly unlikely Khusaaq Sha'ashahn could have made contact, even if—"

"Indeed?" Tarqk scowled at him as he crossed his arms. "And why not?"

"The interference, ta'ahn. Communications with the surface is difficult, even at our low orbit, and tight beam ship-to-ship is sporadic at best. It would be impossible for Khusaaq Sha'ashahn to contact *Acholilah* at its much greater distance and under the present conditions—"

"Somehow Ru'asooli was tipped off!" Tarqk slammed his fists against his desk. "His curt refusal is proof of that!"

Qharubi desperately wanted to enlighten him that Ru'asooli would've refused to take a Matarii *dinsit* from him, someone Ru'asooli considered nothing more than a Khighalli nobody, much less an invitation to such an obvious trap. *You've underestimated Ru'asooli, just like you underestimate all Elkanaghalli'i—*

"How did you know of the contents of the message?"

Qharubi mind snapped back to the immediate and dropped his gaze only to find Tarqk had rotated the pistol with the tip of his finger so that the muzzle of the weapon now pointed directly at him. He tried to look and sound guiltless—it wasn't difficult because at least in this particular instance he was. "Ta'ahn?"

"You heard me. How did you know?"

"I did not know, ta'ahn, I only assumed—"

"You should learn never to assume, Qharubi. Especially never make assumptions about *me*. Just like your kinsman, you've been tripped up by your own stupid attempts at trickery." He shook his shaggy head in feigned sadness as he withdrew a small device from a compartment in his desk, then held it out for him to see. "Do you know what this is?"

Qharubi gave the innocuous looking object a quick look. "No, ta'ahn."

"Neither do I, but we're about to find out. It was recovered from the body of one of those Thalamian smugglers we intercepted. Tu'indai's convinced it's some sort of neural scrambler. Shall we test her hypothesis?" He rose and circled the desk.

Oh, let's not.

"You are a fool, Qharubi. An imbecile. I gave you, an Elkanaghalli, the honor of being my second in command and you repay me by fomenting mutiny?"

"But—"

"Don't deny it. I have enough evidence I could kill you right now and would be found fully justified."

Qharubi swallowed convulsively as Tarqk stopped in front of him.

"Should I kill you? Well? Speak up! Say something in your own defense, Elkanaghalli, or are you so stupid you cannot even manage that?"

"Ta'ahn, I—"

"Too late, Qharubi," Tarqk whispered sweetly and slapped the device against his chest.

— v —

Teague gave his eyes another vigorous rub then squinted at the tactical display. He swallowed, winced, then tried to clear his throat, but it only made the raw tickle worse.

"Sir?"

He turned towards Lesedi's familiar clipped voice. "Yes, Ensign?" he asked in a voice so raspy it startled him.

"Permission to speak freely?"

He stared blearily at the tawny-skinned woman and nodded, albeit very reluctantly. As far as he was concerned, the junior weapons officer had a penchant for speaking not just freely but far too much. The last thing he felt up to was a chat.

"You look terrible, sir. Doctor Amalfitano—"

"I'm just tired, Ensign, nothing terminal, I assure you." *Although Amalfitano has some explaining to do.* He massaged the bridge of his nose. *Twenty four hours, give or take... twenty hours?*

"Yessir." She smiled worriedly then jerked her chin towards the holo. "We can keep an eye on 'em, sir. Why not take a break?"

He turned his gritty eyes to the holographic display and found he could no longer separate the alien vessel's blinking telltale from the glowing grid. All was a uniform, and suddenly painfully bright, blur. *A shower and something to eat, that's what I need. Yeah.* "Yes, all right." He nodded and pushed himself out of his chair. "You have the conn, Ensign."

— vi —

Qharubi opened his eyes. For a moment he wasn't sure where he was, aside from the obvious fact that he was lying flat on his back. So his still addled brain tried to take stock... the last thing he remembered was—

"So, you're not dead."

Qharubi found himself equally surprised by the simple observation. Since his eyes appeared to be the only part of his body under his conscious control, he turned them towards Tarqk's familiar, raspy voice and hoped that was enough to demonstrate that he was still obedient, and attentive. Otherwise Tarqk might find that a good enough excuse to finish the job.

The halting movement of his eye muscles awakened the rest of his body and each muscle, each joint showed its displeasure by sending jolts of agony through him. Neurons screamed. Muscles spasmed. His vision blurred. He blinked and his watery eyes reluctantly refocused on Tarqk.

Tarqk was again seated at his desk, his unhappy gaze fixed on the small device. "Pity." He tossed it onto the desk and added irritably, "Dismissed."

I thought you'd never ask. Qharubi, after several attempts, and by sheer force of will, managed to lurch to his feet without crying out in pain then he grabbed the bulkhead to steady himself as the cabin suddenly began to spin.

"Tell Tu'indai to come to me," Tarqk added, not looking up.

Qharubi nodded dumbly. It was the best he could do. His tongue was still firmly wedged against the roof of his mouth and behaved as if it had no intention of releasing its death grip.

"And one more thing..."

Qharubi tightened his hold on the bulkhead, then managed to turn, just enough, so he could face Tarqk.

"...tell your supporters that the next time I won't be so benevolent. If I hear any more nonsense about mutinying, any more grumblings, any excuses for incompetence, *period*, I will start executing crew—starting with you. Understood?"

He nodded again, fixed his eyes on the door, managed to get a full breath into him then staggered out of the cabin.

Once in the corridor, beyond Tarqk's view, he leaned heavily against the wall and gulping for air, looked down at himself. His mid-thigh length tunic concealed the dampness of his crotch. He tugged at the snug fabric of his trousers as he clung to the small relief that he'd emptied his bladder shortly before Tarqk had ordered him to his cabin. *Could've been worse.* He tried to smile at his pathetic attempt at a private joke. The muscles responded by jerking the whole side of his face into a lopsided, twitching grimace.

He waited until the spasm had passed, took a deep, steadying breath then stumbled back down the corridor, using the wall for support. Just short of the open bridge lock, he stopped and tried as best he could to straighten his disheveled duty uniform. It was pointless. He gave up, satisfied himself by smoothing back his hair, then he clutched his bandoleer with one shaky hand, his weapons belt with the other and stepped unsteadily through the lock.

Eyes turned towards him as he slowly made his way across the bridge. No one spoke; no one rose to offer a hand—no one dared. He ignored the stares, the commiserating winces and as he awkwardly lowered himself down into the command chair he breathed a silent sigh of relief that he hadn't tripped in front of the crew. He took another, deeper breath, hoping it would steady his voice. "S-s-science O-o-officer."

Somewhere nearby, someone giggled.

Chiku!

Tu'indai rose and slowly sauntered over to him. "Y-y-yes, S-s-sha'ashahn?" she mocked.

"N-n-nahru'tzrhi d-d-desires—" He squeezed his eyes shut, concentrated, and then added without a stutter, "—your presence in his cabin." He almost breathed another sigh of relief. *Almost.* He knew his public torment was far from over.

She leaned close and whispered, "And do you know the reason he *d-d-desires* me?" as she ran her fingers down his still spasming arm.

Perhaps to test the scrambler again, just to make sure? "No." He jerked his arm away, but the motion went wild. His twitching muscles overreacted and he hit himself in the opposite shoulder. He grunted and winced.

"Did you hurt yourself?"

"No." For the moment, monosyllabic answers seemed to be the safest way to go.

Undeterred, she wrapped her hand around his arm and gently forced it down into his lap. He fixed his eyes on it, hoping that alone would keep it there, hoping she wouldn't notice the dampness of his crotch.

If she did, she didn't make an issue of it. Instead she continued with her verbal teasing. "I'm sure you do not know why he *d-d-desires* me, Elkanaghalli. Maybe I'll teach you?"

"No."

She grinned. "I'm a most able instructor."

"So... s-so says the s-s-scuttlebutt a-a-among the crew," he hissed through clenched teeth.

"And rumors have it that you're planning a mutiny," she whispered in his ear.

He glanced sidelong at her before he could stop himself then immediately dropped his gaze back to his lap.

She chuckled softly and brushed a tangled lock of his hair from his cheek. "But one mustn't *believe* everything one hears, Sha'ashahn." She stood back and looked him over as he continued to twitch. "You're a mess." She shook her head and added with what sounded to his startled ears like genuine concern, "You should be in sickbay—"

"Nahru'tzrhi is... is waiting, Science Officer."

"How about I help you—"

"Now." He lifted his eyes to the tactical, waiting, and finally heard her walk away. He glanced around. The crew looked to be busy at their stations. *Too busy.*

"Hebaath."

The relief scanner officer twisted in her chair, her tattooed face an expressionless mask—but he'd recognized her giggle earlier. She was one of Tarqk's favorites, right behind Tu'indai, and like Tu'indai, she made little effort to conceal her privileged position.

"Ta'ahn?"

Time to return the favor. He crossed his arms, hoping to conceal his continued muscle jerks. "Any change in interference levels?"

"Only slight fluctuations, Sha'ashahn. Nothing of significance." She started to turn back to her console, dismissive in her tone.

"I'll decide what's significant. Put the data on-screen!"

"Of course, ta'ahn," she replied, still with an underlying tone of conceit. She had good reason to believe his days as second were numbered. Perhaps she even thought she stood a good chance at replacing him.

He managed to thumb a recessed button on the arm of his chair and a small viewer immediately dropped from the ceiling to dangle in front of him at eye-level. For a moment he stared at the display and what was clearly intended to be a confusing mass of raw data. "I see a projected window in the interference." He rolled his eyes towards her. "Has this been confirmed?"

"Confirmed—"

"And this is the window the Coalition captain mentioned, correct?"

Her earlier cockiness began to evaporate. "Correct—"

"Will we within scanning range of the island at that time?"

She blinked. "I'm... I'm not sure, ta'ahn."

"Then I strongly suggest you find out."

"At once, ta'ahn!" She spun her chair around to face her console.

Qharubi pushed down on the arms of his chair, forcing himself to a wobbly stand and the small viewer obediently glided up and out of the way. He arched his back, stretched his strained shoulder muscles and grunted.

Startled, Hebaath jerked her chair around and looked up at him.

"Done already? I *am* impressed."

"Actually—"

"Actually what?"

"Actually, no, Sha'ashahn."

"No? What's the delay?" He jabbed a finger at the suspended viewer. "I can tell just by looking at the figures that we'll be on the opposite side of the planet during the decrease in interference. I only asked you in order to check my own computations."

"But I—"

"You have a regrettable slowness about you, Hebaath. While it's obvious to everyone aboard *Makhaira* that Nahru'tzrhi has been willing to overlook such failings up until now, finding your limited abilities lay *elsewhere*," he glanced down at his crotch and paused just long enough to permit several emboldened crewmen to chuckle softly, "*I* find it a very dangerous flaw for a bridge officer." Satisfied he'd made his point, he smiled then resumed his seat and turned his attention back to the tactical.

— vii —

Teague carefully eased himself down at his desk then tapped in an order for hot tea and toast.

The shower had not had the desired revitalizing effect. He still felt—*and probably looked*, he added to himself—like death warmed over. But at least he was slightly more awake, which was a good thing, he realized as his weary gaze fell on a stack of data discs some thoughtful person had placed on his desk.

With a sigh, he picked up the top-most disc and tried to slip it into the desktop data reader only to find another disc already in the slot.

He pulled out the disc and instantly realized what it was. "Blast it!" He shoved the disc containing the data downloaded from the wreck back into the slot, hit the activator, then, hearing the chime of the servo-door, turned and took his breakfast tray from the small dispenser.

He placed the tray on his desk and taking the cup in one hand, a piece of toast in the other, turned his full attention to the now active monitor.

For a moment nothing happened, then a single, all too familiar symbol swelled to fill the screen: an archaic version of the Rim Coalition's standard.

He lurched forward in his chair. "Hello... what do we have here?"

He hurriedly tapped in a command; the screen obediently scrolled up, revealing a mass of symbols. He keyed in another command, all the while hoping the data locked in code was not so old that its cipher had been wiped from the computer's memory then he returned to his breakfast and quickly washed down the toast with the tea.

The tea did little to soothe this sore throat and he found himself fighting the sudden, tickling urge to cough as he scowled at the data reader. *What's taking so long?*

A soft *bleat* from the terminal brought a smile to his lips. "About time." He leaned forward and began reading the information as it slowly scrolled up the screen.

It wasn't long before his red-rimmed eyes widened. *"Bloody hell!"* He tapped the desk-com. "Sickbay."

A female voice answered, *"Sickbay—"*

"Teague here. I need—" before he could finish, he began to cough.

"Sir...?"

Barely able to catch his breath between violent, hacking coughs, he managed to force out, "Amalfitano. *Get Amalfitano!*"

A moment later Amalfitano's anxious voice asked, *"What is it, Edwin? Rosen said—"*

"Doctor, I've... I've found..." He knit his brows. *Found what?* Try as he might, he couldn't remember. He shook his head to clear it of its sudden fuzziness; instead the small bright world of his cabin began to spin.

"Edwin?" Amalfitano's voice rang in his ears. *"Edwin, what—"*

"I think I'm going to pass out," he murmured in calm astonishment an instant before he slumped forward in his chair.

Chapter 6

Corsali sat cross-legged in the cabin's dappled shade and fanned her face with a scrap of thatching as she gazed out at the deck, and beyond that, the wind-ruffled sea.

Several hours before she'd reluctantly stripped down to her undershirt but had gone no further. She had no place to go except to strip all the way and under the circumstances she was not about to do that. Manatee she might be, but she was *not* about to test the waters.

Now the upper half of her softsuit formed a thick, damp wad around her waist. *Uncomfortable, but...*

The air within the cabin was stifling hot and full of sticky salt spray that formed an irritating rime on anything it touched. Her face and bare arms itched and she tried to remember how it felt to be cold as she wiped another rivulet of gritty sweat from her cheeks, forehead and neck, using the empty sleeve of her softsuit.

Beyond the shelter of the thatched roof of the cabin, the light of first dawn had rapidly turned into a blinding glare as Beta Rasal Ghul rose to join her sibling star. The deck, crisscrossed by bicolor shadows, shimmered and rippled as heat waves danced across it, intermixing the vivid blue-white light of Beta with the dazzling reddish-orange of Gamma. Where shadows cast by the two suns overlapped, the rough wood planking was an eerie pitch black—

The Flammarion effect, a part of her mind whispered.

Who fucking cares? another part replied testily as she gave her sticky cheek another rough wipe with the sleeve while lifting her slitted gaze to the binary itself. The thick layers of the planet's atmosphere distorted and magnified the two stars and the tongue of plasma that bound them together. The suns filled the doorway, a surrealistic painting framed by the rough planking. *Van Gogh, eat your heart out—*

Aquila groaned softly.

She eyed him then, with a weary sigh, scooted closer to him. "Sir, are you all right?"

His only response was another low moan.

"Sir?" She gently touched his cheek and was taken aback by its clamminess. She checked his pulse then his side and her worst fears were confirmed. "I'm going for Suhjai, Commander."

Not sure if he was able to hear her much less understand, she gave him one last worried glance, scrambled to her feet and hurried to the cabin doorway.

Shielding her eyes with her hands, she started across the deck. She felt the suns' burning rays on her face and shoulders and by the time she had reached the far side of the deck she was essentially blind. She found the ladder's handholds by touch alone, and with the warning of the night before topmost in her mind, peered down at the lower deck.

"*Hello?*" she called into the stiff, hot wind. "Is anyone down there?" She waited, tapping her finger on the railing. *Hip deep in yowies and not one within hearing distance?* Not that she could blame the aliens for seeking shelter, presumably below decks. Still…

She tried again, louder. "Sha'ashahn? Suhjai? *Anyone?*"

Yet again she was answered only by the snap of sails and groan of rigging. Then something else: a faint clicking from high above. She glanced up, caught a glimpse of two Blatto clinging to the mast, loops of rigging held in their arms.

"Hey! You!"

They looked down, saw her, and in response quickly scuttled around the mast to disappear behind the sail.

She scowled after them, muttered, "Gee, thanks," then squinted back at the cabin. *You coulda picked a better time to start bleeding again, you know.* She shook her head and took a deep, steadying breath, got a firm grip on the handholds then felt around for the first rung. *Here goes.*

Once her foot was securely planted, she began a slow, cautious descent into the inky shadow cast by the upper deck. She had no sooner planted both feet on the lower deck when tattooed hands grabbed her around her waist. *Yowie hands—gods!*

She stiffened but did not scream, despite the overwhelming urge, and remained stock still as the shadowy bulk of a second trooper stepped into her limited and still sun-dazzled range of view.

He none-too-gently pried her fingers from the ladder. *"Kaa'path-sseh?"* He paused then lifting his gaze, grunted, *"Pak-tu'a."*

The hands that still tightly gripped the folds of her rolled up softsuit abruptly let go and she found herself exhaling the breath she didn't realize she'd been holding.

"Kaa'path-sseh?" he repeated ominously, his feral eyes again fixed on her as he leaned even closer. *"Ithsu baktai—"*

"P-p-please, I… I n-n-need Suhjai," she stammered in a small voice while trying not to grimace at his fetid breath. "I… I m-m-mean the c-c-commander does. He's s-s-started to b-b-bleed again."

"Sa'huri." He again lifted his gaze to the soldier who stood behind her. *"Kuuthok-sseh?"*

He was answered by a perplexed grumble. He looked back down at her and shook his shaggy head.

Her eyes were better adjusted to the darkness now and she could clearly make out his ursine, tattooed and scarified face. She wasn't absolutely sure, but he looked like the same one Aquila had punched in the throat. Hadn't the officer said he was one of his most trusted men? *Gods, I hope you are who I think you are—and you don't harbor grudges.* "How a-a-about, ah… Sha'ashahn then?"

The merc cocked his head to one side and studied her face, then the rest of her and she suddenly wished she'd remembered to get back into the top of her softsuit. *"Please,* t-t-take me t-t-to Sha'ashahn."

He smiled, displaying a mouthful of discolored and chipped teeth.

She instinctively backed up a step, only remembering his companion when she bumped into him. She risked a quick glance over her shoulder at the second soldier then jerked her gaze back to the first one as he grabbed her arm.

She tried to wriggle free of his painful hold all the while trying not to breathe too deeply. "Let m-m-me… *g-g-GO!"*

In reply he wrapped his other arm around her, drew her against his filthy hauberk and ran an equally filthy, tattooed and very smelly finger down her cheek. *"Tawok ta-sseh, kaa-schat? Akanj?"* Using the same finger, he hooked the neck of her undershirt, pulled it out and peeked inside. *"Ta'ath?"* His eyes darted to hers and he grinned.

She squeezed her eyes shut as he forced his hand down the neck opening to feel around. All of the horror stories, the vid-reports of Hahtooshan atrocities came tumbling out of their hiding places, shaken loose by his rough groping.

She gritted her teeth against a scream. *I won't give you that satisfaction!*

"Torliss!" a deep voice boomed, *"Sa'huri!"*

The soldier holding Corsali yanked his arm free, ripping her undershirt in the process and roughly shoved her aside as the other trooper stepped back while muttering under his breath.

Clutching her torn undershirt, she backed into the railing as yet another Hahtooshan stalked across the open deck towards them. *Please be the officer... please!*

It wasn't.

The newest arrival stopped in front of her, grabbed her arm and growled, "I distinctly remember telling you to remain on the upper deck. Explain yourself!"

She cringed back. *Please don't—*

"Answer me!"

She tried but her mouth was too dry.

"I said, *answer* me!" He gave her a shake, strong enough her jaws snapped together.

"Matoosh!"

Keeping his vice-like hold on her, he turned his murderous gaze towards Suhjai's all too familiar sharp voice as she elbowed her way between the two troopers.

She stopped and placing her hands on her hips, took in the scene. "What's going on here, Matoosh?"

"Ask her yourself." The recipient of her question roughly jerked Corsali away from the railing, nearly thrusting her into Suhjai then letting go, he placed himself between Corsali and the ladder, crossing his thickset arms for emphasis. "Perhaps she came looking for her tongue? She appears to have lost it."

Suhjai eyed him then turned her cold gaze on Corsali, giving her ripped undershirt barely a glance. "What are you doing down here? Didn't Matoosh here warn you last night to keep to the upper deck? Ruh'ta'aq was given explicit orders to do so."

Before she could even open her mouth, the trooper in question gave her a shove between the shoulder blades and she stumbled and fell to her knees at Suhjai's feet.

At Suhjai's glare, Matoosh shrugged, "Perhaps all it needs is to be shaken loose?"

Suhjai waited until Corsali had staggered back to her feet then demanded, "Well?"

"I... I—"

"*Tah.*" Matoosh smiled a triumphant smile. "As I suspected. A gentle prod was all that was needed."

Suhjai fixed him with a withering stare then turned it on Corsali. "Explain yourself, Rimmer."

"Yes, *please* do," Matoosh added with a malicious grin and a sidelong, challenging look at Suhjai.

"I... I was looking for you." Corsali gave the troopers a quick, sidelong look only to find them staring back, smirking. There was no point in telling Suhjai what had almost happened; she doubted Suhjai cared a whit. She doubted any of them cared a damn about her. Aquila had some value—at least to the officer. She had none—at least none she cared to think about.

"Me?" Suhjai asked, drawing her gaze. "Why?"

"The commander, he's... he's begun to bleed again, and—"

"He sent for me? I was given the distinct impression he does not think highly of my medical skills." She pointedly ignored Matoosh's muffled snort. "Why the change of mind?"

"He didn't ask me. I just came."

"And you want me to help him, yes?"

She nodded. *"Please."*

"Why should I?"

"Because... because if you don't, he'll bleed to death—"

"It's no concern of mine if he dies. I would've happily fed all of you—"

Matoosh coughed, loudly.

Suhjai scowled up at him then looked back at Corsali. "But Sha'ashahn considers you and your companions of some small worth, and has given me orders to do what I can, and I, for one, do what I am ordered to do." She turned to the temporarily forgotten troopers. "Sa'huri. The Rimmers' medical kit—*be quick about it!* And Torliss..."

The other, the one who had groped her, gave Corsali and then Suhjai a wary look as his companion made good his escape.

"Make yourself useful below decks."

His replied with a curt nod and turned to leave.

"Torliss…?" Matoosh added in a deep, ominous growl, stopping the trooper in his tracks.

"Paq, Ruh'ta'aq?" the alien asked deferentially.

"I will not speak to Sha'ashahn about this incident, but rest assured, if you ever *touch* this female again, in fact if you ever even *look* at her again, I'll take immense pleasure in slowly disemboweling you, then dumping you, *still* alive, overboard. *Understood?"*

The alien trooper nodded vigorously.

"Now get out of my sight." As Torliss hurried away, Corsali's unlikely champion turned to her and pointed to the upper deck. "You, too, Rimmer."

She didn't have to be told twice. She edged around him and choosing speed over modesty, let go of her torn top and scrambled back up the ladder.

— ii —

Ensign Lesedi looked down at herself and gave her command blues a quick smoothing with her hands. *Here goes.* She stepped across the threshold, into the brightly lit sickbay.

The cramped unit looked like the inside of a disturbed beehive: red-suited staff were hurrying about with an air of preoccupied urgency and Lesedi felt like a sore thumb, or, in this case, a bright blue thumb in a sea of red. She also sensed that she was being deliberately ignored and felt an irrational twinge of irritation, but as soon as she recognized the emotion, she squelched it.

She also realized that it had been a mistake to assume that she could just walk in and get an immediate status report from Amalfitano. She started to back out of the sickbay before she got in anyone's way and promptly backed into something—something that grunted loudly.

She spun around and came face to face with a medtech, his hands full of sampling tubes.

"Why don't you look where you're going!" he snapped as he struggled not to drop any of his precious cargo, then his eyes widened. "Oh, sir! I didn't... sir, I mean—"

"It's okay." She flashed him a smile. "I'm looking for Amal—"

"Sorry, sir, gotta get these specimens to the lab!"

"...fitano," she ended as he hurried away.

"Doctor Amalfitano's in there," a familiar female voice said and Lesedi turned towards it in relief.

"Oh, Althea!" she began, spotting the nurse at a nearby console. "Boy, am I glad to see you."

Althea Rosen replied with a harried smile, motioned to the doorway of the lab and said, "Just follow that medtech, sir."

Lesedi knew a 'go away and don't bother me' when she heard it. She nodded and started for the aforementioned door.

As she approached, she overheard Amalfitano's exasperated voice from within, along with Lieutenant Drakin's sharp, slicing hiss. The nurse's voice had always reminded Lesedi of the ominous sizzle of a maser pistol—with a personality to match.

She quickly sidestepped to allow the medtech to hurry by again, this time with an apologetic nod as he exited the lab, then she peered inside the small and very crowded chamber and spotted the doctor and the nurse. Despite almost a year of being posted on the ship together, Lesedi had yet to overcome her unease of the massive reptiloid who bore more than a passing resemblance to a bipedal and slightly more upscale Komodo dragon: over two meters in height with a brown, white and tan chevron-patterned scaly hide, spatulate snout, small, widely spaced emerald-green eyes and a very long, bright blue tongue that behaved as if it had a mind of its own. And surrounding that tongue was a mouth full of razor-sharp teeth. *Glad you're on our side...*

"She puts a whole different spin on the expression man-eater, doesn't she?"

Lesedi glanced over her shoulder.

Rosen grinned and slipped by her, into the already over-crowded room.

Lesedi nodded distractedly as she turned her nervous gaze back on 'Drakin', dubbed such by the ship's quartermaster, McGuigan, because her Eltannian name was unpronounceable by even the most adept human tongue.

"What the hell do you mean, can't I see it?" Amalfitano roared, jerking Lesedi back into the present and the meaty problem at hand. *"Of course I can see it!"*

"Don't get zo damned sssnappy, okay?" Drakin spat back, her bifurcated tongue flicking out to flutter, tauntingly, millimeters from Amalfitano's forehead and he swatted at it as one would do with an overly curious fly.

Lesedi crossed her arms and cocked her head to one side as she watched the two in fascination. It'd be like trying to carry on a serious conversation with someone with a party favor—someone who had the maddening desire to use it at every opportunity. *How do you do put up with it? Then again...* Her eyes darted back to Drakin and her truly impressive mouthful of dagger-like teeth. *What else can you do?*

"I wasssn't sssure if you'd ssseen da sssignificanz of dat—"

"The day I need a goddamned nurse to point out the significance of a piece of data is the day *I retire!"*

Lesedi was impressed by his response, even more so when Drakin tapped his chest with a very business-like talon with enough force to pucker the fabric of his med reds and he didn't even flinch; in fact he appeared as if he hadn't even noticed.

"Remember, *you* sssaid dat." Her tongue flicked out again and this time it tickled the tip of his rather prominent nose. "Not *me.*"

As Amalfitano started to open his mouth for an explosive retort, Lesedi decided it was now or never and cut him off with a hesitant, "Ah, excuse me, Doctor...?"

Amalfitano and Drakin turned, their faces still holding all of their anger and frustration, but as Amalfitano's eyes fell on Lesedi, the icy expression faded.

Drakin however, continued to glare, her beady eyes darting between Lesedi and Amalfitano, clearly annoyed at Lesedi for her untimely interruption.

"I assume you're here for a status report on Teague?" Amalfitano asked.

"Yeah."

"Been real busy. Sorry."

To Lesedi he didn't sound the least bit sorry. He sounded exhausted.

"I kept meaning to give you an update, but—"

"It's okay," she shrugged, "we've all been a little busy the past coupla hours."

"Come into my office, Ife." He roped in her broad shoulders with his lanky arm, "we need to talk."

Lesedi flashed him an apprehensive look. *Uh-oh.*

He maneuvered her out of the lab, through the bustling sickbay and finally into his untidy office, then released his hold and motioned her to a chair. "Take a seat."

She sat.

He circled his littered desk, picked up a report flimsy and glanced at it, then, as he eased himself down into his chair, his eyes came to rest on her.

Lesedi, feeling acutely uncomfortable under his intense gaze, ran her fingers through her close-cropped, curly black hair and forced a smile. "I don't think I'm gonna like what you're gonna tell me, Doc."

"Depends," he replied. By his tone and expression, she had the distinct impression that he was sizing her up, judging her by past performances and Izraad's in-depth psychological profile.

Her brittle smile crumbled. *Bet you found the time to read that.*

Amalfitano continued his silent scrutiny as he reached under a mound of reports and pressed a buried button. The office door closed with a soft *thump.*

An oppressive silence fell on the room.

Teague's dead. Lesedi felt her heart lurch. *That's what you're gonna tell me—*

"You don't think you're ready for command, do you?"

"What?" She flinched, taken off guard.

Amalfitano stared at her with narrowed eyes. "Well?"

"Ah, well it's not that I'm not ready, it's just—"

"What? Just what? This is what you trained for, isn't it? I mean this isn't the first time you've taken the conn."

She wiped her damp hands on her thighs, too late realizing he'd seen her do it.

He picked up a holocube that had been sitting among the clutter on the desk and stared down at the oh-so lifelike, three-dimensional image of a small black dog that had been a beloved childhood pet as he continued, "You need to quit thinking of yourself as the junior weapons officer temporarily acting as captain—you *are* captain.

Don't hope for a reprieve because the chances of us finding Commander Aquila alive, much less able to perform as captain is next to nil. As for Teague…"

"Sir?" Her voice cracked. "He hasn't—"

"Died?" He shook his head. "No."

You mean, 'No, not yet'.

"But he won't be returning to duty for a good long while—he's got DIC, just like Niebuhr."

"But how—"

"Don't ask me, haven't had time to figure it out. That's my problem. Yours is being captain."

"But, sir—"

"But nothing! This is a damned good crew, the best I've ever served with. They deserve the best captain they can get."

"They had the best," Lesedi said quietly as the full import of the situation hit her. *Command. I'm in command—every decision from here on out is mine and mine alone.* She'd been too damned busy to grasp the enormity of what she was facing, until now, and as she stared at her hands, she noticed they were trembling. *Every mistake, every death—*

"Yeah, Gildun Vildur was the best, damned if she wasn't, no argument there. Problem is she's no longer here. So now we need a new captain, one who's every bit as competent. Because not only are we all depending on you, so's Gildun—she's depending on you to get her ship and crew to safety."

"And what if I can't?" she whispered, clasping her hands tightly as if that and that alone could keep her together, keep her from succumbing to total panic.

He fingered the holocube. Keeping his eyes focused on the small dog with the bright red ball in its mouth, he spoke again, but his voice had lost its harshness. "Lemme tell you something. Gildun told me you were the best. The best weapons officer, the best at giving unbiased observations on tactics, and like Aquila, one of the best-damned command candidates she'd ever met. CWO Cooper agreed."

The mention of her mentor, her direct superior made Lesedi wince. George Cooper had been a good man, a brilliant weapons officer, always willing to share his hard-won experience and critical insights garnered over almost two decades in the service—and in the previous two weeks she'd hardly thought about him. *Too busy,* she rationalized. *No, too afraid,* she realized with brutal honesty.

George Cooper had been killed along with Vildur and twenty six others in the Matarran ambush. The crew had been celebrating the captain's belated fiftieth birthday party, a purposefully raucous affair, a chance for the entire crew to let off a little steam after weeks of monotonous patrol duty. As fate had it, just as the party was winding down and the captain was enjoying one last bite of birthday cake, the main conference room and adjoining docking bay were holed, the resulting explosive decompression spewing everything and everyone inside the room and bay into the vacuum of space the instant before the emergency doors sealed off the area.

Had the attack happened a couple minutes later, the captain and Cooper would likely still be alive; had it happened a couple of minutes earlier, the death toll would have been far, far higher. After all, she had been the last one to leave, the last to see Commander Cooper and Captain Vildur alive, laughing loudly at some shared memory; she'd been the last to wish the captain happy birthday before exiting the room mere seconds before the explosion, the force of it literally throwing her to safety just as the emergency doors slammed shut a few scant centimeters from her, cutting her and the rest of the ship off from the merciless vacuum. She'd felt the searing heat, followed in a heartbeat by the burning cold that seemed to grab her, dragging her towards the ragged blackness that had been, seconds before, the conference room, felt her breath being sucked out of her...

She bit her lip, dropped her gaze to her tightly clasped hands and tried not to think about what those who died had felt the instant before their lives were snuffed out, or had they felt anything? This was why she hadn't thought about him; she'd made every effort not to. Lieutenant Izraad and Amalfitano, in the days following the ambush, had repeatedly assured the crew that the blast killed everyone in the conference room outright; they hadn't even known what hit them. *But what if—*

"Were they wrong?"

Wrong? She jerked her head up and briefly met his even stare, for an instant not sure what Amalfitano was talking about, then she remembered: command, and whether she was up to it or not. She again fixed her eyes on her hands, forced out the images of the ambush and focused on what he'd said.

She thought about past experiences when she had been given the conn. She remembered all the times when she had tried to out-think Cooper and Vildur during a crisis, had tried to put herself in the captain's position, only to find that her solution was more often than not the very same one Vildur had settled upon.

Recollections of her days at Cornwallis Base, the grueling command training she'd endured in order to prepare her for this very eventuality swam past, plucking at her consciousness. So involved in her thoughts, she didn't hear Amalfitano tap an order into the desk-mounted servo-panel.

Only when she overheard a soft chime did she return to the present reality.

She looked up to see him taking two steaming cups of coffee from the servo-door. He turned and smiled—a genuine, almost fatherly smile that chased what few remaining self-doubts she had.

"Here." He offered her one of the cups.

As she took it and brought it to her lips, he held up his own in salute.

Lesedi stopped, looked at him, waiting, but the doctor stared back in silence.

"To absent friends," she mumbled before taking a hasty sip of the hot liquid.

"To Captain Lesedi," he countered and swallowed his coffee in several loud, wincing gulps. Setting the now empty cup on his desk, he turned to a stack of flimsies, giving her a chance to absorb what he'd said as she sipped at her coffee.

Finally he leaned forward in his chair, his elbows resting lightly on the desktop. "So, what's your first order as captain?"

She jerked her head up, not sure what to say. It had to be something important, something impressive. Something… *captainly*.

"Well?"

"Ah, well… I think I should convene a department head meeting to discuss the entire situation."

His expression hardened. "You *think* you should, huh? And you want me to tell you if you should or not, right? What the hell have I just been talking about, Ife? Was I talking to myself—or maybe the wall? *Cacchio!*" He shoved himself away from his desk, got to his feet and strode out of the office.

She remained sitting, staring at his empty chair for several minutes then she found her gaze drawn to the holocube and the image of the dog who seemed to be smiling back at her, its eager expression urging her to make her move.

Okay, here goes. She leaned over the desk, pushed the stack of lab reports out of the way and pressed the desk-com button. "C and C?"

"Control. Stoker here—"

"Status."

"Unchanged, sir."

"Good. I'm convening a meeting of all departmental heads at, ah… fifteen hundred, in the starboard briefing room."

"Yessir. Is that all, sir?"

"Yes. Lesedi out." She released the button, looked back at the holocube and smiled.

"That wasn't so hard, was it?"

Lesedi spun around. Amalfitano was leaning against the doorframe, arms crossed and grinning.

She jerked her chin towards the cube. "Cute dog."

— iii —

Corsali knelt beside Gianakis and checked his pulse then pressed her palm to his forehead. Whatever Suhjai had given him and Aquila was still working—both appeared comfortable and by her reckoning, it had to be well past planetary noon.

Her stomach concurred with a grumble of protest and she gave the tray containing the remains of breakfast an unhappy look. While the spheres were quite soft when fresh, they became something akin to rocks in hardness within a matter of an hour or so.

Hungry as she was, she wasn't *that* hungry—and she was certainly not going to go look for anything fresh. One trip to the lower deck was enough for a lifetime—in fact a hundred lifetimes—*a thousand.*

At least Suhjai, during her brief, albeit unhappy house call, had also managed to repair Corsali's ripped undershirt using several self-sealing dressings to do the job.

She looked down at herself, gently test-plucked at one and sighed, "Very fashionable."

She got back to her feet and as she reached up to wipe her sweaty cheek, she caught a white flash out of the corner of her eye, just beyond the doorway.

She turned, squinted into the dazzle then clutching her patched shirt to her, backed up several startled steps as one of the aliens stopped in the doorway of the cabin, his silhouetted bulk nearly filling the opening.

Since childhood she, like all Coalition citizens, had been bombarded with horror stories about the little known alien race. Hahtooshans were the modern day 'Hannibal at the Gates': bogeymen used to frighten both children and adults alike, except these bogeymen were all too real. *Yowies indeed.* Her heart began to hammer against her ribs.

"May I?" He dipped his shaggy head then motioned with his open hand—permission to enter—and she replied with a very uncertain nod.

He stepped into the cabin, out of the near eye-dazzling glare and she almost breathed a sigh of relief as she realized it was none other than the officer rather than the surly Matoosh or worse, one of the grope-grabby troopers.

"I've come to ask if you and your companions would honor Suhjai and me by sharing our afternoon meal."

Corsali looked past him, expecting to see a Blatto laden down with a tray of food or even Suhjai—

"In our quarters... below decks," he added in reply to her furtive glance.

"I... ah," she stammered, "I m-m-mean, oh."

"Suhjai informed me of what happened." He motioned to her shirt without actually looking at it; in fact he appeared to be making a very concerted effort not to look by keeping his strange, pale eyes firmly locked with hers. "Torliss has been... disciplined."

She was briefly tempted to ask what 'disciplined' meant. She hadn't heard any blood-curdling screams or a loud splash of water of something large and squirming being heaved overboard. Perhaps his idea of discipline was more 'creative', less noisy, than his subordinate's?

She gave the officer's impressive personal armory another quick sweep with her frightened eyes. *On second thought, I really don't want to know.* She turned and gestured awkwardly to Aquila and Gianakis. "I... ah, think it would be best if we let them sleep—".

"And what about you, Ensign? You must eat, to keep up your strength, yes?"

"I'm... I'm really not hungry."

"Not hungry, or," he paused, "too frightened?"

She flicked him a sidelong look and bit her lip.

"As I thought," he sighed as he reached for a pouch hanging from his belt.

She countered by backing up another step while tightening her grip on her undershirt. *"Please..."*

He looked up and realizing she'd backed away replied irritably, "I give you my word as an Elkanaghalli and an officer of the Orthodoxy I mean you no harm."

I bet you tell all the girls that, just before— She couldn't help it; her gaze dropped to the dagger. *Gods!*

"You doubt my word?"

Corsali very reluctantly met his gaze; behind the façade of indignation stirred something else: an undercurrent of... desperation? *Perhaps it's all a façade, just like the commander said—a ruse—just like your humanoid form.* She knelt beside Aquila and began fumbling with his blanket. "Ah... well, it's... it's not that."

He squatted beside her and she froze. "What is it then?"

She fixed her eyes on her hands, on the blanket her fingers clutched, focusing on that to the exclusion of all else... like the fact that she had a Hahtooshan—a fully armed Hahtooshan—squatting next her, a scant few centimeters away. Finally she found a voice, although it didn't sound at all like hers: "I... I just don't think I should leave them."

"I could have my second, Matoosh Ruh'ta'aq, stand watch over them if that would ease your mind."

Out of the corner of her eye, she saw him smiling his best smile, which seemed just too guileless to be true, surrounded as it was by his hideous tattoos and elaborate scarification.

She gave her head one quick shake. "They might wake up and if I wasn't here—"

"They might do something… *foolish?*" With that he leapt to his feet and she forced herself to look up at his no longer smiling face.

He exhaled forcefully then shaking his head turned to the cabin's small table and finished untying the pouch that hung from his weapons belt.

What if this isn't a façade? She gave him an unguarded, appraising once-over. *So far you've behaved yourself. Given the choice, as company, you're certainly preferable to your buddies and let's face it you're all that stands between me and them… or the sea.*

She took a deep breath and suppressed a shiver. *If anyone's going to make that choice, it's gonna be me.*

Hoping to rekindle the conversation she'd so successfully squelched, hoping her voice wouldn't crack, she asked, "What's that, um… Sha'ashahn?"

"Food," he replied stiffly as he placed the pouch on the table and pulled it open, revealing several small bluish-green spheres. "Suhjai warned me you'd refuse. I'll leave you to eat when you *are* hungry." He started for the door.

She bit her lip then said, "Sha'ashahn?"

He stopped and looked over his shoulder; she met his sidelong glower and steeling herself, held up her hand.

He stared at her for a moment, clearly surprised, then, even more surprising, he walked back to her, wrapped his fingers—bare fingers this time, like his soldiers, not armored—around hers and gently pulled her to her feet. His hand kept its hold a little longer than needed. Long enough for her to find herself surprised at just how hot his bare skin was. Long enough for her mind to detect the roughness of heavy calluses on his fingers and heel of his palm; that his *very* human-looking hand and fingers were likewise elaborately tattooed—

Realizing she was studying his hand, he abruptly released his hold and again turned for the door.

"Please," she began, "I didn't mean to offend you. Truly. It's just your hands…"

He stopped but this time kept his back to her as he grumbled, "What about them?"

"They…" She took a deep breath, decided to go for broke. "They look so human."

"Indeed?" he replied coldly then held his hands up in front of him and studied them, front and back, as if for the first time. "How terribly shocking—for you." He shot her a sidelong, hateful glance as he dropped his hands to his sides. "Please accept my sincerest apologies."

"Please." She took a step towards him. "I didn't mean that the way it sounded—"

"Indeed? How did you intend it to sound?"

"—it's just..."

"Just what?"

She took a step closer; her heart was thumping wildly now, her lips had gone dry and her mouth felt like cotton. "You have to understand, I was raised to be terrified of Hahtooshans—and here I am, alone with one. I have no idea what you want."

"I wanted to share a meal, perhaps some intelligent conversation—*nothing more*, so don't flatter yourself." He squinted at her, a hard look that seemed to cut right through her then with a jerk of his chin continued, "Does it ever occur to you that I find you and your kind *just* as disconcerting? Just as... repellant? *No?* Of course not! You are human. And humans, as all sentient beings know, are the personification of all things virtuous while we A'tuu'shahn'i are the embodiment of pure evil, the beast that lurks in the shadows. What do your people call us? *Yowies?* Meaning we're brutish creatures, barbarous monsters capable of the most monstrous acts. *Yes?"*

"I'm sorry—" she stopped, snorted softly and shook her head. "I keep saying that, don't I? And then I immediately go and do something else to offend you."

He only shrugged at that, a slight twitch of his shoulders, nothing more.

"My only excuse is that I'm scared, for myself, for them," she motioned to Aquila and Gianakis.

He took a deep, ragged breath then exhaling wearily fixed his narrowed gaze on what lay beyond the doorway.

She almost expected him to say, "I'm scared too." *Are you? What in hell could a Hahtooshan be scared of?*

After another awkward pause, she walked over to the table, hoping he wouldn't take this as a dismissal and leave while her back was turned, and began pulling spheres of bread from the pouch.

They were still warm and soft and she hoped her suddenly growling stomach didn't startle or offend him. "Looks like you brought more than enough for all of us." She turned and was pleased to find he hadn't moved. *Pleased? Okay, maybe not pleased. Surprisingly relieved?*

She smiled, tentatively, and held out a chunk of the bread. "Stay?"

He hesitated, then nodded and as he walked towards her, he produced a small flask from under his hauberk that was, she suddenly noticed, a coppery brown, like old, well-oiled leather, albeit rather grimy leather. In fact his entire uniform, from boots to collar, was the same shade and had been since his unexpected arrival, but she'd been too scared, too preoccupied to notice. Everything else, every appendage, every accessory however, was just *as* she remembered it and *where* she remembered it, as was the constantly changing texture of the bizarre uniform's underlying material.

She raised a quizzical brow. "Your uniform…"

"Yes?"

"Wasn't it black?"

"Last night? Of course."

Corsali eyed him again, reminding herself that he was a shape-shifter after all. Altering the color of his attire and weaponry, in the greater scheme of things, would be a minor case of sleight of hand—certainly less complex than its mutable texture. "You mean it changes color, depending—"

"Upon my surroundings and circumstance—had you noticed my approach, you would have realized it was in fact white before I stepped into the cabin, all the better reflect the suns' rays, but," he made a face, "not a particularly handsome hue. This," he swept his hand across his chest, "is the preferred shade for ship-board attire."

Curiosity getting the better of her, she reached out to touch the hem of the hauberk but its texture morphing suddenly speeded up as if anticipating—dreading—her touch, stopping her just short of making contact. She looked up to find him staring warily at her outstretched fingers.

She quickly withdrew them, adding casually, "How does it change?"

"Color? By the use of imbedded chromatophores, iridophores and leucophores," he replied matter-of-factly, as if it was common knowledge.

"And the changing texture?"

"Electroactive polymers."

"Under your conscious control?"

"Yes." To emphasize the point, his body instantly evaporated as his uniform—including the jewel-colored gorget at his throat and handful of multihued medallions that adorned his hauberk and bandoleer—took on the exact coloring and pattern of the woven backdrop of the cabin wall. It would have been the perfect camouflage but for his bare head and hands, which were now suspended like parts of a disembodied puppet.

Her eyes widened and her jaw dropped in unabashed astonishment. *What the fu—*

"But our duty uniforms such as this, as well as our battle armor have the ability to respond to changing conditions without conscious input from the wearer," he added as the ghillie suit abruptly returned to its earlier coppery and decidedly *solid* shade and the gorget and medallions to their vivid colors. "You do not have such technology." It was said as a statement of fact, rather than a question.

She shook her head as she gave his grubby but nonetheless truly astonishing uniform another look; she knew she was tantalizingly close to solving the mercs' shape-shifting abilities and it had to do with his disconcerting attire—assuming it was a uniform and not his real skin—she just had to keep him talking and with luck he'd let something significant slip, like what he really looked like. He'd clearly sought out her company for a reason; maybe he'd been telling the truth, maybe he wanted nothing more than intelligent conversation... and what could be more scholarly that discussing his ability to shape-shift?

"Your Coalition would deem the use of such... underhanded."

She reluctantly pulled her gaze off the uniform and all it implied; to her chagrin he'd changed subjects, perhaps deliberately, perhaps not, but the last thing she wanted to do was risk his ire again.

Let him talk, maybe he'll come back to the subject of his own accord. "Underhanded...?"

"Most sentient beings have developed a very elaborate code of conduct when it comes to combat: fight or flight, posture or surrender. We A'tuu'shahn'i do not subscribe to those rules. We *don't* run, we *never* surrender and we do not posture. *Well...*" He shrugged. "...I suppose that's not entirely true. Often times the mere mention of us will cause people to rethink their plans and not to press the issue further." He flicked her a sidelong, lopsided, and surprisingly disarming smile, then continued, "But when paid to do so, we fight. To increase our odds of winning for our clients, we use stealth, such as this attire and that makes anyone who deals with us very... *uncomfortable.* But rather than admit that, our enemies accuse us of using unfair, cowardly tactics."

"Like shape-shifting?" No sooner had she said it than she regretted it, realizing she'd just said shape-shifting was a coward's trick...

He stared at her, an odd look in his very odd eyes, but instead of reacting as if he'd just been insulted again and this time deliberately, he replied, "Let's say that we A'tuu'shahn'i pride ourselves on being prepared for any contingency and leave it at that." He popped the stopper of the bottle and took a deep, wincing swig.

"So it would seem," she replied, both relieved and frustrated, as her nose caught a whiff of the distinctive, musty aroma of the native ale.

He wiped the top with his sleeve then held out the bottle, offering it to her.

Corsali again met his gaze. He certainly looked real enough, the human shape he'd embraced appeared solid enough, although the elaborate scarification and overlying tattoos were distracting—calculatingly so, she realized. They were a form of camouflage every bit as effective as his chameleon-like panoply, possibly even integral to his shape-changing abilities. Even this close it was hard to accurately access his features, some were obscured, others, like his nose and browridges were exaggerated by the pattern of inky-black swirls and complex designs carved into his sweat-glossy, olive-brown skin—like mist on water, all the better to conceal any minor flaws, any overlooked details in the underlying façade.

And his eyes... they glittered like polished mica. *One-way mirrors—deliberately impenetrable.*

There's someone very interesting lurking, hiding, back there, isn't there? Maybe you are scared. Of what? Certainly not me.

Corsali suddenly realized she was staring again and this time he was staring back, unblinking, as if challenging her to see past her own reflection, her own preconceptions, her own deeply held prejudices.

She cleared her throat as she looked at the proffered flask. "Thank you, but no."

He shrugged and took another, deeper swig from it.

She offered him the bread again, but he shook his head and as he swallowed his mouthful she said, "You speak trade-standard like an Earther," then she took a bite—a very large bite—of the bread.

"You do not. You speak like a colonist." He cocked his head to one side, studied her for a moment as she chewed, then added: "Selkis?"

Corsali, her cheeks bulging, couldn't help but smile, acknowledging his impressive skill at picking up the fine nuances of accent. Few people had ever heard of Selkis, even fewer able to identify the far-flung colony's particular inflections. She managed to swallow her mouthful then said, "You have a very good ear." She took another bite, smaller this time, forcing herself to slow down, despite her hunger.

"I speak many languages, as well as a number of their dialects like… a native, as do all A'tuu'shahn'i. It's very useful in our line of work. One never knows who one might be dealing with, or working for."

"Ah." Corsali couldn't help but think of the two soldiers, and their very believable pretense at not understanding her. She took another bite, tearing it off the small loaf with unnecessary force. *Yes you did, you fucking bast—*

"And our clients always seem to feel so much more at ease plotting the murder of their neighbors when they can do it in their own provincial tongue." He gave her a sidelong look and his lips drew back into the faintest of wicked grins.

"Very funny," she replied sourly as she wiped some crumbs from her lips.

"Perhaps." He started to bring the flask back to his lips. "But it's also the truth." He took a gulp from the flask.

"You seem to know a lot about us, about the Coalition I mean."

He swallowed then replied, "And that surprises you?"

"No—I mean we know so little about your Orthodoxy—"

"So therefore we should be equally ignorant of you? Your Coalition dominates this part of the rim, encompassing over a thousand worlds. We A'tuu'shahn'i have learned to tread carefully, lest we be crushed underfoot."

Tread carefully? She gave him and his weapon-encrusted chameleon ghillie suit a sidelong look as she nibbled on what remained of the small loaf, reluctant to finish it off and grab another, proving she *was* that hungry... and had lied about it.

"Perhaps you know so little of us because your Coalition never asked, or more accurately did not care to know—so much easier to vilify the strange than the familiar, yes?"

"Well, I'm asking."

"Why?"

He did seem in a chatty mood and she figured what the hell—he'd said he wanted conversation and maybe, just maybe, she could get him back to discussing his uniform... and those other 'unfair tactics' he'd alluded to. "I'm intensely curious. It's not like I get the chance to talk to a Hahtooshan every day."

He eyed her and arched a tattooed brow, almost mockingly, as if to say, 'Are you sure?' and she felt a shiver run up her spine. *Come to think of it, I'm not—*

"So what do you wish to know?"

She blinked, taken back; she hadn't expected him to acquiesce so easily and so foolishly didn't have any questions at the ready. But now he was waiting, apparently willing to talk freely—a truly unprecedented opportunity—and she had to come up with something and quick. She stuffed what remained of the bread into her mouth, using that as a stalling tactic, chewed thoughtfully—longer than she needed to—finally swallowed, then began, "Well, um... okay, for starters, how about your basic political structure?" It seemed a good place to start—a total unknown to her and everyone else in the Coalition... but no sooner had she voiced it than she recalled her father's warning: 'Never discuss religion or politics with anyone who wants something from you or you want from them as it's a sure fire way to kill a conversation'.

To her relief this particular Hahtooshan clearly hadn't met her father or heard of that rule because he answered readily, "Equating your systems of governance to ours is very difficult. But I suppose the closest parallel would be a merit-based oligarchy?"

She absently reached for another loaf of bread as if her stomach was guiding her hands, rather than her brain, too late realizing what she'd done. "And…?"

"Under our system, contracts are awarded by the Q'shaathrah, based on the needs of the client. These days those needs are for ships and soldiers to settle our clients' fights for them."

"These days? Meaning it wasn't always that way?" She tore off another small chunk and stuffed it in her mouth. As ravenous as she was, she didn't want to have a mouth full of food at an inopportune time. Small, easily swallowed pieces for now, while he was willing to talk.

He shrugged, said, "There was a time, thousands of generations ago, when A'tuu'shahn'i were not feared, not shunned, but sought out as the finest engineers, scientists and terraformers—a case of history repeating itself, or, more accurately, *reversing* itself."

She squinted at him, wondering what he meant by that but loath to interrupt.

"Our ships were considered the standard by which all others were judged. Led by the Elkanasu, we were the first to explore the farther reaches of the outer Rim; we even discovered a number of planets your Coalition now claims as its own and many of our navigational maps are still in common use—not that anyone acknowledges their original source. Of course not."

"So, what happened?" Without thinking she popped a large piece of bread in her mouth.

He took another gulp from the flask, winced as he swallowed, then looked down at himself, at his filthy panoply as if in utter disgust. With a sigh, he fixed his narrowed gaze on what lay beyond the doorway and replied simply, "We fell on hard times."

Corsali watched him, waiting, hoping he would elaborate while she quickly and quietly reduced her mouthful to easily swallowable sizes.

But she needn't have rushed. He took several more measured sips from the flask and roughly wiped his mouth with the back of his hand before turning back to her. "So, being A'tuu'shahn'i, we did what we do best. We adapted. We used our superior technology, our superior skills to carve ourselves a new niche, or, I suppose you could say we cleaned out a very old niche."

She arched a brow. *You sure are one for the cryptic remarks, aren't you?* Aloud she replied, "As mercenaries."

"And to you that's deeply repugnant, yes? You look upon us as cold-blooded monsters—butchers for hire."

Before she could deny the obvious, he continued, "You Rimmers have directed all of your energies, all of your technologies towards the goal of killing from a distance, a way of seeking not only new territories, but also *group absolution* for your insatiable avarice.

"You even use euphemisms to further distance yourself—you *eliminate* a target, you *mop up* resistance—but *you* didn't actually see the enemy die, therefore your brain tells you maybe you didn't really kill him, so why feel guilty? Distance killing makes those who engage in it feel less criminal, less culpable, but the dead are still dead, the maimed still crippled," he added with an audible note of bitterness.

"Close-up killing on the other hand, where you see your opponent and he sees you, where you smell his fear mixed with your own... that's considered the act of a monster—a butcher, a... *merc*. To kill close up, to actually watch your opponent die..." He twitched his shoulders and fixed his now slitted gaze on what lay beyond the doorway. A moment passed, awkward and silent, then: "I *feel* the responsibility, the guilt; I acknowledge the simple fact that the enemy is, in truth, no different than me, yet *I* am deemed the monster." He snorted, paused to take another angry gulp then flicked her a sidelong, challenging look as he swallowed, loudly.

Sensing he'd just revealed something critical, accidentally or deliberately, and at the same time feeling the overwhelming need to defend herself, defend her species, the Coalition, she replied: "But Hahtooshans use planet-killers—"

"Only as a last resort when all else has failed. Often just the threat, rather than the deployment of such a weapon is enough to force the enemy into surrendering. In the long run it actually saves lives on both sides, as well as the planet, as that is usually what our clients covet. Regrettably," he sighed, "there is the rare occasion when the only way to settle a quarrel, once and for all, is to remove the object of the dispute."

"By utterly destroying an entire planet."

He dropped his gaze to the flask he clutched in his hand. "While A'tuu'shahn'i are universally reviled for what we do, Ensign, we are very, *very* good at it—we had excellent teachers after all—it does pay handsomely and there is never a lack of willing customers—we're richer now than ever before. Many within the Orthodoxy use that as reason enough that we should never attempt to return to what we once were."

She stared at him, sensing a chink in his intellectual armor. "And you?"

"I fear we are at great peril of becoming victims of our own success, yet another case of repeating hist—"

"Sha'ashahn."

They turned to find Suhjai in the doorway, an expression of feigned surprise on her heavily tattooed face. Corsali wondered how long she'd been standing there, eavesdropping—perhaps the entire time. Maybe the officer had sensed her presence early on and had continued to talk, just to bait her, knowing she'd interrupt before he said anything too revealing. Or maybe this too was all an act; maybe the two had carefully choreographed the whole thing.

"I did not expect to find you still here," Suhjai added as she stepped into the cabin.

"Just as you proposed, she was understandably reluctant to leave her companions…"

Suhjai favored Corsali with a cold stare.

"…so it was decided we'd eat here," he continued. "You're most welcome to join us."

Suhjai looked at the half-eaten piece of bread Corsali held, forgotten, in her hand. Then, fixing Corsali herself with a resentful glance, she said, "Looks like you've already started, or should I say almost finished. Besides, I have work to do."

"Yes, of course," he replied with just the faintest hint of a sneer as Suhjai knelt beside Gianakis. "How *could* I forget?" With that he brought the flask back to his lips and took several deep, and, Corsali suspected, deliberately loud gulps.

— iv —

Lesedi entered the cramped briefing room at precisely fifteen hundred; everyone whose presence she'd requested was already there, seated at the elliptical table. As she walked in, conversation immediately ceased and coffee cups settled on the tabletop.

"Ife?" Amalfitano pointed to the chair next to him, at the head of the table. "Over here."

She felt like an interloper as she slipped onto the chair Vildur had always occupied and Amalfitano, sensing her thoughts, flashed her a reassuring grin and poured her a cup of coffee.

To Lesedi's left was Izraad, and beside her, Stoker, then the tac-op, Zayyad, and helm, Eisele. Next to Amalfitano was Perou, from engineering. Beside him sat the chief scanner operator, Cyllo, and next to her, McGuigan, the quartermaster. At the far end of the table was the head of environmental, Cajori, and the chief navigator, Pardix.

Lesedi had spent most of the day reworking her thought patterns so that she was genuinely beginning to think of herself as the ship's commanding officer. Orders were getting easier to give and delegating duties was becoming second nature.

Now all she had to do was to convince these officers that she was the captain. *Here goes.*

"I called this meeting so that you would all have an opportunity to air your views on our current... predicament. I believe the best way to go about this is to have each department head give us an update for their area then I'll open the meeting up to discussion. But, before we start, I need to say a few of things. First, I am in command. And I, as captain, expect full cooperation from all departments. If I sense any hesitancy on your part, rest assured, I'll deal with it accordingly. Once we leave this room, I will not tolerate anyone second-guessing me in front of the crew. All final decisions will be mine, and responsibility for them will be mine.

"Next, my chief responsibility is the safety of this ship and her crew. After that is my duty to try to locate and recover the missing members of the landing party. If those two duties conflict, let me tell you now that the crew and the ship comes first, Commander Aquila and the other missing second, as I know he would want it. Lastly, Ensign Zayyad, you're to immediately assume the duties of Exec, along with those of tactical officer."

Taken off-guard, Zayyad, who had just taken a gulp of hot coffee, began spluttering then coughing. He stared at her with streaming eyes and managed a curt nod then began coughing again.

"That is of course if you survive inhaling your coffee," Lesedi added. Her off-the-cuff comment had an unexpected effect, everyone smiled or chuckled softly and there was a palpable easing of the tension. "Okay, now on to the department head reports. Doctor Amalfitano?"

Amalfitano acknowledged each officer as his eyes swept the room, then he began. "Lieutenant Teague is suffering from severe hemolytic pneumonia, caused by the aspiration of some very fine dust particles while on the planet. Unfortunately, the dust also contained the same bacterial spores we found in the saliva and stinging organs of the native predators, which means these spores are able to survive in a free, wind-blown state, something we must take into account when planning any future planet-falls. We're now getting positive cultures from his blood, so it's only a matter of time before he'll start displaying the same life-threatening symptoms as Niebuhr…"

And which killed Private Arctoi, Lesedi thought to herself.

"…I've ordered precautionary physical examinations for everyone who came into contact with the lieutenant, along with ordering Environmental to institute a full airborne contaminant protocol. I've also notified all departments of the symptoms to be on the lookout for, but so far nothing's turned up. At this time I don't believe anyone else from the second landing party is at risk. According to Trooper Poole, the lieutenant was having trouble with his visor fogging up, and so cracked the seal to vent the moisture. My staff were closely monitoring the rescue squad's vitals and Lieutenant Teague's respiratory rate was quite elevated at the time, which would account for the fogging issue, and the combination of cracking the seal and his increased breathing rate led to him inhaling a minuscule, but nevertheless very hazardous amount of these spores."

Amalfitano clasped his hands together and met Lesedi's attentive stare. "Niebuhr remains extremely critical and we haven't been able to develop an approach that's effective against the disease organism. Lab hopes they'll have something in the next few hours, so all we can do right now is wait."

Lesedi nodded and turned to Stoker. "What about communication, Ensign?"

"Foldspace capabilities are still impossible due to the present phase in EM output, sir. I can't see any chance of transmitting a message to HQ or even the nearest Coalition planet unless we leave the system's umbrella of interference. Communication with the Hahtooshan vessel will also vary with the intensity of the flare activity."

Lesedi turned next to the head of environmental. "Cajori?"

"So far the radiation screens are holding, sir, but we've picked up some minute alterations in power levels. The screens are weakening, slowly, but weakening nonetheless. I calculate that we can remain here in orbit for approximately forty-eight hours, if the flare activity doesn't intensify, before the screens weaken enough to allow significant leakage."

"Any improvement with the scanners?" Lesedi shifted her gaze to Cyllo.

"No, sir, still too much interference. As you're aware, there's a projected decrease in flare activity in a little over four hours. At that time we should be able to punch a hole in the atmosphere and get some intelligible results."

Lesedi clasped her hands together. "So, in summary, this is our situation: we're in orbit around a planet whose binary is highly unstable, and while the Rasal Ghul system was once claimed by the Coalition, as of the last Determination and Delineation of Borders by the Coalition Central Committee, a little over twenty years ago, it wasn't listed as territory or even a protectorate—"

"Who'd want it, much less fight over it?" Cajori muttered, just loud enough for everyone to hear and respond by nodding.

"Indeed," Lesedi replied. "On this planet are the remains of a wrecked Hahtooshan vessel and six members of our landing party, all of who are presently unaccounted for. They may be incapacitated or dead. They might also be in the hands of any Hahtooshans who survived the crash of their vessel.

"Nearby is a Hahtooshan gunboat, and its captain has already stated its desire for us to leave the area. It may decide to force the issue. And at present, we're unable to communicate with HQ and make our situation known to them.

"Lieutenant Teague made it clear to the Hahtooshans that we would not leave until the stellar activity decreased enough that we could attempt locating our missing. That deadline is quickly approaching.

"We never did get a response to the Lieutenant's suggestion of collaboration, but since the Hahtooshans have made no hostile moves, I feel it's safe to assume that they'll allow us to remain just long enough to attempt retrieval but no longer, at least not without a fight.

"There is also another time factor, one which Ensign Cajori has mentioned, and that's the increasing risk of radiation. We can safely remain here no more than two more days. I doubt however, that the Hahtooshans will allow us to stay that long.

"So, unless someone can offer up a better plan, it's my intention to remain here until the present phase of activity dies down, which is scheduled to reach levels acceptable to resume sensory search by nineteen hundred hours, do as thorough a search as is possible and hope that we're able to locate the missing.

"If we're unable to do so and are ordered by the Hahtooshans to depart, my plan is to break orbit and take the ship to a distance far enough away that we can make contact with Headquarters. We will apprise them of the situation and await their orders. If anyone has a better idea, now's the time to voice it." She looked around to find heads shaking; clearly everyone found the thought of abandoning the missing on the planet abhorrent but also realized that, as a final option, it was the only sensible thing to do—all but one that is.

Pardix was glaring at her with ill-concealed contempt.

Shoulda known. The navigator had been a challenge for her ever since he transferred aboard and his hatred for all things Hahtooshan was a well-known fact. "Mister Pardix, you appear unhappy with the plan I've laid out. I assume you have a better idea?"

"Better than yours of turning tail and running if those mercs cry *boo?* Damned straight I do! That's Commander Aquila down there, and you're seriously thinking about just leaving him to the mercy of those fucking butchers?"

Amalfitano opened his mouth. "Wait just—"

"I say we stay until we find the commander and to hell with the Hahtooshans!" Pardix turned to Zayyad. "A few well aimed seeker missiles up their collective asses will probably bring them around to our way of thinking, don't you agree, Khaleed?"

Zayyad stared back at him.

"Well? *Say something!*" Pardix snarled. "I know you don't agree with this plan of Lesedi's!"

Zayyad continued to stare.

"I see! Now you're second in command, you've suddenly forgotten any allegiance you had to Commander Aquila. *Great!* Well I find it difficult to put my faith, not to mention my life, in the hands of some wet behind the ears ensign with delusions of grandeur and little combat exper—"

"That's enough," Izraad interrupted calmly, but firmly. "Ensign Lesedi was next in line for command. And it would be in everyone's best interest if—"

"*Everyone's?*" Pardix growled as he rose from the table. "How 'bout Commander Aquila? How 'bout the others? I can't see this being in their best interest!"

Lesedi started to respond but Izraad beat her to it and said, "Ensign Pardix, none of us like this plan, not even Ensign Lesedi. No one wants to leave the commander and the others behind. And, if I remember correctly, the ensign did not suggest we just up and leave without a thorough search *first.* Like it or not," she added, "we cannot stay here forever, even if our Hahtooshan friends say that's just peachy with them. We all heard Ensign Cajori's report on the shielding. And there's still the matter of the *Herrick.*"

Lesedi blinked. With everything else happening at once, she'd totally forgotten about the missing liner. Aquila wouldn't have; Vildur *definitely* wouldn't have. *Shit, shit, shit!*

Izraad made brief eye contact with each person seated at the table before she continued, "Captain Vildur is dead. Commander Aquila is missing and Lieutenant Teague is incapacitated. It's now up to us. We must hold this ship together, to function as if nothing is amiss. To do otherwise would dishonor those officers."

She turned to Lesedi. "I, for one, have complete faith in Ensign Lesedi. I suggest that those of you who don't," she shot Pardix a sidelong glance, "at least give her a chance." She leaned back in her chair. "That's all I have to say."

"Thank you, Lieutenant Izraad," Amalfitano said. "You've summed up the situation perfectly. We must provide a united front, for the peace of mind of the crew... and the lack of it for the Hahtooshans."

"What do you say, Tace? Truce?" Lesedi asked but Pardix only stared back in stony silence.

Eisele jabbed him in the ribs and whispered, *"Tace...?"*

"Truce," he finally mumbled.

"Then I suggest we adjourn," Lesedi said then added, "dismissed," when no one moved.

Chapter 7

Lesedi turned to Cyllo. "Any change?"

Cyllo, without looking up from her bank of active screens, said, "There's a definite decrease in Gamma's photospheric granulation, sir, with an associated diminution of plasma transfer to Beta, but the residual EM radiation's still affecting the planet's ionosphere in a way to make it highly reflective to our probes."

Lesedi squinted at her. *A simple 'no' would have sufficed.* "Zayyad," she turned to the tactical officer, "what're our friends up to?"

"So far they've been maintaining their distance, sir. No change in ship's status."

"Stoker?"

"No change in foldspace, sir. But channels are clear to the Hahtooshan ship."

Lesedi turned her attention to the tactical display. *Will they sit back while we search?*

"Sir…?"

She jerked her chair around to face Cyllo.

"Scanners are starting to pick up surface features—sir! For just an instant scanners registered human life form readings, but…" Her eyes crinkled into a puzzled squint as she stared down at the screen.

"But…?" Lesedi prompted apprehensively.

"The readings are located almost two hundred kilometers east south-east of the landing site coordinates."

"Two hundred…?"

"Yessir, off the coast—"

"Is it possible it's due to some sort of atmospheric refraction, giving a false location?"

"Possible, I'll re-calibrate."

"What about the area surrounding the landing site?"

"The site should be coming within range in a little over eight minutes—"

"Sir," Stoker interrupted, "I'm receiving a message feed from the Hahtooshan ship."

Lesedi scowled at the tactical display. *Shit!* Aloud she said, "Let's hear it—*Stoker?* Put a voice imitator on—I wanna sound just like Lieutenant Teague." She looked briefly at Pardix's back. "I wouldn't want 'em to get confused over who's in charge over here. They might get cocky and think they can take advantage."

Stoker ignored Pardix's muffled snort. "You got it, sir."

— ii —

"Ta'ahn?"

Ru'asooli shifted in his chair and reluctantly opened his eyes.

"Ta'ahn?"

He shifted his gritty gaze to Lura'jaii, who, at that moment, was standing next to the communications console and its operator and grumbled, "What?" Only then did he realize he'd been napping, he was sure of it—and on the bridge no less. Perhaps no one had noticed? Even he didn't believe that. No, they'd all noticed. He could tell by their furtive glances. He didn't even want to think about how long he'd actually been asleep.

"Tarqk Nahru'tzrhi has contacted the Coalition vessel."

"What?" Ru'asooli snarled, half-rising out of his chair, his anger at himself, his anger at Lura'jaii for allowing him to be caught napping on duty, shifted, instantly and pinpoint to Tarqk. "Put it on!"

Lura'jaii nodded and tapped the com-op on the shoulder.

There was a burst of static, followed by Tarqk's raspy voice: *"...stellar activity has decreased. We give you two standard hours to locate and retrieve your missing."*

There was a pause, long enough for Ru'asooli to curse explosively, before Tarqk continued, *"Do not interpret our generosity as weakness. We're willing to be patient while you search—but only for two hours. After that we will consider your remaining in orbit a provocative act against the Orthodoxy and respond accordingly."*

"What does he think he's doing?" Ru'asooli bellowed. "Jam their transmission!"

"But—"

"But *what?*" Ru'asooli snarled as he squinted balefully at Lura'jaii.

"Ta'ahn, by doing so, we risk exposing ourselves."

"Tarqk has overstepped his authority for the last time!"

"Agreed, ta'ahn, but if you'll permit me a suggestion?"

Ru'asooli eyed his second, his curiosity piqued. "I'll hear it then decide."

"Override his transmission, ta'ahn, but follow his lead."

"Follow his lead?"

Lura'jaii surprised him again when she stood her ground. "Computations state that the interference will not decrease enough for them to locate, much less retrieve their landing party... even if they knew where to look. By giving them this time, we allow them the chance to scan the area surrounding the wreck for their missing crew—but they will find nothing. We can then order them to leave, thus avoiding further escalating this confrontation."

Ru'asooli thought about what his second had suggested and to his chagrin realized that it made sense. Moreover, it was probably exactly what Tarqk had had in mind, and that only made him angrier... until it occurred to him he could both follow Tarqk's lead *and* teach the upstart who was really in charge. *Oh, yes.*

"Has the Coalition vessel responded?" He looked past Lura'jaii, to the com-op.

"Coming through now, ta'ahn—"

"*...this is the CEFS* Baidarka. *We're aware of the decrease in photospheric activity and are in the process of a scanner sweep. We have no desire to engage in hostilities, but we also have no intention of leaving orbit until we can determine the fate of our missing crewmembers. Once that's been accomplished, we will depart.*"

"Override," Ru'asooli said sweetly.

"Channel open, ta'ahn," the com-op replied as he gave Lura'jaii a sidelong look to which she replied with an equally uneasy stare.

Ru'asooli settled back in his chair and crossed his arms. "You have *two* standard hours to determine the fate of your missing, and two hours *only*." He signaled the officer to cut the link and favored Lura'jaii with an intensely smug smile.

— iii —

"What do you mean transmissions are jammed?"

The communications officer quailed.

"OVERRIDE!" Tarqk bellowed.

The hapless soldier turned back to his console. After a moment of futile effort, he turned back to the enraged officer. "I cannot—"

"Then you die!" Tarqk, his hand shaking in rage, jerked his pistol from its holster and squeezed the trigger. A beam of energy leapt out at the horrified com-op, engulfing him and his scream in a blinding flash.

There was a moment of shocked silence; no one moved.

It was broken by the smack of Tarqk shoving his pistol back in its holster. "Increase ventilation," he grumbled, his nose wrinkling at the stench of ineptitude. "And Qharubi, do something about... *that.*" He waved his hand at the still-smoldering communications seat.

Qharubi, seated at his console, stared at the nearby station in something akin to astonished paralysis.

Summary executions were not unheard of; he'd carried out some himself—for cowardice that cost the lives of others, for losing a contract due to gross incompetence. *But... this? And on the bridge?*

Like most A'tuu'shahn'i, or at least the successful ones, he'd learned to balance perfectly on the knife-edge of obedience and its alter ego, initiative.

Tarqk's increasingly capricious behavior had turned the delicate balancing routine into a frantic act of desperation. The now-pervasive climate of fear aboard the *Makhaira* had effectively hamstrung initiative—crew were too busy trying to outthink their volatile captain, anticipate his mood swings or avoid him altogether. *Tilt too far—*

"NOW!" Tarqk barked, startling Qharubi out of his frozen bewilderment.

He rose and started for the communications console. *You're mad, stark raving mad—*

"I want that override effect neutralized immediately!"

"But ta'ahn, Ru'asooli—"

"DO IT!"

"Yes, ta'ahn." Qharubi eased himself down onto what remained of the ruined chair. The weapon's beam had not only vaporized the communications operator, but had heavily damaged the console as well and he secretly cursed Tarqk—and his bad aim.

After a cursory assessment of the station, Qharubi rose to face his captain. "It's impossible, ta'ahn, without extensive re-routing and repair." He waited, watching as an expression of impotent fury washed over the already enraged officer's face.

"Nothing's impossible on my ship!"

Qharubi took a breath, assuming it would be his last.

"Wait, ta'ahn."

Both Tarqk and Qharubi turned to Tu'indai, equally shocked by her interruption.

"You dare to question my authority?" Tarqk hissed. "You overestimate your value!"

She calmly met his gaze. "Not question your authority, ta'ahn, only your timing."

Tarqk's eyes widened. *"Why you—"*

"To execute him now would be a waste of his expertise," she replied evenly, her eyes never wavering from Tarqk's. "Let him complete the repairs... *then* execute him."

Tarqk stared at her for a moment before bursting into laughter. He slapped the arm of his chair and replied, "Excellent! Excellent, Tu'indai!" He turned to Qharubi and sneered, "You have your orders!"

"Yes, ta'ahn." As he turned back to the console, he caught a glimpse of Tu'indai and her gleeful expression. *You're both mad...* He clenched his teeth, fixed his narrowed gaze on the console and tried to decide where best to begin. *I'm going to need help.*

Indeed you are, another part of his mind replied. *Initiative, Qharubi. Initiative. The situation has tilted too far—*

"What are you waiting for?"

He flinched then realized it was Tarqk who had spoken and looked up. "I will need assistance."

"Then get it!"

"Yes... ta'ahn." Unable to page for the relief, he motioned for two other bridge crew to leave their posts to assist.

— iv —

Lesedi tapped her fingers on the arm of her chair as she waited for the crackle of interstellar static to die down then she turned to Stoker, eyebrows raised.

"I can't tell if they're still receiving, sir. That last burst might've—"

"See what you can do."

"Yessir."

While Lesedi watched Stoker's futile attempts to reestablish contact it struck her that there was something not quite right about the conversation. And the more she thought about it, the more she was convinced that the second voice sounded slightly different—a little deeper, less raspy—than the first. *Why would two speak for one ship?*

A mental warning light flicked on.

Something's very wrong here, but what? Is my nervousness making me hear things that aren't there or are my instincts telling me something? And come to think of it, why are they so damned eager for us to leave? What the hell're they up—

"They're definitely no longer receiving," Stoker interrupted. "I can't tell if it's deliberate, or a problem with their communications equipment. And sir...?"

"Yes?"

"I'd swear the last communication did not originate from the same area of space."

A small, but very cold knot formed in Lesedi's stomach.

"It's almost like two different sources, very close, almost overlapping." He shrugged. "Probably due to the radiation interference. I'll run a cross check on my equipment."

Yeah, you do that. Lesedi gave her belly an absent-minded rub and settled back in the chair. "Looks like we've got two hours, everyone. Let's make the most of it."

— v —

Ten strained minutes later, Cyllo straightened up and looked at Lesedi. "Sir, I've scanned an area one hundred kilometers in circumference surrounding the landing site—*nothing.*"

Lesedi tried not to look—or sound—as disappointed as she felt. "What about those earlier readings?"

"Spotty, sir. Readings suggest a surface vessel of some sort, or possibly a low and slow flying atmospheric craft. Tracking suggests it's heading towards an archipelago some two hundred and sixty kilometers off the coast with an indeterminate but concentrated number of other life-forms—"

"Indeterminate?"

"Readings are constantly being disrupted by some sort of low-level electronic interference—"

"What frequency pattern?" Izraad interrupted.

"One point three to one point six gigahertz, sir."

Izraad nodded. "The same high frequency, low intensity patterns that have been detected in sensor traces of Hahtooshans—"

"Sir!" Cyllo gasped. "I've just got three *human* readings!"

Lesedi leapt out of her chair and hurried to Cyllo's station; Izraad joined them.

"See? *There!* One very strong reading, the other two weak but definitely human!"

Lesedi smiled, but it faded almost immediately. "Only three—*you're sure?"*

Cyllo nodded then she too was struck by the implications of her readings. She checked them, again. "Confirmed."

"And they're located within the Hahtooshan frequency pattern," Izraad added, giving Lesedi a sidelong glance.

"Stoker—"

"Feeding coordinates to flickerstage… now, sir," he replied, and after a pause: "Flickerstage standing by for retrieval."

"Have they locked on to them yet?"

"Not yet," Stoker replied distractedly, eavesdropping on several conversations at once. "Still a lot of distortion, but the flicker chief says it's beginning to clear. Sir," he looked up briefly, "they're having real difficulty fixing the signal due to the surrounding interference." He turned to Lesedi. "Perou's on his way to assist."

Lesedi dropped heavily into her seat. "Now, if those goddamned mercs will just cooperate."

— vi —

Qharubi crawled out from under the console, wiped his stinging eyes then looked up to find Tarqk staring down him.

"Have you affected repairs?"

"I believe so, ta'ahn, but they're temporary at best."

Tarqk huffed irritably and as he turned away, Qharubi slowly got back to his feet then stood rigidly beside the communications station and its nervous relief operator.

"Ta'ahn!"

Tarqk fixed his cold gaze on the scanner officer. "What?"

The soldier glanced at Qharubi, then back at Tarqk. "The Coalition vessel—"

"What about it?"

The officer gave Qharubi another pleading look.

"He will not speak for you, Hebaath," Tarqk growled.

Hebaath's eyes flicked back to Tarqk and she began unsteadily, "Its scanners have located their landing party. Systems are locking on preparatory for... for retrieval—"

"WHAT?"

Hebaath cringed as she looked at Qharubi as if to affix blame as well.

Tarqk also turned to him, eyes blazing. "You said it would be impossible for them to locate them!"

"Ta'ahn, I said it would be highly unlikely, since they would be looking—"

"Khusaaq! He's done this deliberately!"

Qharubi wasn't sure what to say so wisely said nothing.

"Station!"

Qharubi hurried to his console as Tarqk snarled, *"Power up all systems!"*

A moment later, the relief com-op said, "Ta'ahn, I'm receiving a message from the Coalition captain. He demands an explanation for our provocative behavior—"

"Provocative indeed! *I'll* show him provocative. Engage flatspace engines. Prepare for foldspace integration. Plot course away from planet!"

The crew scrambled to obey his rapid-fire orders.

Qharubi stared at his command board, mentally checking off each of the ship's systems as they came on line at optimum levels. As he came to the last of the telltales, he narrowed his eyes and studied the read-outs. "Ta'ahn," he glanced over his shoulder, "may I suggest that tracking computers be disengaged?"

Tarqk eyed him suspiciously. "For what purpose?"

Qharubi felt now was not the time to remind Tarqk that he'd served as the *Makhaira*'s senior weapons officer and had performed in that capacity with such distinction that in recognition he was going to be elevated to the ship's commanding officer—or was, until Tarqk's unexpected, unexplained and very unwelcome transfer. "We sustained some scanner damage that has yet to be repaired, that plus the distortion created by the EM interference could cause false images in the tracking computers, decreasing our weapons effectiveness."

Tarqk stared at him in obvious doubt about his motives, his skills. Keeping his eyes locked with Qharubi's, he snarled, "Weapons officer!"

"Yes, ta'ahn?"

"Do you agree with Sha'ashahn?" His eyes slid to the crewman.

"What he says is possible, but... but I do not believe the damage or distortion will cause the difficulties he perceives."

"If you're wrong...." Tarqk murmured sweetly and the weapons officer swallowed hard as his eyes darted to Qharubi, but seeing no sympathy in the officer's eyes, he looked back at Tarqk and reluctantly nodded.

"Ta'ahn?"

Tarqk turned his exasperated gaze on the com-op. "What now?"

"I'm picking up a tight beam from Ru'asooli Kshira'tzrhi."

"A reply to the Coalition vessel," he growled to no one in particular. "When will that fool stop meddling!"

The officer hesitated then replied, "No, ta'ahn, the message is an encoded—"

"About time he explained himself!" Tarqk leaned back in his chair. "What does he have to say for himself?"

The officer blurted out, "Ru'asooli Kshira'tzrhi is attempting to contact the Orthodoxy, ta'ahn!"

Tarqk blinked then turned to Qharubi, his smug smile replaced in a heartbeat by a wide-eyed stare of apprehension. *"Is that possible?"*

"Acholilah's foldspace com-net and scanners were extensively damaged by the same EM burst that damaged our scanners," Qharubi replied calmly. "At last report, repairs had yet to be completed. Even if they had, the present level of ionic interference would make such contact impossible—"

"But Ru'asooli may not know that, since his scanners were also damaged," Tarqk said with audible relief. "And what's the content of this message?" He turned to the com-op.

"Ru'asooli Kshira'tzrhi is requesting more detailed information on the *Quezhphatanz*—"

"Tah!" Tarqk sneered as he angrily wiped the oily sheen of sweat from his cheek. "The old woman's finally looked at the data tapes." He settled into his chair and smiled. "But it just goes to prove that there's no idiot like a superior idiot."

Qharubi bit his lower lip against an involuntary grin. *No, there certainly isn't… ta'ahn.*

— vii —

"Status, Mister Zayyad."

"Hahtooshan ship's fully powered up main engines, sir. Field generators on line."

Lesedi turned to Stoker. "Any response?"

"Nossir, all hailing frequencies open—*wait!*" He hurriedly turned back to his console and began tapping in commands. "I'm picking up a tight beam transmission… it's very faint and garbled, but—"

"A response to my message?"

"Nossir," he replied distractedly, "it's… it's directed towards the central hub—"

"What are they saying?"

Stoker squinted in concentration as he eavesdropped on the message. "Unable to decipher, sir, but one word keeps being repeated: *Quezhatani*…" He shook his head in exasperation and glanced over his shoulder at Lesedi. "Or it may be *Kusatanzi*? The transmission's extremely corrupted."

Lesedi in turn looked at Izraad, eyebrow arched.

"I'll run a data search." Izraad turned to her console.

"Any way anyone could receive that message?" Lesedi asked.

"No," Stoker replied, puzzled. "All foldspace channels are still whited out. I don't understand it, their communications—"

"Sir?" Izraad interrupted. "Records state a Wuotani freighter by the name of *Quezhphatanz* disappeared in this region of space one hundred and thirty years ago."

"Why would mercs be interested in a Wuotani freighter that vanished over a century ago?" Pardix asked an instant before Lesedi could.

"Hell if I know," Lesedi shrugged.

"Maybe it's not the same ship," Eisele, the helm officer, suggested. "Maybe it's not a ship at all."

Lesedi turned to Stoker. "Anything more from the Hahtooshans?"

"Nossir. All transmissions have ceased. Still no response to our hail."

Lesedi thumbed the com button on the arm of her chair. "Flickerstage… Perou, any luck?"

"No sir," the engineer responded. "Still too much damned interference. We can't lock on to them long enough to commence retrieval."

"Keep trying. We've got a merc with a real itchy trigger finger—"

"*Sir!*" Zayyad interrupted. "The Hahtooshan ship—she's positioning herself to…" His voice trailed off as he stared at the readouts on his console and knit his thick brows.

"To…?" Lesedi repeated impatiently.

His eyes widened as new data filled his screen. "To leave orbit, sir! Flatspace engines are maneuvering her into a polar trajectory, presumably to take advantage of the planet's electromagnetic fields—*sir,* I'm picking up on massive power fluctuations. They're definitely planning on folding."

Lesedi glanced around the control room; everyone was at battle stations, all systems ready.

"Sir! They're folding, *now!*"

Lesedi turned to the tactical display just in time to see the telltale of the Hahtooshan ship abruptly shift position, leaving a glowing trail of ghostly doppelgangers across the gridded projection as the ship folded space around it. Then just as abruptly the telltale and its sensor ghosts winked out.

"What's her heading?"

Zayyad, his eyes glued to his console's screen, watched as the tracking computer traced the Hahtooshan ship's skipping path through space as the vessel briefly flickered back into existence each time it passed over a fold. "Interference is distorting the active tracking scanners. But I think their heading is—*SHIT! They're headed directly for us!"*

"Pardix... give us some room to maneuver!" She turned to Peters. "Weapons?"

"All systems green, sir."

"Sir!" Zayyad interrupted. "She's dropped out—" The deck shook violently as a massive concussion rolled through the ship. He clung to the arms of his chair then added breathlessly, "Glancing particle beam hit on secondary impeller ring!"

"Stoker! I don't care what the hell you have to do but get me that goddamned merc captain!" Lesedi fixed her furious gaze on the tactical display. The Hahtooshan ship, having abruptly dropped out of foldspace and back into flatspace was wheeling around for another run. She drummed her fingers on the arm of her chair, muttered, *"Stoker...*"

"Still no response—"

"Peters?"

"All tracking computers locked onto targets, sir!"

Lesedi watched as the warship completed its turning maneuver. "Fire on my command."

Seconds passed; the Hahtooshan ship raced towards them and still Lesedi remained silent, staring at the screen and the rapidly approaching vessel.

Peters gave her a nervous glance; several other bridge crew did likewise.

As the Hahtooshan ship got to within nine thousand kilometers, a new telltale lit up on the suspended holo: a warning that the caravel's multiple rail guns had activated in preparation to launching a point blank projectile volley at the *Baidarka*.

"Peters! Disengage tracking computers—fire manually!"

"But sir—"

"Do it!" Lesedi barked, adding hastily, "The tracking signals to the computers are being distorted by the interference. Use your eyes and take your best damned guess!"

"Aye sir, tracking computers off!"

She looked back at the tactical display. *"Fire!"*

Peters exhaled forcefully as he punched in the last digit of the firing sequence and the deck below them shuddered as a lethal barrage of particle beam fire lashed out at the oncoming ship.

A moment later the projected image of the warship vanished briefly into a dazzling ball of light.

"Glancing hit on matter intake guide, sir! She's coming about, main particle cannon energizing!"

"Distance?"

"Three thousand and forty five kilometers—*she's fired!* Impact in—"

"Hard about!"

The *Baidarka* shook as it spiraled out of the way of the particle beams and the energy wave sliced through the vacuum within meters of its primary impeller ring.

Even though the beams failed to make a hit, the disruption of particles in the surrounding vacuum caused a vibration that rippled outwards in an expanding sphere, engulfing the ship. Throughout the *Baidarka*, lights flickered and its hull groaned.

"Fire!"

Still tumbling in an evasive belly roll, the *Baidarka* fired another particle volley as the alien vessel swung under the planet's southern pole.

Just before it vanished behind the bulk of the planet, the tactical display registered a faint, telltale flash.

"A hit?" Lesedi looked at Zayyad.

"I think so. *Yessir!* A direct hit on their exhaust guides!"

She squinted at the tactical display, ignoring the loud whoop from Pardix. Instead of feeling elated, she felt the cold knot of dread reform... and grow.

She met Zayyad's equally sober stare. *That was too fucking easy.* She smacked the com button. "Flickerstage, what's your status?"

"Distortion clearing, sir, but we've gotten out of range of the surface coordinates—"

"Sir!" Cyllo interjected. "Photospheric granulation is increasing faster than computer models extrapolated, flaring will reactivate the ionosphere in less than ten minutes."

"Pardix—"

"Way ahead of you, sir. Course plotted and locked in."

Eisele, following Pardix's plot, spun the *Baidarka* around and down towards the planet.

A few minutes later, it leveled off as it dropped into a close, geosynchronous orbit.

"Cajori, how are the radiation screens holding?"

"So far they're holding, but those flares Cyllo spotted are *massive.*"

"How long can we stay?"

"Six hours, tops. After that the screens will burn up, and us with them."

"From the frying pan and into the fire," Izraad murmured dryly as she released the death grip she had on the arms of her chair.

Chapter 8

"Get up!"

Qharubi opened his eyes to find Tarqk, his gaunt face streaked with soot and his arms crossed, standing over him.

What the...? Qharubi risked a quick glance around only to find himself sprawled on the deck not far from his still sparking console. Nearby, stations were dark and the air was tinged with smoke and the pungent stench of cooked flesh—

"I said *get up!*" The snarled command was accompanied by a kick to his booted foot.

"Yes, ta'ahn," Qharubi replied, his blistered lips making anything louder than a raspy mumble impossible. He tried to sit up—and gasped in startled agony. He blinked back a flush of light-headedness then slowly, reluctantly, lifted his head just enough so he could slide his pinched gaze slowly down his soot covered and scorch-marked uniform. Taking stock of the visible damage, he suspected what he couldn't see was far worse.

Dislocated left shoulder... broken arm, badly burnt hands...

He stopped his gruesome inventory, suddenly unable to keep his head held aloft on a neck that felt like rubber, and closed his eyes—his vision was going anyway, graying around the edges. He was going into shock. Worse, he knew he was going into shock. Tarqk wasn't the sort of commanding officers who cared about such trivialities. *He's going to rather put out—*

"Sha'ashahn?"

His eyes snapped open, for an instant thinking it was Tarqk; instead he found relief com-op now squatting beside him.

"Let me help you." The com-op cast a quick, nervous glance over his shoulder before he turned back to Qharubi.

Qharubi didn't really want any help, especially to get up. He wanted to be left exactly where he was until he succumbed to his injuries. *Far less painful that way—or so I've heard.* He even made a half-hearted attempt at willing his duty uniform, which was already reacting to his injuries, stiffening around the fractured bones and pumping painkillers into his bloodstream, to leave him the hell alone. Not that it would listen. At least not under these circumstances, where help was this close at hand. It had its own agenda, and that agenda was to keep him alive until he could be delivered to that help.

"Ta'ahn…?"

He squinted furiously at the relief, or as furiously as he could manage with his sight coming and going, annoyed at the crewman's dogged persistence. He also knew there was no alternative, no relatively painless escape into oblivion. Tarqk was nearby and Tarqk was not about to let *that* happen, oh hell no.

He clenched his teeth as he drew his injured arm against him. Then with a curt nod to the com-op and with the com-op's help, he somehow managed to lurch to his feet. He stood there for a moment, visibly wobbling, eyes squeezed shut and lips clamped tight against the urge to vomit, then, using the crewman's proffered arm for support, he again looked around. What he saw sent his mind and stomach spinning anew: the tactical well was a shambles, bodies were welded to consoles, others, still smoldering, lay in crumpled heaps where they'd been thrown by the massive electrostatic discharge that had almost torn the ship apart.

Qharubi shifted his horrified stare to the com-op and mumbled through blood-sticky lips, "How many… many did we lose?"

"Five on the bridge." The crewman jerked his own badly blistered and bleeding chin towards his dark console. "As for the rest of the ship—"

"Return to your station!" Tarqk's voice barked from behind them.

The relief glanced at Qharubi, a look of pleading in his eyes.

"Go," Qharubi whispered hoarsely. *"Do what you can."*

The relief nodded and avoiding Tarqk's suspicious gaze, returned to his ruined console.

Qharubi steeled himself and slowly turned around, almost falling as he did so.

Tarqk looked him up and down then met his shocky stare. "Go to your quarters and make yourself more presentable."

"Yes, ta'ahn," Qharubi replied hoarsely. Using the wall for support, he stumbled out of the ruined tactical well.

"And seek medical attention," Tarqk tossed over his shoulder as Qharubi reached the airlock. "I want you fully capable to resume your duties when you return. I'll be generous. You have until the end of the watch before I want you back at your post."

Qharubi nodded as he pressed his trembling hand against the lock release.

At first nothing happened as if the lock itself was reluctant to allow him his escape, temporary as it might be.

Finally, the damaged airlock irised open and he staggered inside. The inner lock closed with a protesting groan, sealing him off from Tarqk's pitiless gaze and the stinging smoke and nauseating stench of melted circuits and charred flesh.

He leaned against the lock's wall, took a ragged breath and fixed his blurring gaze on the opposite door. *You can make it.* He took a very wobbly step, then another. *You have to.*

Within reach of the activator, he blacked out.

— ii —

Amalfitano stopped in the doorway of his office, crossed his arms and stared at the results of the ship's roller-coasterish evasive maneuvers. He sighed, shook his head then strode towards his desk, angrily snatching up flimsies as he went.

"Hey, Doc?"

Amalfitano looked up to find a member of the decontamination crew in the doorway. The man had a bloody nose and the start of one hell of a shiner.

Amalfitano gave his own discolored temple a rub as he muttered, "Fleming's tending to the bumps and bruises, Crewman." He turned back to the task of gathering up the flimsies that had been strewn across the floor.

"No, Doc, that's not why I'm here. I wanted to let you know we've finished. Actually, we finished a while ago, but—"

"Finished?" Amalfitano grumbled as he dumped an untidy stack of reports on his desk.

"Lieutenant Teague's cabin, sir? You ordered it decontaminated—"

"So?" he snapped as he stooped to snatch up another handful of reports.

"Well, Doc, I—"

"Look, Salazar, I really don't have time right now, okay?" He knelt, picked up the holocube that had been sent flying and was relieved to find it unscathed.

"But Doc, I came across something that might be important."

Amalfitano rose, started to replace the cube on its usual shelf, next to his prized collection of antique medical textbooks. "Like what?" Having second thoughts, he placed it on the desk and began straightening the stack of flimsies.

The crewman daubed his still profusely bleeding nose on his sleeve before answering, "Well, you see the lieutenant was looking at some data when he took poorly."

Amalfitano didn't look up as he placed the now semi-neat stack near the cube. "So?"

"It was still on his desk-top monitor's screen, Doc."

Amalfitano squatted to retrieve another handful of flimsies but stopped in mid-reach as he suddenly remembered Teague's remark, just before he collapsed, about having found *something*. He looked sharply at the tech. "What did you do with it?"

"I left it alone is what I did," Salazar replied as Amalfitano rose. "Told the others I thought you'd want to see the screen just the way the lieutenant left it—" He hastily stepped aside as Amalfitano hurried by, then followed him with his bemused gaze as he gave his bloody nose another rough wipe. "You're welcome, Doc. *Anytime.*"

Amalfitano hurried up the gentle rise of the corridor, oblivious to the tight smiles of relief from passing crew. Then, taking two steps at a time, he bounded up the emergency stairwell to the main residential deck.

The rest of the de-con crew were gathering up the last of the cleaning equipment as a breathless Amalfitano entered Teague's cabin.

"Everything's back in ship shape, Doc," one said.

Amalfitano didn't hear the comment as he slipped onto Teague's chair, didn't notice the techs file out and close the door behind them. His full attention was riveted on the monitor. Sure enough, the screen was still active.

He gave the information displayed a quick glance. *"Cazzo!"* he whispered as a cold shiver ran up his spine. Not taking his eyes from the screen, he tapped the desk-com. "Control? Amalfitano here—get me Lesedi."

There was a pause, then, *"Lesedi—"*

"Ife, I'm in Edwin's cabin—I've found something you need to see."

"Doctor, I've got a merc warship out there licking its wounds and—"

"Ife, *damn it*, this is important! Get down here—*now!* And bring Cyllo and Izraad with you!" He cut the link then tapped in a request to replay all of the data.

A few minutes later, the door opened.

"This better be damned important!" Lesedi snapped as she stormed in, Izraad and Cyllo on her heels.

Amalfitano rose from the chair and motioned for her to take it. "You be the judge."

Lesedi took the proffered chair and began reading the data displayed in the screen.

Izraad gave Amalfitano a worried glance then joined Cyllo behind Lesedi. Standing on tiptoe, she peered over Lesedi's shoulder.

Finally Lesedi looked up at Amalfitano, wide-eyed. "What have we stumbled on by accident?"

"You can bet the bank whoever bought the Hahtooshans' services knew *exactly* what they were looking for when they sent them here."

Cyllo blinked. "But the risk—"

"Pay those butchers enough," Amalfitano interrupted heatedly, "and no risk is too great."

"Yeah," Lesedi agreed. "And it certainly explains why they're so damned insistent that we leave." She pressed the desk-com button. "C and C?"

"Zayyad here, sir."

Lesedi briefly looked at Izraad and Amalfitano then turned back to the com-unit. "Notify all department heads, I'm calling an emergency meeting in ten minutes in the briefing room. Those unable to attend are to monitor the meeting on closed channels. I'll be in Lieutenant Teague's cabin until then. Notify me of any changes, Lesedi out."

— iii —

Amalfitano, Izraad, Cyllo and Lesedi entered the briefing room and Amalfitano immediately strode over to the main terminal and slipped the data disc into its waiting mouth. Cyllo sat down beside him as he checked to make sure the information was ready to be viewed. Izraad activated another terminal and began tapping in commands. Meanwhile, Lesedi paced the room, her eyes fixed on the floor.

Stoker, Tasende, Cajori and Perou hurried in, followed a moment later by a breathless McGuigan. As they took their seats at the table, each placed an earpiece in his ear so he would be kept informed of the status of his departments, without disrupting the meeting with the flood of continual updates.

Lesedi sat, gave each grim-faced officer a quick nod, then turned to Stoker. "Is that everyone?"

"Those not present will be on closed loop, sir. All have reported in and are waiting."

"Then let's get started. I called this meeting because Doctor Amalfitano just finished reviewing the data recovered from the wreck and has uncovered information that has a direct effect on any command decisions I make from here on out. I now ask Doctor Amalfitano to tell you what he's learned. Doctor?"

"The Hahtooshans," Amalfitano began, "or, more likely, a yet-identified person or government who contracted the Hahtooshans' services, somehow came into possession of information pertaining to a secret military base, a base located on the fourth planet of this system."

"Secret base?" Cajori asked apprehensively. "Whose base?"

"Ours," Lesedi answered sourly.

McGuigan arched a brow and snorted, "There's no secret military base on the fourth planet. If there was—"

"Not now," Lesedi interrupted. "It was abandoned well over a hundred years ago. Doctor, please continue."

"The base was, as I said, a secret. Its location was ideal: an isolated system known for its sporadic and violent flare outbursts—a system any sentient being in their right mind would avoid. And there was the added benefit: the same shielding that protected the base's staff from the intense radiation would have made covert transmissions near impossible—"

"Even if there was a radical decrease in stellar output," Zayyad's disembodied voice crackled from the briefing room's speaker, *"the constant background interference would have masked all but the most powerful of tight-beams. It was only by chance we heard that SOS from the wreck, and only because it was being broadcast from the seventh planet, not the fourth, and we just happened to be in the right place at the right time—"*

"Or the wrong place at the wrong time," McGuigan muttered, to which prompted nods from several seated at the table.

"And all this security was for a damned good reason," Amalfitano replied. "The sole purpose of this base was the creation of biological warfare agents."

Each face that stared back at him registered shock, then growing comprehension.

Cajori muttered a profanity under his breath; Perou mumbled his hearty agreement.

"The Hahtooshan crew of the craft which crashed on the planet below managed to download the base's data banks, which, unfortunately, had survived largely intact—"

"Doctor," Izraad interrupted, "May I add something here?"

"Of course."

"Since Doctor Amalfitano's discovery of this information, I've been running a search for any information on this base. So far I've come up dry, which, if what I believe actually happened did indeed occur, is not surprising. There have been rumors—unsubstantiated of course—for decades about a catastrophic event at a remote outpost..."

There were murmurs of agreement from those around the table.

"...I now believe these rumors were not the result of someone's overactive, or possibly space-happy mind, but based in fact, and the catastrophic event was the accidental release of an infectious agent so virulent the outpost's entire population was wiped out before anyone realized what was happening and could destroy the data banks."

"And who'd want to set foot in the place to make sure they turned out the lights?" McGuigan asked sourly.

Lesedi scowled at him. "This is no time to be flippant."

"Nevertheless," Izraad said, "Mister McGuigan is essentially correct. The data gathered by the Hahtooshans was not complete and it would appear, going by the 'holes', that an attempt was made, sometime after the accident, to clear the banks from the safety of orbit, and when that failed, a volley of seeker missiles was fired. These apparently did succeed in doing significant damage, but... not enough."

"Doctor." Cajori's voice was laced with a note of apprehension. "Do you think there's any connection between this organism and the disease infecting the landing party? I mean could they have picked it up from the Hahtooshan wreck?"

"No," Amalfitano replied. "The agent responsible for the disease infecting the landing party is a bacterium, most likely indigenous to the planet, although it's remotely possible it might been introduced by the base's staff, either accidentally or intentionally."

Lesedi raised her brows. "Introduced?"

"It's possible that Rasal Ghul Seven was used as a testing site," Amalfitano answered. "We've determined that the bacteria infecting the landing party harbor plasmids." He looked at Tasende. "Xosé, this is more your area of expertise...?"

"Plasmids are essentially genetic parasites," Tasende began, "which in turn encode proteins that can break down antibiotics and other therapeutics. The plasmids present in these bacteria have broken down every therapeutic vector we've tried. While plasmids occur naturally, the insertion of plasmids with this resistance inducing capability was a crucial element in developing effective biological weapons. It was considered a fail-safe device."

"Cute," McGuigan grumbled.

"Not only that," Tasende continued, warming to his subject, "but these bugs have an almost uncanny ability to anticipate our efforts at a genetic approach by—"

Lesedi cleared her throat, interrupting him and turned to Amalfitano. "We're a little pressed for time, Doctor, so...?"

Amalfitano nodded, "Of course. The simple answer to Cajori's question is that, while I'd be the last person to deny this bacterium's lethality, I think it far more likely that the culprit responsible for wiping out the base was a virus or proto-virus developed or mutated by the staff for a specific target."

"And this is where that Wuotani freighter, the *Quezhphatanz*, fits in," Izraad said.

"Wuotani freighter?" Amalfitano looked first at Izraad, then Lesedi, then back to Izraad. "What Wuotani freighter?"

"A short time ago Stoker intercepted a transmission from the Hahtooshan ship," Izraad replied. "The name *Quezhphatanz* kept coming up. Turns out a vessel of that name disappeared in this region of space approximately one hundred and thirty years ago." She turned to Lesedi. "Sir, if you'll permit me a bit of speculation?"

Lesedi nodded.

"I will start with some facts. Fact one: while the freighter was of Wuotani registry, its crew was entirely of human stock, as was, by unfortunate, but not surprising happenstance, the population of the base."

Suspecting where she was headed, Amalfitano and Lesedi exchanged apprehensive glances.

"Fact two: the *Quezhphatanz*'s last known port of call was Mirfak Prime, where, records I've managed to uncover state it aroused the suspicions of customs when a doctored manifest was offered up. Cross border smuggling, especially the smuggling of arms was on the rise back then, as were border tensions, and the ship and its crew were held, then suddenly and inexplicably released without further questioning or even a cursory search of its cargo holds.

"I speculate that the *Quezhphatanz* was on the Coalition's payroll as the base's covert supply ship and that its release was as a result of Coalition intervention. I further speculate that it arrived just in time to share the outpost's fate."

"Then how did the Hahtooshans know about it?" Cyllo asked.

"Because," Izraad replied, "I believe whoever contracted the Hahtooshans' services happened across the *Quezhphatanz* and recovered its log, and like us, put two and two together."

Lesedi nodded. "The crew might have tried to get the ship out of the system, beyond the reach of the flares and the interference, to send a S.O.S—"

"Or a warning to keep away," Cajori grumbled.

"And died, leaving the ship to drift," Zayyad added from his location in Control. *"And in a hundred and thirty years it would have drifted a hell of a long way, especially if it was initially left under power."*

"It might have gotten as far as The Barrens, possibly even Matarran held space," McGuigan said, his normally gruff voice edged in growing alarm.

Izraad nodded. "And that brings me back to the significance of the make-up of the freighter's crew and the base's staff. As Doctor Amalfitano has suggested, it's most likely that the weapons they were working on were being tailor-made for a particular target. As I said, the staff and ship's crew were all of human stock, and we know the base succumbed to this organism within a very brief period of time. Possibly a matter of days, even hours."

She hesitated for a moment then continued in a calm, even voice, "We're not simply talking about a weapon that could wipe out the population of a planet, or even that of an entire sector. We're talking about the potential for genocide on an apocalyptic scale, since humans make up over sixty percent of the population of the Coalition, not to mention that of many of the non-aligned systems."

"One of which was most likely the original target," Lesedi added. "If I remember my history, the Coalition was at war with several of them at the time."

"You remember correctly, sir." Izraad continued, "Therefore, it's my recommendation that we stop the Hahtooshans here and now. It's highly likely the crew of the survey ship destroyed the data banks after they'd downloaded the information—Hahtooshans are notoriously thorough about things like that. Unfortunately, we have no idea how much of the data the crew of survey craft managed to transmit to its mother ship before it crashed. Possibly nothing, but we cannot take that risk. Once they're out of the sphere of the system's EM interference and they transmit the data, there'll be no way to stop the weapon's redevelopment.

"Since the data our landing party managed to recover from the wreck did not include the any specific information about the disease itself, we can only speculate. And since we have no idea who's behind this, we have no idea from what direction an attack might come." Izraad looked at McGuigan as he started to open his mouth and cut him off with, "Again, we can only speculate."

McGuigan wisely shut his mouth.

"If there wasn't any data recovered on the identity of the disease," Cajori asked, "what makes you think the Hahtooshans know what it is? Maybe they're as much in the dark as we are, and without the data, they, or whoever contracted them, can't replicate it."

"It would explain why they're still here," Stoker volunteered, glancing around at the circle of apprehensive faces.

"You wanna take that kind of risk?" McGuigan replied. "I sure as hell don't!"

"I agree," Perou said. "If we stop 'em here," he rapped his knuckles against the table for emphasis, "and destroy whatever data they managed to collect, no one'll be the wiser. The Hahtooshans and whoever sent them will just chalk up the loss to one of the binary's flare storms, add the cost to their bill and send another ship—"

"But this time we'll make damned sure those banks are destroyed," McGuigan growled.

"What about the missing?" Pardix's voice crackled from the speaker. *"Do we plan on rescuing them before we try to stop the mercs?"*

Lesedi turned to Cajori. "How long can we remain here?"

"At present levels of radiation, another four hours, max."

"Cyllo, what about the binary? Any hope that this phase of flare activity will die down before then?"

"Doubt it, sir. This phase does seem to have peaked far earlier than the past seven phases, but the mass transfer has been much greater and—"

"Is there any risk to the landing party?" Lesedi interrupted impatiently, looking at Amalfitano.

"From radiation... not yet. The planet has a very dense atmosphere, with an especially thick ozone layer. So far they've not been exposed to dangerous levels of radiation, but the longer they remain on the planet, the greater the risk becomes. Co-incidentally, Xosé's run some sims that suggest that the bacterium's growth rate is greatly slowed by exposure to the levels consistent with surface readings, so it's possible that this radiation exposure many work to their benefit, at least up to a point."

Tasende added, "Dichelazine has been used effectively in cases of such poisoning, in most cases completely reversing the effects of the radiation exposure. So, even if they are exposed to fairly large doses, there's an effective treatment. But the effectiveness of the drug is greatly diminished if treatment's delayed—"

"Delayed?" Lesedi asked. "By how much?"

Amalfitano and Tasende exchanged looks, then Amalfitano replied, "Taking into account how long they've already been there, maybe another three days, five tops. After that... well, there is no effective treatment."

Lesedi looked around the table. "Our mission is now clear. Our first priority is to safeguard the Coalition. We *must* disable or better, destroy the Hahtooshan ship. If we can locate and retrieve the missing without jeopardizing that mission, we will. If not..." She found herself staring at Amalfitano.

He nodded, albeit reluctantly.

She turned to Izraad. "I want a full threat assessment on the merc vessel."

"Yessir."

"But just in case..." Her gaze shifted to the briefing room's speaker. "Zayyad, load a data drone with transcripts of the data recovered from the wreck and of this meeting, and a flag that another ship must be tasked with locating the *Herrick*, and launch towards Mirfak when ready."

"Yessir."

"That's it then. Dismissed." As the others rose, Lesedi added under her breath, "And may luck be on our side."

— iv —

Amalfitano eased himself down onto his desk chair, gave his gritty eyes and haggard face a brisk rub then turned to the desk's servo-panel and tapped in an order for coffee. *Strong* coffee.

"I have a better idea."

He jerked his head up to find Fleming leaning against the doorjamb, her arms crossed.

"Like what?"

She straightened up, started towards him. "Like a nap."

"Like I can take a nap right now."

"And you think you'll have a chance later?"

He shrugged as he turned to the pile of new reports.

"William."

"What?"

She motioned with her chin towards the door of his private cabin. "Come on. You're not doing anyone, especially yourself, any good like this."

He scowled at her; she scowled back.

There was no contest.

With a sigh of capitulation, he rose and followed her into the cabin.

She pointed to the bunk.

He dutifully sprawled back and cradled his head in his hands. "Why do I even bother to argue with you? You always win."

"I've asked myself the same question more times than I can remember."

He scowled up at her.

She smiled as she drew a blanket over him. "Think you can get to sleep?"

"No," he grunted. "Too tired."

"Try, okay?"

He shut his eyes tightly. "Satisfied?"

"Not until I hear that funny snore of yours."

He opened one eye a crack. "I don't snore."

She arched a dubious brow and choosing tact over fact replied, "I'll come back and wake you in say… two hours, all right?"

"Or sooner, if something happens, like we get blown up. Hate to wake up only to find out I'm dead."

"You got it." Fleming walked over to the door and thumbed the light switch.

He waited until her footfalls faded into the ever-present background hum. He waited a few minutes longer, just in case, then tossed the blanket aside and got to his feet.

He ran his fingers through his thick gray hair, walked out of the cabin and directly into the path of the doctor's Medusa-like stare. He froze.

"Just as I thought." She rose from his desk chair.

"But… I mean I thought you'd—"

"Left?"

"Yeah." He smiled feebly. "Can't blame me for trying, can you?"

She stabbed a finger at the cabin door and added in a menacing tone, "Do I have to call Drakin to sit on you?"

He stalked back into the cabin; she followed.

Without being told, he lay back down and jerked the blanket over himself. "You can lead a horse to water…"

She sat on the edge of the bunk. "In this case a stubborn donkey would be more appropriate."

"I think I've been insulted."

"Quit stalling."

He fixed his blood-shot gaze on the ceiling and exhaled. "Listen, Jenna, I can't just go to sleep on command, you know."

She slipped her hand into her pocket. "I anticipated that excuse too—"

He grabbed her wrist just as she withdrew a ject-it. *"No."*

"But—"

"I said no." He abruptly let go of her hand.

"Wanna talk about it?"

"What?"

"You know as well as I do. What's been eating at you. Arctoi. Niebuhr. Now Teague. No one blames you, you know."

"Whose fault is it then? I'm the CMO for god sakes and I can't even stop a goddamned hemorrhage?"

"It's no simple hemorrhage and you're exhausted. You've gotta get some sleep." She began rolling up his sleeve. "This is just enough to take the edge off, help you relax."

"Fine."

He didn't feel the injection but its effects were almost instantaneous. He closed his eyes, felt Fleming rise from the bed then overheard a soft murmur of voices and blinked himself back awake.

Izraad had joined Fleming at the bedside. The two exchanged a few more whispered words then the doctor left and Izraad sat down on the bunk beside his hip.

"Thought you'd be in Control."

"Just on my way." She glanced down at a data disc she held in one hand. "But I wanted to stop by and—"

Say good-bye? "Check up on me?"

"Yes." She slipped the disc into her breast pocket then began unbuckling his collar.

"Planning on taking advantage of me?"

"I'm glad to see that there's still some of the old William I love so dearly in there." She tapped him on the chest.

"Zarijan, would you do me a *leetle* favor?"

"Sure," she replied as she finished loosening his med reds.

"Quit mentioning age and old and that sort of stuff?"

"Feeling your mortality?"

"Aren't we all with a bunch of fidgety, cheesed off and trigger-happy mercs within spitting distance?"

"That's it, isn't it? That's what this is all about, isn't it?"

"I'm not sure I follow—"

"Oh yes you do. You see people around you, all younger than you, dying. And you can't help them. Suddenly you feel old and useless, right? Why them? Why not you?"

Great. I just took a sed and now you want to have one of 'those' discussions. Talk about taking advantage...

He let out a long, ragged breath, rubbed his sleepy eyes, then said, "Those people aren't just people, they're colleagues, friends. Gildun was my age, we shared a common frame of reference, a common set of values. And funny thing, but when I was around Robert, the most vital and energetic man I've ever met, I never felt old—he wouldn't let me."

She caressed his jaw then his lips. "What about me?"

He kissed her fingers, murmured, "You know how I feel about you—I love you—but that doesn't alter the fact that I'm almost old enough to be your father, almost old enough to be the father of everyone on board, well, with the exception of McGuigan and that weird guy in the galley—"

"Well," she huffed and crossed her arms, feigning indignation, "I know you were a busy little bee in your youth, but—"

"You know what I mean," he grumbled. "I'm just too damned old to live this life. Living life on the edge, knowing tomorrow you might get blown to smithereens, or you might have to blow some other poor sap to bits is for the young, not dinosaurs like me—"

"Don't let Drakin hear you say that, besides, what happened to your philosophy that wars should be fought by the old?"

He squinted up at her.

"Now, let me see... I want to get this right." She tapped her chin with her finger and looked thoughtful for a moment. "Ah... yes." She fixed him with her unyielding stare. "Right after the Matarran ambush you said, 'More and more, I'm convinced war should be saved for the old, or at least the middle-aged. We shouldn't be spilling the blood of our youth to soothe the wounded egos of their elders.

"'Make a bunch of forty year olds, better yet, *fifty* year olds repeatedly drop to their bellies and fire off a few rounds, then stagger to their feet, swearing and grunting with the effort—well, I'd wager most wars wouldn't get past the warning shot phase. Everyone would be too damned sore, too tired and grumpy to pursue it any further.'" She paused and cocked her head to one side. "Did I quote you correctly?"

He continued to squint at her as he grumbled, "I had a change of heart. That's why as soon as we get back to an outpost—assuming we survive the next few hours—I'm putting in for a transfer."

"You're joking, right?"

"Already filed the paperwork. If it weren't for the interference, I'd have already sent the request. It's time for me to go home."

"Home? But *this* is your home."

"Jenna's right, better get some sleep." He rolled onto his side, away from her. "Doctor's orders and all that."

She leaned over, kissed him on the cheek, then rose from the bed. "We'll talk about this later, okay?" She activated the bed's grav-net and turned for the door.

He kept his eyes tightly shut, waited until he heard the outer door to his office slip shut.

He lifted his head and looked around his cabin, the only illumination coming from the outer office. Fixing each familiar feature in his mind as if for the last time, then with an exhausted sigh, he tugged the blanket up around his shoulders. "Yeah. *Later.*"

Chapter 9

Ru'asooli strode through the airlock, onto the *Acholilah*'s bridge, threw himself in his chair and gave the chamber and its crew a quick, angry sweep with his blood-shot eyes before he fixed his deeply annoyed scowl on the main tactical display. "So, how badly was *Makhaira* damaged?"

Lura'jaii wet her lips, began, "Exhaust guides suffered a direct hit, ta'ahn, and from the complete cessation of sensory probes, it's reasonable to assume that there was extensive damage to the bridge as well. Navigation also appears to have been affected, possibly even weapons control."

Ru'asooli, after a long, reflective pause, asked, "Life support?"

"Unable to determine, ta'ahn, but most likely... yes."

"And the Coalition vessel?"

Lura'jaii hesitated just long enough for Ru'asooli to notice and look up.

"It's difficult to determine with certainty, ta'ahn."

"Then be uncertain!"

Lura'jaii stiffened and replied crispy, "Readings suggest only minor particle damage to their primary impeller ring, ta'ahn."

Ru'asooli stared, incredulously, at her for a moment. "That's... *all?*"

She replied with an apologetic nod and softly worded, "Yes, ta'ahn."

Ru'asooli shifted his fierce gaze from his perspiring second to the tactical display. *You blithering Khighalli idiot!*

"Shall we move closer and attempt contact, ta'ahn?"

"We'll return for the ship and crew once we've finished the job that imbecile Tarqk started. That should give them ample opportunity to ponder the high cost of disobeying orders." He squinted at the tactical display before adding, "Now, for the Coalition vessel. I want it to be a nice, clean kill, none of this..." he angrily waved his hand towards the projection, "fumbling in the dark. Navigator, plot a course away from this cursed system that maintains our invisibility to the Coalition vessel... then circle back. I want to catch them unawares."

— ii —

Amalfitano awoke to the sound of muffled laughter.

He lifted his head and blearily looked around for the culprit who dared to wake him, only to find that he was alone. "Must've been dreaming." He tugged the blanket over his head and buried his face in his pillow, hoping to recapture whatever it was that his sleep-loosened mind had found so funny. *I sure as hell could use a good laugh.*

A few minutes later, he rolled onto his back and stared up at the ceiling. It was no use. He was wide-awake. Whatever it was he'd been dreaming about was gone, as were the mild sedative's effects, so he sat up and squinted at the bedside chronometer. He'd been asleep a little over forty minutes. He rose from the bed and giving his sweaty scalp a vigorous, two-handed scratch, stumbled into the cabin's small head. He took a long look at himself in the over sink mirror and realized he would be asking a lot from a splash of cold water, so he stripped off his sleep-rumpled med reds and stepped into the shower stall.

— iii —

Lesedi shifted in her chair then asked the question that had been burning a hole in her tongue for ten minutes. "How goes it, Khaleed?"

"Still unable to make direct sensory contact with the Hahtooshan ship. Due to disturbances in the stellar wind, I'd say she's still holding an opposing orbit."

"Any evidence as to the extent of damage?"

Zayyad shifted his gaze back to his console's cluster of monitors. "I'm picking up a slight fluctuation in ionized hydrogen levels. Levels much higher than expected, which might be explained by an imbalance in her foldspace field generators—we may've hit her harder than originally thought."

"But no way to be absolutely sure."

"Nossir."

Lesedi chewed on her lip as she stared at the suspended tactical display. No point putting off the inevitable any longer. "Peters?

Transfer all auxiliary power and any we can spare from the screens and power up all weapons banks. And Khaleed? Make an educated guess as to where our quarry is hiding." She jerked her chair around to face the com-op. "Go from step-down red alert to full battle alert, notify all stations to prepare for imminent combat... and Stoker?"

He looked sidelong at her, his fingers hovering above his console.

"Jettison the log buoy."

— iv —

Amalfitano looked up as the shower's hot, pulsing stream stopped, replaced by the metallic, rhythmic voice of the ship's computer, ordering all crew to battle stations.

"Goddamned fucking mercs!" he snarled as he slicked back his still soapy hair with his hands. *"You just couldn't wait another five minutes to start shooting again, could you?"* He stepped out of the stall, grabbed a towel and began to rub himself dry. *"So much for looking presentable on my way to hell!"*

He'd gotten no farther than his chest when he stopped. His eyes widened. The towel fell from his hands and to the floor, like the red alert and the warning drone of the computer, instantly forgotten.

Without warning, the memory of what he'd been dreaming about—what he'd been laughing about—returned.

"Gods...!" he whispered to himself. "Gods!" He hurriedly struggled back into his rumpled med reds. Still fighting with one sleeve, unaware that his uniform was inside out, he dashed from his cabin, through his outer office, into sickbay.

Chuckling loudly, he headed for the lab, leaving a trail of soapy footprints and bewildered staff in his wake.

Oblivious to the effect his entrance and appearance had on the lab personnel, he dropped into an empty chair at a terminal and began punching in requests for data.

"Come on! Come on, damn you!" he muttered as his twitching fingers hovered millimeters from the terminal controls.

"What the hell's going on?" he overheard Fleming demand. "And why are you—"

"Not now!" he snapped, refusing to take his eyes off the screen as it filled with data.

A moment later, a smile slowly spread across his haggard, soap-streaked face. Then he began to laugh.

— v —

"Any luck pin-pointing the merc ship?" Lesedi fought the urge to get out of her chair and look at the tactical monitors for herself.

"Nossir," Zayyad replied. "Still picking up pockets of ionized hydrogen, but otherwise—"

"Well they couldn't have just vanished," Pardix grumbled.

Zayyad favored him with an icy, over the shoulder squint, but said nothing.

"Cajori," Lesedi ignored the exchange, "what's the status on the screens?"

"Beginning to show definite disintegration, sir. The diversion of power is really beginning to tell."

"How long before total collapse?"

"Ninety minutes, present rate."

"Cyllo," Lesedi swiveled her chair towards the woman's station, "any reduction in ionic activity?"

"None sir."

Lesedi slumped back into her chair and fixed her frustrated stare on the holo. "Keep—"

"*Shit!*" Zayyad slammed his fist down on his console, startling everyone then he looked around, his swarthy face flushed with rage and embarrassment. "Sir... the Hahtooshan ship, she's *gone.*"

"Gone?"

"Must've left orbit using the interference as a blind. I'm still picking up some residual, she couldn't have broken orbit more than fifteen minutes ago."

"Peters, arm and launch a tracer torpedo! Maybe we can still track her."

"Aye sir. Tracer armed. Launching... now."

Lesedi fixed her narrowed gaze on the tactical display as she mentally counted off the seconds. If the missile wasn't able to attain lock-on within one minute, the Hahtooshan ship would have made good its escape. *While we were sitting here, twiddling our thumbs!* She overheard a faint *bleat* and glanced at the weapons officer.

Peters gave her the thumbs up. "Got her, sir! Heading... two two three, mark six. Speed... flat three."

"So much for damaging her engines," Pardix said under his breath.

Lesedi let her breath slowly escape through her clenched teeth before she replied, "Ensign Pardix, instead of stating the obvious, how 'bout you calculate parameters for pursuit?"

"Completing now, sir," Pardix replied as he finished tapping a sequence of commands with an unnecessary flourish. "Transferring to helm." He flicked Zayyad a sidelong, triumphant glance only to find the tac-op's back to him.

"Leaving orbit," Eisele murmured, and the *Baidarka*, with the faintest of shudders, lifted out of orbit and turned towards free space.

— vi —

Amalfitano, realizing he'd drawn quite a crowd, reluctantly looked up.

Fleming eyed him suspiciously. "Why do you look like you just pulled a *very* large rabbit from a *very* small hat?"

"See for yourself." He pointed at the activated screen, then as an afterthought wiped a lock of soapy, wet hair off his forehead.

Drakin was the first to take the bait. She stepped close and peered down at the monitor. Scaly brow ridges crinkled. Talons tapped on the console. Bifurcated tongue fluttered in a non-existent breeze. *"Interessstink…"*

Fleming joined her then everyone hurriedly clustered around to stare at the screen.

"Where'd this come from?" Fleming finally asked, turning to him.

Amalfitano grinned. "From here," he said, tapping his forehead, in the process briefly pinning Drakin's tongue against his soapy skin.

"You may be on the right track." Fleming sat down beside him, studied the display carefully then tapped more requests into the computer. "Let's see if it's really as good as it looks."

As the terminal began displaying its response, everyone leaned forward and collectively held their breath.

Drakin's mouth split into a very toothy grin. Someone behind Amalfitano giggled.

Fleming said simply, "You've done it, William." She rose from the chair. "I'll get pharmacy to work on it right away."

As she hurried off, Amalfitano hit the console's com button. "Control... give me the captain!"

— vii —

"Sir?"

Lesedi glanced at Stoker, eyebrows raised.

"Doctor Amalfitano needs to speak with you—"

"Not now!" She fixed her narrowed gaze back on the tactical display. "Status."

"Still have a lock-on, sir. No evidence that they're aware of pursuit."

Lesedi turned next to the engineer. "Perou, any chance of increasing speed?"

"No, not without increasing structural stress on the impeller rings. Sustained flat three, in my opinion, is not without its risks."

"Noted. Cyllo, any idea how long it'll take at present speed to pass through this area of high particle concentration?"

"Estimate minimum of eleven hours, sir, at present speed."

Lesedi scowled at the tactical display. *It's like chasing someone through molasses, but what choice do we have?* "Maintain present speed."

"Sir?" Stoker prompted.

Lesedi squinted at him. "Yes?"

"Doctor Amalfitano—"

"What about him?"

"He's still waiting, sir."

Waiting? She raised a quizzical brow.

"He said it was most urgent he speak with you."

She motioned to her chair arm com-unit. "Pipe it through." Whatever he had to say, whatever new disaster Amalfitano's page might herald, would be, by necessity, shared with the control room crew. This was no time for the captain to leave control.

"Ife..."

Lesedi looked down at the intercom and braced herself.

"...Stoker tells me we've left orbit?"

"In pursuit of the merc ship, yes. What was it you needed to speak with me about? Stoker said it was urgent."

"We've found a cure," Amalfitano replied simply.

"Cure? What—"

"For the bacterial infection."

Lesedi looked around. Everyone not actively involved in tracking the alien warship was now staring at her. She dropped her startled gaze back to the com-unit. "That's great news!"

"It would've been better if we were still in orbit."

"Agreed. But we have to stop the mercs before they transmit the data—"

"I know. So do what you have to do, Ife... then get the hell back to the planet."

Lesedi almost smiled. *If only it was that easy.* "You got it, doc—"

"Four days, Ife," he added, his sobering tone erasing the slight up-curve of her mouth. *"Without protection from the radiation, they won't be able to survive more than another four days on that gods forsaken planet."*

Chapter 10

Corsali watched in silence as Suhjai ran her hand down the length of Gianakis's mottled and bloated thigh. His breathing too had become noticeably labored.

As Suhjai continued to go through the motions of an exam, Corsali bit her lip and looked up at the officer. He was standing stock-still behind Suhjai, arms crossed, his tattooed face a stiff, unyielding mask—the antithesis of the being who'd intrigued her with his candor and yes, his disarmingly boyish smile only a few precious hours before. Now she was left to wonder if it was all an act, a lie. She darkened her stare to a hateful glower. *I believed you!*

If it had been her hope that he'd shift his slitted gaze to her, possibly even read her thoughts, she was bitterly disappointed. He refused to look at her—deliberately, she realized—which left her feeling even angrier and yes... very, very gullible. *Damn you! Damn you to whatever hell you fucking mercs go to!*

She turned her attention back to Suhjai just as the woman pried up one of Gianakis' eyelids. With the knuckles of her other hand, Suhjai gave his breastbone a vigorous rub, but his ashen face remained slack. She clicked her tongue, turned to the medical kit and, after a quick search of what scant few vials remained, withdrew one and a ject-it. She loaded it, pressed it against his shoulder then rocked back onto her haunches and lifted her gaze to meet Corsali's equally bleak stare. "That should ease his breathing."

Corsali nodded and as she drew the blanket back over him, the officer abruptly pivoted on his heel and walked out of the cabin.

Suhjai wordlessly watched him leave, then gathered up the kit, got to her feet and walked over to Aquila. She knelt beside him, examined his dressings then pressed her ear to his chest. He barely stirred.

She loaded the ject-it with another vial, pushed it against his arm, then rose, kit in hand and started for the cabin door.

"Mihr-Suhjai?"

She stopped but did not look back at Corsali.

"Thank you."

"For what?" Suhjai replied and for once her voice held none of its customary tartness. With a shake of her shaggy head, she strode out of the cabin.

Corsali wearily got to her feet and walked over to one of the open-weave walls. She leaned against a support post and peered through the slat-work as hot tears welled up in her already red-rimmed eyes. This time she made no effort to wipe them away. She was just too tired.

Beyond, the sky had darkened to a dull orange. Only Gamma was visible now, just above the cloud-dotted horizon, its copper-red disc swollen to double its actual size in the dense atmosphere. Above, faint aurora danced and writhed in the electrically charged atmosphere like a host of spectral serpents.

Another night on this hellhole of a planet... how many does this make? She couldn't remember. She knew she was exhausted, emotionally and physically; she also knew she couldn't sleep, not now, not tonight. *Aquila or Gianakis—*

She jerked her mind off that track and forced it back to the brilliant horizon and the choppy sea that glittered like a Byzantine mosaic.

A moment later a gust of salty wind ruffled her hair and brought with it the pungent smells of the evening meal.

Then she heard voices, but these were not the usual grunts and growls of the soldiers or the clicking speech of the Blatto tenders which frequently floated up from below decks. Suhjai and the officer were arguing—*loudly*—and she found herself straining to eavesdrop despite the fact that the two were quarreling in their own guttural tongue.

It didn't take her long to realize who was getting the best of whom: Suhjai's shrill voice quickly rose above the officer's heated snarls and finally drowned them out completely.

Without warning the now one-sided argument stopped and by the silence that followed—even the wind seemed to have been holding its breath—it was obvious to Corsali that everyone on board had been listening to the verbal brawl.

Then, just as abruptly, the usual noises of the boat returned as those below hastily resumed their tasks.

Corsali shook herself out of her own distraction and slowly turned back to the sunset only to find that *Gamma* had followed her sister star and plunged below the horizon, leaving a deep maroon sky liberally sprinkled with stars in her wake.

A long and lonely night lay ahead, one she knew Gianakis would not survive. *As for Aquila....* She hugged herself tightly against the sudden chill.

—ii—

"Sir!"

Lesedi jerked her chair around to face Zayyad.

"We just lost the tracer lock!"

She pushed herself out of her seat. "What?"

"Confirmed, sir... tracer has entered search mode."

Lesedi stalked over to his station and Zayyad hastily rose and stepped aside, allowing her to see for herself.

"We've lost them," she whispered, glaring at the inoffensive screen. *"Shit!"*

"Sir?"

"Not now, Stoker!"

"But—"

She whirled around and snarled, *"I said not now!"*

"But sir," he blurted out, "Doctor Amalfitano urgently requests—"

"Explain the situation to him! Tell him I'm a little busy right now!"

Stoker turned to his console and began speaking in a hushed voice. After a brief, heated exchange, he turned to face Lesedi. *"Sir...?"*

Lesedi flicked him a warning look.

"He says this can't wait sir."

"What's so goddamned important it can't wait?"

"He says he needs to discuss something with you, in private, and immediately."

Lesedi, catching Izraad's pointed stare, exhaled forcefully then growled, "Okay, okay, tell him I'll be right there." She turned back to Zayyad. "These things happen, Khaleed. Sorry I snapped."

"Yessir."

By the tone of the tac-op's voice Lesedi knew that even if she didn't hold him responsible, he did. She gave him a pat on the shoulder, then strode out of control and hurried up the corridor.

She stopped just short of the red-framed sickbay airlock, steeled herself, then stepped through.

Fleming was waiting for her. The doctor stood next to the open doorway of the isolation unit. Beyond, one of the isolation cubicles used to house the injured was brightly lit and though its semitransparent walls Lesedi could plainly see that its narrow bed was empty.

She felt her stomach lurch. *So that's it—*

"In Doctor Amalfitanooz office, sssir."

Lesedi wheeled around.

Drakin stood nearby. She motioned to the open doorway with a taloned hand.

Lesedi walked stiffly into the office and her anxious gaze swept the room.

It too was empty.

Suddenly more angry than apprehensive, she placed her hands on her hips and snapped, "What the hell's going on here?"

"See for yourself," Amalfitano replied as he appeared in the doorway of his private cabin. He beckoned to her. "In here."

"I don't have time for games, Doc."

"Neither do I, Ensign," he replied calmly and motioned again for her to enter.

With an exasperated sigh, she stalked past him, into the cabin... and stopped in her tracks.

"Lieutenant?" she gasped, then gaped at the man seated on Amalfitano's bunk, a meal tray on his lap.

"I'm not a ghost, Ensign." Teague was deathly pale, but he was alive... upright, and talking, albeit in a thin, raspy voice.

"You look more like something the bat dragged in," Amalfitano added as he stopped beside Lesedi. "Not that you were ever much to look at."

"It's *cat*, not *bat*," Teague corrected.

"Not in your case," Amalfitano muttered as Lesedi continued to stare, slack-jawed, at the man.

"Sit down before you fall down," Amalfitano grumbled good-naturedly as he guided her over to his fold-down desk chair.

Lesedi dropped heavily onto the chair and looked up at him. *"Niebuhr...?"*

Amalfitano grinned.

She turned her still stunned eyes back on Teague. "I don't believe it!"

"Believe it, Ife. Now," Amalfitano added, "do you want the explanation for their miraculous recoveries before or after?"

"Before or after what?"

"You turn this ship around."

Lesedi blinked then blinked again. "What?"

"Oh, you mean the rumor isn't true?"

"What rumor?"

Amalfitano and Teague exchanged quick, sidelong looks, then the doctor replied, "That we lost the tracer and any chance of locating the mercs, and now there's nothing stopping us from high-tailing it back to Rasal Ghul."

Lesedi leaned back in her chair, shook her head and chuckled. With a resigned sigh, she reached for the desk-com. She flicked Teague a glance. At his confirming nod, she pressed the activator. "C and C."

"Control," Zayyad replied.

"Prepare to launch another data drone. I want it tagged with a Class One Alert and the frequency of the tracer missile, along with all up-to-date medical and captain's logs."

"Aye, sir," Zayyad replied slowly, his tone betraying his confusion. *"And its destination?"*

"Mirfak Prime, but have it programmed to begin transmitting as soon as it's out from under the interference sphere."

"Yessir." There was a momentary pause. *"The drone's ready for medical log feed."*

"Excellent. And Khaleed, once the drone's been launched, plot a course back to Rasal Ghul, maximum speed possible, and execute when ready."

"Sir...?"

"Get us back to Rasal Ghul Seven, Ensign!" She winked at Teague. "We have a landing party to rescue!"

"Yessir!"

Lesedi cut the link, turned to Amalfitano and grinned. "Satisfied?" She then motioned to Teague. "Now, it's your turn."

"Right." Amalfitano sat beside Teague. "Well, as you know, we tried everything known to modern medicine against those critters."

"Yeah, and nothing worked." She glanced at the doorway to see that quite a crowd had formed. Everyone was grinning. She didn't blame them; it was contagious. "Okay, doc. I'll bite. What did you use?"

"I said *modern* medicine."

She gave him a narrow look.

"You see, there were a lot of drugs, really good drugs, that fell by the wayside as the panacea of gene therapy appeared on the scene."

"And?"

"And we never thought about using them to combat the disease."

Lesedi took a deep breath. Amalfitano was really enjoying this—and he'd certainly earned it. Besides, she had the time. It would be at least five hours before they attained orbit around Rasal Ghul Seven, and while she'd lost the Hahtooshan ship, the data drone, once free of the interference, would begin broadcasting. With luck a Coalition ship would respond, pick up the Hahtooshans' trail and finish what they'd started.

"Have you ever heard of *penicillium chrysogenum?*"

She replied with a blank stare.

"It's a mold."

"Oh. So?"

"So, from *penicillium chrysogenum* comes penicillin, and penicillin is real bad news to actively multiplying bacteria."

Fleming squeezed through the grinning mob at the door and stepped into the small room to add, "It inhibits the bacteria's metabolic functions vital to cell wall synthesis. Basically, they go *poof.*"

"Poof?" Lesedi raised her brows as her eyes darted between Fleming and Amalfitano.

"We didn't think of it sooner," Fleming continued, "because it hasn't been used in, well, centuries. All bugs known at the time had become resistant to it, and then to its derivatives and its derivatives' derivatives, and so forth. Which was why gene therapy and its spin-offs ended up the treatment of choice."

"Ah," Lesedi replied with a less than certain nod. "Okay—"

"But those critters on Rasal Ghul had never seen the likes of it," Tasende said, peeking around Drakin, to which the nurse nodded her scaly snout in hearty agreement. "They never knew what hit 'em." He smacked his fist into the doorframe for emphasis. "Which lends some credence to the chief's theory that the bacterium might indeed have been introduced to the planet by the base's staff."

Lesedi looked back at Amalfitano. "Those plasmas you were talking about."

"*Plasmids*, yes," he corrected. "Not only are these bugs able to outsmart every genetic trick in the book, something that would be highly unlikely in a naturally evolved bacterium, but they're resistant to all the modern quorum quenching and phage therapies, all of which are, in one way or another, derived from antibacterial technologies in common use—"

"A little over a hundred years ago," Lesedi finished for him. "In other words, while the base was still operational."

"Exactly," Fleming agreed. "That's what was so baffling at first. At least one of the antimicrobials we tried should have worked since these bugs, even with naturally occurring plasmids, shouldn't have had a built-in resistance, but they did."

"Ditto any gene-based approach," Rosen said. "They seemed to anticipate every therapy we tried, and react accordingly."

"Those researchers thought of just about everything," Lesedi interrupted, "didn't they?"

"Not everything," Amalfitano said pointedly.

"That should have clued us in that something wasn't right," Fleming continued. "If William hadn't thought of penicillin—"

"Goes to prove advanced age has its benefits," Teague muttered under his breath, then gave Amalfitano a sidelong wink.

Fleming smiled. "I'd have never thought of it in a million years. It was never mentioned in any of the modern medical texts."

Amalfitano squinted at her. "I'm not *that* old."

"But those medical texts you collect certainly are," she shot back, to which his gathered staff laughed.

Amalfitano shrugged good-naturedly.

Lesedi slumped back in her chair and shook her head. "Smart bugs... but with an Achilles' heel."

"Yup," Amalfitano agreed.

Lesedi turned her relieved gaze back on Teague and noticed how suddenly exhausted, how frail, the man looked.

Amalfitano had noticed too. "Okay, Edwin," he said gruffly as he got back to his feet, "snack time's over." He handed the tray to Fleming. "Time for bed."

"I'm on a bed."

"Yeah. Mine."

"Oh. Yes. Quite," he replied and with Amalfitano's help got to his feet.

Lesedi rose and stepped aside, then watched as Teague, leaning heavily on Amalfitano, made his slow, shuffling way out of the cabin, through the parting gauntlet of grinning staff and into the main sickbay. "What can I say?" She turned to Fleming. "Congratulations doesn't seem enough."

"No congratulations necessary. William got what he wanted and needed, we all did."

Lesedi smiled. "You can say that again."

— iii —

Lura'jaii shifted in her chair as she swept the bridge with her gritty, burning eyes. It had been a long watch trailing the Coalition ship, waiting for just the right moment to pounce. Ru'asooli had been very clear on that: he wanted a nice, *clean* kill and as far away from Rasal Ghul Seven as possible so as not to draw unwanted attention from anyone who might come looking for an explanation for the patrol ship's disappearance—assuming any searchers would even give the unstable system itself more than a cursory scan. Ships disappeared all the time, especially in this region of space that was so close to a number of ever-changing borders—

"Ta'ahn?"

She squinted at the scanner officer and asked in a hoarse voice, "What?"

"The Coalition craft has launched a missile."

"Another tracer?" Lura'jaii straightened up in her chair.

"No ta'ahn, energy patterns are not consistent with a tracer... or a seeker torpedo," he added, answering Lura'jaii's next question before she asked it.

Lura'jaii relaxed her tense posture somewhat. "A data drone then."

"Indeed, ta'ahn, the energy print is consistent with that of a Coalition data drone."

She absently rubbed her nose. "Heading?"

"The same as the Coalition vessel, ta'ahn."

Lura'jaii knit her brows. *That doesn't make sense. Why would they launch a drone when the machine would not arrive any faster than the vessel, possibly taking even longer to reach—*

"Ta'ahn, the Coalition vessel… she's *disappeared!*"

"Disappeared?" Lura'jaii rose from her chair; at the same moment the airlock irised open and Ru'asooli stepped onto the bridge.

Lura'jaii silently cursed the officer for his impeccable timing as she pivoted smartly on her heel to face him.

"What's disappeared?"

"The Coalition vessel, ta'ahn," Lura'jaii replied.

"Indeed?"

"I believe I can explain, ta'ahn," the scanner officer offered hastily.

Ru'asooli eased himself down into the contoured command chair. "Then do so."

"The data drone—"

"Data drone?" Ru'asooli looked up at Lura'jaii, who had taken up her customary spot, standing at rigid attention beside his right arm.

"The Coalition vessel launched a drone—"

"Why was I not informed of this?"

"I was about to notify you when—"

Ru'asooli dismissed further explanation with an impatient wave of his hand as he peered the scanner officer. "Continue."

"Ta'ahn, I believe the Coalition vessel launched the data drone in preparation for returning to the planetary system."

Lura'jaii nodded. *It made sense, except—*

"Why would the Coalition vessel return to the system?" Ru'asooli asked, voicing Lura'jaii's own thoughts.

Not hearing an answer, Lura'jaii suddenly realized that the question had been aimed at her. "I don't know, ta'ahn."

"Then perhaps we should find out?" Ru'asooli settled back into his chair. "Navigator. Plot a course back to the system and *this* time keep us hidden in their wake, understood?"

The navigator gave the officer a quick, over the shoulder glance. "Understood, ta'ahn."

He turned next to the tactical officer. "Can we destroy the drone without alerting the Coalition ship?"

"I believe so, ta'ahn—if we wait until it's beyond their limited tracking abilities."

"Then do so—but to be on the safe side make it appear it regrettably collided with some Oort debris."

The tactical officer nodded.

"Weapons?" Ru'asooli asked, settling back into his chair.

"All systems at optimum levels, ta'ahn," Lura'jaii replied eagerly, "awaiting your command."

"Patience, Lura'jaii," Ru'asooli murmured. "Let's first see what they're up to, yes?"

Chapter 11

"Huh?" Corsali lifted her head from the sweaty cradle of her arm and looked around. It took her still groggy mind a moment to grasp that she'd been fast asleep and that it had been Aquila's restless mumblings that had awakened her. She rolled over, reached out and touched his arm. "Sir?"

He flinched and his eyes snapped open. *"Wha...?"*

"Just me, sir."

He winced, more in anticipation than actual pain and tried to sit up.

She planted her palm squarely on his chest. "I think it best you just lie still."

He lay back, muttered, "Think you're right," then ran a gummy tongue over his equally gummy lips.

"Thirsty?"

He replied with a feeble grin and: "I'd give a month's pay for a cold beer."

She lurched to her feet, hurried over to the cabin's small table. "Best I can do is some of the native ale." She picked up the pitcher and mug a Blatto had brought just after sunset and returned to his side.

"Gianakis?" he asked as she filled the mug.

She risked a sidelong glance at the crewman and assured herself that he was still breathing, if barely. "He's asleep, sir." *Not quite a lie.* She knelt beside him, slipped her hand under his head and brought the mug to his lips before he asked any more questions.

He took a small sip, then another.

"More?"

He gave his head a slight shake.

She slipped her arm from under him and placed the mug beside the pitcher, then turned back to find him staring up at her with sunken, feverish eyes.

"And what about you, Ensign?" His voice was thin, weak, each word spoken with some effort.

"I'm fine, sir."

He mustered a lopsided smile. "You never were a good poker player."

"How 'bout a little more to drink?" Not waiting for a reply, she reached for the mug but as she brought it towards him, he wrapped his fingers around her wrist.

"I'm counting on you to do the right thing, Ensign."

"Sir?"

"Study this proof he keeps on about. Maybe he *is* telling the truth, maybe... maybe it does pose a threat—convince.... convince him to... to contact the *Baidarka*. Warn... the Coalition."

"Sir, when we reach the island, you—"

"No!" He winced then added in a tight whisper, "I'm relying on you—the Coalition's relying on you."

She hesitated before answering, "You can depend on me, sir."

"I know I can." He gave her wrist a half-hearted squeeze, then let go, exhausted.

She drew the blanket up around his shoulders. "Try to get some rest."

He nodded and closed his eyes.

She waited, watching him while blinking away the tears, and finally satisfied he'd indeed fallen asleep, she rocked back on her haunches and wiping her face, lifted her gaze to the doorway. *I'm counting on you to do the right thing, Ensign*, Aquila's voice echoed in her mind.

And she knew what that *thing* was. Damned right she did. *Besides, what's the worst that can happen?*

The answer came too quickly: *I'll get us all killed.*

She looked at Gianakis then at Aquila. *But if I don't try, Nico will be dead in a matter of hours and you by morning.* She took a deep breath and rose, slipped her arms into the sleeves of her softsuit, pulled the fabric up around her shoulders and fastened the collar as high as it would go, then squared her shoulders and marched out of the cabin.

Once out on the star-lit deck, beyond the cabin door's rectangle of pale green lamplight, she stopped to allow her eyes to adjust to the relative darkness and her legs to the rolling motion of the boat as it tacked into the brisk wind.

Here goes. She started across the deck but half way to the ladder, she heard a soft groan—and it hadn't come from the cabin. She stopped, peered around and finally spotted a figure braced against the starboard railing.

She squinted at the silhouetted form. *Too tall and heavy for Suhjai. Long hair. Only the officer, the one Suhjai called Matoosh and the one Aquila had punched in the throat had long hair, at least those are the only ones I remember…*

She took a step closer. As she did so she caught a glimpse of the Hahtooshan's face and confirmed that it was the merc officer.

Just who I was looking for! She smiled in relief, took another step, then stopped in her tracks as he leaned over the railing and began to retch, loudly.

Gods! She turned away and fixed her pinched stare on opposite horizon as she tried not to let the noises stir up a similar reaction in her own stomach. *Great. Just… great. It's kinda hard to do the right thing when the key to doing that is currently puking his guts out.*

An especially loud, agonizing groan drew her eyes back to him; he was doubled over and clutching his stomach with one hand, the railing with the other and his knees were buckling and she felt a pang of sympathy. *Damn!* Then another thought: *Maybe it wasn't Aquila's mumblings that woke me up…*

She took a cautious step, and another, all the while painfully aware of his deep, gut wrenching gagging.

Ah… I think this is close enough. As she waited for the spasm to pass, she mulled over various approaches. *Please, Sha'ashahn…* She shook her head. *No. The direct approach. Respectful, but direct. Maybe he doesn't realize how serious the situation is—maybe Suhjai's deliberately misled him. Or maybe he's stopped listening to her?*

Realizing he'd stopped retching, realizing her heart was thumping against her ribs, she took a deep, steadying breath. *It's do or die… literally.* She took a step closer and the deck beneath her foot squeaked. *Oh, shi—*

He glanced over his shoulder, fixed her with a scowl and rasped, "You're supposed to be asleep."

"I… I was, but… um…" She motioned to his stomach.

He replied with a grunt and grabbing his belly, hurriedly turned back to the railing as he succumbed to a violent fit of dry heaves.

She cautiously walked over to the railing, a prudent distance *upwind*, grasped the rough plank guardrail with both hands and politely ignoring his labored gagging—not for his sake, but for hers—fixed her gaze on the choppy sea as a gust of wind ruffled her salt-stiffened hair. What had begun as a balmy evening was beginning to unravel. The thin, wispy clouds that hugged the horizon for most of the day had suddenly turned thick.

Finally he stopped retching, and the moment he did he withdrew a small flask from hidden pocket and took a swig, swished the fluid around his mouth then leaning over the railing, spat it out, into the roiling sea below. He gave her a sidelong look, asked in a gruff voice, "What do you want?" then took another gulp from the flask.

"You have to contact our ship."

This time he swallowed his mouthful with a startled wince then replied huskily, "I do, do I?" He roughly wiped his mouth with the back of his hand. "Why?"

"Commander Aquila is—"

"Dying," he interrupted flatly. "As is the corporal—"

"And you're just going to stand there and do... *nothing?*"

As a reply, he brought the flask back to his lips.

"What about this proof you so desperately wanted him to see? Let me contact the *Baidarka,* get them to flick us aboard, then you can show us anything you want—we could even send another landing party down to this island..." her voice trailed off as she realized he was squinting up at one of the planet's bright moonlets, not sure if he'd even heard what she'd said. He abruptly swallowed his mouthful and she found herself wanting to grab the flask and hurl it into the sea. *And you with it, you fucking merc bastard!*

Instead she looked away as she forced down her mounting desperation. She cleared her throat then in the calmest voice she could muster, said, "Please..."

He looked at her out of the tail of his eye—a very bloodshot eye she noted.

"...you can't let them die."

"I'm A'tuu'shahn. Or have you forgotten?"

She squinted at him. *Pretty damned difficult to forget what the hell you are.* "Then why'd you go to all the trouble of rescuing us?"

He again brought the flask back to his lips. "Suhjai was right—yet again. I should've just left you to those beasts." He took a sip, swallowed.

"But you didn't."

He shrugged, replied, "Another bad decision," and took another cheek-bulging swig from the flask then swallowed as his slitted eyes searched the darkening horizon. "I make a lot of them," he added huskily, "always have."

She scowled. *Maybe 'cause you drink too damned much.* "You didn't think it was a bad decision yesterday."

"That was yesterday, now go away."

"No."

He favored her with a sidelong look. "Are you always this impertinent with your superiors?"

By his tone, it was obvious that his choice of the word 'superiors' had nothing to do with rank. But she wasn't about to give up, not now. He hadn't thrown her overboard and she had him talking. When dealing with a Hahtooshan, that had to be considered two steps in the right direction.

"Not usually. I've never had to deal with anyone as pigheaded as you." *Not exactly true, but—*

"*Pig*... headed?"

"Obstinate? *Stubborn?*"

"Ah." He nodded his understanding. "Well, if it's any consolation, I've never dealt with a Rimmer quite like you."

"I'll take that as a compliment."

He almost smiled—*almost*, then replied, "As it was intended."

She met his gaze squarely and for an instant—just an instant—before he again turned back to the sea, she found she could actually see through his grotesque tattoos to the being behind the hideous façade.

She also saw her opening. "Want to talk about it?"

"Talk about what?" he muttered, this time refusing to look at her.

"I dunno. You tell me. You clearly wanted to talk yesterday—you said so yourself. And you could've just as easily puked overboard from the deck below. But you came up here. I have to presume you were hoping I'd be awake?"

"You presume wrong. I assumed you'd be asleep—and just for future reference, when I find I need to vomit, I prefer to be alone. Less embarrassing that way."

"Uh-huh."

He pursed his lips, kept his eyes fixed on the horizon, then finally: "Besides, talking will do no good."

"Then why do *you* stay? Why don't you leave if you want to be alone?"

He looked at her, surprised.

Gotcha.

With an annoyed grunt, he turned back to his distracted scrutiny of the sea. "You would not understand."

Another step, good. Just keep him talking. "You don't know that. I might surprise you."

"Of that I have no doubt." He tilted his head back and gave his collar an angry tug, briefly exposing his heavily tattooed throat. The underlying skin had been rubbed raw.

Wait a minute... Her eyes darted back to his face.

Despite the brisk night wind, his forehead, cheeks and chin glistened with an oily sheen of sweat. And his exposed skin, in patches, was starting to peel. Something about his appearance, Suhjai's too for the past few days had been niggling at her—she'd shrugged it off as minute lapses in their shape-shifting—or another ruse, one to subtly imply seasickness and sunburn. But now it was so damned obvious.

"You're... you're not a shape-shifter, are you?"

He jerked his eyes back to her.

"You really are *exactly* as you appear, meaning you're *humanoid.*"

He stared at her for what seemed like an eternity before replying simply, "Yes."

She blinked; everything she knew—everything she thought she knew about Hahtooshans had just been turned upside down and inside out and it took a moment for her to reclaim her bearings. And true humanoids made up less than one hundredth of one percent of known sentient and semi-sentient species. In fact there were only three known humanoid species in the Rim with humans being the most populous. "But... but everyone thinks you are—shape-shifters that is."

"So now, along with being responsible for every heinous crime—the more sensational the better—any mysterious disappearance, all unexplained bumps in the night, we're also to blame for misinformation guised as fact?"

"Misinformation that conveniently works to your advantage."

He tried and failed miserably to look taken aback at the underlying accusation, then: "And your point is?"

She ignored the question by asking another: "So, who was the source of this… misinformation? *You?"*

"Me, personally?" he replied, pointing to himself, "No," he shook his shaggy head and brought the flask back to his lips.

"I didn't mean *you*, personally. I meant your Orthodoxy."

He roughly wiped his mouth on the back of his hand, in the process opening a blister on his lower lip which immediately started to bleed then he took another gulp.

Frustrated, painfully aware of the urgency of her mission, she blurted out, "Getting drunk isn't going to solve anything, you know. In fact it'll only make the symptoms worse as I'm *sure* Suhjai's told you."

He pointedly and loudly swallowed his mouthful, then: "Suhjai says many things, but I've stopped listening to her."

"Well in this case she's right." She motioned angrily to the flask. "It might have dulled the pain at first, but I doubt if it does now."

He scowled sidelong at her as he dabbed at his bleeding lip.

She crossed her arms and threw caution to the stiff wind. "You're suffering from radiation poisoning and fairly advanced poisoning too, by the looks of you."

The quickly concealed look of surprise in his pale eyes was all the confirmation she needed. "And as every *smart* humanoid knows, the worst thing any *smart* humanoid can do is drink alcohol when they're suffering from radiation poisoning—since one of the first organ systems to be adversely effected is the gut lining. Which means even *you* should know it, too."

"You're assuming I'm smart."

"You're telling me you aren't?"

"I thought our current predicament would speak for itself."

"I don't follow—and you're being evasive."

In response and to her surprise he stuffed the flask back into its hidden pocket, under his hauberk then flicked her another sidelong look. "We were marooned here."

She blinked. "Marooned...?"

"Abandoned. Left to—"

"I know what the hell marooned means. Why?"

"Does it matter? To you we're nothing more than a bunch of murderous thugs—I would've thought you would have thought it ironic justice that we've been left here to die by our own."

"Then you thought wrong. And I think the reason matters a great deal. So, why?"

"You wouldn't understand."

"Is that your answer to everything?"

He looked thoughtful for a moment, tapping his finger on his blood-smeared chin then he nodded, "Yes."

She exhaled explosively, drawing his guarded stare. "Well, dammit, I *want* to understand."

"Why?"

"Because if I understand, then maybe I can convince you to contact the *Baidarka* and get us all the hell outta here."

He shifted his narrowed gaze back to the horizon. "Unlikely."

"Unlikely that I'll understand or that you'll contact my ship?"

He shrugged again, little more than a slight twitch of his ghillie-suited shoulders. "You choose."

Like hell! Aloud and calmly she replied, "Try me."

He closed his eyes and took a deep breath. The fingers of his right hand brushed across the gorget at the base of his throat then he wrapped his hand around the grip of his dagger. "I'm a foolish Elkanaghalli."

His tone suggested that was answer enough.

She gave the archaic weapon a quick, uneasy glance. "Oh."

He opened one eye a crack to peer at her. "I told you, you wouldn't understand."

This time she let her annoyance taint her voice: "And you're not giving me much of a chance, are you?"

He suddenly grasped the railing in one hand, his belly with the other, and as his face tightened into a grimace he again searched the wind-ruffled sea with watery eyes.

Despite her frustration, her sense that he was deliberately stalling, making a macabre game out of her desperation, his own agony, she found herself wanting to reach out to him, touch him, offer the basic human need of comfort in the form of physical contact—*but you aren't human, are you?* And, she reminded herself, that almost instinctual response might in fact be the worst thing she could do—in her admittedly brief interactions with them, she hadn't seen any evidence that Hahtooshans were a touchy-feely sort of species, quite the contrary—

Another stifled groan drew her attention back to the matter at hand and as she stared up at his strained, sweat-streaked face she couldn't help but wince in sympathy. *Gods, you're really ill. How long've you been here? At least a week. Two? Longer? Helluva place to be dumped—what the hell did you do?*

She gave him another pinched look as he succumbed to another fit of retching. *And I wonder how the revelation about Hahtooshans being true humanoids is going to be received when word gets out? There are a lot of experts who've staked their entire careers, their illustrious reputations on the firmly held belief that your kind is some truly alien creature, possibly not even native to the Rim, able to shape-shift into any other creature at will—the ultimate bogeymen—*

He briefly straightened up, took several labored gulps of air then suddenly resumed his violent retching, utterly consumed in the involuntary act of ridding his body of the alcohol in the most expeditious and agonizing means.

Corsali winced in sympathy; there nothing else she could do except stand and watch. So she did exactly that... and suddenly realized that she was close enough she could grab his pistol, disarm him while he was incapacitated, never mind that the pistol was only one weapon in the full arsenal at his disposal—*but then what? Shoot him while he's busy puking? Shoot all of them? Then what?*

Then there'd be no hope of getting Aquila and Gianakis the medical help they need—and I'd be marooned here until the radiation poisoning kills me, too—

Suddenly it dawned on her that this in fact very well might be her fate regardless of her actions. *Which means this politically explosive bit of intelligence is very likely going to literally die with me—*

She eyed her now dry-heaving companion. *Of course maybe that's why you're willing to admit you aren't shape-shifters—you know I'll be taking your secret to my grave.* She turned back to the surrounding ocean. *And likely a watery one at that.*

His dry retching ever so slowly turned to ferocious hiccups and finally, blessedly, stopped altogether. He leaned heavily on the railing for a moment, utterly exhausted by the spasms then he slowly, carefully straightened himself up and wiped his still bleeding lip with the back of a very shaky hand as he favored her with a sidelong look, clearly bracing himself for a wholly unsympathetic response.

She was tempted, direly tempted to say "Told you so", but held her tongue. After an awkward moment of mutual and silent scrutiny of him waiting for her expected reply and her waiting for him to acknowledge it without her actually having to say it, he looked away. She followed his blood-shot and watery gaze only to find that towering clouds now dotted the horizon and the stiff, icy wind that blew around them held the hint of rain.

Maybe this is all part of a ruse, Aquila's voice whispered.

She clenched her teeth against a shiver. *Damn. What if it is?* She squinted sidelong at him. *You can't fake radiation poisoning—well, maybe you could, but to what point? So, assuming you aren't faking, maybe you and your buddies are just an expendable diversion? If that's the case, it might work in my favor—*

"It would appear that we're in for some rough weather," he said hoarsely.

She started to nod distractedly when it struck her that sometime along the way, he'd begun to inflect his voice with a Selkis accent—deliberately, as a subtle effort at putting her at ease, or purely subconsciously, she wasn't sure.

Perhaps it's just habit, just ingrained training, nothing more. *Perhaps I'm reading too much into it.* She looked up at him—his pinched stare was still fixed on the horizon. *Then again...* "I really do want to understand."

He dropped his gaze to her. "Why?"

"I told you why. But let's put it another way. What do you have to lose? And you really look like you need to talk to someone."

He braced his hip against the railing, crossed his arms and staring down at her, arched his brow and replied dubiously, "Meaning you. A female, a... *kaa-schat.*"

She forced herself not react to his sneering tone. Instead she glanced around at the otherwise deserted deck before returning to his piercing gaze. "Yup."

He continued to stare down at her and through his narrowed eyes she watched the inner war his mind was waging against itself.

Come on—let down your guard! You've gotta step out of that uniform some time. "I'm a very good listener," she prompted. As the balance suddenly appeared to shift in her favor, she gave him a mental nudge. *Come on, you can do it, just—*

"It's very complicated." He wiped his sweat-beaded cheeks and forehead with the back of his hand then startled her by admitting, "But you're right. I no longer have anything left to lose." He withdrew the flask.

She started to say something, but thought better of it. *If the liquor helps lubricate your tongue—*

"A little over three Standard weeks ago the Orthodoxy entered into a contract to locate and retrieve all data from the Coalition's abandoned military base on Rasal Ghul Four."

"Contracted with whom? The Matarrans?"

He gave her a sidelong, suspicious look. "I don't know."

Truth? Hard to tell. Not important right now. Move on. "So...?"

He took a sip from the flask, swallowed. "The contracts were awarded, and *Acholilah* and *Makhaira* dispatched. Ru'asooli Kshira'tzrhi, upon our arrival—"

"Excuse me. Rooah... who?"

He looked at her as if she'd said something very silly. "Ru'asooli Kshira'tzrhi, commanding officer of *Acholilah*, and of the overall mission."

"Oh," she murmured and filed the name away. *"That* Ru'asooli. So, upon your arrival...?"

He eyed her for a moment. "Upon our arrival, Ru'asooli ordered a scout into the system to reconnoiter, while *Acholilah* and *Makhaira* remained at the edge the binary's interference sphere. The scout located the base, made planet-fall and the crew made a preliminary data recovery then rendezvoused with *Makhaira* and *Acholilah*. When the data was analyzed, it was discovered that a handful of the base's staff had fled to this planet after an accident that claimed the lives of the rest. Tarqk convinced Ru'asooli—"

"Wait. Now who's this Tarqk?"

"Nahru'tzhri of *Makhaira*," he explained with a trace of annoyance.

She nodded. *Another piece of the puzzle. Move on.* "Okay, so he convinced—"

"Ru'asooli."

"Yeah. Got that. So this Tarqk convinced Ru'asooli—"

"Tarqk convinced…" He held up his forefinger, signal to wait and she stared back, baffled, then he grimaced, hurriedly turned back to the railing and retched explosively.

Coulda told you, she thought to herself while wincing in sympathy.

Clinging to the railing, he took several deep, ragged breaths, angrily wiped his lips, his chin then slowly turned back to her and continued huskily, "Tarqk convinced Ru'asooli that the survivors might have brought their research data with them, and since this planet is more… *hospitable,* he further reasoned that this data would be easier to retrieve. I was… chosen," he added after a moment's hesitation, "to lead the landing force…."

Chosen. Perhaps you knew ahead of time you were going to be marooned? No wonder you didn't volunteer—

"…but my superiors," he continued, his voice now stronger, less raspy, "wishing nothing to be left to chance, ordered the scout back to the fourth planet, to make another attempt at downloading all the data and then to destroy the computer banks—"

"So no one else would recover the information." She hugged herself against the now bitingly cold wind.

"Of course," he replied and motioned to a sheltered corner of the deck next to the cabin. "Perhaps…?"

Corsali nodded eagerly then walked beside him, finding herself ready to steady him if needed, as he continued, "We were paid to obtain the information for the exclusive use of our clients. It would be of little value if others obtained it as well."

As she passed by the door to the cabin her chilled ears picked up Aquila's soft snoring and, fainter still, Gianakis' labored breathing. *You're both still with me… good,* she nodded, relieved. *Just hold on, just a little longer, please. A little longer and I think he just might—*

"Here?" He motioned to a wind-protected spot next to the cabin.

She sat, cross-legged, then braced her back against the cabin's woven wall. "So, the scout went back to the fourth planet while you came here."

Cradling his rebellious belly in one hand, the flask in the other, he slowly eased himself down a mutually comfortable distance from her, his back also to the cabin. "Yes. The scout crew accomplished their mission, but shortly after lift-off the scout was caught by a massive flare surge. The pilot, realizing she could not reach the rendezvous point and knowing there was a landing force on this planet, tried to make planet-fall—"

"And crashed in the desert."

He wiped his glossy forehead with the back of his hand. "Yes."

"And you were on your way to rescue the crew when we arrived?"

"We knew none had survived."

"Then why—"

"*Makhaira* picked up your ship's arrival in the system. As soon as Tarqk realized your vessel's scanners had located the wreck and was preparing to enter orbit, presumably to investigate, I was ordered to make sure that you did not recover the scout's data banks—"

"But you disobeyed orders."

"As I told your commander, at the time I deemed it to be in our own, long term interests."

At the time? What's happened to make you change your mind? Move on, Sirin! "So that's why you were marooned?"

He shook his head as he intently studied the flask he still clutched in one hand as if it was the sole object of his interest, the topic of their discussion. "Tarqk had many reasons for wanting to be rid of me. This situation just provided a welcome opportunity." He brought the flask to his lips and took a deep, wincing gulp.

She couldn't help but cringe, knowing full well what his reckless action would trigger. "Because you're... you're Elkanaghalli," she replied, awkwardly aware of her own ignorance but hoping it was the right thing to say.

"That was one reason, a very good reason, perhaps reason enough for Tarqk." He tugged at his stiff collar then angrily wiped his sweaty forehead with his fingers. "But I'd provided him with *so* many others."

She cautiously scooted a little closer to him, hoping to take full advantage of his suddenly talkative frame of mind while at the same time taking advantage of some of his excess body heat—well aware she was risking him puking on her... or worse. "Like what?"

"The simple answer is that he wanted my bond-mate, Tu'indai."

"Your bond-mate?"

"A'tuu'shahn'i are not so vastly different from Rimmers, you know," he said with an audible trace of annoyance. "We marry, have families. We're not just mindless butchers, hired by the likes of your genteel Coalition to do its dirty work."

"That wasn't what I meant—"

"In our case, Tu'indai is my bond-mate, my *wife* in name only." He again fixed his gaze on the flask he held in one hand and said quietly, "It was an arranged joining."

"Oh," she answered uneasily as she noticed that his other hand was now lightly caressing of the dagger's grip. *Gods, I sure hope that's just a nervous habit.* She looked up at his face to find that new beads of sweat had formed on his forehead and as she watched, one trickled down his gaunt cheek, following one of the deeply cut scars to the corner of his sun-blistered mouth.

"She," he continued as he angrily wiped it away, "like Suhjai, is Taqlth-khu of the Shar'ataan, the lowest of our nine castes, and as with any joining to an Elkanaghalli, it brought her family much prestige."

"And you?"

He chuckled again, and dropped his hand to his belly and she breathed a silent sigh of relief. "The joining was intended to humiliate me, all done and finalized before I even knew what was happening, by those whom I'd offended when I refused to be exploited for their material gain."

"Did it work?"

He paused then shook his head. "No. My purpose in life was never to make anyone rich, not even myself. I have sworn myself to uphold other values—they simply forgot that, forgot that I am Elkanaghalli of the old order."

"So this Tarqk chap wanted your wife—"

"Yes. Had he just *asked*, I would have happily given her to him as she gave me nothing but aggravation. I'd be lying if I said I wouldn't have been pleased to see her do the same to him." He favored her with a sidelong look.

"If Suhjai's an example of a taath... tak—"

"Taqlth-khu," he corrected then abruptly looked away as his face tightened into a wince.

"Well," she smiled thinly, bracing herself for what might come next, "I can see why."

He leaned back against the cabin wall, arched his head back and took several deep breaths, then said, "Yes, Suhjai can be almost as exasperating as Tu'indai. Over the years I've come to realize that it's a dominant Taqlth-khu trait."

"Almost as exasperating?"

"I did say I would've happily given her to him." He let out an exhausted sigh, muttered, "Why he would wish to trade one for another..." as he rubbed his belly.

Her eyes widened with sudden comprehension. "You mean Suhjai was his—"

"Let's say that Suhjai, like me, had become an unwelcome impediment."

"Which is why he picked her to accompany you."

He chuckled. "Actually, she volunteered for the mission."

"Volunteered? To be marooned?"

"No, to keep an eye on me."

"You mean to spy on you?"

"To make sure I carried out my orders—and that I'd reveal to her the names of those who were planning a mutiny against him."

"Mutiny?

He shrugged. "Rumors only, although in truth it I wouldn't blame the crew for wanting to rid themselves of Tarqk."

She paused then replied, "Only she really was being marooned with you."

"Thus solving two dilemmas at once. She was quite... perturbed when I informed her of the truth."

"I think I might be a bit on the testy side too, if I were her."

He only shrugged as he continued to massage his stomach.

She pressed her ear against the cabin wall. Several seconds passed before she again overheard a soft grunt of a snore. Relieved, she exhaled and cautiously edged a little nearer to him. "So, what's the complicated answer?"

He looked down at her and by his expression was clearly surprised to find her now seated so close to him.

And seeing his expression, she realized she was equally startled by her brashness. *Maybe it's the Selkis accent,* she rationalized, *maybe knowing that he really is humanoid, not some... alien monster.* Whatever it was, she realized she was no longer terrified of him, which, she realized, might *cut* both ways. "You said that was the simple answer," she replied hastily as she hugged herself, hoping to hide her own surprise. "Which means there's a complicated one too."

He studied her for a moment, clearly not taken in by her ruse and said, "Are you *still* cold?"

"Yes," she replied quickly because she was that, too. *"Very."* She pulled her softsuit's collar tightly around her throat for emphasis.

He slowly and cautiously lifted his arm to expose his flank, then, at her hesitation, added, "I give you my word it will go no further. Come. You're cold. I'm not." And before she knew what was happening and could react, he wrapped his arm around her and tugged her tight against him.

"Ah...." She looked up to see him staring down at her and tried not to grimace at the creepy feel of his uniform morphing against her, the decidedly strange sensation only slightly moderated by the softsuit. It was, she realized, akin to lying in a bed of snakes, and she briefly wondered if it felt the same to the wearer. *Ugh...*

"As I have repeatedly assured you," he said with an underlying note of exasperation, "I am Elkanaghalli," he lightly touched the enameled gorget, "defender of the true faith, keeper of the past and as first caste, beloved servant of the Elkanasu." He dropped his gaze to the dagger as his fingers lightly stroked the haft. *"Elkanasu toq-bhir,"* he murmured with a faint smile. Then, looking back at her, he added, "We Elkanaghalli are, to the Elkanasu, the *genuine* people, or, more formally, 'The Divine Light and The Image Of Perfection, Revealer of the Truth and Sole Representation of Real.' As such have taken a vow to remain pure, of mind... *and* body—the latter being far easier than the former, let me assure you." He smiled, clearly his attempt at a joke that in fact was no joke at all.

Are you suggesting what I think you're suggesting? "You mean—"

"The closest analog in your language would be a... celibate?"

"Oh." It wasn't the most inspired response but the best she could do on the spur of the moment. She looked away to conceal her surprise and immediately set about trying to figure out how this critical—and totally unexpected—piece of a rapidly enlarging and very complicated puzzle could be put to use. *It certainly explains why your wife's a tad testy. Being married off to a monk as part of a personal vendetta—*

"I should not have expected you to recognize the unique status of Elkanaghalli'i—most A'tuu'shahn'i do not, or, more accurately, *will not.*"

Hearing the sudden bitterness in his voice, she looked back up at him. The smile was gone.

"Perhaps they are right," he muttered angrily as he slid the dagger from its scabbard. "Perhaps Elkanaghalli'i *are* a painful reminder of something best forgotten."

She nervously wet her lips as she stared, wide-eyed at the blade that now gleamed menacingly in the starlight a scant few centimeters from her face—and throat. Suddenly his embracing arm took on a far more sinister context. *Gods...!*

"This brands me," he whispered, his feverish eyes meeting her wide-eyed stare, "this brands all Elkanaghalli'i as something most A'tuu'shahn'i would rather forget, a living reminder of a glorious past that they'd prefer to ignore—a time when A'tuu'shahn'i served only the needs of the Elkanasu, instead of now, when we're slaves to our greed and the greed of others, when we do their bidding, no matter how... dishonorable."

He exhaled and shaking his head, dropped his gaze to the knife. *"Siah'ushu..."*

Corsali too found her eyes draw to the weapon and the elaborate motif etched into the flat of the blade appeared to move, to... *slither* across its mirror-like surface and towards the grip, towards his encircling, tattooed fingers. *What the—*

"Beautiful, yes?"

She glanced up at him and then gave the curious dagger another wary, sidelong look only to find the polished surface now devoid of all design and she felt her skin crawl. *More like fucking creepy—and here I thought your uniform was damned unnerving.* "Uh… well, yes I suppose—"

"I was taught from childhood that Siah'ushu," he jerked his tattooed and scarified chin toward the dagger, "is what makes me who I am, it is all I am, all I will ever be, that through Siah'ushu—in that instant between life and death—I will experience all that has gone before and all that has yet to happen; I will see all, do all, feel all that has occurred and will occur." He paused, smiled down at the massive knife. *"Our presence, all that we do, everything around us is ephemeral—nothing more than a flash of luminescence in the greater darkness,"* he whispered as if by rote, *"this… this is everything, the only true light of permanence…"*

He stared at the dagger, transfixed, then startled her by continuing in a slightly stronger voice, "I took immense pride in the fact that I was Elkanaghalli—I took pride in the fact that we kept the ancient ways, the ancient beliefs alive, kept the flame alive, that in doing so, we were a living link to that far distant past and a reminder of what we might be again." He paused again before adding bitterly, "I used to believe if that flame was ever extinguished, even for an instant, we—meaning everyone *and* everything—would be swallowed whole by *Ha'antoorethah*—The Big Dark—what you call The Barrens, never to escape…"

She risked another quick glance at the dagger, then back up to his face only to see sheer desperation in his pale eyes—and not just about the potential of the disease. Not just of being marooned, but of being utterly abandoned… totally *alone*. Lost forever in his greater darkness.

"No matter." He flashed her a clearly staged and dazzling smile and slid the dagger back into its scabbard then fixed his narrowed gaze on the horizon.

She breathed a silent sigh of relief that at least that particular distraction was gone, while wishing she knew what to say. *But what?* Talking to him was like walking through a minefield. *Say the wrong thing….*

Deciding actions did indeed speak louder than words she slipped her arm behind his back and wrapped it around his waist. Despite the fact that he reeked of alcohol and vomit and that his filthy, constantly writhing uniform was damp with sweat, it seemed the right thing to do—

His entire body stiffened.

Okay, not the right thing. "I'm sorry, Sha'ashahn." She started to withdraw her embrace. "I didn't—"

"No." He leaned back, gently pinning her arm in place.

"No?"

"You… you just took me by surprise."

"Oh." She almost smiled as she felt his rigid back muscles relax just a little. *Now, if I can just get you to relax your guard a little more—*

"And it's Khusaaq."

"Koo…?"

"Khusaaq. My…use name. Khusaaq."

"Oh," she replied, then, realizing he was waiting for her to reciprocate, said, "Mine's Sirin."

"Seer… *in.*" He rolled the name around on his tongue, murmured, "Sir-*in,*" then repeated with more certainty, "Sirin." He nodded to himself. "Yes. A very nice name."

Glad you approve—

"Now, the complicated answer, yes?"

She looked up at him to see his pale eyes fixed on the sky above, searching. *But for what? Your ship? Home? Redemption?* She tightened her hold on his hip and found herself immensely pleased, and at the same time startled at her own response, when the gesture failed to elicit more than a minor muscle twitch. "Yes."

He brought the flask back to his lips, then, realizing it was empty, irritably tossed it aside. "I, along with *Makhaira*'s medical officer, Ouda'yai, and the ship's second, Qharubi, studied the preliminary data the scout had recovered on the weapons that had been created at the base. We recognized the true potential, as well as the potential risk of one, and voiced our opinions to Tarqk."

"And he—" Corsali, overhearing his sharp intake of breath and feeling his entire body convulse against her encircling arm, glanced up to find his eyes tightly shut and his lips drawn back against his teeth. She waited a moment, but when he groaned then began to frantically gulp for air, she jerked her arm free and got to her knees. "I'll get Suhjai!"

"No…!"

"But—"

"It… it will… *pass.*"

She dropped her worried gaze to his belly as his fingers dug into his uniform and realized for the first time that his fingers were bloodied, his fingernails torn and frayed from their futile efforts at reaching the searing pain.

"You need medical attention!"

He grabbed her wrist as she started to scramble to her feet and roughly jerked her back to her knees. *"No...!"*

Her startled eyes darted between his taut, sweat-streaked face and his painful hold. "But Suhjai—"

"There... there's nothing... she... she can do." With that, he abruptly let go of her and sagged back against the wall.

Corsali had a sudden, horrible thought. "She's been treating the Commander and Gianakis while you and the others... went without? But—"

"You... you said you wanted to understand, so... *so let me finish!"*

"Fine. *Then* I'll get Suhjai. There's gotta be something she can do to ease the pain—"

"Tarqk... Tarqk plans to... to keep the weapon."

"What?"

He took several deep, steadying breaths then answered in a slightly stronger voice, "He plans to keep the weapon—*test it*. He believes the Orthodoxy will... will then be in a position to demand a higher price for something of this magnitude of sheer destructiveness, or perhaps... perhaps even to keep it for ourselves."

"Where? Where's he going to test it?"

"Does it matter? Nothing—" He winced, clutched his belly and continued tightly, "Nothing can be... be done to stop him now and once it's released, there'll be no stopping it. I tried to warn him of this, we all did—that was his *mutiny*—he was afraid we were going to claim credit, take his glory away from him, but he would not—" He shut his eyes, clenched his teeth and grabbed his belly with both hands.

"But he has to be stopped!"

"It's too late," he forced out.

"No, it's not! Give me one of our tac-pacs!"

He squinted up at her, his face contorted in a grimace.

"He has to be stopped! You want him stopped, together we can, but only if you give me a tac-pac!"

"It will do no good—"

"Damn you, you—"

"It's too late—"

"Meaning you're just going to do nothing!" She leapt to her feet and stepped back, just in case he had a mind to grab her again. "You're going to let him do this, just like you're going to let Commander Aquila and Nico die and who knows how many others! What about your men? Suhjai? Don't you want to save them? You *want* them to die?"

"They're A'tuu'shahn—"

"Stop hiding behind that bullshit! I don't give a damn what they are—what *you* are! We've got to get off this planet—*we've got to stop this!* This is why you rescued us in the first place, remember?" When he only stared up at her, she snorted in disgust then turned away and tried to sort out her roiling thoughts. *Gods, what am I going to—*

"Here..."

She slowly turned around to find him holding up a tac-pac.

"Take... it."

She searched his exhausted eyes as she warily stepped closer, not sure if this was a trap or not.

"Take it!"

She snatched it from his blood-sticky palm and hurriedly backed up, again out of easy reach, then, under the guise of fumbling with the activator, her heart hammering against her chest, she triggered the emergency retrieval as she brought the small device close to her mouth. *"Baidarka,* this is Ensign Corsali! *Baidarka...* come in!"

The only reply was the rustle and snap of static.

She wet her lips and tried again. *"Baidarka,* come in! This is Ensign Corsali, *Baidarka.* Respond! *Please,"* she whispered desperately as her fingers tightened their hold, "answer me! Please!"

She pressed the tac-pac to her ear, straining to hear something—anything—over the rush of the water and the wind. *Nothing.*

She tried again, this time making no effort to keep her voice steady. *"Baidarka,* you've got to answer! You've got to!"

"I fear I've succeeded in outsmarting myself," he whispered.

She wheeled around to face him. "What?"

"I thought my plan was foolproof. I thought we'd reach the island in plenty of time." He shook his head. "Now Tarqk will succeed, my family—all Elkanaghalli'i will be disgraced. All... *all for nothing.*"

She swallowed convulsively and looked up. "You wouldn't have left us behind..."

As if in reply, an especially bright auroral curtain snaked overhead, hissing and crackling across the cloud-smeared starfield.

She followed it with her blurry gaze until it vanished behind a thick bank of clouds, then she looked back at the silent tac-pac. *Wait a minute...*

Her eyes slowly widened. *"Of course!"* She dropped her gaze back to him. "They haven't left, they're still in orbit! It's the radiation, that's what's—"

"No," he interrupted quietly and with an expression of such absolute certainty that it sent a cold shiver up her spine. "Your ship has left or was destroyed—"

"But... but you don't know that! You don't—"

"I've already made a number of attempts at contacting your vessel, using both your communicating device and mine."

"What?" She dropped her stunned gaze to the tac-pac. "Then why—"

"I told you it was no use but you refused to believe me. You needed to try for yourself."

The revelation left her feeling as if the air had been knocked out of her and she fell heavily to her knees beside him. *"No..."*

"Yes," he replied wearily as his face began to twist into yet another wince. "You've been marooned here, just... just as I've been. And like me, you'll die here."

Chapter 12

"Cajori, what's the status on the screens?"

"Holding, sir, at eighty-seven percent."

Lesedi turned next to Cyllo. "EM output?"

"Gamma's presently in one of its quiescent phases with granulation nearing minimum. Based on prior cycles, this shouldn't last for more than three hours—four, tops—before convection cells within the photosphere re-energize and produce plasma bursts along the contact ribbon, which will white out our scanners—"

"Not to mention burning up the screens," Cajori interrupted. "They won't be able to diffuse another massive outburst."

"Sir?"

Lesedi glanced over her shoulder at the relief com-op, Masursky. "Yes?"

"Doctor Amalfitano said to tell you that he just finished questioning Crewman Niebuhr." Masursky's eyes darted to Cyllo then back to Lesedi. "Niebuhr verifies that three of the landing party were attacked and presumably killed by the same predators that attacked—"

"Which three?"

He hesitated then replied, "Medtech Jarvis, Private Gislasen and... and Corporal Lundgren."

Lesedi glanced at Cyllo but the woman's back was to her, her reaction to the news hidden, just as she'd kept her personal fears concealed behind a professional mask.

It had been a well-known bit of shipboard gossip that Cyllo and the gregarious Lundgren were more than just friends. *Damn... I never once thought to talk to you privately about this very possibility. Vildur would have found time, regardless of the situation. Aquila would've too. I was too busy being... captain—*

"Sir." Cyllo's voice was all business but she kept her back to the control room, "I'm starting to get some intelligible readings from the planet's surface."

Lesedi made a mental note to take the woman aside, later—give her some time off. ETA?"

"Twelve minutes."

She turned to the tactical display. "Go to yellow alert."

— ii —

A hand lightly grasped Corsali's shoulder, followed by a whispered, *"Ensign...?"*

"Go away," she mumbled and tried to twitch off the hand's grip.

The fingers tightened their hold, followed by a more insistent, *"Ensign, wake up!"*

The demand was punctuated by a shudder that ran through the decking below her, jolting her to full wakefulness. Her eyes snapped open. Above her hovered a swarthy, tattooed face bathed in the flickering green glow of a lantern.

"Khusaaq?"

At his curt nod, she glanced around to find that she was back in the cabin, covered in a blanket and a lit lantern sitting on the deck beside her. Her last memory was of huddling against the outer cabin wall, watching over him after he lapsed into a fitful, exhausted sleep.

"How did I get—*what's happened?"* she hissed as she suddenly noticed the odd look in his pale eyes. *Aquila!* "Commander—"

"He's still alive," he interrupted as he lurched back to his feet, taking the lantern with him, "as is your crewman—but we must get you to the bow of the boat."

She sat up and realized that he was not alone. Three wind-blown and grim-faced troopers stood just behind him. She tossed the blanket aside and scrambled to her feet. "What's happened?"

"The storm—it's almost upon us." He grabbed a roof pole with his free hand to steady himself as the deck heaved again, accompanied by a distant, rolling peal of thunder, then he jerked his chin towards the soldiers. "They'll carry your companions. Sa'huri, Gienah, *vott!"* He motioned to Gianakis and Aquila and two of the troopers stepped forward. *"Kaahath!"*

"Be careful!" she snapped as the one she recognized as the one Aquila had punched in the throat roughly scooped up Gianakis' limp body in his arms.

As the second trooper knelt to gather up Aquila she briefly met his brutish gaze and instinctively backed up a step as she realized he was none other than the churlish accomplice of the soldier who'd groped her. Then the third stepped forward—she recognized him, too.

"Matoosh will help you down the ladder," Khusaaq explained. "Go," he gestured with the lantern to the doorway just as another shudder ran through the boat, *"hurry!"*

"But what about you—" she was cut off as Matoosh's armored fingers locked around her wrist.

With a determined tug, he started after the two soldiers as they vanished into the gusting darkness beyond the cabin's doorway. She glanced helplessly back Khusaaq. "But—"

"I'll be right behind you," he urged, *"now go!"*

A curtain of wind-driven rain struck the boat broadside just as she and Matoosh reached the ladder and if he hadn't had such a firm hold on her she would have gone sliding across the deck... and right off the edge into the churning water below.

As if sensing her panic, he wrapped his arm around her, grabbed the top of the ladder with his other hand and together they hung on for dear life—he onto the ladder and she onto him—as the boat lurched violently then yawed hard to starboard.

The moment the boat righted itself she risked a look up at Matoosh's rain-slick and gale-battered face then followed his narrowed gaze and peered into the downpour. At first she saw nothing—then a dazzling flash of lightning briefly lit up the deck. In that instant she spotted Khusaaq staggering towards them, a thick coil of rope slung over his shoulder. He finally managed to reach Matoosh's side, breathless, then, over another rumble of thunder—this one much louder—along with the roar of the rain and wind, yelled, "Can you climb down on your own?"

Corsali gave the heaving and wave-sluiced deck below a wary look. The alternative—being carried by Matoosh—was even less appealing, especially when she met his decidedly unenthusiastic gaze. *Who'd be the wiser if you just 'accidentally' let go? Me, that's who, at least for a few seconds.* She nodded.

"Good." He managed a nervous smile and motioned to Matoosh.

The trooper went first and then with Khusaaq's help, she carefully eased herself onto the top rung only to find Matoosh waiting just below, ready to offer his body as a shield against the vicious pummeling of the squall. She carefully eased herself down the ladder and into his protective embrace and together they began the descent.

Half way down, the ladder shook as Khusaaq began his own precarious climb down the slippery rungs.

As her foot touched the deck, Matoosh tugged her away from the ladder. Having lost all reticence about him, she again wrapped her arms around his waist and like him peered upwards. Through the hammering rain, she saw movement: soles of boots as they briefly appeared suspended within the maelstrom, the flash of lightning off Khusaaq's hauberk, loops of rope flapping wildly in the wind.

Then, to her immense relief, he too stepped onto the deck.

He leaned close and between labored, sodden breaths, gasped, *"Go... with... Matoosh!"*

"But—wait, damn you!" She made a grab for his bandoleer but missed. *"Where the hell're you going?"*

He angrily wiped a lock of sopping wet hair from his eyes. *"The rudder!"*

"But—"

"The Blatto abandoned ship the moment they saw the storm coming—someone must steer the boat or we'll surely capsize!" He adjusted his hold on the coils of heavy, rain-soaked rope and jerked his chin towards the bow. *"Go!"*

Matoosh gave her arm an insistent tug and using the mainmast's boom to guide him, started across the pitching main deck as Corsali stumbled alongside. High above, lightning exploded in the already highly charged atmosphere and thunder boomed in response, the cacophony vibrating though the deck, through her bones.

Within sight of the forecastle they both heard a loud, ominous *crack* from somewhere behind them, followed by a deep, shuddering groan of decking giving way.

Matoosh dropped his horrified gaze to her and, over the rapid-fire *snap-snap-snap* of the sodden main sail torn loose, shredded and flapping wildly in the gale a meter above him, bellowed, *"I must help Sha'ashahn!"* He pointed to the forecastle. *"Can you make it the rest of the way on your own?"*

She grabbed a stanchion and yelled back, *"I... I don't think so!"*

He swore—at least he looked like he swore to her—but his words were ripped away by the fierce wind before they reached her ears.

Matoosh unbuckled his weapons belt, threw it around her and the stanchion, grabbed the ends, buckled it around her waist and firmly clinched her to the pole. He shouted in her ear, *"I'll return for you!"*

Not waiting for her reply, he hurried back the way they'd just come, vanishing into the wind-whipped downpour.

"You damn well better come back for me!" she yelled after him as she realized he'd placed the belt's unfamiliar buckle where she couldn't reach it. *You fucking bastard...! You did—* She lifted her gaze as she heard an odd noise, like a muffled cry, almost lost within the howling wind and roaring rain. She hoped to spot Khusaaq or even Matoosh returning: instead the curtain of rain parted just long enough for her to see a wall of water engulf the entire stern and she screamed, *"NO!"*

— v —

"Entering planetary orbit, sir."

Lesedi nodded to Eisele then turned to Cyllo. "Anything?"

"There's a lot of electrical activity going on down there, sir. Surface storms—they're causing a lot of sensory arti—*I've got a retrieval beacon!* Almost directly below us, within a storm cell—"

"Full stop!"

"Full stop, aye sir," Eisele replied calmly as her fingers tapped out a soft cadence on her helm control panel.

Lesedi smacked the com button. "Flickerstage, prepare to lock onto signal."

"Sir," Cyllo added, glancing over her shoulder, "scanners are picking up definite human readings... but they're still within those high frequency, low intensity—"

"Hahtooshans." Lesedi turned to Izraad.

Izraad nodded. "It would appear so—"

"Sir! The surface craft—"

"What about it?"

"It's... it's breaking apart!"

"Perou!"

"Locked on—"

"Flick up the whole boat. *Now!"*

He jerked around in his chair to face Lesedi, eyes wide. *"The whole boat?"*

"The whole fucking boat! No time to sort out human from Hahtooshan—use the main cargo bay—it'll fit won't it?"

"Just barely, but yessir, it'll—"

"Then do it!" Lesedi barked, rising out of her chair. "Khaleed you have the conn!"

"Medical and security notified, sir, both have dispatched teams to the cargo bay," Masursky called after her as she dashed through the airlock.

— vi —

Lesedi arrived at the cargo bay's main airlock to find a large, heavily-armed and armored contingent of marines waiting for her.

The team's sergeant, Delatorre, handed her a filter mask and goggles with a muttered, "Doc's orders."

Lesedi nodded, slipped the mask and goggles into place then accepted the shocker Delatorre held out for her. She checked it, then turned to the surrounding men and said, "We have no idea how many mercs we might be dealing with—assuming we're dealing with mercs at all—so don't take any chances. See something you don't recognize as one of our crew, shoot—" She overheard the clatter of feet echoing down the corridor and turned.

Amalfitano, leading his triage team, smiled tightly as he trotted towards her. He opened his mouth to say something just as the cargo bay klaxons began to howl and warning lights flash.

Lesedi turned back to the doors and on tip-toe, peered through one of the airlock's small glass ports at the brightly lit bay beyond as a computer voice boomed over the klaxons: *"Danger! Danger! Flickerstage now in effect! Exit the cargo bay immediately!"*

Amalfitano, rocking nervously on the balls of his feet, looked over Lesedi's shoulder as Delatorre stared anxiously through the other port while fingering his shocker.

Others quickly joined them, crowding up against the doors and craning their necks. Lesedi tried very hard not to notice that Drakin stood beside Amalfitano and behind her, and that the nurse's bifurcated tongue kept flicking past her ear.

The cargo deck vibrated noticeably while the whine of the flickerstage became audible to those in the corridor.

"Here she comes," Perou's voice echoed from the overhead speaker as a ghostly outline formed in the center of the bay.

A series of even fainter outlines quickly appeared within the first, each one smaller and seemingly farther away. Then, with a brilliant flash, the multiple images rushed together, abruptly coalescing into an unrecognizable mass of tangled rope, fabric and wood.

For a moment there was only stunned silence then Delatorre asked, "That's a boat?"

"Was a boat," Lesedi replied. "Cyllo did say it was in the process of breaking apart."

"You can say that again," Delatorre muttered.

"Okay," Lesedi said. "Everybody step aside." She turned to the marines. "Don't take any chances. See anyone other than our people, hit it with everything you've got until it drops in its tracks."

There was a murmur of hearty agreement from the marines.

"Perou?"

The engineer's disembodied voice replied, *"Yessir?"*

"I want the locks sealed once we're all through.

"Khaleed?"

"Yes, captain?"

"Open them only on my voice-imprinted code. Understood?"

"Yessir."

As Lesedi dropped her gaze from the overhead speaker, she noticed Amalfitano's stare. "I'm damned well not gonna risk a bunch of mercs taking control of the *Baidarka*. I'd rather space everyone in the bay."

Behind her, Drakin lisped, "Dere waz no mention of dat in da party invitation."

Amalfitano nodded his unhappy agreement then turned to the group. "Masks—goggles."

Once everyone had complied, Lesedi hit the release and the outer double doors opened, followed, an instant later, by the bay's interior doors.

Delatorre was the first through, followed by his team. As they fanned out, Amalfitano started for the lock, but Lesedi blocked his path.

He looked at her. "But—"

"Not yet. Let Delatorre and his men secure the situation first. Remember, somewhere in that," Lesedi waved her hand towards the groaning pile of water-logged wood and shredded sail, "are who knows how many mercs."

"Sssnackz," Drakin lisped softly, rubbing her taloned hands together. Then, noticing Lesedi's sidelong stare, she tried to look contrite.

"And I've got badly injured people up there!" Amalfitano said. "Cyllo said two of the human readings were extremely weak and that was hours ago!"

"As soon as the wreck's secured, you can go in. But *not* until I say so."

Amalfitano glared at her.

"Sir!" one of the marines called out. "We've located two human life readings!"

"Make that three!" another voice yelled from somewhere behind the wreck.

Lesedi hit wall-com button. "C and C!"

"Control, Zayyad here—"

"We got them!" She glanced back at Amalfitano as she overheard an eruption of cheers from the ceiling-mounted speaker. "Now get us the hell outta here!"

"Sir!" Delatorre yelled, "We're picking up on a lot of that interference—we got mercs, captain, lot's of 'em!"

"Sir!" another marine yelped, "this heap's breaking up, *fast!*"

Amalfitano turned to Lesedi. "Ife—"

"Okay, go—but don't get out of sight of Delatorre and his men."

Amalfitano didn't need to be told twice. "Come on!" he motioned to his team then dashed through the airlock, onto the broad, brightly lit expanse of the cargo bay floor and through the cordon of wary-eyed marines.

The boat, never designed to sit on solid ground, creaked and groaned as it sagged, drooping and distorting under its own sodden weight while all around it a rapidly enlarging pool of foul-smelling, muddy, yellow-green water formed.

Lesedi, Amalfitano and Drakin stopped beside Delatorre and looked up.

"How da hell do we get up dere?" Drakin lisped as she eyed what remained of the main deck, some four meters above the cargo bay floor.

"Over there." Delatorre pointed to a tangle of rigging and sail hanging from the port side of the boat. "Not much, but it'll have to do—"

He was cut off by a muffled series of snaps from somewhere deep within the hull.

Drakin took a hasty step back. "I tink I'll ssstay down here, triaging, if itz all da sssame to you."

"I was about to suggest the same thing," Amalfitano said as Rosen, two medtechs and another marine joined them.

Delatorre went first, deftly climbing the snarl of rigging like a child in a favorite tree. As soon as he gave the all clear, the marine followed. Then Lesedi began her climb, followed less adroitly by Amalfitano, Rosen and finally, the medtechs.

"Captain." Delatorre touched Lesedi's arm as she started to towards the stern. "Best stay here 'til we secure the area."

"Yeah. Okay." She nervously fingered her shocker as he crept towards the stern, then, hearing a telltale creak of the deck boards, she glanced over her shoulder. "That goes for you, too, Doc."

Amalfitano scowled at her then at Rosen. "I don't know about you, but I'm getting a wee bit—" He was cut off by the loud, staccato *poppoppoppop!* of shocker fire.

"Down!" Lesedi hissed and they dropped to the buckled deck then nervously glanced around.

A moment later Delatorre called out, "Captain! Over here!"

Rosen gave Amalfitano an apprehensive glance as they scrambled back to their feet. "A case of being careful what you ask for?"

"Too late now," Amalfitano replied. "You," he pointed to the medtechs, "best stay here. Althea, with me."

Together they cautiously followed Lesedi as she began picking her way across the warped, debris-covered deck, towards the sail-shrouded ruins of the stern castle.

"Doc!" another voice called out. "We've found Ensign Corsali!"

Amalfitano looked at Rosen.

"Go," she said, "I'll check this one out."

He nodded and began retracing his steps as Lesedi and Rosen continued on to where Delatorre and the marine stood beside a section of fallen mast.

"What is it?" Lesedi asked.

Delatorre pointed with the muzzle of his shocker.

Pinned under the mast was a humanoid body, the lower half largely hidden under loops of frayed rope and shattered timber, the upper half shrouded by more tangled rigging and a tattered piece of sail. Only an arm and gauntleted hand were fully visible.

Rosen looked at Delatorre and whispered, *"Hahtooshan?"*

He tapped his hand-held scanner. "This says *that,"* he pointed at the body, "is a source of some of that interference Lieutenant Izraad says is associated with Hahtooshans, and what I can see of the uniform certainly matches those Looper accounts."

"Don't worry, ma'am," the burly marine said to Rosen as he kicked the lifeless arm with his boot, "we shocked whatever it is but good."

"I certainly hope so," Rosen said, then after a moment's reluctance, knelt, scanner in hand and held it as close as she dared.

"Well?" Lesedi asked impatiently. "Is it alive?"

Rosen nodded distractedly. "The scanner may be playing tricks on me, with all this interference..." She rose, slowly, her dumbfounded gaze fixed on the body at their feet. "But—"

"But what?" Lesedi snapped.

She met Lesedi's gaze. "This," she tapped the scanner, "says our Hahtooshan here is... *human."*

PART II

Chapter 13

The *Baidarka*'s sickbay was ominously silent except for the ever-present hum of machinery. A sense of expectancy, and dread, hung in the antiseptic-tainted air as red jumpsuit-clad staff coalesced around the empty triage bays—then the main doors snapped open and the quiet was shattered by the bark of rapid-fire orders as the first stasis-board was escorted in.

Amalfitano, who'd accompanied the board carrying Aquila from the cargo bay, stepped back only long enough for two medtechs to slide Aquila onto a trauma bed. Then he elbowed his way to the bedside, his eyes fixed on the bank of diagnostic monitors as they came alive with data.

A nurse positioned himself across from Amalfitano and began quickly but carefully peeling back the tattered and blood-caked dressing that covered most of Aquila's swollen flank. Other staff began filing into the small bay, each with a task to perform, which they did wordlessly and quickly.

Oblivious to the activity around him, Amalfitano palpated the wound and privately winced. "Sensitivities?"

"Negative," the nurse replied.

"Then fill him with as much penicillin as his cells can hold."

"Yessir," he replied as he grabbed a waiting ject-it and vial.

"I'll take over, William." Fleming stepped into the bay. "Meerut needs you in bay three—Gianakis."

Her tone left little to the imagination. He nodded as he wiped his hands on his med reds. "Lemme know as soon as he's prepped." Not waiting for an answer, he strode out of the bay.

Rosen appeared at his side. "Chief, we need to talk—"

"Not now!"

"But this is really important."

"And this," he angrily waved his hand around, *"isn't?"* as he stepped into the next triage bay, leaving Rosen to stare after him. There he found Meerut and two medtechs working furiously, stripping Gianakis of his drenched and tattered softsuit.

Amalfitano gave the overheads a thorough study then dropped his gaze to the marine's deathly pale face.

"I've begun DIC protocol," Meerut replied to his unspoken question.

"Stems?"

"Replicating as we speak—and he's negative on the sensitivities."

He turned his attention to the crude splint and Gianakis' bloated and mottled leg.

"Almost total loss of peripheral circulation below the groin," she continued. "Minimal collateral build-up."

Amalfitano nodded as he ran his hand over the man's swollen thigh and felt a telltale *crackle* under his fingertips. "Late stage gas gangrene."

"With associated systemic toxemia," Meerut added grimly. "Xosé promised a preliminary report on any antigenic toxins within five minutes."

"Have pharmacy prepare a polyvalent antitoxin, just in case, along with a polyvalent heterologous antiserum as a back-up in case the penicillin doesn't do the trick—"

"Already done, sir."

"Once you're finished, get him into stasis. I want him stabilized before we take him to surgery."

"You got it, chief."

Realizing the nurse had left little for him to do, and wanting to get the full scope of what they were dealing with, he murmured, "Excellent," then walked out and into the last of the occupied triage bays.

The medtech looked up from cleaning the gash on Corsali's forehead, flashed Amalfitano a tight smile then returned to his work.

Amalfitano gave the unconscious woman a quick once over, then looked at the monitors and breathed a silent sigh of relief at what he saw: moderate concussion, facial and upper body contusions, superficial cut across the forehead, aspiration pneumonia and four broken ribs.

He muttered, "You were damned lucky," then left to prepare for surgery.

— ii —

"That's the last of 'em," Delatorre said as he and Lesedi watched two marines frog-march a still shock-stunned and rubbery-legged Hahtooshan away from the wreck.

Lesedi shifted her gaze to the group of eight bedraggled Hahtooshans who stood huddled together, naked, shivering and shackled and wrapped in thermo-blankets, next to the main bay airlock under the watchful eyes of Delatorre's team. "You say that one," she pointed to the smallest, "is a *female?*"

"That's what Althea's scanner said, for what *that's* worth!"

Lesedi gave him a sidelong look.

"It's going to take a helluva lot more than a medical hand scanner with a severe case of the hiccups to convince me they're human. Superficially humanoid, yes—they're goddamned shape-shifters after all—"

"But—"

"But *human?*" Delatorre gave his head a vehement shake. *"Nossir!"*

She sighed and shook her head. She didn't want to think it was true either.

"A case of seeing is deceiving?" Perou smiled as he joined them, oblivious to the frigid stare Delatorre gave him. "Don't look like much of a threat, do they?"

"Don't be fooled by appearances, *sir,"* the stocky marine sergeant growled. "Give any of 'em an opportunity and they'd happily slit your throat as thanks for saving 'em from drowning." He pointedly shifted his gaze to the nearby piles of confiscated weapons and uniforms—waterlogged mounds guarded by two marines whose grim faces mirrored Delatorre's. "If it'd been up to me," he continued, "they'd be treading water right now—or better yet, *spaced!"*

Perou, flush-faced by the sergeant's unexpectedly heated reaction to his off-the-cuff remark, followed Delatorre's furious stare as the sergeant kicked at the heap of uniforms for good measure.

"And as soon as medical gives me the okay," Delatorre continued, hooking his thumbs into his weapons belt, "I'm taking 'em to the brig and getting 'em under lock and key before they can get any ideas about doing just that!"

Lesedi flicked Perou a less than sympathetic look, then turned to the two Hahtooshans they'd pulled from the ruins of the stern castle. They were now strapped to stasis boards and at that moment being tended to by Drakin and three medtechs. "I want two guards assigned to each of them, at all times, Sergeant, until Amalfitano gives the okay for them to be transferred to the brig."

"Already done, sir. I also notified sickbay to make two isolation cubicles ready. We felt they'd be the securest place to keep 'em."

"Agreed."

"Sir?"

Lesedi turned to find one of the remaining triage members approaching her.

"Sir, I've cleared the prisoners for transfer to the brig. All their injuries are relatively minor and can be tended to there, besides, the female's claiming to be a medic, so maybe she'll help—"

"I wouldn't count on it," Lesedi grumbled, then looked pointedly at Delatorre.

He pulled his shocker from its holster. "If you'll 'cuse me, sir?"

Lesedi nodded and as Delatorre and the medtech walked away, Perou leaned close. "What the hell'd I say?"

"Paul's sister and her family were aboard the *Perrault.*"

"*Perrault.*" He knit his brows. "Sounds vaguely—"

"Passenger liner," Lesedi interrupted. "Three hundred colonists, fifty four crew. Crippled, boarded and all aboard *massacred* by mercs. And just for future reference, my father was the *Perrault's* first officer."

Perou's mouth formed a silent, '*O*'. Then he cleared his throat, added quickly, "Sir, I've had a chance to do a very preliminary analysis of their uniforms with an eye as to how they've so successfully managed to hide that they are in fact humans, not—"

"And?"

"Those high frequency, low intensity patterns associated with Hahtooshans? Seems they not only mask their true number, but they're also an extremely effective baffle for even the most powerful sensors. Only at very close range—less than a meter—can a scanner actually identify them as human, and let's be honest, who would, in their right mind, ever want to knowingly get that close to a Hahtooshan?"

Lesedi looked around her. "Who indeed."

"But in fact it's not the uniform that's generating the patterns, it only enhances them."

She looked back at him, eyebrows raised. "Then...?"

"Don't ask me how," Perou replied, "but the Hahtooshans themselves are the source."

"That's a hell of a thing," Lesedi admitted.

"Yeah. I'll get you a more detailed report hopefully in a few hours, but I need medical involved—right now they're a wee bit busy."

Lesedi nodded, then asked, "What's the hold up?" as she noticed that Drakin was still fussing over her unconscious, and, she noted, still fully clothed charges.

"Assside from da fact dat our ssscanerz refooz to cooperate?" Drakin grumbled as Lesedi walked towards her; with a shrug, Perou followed.

"Why weren't they stripped like the others?" Lesedi asked the nearest marine.

"Ask her, sir." He jerked his chin towards Drakin. "She's the one who countermanded your order, sir."

What the hell? Lesedi's expression darkened as she turned to the nurse. "You don't have the author—"

"I can't tell if diz iz hiz ssspleen," Drakin interrupted as she turned to the nearest Hahtooshan and fingered a shiny, purplish-red mass that hung from a gaping wound which encompassed most of his lower torso, "or part of hiz uniform. Wat do you tink, *sssir?*" She grabbed it, flapped it about as she fixed Lesedi with an innocent look that to Lesedi was anything but innocent. Challenging was far closer to the mark.

Lesedi glanced at what the nurse was holding, then immediately fixed her bulging gaze on the wreck. "Ah... I have... no idea what it... it is."

Undeterred, Drakin gave the object in question a gentle tug. "Humm..." She leaned closer, her masked snout millimeters from the merc's mangled belly. "It appearz to be attached to sssometing—"

"Then maybe you shouldn't pull on it?" Lesedi offered as she envisioned the entire merc unraveling in front of her—and the paperwork *that* would incur.

"Diz iz odd..."

Lesedi clenched her teeth and turned back to the nurse. "What's odd?"

"Hiz uniform."

"Of course it's odd, it's damned odd—it's merc—"

"I don't mean dat. I mean da whole ting haz ssstiffened up."

Lesedi risked a quick feel of the closest piece, in this case the fabric that encased the Hahtooshan's upper arm. And Drakin was right: it had become almost rigid. *How... odd indeed.*

"In my humble medical opinion, removing it will have to wait—da udder one too." She jerked her snout towards her other charge. "Too many fracturez... too many," she wiggled her taloned fingers, "dangly bitz. But of courz itz your call, *sssir,*" she added sweetly.

Lesedi hesitated at the nurse's tone, then nodded, very reluctantly. "Agreed."

Drakin activated the stasis field and restraint web then stepped back and motioned to one of the medtechs. "Go."

"Sir! Look at this!"

Lesedi swallowed hard. *Oh please... my stomach can't handle any more show and tell.* She reluctantly turned to one of the marines who was guarding the remaining merc and replied with equal reluctance, "Yes, Private Lhota?"

To her relief he only brushed a tangled mass of long, sopping wet hair away from the remaining Hahtooshan's slack face and neck, exposing his collar, gorget and insignia-encrusted bandoleer.

The novelty—the shock—of looking upon the true face of a merc had already started to wane. Nevertheless, Lesedi found the mixture of grotesque scarification and tattooing in combination with all-too human features extremely disquieting.

She'd assisted in the hurried pat down of their shocker-stunned prisoners—leaving the actual stripping of arms and uniforms to the marines and medical—and in the process discovered that Hahtooshans were—at least superficially—human in *every* respect.

Now, as she stared at this particular mercenary's face, her mind recoiled at the idea that these dreaded aliens weren't shape-shifters—weren't, in fact, *aliens* at all.

She fixed her eyes and her attention on something only slightly less unsettling: the merc's truly extraordinary uniform.

As part of her training, she'd watched over and over the vid-images of the one documented time humans had met Hahtooshans face-to-face, so to speak—the now infamous Cotopaxi award ceremony—grainy vid-images that showed little more than wraithlike shadows and which were considered highly suspect by the experts; she'd studied what little was known of their battledress, gleaned from sketchy accounts from even more questionable sources, but nothing had prepared her for this: the iridescent black uniform faintly shimmered and flashed in eerie, multicolored pulsations as if it had a life of its own and its surface... it kept shifting from smooth to bumpy, to covered in what looked like tiny wriggling tentacles and then back to utterly smooth. It made *her* skin crawl. She'd seen a lot of high-tech ghillie suits before, but this one beat them all, hands-down, by the proverbial mile.

Lhota, who, along with his companion Tanser, had been busily stripping their charge of anything that looked even remotely like a weapon, said, "I'm impressed."

Lesedi started to nod distractedly while she took in the array of colorful campaign medallions that encrusted his bandoleer—then her eyes widened as they came across one particularly elaborate medal of green and gold high on his shoulder. *Gods!* Aloud she replied, "As well you should be. We've got ourselves a real prize here."

"Ssspeak for yousssef," Drakin lisped irritably as she went about assessing and cataloguing the mercenary's extensive injuries.

Lesedi, still staring at what she had immediately recognized as a high rank insignia, rummaged through her mental files on Hahtooshans, information yet again gleaned from very dodgy sources. "He's a... *Sha'ashahn*—I think." She shrugged. "Definitely an officer of some sort."

"Shah ah... *what?*" Perou asked as he appeared at her elbow to peer more closely at Lesedi's unexpected find.

"Sha'ashahn," Lesedi replied with more certainty as she continued to scan the impressive array of insignia. "It's equivalent to a full battle commander. One of the xenoethnography instructors at the academy..." Her voice trailed off as she stared at the cobalt and vermilion gorget at the base of his throat, revealed when one of the marines drew a lock of hair aside, looking for more weapons. Momentarily forgetting all about any reservations she might have about getting so close to even an unconscious Hahtooshan, she leaned even closer.

"What is it?" Perou asked, following suit.

"I have no—"

"Sir!" Tanser gasped.

Lesedi flinched violently, bumping into Perou in the process then she glared at the marine. "What?"

Tanser pointed to another medal that had been hidden behind the wide bandoleer and exposed only when he tried to pull the dagger from its water-swollen scabbard. "Isn't that... a Coalition Battle Commendation?"

Lesedi stared at the small, and compared to the rest, rather plain medallion. "It certainly looks—" Her eyes widened and she gasped, *"From Cotopaxi!"*

"Why would he hide it like that?" Perou asked as he stared at the highly prized and rarely awarded medal.

Lesedi shrugged irritably, "Hell if I know."

"Didn't think the Coalition awarded the commendation to anyone but Expeditionary Force members," Lhota said. "And to a yowie of all people?"

"Cotopaxi was an exception," Lesedi replied as she straightened up. Recovered from her initial shock, she stared down at their prisoner with a mixture of absolute loathing and bitter curiosity; rumor had it none of the Hahtooshans who'd attended the ceremony had survived what followed, so... either the rumor was wrong, or this merc was boasting someone else's award.

Neither option sat well with her and she shifted uneasily. "Basically the Orthodoxy blackmailed the Coalition into it, demanding it as part of their payoff, and with the Matarrans breathing down our necks, we didn't have much choice—"

"Now, correct me if I'm wrong," Perou interrupted, "but I was under the impression that the Hahtooshans had been *hired* by the Coalition to protect the Cotopaxi colony—"

"Some protection!" Lesedi snorted. "Every last colonist was killed."

"As were all but a handful of Hahtooshans," Perou replied pointedly, "by the Matarrans—our friend here clearly being one of that handful. Except... weren't the survivors supposedly killed in an accident shortly after the award ceremony?"

Lesedi scowled at him. "Yeah. *Supposedly.*" Then she turned back to a more sympathetic audience: Tanser and Lhota. "It wasn't until much later, when it was too damned late to tell the mercs to go stuff themselves that the atrocities at the Chhotri and Tharus camps came to light and the Coalition finally came to its senses and outlawed the use of mercs." She shook her head, muttered, *"Fucking butchers,"* then happened to catch Drakin's oblique frown.

Lhota glanced sidelong at Perou then motioned to the heap of weaponry at his feet. "I think that's it, sir. Except that," he pointed to the dagger, still in its scabbard. "It won't budge."

Lesedi grabbed the knife's grip and despite its odd, sticky feel, gave it a two-handed tug herself with the same result. She quickly released her hold and without realizing it, wiped her hands on her thighs.

"I'll collect it once he's been stripped him in sickbay," Tanser offered.

"Just make damned sure you do," Lesedi replied irritably, still wiping her hands.

Lhota, his gaze again fixed on the prestigious medal, added, "Bet he could tell some tales."

"Da only perssson he'll be talking to iz da devil if you don't get out of da way!" Drakin gave the restraint webbing one last tug with a talon and, satisfied her patient was properly secured, began guiding the board towards the airlock, Tanser and Lhota in tow.

— iii —

"Chief...?"

Amalfitano looked up from the stack of reports to find Meerut standing in the doorway; he started to rise from his chair. "Ready?"

"Not quite."

"What's the problem? Has Robert—"

"No... no, the commander's almost ready. Doctor Fleming said to tell you another ten minutes at most, they're just finishing up with his de-con."

"Lemme know when he's prepped." He resumed his seat and turned back to the reports.

Meerut hesitated then asked, "Uh, Chief... has Althea had a chance to talk to you?"

"About what?"

"About the Hahtooshans, sir."

"What about 'em?" he replied distractedly as he thumbed through the report flimsies.

"About the scanner readings—"

"Which says they're human?" he interrupted, not looking up.

Meerut took a relieved breath. "Yeah, I mean, I thought—"

"Don't believe it."

"But—"

"But what?" He leaned back in his chair and fixing his gaze on the young nurse, added ominously, "The scanners are *wrong.*"

Meerut surprised him when she stood her ground. "I respectfully disagree, Chief. I just received one in triage four. He's in *really* bad shape. Doctor Fleming said to come get you—"

"Cacchio!" He lurched to his feet, snatched the filter mask she offered him and stormed from his office, into the main sickbay and then into the nearest triage bay.

There, on the trauma bed, lay a Hahtooshan.

Two marine guards, likewise masked and their weapons drawn, stood off to one side while a medtech busily pulled needed supplies from a nearby locker.

Amalfitano, cautiously stepping over bits and pieces of the merc's blood-soaked uniform that had been hastily cut and stripped from his body, barely gave the massive soldier himself a glance. He turned his full attention on the bank of monitors. After a moment's study of the wildly erratic read-outs, he grumbled, "I can't tell if he's dead or doing hand-springs, much less if he's... *human.*"

"Then don't look at *them,*" Meerut replied simply. "Look at *him.*"

Amalfitano squinted furiously at her, then *very* grudgingly did as she suggested.

Crossing his arms, he took in every square centimeter of the soldier's naked, tattooed body and found himself grimacing at what he saw. The pale pink of shattered bone and the glistening purple of organs never meant to see the light of day was always unsettling—even to him after all these years—and even more so now, surrounded as they were by ruptured, tattooed skin the color of wood ash.

He needed no trauma bed or computer to tell him the creature was critically, if not fatally injured.

No... not a creature. Meerut was right. One look at the Hahtooshan's violently exposed internal anatomy was evidence enough. *Not an alien. Not a shape-shifter. Human.* He tried to get his mind around that stunning revelation. He found he couldn't, despite the very graphic evidence before him.

Later. I'll deal with this later. He exhaled forcefully. "Shut off the machines."

She stared at him in disbelief. "Chief? We can't—"

"The monitors! Do what you told me to do: *use your eyes!* Until we can neutralize this... *whatever this is,*" he gestured irritably at the nearest monitor, "they're about as useful as a blindfold! And you," he fixed his piercing stare on the two marines, "get the hell out of the bay!"

"But sir," one began, "Ensign Lesedi gave strict orders—"

"I don't give a damn who ordered what! He sure as hell isn't going to be causing any trouble and you're in my staff's way. *Out!*"

Amalfitano watched as the guards reluctantly shuffled out of the bay and positioned themselves just outside then he turned back to Meerut and the medtech and growled, "I want a detailed assessment of his injuries as soon as possible."

Meerut and the medtech looked at each other, then at the huge mercenary and finally back at him.

"Might take a while, Chief," she said.

The medtech only smiled feebly and murmured, "Yessir."

With an annoyed grunt, Amalfitano started to leave then stopped and turned back to the two. "Run a full check his sensitivities—and tell Xosé he needs to concoct a compatible blood expander and yeah, he'd better get started on stem replication, too, then get him prepped, de-conned and into stasis. Once we've finished with the commander and Gianakis, we'll take him to surgery and if he has

any, may *his* gods help him!" With that he strode out of the triage
bay and almost collided with Drakin as she guided the last stasis
board into sickbay. He glanced down at its burden and inwardly
cringed. *Gods, not another one...* He hadn't thought to wonder if any
of the Hahtooshans were injured seriously enough to require his
services—hadn't cared to wonder, truth be told, leaving the triaging
of their prisoners up to his staff. Aquila, Gianakis and Corsali had
been his primary—his only worry.

She beckoned to him. "Come wit me."

"Cazzo!" he swore, but dutifully followed her, along with the
marine guards, into a brightly lit triage cubicle. "I'm expected in
surgery any minute, so make it quick."

Drakin slid the Hahtooshan's strangely stiff body from the board
and onto the bed, then, "Diz, ma dear Doctor, iz a Hattoosssin of
high rank! A Sssha ah... sssometing. Aren't you impresssed?"

"He's rank all right," a medtech muttered as he slipped between
the two marines and into the small bay. *"Pee-hew!"* Then his gaze
fell to the floor and the trail of smelly, blood-tinged green water left
in Drakin's wake. "You could've at least dried him off!"

"I did tink about wringing him out, but by da lookz of him, he
already got wrung," Drakin pointed to the decidedly unnatural twist
of the merc's right leg.

The medtech, Rafe Pierson, winced. "Oh... ick."

"Waz da matter? A few compound fracturz make you queasssy?
Tut, tut. Now, hep me get diz creature peeled, de-bugged and into
ssstasssiz before he decidez to go belly up."

Pierson glanced down at their supine patient and arched a brow.
"He's already belly up."

Drakin stopped fumbling with the buckle of the Hahtooshan's
weapons' belt long enough to give him a sidelong glance. "I meant
check out."

"Check out?"

"Croakerz. Cold meat. Bite da dussst. Go... *wessst,"* she grunted
as she figured out the buckle, unfastened it then tugged the belt from
under the Hahtooshan's heavy, rigid body, seemingly unfazed by the
uniform's strange and rapid texture changes. To Amalfitano the
effect went beyond disturbing to the downright hair-raising and was
happy to let Drakin do the honors of stripping the merc to the nurse.
"Peg out, pop off, go out wit da tide." She dropped the sodden belt

to the floor then kicked it towards the nearest marine, who hastily side-stepped to avoid it. "My complimentz to Enzen Lesssedi," she replied to the man's less than appreciative response.

Drakin paused, hands on hips and stared down at their slack-faced patient. "And he would've, if it hadn't been for hiz uniform turning into a compresssion sssuit."

"A what?" Amalfitano replied and touched the Hahtooshan's cast-like trouser leg. "Well, I'll be damned."

Pierson looked at Amalfitano, then back at Drakin. "Uh... still not following here."

Drakin favored him with a look she normally saved for Amalfitano and small, edible creatures and replied in a slow, measured voice, "A compression sssuit iz—"

"I know what a compression suit is," Pierson grumbled testily, "I meant—"

"Kick. Da. Bucket?" she asked as she unbuckled the bandoleer, yanked the wide strap free, then tossed it under the table this time, out of the way, as Pierson shook his head, completely confused; a sidelong glance at the marines suggested he wasn't alone.

"Cock *off,*" she grunted as she peeled up the rigid lower lip of the waterlogged hauberk, then began hunting for a way of separating her patient from his form-fitting and now equally rigid trousers. "Ooo... peekie-boo," she murmured, prying up the waistband and peering inside. "Oh... mah." She gave Amalfitano a sidelong glance and wiggled her browridges. "Hez even got tattooz on hiz—"

"Cock... off?" Pierson's eyes widened. "Oh, you mean—"

"Ceez to exissst." She straightened up. "Curtainz. Done for. Drop off da twig."

"In other words, *dead.*"

"Dat's what I sssaid."

Pierson shook his head. "You really must stop reading those cheap detective novels."

"And if you don't get your sssweet little butt in gear, he'll be one corpoooz delicti and quick."

Pierson took in their latest patient and made a face. "I think a corpus *un*-delicti is more like it."

She grabbed the heel of the Hahtooshan's right boot, and bracing his upper leg with the other hand, managed to pull the boot free without taking his fractured leg with it. It followed the bandoleer under the table. "A puz only a massser pissstool could love, yez?" She met Pierson's gaze. "Well sssorry to sssay diz, but you ain't zo cute yousssef, Rafe." She quickly repeated the procedure with the other boot.

Pierson looked wounded as she turned back to the business at hand.

"Cutters?" Amalfitano asked, offering her a set from the bedside tray.

"Tanks, but I brought mah own." Drakin clicked the tips of her razor-sharp talons together, then as Amalfitano, Pierson and the marines watched in decidedly uncomfortable silence, she made relatively quick work of separating her charge from his hauberk and trousers.

— iii —

Amalfitano stepped out of the operating room airlock, stripped off his soiled surgical gown and stuffed it in the disposa-chute.

"Coffee, Chief?"

He lifted his exhausted eyes to find Pierson offering him a steaming cup, along with a dish of his favorite anisette cookies. He took the offerings with a weary smile and a murmured, "Thanks," then he wandered—wobbled—over to the nearby nurses' station. He set the cookies on the console, and, with a grateful sigh, eased himself down in a chair.

"Uh, Chief?"

He reluctantly looked up from the untouched cup of coffee he now held in both hands to find Meerut standing in front of him, a flimsy in her hand. He blinked back a yawn. *"Huuuuh...?"*

"You wanted a detailed assessment."

"I did?"

"Yessir, on the injured Hahtooshans, sir."

He stared glumly at the flimsy, realizing unhappily that his order had boomeranged. "Uh, thanks." Then, hearing the nearby airlock snap open, he looked up to see Fleming stagger out while fumbling with her surgical gown. "Over here, Jenna." He crooked his finger at her.

"Why do I sense I'm not going to like what you're going to tell me?"

"Blame her." He jerked his chin towards Meerut as he brought the cup to his lips. "She's the one with the bad news."

Fleming gave up on the gown, grabbed a cookie instead and snuffed it in her mouth as she turned her tired eyes on the nurse.

Meerut managed a contrite smile. "I was about to give Doctor Amalfitano a report on the two critically injured Hahtooshans."

"Two?" Fleming muffled through her mouthful and turned her now accusing gaze back on Amalfitano. She swallowed, hard. *"You said there was only one."* She snatched the cup from his hands and took an angry gulp.

"No, I only *mentioned* one. I thought I'd surprise you with the other." He smiled thinly. *"Surprise."*

Fleming's sour expression soured further.

He offered her the plate of cookies.

Her expression turned down right frigid.

He shrugged and motioned unenthusiastically to the flimsy. "Read it. I'm too damned bushed."

"The soldier—the one I showed you," Meerut began, "is the worst off..."

"Anything fractionally worse and he'd be dead," Amalfitano muttered under his breath.

"...depressed right temporal fracture, and hairline occipital—"

"Any sign of primary brain stem injury?" he asked as he regained ownership of the coffee cup.

"Have you seen their skulls?"

He took a sip then squinted at her as he swallowed. "Been *just* a tad bit busy, so... no."

"Well, the simple answer is no."

"What else?" He grabbed a cookie and took a bite, suspecting it was going to be the only meal he was going to get for a while then washed it down with another gulp of coffee.

"Massive crush fractures of his pelvis and lower spine—"

"Anything salvageable?" Fleming asked.

Meerut shook her head. "Nope."

"Hope you've been busy replicating all the seed bone we'll need," Amalfitano said.

She nodded. "And Xosé says we can use existing skeletal matrix, with some modification based on a scan we took of another mercenary of the same height and weight—he just finished."

"Go on," he said with obvious reluctance, knowing there was more, lots more, and not one bit of it good news.

"Both femurs also sustained multiple fractures and there's associated internal injuries and numerous deep abdominal lacerations from mid-chest down..."

"Cazzo," Amalfitano muttered, to which Fleming nodded her agreement.

"...his lower back took the full brunt of that mast when it toppled. If he'd been a human—" Meerut bit her lip and glanced at him.

"Havin' the same problem."

"Lieutenant Perou says he thinks that some credit can go to their uniforms—seems they can form—"

"A rigid sheath around the wearer, yeah, I know, and in the process act like a compression suit. Damned clever, if I say so myself." Amalfitano paused, heaved a weary breath, then added, "Dare I ask, anything else?"

"Yeah, a dislocated jaw and fractured left zygomatic."

"Wonderful." He polished off the cookie and grabbed another.

Fleming did likewise then stole another deep gulp of coffee from the briefly unguarded cup, draining it. Amalfitano retaliated by grabbing the last cookie.

Meerut sighed, then leaned over the console and thumbed the intercom. "Rafe? More coffee—on the double... and another cup, please—"

"And more of *my* cookies!" Amalfitano added tartly as he glared at Fleming.

"And the other merc?" Fleming asked as she brushed the evidence from her chest.

"Moderate concussion secondary to blunt force trauma to his right parietal, five fractured ribs with associated pneumothorax, severely lacerated liver and ruptured spleen. And a real nasty compound fracture of the right femur, dislocated left shoulder and a greenstick of the left mid tib-fib."

Amalfitano gave his pounding temples a vigorous rub as he visualized the work ahead and asked with audible reluctance, hoping Meerut would take pity on him, "Anything else?"

"Both were suffering from moderate hypoxemia due to laryngospasm secondary to near drowning, along with chemical pneumonitis—"

"Electrolyte imbalance?" Fleming asked.

"Mild elevation of chlorine and sodium… the water they inhaled was exceedingly salty.

"Lucky for them," Amalfitano muttered. "Anything *else?*"

"All of 'em are all suffering from second stage radiation poisoning. Those uniforms of theirs do a helluva job protecting the wearer from short-term exposure, but you'd think they would've taken the risk of prolonged exposure into account before they—"

"Do a sensitivity," he interrupted as he wearily pushed himself away from the console, "then start 'em all on dichelazine." He rose, then looked around, arms akimbo. "Where's that damned coffee?"

"Sensitivity's done," Meerut replied. "Only one *teensy* problem."

Amalfitano eyed her. "And that is?"

"They refuse treatment."

"Refuse?"

"Yup. All ten of 'em—well, actually only eight of 'em cuz the two we have in sickbay are unconscious and therefore can't tell me to go stuff—"

"That's merc gratitude for you." Amalfitano rubbed his forehead. "You got that on vid record?"

"Of course. In fact each one was more than happy to tell me and in perfect trade-standard no less—if you'll excuse me for saying so—to go fuck myself, and on the record."

"Well, then that's their funeral and good riddance."

Pierson appeared, carrying another cup, a decanter and more cookies, lots more and on a platter this time.

Amalfitano helped himself to a handful before Pierson could even place the platter on the console, ate several in quick succession, then followed up with a deep gulp from his replenished cup.

"Cook says she'll have a fresh batch in about an hour," Pierson said then without being asked, helped a grateful Fleming out of her heavily soiled gown.

"Fat lot of good that will do me," Amalfitano growled and stuffed one, whole, into his mouth.

Pierson pushed the gown into the disposa-chute, said, "I'll tell her to keep 'em warm for you," then grabbed a cookie for himself and hurried off.

Amalfitano finished off his coffee as he waited for Fleming to get a few cookies and a full cup of coffee in her then he said, "What say we take the more critical one first?"

Fleming shrugged. "I was going to suggest we take the less critical one first and work our way up, but… hell, why not."

Meerut said, "He's prepped and waiting for you in Op Room Three."

Amalfitano scowled at her. "You thought of just about everything, didn't you?"

Meerut snatched a cookie from the platter. "You don't know the half of it."

"Do I want to know what you mean by that?"

Meerut ate her cookie in two bites then started for the operating room. "You'll find out soon enough, Chief."

Amalfitano and Fleming exchanged worried glances as they trailed a few unenthusiastic paces behind. They each donned a fresh gown and mask, then Amalfitano pressed the release. The lock opened and they crowded inside.

As the airlock obediently went through its cycle, Amalfitano tapped impatiently on the wall. When the inner door opened, Amalfitano was the first to step out.

Within the operating room and clustered around the surgical table and the drape-shrouded body of their Hahtooshan patient stood three op-techs and two marines, masked and the marines wearing gowns over their body armor.

Amalfitano's eyes darted to the guards. "Are they really necessary?"

The airlock door opened again and Rosen entered followed by yet another marine.

"All right, enough!" Amalfitano snarled. "One guard maybe, but two? And now three?" He pointed his finger at their patient, who was held in the eerily cold glow of the stasis field. "He's no threat to anyone in his present condition and I need some elbow room," he demonstrated by jabbing outwards with said elbows, forcing the marines to edge away, "so all of you, get the hell—"

"They aren't just for him, Chief," Meerut said, "but for her."

"Her...?" Amalfitano asked as he and Fleming followed Meerut's gaze.

Inside the open lock, standing stiffly in front of a fourth marine was a figure clad in a baggy, highly reflective yellow maintenance jumpsuit, the sort designed to fit over a space suit. It made anyone wearing one far more visible, a good thing if you somehow got separated from your tether and found yourself floating around in space, hoping to be rescued before your air ran out. But inside, under the glare of the lighting, it was nothing short of a shock to the eyes.

He flicked Meerut a sidelong look. "What the hell?"

She leaned close. "The brig jumpsuits didn't fit the soldiers—too small."

It wasn't the attire that he'd questioned, and he knew Meerut knew that. *Two can play this game.* "The soldiers or the suits?" he whispered in kind as he turned his gaze back to the newest arrival to find the merc looking around the room with a mixture of intense curiosity and lip-curling contempt.

"What do you think, Chief?"

"So they all wanted to be dressed in matchy-match maintenance suits?"

"I don't think they were given the choice," she replied as the marine gave the newcomer a not-so-gentle prod between the shoulder blades with the muzzle of his shocker; she flicked him an over-the-shoulder look baleful enough to cause him to reflexively step back. Point made, she then stepped out of the airlock and into the operating room.

"Doctor Amalfitano, Doctor Fleming," Meerut continued in a slightly louder voice, "I'd like to introduce you to—"

"Mihr-Suhjai'baldah," Suhjai said coldly, "Junior Medical Officer of the A'tuu'shahn Orthodoxy vessel, *Makhaira.*"

Amalfitano blinked again, then shook himself out of his momentary shock and turned to Meerut. "Okay, joke's over."

"Chief, she really is *who* and *what* she says she is."

He stared at the nurse, then at the Hahtooshan as a vague memory surfaced, of one of his staff—or was it one of the marines?—mentioning in passing something about one of the captured mercs claiming to be a medic. At the time he'd been desperately trying to salvage what he could of Gianakis' leg and it hadn't seemed the least bit important.

Now, as he looked at her, what he saw looked downright laughable—at a distance and that distance being well beyond the length of her reach, with the operating table, its burden and two armored marines between them for good measure. The over-sized jumpsuit nearly engulfed her frame. Sleeves and cuffs had been rolled up into thick wads at wrists and ankles, the rest hung in voluminous folds from her waist and shoulders making her look like a child playing dress-up.

Only this child's face was covered in elaborate scarification and inky-black tattoos and bore a very un-childlike hateful stare, a stare that instantly reminded him of a viper with its fixed and chillingly predatory gaze.

"You sure as hell don't look like a medical officer."

"Neither do you," she sneered.

Amalfitano forced a smile, murmured, "Charmed, I'm sure," and turned his own piercing stare on Meerut.

She replied hastily, "It was obvious that the commander and Corporal Gianakis had been provided with rudimentary medical care, so—"

"I was only following Sha'ashahn's orders," Suhjai growled, then, at the guard's pointed but slightly more circumspect urging, shuffled towards the table.

"Who?"

Meerut leaned close and whispered in his ear, "The merc officer."

"Oh." Amalfitano looked at Suhjai, who scowled defiantly back at him. "Well, remind me to thank him." He shifted his gaze back to Meerut. "And you too."

"Sir," Meerut began, "I thought it would increase the likelihood of saving—"

"Matoosh!"

Startled, Amalfitano turned to Suhjai. "I beg your pardon?"

She jerked her slitted gaze off the battered face of the soldier and fixed it on Amalfitano. "Matoosh!"

He squinted at her, not sure if he'd just been insulted, or she had an explosive case of the sneezes.

"I was told you needed my assistance with Sha'ashahn, not Matoosh—"

"You mean to tell me you're refusing—"

"I will assist with Sha'ashahn—*first.*" She crossed her arms, but the effect of her defiant gesture was lost when her arms vanished into the loose folds of fabric.

"Look, I need..." He clenched his teeth before finishing, "I need your help to save him."

She mimicked his expression perfectly before replying, *"First* Sha'ashahn. *Then* him."

"I see. Well, there's no reason for you to stay, is there?" He motioned to the guards. "Take this... *creature* back to its cage."

As one grabbed a handful of her jumpsuit her gleeful smile vanished, replaced by wide-eyed astonishment. "But... but what about Sha'ashahn?"

"What about him?"

"I was told he was seriously injured and—"

"He is, but not as critically as this one, and in my sickbay, priority of care is based on need, not who, or, in this case, *what* you are." So that wasn't entirely true, he admitted to himself. He'd taken Aquila and Gianakis before the mercs and this one was definitely the most gravely injured, but—

"In mine it goes by order of rank and—"

"Well fortunately for this particular merc, we're in *my* sickbay, not yours. He goes first. Get her outta here—*now!*" Amalfitano lifted his own hard gaze to the marines then ignoring what he assumed was an outburst of Hahtooshan profanities, fixed his red-rimmed eyes on the surgical table and its burden.

As the airlock closed, abruptly cutting off the verbal assault, he looked up to meet Meerut's apologetic stare.

"Sorry, Chief. I thought—"

"I'd have done the same thing." With that, he turned back to the operating table, exhaled, "Let's get to it."

Fleming pulled the surgical drape aside.

He grimaced at what he saw, then, out of habit, turned to the bank of diagnostic monitors. They were dark.

"Cazzo!" He jabbed an angry finger at the monitors. "Haven't you found a way to neutralize this yet?"

"Cyllo and Perou have been working on it," Meerut replied, "but so far—"

"Then I guess we do this the old fashioned way, by guesswork and a hell of a lot of luck." He turned to the body on the table and noticed that his patient was shackled, ankle and wrist, to the operating table, despite his lower body and legs being little better than jelly.

He looked at the nearest guard. "Afraid he'd gonna run out without paying his bill?"

"Captain's orders," the marine answered, stone-faced.

"Overkill," Amalfitano countered as he circled the table, taking in and mentally ordering the work ahead.

Meerut was right. No human—no *normal* human—could have survived such injuries.

He shook his head, then, as he stopped where he'd started, at the head of the table, he found his gaze drawn to the soldier's disfigured face. At first all he saw were fresh, bone-deep gashes and the hideous combination of scars and tattoos, but the longer he stared the less he could see the injuries and the grotesque patterns.

All he saw was the face—*a human face*. And now he had a name. *Matoosh*.

At Fleming's pointed cough, Amalfitano looked up. "Well?" he snapped. "What the hell are we waiting for?"

Chapter 14

Amalfitano stumbled out of the operating room airlock. He somehow managed to strip off his soiled gown and toss it in the general direction of the disposa-chute. That done, he trudged over to the nurses' console, where he promptly flopped down into a chair, dropped his head into his hands and let out a long, exhausted sigh.

"Doctor?"

He lifted his head to peer muzzily at whoever dared to disturb him.

Izraad smiled a sympathetic smile as Lesedi said, "Is this a good time for a status report?"

"Oh, Ife, Zarijan. Ah, I... ah, I was just going to page you." He wearily heaved himself back to his feet. "My office—I'll order up some coffee. Don't know 'bout you, but I could sure use some."

Lesedi glanced at the operating room. Within, beyond the semi-transparent wall, she could see movement. "Have you been at it all night?"

"And all the evening before and most of this morning," one of the op-techs muttered as he hurried by, flashing Amalfitano a sidelong, commiserating smile.

Amalfitano, for his part, only stared, bleary-eyed, at Lesedi, then shaking his head, shuffled towards his office as he grumbled under his breath about inconsiderate commanding officers.

Once inside he motioned to two chairs, grumbling, "Take a seat," as he circled his report-strewn desk. He tapped an order into the desk's servo-panel, sat with a grimace, and bracing his elbows on the desk fixed Lesedi with a decidedly glassy stare. "The commander's stable."

"Corsali?"

"Sirin's gonna be fine—" He scowled at the wall-mounted dispenser. *"Where's that damned coffee?"*

Izraad rose from her chair and murmured, "I'll get it," just as the dispenser chimed.

"—right now what she and Robert need most is rest."

"Ditto for you," Izraad said she pressed a steaming cup into his hands.

"Cook promised fresh cookies, too," he griped.

Izraad nodded, tapped in an order then handed Lesedi a cup.

"And Gianakis?" Lesedi asked.

"Not good. Not good at all, in fact. I'll have a better idea of his prognosis in twenty-four hours but I wouldn't hold out a lot of hope. Hate to admit it, he'd be dead already had it not been for that so-called merc doctor."

Lesedi shifted uneasily. "And the two injured mercs?"

He brought the cup to his lips, took a sip, swallowed. "The officer's injuries are extremely serious but not life-threatening."

Lesedi smiled. "HQ Intelligence will be real pleased to hear that."

Amalfitano stared at her for a moment. In all the rush and confusion, it had never dawned on him the officer's potential worth as a source of intelligence—until now. *I think you just bagged yourself a promotion, Ife.* "Just to be on the safe side I want to keep a very close eye on him for the next ninety hours, give or take. To be honest, the faster I get them both outta my sickbay, the happier I'll be."

"Me too," Lesedi said as Izraad placed a plate of warm cookies in front of Amalfitano. She waited until he inhaled three, followed by a deep gulp of coffee. Then she asked, "And speaking of, what about the other one?"

He sighed as he picked up another cookie, then dunking it in his coffee, shook his head. "Massive crush injuries and lost a hell of a lot of blood, more than a human..." He caught himself, just as Meerut had caught herself... how many hours ago?

Izraad smiled. "It's going to take some time for all of us to come to terms with the unsettling fact that *we're* not the measure of what it is to be human."

Lesedi and Amalfitano glared at her.

"Like it or not," Izraad continued undaunted, "Hahtooshans *are* fully human, they're just not..."

"Not what?" Amalfitano and Lesedi snapped in unison.

"They're just not us," Izraad replied, looking first at Lesedi, then Amalfitano.

Amalfitano squinted at her and finally muttered, "Be that as it may…" and started to bring the forgotten cookie to his mouth. Realizing most of it had dissolved into his coffee, he shrugged, tossed what remained in his mouth, drained his cup then set it on his desk and stared, red-eyed at it. "If we hadn't discovered that the interference pattern they emit stops at their skin—"

"What?" Lesedi looked at Izraad, then back at Amalfitano.

"Yeah. Seems those tattoos and skin engravings aren't just ornamentation, maybe not ornamentation at all. Together they form an interference pattern coincidental with the interface between the epidermis and dermis." He wearily ran his aching fingers through his disheveled hair. "I'll be the first one to admit that by the time I got to the soldier, I was pretty tired, or should I say I *thought* I was tired."

He yawned and knuckle-rubbed his blood-shot eyes. "But without immediate intervention…" He shrugged. "Anyway, about thirty minutes into it, thinking it was pretty much a foregone conclusion we were gonna lose him, I inserted a bio-probe into his abdominal cavity, out of sheer desperation, if you really want to know—the instant he was released from stasis he started going downhill fast and I couldn't locate all the bleeders—and damned if the interference didn't stop. Just like *that*." He tried to snap his fingers. "Well, sorta like that."

Amalfitano shook his head. "Sure would have made things a helluva lot easier had I known that earlier. And going strictly by the lot we have on board, which I'll admit might be too small a sample to make broad generalizations, it would appear each has his own pattern of frequency shifts, but they're all well within—"

"Lemme guess," Lesedi interrupted. "One point three to one point six gigahertz."

"Yeah," Amalfitano stifled another yawn. "How'd you know?"

"They've been detected in Hahtooshan sensor traces," Izraad answered, "but no one ever knew what was generating them—"

"Ensign Lesedi," Zayyad's urgent voice crackled from the desk-com. *"Please report to C and C."*

Lesedi leaned forward and thumbed the activator. "Lesedi here."

"Sir, scanners just detected a faint energy burst, dead astern."

"Speculation?"

"It could be a reflection. The high levels of free energy in this area of space can cause a prism-like effect, which, in turn, might have distorted our own image and reflected it back on us—"

"But not damned likely."

"No. If you want my gut feeling—"

"Always, Khaleed."

"We're being followed, sir, and what the scanners detected was a bow shock wave."

Amalfitano felt a cold shiver race down his spine. He glanced at Izraad. Her expression did nothing to ease his apprehension.

"What's our present speed?" Lesedi asked.

"Flat one, sir."

"Can we initiate foldspeed?"

"Nossir... not until we escape Rasal Ghul's interference sphere—"

"Then go to flat two."

"Yessir—"

"And go to yellow alert. I'll be right there, Lesedi out." She started to push herself out of the chair.

"Sir?"

Izraad's tone stopped Lesedi in mid-push.

"What if those frequency patterns act as homing signals?"

Lesedi stared at her for a moment then said, "I want signal suppressers put on each of the prisoners immediately!" She hurried out of the office.

— ii —

"There," Zayyad pointed. "Another flare."

Lesedi had been staring intently at the tactical display and had also seen the brief burst of light. It was also noticeably brighter than the last one. "Go to red alert." She looked over her shoulder as she heard the airlock open and nodded to Izraad as the woman stepped into the control room. "How're you doing on the signal suppressers?"

"Just finished, sir."

Lesedi swiveled her chair around to face Cyllo. "How long before we clear Rasal Ghul's interference sphere?"

"At present speed, nine minutes."

Lesedi turned next to the helm officer. "I want to be well out of range of the Hahtooshans' weapons when we clear the interference. Can we safely increase speed to flat three?"

Eisele queried her console computer and nodded. "Aye sir. Increasing to flat three."

Lesedi settled back in her chair and fixed her eyes on the navigator. "It's up to you now, Mister Pardix."

The navigator grinned. "Yessir. Don't worry, sir, I'll lose 'em—"

"I *don't* want to lose them—I just want to make sure they don't find us *first*. Understood?"

"You got it, sir."

A few minutes later, Zayyad said, "It's not working." His narrowed eyes darted to Pardix before he added, "We gained a little time, that's all." He jerked his gaze back to his board as a telltale began to flash. "Sir! I'm picking up a massive energy build-up dead astern—" he was cut off as the ship shuddered violently. *"Explosion to starboard!"*

"Hard to port!" Lesedi barked. "Peters, prepare seekers for launch!"

— iii —

Ru'asooli fixed the *Acholilah*'s gunner with his most frigid stare. "You... *missed.*"

"Ta'ahn, the energy flux causes some drift in trajectory. Targeting was not to blame!"

"Ta'ahn," Lura'jaii said, drawing Ru'asooli's fierce gaze, "the Coalition vessel has taken evasive maneuvers, what are your orders?"

"Re-calibrate and shift to active tracking. Target their primary impeller." He dropped his gaze to the gunner. "No errors this time, understood?"

The gunner nodded vigorously and turned back to his console.

— iv —

The *Baidarka* lurched to port and the hull groaned in protest as the screens sizzled under the intense blast.

"Damage report!" Lesedi barked.

"Grazing hit, primary impeller ring… screens badly buckled. No damage to the bulkheads—"

"Sir! She's fired another barrage… impact in seven seconds!"

"Evasives!"

The ship banked to starboard.

Lesedi tightened her hold on the arms of her chair. "Zayyad! Target that goddamned ship and fast!"

"I'm trying to, sir, but the main scanners are out—"

"Can we increase speed?" she looked at Perou.

"The ship can barely handle the stress now, sir."

"Zayyad?" Lesedi turned back to him.

"Still unable to locate her—"

"Peters, plot out a random pattern of fire, seekers set to acquire any target in range!"

"Aye sir—"

"Main scanners back on line," Zayyad interrupted.

"We're now free of the interference," Cyllo added with a sidelong glance at Zayyad.

He turned to his console. "Reacquiring target…"

Lesedi turned to the suspended tactical display as it sparkled back to life—accompanied by a new chorus of alarm klaxons and the flashing marker of the Hahtooshan battle ship headed right towards them.

"Hard to starboard!" Lesedi instinctively pressed back into her chair. *"Fire!"*

A moment later Zayyad said, "More incoming fire, random pattern. That last hit must've affected their tracking scanners' abilities to lock on—"

"Peters," Lesedi interrupted, "attempt to pin-point their location by backtracking the weapons trajectories."

"Way ahead of you sir… sir! Just got a definite fix! Particle cannon locked on target—"

"Sir!" Zayyad interrupted. "Incoming rail—"

"Evasive!

Eisele, her eyes darting between the tactical display of the approaching weapons' track and her console, plunged the ship into a steep, counterclockwise spiral.

The rail projectile grazed the secondary impeller as it raced by and the *Baidarka*, its downward plunge rapidly increasing, quivered then steadied under the helm officer's hand.

Around them the stars spun more and more slowly as the ship, in an ever-enlarging spiral, dropped below the Hahtooshan vessel.

"There she is!" Zayyad pointed to the tactical display as the warship's computer generated image swam into view directly above them.

"Fire particle cannon!"

"Firing, sir!"

A hush fell on the control room crew as they all watched the barrage tear towards the underbelly of the Hahtooshan ship. An instant later, the warship vanished, the area of space it had occupied suddenly filled with a massive explosion.

Unable to compensate, the tactical display briefly whited out.

Lesedi flinched reflexively then squinted at the suspended holographic display as it shimmered back into grid-lined solidity. It registered no warning telltales.

She risked a quick, querying glance at Zayyad.

"I think we got'em, sir!"

There were a few muffled cheers, then the chamber became deathly silent as the warship's marker abruptly reappeared, and by its accompanying readouts apparently none the worse for wear.

Zayyad gaped in astonishment, then: "The particle stream must've hit a plasma pool the scanners didn't detect—" An alarm bleated on his board. "Incoming fire! They've locked onto us!"

Eisele, watching her schematic, stared at the tiny dots that marked the course of the incoming barrage, and made efforts to get the ship out of their path.

"They just folded!" Zayyad barked, grabbing his console as the ship shuddered again. "Grazing hit... shields holding...."

Lesedi scowled at the tactical display. "Tracer—"

"Impossible sir, tracer tubes were severely damaged—"

"Pardix, calculate fold parameters for pursuit—"

"Sir," Cyllo twisted in her chair to face Lesedi, "the combination of energy pools and the inability to pin-point the exact location of the Hahtooshan ship makes the risk of folding into them—"

Lesedi silenced her with one frigid glare. "We lost 'em once, I'm not gonna lose them again! *Do I make myself clear?*"

"Fold parameters complete, sir," Pardix reported.

Lesedi took a deep breath. "Execute."

The ship lurched forward. The shock wave created as it plunged into the dissipating folds left by the Hahtooshan ship sent a violent shudder through the *Baidarka*.

Then, with another wrenching jolt, it too folded, leaving behind a trail of quickly fading after-images.

Chapter 15

"Sir?" a distant voice called. *"Sir... can you hear me?"*

Lesedi opened her eyes and a face, a very worried face, slowly came into focus. She squinted up at it. "Stoker...?"

His mouth broke into a decidedly relieved grin. "Yessir."

She blinked, then looked around and found herself lying on the deck not far from her chair. Stoker knelt beside her, and as she turned back to him, she realized his nose, upper lip and cheek were smeared with blood.

"What happened?"

"Not sure yet," he replied as he helped her into a seated position. "The scanners aren't functioning."

"Life support?"

"On auxiliary power. Like everything else."

She glanced around again. The control room was a shambles; only a few of the more vital consoles were manned. Most of the stations were empty, their controllers in the process of getting to their feet, some, like her, requiring the assistance of others.

"How are you feeling, sir?" Izraad asked as she squatted beside Stoker.

"Okay, I think." Lesedi gingerly rubbed the back of her head, wincing as her fingers touched an especially tender spot. "And the rest of the crew?"

"We've been unable to get a complete casualty report, sir, but so far no fatalities." Stoker got to his feet and offered her a hand up.

Lesedi smiled and he pulled her to a wobbly stand.

"Maybe you should sit down?" Izraad suggested, grabbing Lesedi's elbow as she took an unsteady step.

"Excellent idea." Lesedi eased herself into her chair then gave the control room another sweep with her eyes, stopping at the engineering console. "Status report."

"We should have all major ship systems back on line in a matter of minutes, sir."

Lesedi turned to the tactical station as Zayyad, clutching his right arm, carefully lowered himself into his chair. She gave him a moment then asked, "Any idea what might have happened to our 'friends'?"

"Nossir."

"Scanners are back on line," Cyllo reported. "Instituting a full sweep."

"Sir," Zayyad looked up from his console just as the main tactical display sparkled back to life. "No sign of the Hahtooshans."

Lesedi cursed under her breath as she took in the holographic projection. It now displayed a slightly different starfield than the one she remembered and she raised a quizzical brow. "Pardix, any idea where in the galaxy we are?"

"No, sir. But I've got the nav-comp working on it."

"Is the ship maneuverable?"

Eisele nodded. "Yessir."

"Now if we just knew where we were, we'd know where to go," Lesedi muttered to herself, but Eisele, overhearing her, glanced over her shoulder and managed a feeble smile.

"Sir," Perou said, "all navigational systems are now back on line."

"As soon as possible, I want a full damage report."

"Sir?" Pardix said. "The nav-comp says we've been thrown approximately nine light days from our original location. We're now, essentially, on the opposite side of the Rasal Ghul system."

"And the mercs?" Lesedi asked, swiveling her chair back to face Zayyad.

"Still no trace of 'em."

"Peters, what systems do we have?"

"The forward particle cannon and aft rail are still up, along with all seeker batteries."

"Screens?" Lesedi asked Cajori.

"Holding, at seventy eight percent."

"Stoker, what about foldspace? Any hope of getting a message to HQ or Mirfak Prime?"

"No, sir. There was extensive burn-out in the foldspace circuit loop—"

"Repairable?"

"Yessir, but it'll take time."

"Sir," Perou said. "Reports are coming in. We've got a breach on deck two. The forward rail projector is completely inoperable—"

"Any chance we can get them back on line?"

"Damage, on top of what we'd already incurred during the ambush, is just too extensive. We'll need the services of a space dock." He looked back at his console and added, "We've also got minor structural damage to the primary and secondary impellers, connecting intake guides and auxiliary energizers."

"Are we foldspeed capable?"

"Yessir, but I wouldn't suggest folding until I've a chance to run a full diagnostic on the field generators—"

"Sir," Stoker interrupted, "Medical is reporting five confirmed fatalities, four from the area around the breach on deck two, and one from the rail bay."

Lesedi smacked her fist on the arm of her chair. *"Damn it!"* She jerked her chair back to face the tactical display. "Cyllo, I want an explanation of what the hell happened to us—and to the goddamned mercs!"

— ii —

A steady stream of damage updates and casualty reports punctuated the next ten minutes, then, finally, Cyllo turned to Lesedi. "Sir, I've been reviewing the sensor data—"

"And?"

"If our bow shock wave and the fold wake created by the Hahtooshan ship converged over a plasma pool, it's possible it created a temporal distortion great enough to explain our spatial displacement."

"And the mercs?"

"Most likely they experienced the same kind of violent displacement we did and were thrown in the exact opposite direction we were."

Lesedi's eyes darted to Perou. "How are those diagnostics proceeding?"

He watched as two more telltales came alive on his console. "One generator's offline. The rest check out." He looked at her. "We're good to go, sir—literally."

Lesedi shifted her gaze to Pardix. "Ensign, plot out the reciprocal line and lay in a course. Eisele? Fold two." She rose, stiffly, and walked over to the tactical station.

Zayyad looked up and smiled thinly. His normally swarthy face, Lesedi suddenly noticed, had taken on a rather odd, pasty hue.

"You okay?" She dropped her worried gaze to his right arm and grimaced as she realized it was badly broken. "Shit, Khaleed, why didn't you say something?" Not waiting for an answer, she glanced over her shoulder. "Stoker, get the tactical relief up here on the double!"

Izraad joined them. "Can I help?"

Lesedi turned back to Zayyad. "Think you can get to sickbay under your own power if the Lieutenant helps you?"

"Yeah," he replied with some uncertainty.

"Then get going." She jerked her chin towards the airlock.

"But—"

"I'll take over until your relief gets here." She grinned at his hesitation. "I think I can manage."

Zayyad nodded and, with Izraad's help, he got to his feet. Together they started for the airlock while Lesedi slipped onto his now vacant chair and gave the console a quick once over with her eyes, re-familiarizing herself with the layout… just in case.

— iii —

For the next six hours the control room crew was treated to a steady stream of damage reports from various departments.

To Lesedi the soft drone of voices slowly merged with the background hum of the engines, producing a strangely soothing cadence. There was nothing for her to do but sit and wait… and hope.

She even allowed herself to drift off a couple of times.

"Sir…?"

Lesedi blinked, then, realizing it was Cyllo who had spoken, straightened up in her chair, instantly and fully awake. "Yes?"

"Extreme long range scanners have detected something dead ahead—"

"Something…?"

"Impossible to be more specific at this range and speed."

"Screens up. Drop to flat one."

"Aye... dropping now," Eisele replied and the ship quivered as it fell out of its self-generated spatial displacement.

Lesedi waited, giving Cyllo a chance to study the raw, incoming data then prompted, "Well?"

"Preliminary spectrographic analysis is registering concentrations of metallic matter... but no silicaceous bodies... spread over a large area." She shifted her gaze to another monitor. "I'm also picking up a residual plasma charge emanating from the metallic objects."

"Mines? That's common merc tactic—"

"Yessir, I know, but..." Cyllo's eyes darted from one monitor to the next, "no... or should I say doubtful—" A bleat drew her gaze to yet another monitor; she gave the data a quick study, then with an over the shoulder glance at Lesedi, added, "It's the Hahtooshan vessel, sir—or should I say what's left of it. Spectral analysis and the combined mass of the debris field matches that of a destroyer class—"

Pardix let out a loud whoop and smacked his hands on his console. *"We got 'em!"*

"Ensign...." Lesedi warned half-heartedly then her eyes narrowed. "Wait." She glanced back at Cyllo. "You said D-class—you're sure?"

"Yessir. She must've been more severely damaged than we were, or possibly struck a plasma pool when she was thrown clear of the temporal distortion."

"Yeah," Lesedi nodded distractedly as she turned back to the tactical display. *The original ID must've been wrong. Gotta be it. C and D classes aren't all that different... an easy mistake, especially with all that interference.* She gave her stomach a distracted rub. "Stoker, see if you can pick up any distress calls," she said, more by habit than desire. "Cyllo, scan for life sign readings."

Stoker looked up. "Nothing, sir."

Lesedi looked at Cyllo; she shook her head.

"There but for the grace of—"

"Enough," Lesedi snapped, flicking Cajori a silencing scowl before fixing her gaze on the tactical display. *It's over. You did it.* To her surprise, she felt no relief, no pleasure, which only added to her unfocused unease and mounting anger. *Maybe it was just too damned easy. Maybe.* Her preoccupied squint crumbled into a

frown. "Let's get the hell out of here. Pardix, plot a course to Mirfak. Eisele? Best speed."

As the two acknowledged the orders, she shoved herself to her feet. "And Pardix? You've got the conn. I'll be in sickbay checking on our injured." She gave the tactical display one last accusatory glance then stalked out of the control room.

She stopped just short of the main sickbay airlock, took a deep breath, then stepped across the threshold and headed directly for Amalfitano's office. When she reached the doorway she found Fleming seated at Amalfitano's desk, staring intently at a flimsy.

Lesedi cleared her throat and Fleming looked up. "Here for a casualty update, sir?"

"Yeah, Doc."

"Take a seat."

Lesedi looked past her to Amalfitano's private quarters. The door was open, the room beyond dark.

"The chief's in surgery," Fleming explained. "I can give you the information, but if you'd prefer to wait—"

"No, let's hear it." Lesedi picked up a pile of flimsies that had been hastily dumped into the nearest chair, placed them on the floor and sat. *I want this over with—*

"We have nine confirmed dead."

"Nine?" Lesedi felt as if someone had punched her in the stomach.

"Of the twenty three, correction, twenty *four* injured," Fleming interrupted, "including Ensign Zayyad, one is currently in surgery, three are in critical condition with radiation burns, and six others are in serious, but stable condition. The rest, including two Hahtooshan prisoners in the brig, are suffering from fractured bones, bumps and bruises, nothing major. In fact most our injured have already been released." She leaned back. "We were incredibly lucky, considering, if one can call nine fatalities 'lucky'."

"Yeah."

"Doctor Amalfitano?" a male voice boomed from the desk-com.

Fleming pressed the desk-com's activator. "Jenna here, Xosé, what's up?"

"The chief asked to be notified of the path reports on Corporal Gianakis."

"Be right there." Fleming rose. "If you'll excuse me, sir?"

Lesedi also got to her feet. "Where's Khaleed?"

"Ward one, first bed on your right." With that, Fleming hurried out of the office.

Lesedi followed, then wandered into the ward. Spotting the tactical officer propped up on pillows on a nearby bed, she smiled. "Khaleed, how'ya doin'?"

He held up his immobilized right arm, in the process revealing his bandage-encased chest.

"What the...?"

"Doc says I broke a coupla ribs—go figure."

"Along with your arm."

"So much for my cat-like reflexes."

She couldn't help but laugh.

His full lips parted in a broad grin. "I hear the Hahtooshan ship was destroyed?"

She sat on his bunk, next to his hip. "You heard right. Cyllo thinks it struck a plasma pool. Maybe we hit it hard enough it couldn't withstand the force of being thrown out of the temporal distortion. Who knows and at this point, who cares? We stopped them. That's all that matters."

He leaned close, winced, then leaning back whispered tightly, "Between this and nabbing yourself a merc officer, you're gonna get your own command outta this, Ife. Guaranteed."

"We'll see," she shrugged, feigning indifference even though the same thought had already occurred to her. "To be honest, right now I'd settle for a hot shower and a nap. I'm bushed."

"Sir?"

Lesedi twisted around to find Corsali standing in the ward doorway, clutching the frame with one hand. "Sirin! I didn't know you were up and about."

"I'm not supposed to be, sir, but I need to speak with you."

"Of course." She gave Zayyad a pat on the thigh, murmured, "See ya later," rose and started towards Corsali.

The woman looked terrible. Her normally pale skin was peeling, revealing raw red patches underneath and she was even thinner than Lesedi remembered, with haunted, sunken eyes and livid bruises on her face, forearms and throat. It was what Lesedi couldn't see that worried her even more. Something she hadn't dared think about, much less have time to raise with Amalfitano.

If I find out one of those mercs laid a hand on you, I'll personally space him—in fact I'll space the lot.

"Sir, the Hahtooshans…"

"What about 'em?"

"I overheard one of the staff saying that one of the Hahtooshan ships had been destroyed?"

"Yup!" Lesedi smiled, then just as abruptly, it vanished as she felt the bottom fall out of her stomach. *Ohmagod. "One?* You mean there *was* more than one?"

"Yessir. I—"

"Shit!" She grabbed Corsali's elbow as the woman started to wobble. "Think you can make it to the doc's office?"

"Yessir."

"Then come with me." She wrapped her arm around Corsali's waist, then forced herself to make the short trip at Corsali's slow, shuffling pace rather than a dead run.

Once inside the cluttered room, Lesedi helped Corsali to a chair then smacked the desk-com button. "C and C… Stoker? Have Lieutenant Izraad report to Doctor Amalfitano's office on the double." She cut the link and turned back to Corsali.

Lesedi gave the woman a moment to recover, then, unable to wait any longer, asked urgently, "Now, just how many ships are we talking about?"

"Two," Corsali began just as Fleming entered, a flimsy in her hand.

"Sir, I didn't realize you were still…" Her gaze fell on Corsali and her quizzical expression darkened to a scowl. "What are you doing up, Ensign? I told you strict bed—"

"I brought her here," Lesedi interrupted; before she could explain further, a breathless Izraad arrived.

"Sir, Stoker said—"

"There were *two* merc ships," Lesedi broke in.

"What?" Izraad and Fleming gasped in unison then Izraad added, "Are you sure?"

Lesedi turned to Corsali. "Ensign?"

"Take it slow, Sirin," Fleming warned, with a sidelong look at Lesedi.

Corsali, her eyes darting between Izraad, Lesedi and Fleming, began, "Uh, well… Khusaaq—"

"Who?" Lesedi asked.

"Khus… I mean the Hahtooshan officer," she corrected herself as Lesedi raised her eyebrows, "he told me two ships had been sent to the Rasal Ghul system to retrieve information from an abandoned Coalition base—"

"We know about the base," Lesedi interrupted impatiently, "but go on, what else did he tell you?"

"He said one weapon the base had been working on had an incredibly destructive potential and his captain was going to keep the weapon for himself… he was going to test it on an inhabited planet."

Izraad blinked; Fleming swore under her breath.

Lesedi hesitated only an instant before asking, "Did he say which planet?"

She shook her head. "No, sir—"

"This merc," Lesedi interrupted, shifting her unblinking stare to Fleming. "Is he capable of answering questions?"

"He's heavily sedated. Doctor Amalfitano thought that would be the safest—"

"Wake him up."

Fleming hesitated.

"That wasn't a request, doctor, but a direct order—*do it!*"

Fleming replied with a curt nod, pivoted on her heel and hurried from the office.

"Sir?"

Lesedi looked back at Corsali. "Yes?"

"Khusaaq rescued us because he hoped by doing so, we could help him stop his captain. That was always his main focus—stopping him from unleashing this weapon. I'm sure he'll tell you everything he knows."

Lesedi favored Izraad with a sidelong look and replied dubiously, "Let's hope so."

"Just give him a chance, sir, please."

"Of course," Lesedi replied with a tight smile. *I'll give him just as much of a chance as the mercs gave the crew of the Perrault.*

Chapter 16

Izraad, an unwilling, albeit passive participant in Lesedi's roiling emotions, surreptitiously studied the younger woman's down-turned face as they waited for the isolation unit's airlock to complete its cycle. "Sir, Sirin's an excellent judge of character, in fact she—"

"We're talking about a merc here," Lesedi growled, keeping her eyes fixed on the door, "and she was clearly under duress. I consider her judgment, under the circumstances, questionable at best." The inner door snapped open and she stalked out.

Izraad followed—after a moment's hesitation and a muttered, "Yessir, of course sir, far be it for me to make any pertinent observations, sir."

Fleming looked up from the drug cart as they entered the dimly-lit cubicle and acknowledged Lesedi with a frosty, "Sir."

Lesedi ignored her, her full attention fixed on the Hahtooshan lying restrained on the trauma bed.

Fleming murmured, "Lights, twenty five percent," and the room brightened accordingly. "I've just given him a counteractant but I can't guarantee he'll be able to understand, much less—"

"Understood," Lesedi cut her off.

Izraad risked a sidelong glance at Lesedi as Lesedi's emotional turmoil abruptly distilled into one overwhelming reaction: murderous hatred.

Izraad looked down at their prisoner. Clad only in a pair of ship-issue exercise shorts and a patchwork of dressings with his right leg encased in a hip to ankle immobilizer, he looked far less imposing than she remembered from her brief glimpse in the cargo bay. His exposed skin was smeared with yellow burn salve which effectively camouflaged his tattoos, leaving him looking completely human—if one ignored the still visible pattern of elaborate facial scarification. *But not just a bizarre form of personal adornment, perhaps not even adornment at all. Homing signals—and who knows what else.*

Fleming gave the bed's restraint web a quick tug. "It shouldn't take more than a few sec—"

The mercenary groaned softly, prompting her to jerk her hand away and the two marine guards to raise their shockers.

Izraad gave the over-bed med-comps a quick scan. Cyllo's hastily designed nullifiers and surgically implanted micro-sensor heads—Fleming's idea—were working perfectly, as was the counteractant.

Her gaze returned to the Hahtooshan's face as she suddenly sensed *him*, the being behind the unsettling façade, as his mind slowly, sluggishly, crawled from its drug-induced stupor.

As he struggled towards wakefulness, she found herself awash in a chaotic mix of fragmented thoughts and jumbled emotions—*memory confetti*—that swirled around her as if blown on a gentle breeze. It was all so familiar, all so human, and yet... *not*.

"Sha'ashahn?"

Izraad felt his mind turn towards Lesedi' sharp voice, blindly grasping for it as a drowning man would reach for a life preserver. *Come on... reach.*

"Sha'ashahn?" Lesedi repeated coldly.

His eyelids fluttered.

Izraad urged, *Reach... yes!* and he opened his eyes.

As the Hahtooshan stared dully at the ceiling, Izraad caught glimpses of random thoughts that were swimming around in his mind, seemingly with no permanent home. Then they began to coalesce, to precipitate out of the murk of his heavily drugged state as the counteractant took hold.

Mind and body were integrating. She could almost feel the pieces snapping back into place.

"Sha'ashahn?" Lesedi prompted impatiently, tapping her foot for emphasis.

Despite his dazed expression, and the restraint webbing, Izraad sensed Lesedi's sudden, strong urge to back up a step as the mercenary's pale eyes slowly came to rest on her. To Izraad the outward appearance of grogginess was just that; he was now wide-awake. *Clever boy.*

"Sha'ashahn, you're in possession of information we require."

His only response was to blink and Lesedi flicked Fleming a quizzical, bordering on accusatory glance.

"Perhaps he doesn't speak Standard," Fleming quipped irritably.

Izraad felt like interjecting that he did, he understood perfectly but something held her back. Perhaps it was Lesedi; perhaps it was the Hahtooshan himself. Perhaps it was simply that she didn't want to tip her hand too quickly—to the Hahtooshan, or, she realized to her surprise, Lesedi.

Lesedi turned back to him. "Fine. Sha'ashahn, ah... Pay-too... ah..." She paused to sort through her long neglected Hahtou vocabulary. Finally, with more certainty she said, "Pay-toot-say?"

His blank stare sharpened, and for a moment he regarded Lesedi with utter revulsion. He parted his blistered lips and in an oddly cadenced voice barely above a hoarse whisper, replied haltingly, "I understand... your tongue, Rimmer, so... so there no need to... to butcher mine."

Lesedi smiled coldly. "I'm so glad to hear it. It'll make things that much easier."

As she spoke, he took in his alien surroundings and the faces of those clustered around his bed without so much as a blink. His strange eyes brushed past Izraad, then jerked back to her. He gave her Intelligence grays and her collar's distinctive, Wajet eye insignia—marking her as a chempath—a quick, confirming glance, then he locked gazes with her and she felt her skin prickle. *So, you know who, and, more importantly, what I am. Good. Perhaps that will be enough.*

As if sensing *her* thoughts, he quickly turned back to Lesedi and asked in a stronger, albeit more wary voice, "Where... is this?"

"You're aboard the Coalition patrol vessel, *Baidarka.*"

"*Baidarka...?* But—" He tried to sit up; the restraint web responded by tightening, tugging at his blistered and bandaged skin. He looked at it, then back at her, clearly surprised. "What—"

"That's for our protection, Sha'ashahn, as well as yours."

"I'm a prisoner? Where's Aquila?" He tried to look around Lesedi. "I demand to speak with him!"

"I'm the one asking the questions here," Lesedi replied stiffly. "And you're in no position to demand anything."

He fixed her with such a malignant scowl even Izraad found it unsettling, despite the restraint web and armed guards. "And *who* are you?"

"I'm Ife Lesedi, commanding officer of the *Baidarka—*"

"Commanding officer?" he repeated as he dropped his gaze to her uniform's rank insignia. "You're an ensign."

"—and this is my Intelligence Officer, Lieutenant Izraad." Lesedi jerked her chin towards Izraad.

His eyes cut to Izraad. *Betrayal.* The instant their eyes locked she tasted the overwhelmingly bitter tang of betrayal. *You think you've been deceived, tricked... by Robert?*

"We have some questions for you, Sha'ashahn," Lesedi began, again drawing his hateful gaze. "I strongly suggest that you cooperate—"

"But if I do not, your chempath will strip my mind, yes?" he growled, but to Izraad his menacing tone was all bluster.

Just the suggestion of a mind-strip terrifies you. She arched a brow in surprise. It was not the reaction she'd expected. Anticipatory fear, yes. That was a near-universal response. *But terror? In a Hahtooshan? What are you hiding?*

"Does your commanding officer know you're playing captain?" he taunted. "Or perhaps you led a mutiny in his absence—"

—Or he's dead, Izraad caught the sudden, stray thought that sent a fresh ripple of alarm through the Hahtooshan. *Maybe they're all dead, all drowned—*

"I'd prefer it to be voluntary," Lesedi continued, pointedly ignoring his baiting remarks, "but I'll have the information I need, one way or another. I'm giving you the opportunity to cooperate—"

"What about my escort?" he interrupted, putting voice to his urgent fears. "Are they alive? Did you take them captive as well?"

Izraad glanced sidelong at Lesedi, mentally prompting the woman to give him that much.

"Answer *my* questions to *my* satisfaction," Lesedi replied, "and I'll *consider* answering yours, merc."

His eyes flashed; he clenched his teeth. But instead of the expected enraged reaction, Izraad sensed something very different, something she hadn't anticipated: *intense remorse.*

"So, we know about the base," Lesedi crossed her arms. "We know your Orthodoxy was contracted to retrieve the data on the biological weapons—"

"Why do you need me?" he sneered in an attempt to shore up his intimidating Hahtooshan persona, both to Lesedi and, Izraad realized, himself. "You *know* everything."

"Not *everything*, merc. Now, are you going to cooperate and answer my questions, or...?" she jerked her chin towards Izraad.

His menacing scowl deepened but despite his best efforts, a stray thought, more a desperate plea for help, escaped. *Sirin!*

Sirin? Izraad raised a brow. *Our Sirin?* She glanced back at the doorway. *Perhaps—*

"What... what do you wish to know?" he grumbled, drawing Izraad's preoccupied gaze.

Lesedi stared down at him, surprised and every bit as wary by his sudden capitulation. She'd clearly envisaged bravado, maybe even a berserker reaction—they all had—he was a merc after all, with a merc's reputation of brutish, ferocious behavior.

But to Izraad, his startling acquiescence wasn't a simple, straightforward attempt to avoid the dreaded mind-strip. That was part of it to be sure, but there was more. His sense of guilt over the presumed deaths of his escort was growing, clearly building upon a long-standing mindset, now fed by the internal mantra, *It was all for nothing...*

And there was something else, every bit as intense as his fear and his guilt: a strong, almost overwhelming sense of duty. *But... not to the Orthodoxy.* Izraad was sure of that. *At least not primarily, which begs the question, duty to whom?* Puzzled, she again took in their captive, from head to toe. Human he might be, but he was also very, very alien in so many ways. *Maybe Sirin was right, maybe you really do want your captain stopped, but why—*

"Ah... well, for starters, exactly how many of your ships were sent to Rasal Ghul?" Lesedi asked, drawing Izraad back to the matter at hand.

He hesitated, and with another flicked glance at Izraad, answered, "Two."

"Only two?"

"That *is* what I said."

"Sure?"

"Yes."

"Who contracted your services?"

"I was never told."

Lesedi snorted her disbelief. "And you weren't even the slightest bit curious?"

"We weren't paid to be curious. We were paid to recover—"

"But there was a plan to test the effectiveness of the weapon uncovered on Rasal Ghul Four on a populated planet?"

"Not one sanctioned—"

"Just answer the damned question, yes or no!"

He squinted up at her and hissed, *"Yes."*

"What planet?"

"I don't know."

Emboldened, Lesedi leaned close to his ear and whispered, "Yes, you do."

He glared at her out of the corner of his eye. "No, I *don't.*"

She straightened up. "I give you one more chance. Tell me, *what* planet?"

"I don't know!"

"You're *lying,* yowie."

He spat in her face.

Startled, Lesedi stepped back; the closest guard grabbed his jaw and slammed his mouth shut with enough force Izraad could hear his teeth crack together. He tried to shake the man's grip loose, his snarls muffled by the man's vicious hold.

"Enough!" Izraad ordered just as the other guard moved in to help subdue him. "Let him go!" She motioned for everyone to step back as the marine unhappily released his hold, but she knew it was too late. They'd done exactly as he'd expected—the razor-thin chance they had at getting him to divulge what he knew voluntarily had been lost.

"Don't touch him," Izraad warned as the Hahtooshan, now free of the guard's hold, hurled obscenities through freshly bloodied lips while he struggled to pull his arms and legs free of the sticky net. He succeeded only making it cling even tighter, scraping his skin free of the salve and tearing open scabbed over blisters as it did so, dislodging dressings and causing his immobilized thigh to bow in a way that made Izraad's stomach flutter.

A sidelong glance at Fleming and seeing the look on her face as the doctor studied the closest monitor's readouts, hearing his now frantic, gasping, *"Qusheh-ne!"* as he continued to struggle, heedless to the damage he was causing himself prompted Izraad to grab Lesedi's arm, briefly drawing the woman's gaze.

"Sir..." She motioned for Lesedi to follow her. *"Outside."*

Lesedi remained where she was.

"Now, sir," Izraad hissed in her ear then walked out of the cubicle.

Lesedi stalked angrily after her and once they were in the corridor, the door to the cubicle closed, she snapped, *"What?"*

"We're not getting anywhere like this—let him calm down."

"We don't have that luxury, Lieutenant."

Izraad fixed her with an exasperated stare, "I fully understand the time constraints, Ensign, but what we need most *accurate* information. Right now I wouldn't trust anything he says. So, I am telling you to give him a chance to calm down, and while he's doing that, I think it would be wise to talk to Sirin, perhaps even—"

"Sirin? But you saw what she looks like!" Lesedi jabbed her finger towards the main sickbay. "Don't you think she's been through enough?"

"Agreed. But let's not forget that she was able to get him to freely divulge some critical information. Perhaps she can do it again. I sense a very palpable sense of betrayal—"

"Betrayal, by whom?"

"Us—or, more accurately, he believes by the commander."

Lesedi snorted, "Any promises Commander Aquila made while being held captive by this merc were clearly made under coercion!"

"I fully appreciate that, Ensign. I'm just telling you what I'm sensing. He believes he's been lied to, tricked. Sirin said he wanted his captain stopped, which is why he rescued—using *her* word," she added hastily as she saw Lesedi rising to the bait, "—them. And I sense he's telling the truth about that—or at least he's not purposefully lying about it. Perhaps we can get more useful information out of him if we first establish that we haven't lied to him, that whatever understanding he had with Aquila will be honored. Sirin, I believe, is the key to that—"

"That's a goddamned merc—" Lesedi jabbed a finger at the isolation unit, "—you trust what he says?"

"I didn't say that. I trust what *I* sense he's thinking and his underlying emotional state. And he believes he's been tricked."

"We don't have time to mollycoddle a merc, Lieutenant. And to be blunt I don't give a damn what he *thinks*. Every minute, every second is critical. I need whatever information he has, and I need it *now*, not hours or days from now, after we've convinced him we aren't *lying* to him—for all we know, this could just be a stalling tactic!"

Izraad opened her mouth to reply just as the cubicle door snapped out and Fleming stepped out, a ject-it in her hand.

"Sir," Fleming began, "I really must insist—"

"I want him mind-stripped, immediately," Lesedi said and in a voice deliberately loud enough to be overheard by the Hahtooshan.

"What?" Fleming gasped and hit the door release. She waited until it had closed again, then said, "Absolutely not! I agreed to you questioning him, but he's in no shape to be mind-stripped—"

"We have to know what planet they've targeted!"

"But sir," Fleming persisted, "if you could just wait a few hours—"

"We don't have a few hours!"

"But—"

"Would you rather lose the entire population of a planet?"

"Of course not!" Fleming said. "It's just—"

"Need I remind you that *that*," she gestured angrily to the cubicle, "is a *merc?*"

"Sir, I'm well aware of who and what he—"

"Your concerns have been noted," Lesedi cut her off, "but my decision stands—"

"And what decision is that?" a sleep-rumpled Amalfitano interrupted as he stepped out of the airlock.

"The prisoner's refusing to divulge vital information," Lesedi replied heatedly. "That leaves me no option but to have him mind-stripped."

Amalfitano turned his piercing gaze on Fleming.

"I warned the Ensign that he's in no condition, that it might—"

"I'm well aware of the risks," Lesedi fired back, "but this has to be done. Too much is at stake."

"Can't this wait?" Amalfitano asked. "We didn't just spend—"

"You tell me," Lesedi snapped. "You see, there were two Hahtooshan ships, not just the one."

"Two?" He looked at Izraad; she nodded unhappily.

"And according to Ensign Corsali, the mercs plan on testing whatever the hell they found on a populated planet."

Amalfitano looked away and running his fingers through his hair, swore, *"Cacchio—"*

"We have to know what planet, and I'll give him *one* more chance to freely tell us, but if he still refuses…"

Amalfitano blew out his cheeks, shook his head.

"I'll accept full responsibility," Lesedi added with a silencing glance at Fleming. "Doctor Amalfitano, I request your presence as well, just in case we run into complications, but I will not order it."

"Yes, of course." He turned to Fleming. "No need for you to stay, Jenna, besides, someone needs to make rounds. Drakin warned me there're a bunch of cranky people out there who wanna be discharged."

She glanced back at the cubicle. "I just gave him a relaxant—"

"You did what?" Lesedi hissed. "On whose authority—"

"Mine," Fleming snapped. "You won't get much information out of him if he's dead." She turned to Izraad. "It was a mild *muscle* relaxant only, Lieutenant—not enough to cause any effect on you questioning him, but in my *medical* judgment it was absolute minimum necessary to prevent further harm." She handed Amalfitano the expended ject-it, added, "He's *extremely* agitated," then favored Lesedi with one last icy look before she stepped into the airlock

Amalfitano waited until the lock closed behind her then he looked sharply at Lesedi. "Doctor Fleming's just doing her job, Ensign."

"Too well, if you ask me."

Izraad eyed her. *Same could be said for you… sir.*

"I thought you," Lesedi continued, arms akimbo, "of all people would—"

"Happily wish every damned merc dead?" Amalfitano finished for her. "Look, Ensign, let's get a few things straight, here and now. As a species—" At Izraad's soft cough, he quickly amended himself, "I mean, as a *society*, I consider them to be nothing more than cold-blooded thugs-for-hire, but I'm also a doctor—a goddamned good one if I say so myself—and I just pieced this particular merc back together and I'm in *no* mood to do it again. Plus, correct me if I'm wrong but I thought you were after information, not retribution." He crossed his arms. "Tell me I'm wrong. Because if I'm not, I want no part of this."

"Neither do I," Izraad added for good measure.

Lesedi's jaw muscles bunched, her dark eyes darting between the two in impotent rage, then: "All I want is to know which goddamned planet they're going to target so perhaps we can beat them to it and, oh, yeah, while we're at it, save a few million innocent lives!"

"Fine," Amalfitano grumbled, "then let's get this the hell over with."

Lesedi nodded and started for the cubicle.

"But before we do," Izraad said, stopping Lesedi in the tracks and fixing her with a cold stare, "understand one thing about mind-stripping, Ensign: the subject cannot lie—"

"I *know* that—"

"When asked a *direct* question," Izraad continued, undeterred by Lesedi's indignant tone. "So keep your questions simple and to the point."

"Understood." Lesedi smacked the door release, then spun on her heel and strode back into the cubicle.

Izraad and Amalfitano, after exchanging exasperated looks, followed.

The object of their heated discussion watched them file into the cubicle in unblinking bravado. Fleming's mild relaxer had had the intended effect. He was no longer fighting the restraints; even his breathing had slowed and deepened, but the damage, superficial as it might—or might not—be, had been done by the looks of his bleeding skin and the tattered dressings, his freshly bloodied lips... and the sheer, unadulterated hatred in his eyes.

Amalfitano took in the look of his patient with a wide-eyed stare then flicked Izraad a sidelong, accusative glance. She only shrugged.

As he turned back to Khusaaq, Khusaaq's eyes briefly locked with Amalfitano's and Izraad could sense the doctor's immediate, heart-thumping response. It was one thing to perform surgery on one of the feared mercenaries, but to have one actually look directly at you, well... that was something altogether different, and clearly the truly blood-chilling stare this mercenary was using on Amalfitano was a well-honed technique.

Satisfied with Amalfitano's reaction, he shifted his gaze to Lesedi and in a voice that belied his murderous expression, asked sweetly, "Back so soon?"

To Izraad his response was a case of very bad judgment: he'd clearly overheard at least some of their angry conversation, just as Lesedi had hoped. Instead of reacting the way she'd assumed he would, he'd drawn a very different conclusion from their heated remarks. Lesedi, he perceived, was not fully in command, that the three were not a united front; chinks he clearly planned to use to his advantage.

"Okay, merc," Lesedi said, crossing her arms, "let's start where we left off."

"Let's not," he sneered, mimicking her clipped accent exactly.

She squinted at him. He grinned back at her, challenging, baiting, probing for a reaction—perhaps even hoping to goad her into overreacting—anything to stall the inevitable.

Realizing what he was up to, Lesedi smiled back at him, asked politely, "Just answer one question, merc. What planet? Give me a *name*. That's all I ask."

"And I've already told you, I don't know," he replied casually as he let his gaze wander around the cubicle, a deliberately dismissive gesture, as if his curious, alien surroundings were his primary, his sole, concern.

"My Intelligence Officer begs to differ. She tells me you're hiding something—something *very* important. Now, what would that be?"

He snorted as his narrowed gaze returned to her. "You tell me."

"I'm in no mood for games, merc, and we're running out of time. Tell me the truth, voluntarily, or I'll have my chempath obtain it by force."

He laughed, an oddly barking and decidedly forced laugh, then his eyes narrowed to slits and his snarled, "You have no idea who you're dealing with, do you?"

To Izraad the response was more than just a challenge, more than just a statement of the obvious. He'd let something slip, something critical—

"And you're wasting our time," Lesedi fired back.

"I've told you what I know—"

"You haven't told me what planet!"

"I. Do. Not. Know."

She gave Izraad a sidelong look.

Izraad replied with a slight shrug. He was suddenly doing a much better job at safeguarding his thoughts and she found herself unable to sense anything beyond his cold-blooded hatred for Lesedi, his overwhelming dread at the prospect of a mind-strip—and the growing awareness that he'd grossly misjudged the situation.

"How's that possible? You're a Sha'ashahn—that's equivalent to our rank of battle commander, isn't it? Which means you can't be *that* stupid." Lesedi stepped back, away from the bed, motioning to the guards to do the same. "Or maybe you are. I guess we're all about to find out."

He looked up at Izraad as if still clinging to the crumbling belief it was all a bluff, all a game, but what he saw in her eyes sent him to the edge of total panic. He risked a sidelong glance at Lesedi, having dropped all pretense, his raspy voice now betraying renewed alarm. "I don't know what planet! I was never told... I'm telling you the truth!"

"Not the whole truth," Lesedi replied coldly.

He swallowed convulsively, licked his blistered and blood-sticky lips then fixed his menacing stare on Izraad, clearly hoping that and that alone would keep her at bay, and had the situation been any less dire, it might have. Just the thought of actually touching him, touching his thoughts, submerging herself completely in such a hate-filled, panicky mind suddenly left her feeling decidedly unsettled. She was a veteran of almost a thousand mind-strips... but none, she knew, could prepare her for what she was about to experience. *He's human—just keep reminding yourself of that. He isn't an alien.*

It didn't help. He might *be* human, but he wasn't *a* human. He was a Hahtooshan, and a terrified, murder-minded one at that.

Let's get this over with. She braced herself as best she could, then taking advantage of his preoccupation with the anticipated physical contact, selected and then slowly began exuding a pheromone, careful to regulate its potency so as not to affect the others in the small room. "It will be far less unpleasant if you don't fight—"

"Don't!" he hissed through clenched teeth, his rigid body pressed against the trauma bed. Then he caught a whiff of an odd, sweet odor and he shook his head in a futile attempt to dissipate the pheromone.

"Sha'ashahn," she murmured, "don't fight me."

His pupils were dilating and she nodded to herself. She had chosen well. The first barrier had been breached.

"*Qushah-ne…*"

"Sha'ashahn," she said in her most soothing voice, "if you fight, it will—"

"*Chulh!*"

Izraad, using her sleeve, roughly wiped his cheek free of as much of the salve as she could. Then, bracing herself, she pressed her palm against his exposed skin.

He violently flinched at the direct contact and stared up at her, eyes wide, his breathing now coming in short panicky bursts.

Out of the corner of her eye, she saw Amalfitano grab a wash cloth, slosh something on it, then offer it to her, knowing better than to do the job himself.

Keeping her eyes locked with Khusaaq's, her one hand pressed to his cheek, she took the cloth and quickly wiped the salve from his other cheek, forehead and throat.

He stared up at her, managed between breaths, *"Toh… tohiss-mat…"*

"It's not too late…" she murmured, placing the cloth within easy reach while the pores in her palm released another pheromone, one that she hoped would quickly break down his resistance.

It didn't; she pressed harder.

"Chulh!" He managed to jerk his head away, briefly breaking contact. *"Tu-mazneri!"*

She grasped his head in both hands, and, after a moment's struggle, roughly jerked his face back to her. *Stop fighting me!*

He squeezed his eyes shut. *Chulh!*

She pushed even harder.

Suddenly she felt something give, something *rip* open. *Yes.* She almost smiled as she slipped through, into his mind.

He screamed and, taken aback by the raw agony of it, Lesedi backed up a startled step and bumped into Amalfitano.

To the others in the room, his screams rapidly dissolved into chest-heaving gasps, but to Izraad, he continued to shriek at the top of his lungs as his mind clawed at hers in utter terror. Murderous hatred, almost bestial in its mindlessness, lunged at her from every direction. Excruciating pain knifed through her.

She tensed against the onslaught, but kept her palms pressed firmly to his sweat-slick cheeks. *It's not supposed to be like this… it's not supposed to hurt this much—STOP FIGHTING ME!*

Part of her was also dimly aware of Amalfitano, somewhere within the maelstrom of fury and searing pain that raged around her.

He knew better than to touch her but he had moved closer and she sensed his growing concern. A witness to numerous mind-strippings, he too realized something was wrong. *Very wrong.*

"Chulh!" Suddenly unable to control his neck muscles, his head lolled forward, into her cradling palm. *"Chuuulhhh…."*

Izraad nodded to herself. Another barrier had been broken. Even if he thought to hold his breath now, he'd inhaled enough.

"Tuuu-maaaz… mazneri," he slurred as he strained sluggishly against the restraint web. *"To… tohiss-maaat. Chu… chuuulhhh…"*

Izraad watched his increasingly feeble struggles with detachment as she assessed his body's growing weakness. The overwhelming terror and pain had begun to subside, like a retreating tide, his mind and body close to utterly spent.

Still cupping his chin in her palm, she gently turned his head to the left, then the right—there was simply no resistance, physical or mental. She tilted his head back and stared into his eyes. His pupils were now deep, inky pools surrounded by only the thinnest ring of bluish-gray. *Excellent. "Sha'ashahn, pa'-tu-kaat?"*

She felt the ever so slight stir, somewhere deep, deep within his subconscious mind. She'd reached the desired level, where there were no secrets, no places to hide, in the process sending his conscious mind into a state of shocked paralysis, where it would stay until she withdrew.

She murmured, *"Maz-akanj,"* and using her thumb, gently wiped away the thin rivulet of blood-tinged saliva that had dribbled from the corner of his slack mouth, a signal to Amalfitano, then using the cloth, gave his face another quick wipe, freeing the pattern of deep scars of the last of the salve.

Knowing his part, Amalfitano stepped close, applied a small amount of lubricant to his patient's eyes, then he quickly snaked a small suction tube to his mouth and part way down his throat. Satisfied with the placement, Amalfitano affixed it to the corner of his mouth with a small clip.

At Lesedi's curious stare, Izraad explained, "In his current state he's incapable of blinking and he's lost his gag reflex as well—without the tube he'd aspirate his own saliva."

Lesedi's only response was a silent, *'O'*.

Amalfitano then stepped back, out of the way and Izraad turned back to the business at hand.

"*S'sarhi-sseh?*" she asked then waited as his blistered lips tried to form words, but all that came out was a soft gurgle. *What's your use name?* she mentally prompted. A baseline. A known fact. A point of reference... a safety line. An umbilical cord.

Finally the answer she was seeking surfaced. *Khusaaq...*

Very good. She ran her fingers of her other hand across his sweat-glossy, scarified, and bruise-darkened forehead. "Aganreka'a, Khusaaq. *Qu'sahtoq.*" She kept her eyes locked with his and continued in the same soothing tone, "He will answer you now, sir, but ask only one question at a time."

She waited then risked a sidelong glance at Lesedi to find the woman staring down at him. Lesedi looked, to Izraad, as if she was about to be physically ill. *Good.*

Amalfitano gave Lesedi a less-than-gentle prod and whispered, "*Ensign?*"

"I... I had no idea," she stammered, "I didn't think it would—"

"I can't maintain this state of receptivity for more than a few minutes, sir," Izraad prompted coolly. *Not without doing permanent damage.*

Lesedi swallowed hard, and replied unsteadily, "Yes... yes, of course." She wet her lips. "Ah... all right. Let's, ah, let's establish the facts, first. Ask... ask him how many ships."

Izraad again swept her fingertips across his forehead, over the elaborate scars, the tattoos as she repeated the question in Hahtou. He stared up at her... and blinked.

In the instant she'd been distracted, he'd somehow mustered a weak resistance, regained some control.

Damn you, Ife! If you didn't have this stomach for this.... She took a deep breath and put her full concentration back to the task at hand. She ran her palm down his cheek, pressed it against his rapidly pulsing carotid artery just below the jaw and soothed, "Maz-akanj, Khusaaq."

The feeble barrier collapsed.

She repeated the question, repeated it again more firmly, and finally, to her immense relief, he replied in a slow, deliberate tone; finished, he absently tongued the suction tube.

I know it makes it hard to speak, but it's there for your protection—now leave it alone.

He obediently stopped tonguing the tube.

She smiled, *Excellent,* and stroked his cheek as she spoke softly, "Yes, there were two ships. *Acholilah*, commanded by a Ru'asooli Kshira'tzrhi, and *Makhaira*, captained by Tarqk Nahru'tzhri."

"Was there a plan to test the weapon on a planet?"

Izraad relayed the question, listened to his halting response, and answered, "He says Tarqk felt the weapon was worth far more than they'd been paid, and to prove it, he wanted to test it."

"Which planet—"

"What about the weapon itself?" Amalfitano interrupted. "Does he know what it is? What's its mode of transmission?"

"One at a time." Izraad eyed them both. "I suggest we build up slowly to your question, Ensign, by obtaining information he is more willing to supply." *Or is more certain about.*

"Fine," Lesedi grumbled.

Izraad ran a slender fingertip along his jaw as she mentally rephrased Amalfitano's questions in Hahtou, then, one at a time, she murmured them to him.

Out of the corner of her eye, she saw Amalfitano lean closer, visibly straining to catch an understandable word here or there, to give him some hint as to what, exactly, they were up against.

But by his expression, what he heard was, to his ears, nothing more than gibberish, and slurred gibberish at that. "Well?" he asked the instant Khusaaq stopped mumbling.

"Shhh," Izraad warned, then answered, "He says that there were two viral agents." She paused as she overheard Amalfitano's muffled obscenity. "One was..." She knit her brows as she mentally translated his answers from Hahtou into Standard. "A nonsegmented... negative stranded ribonucleic acid virus... capable of rapid spike mutation?" She risked a quick, sidelong glance at Amalfitano.

Lesedi too turned her baffled stare on the doctor. "What the hell does that mean?"

"Sounds like *filoviradae*. Maybe *paramyxoviridae* or even *rhabodoviridae*. All were mentioned in the data we recovered from the wreck and a mutant strain of Faget's Songo would be an excellent candidate for a biological weapon—"

"Faget's… what?" Lesedi said.

"Faget's *Songo*, maybe. But it might be a whole host of other critters. The *filoviridae* are one hell of a big family, with a large recombinant factor."

"Deadly?" Lesedi asked.

"If it's a strain of Songo, very, and highly contagious."

"Curable?"

"If it's Songo, or some other strain of filovirus, then yes, in most cases and if caught early enough, but—"

"Doctor, Ensign," Izraad interrupted, softly but firmly, "perhaps we could continue this discussion later?"

Lesedi nodded. "Yes, yes of course."

"And the other agent?" Amalfitano asked apprehensively.

Izraad repeated the question and listened to his softly slurred response. "The other is an easily aerosolized, helical ribonucleic acid virus with highly adaptable surface antigens?"

"Most likely *orthomyxoviridae*," he muttered. "It's a commonly used vector—"

"Enough to go on?" Lesedi asked.

"Not by half, but…" Amalfitano gave the bank of over-bed medical monitors a glance. He'd been an eyewitness to enough mind-strippings to recognize the terrible toll this particular interrogation was taking. "It gives me some place to start." He turned to Lesedi. "Go ahead, Ife, but make it *quick.*" He jerked his thumb at the monitors. *"Real* quick."

"Were both captains in on the plan, to release the disease on a planet?" Lesedi asked.

After another agonizingly slow exchange, Izraad replied, "He has no first-hand knowledge, but doubts Ru'asooli would've gone along with Tarqk's plan—it was not what they were contracted to do."

"Who contracted them?"

Izraad relayed the question, pursed her lips at his halting response and flicked Lesedi a sidelong look. "He was not told, he was not in a 'need to know'—" She turned back to him and narrowed her eyes as a gauzy image, a stray thought and strangely not feeling fully his briefly wound around her, like a wisp of smoke—and then was gone. *"Matarrans,"* she whispered, suppressing a shiver, but whether it was a response to the expected revelation, or to the odd sense of another presence she wasn't sure. "He believes it was the Matarrans."

Lesedi and Amalfitano exchanged looks then Lesedi edged a little closer to the bed and stared down at him, taking in every centimeter of his sweat-glossy face before asking her next question. "What class of warship is the *Makhaira?"*

This time Lesedi needed no translation as she heard his whispered answer: *"Loh'raath."*

"C-class," she said, more to herself than to the others. "And the ship that was destroyed was a D-class."

Izraad nodded.

Lesedi slammed her fist down on the bedside drug cart. *"Bloody hell!"* Then she looked back at Khusaaq to find him staring directly at her, bewildered and clearly very frightened as his mouth worked feebly against the tube.

Izraad wrapped her fingers around his chin, in the process drawing his wide eyes back to her and murmured sweetly, "Maz-akanj, toqtuq bah'dei-qu'… qu'sahtoq." *Don't be afraid, it's not your fault.*

The fear slowly drained from his eyes and he stared up at her, an almost imbecilic smile on his mouth.

In the same quiet, soothing voice, Izraad said, "Sir, please. *Be careful."* She caressed his jaw, his cheek. "He responds to any emotional outburst as if it were aimed at him, and since in his present state he wants desperately to please, your perceived anger at him is both terrifying and confusing."

"And we need to speed this up," Amalfitano whispered as he opened the drug cart and began pulling out vials. "His vitals are going off scale."

Lesedi glared briefly at him then turned back to Izraad. "What planet? What's the target?"

Izraad leaned close and fed Khusaaq the question, then encouraged him with a warm smile as he struggled to form words.

When he finally managed to speak, his reply was so weak only she heard him, much less understood him.

She blinked. *Gods...*

"What did he say?" Lesedi demanded in a strained whisper as Amalfitano turned to Izraad, a fistful of vials in one hand, a ject-it in the other.

"He *was* telling the truth, he was never told—"

"Tell him to make an educated guess!" Lesedi snarled.

Izraad leaned closer, her eyes, her mind searching his for any stray thought, anything to go on. *Help me...* She reached out, mentally shifting through the swirl of disjointed and long-buried memories, faces, snatches of conversation, sights, smells that bobbed and surged around her like flotsam caught in a whirlpool.

Sirin said you wanted to stop him—help us do just that. She lightly stroked his cheek, his jaw as she tried to ignore his shallow, erratic breathing, the ominously glazed look that now clouded his eyes, the rapidly gathering darkness that had begun to infiltrate even this deep into his subconscious mind. *Tell me what you think. Please... try.*

She opened her mind to his, inviting, encouraging—a welcome and safe haven to any stray image, any half-forgotten rumor, any whispered speculation—it was an enormous risk, but one, under the circumstances she felt she had no choice but to take. *We have to know...* And as she did so, she found she couldn't shake the very peculiar sense of being shadowed, of someone or *something* padding silently alongside her in her wanderings, just out of view—a sensation she'd felt almost from the start, but now it was becoming stronger with each passing second.

She felt if she reached out she could touch whoever, whatever it was, but something held her back: *fear*, but whether it was her own or not she couldn't say. She also sensed she was being watched, of multiple eyes peering out at her from the murk of his subconscious, of sudden and startling lucid images, so shocking, so truly horrific she found herself mentally stumbling back; of being carried along on wave upon wave of stomach-turning guilt coupled with unfocused rage—

The stripping was starting to unravel, her gambit had failed, and she struggled to regain control before it was too late—for both of them.

She began to withdraw before his already weakened body succumbed to the physical and psychological trauma of the mind-strip, before she found herself succumbing as well when something lightly brushed against her then was gone, drawn back into the surrounding and increasingly murky and fast moving eddies. But it was enough for her. An icy shiver ran down her spine.

Kakkab-Ta'abi. She took several steadying breaths as she continued her slow, cautious retreat, and managed, "He believes his captain would target Kakkab-Ta'abi."

"Never heard of it," Lesedi snapped.

"Anger, Captain," Izraad warned softly as she stroked Khusaaq's ominously clammy cheek. "Kakkab-Ta'abi—it's their name for the Tangaloa-Tuli system. I agree—it would make an ideal target."

"But... but Tuli's an unarmed planet, purely agrarian!" Amalfitano blurted out.

"Shhhh," Izraad murmured over Khusaaq's increasingly noisy, labored breathing; she was almost free...

"Exactly," Lesedi replied. "Isolated, with a large human population—*dammit to hell!"*

"If that's all, sir?" Izraad prompted with an audible trace of exasperation, Lesedi's snarled obscenity having stirred up Khusaaq's subconscious like mud in a pond.

Lesedi nodded, then jerked her eyes back to Khusaaq and hissed, *"You goddamned fucking butchers, I hope you all burn in hell!"* She spun on her heel and stalked from the cubicle.

Izraad scowled after her. Once the airlock snapped shut, satisfied Lesedi and her explosive outbursts were gone, she gave his jaw another gentle, lingering caress as she mentally staggered, totally spent, from his mind. She ran her fingers down his hollow, blistered cheek and in a voice barely above a husky whisper, said, "Ishahq, Khusaaq. Ishahq." *Go to sleep now.*

His eyelids fluttered; a moment later they closed.

Amalfitano pressed the ject-it against his left shoulder, quickly reloaded it and pressed it against his thigh. As he loaded a third vial, he glanced sidelong at her, and realizing she was leaning heavily against the bedside table, asked, "You okay?"

One of the marines stepped forward, offered her his arm for support, but she waved him off. She took several deep, steadying breaths and wiped her own sweaty forehead with the back of a very shaky hand. "Never... never better."

Amalfitano replied with a worried grunt as he studied the monitors. "There must be ten million people on Tuli."

"At least." She stared at Khusaaq's gaunt, sweat-streaked face, unable to shake the nagging feeling that she had not uncovered all, that something important—something critical—*someone* critical was still lurking within the shadowy and unfathomable undercurrents of fear and hatred. Something, someone utterly alien.

Feeling a sudden chill, she gave her goose-pimpled upper arms a brisk rub. *But what?*

"Even if I knew exactly what we were dealing with," Amalfitano continued, drawing her distracted stare as he circled the bed to get a better look at the monitors' read-outs, reloading the ject-it as he went, "there'd be no way in hell to vaccinate the entire population in time—"

"Chief?"

They both looked up as Meerut entered the small cubicle.

"Yes?"

"I'm sorry to interrupt, but—"

"We're almost done here," he replied, pushing the ject-it and its heavy sedative load against Khusaaq's right shoulder. "What's up?"

"We have those lab results on Commander Aquila you've been waiting for."

"Go on, William," Izraad said as Meerut slipped between him and the bed. "We can finish up without you."

"Sure?"

"Yeah."

"Promise me you'll get some rest as soon as you're done here? You look positively done in."

"Promise," Izraad replied wearily.

He turned to Meerut. "See she does."

"Yessir."

He gave the monitors another glance. The potent sedative and painkillers were already having a noticeable—positive—effect. Mollified with the read-outs, he handed Meerut the expended ject-it and handful of remaining vials then turned for the door. "But first I need to see a man about a bug."

— ii —

Lesedi strode over to the main sickbay station and smacked the com-unit. "Control."

"C and C, Pardix here—"

"Tace, change course for Tangaloa-Tuli, maximum fold factor."

"Sir?"

"I'll explain when I get there—just do it!" She cut the link then hurried out of sickbay and towards the control room as images of the mind-strip warred with visions of Tuli under attack. *It had to be done! Goddamned bastard left me no fucking choice!*

The airlock snapped opened in front of her and she stepped through.

Pardix rose from the command chair and his eyes widened when he saw her expression. "Sir—"

"ETA to Tangaloa-Tuli?"

"Fifty two and half hours, sir, present speed."

Lesedi turned to the com-op, Stoker. "How long before we can transmit a foldspace message to Tuli?"

"The repairs will take at least another seven hours, sir."

"Damn!" Lesedi threw herself down in her chair.

"Sir...?"

She looked up. Pardix was now standing beside her. His usual smug sneer had been replaced by an apprehensive stare.

"There were *two* Hahtooshan ships."

His full lips parted in stunned disbelief as Cyllo swiveled around in her chair and repeated, "Two?"

Pardix blinked, then began, "And the other one—"

"Is most likely on its way to Tuli," Lesedi finished for him, "to test the weapon they recovered from the base."

"Holy shit," he whispered.

"Sir?"

Lesedi, alerted by the tone of Stoker's voice, braced herself.

"I've just checked the directory. Tuli doesn't have a foldspace net." Stoker looked at the data disc he held in his hand, as if to direct Lesedi's baleful gaze away from him. "They use the Kornephoros-Alchete relay—"

"That'll take hours!"

He nodded grimly. "At the very least—"

"On top of the seven hours it'll take to finish repairs!" She smacked her fist on the arm of her chair. "We've got to find a way to warn them!"

"Agreed, sir," Pardix replied. "But how? For all we know, the other warship's entering the Tangaloa system as we speak."

Lesedi glared at him. "Thanks, Tace. That possibility hadn't occurred to me."

Chapter 17

Amalfitano leaned back in his chair and tried to savor the first five minutes of down time he'd had in…. He knit his brows. *Can't remember.*

Fleming sat across from him, her bare feet propped on his desk, a cup of coffee clutched in her hands. "I don't know about you, but I'm pooped."

"I passed pooped days ago."

She managed a feeble chuckle. "Lucky you."

He eyed her as he reached for his own, forgotten cup of coffee.

"So," she asked, "you think this weapon might be a form of Songo?"

"The description fits, but it fits a whole host of bugs, too. Songo's the most plausible, it's an ideal agent for a weapon, easily spread and extremely virulent, and the data from the base prominently mentioned filoviruses. Clearly they were considered one of the more promising lines of research. I can't discount the possibly of it being one of the *myxoviridae*, but my gut tells me *filoviridae* and Xosé agrees with me—*hell*, I'm beginning to think we're grabbing at straws."

"At least it's something."

"But what if it's the *wrong* something?"

"Then we pray our illustrious acting captain stops the Hahtooshans before they reach Tuli—assuming Tuli is, in fact, the target."

He eyed her. "Don't think much of Ensign Lesedi, you do?"

"She's far too gung-ho for my tastes."

"She's young. Needs some seasoning. If you remember, Robert wasn't all that much different when he came aboard."

She replied with a non-committal grunt.

He took a sip of coffee, swallowed. "Been meaning to tell you, I was really impressed with your work on the soldier."

"It was a team effort. You—"

"No. If it hadn't been for you and your micro-vascular work, we'd have lost him for sure. And those micro-sensor heads? Brilliance. Pure brilliance."

She blushed then chuckled at her own embarrassment. "Maybe you should hold off your compliments until you've met him."

"That bad, huh?"

She pointedly massaged her forehead. "Think of a constipated two year old on steroids."

Neither, in truth, had had much experience with toddlers but the analogy still struck a chord and left him privately wincing and also secretly relieved that the soldier's injuries had left him temporarily a paraplegic and therefore limited as to what he could do as far as mayhem—*although with Hahtooshans one should never make any assumptions*, he quickly reminded himself. He cleared his throat, shifted in his chair. "Something to look forward to, then. But back to you. I plan on making my opinions about your skills official, in my log, as soon as I get a few spare minutes."

"Thank you. And I've been meaning to ask if you'll teach me that ganglion-wrap technique?"

"Anytime."

"Not right now." She slumped back into the chair, wiggled her toes and yawned. "Maybe... tomorrow—"

"Doctors?" Meerut asked as she entered, a flimsy in her hand.

Amalfitano gave Fleming a sidelong look and muttered, "Uh-oh."

"I warned you we shoulda locked the door," Fleming grumbled as she set her cup on the desk and dropped her feet to the floor, scowling sidelong at the nurse as she did so.

"The Hahtooshan officer..."

Fleming groaned loudly and snatched up her discarded grip-boots.

"What about him?" Amalfitano straightened up.

She held out the flimsy. "You'd best see for yourself."

He took it, and as he skimmed down the sheet of read-outs, his brow crinkled into an accusative glower. "When did this start?" He handed the flimsy to Fleming.

"I noticed a discrete change in his respiratory pattern and cardiac output shortly after Lieutenant Izraad left, but—"

"I don't believe it!" He lurched to his feet, adding, "I sit down for one goddamned second and this is what happens!" He stormed from the office.

Meerut and Fleming caught up with him in the isolation unit, where Meerut added, "The Lieutenant warned me that the state of post-strip sleep she'd induced would be very deep, and that, along with the heavy PK and sed load—I wasn't immediately concerned, but now…"

He sat at the unit's console and stared at his unwelcome patient's latest readouts on a monitor.

"I've notified the lieutenant," Meerut said. "She's on her way."

Fleming, still clutching the flimsy, slipped onto the chair next to Amalfitano. "Maybe she's seen this kind of response before."

"Seen what kind of response?" Izraad asked as she entered the unit.

"*This!*" He snatched the flimsy from Fleming's hand, rose and shoved it into Izraad's. "The merc officer—"

"Khusaaq. His name is—"

"I don't give a damn what his name is! What I do give a damn about are these readings!"

Izraad took a moment to study them.

"Well?" he demanded as she finally lifted her gaze.

"You think this was the result of the stripping."

"What else could it be? He suffered no major head trauma. Moderate concussion, yes, but that was it—believe me, I checked, thoroughly." He jabbed an angry finger at the flimsy. "And there's no way you're going to tell me this is a result of a goddamned concussion!"

"I'm not trying to tell you anything. I was just trying to say that while Hahtooshans are clearly human, there's a hell of a lot we don't know about them, especially the way they react physiologically and psychologically to extreme stress or—"

"Mind-stripping?"

"It had to be done, Will—"

"Don't you *dare* give me any crap about me, of all people—"

"I had no intention of saying that you, of all people, should be thrilled that a Hahtooshan's health has taken a sudden, dramatic turn for the worse." Izraad crossed her arms. "I fully appreciate the tremendous loss you suffered at their hands so I've always excused your rather... well, knee-jerk hatred of them. It's completely understandable. But—"

He opened his mouth, but she cut him off.

"*But* I know you. To you, at this moment, he's not a Hahtooshan. He's your patient. Hate what he represents? Certainly. Abhor what he does for a living? Of course. But hate *him?*" She shook her head. "That's not the William Amalfitano I know. But I'm not a doctor. I work for Coalition Intelligence and to me he's not just a Hahtooshan, or a Hahtooshan officer, a rare prize, a potential windfall for Intelligence no matter how you slice it, he's also the only one who could tell us what his captain is up to in time to stop him.

"When Ensign Lesedi initially questioned him, it was obvious to me that he was hiding, *protecting* something—I couldn't tell if it was about the planet, or something else, so anything he would have told us, voluntarily, would have been suspect. He had to be mind-stripped, we had to know the truth—"

"But we still don't know the truth!" Amalfitano interrupted. "We still don't know for sure what we're dealing with or what planet they've targeted, we only have his 'gut feeling'—"

"Which is more than we had to go on before. I'm sorry, William, but if this," she tapped the flimsy with her fingertip, "is the direct result of the stripping, if he dies," she tossed the flimsy onto the nurses' station, "well, to be totally brutal about it, while HQ will likely be mightily put out, I can live with it."

"Even if we got it all wrong?"

"Yes," she replied simply.

He stared her for a moment then abruptly looked away, embarrassed at his outburst, not to mention his irrationality. *He's a goddamned merc after all. For all I know, he might have been the one who pulled the trigger—*

"Back in a minute." Izraad started to walk away.

"And where the hell're you going?" he snapped, addressing her retreating back. "In case you forgot, our problem is in there." He jerked his thumb towards the row of isolation cubicles.

"I know," she tossed over her shoulder. "Won't be long."

Amalfitano fixed his quizzical stare on Fleming.

"Hell if I know," she grumbled wearily.

He sighed, muttered, "Bring me a goddamned neural stimulator, will you?" then stalked over to airlock and smacked the release. The door opened, he stepped inside, and then drummed his fingers impatiently on the wall as the small chamber cycled.

"This is just what I needed! *Cazzo!*" He slammed his fist against the wall just as the inner door opened.

Nursing his skinned knuckles, he entered the first cubicle. He acknowledged the guards with a curt nod, gave each monitor a thorough study then looked down at his patient.

Going sour isn't the way you thank me you know. It fact it's goddamned rude! He scowled furiously at the Hahtooshan for emphasis, then, overhearing a plaintive, warning *bleat* from one monitors, shook his head and let out an exhausted sigh. *Hell, maybe she's right. Maybe I missed something, something vital—but dammit, I haven't slept, barely ate...*

He rubbed his burning eyes then stared up at the bank of monitors. *Now there's an irony: to be drummed out of the service because I can't save a fucking merc—stop!* He shook his head, hoping to clear it. *This isn't getting you—or him—anywhere.*

He blew out his cheeks, *Now where was I?*

Something vital, yeah. He carefully pried up the mercenary's right eyelid and peered at the fully dilated pupil, then counted off the seconds as it ever-so-slowly responded to the ambient lighting.

He released his hold on the eyelid, drew the thin drape aside, then walked down to the foot of the bed as his trained eye searched his patient's body for anything that might explain what the machines were telling him. *Something that didn't show up in the tests or during surgery.*

There's no point in denying it. Something was overlooked, and I'm the one who overlooked it. Maybe even something obvious... His eyes darted back to the Hahtooshan's slack face. *Maybe that's it. Somewhere along the line, without realizing it, I stopped thinking of you as a merc, started thinking of you as human. But you're not, are you? At least not exactly like us, physiologically or psychologically just like Zarijan said. And maybe those small differences....*

He ran his thumbnail up the bare, salve-greasy and tattooed sole of his patient's right foot, but the action didn't elicit even a minor twitch of a toe. He sighed and shook his head.

Meerut entered the cubicle, holding the requested neural stimulator. "Here you go, Chief."

"Thanks." He wiped his hands on his medreds, took it from her then blinking back the urge to yawn, walked up to the head of the bed.

She gently turned their patient's head to the side and parted his thick, filthy and tangled hair, exposing the base of his skull.

Amalfitano carefully positioned the small device, turned his attention to one monitor and pressed the activator. The screen immediately sparkled to life then rapidly filled with data.

What he saw did not look promising. In fact it looked anything *but* promising.

He flicked Meerut a sidelong look; she replied with a noncommittal shrug.

He gave his red-rimmed eyes another vigorous rub with the heels of his hands, and then, overhearing the airlock's inner door snap open, turned towards it and through the semi-transparent divider, saw two figures step out.

A moment later, Izraad and a grim-faced Sirin Corsali appeared in the cubicle's doorway and he raised a startled brow.

Izraad turned to the marines. "You two can stand guard just as effectively just outside."

They looked at each other and then back at her and one began, "But sir—"

"I'll take full responsibility. Out."

"Yes, ma'am," one murmured as they reluctantly slipped past her and out of the cubicle.

Meerut too took the hint. With a sidelong, 'Hell if I know' glance at Amalfitano, she withdrew.

"Okay," Amalfitano began, "now what the—"

"William, Sirin and I were having a talk when Meerut called me."

"I thought you were going to lie down."

"Change of plans."

He inhaled through his nose, exhaled the same way. She still looked like hell, but there was simply no point in arguing the issue with her. "And?"

"And based on what Sirin told me, I thought she'd be of great help."

Overhearing a soft intake of breath, Amalfitano shifted his quizzical gaze to Corsali staring down at Khusaaq, her hand to her mouth.

"This wasn't supposed to happen," she said softly, then looked back at Amalfitano and Izraad. "I told Ensign Lesedi he wanted to cooperate..." She bit her lip as she cautiously touched Khusaaq's bare shoulder with her fingers and chided softly, "Why didn't you tell them what they wanted to know?"

Amalfitano leaned close to Izraad's ear. "I don't think this is a good idea. She's been traumatized enough. To force her to—"

"I didn't force her to do anything." Then, in a louder voice she said, "Here Sirin," as she pulled down the wall-mounted fold-down chair next to the bed. "Stay as long as you want. Buzz the nurses if you need anything, and the guards are just outside, okay?"

Corsali nodded as she sat, murmured, "Thank you."

"Talk to him, Ensign," Izraad continued.

Corsali looked up at her with glistening eyes. "About what?"

"Anything—your childhood, your life on Selkis, how you came to be stationed on the *Baidarka*... trivial stuff, anything that comes to mind. Maybe things you talked about while on the planet. It'll give him a lifeline—something to help him find his way back."

"Yes, ma'am." She slipped her hand through the restraint web and wrapped her fingers around Khusaaq's wrist and Izraad gave her shoulder a squeeze. "I'll be back to check on you in a little while—sure there's nothing I can bring you?"

Corsali refused to look up this time as she shook her head.

Amalfitano began, "But—"

Izraad put her finger to her lips, then crooked the same finger at him, dimmed the lights and quietly backed out of the cubicle.

He trailed after her. "But..."

"But what?"

"I don't think we should leave her alone—"

"I do." She slipped between the two marines and stepped into the lock. "Coming?"

He hesitated. "But... but you're seriously suggesting we leave her alone with... *with a merc?*"

"In his present condition and with the restraint webbing, is he a physical threat to her?"

"Well, no, but can you imagine what HQ would say? What Lesedi would say?"

She grinned. "Yes, as a matter of fact, I can."

"Then—"

"Do you know what's wrong with him?"

"Not yet," he replied defensively. "I haven't had time to—"

"Well, I think I do. And if I'm right, this can't hurt, in fact it might be his only chance."

"You said you didn't care if he died."

"I said I could live with it if he did, but that doesn't mean—"

"But...." He looked back at the cubicle door. "But—"

"You're repeating yourself, William."

"But..." he began then scowled at her as she held up her forefinger.

"No more buts, okay? Give me, say… six hours. If his condition hasn't improved, he's all yours. Deal?"

"At the rate he's deteriorated in the past fifteen minutes, he'll be dead in six hours, or less. A *lot* less."

"All right, give me three."

"This isn't a damned game, Zarijan!"

"I know. Trust me on this."

"Do I have a choice?"

"Not really. Now, are you coming?"

He looked at the other occupied cubicle and answered, "Mm, no. While I'm in here, I might as well check on the other one." *And get the belated introductions over with.*

"When you're finished, how 'bout dinner?"

"And a chat?" He gave the darkened cubicle they had just left a pointed glance.

"Sure. But don't be long." She hit the release and the airlock closed.

He fixed one guard with his gritty-eyed stare, then the other. Both had the sense not to say anything. He shook his head, then blinking back a sudden yawn, he walked down the short corridor of the isolation unit and into the next, brightly lit cubicle.

"Evenin', Chief," Drakin lisped as she looked up from adjusting a sensor lead.

"What are you doing here at this hour? You should have gone off shift—"

"I'm ba-bee sssitting."

"Baby...?" His eyes flicked to the requisite guards, but just like their fellows he'd left behind in the corridor, their expressionless faces were of no help. He then looked down at the bed.

The soldier was awake and staring at him, one fierce eye glittering. The other was swollen shut and surrounded by a very angry bruise that had discolored the entire left side of his puffy, tattooed and scarified face.

"Matooz, diz iz Doctor Amalfitanooz," Drakin said. "Now be a good boy," she gave him a rough pat on his shaggy head, "and sssay hello—"

"CHIKU!" he roared, jerking his head out from under her talons, his fists balling under the restraint web.

Amalfitano instinctively backed up a step as a part of his mind hastily reminded him he was dealing with a paraplegic—*not* quadriplegic.

Startling as the trooper's explosive reaction was, it was more in line with what he expected from a merc. It was, in a strange way, comforting.

He cleared his throat. "Ah... Matoosh, isn't it?"

"I'm paralyzed!"

"Ah, Matoosh... listen to me—"

"CHULH!"

Amalfitano turned to Drakin, eyebrow raised.

"Sssee? Ba-bee sssiting. No one elssse volunteered."

"Gee, I wonder—"

"YOU DID THIS TO ME!" Matoosh bellowed.

Amalfitano winced then asked evenly, "Now why would I do that?"

"I'm A'tuu'shahn!"

"Yes, you are... unfortunately. But I don't see—"

"You're Rimmer!"

"Okay, I'll grant you that, too. So?"

Matoosh tried to jerk one massive arm free; the webbing tightened in response. *"You did this to me!"*

"Don't sssay I didn't warn you," Drakin muttered as she busied herself with the drug cart.

Amalfitano sidled close to her, glanced at their patient, who, he noticed was still glaring malignantly at him with his one good eye and whispered, "How long has he been like this?"

Drakin looked past him to Matoosh and replied in a normal voice: "You mean diz ornery? It comez zo naturally, I sssussspect sssince he waz born. Da midwife probably ssslapped hiz faz inssstead of his butt and he never got over da indignity."

One of the marines made a strangled noise, briefly drawing Matoosh's murderous glare.

Drakin shrugged, adding, "Den again, he iz a butt-ugly Hattoosssin—it would be an eassssy missstake."

"Yeah." Amalfitano turned back to Matoosh to find him staring back at him, the venom in his eye undiminished. "Listen," he began then held up his hand as Matoosh started to open his mouth. *"Just listen, damn you!"*

Matoosh clamped his mouth shut and squinted malevolently at him.

"Much better. Now, while you probably won't believe me, I'm telling you the truth. You suffered massive crush injures to your lower back and legs, but we repaired *everything*. I fully expected some residual, but *temporary*, paralysis, so just calm down, all right? No one here wants to hurt you, I promise—"

"Tah! The promise of a Rimmer!"

Suddenly recalling Fleming's very unflattering description of the trooper, realizing she hadn't been disparaging enough—no way near enough—he replied with obvious exasperation, "No, the promise of your doctor. But if you keep fighting the restraints like that," he added, suddenly more angry than frightened by Matoosh impressive display of upper body strength which was clearly testing the restraints to their limit, "I won't promise anything."

Matoosh hissed, *"Get out!"*

"No."

"Chekq-mat!" When Amalfitano only replied with a baffled stare, he repeated the threat in Standard, *"Then I'll kill you!"*

Amalfitano replied quietly, "Rather difficult under the circumstances, don't you think? Besides, that's not a very grateful reaction. I saved your life—"

"I'd rather be dead than in the hands of Rimmers! To be tortured—"

"Tortured?"

Matoosh's eye narrowed to a menacing slit. "A'tuu'shahn'i know what happens if we are captured by Rimmers. *Don't deny it!*"

"Look, I don't what you've been told, but we don't—"

"I *heard* Sha'ashahn's screams—"

"It isn't what you think—" Amalfitano began, *–Or is it?* He tried again, "Matoosh, no one here is going to hurt you—"

The mercenary spat in his face.

Amalfitano backed up a startled step, then after a moment of mutual scrutiny, pointedly wiped his cheek and said with a calm he didn't feel: "Drakin?"

"Yez?"

"How 'bout you get our young guest some food?"

"Sssure ting."

As she shuffled by him, winking, Amalfitano suddenly had the feeling that he'd just set up the soldier for something very unpleasant. *Not that you don't richly deserve it—*

"Food?"

The Hahtooshan's rage had crumbled into confusion and, Amalfitano realized, overwhelming fear. His smug smile vanished.

Behind the muscle-bound bravado, beneath the grotesque scarification and tattoos was a terrified teenager, no different in reality to the scores of terrified teenagers who'd passed before him during the war. *No different at all, except unlike most of them, you have a name—*

"You mean you're going to poison me!"

"No. I mean I want you to eat." He made a gesture of placing something in his mouth then motioned expansively to Matoosh's body. "A big, strapping boy like you—bet you're hungry."

"I'm paralyzed!"

Amalfitano sighed wearily. *Great. We're back to this again.* "Yes, I know, but only your lower back and legs. Not your stomach." *Or, unfortunately, your mouth.* "And tomorrow morning, bright and early, we'll start you on therapy, all right?"

Matoosh's expression snapped back into total bewilderment. "Therapy...?"

"Exercise. Until then, I want you to stop fighting the restraints," he added as Matoosh's chest and shoulder muscles bunched, "and eat everything Drakin brings you." *And your gods help you if you don't.*

Matoosh shook his head. *"Tuh maztsaeh...."*

"You don't have to understand. You just have to do exactly what I tell you to do, what the nurses tell you, and we'll have you up and walking again in no time." *And the hell outta my sickbay.* "Agreed?"

Matoosh only stared up at him.

Amalfitano grinned. Izraad had the market cornered on mind-stripping, but he was no slouch when it came to confusing the hell out of a Hahtooshan. "Excellent." He started to give him a pat on the arm, but seeing the sudden, homicidal look in the trooper's eye, realizing he should quit while he was ahead, and still had a head, he turned and walked briskly out of the cubicle.

He resisted the temptation to peek in on Corsali.

Instead he strode by the darkened cubicle, by the two guards and into the awaiting airlock.

A moment later the outer door opened and he stepped out and almost ran into Drakin and the covered tray she held in one hand.

They smiled at each other and Amalfitano lifted the cover. One look and he quickly replaced it. "And do something about that... smell, will you?" He wrinkled his nose. "We did what we could in surgery but he still stinks to high heaven."

Her expression brightened. "You mean... a bed bat?"

"Ah... yeah," he replied warily. "I suppose I do—the other one too, when you get the chance."

"Bot?"

"Yeah... both. If you don't mind. And the officer needs his wounds redressed."

She replied with such a toothy grin that he felt a very brief twinge of pity for the luckless soldier, who, unlike the officer, would be awake for what promised to be an arduous if not altogether degrading procedure—then he rationalized to himself that Drakin was the best choice for the job. Few patients would be foolish enough to argue with her, no matter the provocation and even if the soldier was that foolhardy, it wouldn't matter; Drakin had a way of getting done what needed to get done, one way or another. One could say her methods were akin to making sausage: it was best to be ignorant to the actual process otherwise it was hard to appreciate the results.

"Right away!" She hurried into the airlock, her wicked grin, like the Cheshire Cat's, lingering in Amalfitano's mind long after the door had closed.

He gave himself a shake. *Cacchio!*

"Doctor?"

Gods, now what? He pulled his thoughts off the mental image of the soldier being put through a meat grinder and turned to the familiar voice.

Meerut rose from the console. "I don't know what you and the Lieutenant are up to, but it's working."

"Working?"

"On Khusaaq."

He scowled at her. *Don't you start—*

"Cardiac output, blood pressure, respiratory rate and—"

"Lemme see." He stalked over to the console.

"There, see?" She pointed to a monitor. "So, does the lieutenant have those three hours?"

He squinted at the readings. Hate as he did to admit it, there was a noticeable, albeit very small, improvement across the board. It was too early to say it was significant, but at least it was a change, and for once in the right direction. "Yeah, suppose so. Meanwhile, I want every diagnostic test in the book run on him." He started for his office, tossing over his shoulder as he reached the doorway, "And I want the results yesterday!"

He walked over to his desk and sat down, then stared, bleary-eyed at a new pile of flimsies that had appeared on his desk during his brief absence. *I swear these things breed when no one's looking.*

As he made a feeble effort at putting some order into the untidy mound, a metallic flash caught his eye. He carefully shoved the fresh stack of flimsies aside and his eyes widened as they fell on an ornate and enormous dagger. "What the hell?"

He carefully picked it up and using his elbow, tapped his desk-com. "Meerut?"

Pierson's voice responded, *"She's in with the Hahtooshan officer, Chief, something about stat lab—"*

"Then *you* get the hell in here."

A moment later the medtech appeared in the doorway. "Chief?"

Amalfitano held up the dagger. "Maybe you can tell me what this is, and what the hell it's doing on my desk?"

"Drakin's idea of a toothpick?"

Amalfitano's face puckered into a weary frown. "Not in the mood, Rafe."

"Sorry, Chief. Truth is the de-con crew found it while cleaning one of the triage bays—"

"Not exactly standard issue triage equipment," Amalfitano grumbled as he eyed the knife.

"Belongs to the merc officer, sir. It was mixed in with what Drakin left of his uniform. Lieutenant Perou took the uniform, said he wanted to run tests on it, but the de-con crew weren't sure what to do with that. Or *that.*" He jerked his chin to a nearby chair. Draped over it was a wide, grubby brown strap covered with colorful medallions and, Amalfitano noted, sporting an empty scabbard.

"So they thought I'd want them, what, as trophies?"

Pierson smiled. "Nossir. Security's been notified to come collect 'em, but—"

"But?"

"The Hahtooshan medic—"

"You mean quack."

Pierson smiled thinly. "Yessir, the *quack,* well… Chief, she's been creating quite a ruckus, claiming we haven't provided adequate medical care guaranteed by treaty and—"

"What treaty? We don't have any treaties with the Hahtooshans."

"I dunno, Chief, I'm just telling you what—"

"Never mind. They're safe here for the time being—but remind Security to come collect them. Go back to whatever you were doing." Amalfitano looked back at the weapon and made a face. The intricately carved, glossy black grip had an odd, sticky feel to it and he handled it gingerly. *I wonder how many people you've killed with—*

"And what, pray tell, do you have there?" Izraad asked as she and the departing Pierson slipped around each other in the doorway.

Amalfitano held up the dagger and as he did so, he turned it slightly. The overhead lights washed over the flat of the blade, revealing convoluted designs etched into its surface of sinuous, entwined bodies capped by anthropomorphic faces with spiral horns, curled snouts, and long, fanged mouths with protruding tongues.

As his eyes followed the intricate pattern, the monstrous beings suddenly appeared to move, to *slither* across the blade, into its blood channel, as if trying to flee from the light—or his curious gaze. *What the hell...*

He blinked and looked again. He wasn't sure, but the swirling pattern did appear slightly different than before. *Light must be playing tricks on my eyes—or more likely I'm just that damned tired.* He cleared his throat. "Rafe tells me it belongs to the officer—"

"Khusaaq."

He squinted up at her. "Stop doing that."

"Doing what?"

"You know damned well what." Using the dagger, he motioned angrily in the general direction of the isolation unit. "He's not some stray puppy. He's a goddamned yowie—"

"With a name. And that name is Khusaaq. Would you prefer I refer to him as 'that goddamned yowie'?"

"As a matter of fact, yeah—'cuz he is. And while you're at it, stop encouraging my staff to—"

"Humanize him?"

"Yeah."

"Well, I won't. He is, after all, human. So live with it."

He scowled at her.

"Now, about that," she pointed to the knife. "May I?" She held out her hands.

He carefully placed it across her open palms, then without consciously realizing it, roughly wiped his own hands on his chest. "Seems sort of... well, anachronistic, doesn't it? I mean, these guys are the galaxy's high tech hit men—and they carry daggers?"

Izraad visibly grimaced as she wrapped her fingers loosely around the grip. "Has a creepy feel to it."

"Gee, I wonder why?"

"No, I mean... oh, never mind. But back to your question. From what Sirin's told me, only the Elkanaghallis carry these."

"The... *what?*"

"The Elkanaghallis—Khusaaq's clan, or caste. And its purpose, I suspect, is more ceremonial than functional—a modern day *adh-dhame* or *athamé* I suppose one could say."

"One could, if one knew what the hell you're talking about."

She chuckled softly. "What I mean is that it's a ritual dagger—not something used in everyday life." She gently placed the knife on his desk, then making a face, absently wiped her fingers down her thighs as she asked casually, "And speaking of, how's he doing?"

"I was wondering when you'd get around to gloating."

"Me? Gloat?"

"Don't play innocent with me, Zarijan. Meerut's already told you."

She sat on the corner of his desk. "Okay, a little gloating. So, do I have the whole three hours?"

"I'm sure Meerut answered that, too. Now, before you buy me dinner—" He clapped his hand over his mouth as he yawned.

"Maybe you should skip dinner and go straight to bed."

"Gonna join me?" he asked hopefully.

"I wish."

"Yeah, not sure I'm... well, up to it right now anyway." He straightened up in his chair and cleared his throat. "Now, how 'bout an explanation for this so far miraculous turn-around."

She folded her hands together and fixed her eyes on the age-worn bandoleer.

It was not like her to be coy and he prompted warily, "Zarijan?"

"As you know," she began, still not looking at him, "the technique of mind-stripping, while using little physical force, is still perceived as a profound violation of the subject's image of 'self'."

"I understand that—"

"And the intensity of the reaction to this violation, this... defilement," she continued, "depends upon the strength of the subject's ego-construct. No one comes out of a stripping without some feelings of humiliation, but most rationalize that they were not to blame, that they were helpless to stop it. Some even go so far as to deny it ever happened—"

"Are you trying to tell me that mercs have a psychological glass jaw?"

"No." She took a deep breath then turned to face him. "What I'm trying to tell you is that he's an Elkanaghalli, a Hahtooshan religious caste, and the Elkanaghallis are, for lack of a better term, monks."

He laughed, "What?"

"Sirin said he told her that the Elkanaghallis believe they are the image of perfection and as such take a vow of physical and mental *purity*. If either of those is violated, their entire self-image, their ego-construct, shatters."

His laughter died on his lips as the full ramifications of her remarks hit home. He dropped his no longer amused gaze back to the dagger and managed a tight, "Oh."

"Sirin was somehow able to establish a rapport with him while on the planet by seeing him for *who* he is, not *what* he is. From everything she's told me, and clearly from the actions he took on the planet, he doesn't exactly fit our entrenched image of the stereotypical Hahtooshan killing machine, maybe none of them do."

He gave her a very dubious look. "Remind me to introduce you to Matoosh—"

"This isn't a case of Stockholm syndrome, William. It was never a hostage situation. He made it clear from the get-go that as far as he was concerned, he rescued them and treated them accordingly—"

"But Sirin—"

"Was she raped?"

"No—"

"Did you find any evidence that she was in any way physically abused? Or that Robert or Gianakis were abused?"

"No, but that doesn't mean she wouldn't have felt constantly threatened. Have you seen the size of those troopers? They're *huge*. Even the officer's damned imposing. She also couldn't have failed to realize that he was the key to her survival and—"

"True, but in talking with her earlier, I didn't sense anything but genuine concern for his welfare. Which is why I agreed when she asked if she could see him. It was as much for her sake as his."

"Even so—"

"Even you've admitted that Robert and Gianakis would have died if it hadn't been for their doctor's intervention—to the detriment of the Hahtooshans, I might add."

He arched a brow. "I don't follow."

"Sirin told me that Suhjai kept them alive by using what few medical supplies she had left, in the process denying much needed care to her fellow Hahtooshans."

He chewed on what she'd said for a moment and realized he found it just as hard to think of Hahtooshans as humane as it is to think of them as human. *Maybe even harder.* "Yeah, but—"

"And he trusted her enough to tell her what I've just told you."

"Assuming it's the truth."

"It is. Before the mind-strip, I could tell he was desperately trying to hide something—no, not hide, *protect* something." She hugged herself tightly. "I've never encountered such terror, such... *pain.*"

Amalfitano couldn't help but wince as he too recalled the agony of Khusaaq's screams. "If we'd known, if he'd just told us—"

"We would have gone ahead anyway," she countered with unexpected harshness. "We *had* to know. We couldn't take the risk that he was lying to us."

"Yeah... I suppose so."

"And... and something else. I... I felt the presence of something—no, some*one* during the mind-strip."

"Someone—you mean someone other than him?"

"I can't explain it—the best I can do is describe it as feeling as if someone was standing nearby, hidden in the shadows, watching—not interfering, not reacting, just... *watching.*" She visibly suppressed a shiver. "I've never experienced anything like that during a mind-strip—really, *really* creepy." She licked her lips, met his gaze. "They may be human, William, but there's a lot about them that is truly alien—surprisingly so. So it's possible what I was sensing was part of his conscious mind, still fully aware."

"I didn't think that was possible."

"Neither did I—but if true, if they can compartmentalize their consciousness, it might add to why he had such an alarming response to the mind-strip. It would be akin to waking up in the midst of surgery but being unable to let anyone know. He's also suffering from long-standing and quite profound psychological trauma—I could sense it even before the stripping. There's this... this unceasing sense of grief, of rage and remorse over—"

"He butchers innocent people for a living! I'd be surprised if—"

"That's part of it, certainly, but Hahtooshans would've had to find some way to come to terms with the brutal reality of their chosen profession, accept it, even embrace it, otherwise it could have serious ramifications for their society as a whole, eating away at it from the inside. They've held this specialized niche, as the Rim's mercenaries of preference, for thousands of years, and that wouldn't be possible if they all suffered from crippling self-doubt and guilt over what they do. No..." she shook her head. "It's more than that. Something, I sense, specific to him, something he's had to hide from his fellow Hahtooshans." She hugged herself, then got up, walked over to the chair and picked up the bandoleer.

He eyed her as she studied it, studied the medallions, then he eyed the dagger, not sure what to say. It was obvious the mind-strip had had a profound effect on her, but he knew better than to press the issue. If she wanted to talk, she'd talk. After an awkward moment he switched back to Corsali. "So, because of this rapport, you surmised that she might be able to reach him?"

She draped the bandoleer back over the chair then turned to face him. "I felt we had nothing to lose and she was willing to try."

"Then you weren't absolutely sure."

"Nope."

"Well, you certainly had me fooled, and it, in combination with the stimulator, does look like it's working."

"So far."

"Our Sirin, spit and polish, never crack a smile, always has the answers Ensign Corsali... and a merc."

"And not just any merc, but—"

"A merc monk."

Izraad giggled. "Yup."

"And a psychologically maladjusted merc monk to boot." Amalfitano made a face. "Either I'm getting old, or this universe is getting stranger and stranger."

"I'd say both."

He fixed her with a wounded stare. Point made, he asked, "What if he dies? That's still a distinct possibility—in fact more like a high probability."

"You mean how will Sirin react?"

"Yeah. I mean, we've put her in a position where she'll feel responsible—"

"Don't underestimate her, William. Or him for that matter."

He dropped his gaze to the dagger. The mirror smooth surface of the blade was now utterly devoid of any decoration. *Cazzo. I definitely need some sleep.* He reluctantly picked it up with two fingers, opened the top drawer and dropped it on top of a stack of papers, "I don't know about you, but this thing gives me the heebie-jeebies."

Chapter 18

Amalfitano, fresh from a shower and five hours of blissfully uninterrupted sleep, slipped onto his office chair, then, as he let out a long, almost satisfied sigh, he happened to notice the bandoleer, which had been draped over the nearby chair, was gone. '*Bout damned time they came and collected that stuff.* But in the bandoleer's place was a fresh pile of flimsies. *Cacchio...*

"I can save you some time."

He looked up.

A not-so-fresh looking Fleming stepped into his office, continuing, "The commander's awake and demanding to see you, we just got Gianakis' latest culture results back and Matoosh is refusing to eat."

"And the officer?"

"You mean Khusaaq?"

"Why does everyone insist I call him by name? Or call any of them by name? I don't want to know their goddamned names! I don't want to know anything more about them than I already know, *damn it!*" He slammed both fists on his desk for emphasis.

Fleming chuckled, "Good try. You're just as intensely curious about them as the rest of us."

"No, I'm *not.*"

"Yes, you *are.*"

He scowled at her.

She shrugged, unfazed. "Okay, if you insist, the merc's showing substantial improvement."

"How substantial—*wait.*" He pushed himself away from the desk. "If you don't mind, I think I'll go see for myself."

She grinned. "Told you so."

He glared at her, adding, "And I want to see those culture results, too!" He stalked past her, out of his office and into the main sickbay.

Rosen looked up from her console. "Doctor, Commander Aquila is asking—"

"In a damned minute!" He continued on, into the isolation unit and over to the airlock. He tapped the release, then, as he stepped inside, he heard Meerut's voice from behind him say, "Hold!"

He grabbed the lock door, held it open for her as she stepped in beside him. He looked down at the covered tray she held. "I smell poached eggs and toast." He let go of the door, lifted the cover and scowled at her. "I don't care if the soldier is refusing to eat—he eats bland liquids only or he doesn't eat, period."

"This isn't for Matoosh." The inner door opened and she stepped out. "It's for Sirin."

"Sirin...?" He followed her, past two new stony-faced guards two stood on either side of the first cubicle's doorway, one of whom replied to his questioning stare with a weary, 'Don't blame us' shrug, and into the cubicle itself. Corsali was sound asleep in the fold-down chair beside the bed, her fingers curled around the Hahtooshan's wrist, her head pillowed on a folded blanket next to his bruised, blistered and heavily tattooed shoulder.

Amalfitano sidled over to Meerut and whispered, "Has she been here all night?"

"We didn't think you'd mind," she replied in kind, "and her presence has certainly had a positive effect."

"Yeah, Jenna told me." He reached for the tray. "May I?"

She placed it in his hands. "Softie."

He shrugged, then, as she left and he started to set the tray on the bedside table, he noticed a portable data reader and two discs spread across its surface.

He nudged them aside, set the tray down, then picked up the reader and its tiny screen brightened in response to his touch. He looked at the display: it contained information on Tuli.

He grinned then murmured, *"Sirin?"*

Instantly awake, she lifted her head and looked at Khusaaq's face. Then, realizing the voice had come from behind her, she glanced over her shoulder. "Oh... Doctor."

He motioned to the tray. "How 'bout some breakfast?"

"Breakfast?"

"It's a little past oh-six hundred."

She immediately straightened up in her chair then clearing her throat, tugged her sickbay robe more tightly around her.

"How's he doing?" he asked as he gave the bank of monitors a quick study.

"I... I was hoping you'd tell me, sir."

"The med-comps can tell me a lot, but," he smiled as he noticed she was still holding his patient's wrist, "but basic hands-on, so to speak...."

She lifted her gaze as she self-consciously released her hold.

"...can be even more important."

"Well, he did move his fingers a couple times during the night. And once, while I was helping Drakin..." She abruptly looked away.

He raised his brows as he realized her cheeks had darkened. Helping Drakin do what? With Drakin the choices were limitless—

"Uh... well, clean him up a bit... he mumbled something."

Likely telling the two of you to fuck off. He stepped closer to the bed, recalling his earlier order about bed baths; his patient did look cleaner—and he certainly smelled better. A whole helluva lot better. Gone was the sickly sweet, telltale stink of advanced radiation poisoning, replaced by the astringent odor of burn salve and antiseptic.

"Those are good signs." He pinched the skin just under Khusaaq's right collarbone and nodded as he saw his right wrist arch against the webbing in response. "Very good signs indeed." He slowly walked around to the far side of the bed as he gave his patient a complete head to toe visual exam.

Stopping at the head of the bed, he again pinched the skin, this time just below Khusaaq's left collarbone and smiled as he got the same response from his left wrist. "He's coming out of it." *Whatever it is.* "Thanks in large part to you, Ensign."

Instead of greeting the news with relief, she asked, "What's going to happen to him? Assuming he does recover?"

"I don't know." *Not quite a lie,* he assured himself. *I'm not sure, although I can make a pretty good guess.* He turned Khusaaq's head then gently detached the stimulator from the base of his skull, in the process noticing that they'd even managed to wash his filthy hair. "I think we can get rid of this, let him wake up at his own pace." He placed it on the drug cart.

She nodded, then leaned forward and, using her crooked forefinger, lightly stroked his elaborately scarified, salve-greasy cheek. "Maybe this is a terrible mistake."

"Mistake?"

"Trying to bring him back."

Amalfitano felt his chest muscles tighten.

"May I stay a while longer?" She lifted her gaze. Her eyes were glittering.

He pretended not to notice as he gathered up the stimulator. "I suppose so, but not all day, okay? You need your rest, too. And eat your breakfast before it gets cold." He gave her shoulder a light squeeze and quietly withdrew.

Once inside the airlock, cut off from her questions as well as the demands of sickbay, he rubbed his suddenly pounding forehead as he tried to reconcile his long held hatred for anything Hahtooshan and the look in Corsali's eyes when she looked at... *Khusaaq.*

He found he couldn't. He hadn't even come fully to grips with the knowledge that Hahtooshans were human, not alien. *If we were so wrong about that...*

He squeezed his eyes shut, hoping to stop that line of thinking in its tracks.

It worked, only because it prodded loose another.

And what if I'm wrong about the virus? What if it's something else entirely? Something obvious, something I overlooked... again?

The answer was immediate: *Then millions of people will die.*

The outer doors hissed open and he pushed himself away from the wall.

Fleming rose wearily from the unit's central console as he stepped out of the airlock and greeted him with a broad, albeit tired smile. Seeing the look on his face, that smile faded to a concerned stare. "You all right?"

"Ever question why you ever became a doctor?"

She ran her fingers through her mane of fiery red hair and replied, "Every time I walk into Matoosh's cubicle, why?"

He shook his head, muttered, "Never mind," then noticed she was holding a couple of flimsies. "What do you have there?"

"The latest path reports on Gianakis—"

"Thanks," he grumbled as he traded them for the stimulator.

"I've adjusted the protocol accordingly." She placed the stimulator on the console.

He nodded distractedly and handed the flimsies back to her, unread.

"The commander's asking to see you."

He nodded again and walked away.

— ii —

"Heard you were up."

Aquila looked up to find Amalfitano standing in the doorway of the private sickbay cubicle. "Will!"

"Didn't know you had company, though," Amalfitano said with a nod to Izraad, who stood at the foot of Aquila's bunk, and Teague, who was wearing a robe and pajamas and seated on a fold-down chair.

"Just updating the commander on everything that's happened," Izraad replied.

Aquila grinned. "Seems I missed all the excitement."

Amalfitano answered with a lackluster, "Lucky you."

"Pull down a chair. I wanna hear everything."

Amalfitano instead remained where he was, shoulder braced against the door frame. "Can you be a little more specific?"

"Well, for starters, how's Khusaaq? Any improvement?"

He sighed and rubbed the back of his neck. "I just looked in on him, and he's showing some improvement. I'll have a better idea as to whether any permanent damage was done later today or more likely tomorrow, once he wakes up."

Aquila leaned back into his pillow. "He's a very interesting individual, we could learn a lot from him."

"I thought we already did," Amalfitano growled.

Aquila knew that tone of voice. It did not bode well. Amalfitano had a well-documented tendency to become overly protective of his patients… *but a merc?* "Will," he began, "Ensign Lesedi did the right thing under the circumstances. Corsali was right—he told me, told us that he rescued us in hopes we could help him stop the release of this weapon, so if I'd been able to question him, we might have been spared this, but I *wasn't*. Lesedi made a command decision—"

"I understand that—I agreed to it, remember? I was *there*. But what if what he told us is wrong?"

"That's impossible," Izraad replied. "A subject under mind-strip is incapable of lying. Hide a critical truth, as he did, yes, but not lie when asked a specific question—"

"I don't mean that," he interrupted with an impatient wave of his hand. "He said he was never told *which* planet was the target; he just suspected this captain of his would target Tuli. There're at least five other human-inhabited planets within this sector. What if it's one of them instead?"

Aquila began, "Will—"

"And what about the plague itself? Maybe it isn't a filovirus. Maybe it *is* an *orthomyxoviridae* or even something we've never heard of—what if we've got the wrong goddamned planet and the wrong goddamned bug? Then what? There are a hell've a lot of 'what ifs' here, too many lives at stake if any one of our assumptions is wrong—"

"What do you want me to say?" Aquila interrupted, exasperated. "I don't know what we'll do. Ensign Lesedi's fully apprised HQ of the situation and standard procedure would require them to alert every planet within the Hahtooshans' potential target area—including the non-aligned worlds. The entire sector should now be on full alert. If they try for any other planet, they'll find themselves running up against a prepared defense."

Amalfitano scowled at him. "And Tuli?"

Aquila massaged his temple. *You sure can be a pain in the butt at times, you know that?* "That's why I agree with Khusaaq. It has a large, mostly human population, and it's a well-known fact that Tuli's unarmed. It feeds anyone who comes asking, whether they can pay or not, it needs no defense—"

"Except against a madman," Teague muttered, drawing everyone's gaze.

Aquila nodded, "Yeah," and looked back at Amalfitano. "We're doing everything we can to stop them—"

"And if we can't?"

"Then we can't," Aquila replied testily. "It's as brutally simple as that." *Satisfied?*

Amalfitano abruptly fixed his heated gaze on his feet.

After a prolonged and uncomfortable silence, he lifted his hooded gaze and said, "You're right," but his tone was far from convincing. "Sorry I blew up."

"Forget it."

Amalfitano glanced over his shoulder. "Best go make rounds. Got people to discharge."

"Ah, how about me?" Aquila asked hopefully.

"Let's see how you do today, okay?"

"But I feel—"

"No buts. You've been through a hell of a lot, and I'm not going to discharge you until I'm convinced you're sufficiently recovered."

"You really can be a *pain* in the butt, you know that?"

"So can you." With that, Amalfitano strode out of the room.

Aquila sighed then turned to Izraad. "He's going to hold himself solely responsible if the worst happens, isn't he?"

She nodded. "'Fraid so."

Chapter 19

Lesedi sat down on the edge of her bunk and let out a long, exhausted sigh as she debated whether to order up a bite to eat or take advantage of every minute to catch up on her sleep. She'd need it. In less than fifteen hours they'd reach Tuli.

Realizing she wasn't in the slightest bit hungry, she sprawled back on the bunk, closed her eyes and tried to relax while painfully aware that she wasn't the least bit sleepy, either. *Too damned bone-tired to be sleepy—*

"Ensign?" the swing shift com-op's voice boomed unexpectedly from the bedside com unit's small speaker, startling her.

She sat bolt upright and hit the com-toggle. "Yes, what is it?"

"Doctor Amalfitano asks that you please report to his office, sir."

Her brain swiveled on its hinges, rapidly shifting from heart-thumping alarm over what new disaster might have befallen them in the brief time since she'd left the bridge, to what Amalfitano could possibly want to tell her... in person.

A cold knot of dread formed in her belly. *Can't be good news.* "What's up?"

"Don't know, sir," Masursky replied. *"He just said to report to his office immediately."*

The cold knot cinched tight as she lurched to her feet. "On my way." She cut the link, muttered, "Whatcha bet it's about that goddamned merc," as she ran her fingers through her close-cropped curly black hair. She glanced down at her wrinkled command blues. "Hardly presentable, but it'll have to do." With a tug here and a yank there, she started for the door.

— ii —

Amalfitano managed a tired laugh at Teague's equally tired joke, rocked back in his chair and smiled. It was almost like old times. *Almost.* Aquila was seated in his customary spot, to the left of Amalfitano's desk. Izraad was seated to Amalfitano's right, and beside her, Teague, but between them was an empty chair. *Gildun's chair.*

Amalfitano's smile faded, then, sensing he was being watched, turned to the doorway of his private office. "Ife." He rose from his chair and motioned to her. "Please, come in."

Lesedi, clearly surprised by the gathering, stepped into the room, nodded to each officer in turn then looked expectantly at Amalfitano. "You wished to see me, sir?"

"Not me. *Him.*" He jerked his chin towards Aquila.

Lesedi turned her apprehensive gaze to the officer. "Sir?"

Aquila patted the arm of the empty chair beside him. "Please, Ensign, take a seat."

She sat and clasped her hands in her lap.

"There's no need to look like you're headed for your own execution, Ensign," Aquila added.

"Yessir," she replied with little enthusiasm.

"From what I've been told," he continued, "you've done a remarkable job as captain. Doctor Amalfitano, Lieutenant Izraad and the command crew have placed depositions on record stating that…"

Amalfitano felt a twinge of sympathy. Lesedi's apprehensive stare spoke volumes: *Here it comes.*

"…and I intend on making sure HQ is aware of just how important your actions have been in safeguarding Coalition interests against a very devastating external threat."

Lesedi smiled, briefly, and answered with a clipped, "Thank you, sir."

"That's why I hate to say what I'm about to say. It's like I'm kicking your legs out from under you after giving you a pat on the back."

"Sir…?"

Amalfitano watched Aquila with a very critical eye as the man rose stiffly from his chair. *I sure hope this isn't a mistake—*

"I'm resuming command. As of now."

Lesedi blinked then blinked again. "Sir?"

"Will's given the go ahead." He gave the doctor a quick, sidelong glance.

Amalfitano nodded, albeit reluctantly. *Like I had a damned choice—it was that or put up with you badgering me every five seconds.*

"I've recovered enough to take back command of the *Baidarka*. I hope you understand just how important this is to me—it has nothing to do with your competence. It's just that...." his voice trailed off as he realized Lesedi was grinning. He looked sharply at Amalfitano to find the doctor grinning as well. "Did I say something funny?"

"I think what you see there," Amalfitano winked at Lesedi, "is the look of total relief. Am I right, Ensign?"

"Yes, sir!"

Aquila turned back to her. "But... I thought you'd, well..."

"Sir," she began, stopped, and started again, "Sir, I understand and really appreciate your concern, but you see, I never felt as though this was my command—I knew that when I took over. Must admit, I did find the experience a challenge, but believe me, I *am* relieved, in more ways than one."

Aquila gave her shoulder a squeeze. "You're one hell of a fine officer, Ife. You deserve a ship of your own and I intend on telling HQ that, even though that would mean the *Baidarka* would lose the best weapons officer in the fleet."

Lesedi's tawny cheeks darkened to a deep, rosy brown. "Thank you, sir. But for right now, I'm perfectly happy where I am—"

Amalfitano cleared his throat. "Ah, if you two don't mind me breaking up this mutual admiration get-together, I believe dinner should be ready just about now." He rose, turned to the doorway. "Ah, yes, here come the appetizers."

"Dinner?" Lesedi asked.

"Yeah," he replied, "I felt Robert here deserved a welcome back dinner, hope you don't mind?"

"Oh, not at all, sir." She started to push herself out of the chair.

"Where the hell do you think you're going?" Amalfitano asked, arms akimbo.

"Ah, back to my cabin, sir?"

"Not sticking around for the celebration?"

"Ah, well, I didn't realize I was invited—"

"Sit your butt down!" Amalfitano snapped, pointing to the chair.

Lesedi resumed her seat.

"Always said," Aquila replied with a wink at Izraad, "Will here knows how to speak to a lady."

Amalfitano shot him a piercing look as Pierson entered, carrying a large, heavily laden tray.

The medtech placed the tray on the desk, unloaded a plate of appetizers, a bottle and five glasses, then with a sidelong look and a nod at Amalfitano, withdrew.

"Those look good," Aquila grinned as he reached for an appetizer.

"Yeah, they're a little something Drakin whipped up," Amalfitano answered nonchalantly. "Some sort of traditional Eltannian dish. Her way of saying welcome back—"

"Drakin, huh?" Aquila replied and hungrily stuffed the hors d'oeuvre in his mouth, but as he began chewing, he happened to notice Izraad's expression. "Something wrong?" he muffled.

"It's just good to see you've regained your appetite, sir."

"Never lost it, despite Will's best efforts."

Izraad looked at Amalfitano. "I had no idea Drakin was into haute cuisine."

"She's a woman of many talons," he grinned.

The intelligence officer winced.

"Well," Aquila replied as he grabbed another, "tell her for me these are real tasty." He devoured the snack in two bites. "Interesting taste… can't quite place it."

Izraad gave the tray a pointed look then whispered to Amalfitano, "Have you checked the whereabouts of Matoosh lately?"

He bit his lip against a snort, remembering his analogy to sausage then concealed his reaction by pretending as if he'd almost sneezed. "Come to think of it, nope." He picked up the tray and held it in front of her. "Care for one?"

"Thanks. I'll pass."

Amalfitano shrugged, offered it next to Lesedi, who also declined then, as he placed the tray back on his desk, Aquila grabbed another appetizer. "I'd take it easy on those, Robert."

"But these are the first tasty things I've had to eat in over a week!"

"Exactly."

Aquila pointedly shoved it in his mouth.

Amalfitano sighed, "Be it on your own stomach lining then."

Aquila took two more. Teague managed to grab the next to last one from the tray before Aquila's hand was back again.

Amalfitano picked up the bottle and a glass. "How 'bout something to wash them down with?"

Aquila, cheeks bulging, nodded eagerly. It was a poorly-kept secret that Amalfitano kept a private and rather large stash of vintage liquor and was willing, on special occasions, to share, and share quite generously.

"Sparkling water," he added and Aquila's keen expression vanished as Amalfitano handed him the glass. Moving on, he filled the others' glasses then sloshed some into his own.

He turned to Aquila and held up his glass. "To Commander Aquila."

"To Commander Aquila," the others echoed.

"To Ensign Lesedi, Doctor Amalfitano, Lieutenant Izraad and the crew of the *Baidarka*," Aquila countered, then, holding up his glass added with a private smile, *"Prosit."*

Amalfitano arched his brow in begging curiosity, but before Aquila could explain, Teague said, "Hear, hear," touching his glass to Lesedi's.

"And to those we left behind," Izraad murmured as she tapped her glass against Amalfitano's.

"Yeah," Aquila agreed softly and gave his side an absent rub.

Amalfitano gave him another critical once over as he questioned for the hundredth time his decision to accede to Aquila's unrelenting demands to be declared medically fit to resume command.

The man looked awful. His face was puffy and piebald with bruises and peeling skin, his sickbay jumpsuit-clad torso was abnormally bulky with dressings and by his constant fidgeting sitting upright was clearly uncomfortable. But Aquila also looked like the proverbial cat that had just eaten the canary—or, in this case, all but one of the appetizers.

Amalfitano shook his head and turned his attention on the doorway. "Looks like dinner's been held up."

"Maybe the galley assumed we'd take longer with the hors d'oeuvres?" Izraad replied with a sidelong look at Aquila.

Unfazed, Aquila turned to Amalfitano. "Gives us a few minutes, and I've been wanting to ask you—Zarijan tells me the Hahtooshans are, without a doubt, human?"

Amalfitano hesitated; he hadn't planned on revealing the full truth until he was one hundred percent positive. *I guess ninety-nine percent is good enough—it'll have to be good enough.* He smiled, a small smile. "They've been highly specialized through aggressive bio-engineering, but yup, they're still one hundred percent human."

"How's that possible?" Aquila interrupted as he repositioned himself in his chair.

Before Amalfitano could answer, he happened to catch Izraad's odd look. She knew something was up, she just wasn't sure what that something was. *You will soon enough—but I'm gonna enjoy myself, first.* "You mean how's it possible that they're human?"

Aquila nodded as he sipped at his water.

"All I know is that sequencing from the globin gene clusters prove what the scanners and our eyes were telling us from the start." He paused, took a gulp of water then flicked Izraad a sidelong look as he swallowed. "But there's more to it, *a lot more.* Xosé's still in the process of running a complete DNA analysis on each of the ten Hahtooshans we have on board, but preliminary base sequencing assays on samples taken from each have proven to be extremely interesting—not to mention wholly unexpected."

"More unexpected than proving they're human?" Teague asked sourly.

"Yeah... you could say that, Edwin."

Aquila raised his brows while Teague and Lesedi exchanged unhappy glances. Izraad just looked increasingly worried.

Amalfitano steepled his hands and began, "Excluding seven, the female..."

"Suhjai," Aquila grumbled and took another sip to wash away the distaste.

"...and six of the soldiers, the remaining three are genetically very closely related."

"Siblings?" Izraad asked.

"Essentially yes, but clearly their genetic interrelationships are far more complex than ours."

"The family that slays together stays together?"

Amalfitano pointedly ignored Aquila's muttered remark. "For example, Khusaaq and Matoosh are genetically almost indistinguishable, except that Khusaaq's seven standard years older than Matoosh, and one of the soldiers... one of the guards told me his name is *Gienah?* He's also very close, genetically, although not as close as Matoosh, and he's even younger—and something else. Even with the slight variations, and admittedly, based on the very small sample we have of the Hahtooshan population, I think it's highly likely that they're all descended from an exceedingly small number of individuals."

Aquila squinted at him. "And?"

"And there's only a minor diminution of the genetic 'message', for lack of a better term, in their mitochondrial DNA."

"So?" Aquila prompted.

"So, what I'm saying is that they're of human stock, we've established that beyond a doubt—"

"Got that," Aquila nodded impatiently. *"And?"*

"And they have an extremely small gene pool with surprisingly few recessives—"

"Meaning they're all kissing cousins without the idiot factor," Aquila interrupted before taking a deep gulp of water.

Amalfitano sighed, "Not exactly." He took a sip from his glass. "Although it does make them rather... well, fragile—"

"Fragile?" Aquila repeated with a snort of disbelief. "Have you taken a good look at those troopers? Even Khusaaq—"

"Not fragile to look at," Amalfitano replied irritably, "or physically, no—quite the contrary. One could reasonably describe them as physically very robust—and many have, just without realizing it." He grinned and took another sip from his glass.

Izraad and Aquila looked at each other then back at Amalfitano, sensing the last remark was clearly his idea of a private joke.

"I'm speaking strictly on a chromosomal level," he continued. "Which is bad news for them, and probably sooner rather than later as the number of alleles at each locus shrinks. But, as I was about to say, most importantly, while there's obvious evidence of genetic tinkering, tinkering that's effected things like their heightened acuity of the senses, their physical strength and the density of their bones and their truly astonishing ability to heal from injury, their mitochondrial DNA is, essentially, untouched."

"I don't mean to sound like an idiot myself," Teague said with just a hint of annoyance, "but so?"

"So mitochondrial DNA undergoes natural mutation much more rapidly than the DNA that's found in the chromosomes. And there's only the teensiest difference between their mitochondrial DNA and—"

"So," Aquila interrupted impatiently, "by cross referencing the mitochondrial 'drift', it would be possible to determine how long they've been isolated from the rest of humanity."

"Yeah, you could say that," Amalfitano said, then smiled in a way that left Aquila with the distinct feeling that it wasn't that way at all.

"And when you say isolated," Teague said, "what you mean is taken from Earth."

Amalfitano nodded. "And here's where it gets truly interesting. We did just that, date by the degree of mutation—"

"Get to the point," Aquila said as he shifted again in his chair, clearly uncomfortable and now more than a bit annoyed.

"Okay, here it is. Khusaaq and the two closely related to him? Their ancestors were taken from Earth three hundred and seventy thousand years ago, give or take a few thousand years. Two other troopers, the biggest of the lot, two hundred forty-five thousand years ago, or thereabouts, three others, between two hundred and thirty-eight and two hundred thousand, the last soldier, one hundred and eighty-five thousand—"

"And Suhjai?" Aquila asked warily.

"Thirty thousand, tops." Amalfitano paused and looked at each of his dinner companions. He'd just dropped a bombshell, but by the blank looks Aquila, Teague and Lesedi were giving him, clearly only Izraad, with her wide-eyed stare, had heard it go off.

He stared back at her, waiting, watching as she rapidly put the pieces together, just as he, Fleming and Xosé had done only a few hours before, and like them, she was clearly coming to the same startling conclusion.

"So they were all taken from between three hundred and seventy thousand and thirty thousand years ago," she repeated. "You're absolutely sure."

"Within a few thousand years or so, yeah. Ninety-nine percent sure. It's likely that there are far older, let's call them 'take-dates', within the Hahtooshan population, but I'd wager a month's salary that there aren't dates much younger than say…"

"Twenty thousand?" Izraad replied.

Aquila wriggled in his chair as his eyes darted between Izraad and Amalfitano. "Would one of you please enlighten the rest of us as to what the hell's going on?"

Amalfitano smiled and gestured to Izraad. "I think it only fair you do the honors, Zarijan, since you had it right from the start."

She squinted at him. "I don't follow...."

"You said, 'Like it or not, Hahtooshans *are* fully human—'"

"They're just not us," she finished for him.

He nodded. *"Bingo."*

Izraad turned to Aquila. "They're Neanderthals."

Aquila's jaw dropped. Teague's eyes widened, then *his* jaw dropped. Lesedi just stared, mouth agape, her forgotten glass of water held halfway to her lips.

"...which makes them fully human," Izraad continued, "just not... *us."*

Aquila was the first to recover and gasped, "Are... are you sure?" as he turned his wide-eyed, unblinking gaze on Amalfitano.

"Yup. They've been heavily bio-engineered, but the mitochondrial DNA results are conclusive. So it would seem Neanderthals didn't go extinct as a separate species after all, they just went, well... off planet."

"But... but they look just like us!"

"Robert, if I were to put a Neanderthal up against an ancient, but anatomically modern human you'd be hard pressed to notice a major difference; not surprising since most of us carry some Neanderthal genes. There was clearly a lot of cross-breeding going on way back when, and it's pretty conclusive that we, meaning modern humans, didn't hunt Neanderthals to extinction—at least not everywhere—we mated with them and eventually so diluted their genetic makeup they simply ceased being Neanderthals.

"That being said, there are some distinctions—and strangely, those tattoos of theirs work in two seemingly opposing ways, first by concealing just how human they are in physical appearance and then obscuring most of the more obvious outward differences, like the ratio of arm to leg length, the shape of the ribcage and pelvis, the thickness of the browridge, size and shape of the nose and greater sturdiness of the jaw. Xosé was the first to get suspicious, when he was creating a skeletal matrix for Matoosh... something was off, and yet vaguely familiar about the shape of their pelvises and femurs.

"But there are other internal differences, such as their hemoglobin, which carries a dominant allele for higher oxygen saturation or that their liver is a major producer of antibodies. Or larger brain capacity—theirs is larger than ours, by the way, just as ancient Neanderthals' brain capacity was larger, and their skeletons are far more what anthropologists refer to as 'robust', to carry the greater muscle mass, just as their ancestors' skeletons were stockier and for the same reason, which makes them incredibly strong—no genetic enrichment needed in that department, although Xosé says he's found evidence that there was some enhancement done when it comes to recovery time in muscle fatigue, which would give them far greater endurance."

Lesedi and Aquila exchanged startled looks as Amalfitano continued, "Overall they are taller, perhaps a little more elegant for lack of a better word, than their distant ancestors—but then again, we're dealing with highly evolved Neanderthals."

"Or were provided with some evolutionary assistance," Lesedi muttered.

Amalfitano shrugged. "Someone who knows far more than I do about genetic drift among Neanderthals could pin down the dates to less than a century, possibly even a decade or so and pinpoint the exact locations from where their ancestors were taken to within a few kilometers, which could be a boon to paleoanthropologists by providing more data on the true extent of their range—and something else. Khusaaq, Matoosh and the other, genetically related soldier, Gienah? Many of their engineered characteristics are more, well..." he shrugged, "more primitive?"

"Primitive?" Aquila repeated.

"Not as highly specialized?" Amalfitano shook his head. "I can't explain it any better, but my gut tells me Khusaaq and his kin's ancestors were the first, or some of the very first Neanderthals to be successfully bio-engineered. Not only that, but the three are—what did you say his caste was called?" He looked at Izraad.

"Elkanaghalli."

"Yeah, *that*." He motioned to her. "Once their lineage with its desired enhanced characteristics was established it wasn't tinkered with except through natural mutation and drift."

Izraad leaned forward in her chair. "That fits with what Sirin told me Khusaaq told her, that there are nine castes in all, and that the Elkanaghallis are considered... well, *anachronistic* by other Hahtooshans, although—and this is telling, Elkanaghalli in Hahtou means 'the genuine people' or 'the first people'—but she assumed he meant in a purely cultural or refined sense, not physical, or, in this case, chromosomal sense."

"They certainly don't look any different," Lesedi said.

"Actually, they do," Amalfitano replied. "Granted, most of the differences are very superficial, such as the Elkanaghalli wear their hair long, and the tattoo patterns clearly vary from caste to caste—Khusaaq's facial tattoos are by far the most elaborate, and coincidentally, he's the oldest—approximately twenty-six in Earth-years—but unlike the others, his tattoos share the same basic underlying pattern as Matoosh and Gienah.

"And of the others who share the same take-dates, well, they have almost identical facial tattoo patterns, so it's reasonable to speculate that facial tattoo design is a mark of caste affiliation and the complexity, or lack thereof, a sign of relative age. And curiously the tattoo pattern on each Hahtooshan's right arm and leg is very different than those on the left. The design on the right side is sinuous, almost delicate, while that on the left is bolder and far less elaborate, even on Khusaaq. Plus, according to Delatorre, there are slight differences in uniform and personal weaponry, but—"

"Now we know the differences are more than just skin deep," Izraad said.

"Yeah," Amalfitano nodded. "And speaking of uniforms, we also discovered something really fascinating about theirs—"

"And that is?" Aquila prompted.

"It's a pharmacy unto itself—stimulants, painkillers, clotting agents, antimicrobials—even wound fillers, you name it, they've been impregnated into any part that comes into direct contact with their skin, plus, as I witnessed firsthand, it reacts to injuries, like broken bones or internal bleeding by becoming a compression suit. And my best guess is that all of this doesn't have to be under the conscious control of the wearer."

Aquila, Teague, Lesedi and Izraad looked suitably impressed.

"Definitely something our people should look into," Aquila replied.

Amalfitano nodded, "Yeah, my thoughts exactly."

"But sir," Lesedi said, "getting back to the Hahtooshans themselves, the Loop Confederation has detailed records of using them against the Dabih Negus during their High Chankka War, and that was almost four hundred and fifty thousand years ago—in other words, eighty thousand years before your earliest 'take date', which means maybe there are even older lineages?"

Amalfitano crossed his arms. "That's possible, of course. Neanderthals were certainly around that long ago, but Xosé has a theory about that, and it involves those tattoos of theirs. As you know, Xosé fancies himself an authority on the Dabih Negus, has studied 'em for years, even has a decent collection of their artifacts—"

"He's certainly dragged me into some pretty rough areas of Mirfak on the hunt for authentic pieces," Lesedi grumbled, rubbing her jaw for emphasis.

Amalfitano saw heads nodding as those present recalled the unfortunate events leading up to Delatorre leading a squad of marines on a 'rescue' mission when one of Tasende's adventures in the less savory districts of Mirfak turned ugly. Lesedi had accompanied the pathologist, as she often had, reasonably concerned that his single-minded desire to find artifacts to add to his collection more often than not trumped his awareness of his personal safety. With a muscular physique she kept in peak form, Lesedi was a force to be reckoned with and few, once they sized her up, dared to try. This time she was doubly concerned as his plan was to return an object he'd bought only the day before. He'd spent the night studying his prize only to determine that the Negan middle empire stele that had cost him a month's salary was in fact a fake and a rather bad fake at that.

It took a lot to get Tasende angry, but being duped about one of his passions was a sure fire shortcut to his bad side. So, when the less than reputable dealer, not surprisingly, took offense that Tasende knew enough to realize he'd bought a forgery and demanded his money back, and in turn had accused Tasende of trying to pawn off a fake in order to get his money back while keeping the real item, Lesedi was forced to keep the dealer's hooligans at bay until Delatorre and a squad of marines arrived. Her protection had cost her a fair amount of skin, not to mention a dislocated jaw, a few teeth and several cracked ribs. The incident had also forced Captain Vildur to pay the spaceport's irate authorities an official apology and in person, but, by doing so, she spared Tasende a hefty fine and a lengthy ban from setting foot inside the *Baidarka*'s main R and R port.

Tasende, for his part, lost both the fake and his money—adequate punishment according to Vildur—which put only a temporary damper on his passion and his quest for more artifacts.

"You see," Amalfitano continued, "aside from creating an interference pattern that effectively camouflages their exact number and a whole host of other purposes I can only guess at, the tattoos also have a distinctive visual pattern, but you don't see it until you see it in its entirety."

"And that is?" Lesedi asked uneasily.

"Tasende says they look just like extremely archaic circuitry patterns—the really ancient liquid circuitry patterns specifically, in common use by the Dabih Negus thousands of years before the Chankka Wars. Perou agrees."

Aquila leaned back in his chair and crossed his arms. "So?"

"So, those four hundred and fifty thousand year old records Ife mentioned, about the Hahtooshans? Well, Tasende's done some research and it turns out there are other, even older chronicles that claimed Hahtooshans were actually organic machines. Some, like the Thalamians, still believe that's true. Others believed they were a heretofore unidentified and highly advanced alien race, possibly even from outside the Rim, capable of shape-shifting—"

"Among other equally unpleasant surprises," Teague muttered.

"Yeah," Aquila agreed. "Made 'em very popular as mercenaries."

"Which takes us back to Xosé's theory," Amalfitano said.

"Which is?" Teague asked.

"What if whoever or whatever took the ancestors of modern Hahtooshans really were organic machines?"

Aquila raised his brows in begging interest.

"As I said," Amalfitano continued, "mitochondrial analysis is absolutely conclusive, and that's just what we've learned from the individuals we have on board. As I mentioned earlier, it's highly likely others have other 'take dates'."

"So," Aquila picked up the water pitcher and refilled his glass, "you're suggesting that someone or some*thing* came around collecting Neanderthals, or at least Neanderthal genetic material over the space of almost four hundred thousand years?"

"And for what purpose?" Lesedi asked, her eyes darting from Aquila to Amalfitano. "To genetically manipulate them into biological analogs of themselves?"

"Maybe it was nothing more than a hobby," Teague quipped, "like Tasende's collection."

Aquila flicked the man a sidelong squint, clearly annoyed that he was being flippant. "Hell of a long time to maintain an interest in a hobby, don't ya think?"

Teague only shrugged. It was a well-known fact that pride of place in his cabin was held by a very impressive bonsai, a tree he'd carefully tended to since childhood, a gift from his botanist mother, and one with an estimated age of well over three hundred years.

"Maybe they viewed sentient biologicals the same way we view smart machines," Izraad offered.

"Meaning *expendable,*" Aquila replied. "Again, making them the perfect mercenary, and being sentient and self-replicating, they'd be ideal for other pursuits, like multigenerational exploration and first contact with other biologicals—call 'em a 'friendly face' rather than a machine saying 'take me to your leader'."

Lesedi made a face, and not a very friendly one at that, causing Aquila to chuckle.

"Okay," Aquila said, "I grant you that, but the point remains, another biological would likely be perceived as marginally far less threatening than a sentient machine."

Lesedi, clearly unwilling to concede, replied, "Until you realized just what these friendly non-threatening faces were capable of doing."

Teague offered, "And it wasn't like there was anyone around to tell them they couldn't just come harvest Neanderthals any time they wanted and use them for whatever they wanted—rules about collecting unique genetic material, especially from sentient species have never been rigorously enforced, even now despite all members of the Coalition along with a number of non-aligned systems having signed an accord stating exactly that."

"But why Neanderthals?" Lesedi asked. "Why not some other species?"

Amalfitano eyed her, knowing what she was really suggesting and found himself mildly amused that she was actually offended. "You mean, why not *us?*"

She met his gaze squarely, almost defiantly. "Yeah."

"Understand, Ife, Neanderthals were highly specialized and incredibly successful as a species—they were certainly around a lot longer than modern humans have been around and maybe it was that specialization that made them, in the eyes of the beings who collected them, the better choice for their purposes."

"Meaning as mercenaries," Lesedi replied.

"Not necessarily," Izraad said. "Sirin told me Khusaaq told her that his people hadn't always been mercenaries—she said he told her that at one time, thousands of years ago, they'd been looked upon as the finest engineers, terraformers and explorers by the then foremost civilizations of the Rim—"

"And if they were considered 'expendable'," Aquila interrupted, "they could have been hired out by their masters for tasks deemed too risky for others to undertake, and if that were the case, it wouldn't be a huge leap to go from surveyor to soldier."

Izraad nodded. "Exactly—Khusaaq mentioned to Sirin that the Orthodoxy had 'fallen on hard times', and said that this was the rationale for becoming mercenaries in the first place. He didn't elaborate, but it's possible they were forced back into the same niche held by their masters eons before—from which has come those accounts of Loopers employing Hahtooshan mercenaries—they just weren't the same Hahtooshans, meaning they weren't Neanderthal in origin but rather something else, perhaps not biologicals at all, but rather sentient machines just as Tasende suggests.

"Interestingly," she continued, "while the Loopers are credited with coining the name Hahtooshan for these mercenaries, the Dabih Negus referred to these alien soldiers as *Akkansah*, which, per the records left by the Negan chroniclers, was the was the name these aliens used to refer to themselves, not Hahtooshan, but the name Hahtooshan, or, more correctly, *A'tuu'shahn* isn't of Looper origin either, in fact it has no connection to any word or term in the Looper vocabulary, ancient or otherwise. And Sirin said Khusaaq repeatedly mentioned beings he called the *Elkanasu,* beings he referred to as their masters, and beings he clearly considers as divine."

"So perhaps these Akkansah and Elkanasu are one and the same, and as such could very likely be the beings who created Hahtooshans as we know them?" Amalfitano suggested.

Izraad only shrugged, then picked up her forgotten glass and took a measured sip. "You'd have to ask Xosé if there's a reasonable correlation, as he's extensively studied Negan language and phonetics, but they certainly sound similar and look even more alike when transcribed into Negan glyphs."

Amalfitano gave everyone a few minutes to absorb all that information—along with the possible ramifications—while he eyed the doorway. Dinner was definitely taking far longer than he'd anticipated. He pressed the desk-com. "Galley?"

A moment later the disembodied and decidedly harried voice he recognized as the one of the cooks, Montoya, replied, *"Galley here—"*

"This is Amalfitano, Josada—what's the hold up? We're all starving up here."

"Ah, doc. Sorry—bit of a mix up. But dinner will be up in a jiffy—another ten minutes, tops."

"Fine." He released the com button, turned back to his companions and shrugged apologetically. "You heard the lady."

"Since we have a few minutes..." Izraad began and everyone turned expectantly to her, "I've also come up with an explanation as to how the rumors about their supposed shape-shifting abilities started."

"Indeed?" Aquila replied as he shifted around, clearly trying to get comfortable in the chair.

"It has to do with those truly remarkable uniforms of theirs," Izraad continued. "Not only is it a mobile pharmacy and who knows what else," she nodded to Amalfitano, "Sirin told me it also has the ability to not only change color and texture, but it can perfectly mimic its surroundings using leucophores, chromatophores and iridophores for color change and electroactive polymers for the alterations in texture which in turn are imbedded in the uniform's composite; she said she witnessed this firsthand when Khusaaq demonstrated its astonishing abilities for her.

"She said if he hadn't been bareheaded at the time, he would have been completely invisible and she said she was standing no more than a meter away from him at the time. I've had Perou and his engineers run tests and the uniform material definitely has the ability to completely conceal the wearer from any sort of sensing device, even close up—"

"Which supports what was seen in those long-disputed images from the Cotopaxi ceremony where all you could spot was an almost imperceptible ripple effect." Aquila looked sidelong at Teague. "Maybe those images weren't doctored for propaganda purposes after all. Maybe they were authentic."

Teague nodded.

"But what about those interference patterns?" Lesedi asked. "Doctor, you said they were was emitted by their skin?"

Amalfitano nodded. "Their tattoos and skin engravings form an interference pattern coincidental with the interface between the epidermis and dermis—"

"So why didn't their uniforms conceal them," Lesedi asked, "or at least conceal their interference patterns, from our sensors?"

Izraad smiled. "I wondered about that too, wondered why these patterns have been picked up before and were always associated with known Hahtooshan activity—until Sirin mentioned that for the entire time she was in their company, none of the Hahtooshans were wearing helmets. Lieutenant Perou believes the wearer has to be completely encapsulated in order to eliminate any... bleed. It's also very possible they have conscious control over the interference they emit; maybe they were purposely emitting it in order to provide constant positional information for each other as well as their ships in orbit—"

"Or to jam our abilities to locate and retrieve our missing?" Lesedi offered.

She nodded. "Or both."

"Interesting stuff," Aquila said as he again shifted in his chair. "Damned interesting..."

Amalfitano watched him unhappily then shaking his head, happened to notice that Izraad was grinning at him. "What?"

"Something just occurred to me."

"What?"

"That you referred to Khusaaq by name at least a dozen times in the past few minutes. Not to mention mentioning Matoosh, Suhjai and Gienah by name—"

"So?" he interrupted defensively.

"So... nothing. Just an observation." She smiled sweetly.

Amalfitano squinted at her, then, overhearing approaching footsteps, turned, fully expecting to see the main course arriving. Instead he saw Pierson. The medtech had stopped short of the door, beyond the others' view, and was now motioning anxiously to him.

Amalfitano smiled at his dinner companions. "I think I best go see in person what's holding up our chow." He rose and casually strode from the office.

Pierson waited for him beyond earshot and the view of those in his office.

"What's up?" Amalfitano asked in an urgent whisper as he approached him.

"Khusaaq, Chief. He's waking up."

"Is Sirin still with him?"

"No—she left a coupla hours ago. Drakin managed to convince her to go back to her cabin, get some sleep. Want me to call her back?"

"No. At least not until we see where we stand," he tapped the side of his head, *"upstairs."* He glanced back at his office and overheard the muffle of conversation and laughter. Satisfied he wouldn't be missed for a few minutes, he hurried into the isolation unit, through the airlock, and finally into the dimly lit cubicle that held his star patient.

Amalfitano glanced down at him then swept his eyes across each of the medical monitors. They confirmed that Khusaaq was indeed waking up. *About damned time...* He turned to Pierson. "Got any bright ideas about speeding things up that won't risk life and limb?"

"Poke him in the ribs then run like hell?"

"You're a big fat help."

Pierson shrugged. "Never thought I'd be in this position, Chief, or I'd have studied up on it—thoroughly."

"You and me both." Amalfitano gave the restraint web a test tug. Satisfied, with a muttered, "Here goes," and a nod to the nearest guard, he lightly touched Khusaaq's shoulder. "Sha'ashahn...?"

Khusaaq moaned softly.

Amalfitano, emboldened by his patient's less than spectacular reaction, gave his shoulder a gentle shake. "Sha'ashahn? Ah... *Khusaaq?"*

This time his only response was to smack his lips then sigh heavily.

Amalfitano gave the monitors another look, said, "Come on, you're almost there," and tried again, this time with a firmer shake. "Wake up!"

Khusaaq grunted and tried to roll away; the restraint webbing tightened in response.

Amalfitano gave Pierson a sidelong, exasperated look. "Got any better ideas?"

"Don't need any." He motioned with his chin to their patient. "Yours did the trick."

Amalfitano dropped his gaze. Khusaaq was now staring up at him with a decidedly vacant expression.

"Will?"

Amalfitano flinched and wheeled around to find Aquila standing in the doorway, arms akimbo. "Oh... Robert," he began as Pierson hastily stepped aside.

"Dinner conveniently arrived right after you left."

He looked down at Khusaaq, then back at Aquila. "Oh."

"Aren't you going to join us?"

"I was... but Khusaaq had other ideas."

"He's awake?"

"Yeah." He motioned for Pierson to leave. "I can take it from here, Rafe. Thanks."

As Aquila joined him at the bedside, Amalfitano took the opportunity to give the bank of monitors another study. *So far so good, but a little nudge can't hurt.* He opened the drug cart drawer, pulled out a ject-it and vial, loaded it and pressed it against Khusaaq's thigh.

"You two," Aquila motioned to the guards. "Outside. And close the door after you."

One guard began, "Sir, Ensign Lesedi—"

"I resumed command twenty minutes ago. Now... *out!*"

The guards left without further protest or delay, easing themselves around Aquila and Amalfitano and out into the corridor.

Aquila waited until the cubicle's door closed with a muffled *thump* then he turned his full attention on Khusaaq. After a moment, he murmured, *"Neanderthal,"* then shot Amalfitano a sidelong look. "It truly boggles the mind."

"You're telling me. And speaking of, telling people that Hahtooshans are human was going to be hard enough, but telling them they're Neanderthals? I don't envy someone their PR job and woe be it to anyone who stupidly calls a Hahtooshan a cave-man to his face." Just uttering the phrase brought a host of very ugly images to Amalfitano's mind; while Neanderthals had certainly undergone a make-over in the centuries since their discovery, the earliest images of slavering, slump shouldered brutes remained and he knew it wouldn't be long, once word got out, that such images would reemerge, spurred on by the pervasive hatred and fear of all things Hahtooshan. Never mind that Hahtooshans were anything but slavering, slump shouldered brutes.

Amalfitano shook his head as he gazed at the empty ject-it. Then placing it on the drug cart he added, "Humans have seen themselves as the only child for twenty thousand years; and like any only child, something tells me our species isn't going to be too happy to find out we have an older, much bigger brother."

"Agreed, and if given a choice *I'd* prefer the prodigal sons not return as top tier mercenaries with a serious grudge, if it's all the same to you."

Amalfitano managed a soft chuckle, then more seriously: "It's going to change everything you know, Robert. *Everything.* From our view of our own past, to what it is to be human... to... well, everything."

"And the hard sell is going to cut both ways you know."

Amalfitano stared at him.

"You think the Hahtooshans are going to be any happier when *they* learn the truth?"

Amalfitano blew out his cheeks. He hadn't thought of that angle. And now that it had been brought to his attention—*what was it Zarijan said Sirin said Khusaaq had said, that the Elkanaghallis considered themselves the image of perfection? Talk about a hard sell—*

"Does Corsali know?"

Amalfitano turned to him, briefly baffled. "Know?"

Aquila lowered his voice before answering, "What he is."

"You mean Neanderthal."

"Yeah."

"No, or, should I say I haven't told her but she knows he's human—"

"I want you to leave her to Izraad—let her tell her."

"Why?"

"Because she's a trained professional in such matters?"

"And I'm not?"

"On this scale?"

"Okay, maybe not," Amalfitano conceded, "but then again, who is?"

"Okay, maybe no one. But the fact remains, this is Izraad's area of expertise and after you left and just as dinner arrived she raised the idea that she should start formulating a plan on the best way to break the news—to everyone, Hahtooshan and Coalition. I agreed and she suggested she should start with Corsali, and then him," he motioned with his chin to Khusaaq, "use 'em as test subjects."

Amalfitano exhaled then nodded. It made sense—if not handled carefully, things could go from bad to worse in a heartbeat. Telling Corsali seemed straightforward enough; he hadn't even gotten around to considering how or when he'd inform Khusaaq. And it never occurred to him that once they knew, it wouldn't be long before the entire crew knew. And then it would spread from there, leaving chaos in its wake. The news was indeed going to change everything, and, he realized, not for the better. *Definitely not.*

"So mum's the word until Lieutenant Izraad speaks to them, either together or separately—her call. Agreed?"

"Agreed." Then a new worry: "What about Ife? She knows too and—"

"I swore Ife, Edwin and while it's totally unnecessary, Zarijan, to secrecy. Told them if I learned they'd spoken to anyone about this, I'd toss 'em in with Suhjai and her buddies and throw away the key. The comp-ops were already functioning under a total communications blackout to avoid word leaking out Hahtooshans were human—no out-going transmissions of any sort. So even if word does get out among the crew about them being human, much less Neanderthals we'll be able to contain it to the ship until HQ figures out what to do. Speaking of, what about your staff? Who knows?"

"Fleming, Drakin... and Xosé of course."

"That's all? Might they have said something to someone else? I mean, this is extremely explosive stuff we're talking about."

"I told them all to keep it to themselves until I'd notified the command staff, and then Sirin. When I'm done here, I'll talk to them, tell 'em not to say anything, not even to other medical staff—trust me, they won't."

Aquila leaned close. "Speaking of, can he understand us?"

A little late to be asking, don't you think? Amalfitano thought as he mentally kicked himself. Aquila wasn't the only one who'd totally forgotten that they weren't alone. "Not sure, too soon to tell, really. According to that," he used the expended ject-it to motion to one of the monitors, "he hears us talking, but as to whether he can comprehend what he's hearing—"

"Will, anything he can tell us about this captain of his is vitally important."

He tossed the ject-it back into the open drawer, replied irritably, "Gimme a minute."

Aquila scowled at him, but said nothing.

Amalfitano turned back to his patient and lightly touched his shoulder. *"Pa'-tu-tsaeh?"*

Khusaaq's disturbingly placid expression remained unchanged.

Like hell you understand me. He gave his shoulder a gentle shake and tried again, louder, firmer, his tone a command in any language. *"Pa'-tu-tsaeh? Ithsu baktai!" Answer me, damn you!*

"Maybe he—"

"Be quiet," Amalfitano whispered out of the side of his mouth.

Khusaaq's gaze drifted to Aquila and then back to Amalfitano during the brief exchange and Amalfitano, keenly aware of his eye track and focus, felt a twinge of hope. *Good. That's a step.* *"S'sarhi-sseh?"* he prodded then repeated in Standard, "What's your name?" He waited. *Nothing.* The glimmer he thought he'd seen in Khusaaq's eyes had faded—or, he realized, was likely never really there.

"Didn't know you were fluent in Hahtou," Aquila said softly.

"Wasn't. Zarijan's been tutoring me, thought it might come in handy." He looked around the small room, hoping something useful might present itself. It did. He walked over to the far corner, grabbed an unused monitor and guided it back to the bedside.

"What's your name?" Amalfitano repeated as he tapped the monitor, its dark screen an effective mirror. "See anyone you recognize?" *Look, damn you!* He tapped the screen again, harder, finally drawing Khusaaq's dull gaze. *"S'sarhi-sseh?"*

Khusaaq stared at his own reflection, but Amalfitano saw no reaction, no flicker of comprehension. He exhaled and shook his head. "I dunno."

"Now can I try?"

"Be my guest."

"Thanks." Aquila turned to Khusaaq. *"Sha'ashahn? Pa'-tu-tsaeh?"*

Khusaaq slowly pulled his eyes off the monitor and looked up at Aquila.

Aquila shifted his weight, winced, then lightly gripping his flank added, *"Pa'-tu-prahaj?"* Exhausting his own limited Hahtou vocabulary, he too switched to Standard. "I'm Robert Aquila, commanding officer of the *Baidarka...*"

"Here," Amalfitano murmured as he pulled down the folding chair.

Aquila smiled his thanks, sat and turned back to Khusaaq. "Sha'ashahn, you rescued me while we were on Rasal Ghul Seven, remember?"

Khusaaq's gaze drifted back to Amalfitano and this time Amalfitano did see something stir behind his pale eyes—this time he was sure of it. *Dim recollection?* He murmured to Aquila, "You're on the right track... take it slow. Keep repeating things, names—"

"Aquila, remember?" he said, in the process drawing Khusaaq's gaze. *"Ah... a'-tu-tsaeh?* Robert Aquila. The *Baidarka*. We were on Rasal Ghul. You saved us. Remember—*pa'-tu-prahaj?"*

Khusaaq stared at Aquila's face as he spoke, first abstractedly and then, ever so slowly, more intently. He blinked, blinked again as if trying to clear his vision. Then his blistered mouth began to work, but after a moment of struggle, all he managed was a strained gasp.

Amalfitano, after a glance at the monitors, placed a reassuring hand on his shoulder.

Khusaaq jerked his eyes off Aquila and looked up at him.

"Take it slow, son. It'll all come back, just don't force it."

As Khusaaq turned his now-alert gaze back to Aquila, Amalfitano looked down at his hand... *on a merc's shoulder. And I just called him... son!* He started to withdraw his grasp, but to his surprise, his hand refused to budge. *Hell of a thing.*

"Rasal Ghul Seven... the weapon," Aquila prompted. "Remember? You said you wanted to stop Tarqk, you asked for my help—"

"Ah queelah...?" he whispered thickly.

Amalfitano breathed an audible sigh of relief.

Aquila grinned triumphantly and nodded vigorously. "Yes, Sha'ashahn! Robert Aquila. And this is the *Baidarka*'s chief medical officer, William Amalfitano."

Khusaaq glanced at Amalfitano then took in his surroundings. *"Baidarka,"* he rasped, then after a long pause, "I'm... aboard your ship?

"In our sickbay, you were seriously injured and—"

"But... *Tarqk!"* He tried to sit up.

Amalfitano tightened his hold, stopping him before the restraint web responded. *"Easy,"* he murmured. "Take it easy."

"But you must stop him!" He turned back to Aquila, his voice hoarse, panicky. "He plans to keep the weapon—"

"We know all about Tarqk," Aquila replied, "and his plan to test the weapon on Tuli. We're hot on his tail."

"Tuli...? *Tuh maztsaeh,"* he shook his head, "I... I do... do not understand."

"What did Zarijan say you Hahtooshans call the system?" Amalfitano knit his brows and Khusaaq looked up at him, anxious. "Oh... yeah. Katab tah ba...?"

"Kakkab-Ta'abi?" Khusaaq replied, clearly puzzled.

"Yeah, that's it." Amalfitano nodded. "If you hadn't told Ensign Corsali...." He stopped as he realized that Khusaaq's bewildered gaze had suddenly turned inward.

Amalfitano risked a sidelong look at the monitors, saw every readout shoot up then turned back to him just in time to see his face contort in an agonized grimace. "What the—"

"Chulh!" He squeezed his eyes shut and shook his head violently, then forced out through clenched teeth, *"Chulh...!"*

Aquila leapt from his chair and stepped back. "What the hell's happening?"

"I don't know!" Amalfitano snarled. *"Give me a goddamned minute!"* He gave the monitors and their wildly erratic readings another glance then turned back to Khusaaq. "What's wrong—"

"Chulh!" he groaned as his body convulsed against the webbing.

"Answer me, damn you!" Amalfitano gave his shoulders a rough shake. *"Tawok ta-sseh? Ithsu baktai!"*

Khusaaq's eyes flew open and he began to fight against the webbing. It responded, tightening its grip, making him struggle all the more. *"Chulh!"*

Aquila reached for the door release, clearly intending on recalling the guards, but Amalfitano angrily waved him off. "No!"

Instead he again grabbed Khusaaq's shoulders, roughly shoved him back against the narrow bunk and held him there, confirming what he was seeing was no seizure. If it had been, he wouldn't have been able to keep him pinned to the bed, but that left a host of other possibles, none of them good. *"Tell me! I can't help you if I don't what's happening to you!"*

"CHULH!" Khusaaq shrieked as he continued to fight against the webbing, against Amalfitano's hold.

Amalfitano risked a quick glance at the monitors. *For gods' sake stop before you rupture something!* He tightened his grip... and to his immense relief, Khusaaq suddenly stopped fighting the restraints, stopped fighting against his hold, having utterly exhausted himself.

Amalfitano held onto his shoulders a moment longer then letting go snarled, "What the hell was that about?"

Khusaaq stared up at him in gasping horror. "I... I spoke the... the truth!" His wild eyes darted to Aquila. "I... spoke the truth... but... but you were... not there. I... I thought you were dead. And she... would not... not listen!"

"Cacchio!" Amalfitano looked sharply at Aquila as he jerked open the drug cart drawer. He snatched up another ject-it, loaded it with a potent tranquilizer and pressed it against Khusaaq's knotted upper arm. He then used it to point to the door. "Out."

"But—"

"Out!" Amalfitano barked.

Aquila looked back at Khusaaq to find him staring up at him in such raw agony that he found himself unable to think of anything to say except a terse, "Keep me informed." He thumbed the door release, stepped out, then, after muttering something to the waiting guards, disappeared into the unit's airlock.

Khusaaq, still laboring for each breath, stared after him he whispered, *"I... I spoke... I spoke the truth..."*

Amalfitano acknowledged the two guards as they quickly and silently resumed their positions at the foot of the bed, then turned back to Khusaaq. "I'm sorry, really I am. We didn't know, you see."

He frantically searched Amalfitano's eyes. *"Know...?"*

"We thought you were hiding information about Tuli, not about… what you are."

Khusaaq looked away, fixing his eyes on the far wall as he visibly struggled to get his breathing under control, then, in a slightly stronger voice, said, "Ensign Corsali, she… she told you *everything?"*

"She did what she had to do, you must understand that. We were desperately trying to save your life…"

He clenched his teeth as his bandaged chest continued to heave against the webbing.

Amalfitano turned to the cart and busied himself with its contents. "I'm going to give you something for the pain and—"

"I'm A'tuu'shahn," he growled hoarsely, but with little conviction as he warily watched him load a ject-it. "I need none of your drugs."

Amalfitano checked the dose. "Bullshit."

"Tuh maztsaeh."

"Yes you do. You understand perfectly. So drop the pretense. You're in pain, a hell of a lot of pain by the looks of it—and need I remind you that you don't have the pharmacological benefits of that uniform of yours. On top of that you've just suffered a tremendous shock to your psyche, so I'm going to give you—"

"Chulh!"

"Dammit! I'm just trying to help you, so how 'bout a little cooperation?"

"How 'bout you leave?"

"Listen, you goddamned stubborn son of a bitch—"

"Praise will not sway my decision."

Amalfitano's eyes bulged; he started to make a tart reply, but not sure what to say, settled for scowling at him.

"I do not wish to be uncooperative, but neither do I wish to be unconscious. For now the pain is… bearable. I will tell you when it isn't. Is that agreeable?"

"Not by half," he glanced at the monitors, then back at him, "but I guess I better take what I can get."

"Good. Now leave." He tried to roll onto his side but was stopped by the webbing. He looked down at it, then pointedly at Amalfitano.

"I'll take the restraints off if you give me your word you'll behave."

"You would take the word of an A'tuu'shahn?" he sneered.

"I'll take your word, let's leave it at that, all right?"

He squinted up at him then grumbled, "Then I give you my word that I will… *behave.*"

"Good." Ignoring the less than subtle throat clearing of one of the guards, he tapped the deactivator then, as carefully as possible, peeled off the webbing, wincing as it took sizable bits of skin and blister-scabs with it. "Better?"

Khusaaq gave his upper arms a brisk rub despite the reopened blisters, cautiously stretched then startled Amalfitano by nodding and saying, "Thank you."

"Ah… you're welcome. Now… uh, the guards have to stay, so don't try anything, all right? They have their orders and I sure as hell don't need any more patients."

"I already gave you my word that I would behave."

"Yes, you did. Sorry." Amalfitano cleared his throat, then added, "If you need—"

"I… I'll notify the guards."

The doctor, hearing what sounded like a note of hesitancy in his hoarse voice, asked, "Is there something else?"

"My escort… were they taken prisoner as well?"

"We rescued ten of you from the boat. All but you and one other—ah, Matoosh?"

Khusaaq nodded.

"—suffered only minor injuries, and Matoosh is now in stable condition."

He looked briefly, intensely relieved, then asked, "And from the island?"

"Island? We didn't pick up any Hahtooshan readings except those on the boat." *Not that we looked any further. Not that it would have mattered, even if we had.*

Khusaaq stared at him, clearly unsure if he was telling the truth, then he abruptly looked away as his hands clenched into fists. *"The diffusion screen...!"*

"Diffusion screen?" Amalfitano asked while keeping a wary eye on his hands.

"On the island... we... we managed to power up its diffusion screen." He shook his head and muttered angrily, "It would have blocked your sensor sweeps. I should have taken that into account—*chooslah!*" He smacked his fists on the bunk with enough force to make Amalfitano flinch and the guards jump.

Amalfitano nervously cleared his throat then said, "I'll notify the commander. Right now he's got your captain to worry about, but as soon as he can, he'll contact HQ about them." He hoped he sounded more confident than he felt, but as Khusaaq looked back at him, he felt as if he was looking right through him. "How many?"

"There were five." Khusaaq fixed his slitted gaze on the far wall, took a deep, ragged breath, added, "I don't know how many now," then, turning back to Amalfitano asked, "and what about the planet?"

"Tuli? They've been alerted. And we're on our way there. With any luck, we'll be waiting for your captain Tarqk when he gets there. He won't succeed, Commander Aquila will see to that."

Khusaaq replied with a slight, less-than-convincing nod.

Amalfitano tossed the unused ject-it back into the cart, then studied the monitors' readouts and was relieved that the tranquilizer had finally begun to take effect; now it was his turn to hesitate. "May... may I ask you a question, uh, Sha'ashahn?"

Khusaaq rubbed the bridge of his blistered nose with his fingertips and, with a sidelong glance at Amalfitano, grumbled, "You may ask it. I make no promise to answer it."

"The weapon." He paused before continuing awkwardly, "Your description, during... during the... uh... interrogation—"

Khusaaq's eyes narrowed to baleful slits.

"It was a bit vague," Amalfitano added hastily. "Do you remember anything specific?"

He was clearly trying to continue to glare menacingly at him, but the powerful drug coursing through his bloodstream was making his eyelids heavy; his breathing too had finally slowed, less panicky now, along with his heart rate.

Amalfitano judged that within a few minutes, the tranquilizer would completely take hold, and any chance at getting even a scrap more of useful information would be gone, at least for the time being, and time was one commodity in very short supply. "Look, I know I'm asking a hell of lot, but Ensign Corsali told me you wanted to stop its release. If we knew exactly what we're dealing with, it could save millions of lives."

Khusaaq chewed on his lip for a moment, his gaze taking on a decidedly glassy appearance. And when he spoke, his voice was halting, thick, almost but not quite groggy, "I... I was permitted only the... the most cursory analysis of the data. It was... not my area of... expertise. And Tarqk... Tarqk had use for me... elsewhere..." His voice trailed off, his eyelids fluttered, and Amalfitano thought he'd finally succumbed to the drug.

His shoulders sagged as he realized he'd been defeated by his own efforts to do the right thing. He started to turn away.

"But...."

Amalfitano wheeled back. *"Yes?"*

"On... the island. We... located more... more information. Most of the data—" Khusaaq gave his head a shake to clear it, then continued more steadily, "Most of the data had been corrupted, most likely when the diffusion screens were shut down, and before I had a chance to thoroughly study what information had survived I was ordered back to the mainland." He gave him a sidelong look, suddenly and fully awake now, and added with deliberate harshness, "To ambush and kill your landing party."

Amalfitano blinked. *And here I almost forgot whom I was dealing with—*

"Had you rescued all of us, those whom I'd left on the island could, undoubtedly, provide you with more specific information, since I'd left them with orders to continue their efforts to retrieve and analyze the data. Pity you were... *unaware* of their presence."

"Yes," Amalfitano agreed, hoping his irritation and impatience hadn't tainted his voice and at the same time concerned that the tranquilizer, which was enough to knock out a healthy man for several hours, had clearly peaked and was now rapidly starting to wane. He'd hesitated at the dose, fearful of overdoing it. Underdoing it hadn't occurred to him— "A truly unfortunate oversight, and, as I said earlier, one we will rectify as soon as we can, I promise you. But—"

"In my limited review of the data, I found one organism mentioned repeatedly. A modified..." he knit his brows then added with less certainty, "filovirus?"

"That's a huge help, thank—"

"Is that all?"

"Uh, yes, I—"

"Then leave." He wrapped his hands around his immobilized right leg and carefully rolled onto his side, away from Amalfitano, away from the guards. "I wish to sleep."

Amalfitano glanced at the monitors which told him a very different story, then said, "I'll be back to check on you in a little while," as he locked the drug cart. *Just in case you get any bright ideas.* He gave the bank of monitors another sweep with his eyes, shook his head, and walked out of the cubicle, dimming the lights as he went.

— iii —

Corsali entered the isolation unit just as Amalfitano stepped out of the airlock.

He stopped as he saw her. "Oh, Sirin... uh—"

"I heard Khusaaq's awake?"

"Hmm, yes. Just woke up a little while ago." He slipped onto a chair at the isolation unit's horseshoe-shaped console.

Corsali's eyes darted to the row of darkened cubicles then back to him. "May I see him?" When he hesitated, her hopeful smile vanished. "Is something wrong? Is he—"

"I just think it'd be best if you waited a little while. He knows he was mind-stripped, he knows we know what he is, and he knows you're the one who told us."

She felt like someone had just kicked her in the stomach and managed a soft, *"Oh."*

"Give him time to come to grips, all right?"

She knew he was right, but... "I need to see him, sir. Please."

Amalfitano leaned back in the chair and crossed his arms. "Wouldn't advise it."

"Just for a few minutes?"

He studied her face for a very long time, long enough for her to begin to squirm, feeling as if he was examining her entire soul in an attempt to understand why anyone in their right mind would befriend—*no, be honest here Sirin, become emotionally attached to a Hahtooshan.*

Finally he exhaled and nodded, "All right, but *just* for a few minutes. A quick hello, how'ya feeling, then good-bye and *out.* Understood?"

"Yessir—"

"And if by some miracle he has fallen asleep, I don't want you waking him up—whatever you need to say can wait."

"Of course, sir." She started for the lock.

"Sirin."

She stopped, reluctantly looked back at him. "Yessir?"

"He's... he might not be the way you remember him from Rasal Ghul."

"Understood," she replied, when in fact she didn't and they both knew it. She had no idea what she was walking into, no idea who she'd meet... if he would even acknowledge her. He had every reason to ignore her, hate her.

All she knew was that she had to see him, regardless. She had to know.

"And Sirin? Do me one big favor?"

"Sir?"

"Don't get too close..."

She felt her pulse jump.

"...I took the restraints off."

"Oh. Yes, of course sir." She turned to the airlock control and with a very shaky hand tapped the release. The door opened and she stepped inside.

Using the same trembling hand, she tucked an unruly lock of white blonde hair behind her ear as she stared at the inner lock. *Don't get too close.* She bit her lip. *Too late.*

The door opened.

He knows he was mind-stripped… he knows we know what he is, and he knows you're the one who told us, Amalfitano's voice echoed in her mind. He might not be the way you remember him….

That's gotta be the understatement of the year. She took a deep breath as she stepped out, muttered, "You can do this," and walked into the isolation cubicle.

She acknowledged the two guards with a nod before turning her attention to the bed and its occupant. Khusaaq was on his side, his back to the door and to her. *Asleep?*

She hesitated. *Maybe—maybe not.*

She stepped closer to the bed and as she got a better look at his exposed back, she found herself wincing. The combination of burn salve and tattoos could conceal only so much.

His peeling, tattooed shoulders were pockmarked with blisters, some freshly opened and oozing, others crusted over. While his torso was wrapped in dressings, his lower back was bare and so darkly bruise-mottled she was hard pressed to see his tattoos—he looked worse than when she'd helped Drakin clean him up only the day before, although in truth when it became obvious just how thorough Drakin planned to get, she'd suddenly remembered she needed to look up information on Tuli.

And his breathing… instead of soft and regular, if asleep, or even rapid and shallow, as she'd expected if he was still angry, it was labored, hoarse. *Oh… gods. Not anger. Grief.* Now that she was this close it was palpable and she felt like an intruder. *But if I leave, if I turn my back on you now…* "Sha'ashahn?"

He didn't react immediately, as if reluctant to let anyone interrupt, or share, his personal anguish.

Finally he grumbled huskily, "What do you want?"

"I wanted to see how you were doing."

"Ask your medical officer."

"I did. But… I wanted to see you." *Needed to see you.*

He slowly, carefully rolled into his back, then propped himself up on an elbow and took in every inch of her crisp uniform and finally, her freshly scrubbed face. He roughly wiped his nose with the back of his hand and managed a sneering, "You've changed much since I last saw you, Ensign. Yes, definitely a change."

She felt her cheeks flush deeply as he gave her another, this time far more thorough once-over with his bloodshot, glittering eyes.

"I've changed too, yes?" he added, his voice suddenly brittle.

"Khusaaq, I—"

"I trusted you. I trusted you and you *betrayed* me—"

"I had to tell them what you told me—"

"You didn't have to tell them everything."

"If I hadn't, you would've died—"

"And this is preferable?"

Corsali followed his puffy-eyed glare and glanced over her shoulder. She'd totally forgotten about the guards. She turned back to him. "I did what I had to do, can't you see that?"

"You did what you did to save yourself, your commander and your Coalition—yes, I see that all too well, now."

"Of course I did! Just as you would've done had the situation been reversed, but I did what I did to save you, too—"

"Get out."

"No!"

"Tah! The insubordinate ensign from the boat reasserts herself." He slowly eased himself back down onto the bunk and fixed his eyes on the ceiling as his right hand tightly clutched his immobilized thigh. "Go away, kaa-schat," he growled through clenched teeth. "You no longer amuse me."

"Why are you behaving like this?" She took a step closer. "I know you're—"

"You have no idea what you've done, do you? And I'm acting like what I am, an A'tuu'shahn." He squinted sidelong at her. "This is the real me. Don't confuse my behavior back on the Blatto boat with who I really am. I had a momentary lapse—"

"Meaning you believed we were all going to die, so you let down your guard? Meaning you were scared, just like I was scared. And you're still scared. Except now you're scared you're going to live."

"Do not think that you can trick me again, it could get you..." His eyes flicked to the guards as they both fingered their holstered shockers. He glared fiercely at one, then the other before looking back to her. "Get. *Out."*

"I'm not leaving until you answer me."

"You wouldn't want to hear my answer. Guards—"

"Why?" she snapped, holding up her hand to the two marines. "Afraid you'll show some honest emotion like you did back on the boat? Afraid I'll catch another glimpse of the real you instead of the image you're trying to recapture of the pure, untainted Elkanaghalli?"

His eyes widened and his blistered mouth opened then snapped shut.

Gods! She clapped her hand over her own mouth, horrified at her own words then stammered, "Oh... I didn't mean that!" She stepped even closer. *"I'm so sorry!"*

After an awkward silence, he replied softly, "Why? It's the truth. All I had was what I was, and now even that's gone, stripped away as effectively as my uniform." He took a deep, ragged breath, exhaled and closed his eyes. "I'm very tired, Ensign. Please go away and... and don't come back."

She stopped beside the bed, tempted to touch him, to reach out to him. When she finally spoke, her voice was barely above a whisper: "Is that what you really want?"

He swallowed convulsively then meeting her gaze replied softly, "What I really want is for things to be as they were before I'd ever heard of Rasal Ghul. I want to be back on my ship, with my people, where I belong."

She carefully eased herself down on the edge of the bunk beside his hip, ignoring the less than subtle throat-clearing cough of one of the guards and his uncertain, very suspicious stare. "I know, and I wish that was possible." She cautiously wrapped her hand around his, privately relieved when he didn't pull away, and gave it a squeeze. "Really I do."

He closed his eyes, took another deep, unsteady breath then exhaled wearily. *"You should've let me die, Sirin,"* he whispered as his fingers curled tightly around hers. *"You should've let me die."*

Chapter 20

Aquila stopped in front of the blue-framed airlock that gave access to the *Baidarka*'s control room.

Beside him, Teague reached for the lock activator. "Ready?"

Aquila looked down at himself. He'd checked his command blues at least six times since leaving his cabin. *One more time can't hurt.*

Satisfied, he lifted his gaze and nodded.

Teague thumbed the activator, the airlock door opened and the two officers stepped through only to find the entire bridge crew standing at attention.

"Captain and first officer on the bridge," Stoker announced with uncharacteristic formality. The crew, as one, saluted.

Aquila and Teague returned the salute then Aquila murmured, "As you were," as his bright eyes swept the familiar chamber. His gaze finally came to rest on Izraad and he winked at her; she grinned.

Lesedi, who stood at attention beside her weapons console, smiled broadly. "Welcome back, sirs." Then she began to clap and the rest immediately joined in; some left their posts to grab Aquila's shoulder, to shake Teague's hand; everyone was grinning.

Aquila flushed deeply, gestured for silence and said, "Thanks... to all of you. If it hadn't been for each and every one of you," he said as his eyes briefly lingered on each of his command crew before coming to rest on Lesedi, "I wouldn't be here."

"Neither would I," Teague echoed.

Aquila looked at Teague. "And we'll never forget that."

"Not to worry, sirs," Pardix said with a chuckle, "we won't let you."

Aquila laughed and motioned for everyone to resume his or her seat. Then, as Teague walked over to his own station, Aquila eased himself down at the command console and with a sigh that sounded decidedly pleased, leaned back into the contoured chair. He ran his fingers over the well-worn armrests and smiled at all it implied. As he lifted his gaze to the suspended tactical display, his expression abruptly darkened. Homecoming over, it was back to business. "ETA to Tuli?"

"One hour, fifty four minutes, sir, present speed."

He looked to Cyllo. "Any sign of the Hahtooshans?"

"Nothing on long-range sensors, sir."

He turned next to Lesedi. "Weapons systems?"

"All systems but forward rails show green."

He replied with a curt nod and a grim, "Then let's get to it."

— ii —

Qharubi watched the raw data flow across his console's main screen with detached curiosity: *Makhaira* was literally falling apart around them. It was a testament to Elkanasu design, not to mention A'tuu'shahn engineering that she'd survived, largely intact, for this long and at such high fold speeds. *The planet, just... just reach the planet... then—then what?* He wasn't sure. He wasn't even sure who had given the order to attack the planet. He massaged his forehead. *Tarqk? Ru'asooli? Or the Q'shaathrah itself?* He tried to concentrate, tried to recall, but everything was a muddle. Only one thing was clear: *reach the planet*. Nothing else mattered.

He fixed his blurry gaze on his control screen, stared at the read-outs that ticked off her slow death. He was only minimally aware of the muffled coughs of the skeleton bridge crew. Now only the most vital consoles were manned.

He rubbed his burning eyes and tried to remember when he'd last slept—aside from brief snatches on the bridge—and found he couldn't. Like everyone, he'd been at his post since exiting the Rasal Ghul system, leaving only briefly to relieve himself or grab something to eat or drink from the bridge's small satellite galley. He had no appetite, hadn't for days—it was also a common, muttered complaint among the rest of the bridge crew. Everything tasted odd or had no taste at all, but he knew he had to eat, had to drink, knew the others did too and so kept reminding them, all the while aware that stocks were starting to run low and no one could be spared to replenish them.

Worse, his joints ached, it hurt to breathe and his head throbbed continuously, almost blindingly and to the point it made any thinking, much less trying to outthink Tarqk, more effort than it was worth. His only comfort, such as it was, was that he wasn't alone in his suffering. Everyone on the bridge, including Tarqk, had voiced similar ailments or worse. The medics, while making rounds to hand out stimulants to the bridge crew, would do their best to knock down the pain without knocking the person out, but those visits were becoming fewer and farther between—yet another ominous sign. No one needed to tell him that life support was failing ship-wide—had been failing since their encounter with the Coalition vessel. The air on the bridge was foul and uncomfortably hot. Conditions were likely even worse elsewhere on the ship—no one knew because Tarqk had stopped requesting updates. The news was never good, always grim and getting grimmer.

Qharubi managed to turn his head, just so, and glance over his shoulder without a grimace; Tarqk was still napping, slumped in his command chair and snoring fitfully. He turned back to his console, fixed his blurry gaze on the readouts and tried to remember what he'd just been doing. Then he remembered. He'd been watching *Makhaira* die with a sense of detached curiosity—

"Ta'ahn..."

Tarqk snorted and flinched awake, jerked his head towards Qharubi, then followed Qharubi's equally startled gaze to the sensor-operator as she continued, "Kakkab-Ta'abi system on long range sensors. ETA—"

"On tactical," Tarqk muttered huskily as he straightened.

Qharubi twisted in his chair and squinted at the suspended image. Only the innermost of the massive system's twenty-three planets, Tuli, was inhabited. In order to reach it, *Makhaira* would have to run the gauntlet of its immense and unusually dense Oort cloud then dodge the deep gravity wells of the outer gas giants.

The tactical display's multitude of critical read-outs blurred and Qharubi rubbed his burning eyes then squinted again. It didn't help.

"Ta'ahn!"

Tarqk, who'd just slumped back into his chair, clearly intent on resuming his nap, scowled at the now wide-eyed sensor officer. "Now what?"

"A ship approaches!"

"Show me," Tarqk grumbled and tugged his rumpled duty uniform into place.

The tactical display quivered, briefly, as one computer-generated view of space was replaced with another.

As the new image steadied, everyone's eyes were drawn to a flashing marker that was moving rapidly across the artificial starfield.

"Identify."

Qharubi made a quick study of the read-outs, felt his heart sink then turned to face Tarqk. "It's the Coalition patrol craft, *Baidarka*."

Tarqk stared at him for several heartbeats in open-mouthed shock, then he gasped, *"Khusaaq!* He's... he's betrayed us to the Coalition!"

"She's gaining on us, ta'ahn," the sensor officer reported.

"Increase speed!"

"Impossible," Qharubi replied. "Power reserves are dropping rapidly. At present rate, we will be forced to drop in—"

"Sensor shroud!"

"Also impossible. The mechanism was damaged beyond repair during our last skirmish with the Coalition ship. As were full rail capabilities. Aft rail banks are only fifty percent, forward less than forty."

"Seekers?" Tarqk asked with an audible note of desperation.

"Still operational, ta'ahn."

"Divert all power to tubes! Prepare to launch on my order!"

— iii —

"Sir!" Zayyad glanced at Aquila. "Hahtooshan craft, bearing seven two six, mark five—"

"Definite C-class," Cyllo added, "analysis of ionized hydrogen trail matches—"

"Battle stations," Aquila interrupted calmly as he pushed himself back into his chair.

"Intercept course plotted and laid in," Pardix said.

"Altering course now," Eisele responded an instant later.

"Launch tubes powering up," Lesedi reported.

Cajori added, "Screens fully energized—"

"Sir," Zayyad interrupted, "she's taking evasives, changing course to—she's dropped!"

Aquila turned his even gaze on Eisele. "Helm..."

"Dropping now, sir," she replied, anticipating his order.

He felt a familiar quiver run through the deck below his feet as the *Baidarka* dropped into normal space. "Tactical."

The grid-lined holo shimmered into existence a meter in front of him.

The massive sun, Tangaloa, and its twenty-three planets appeared as pale yellow spheres; the thick Oort cloud was a milky haze of tiny white dots; and the Hahtooshan ship was a pulsing red dot racing across the faint blue background grid.

At the top of the display was the computer's marker for the *Baidarka*: a bright green spot that sped across the schematic void in a headlong plunge towards the onrushing red dot.

"Time to intercept?"

"Nineteen minutes, forty seconds," Zayyad replied, "if their present course and rate of deceleration are maintained."

"Lock tracking computers on target."

"Computers locking," Lesedi said. "All weapons systems but forward rails fully operational."

"She'll be within maximum weapons range in sixteen minutes," Zayyad added.

"Stoker, open a hailing—*wait*, belay that." Aquila twisted in his chair to face the com-op. "Get Amalfitano. Tell him I want to speak with Sha'ashahn."

— iv —

Amalfitano hesitated at the doorway of the isolation cubicle, plastered on a positive face, then clearing his throat, stepped into the darkened room.

"Shhh," came a familiar female voice.

"Sirin?" Amalfitano whispered, feigning surprise. He'd known of course; Drakin and Meerut had kept him informed of what they found when they made rounds and based on what they'd told him, what the monitors had told him, he'd given his tacit approval of leaving matters as they were, but not without serious mixed feelings.

His eyes, now adjusted to the gloom, saw that she was seated cross-legged at the head of the narrow trauma bed, her back braced against the wall. Khusaaq was curled up on the bed in front of her, his head cradled on a pillow in her lap.

"I distinctly remember saying you could visit for just a few minutes," he added softly but firmly as he stepped closer. "That was... what, fourteen hours ago?" *Not to mention warning you not to get too close....*

"I know, but... he did ask me to stay, sir." She placed the portable data reader she'd been holding on the bedside table. "I couldn't refuse. I'm sorry—"

"Don't be. Going by those," he jerked his chin to the monitors, "you made the right call." He dropped his gaze. Khusaaq's face, in fact his entire body was completely relaxed, and that meant only one thing: he felt safe in her embrace, safe enough to fall into a deep, natural sleep—going by what the nurses had reported, almost thirteen hours of uninterrupted sleep, sleep without the aid of drugs, sleep his body desperately needed.

Cacchio. "We've entered the Tangaloa system... and just made sensory contact with the Hahtooshan ship." He caught the flicker of unease in Sirin's eyes, saw her fingers tighten their protective hold on Khusaaq's bare shoulder. "The commander's hoping maybe he can talk his captain into breaking off the attack now that he's been found out."

Sirin nodded then murmured, *"Tanhah,"* as she gave Khusaaq's shoulder a gentle shake. *"Wake up..."*

Khusaaq stirred, grunted irritably, then opened one bleary eye and mumbled, *"Sseh...?"*

"Doctor Amalfitano's here."

He turned his still groggy gaze towards the doctor. He squinted at him, wet his blistered lips then rasped, "I did not call for you."

"I know. And I'm very sorry to awaken you, but—"

"What do you want?" He carefully, reluctantly, pushed himself out of Sirin's lap and to a seated position beside her, wincing and clutching his thigh as he did so.

"Commander Aquila wishes to speak with you."

"May I ask the reason?" he asked as he rubbed his still sleepy eyes.

"I think it would be best if he tells you himself." He tapped the light switch and the room brightened.

Khusaaq dropped his hands away from his haggard face and looked expectantly at the doorway, then back to Amalfitano.

Amalfitano pointed to the wall-mounted intercom, adding, "Stay put. You can speak from there."

Heedless, Khusaaq eased himself off the bed and as he put his full weight on his feet, his right leg, despite the immobilizer, buckled. He caught himself, then grimacing, slowly straightened up.

"That's why I told you to stay put—it's not a walking brace," Amalfitano chided as he stepped forward and offered his arm for support.

"Obviously," Khusaaq replied, but waved off the proffered arm.

Amalfitano eyed him critically. "I'll give your bio-engineers credit, you're healing faster than anyone I've ever seen, but now that you're medically stable, I want to replace that femur. I have the skeletal matrix ready—"

"No."

"No? But—"

"It will mend. It always has in the past."

"That's all well and good," Amalfitano replied, having seen the tell-tale evidence of numerous previous injuries etched on his bones himself, "but as your doctor, I'm telling you that you've far surpassed its warranty."

"Warranty...?"

"Don't tell me your people don't use organ replacements and bone matrix."

Khusaaq looked at him out of the corner of his eye as he braced one hand against the wall. "A'tuu'shahn'i... *yes*," he said then began hopping slowly, painfully, towards the wall unit. "Elkanaghalli'i... *no*. We live and die with what we were born with."

Uh-oh. Amalfitano couldn't help but flick a glance towards Matoosh's cubicle as he thumbed the activator. "C and C?"

"Aquila here."

"Sir, I have Sha'ashahn here with me."

Khusaaq edged closer to the speaker as Aquila said, *"Sha'ashahn, we've made sensor contact with your ship. She's just entered the Tangaloa system. I'd rather end this peacefully..."*

Khusaaq flicked Amalfitano, and then Sirin a sidelong look of genuine surprise.

"...I thought perhaps if you spoke with your captain," Aquila continued, *"you might convince him—"*

"I will of course do what I can, Commander."

"Good. The doctor will escort you to Control."

"Control?" Khusaaq blinked in astonishment. "Yes... yes of course."

"And Will?"

Amalfitano, his gaze never leaving Khusaaq, leaned close to the speaker. "Yes?"

"On the double."

"Understood." He cut the connection, turned to Khusaaq and gave him a skeptical once over. *You look like death warmed over—and I seriously doubt you're in much better shape upstairs.* "You really don't have to do this—"

"You would have me do nothing?"

"No, I'm just—"

"Your commander has offered me one last chance to fulfill what was my goal from the start, to stop Tarqk from unleashing this weapon. I can hardly refuse." He looked down at himself and the ship-issue shorts he was wearing then back at Amalfitano. "Perhaps you have something more suitable I might borrow?"

Amalfitano briefly wondered what would be appropriate under the circumstances. Then it came to him. *Of course!* He tapped the wall-com's activator again. "Rosen?"

There was a pause then the nurse answered, *"Yessir?"*

"Has Sha'ashahn's uniform been repaired?" He winked at Sirin.

"I... think so, Lieutenant Drakin was—"

"Then collect it and bring it here—right away."

"Chief...?"

"Just do it!" He released the button and looked back at Khusaaq to find him slowly hobbling back to the bed.

"Thank you, Doctor," he said as he eased himself down on the edge of the bunk.

"Let's say it's the least I can do."

Khusaaq nodded gratefully.

Sirin scooted close to him and without being asked, began combing his long, coarse black hair with her fingers.

Khusaaq closed his eyes, tilted his head back and smiled contentedly as she made quick work of the tangles, then began to plait his hair.

One of the guards, taking advantage of their mutual preoccupation, sidled over to Amalfitano and whispered in his ear,

"Sir, I don't think this is a good idea." He gave his holstered shocker a pointed glance.

"I do." Amalfitano walked over to the bed. "How 'bout I give you a mild painkiller, Sha'ashahn? It's not a long walk to Control, but—"

"No."

"Sure? That uniform of yours can't help you..."

Khusaaq opened one eye a crack to scrutinize Amalfitano.

"...if that's what you're counting on. And yeah, we know all about its... shall we say, unique properties?"

Khusaaq continued to stare at him, one-eyed. Then upon hearing the outer airlock snap open, he shrugged and turned his attention to the doorway just as Rosen appeared, the heavy hauberk, bandoleer, belt, trousers and boots in her arms. Everything was clean and glossy; the uniform's sandy color bore no trace of the blood, grime or stench that had coated the age-worn panoply when its wearer had been brought to sickbay.

Rosen draped it across the foot of the bed next to Khusaaq then placed his boots on the floor.

Khusaaq smiled at seeing his refurbished uniform and murmured, *"Jaas-nhe,"* to Rosen as he eagerly ran his tattooed fingers over it.

"You're... ah... welcome?" she replied with a quizzical glance at Amalfitano.

The doctor nodded and grinned.

With a baffled shake of her head, Rosen withdrew.

Khusaaq cautiously eased himself off the bed, onto his good leg, then removed the immobilizer and placed it on the bed.

"Ah, that's not a good idea," Amalfitano said, eyeing the discarded brace.

"You said it wasn't a walking brace," Khusaaq replied then without further ado, stripped off his shorts.

Sirin's eyes widened, then she jerked her gaze off him and hurriedly rose from the bunk as she stammered, "I... uh... I better get to Control myself."

Amalfitano tried not to grin at her flushed expression, or her quick, sidelong glance back at Khusaaq as the doctor stepped aside for her to slip around him. He walked over to the drug cart and unlocked it then, under the guise of casually checking its stocks and giving Khusaaq some semblance of privacy even if he didn't appear the least bit self-conscious, he grabbed several vials and a ject-it and slipped them in his pocket. He then reached up and, taking his time, turned off each of the monitors.

Finally, he turned back to Khusaaq to find him grimacing as he struggled to tug on his right, knee-high boot while his thigh bowed noticeably.

Amalfitano inwardly winced, then, shaking his head, gave him another quick visual once over. The rest of the crew might not appreciate his choice of attire, but it seemed only fitting. *In more ways than one. Not sure how you're gonna walk, though.*

"Now, about that painkiller..."

"No, I will manage." With that Khusaaq rose unsteadily from the bunk. The trouser fabric that encased his right thigh instantly formed a snug, rigid sheath far more effective than the bulky immobilizer.

Amalfitano raised his eyebrows. *Well, I'll be damned.* Aloud he said, "Ready?"

Khusaaq drew himself up to his full, and decidedly impressive height—up to that moment Amalfitano had only seen him in the horizontal and had been impressed. Seeing him completely vertical *and* in uniform was a whole different matter—a very unnerving matter. A sidelong glance at the two marines left little doubt they felt the same way, and it didn't help, not one bit, when his sandy colored uniform abruptly darkened to a rich, iridescent black as its overall texture morphed from completely smooth to covered in tiny, peaking bumps, then back to utterly smooth.

Minchione. Amalfitano blinked then risked another sidelong glance at the equally startled guards.

Khusaaq adjusted his medallion-encrusted bandoleer and seemingly oblivious to the stunned reaction of those around him, turned to Amalfitano and said, "Yes."

— v —

Amalfitano kept his concerned gaze on Khusaaq as he, Khusaaq and the guards made their way from the isolation cubicle to the control room airlock.

It was obvious to Amalfitano that Khusaaq had gun-barrel vision. He wasn't seeing or hearing what was going on around him: the startled looks of passing crew, the open-mouthed shock at the rapidly changing texture of his glimmering black ghillie suit, the whispered remarks and hate-filled stares that followed him. He was focused on one task and one task only: putting one foot in front of the other, of reaching the ship's control room without tripping or falling in front of what was, in essence, a captive and very hostile audience.

Each step took its toll, and by the time they were within sight of the blue-framed airlock, Khusaaq was unable to lift his right leg from the deck and had resorted to a slow, but determined shuffle.

He stopped before the lock, shaking, his breath coming in short, sharp gasps and gave Amalfitano a sidelong, pinched look as one of the guards cautiously edged around Khusaaq and tapped the activator. But as the airlock opened, he wiped the grimace from his face, took a deep, steadying breath then stepped though and into the *Baidarka*'s control room without even the barest hint of a limp, only to be greeted by more sharp intakes of breath and gulps of horrified astonishment.

Amalfitano and the guards followed, then as the two marines took up position on either side of the airlock he stopped to stand not quite shoulder-to-shoulder with his slightly taller patient. As he did so, he caught Aquila's stunned blink and felt perversely pleased by it. *Talk about making an entrance...*

For a moment the crew stared unabashedly at Khusaaq, each taken aback and drawn in by his undeniably sinister appearance, from his eerily glimmering ghillie suit with its colorful campaign medallions and insignia, to his heavily tattooed, scarified and blister-pocked face.

Khusaaq, his nostrils flaring, swept the chamber with an outwardly calm, undeniably arrogant stare of his own, clearly aware of its unsettling effect. Even Sirin garnered no overt reaction as he briefly made eye contact with her. Then his gaze happened upon Lesedi and he drew his full lips back into a cold, unpleasant smile.

"Welcome to C and C, Sha'ashahn," Aquila said, breaking the strained silence.

Khusaaq casually shifted his gaze from a now thoroughly unnerved Lesedi and fixed it on Aquila.

Aquila, oblivious to the exchange, shook his head. "I never, in my wildest dreams, thought I would ever hear that, much less say it."

Khusaaq nodded, then, clasping his hands behind his back, looked past him to the tactical display as Zayyad said, "Sir, she'll be within weapons range in five and a half minutes."

"Hail them."

"Aye, sir." There was a pause then Stoker added, "They've acknowledged and are receiving, sir."

Amalfitano instinctively edged a little closer, ready with the steadying arm or a quick grab if his knees started to buckle, but if Khusaaq noticed, he didn't show it. His gaze remained fixed on the rapidly changing tactical display.

"Hahtooshan vessel," Aquila began, "this is the Coalition patrol ship, *Baidarka*. State your reasons for being here." He waited, counting off the seconds as he tapped his finger on the arm of his chair. "Hahtooshan vessel—*I repeat*—state your reasons for being within this system."

"Sir, I'm receiving a response—audio only."

There was a faint rustling sound, then a harsh voice crackled from the overhead speaker, *"This is the A'tuu'shahn Orthodoxy vessel,* Makhaira... *"*

Amalfitano, watching Khusaaq out of the corner of his eye, saw him visibly stiffen at the sound of the raspy voice.

"...to whom are we speaking?"

"This is Commander Aquila, Captain of the Coalition Expeditionary Forces Ship *Baidarka*."

"Captain? Are you sure?" the voice sneered. *"I was under the impression... well, I suppose your rotating command structure is neither here nor there. This is Tarqk Nahru'tzrhi, and I see no reason to state the obvious. Your presence here is proof enough that you know our purpose."*

"I do indeed, Nahru'tzhri, and if you do not immediately abort this mission, I'll have no choice but to destroy you—"

"Destroy me?" He chortled. *"You seriously believe that your pathetic little patrol boat poses a threat to me?* Makhaira *is no Matarii border raider!"*

"Neither is the *Baidarka.* Nahru'tzhri, I ask again, abort your mission—"

"I strongly suggest that you do as Commander Aquila says, Nahru'tzhri," Khusaaq interrupted, drawing every eye in the control room.

There was a very long pause before Tarqk sneered, *"Ah, Sha'ashahn. What a... surprise. I thought you were dead."*

"You should have made sure—"

"Well, rest assured, I'm about to rectify that oversight."

"Sir," Zayyad whispered, "they're coming about and will be within weapons range in less than three minutes."

Aquila turned back to the tactical display. "I give you one last chance, Nahru'tzhri, abort your mission or surrender—"

"Surrender? Do not judge all A'tuu'shahn'i by your Elkanaghalli pet, Commander. A'tuu'shahn'i do not surrender and I have no intention of aborting my... 'mission'. But... before we blow you to plasma—"

"Sir?" Stoker said, "they're requesting visual feed."

Aquila glanced back at him. "Visual?"

A bleat from Stoker's console drew his attention and he blinked in astonishment. "They're transmitting on visual now, too, sir."

"Do it."

An instant later a totally unfamiliar Hahtooshan face and equally alien backdrop replaced the suspended three-dimensional tactical display.

"Ah, Commander Aquila, I presume?"

Aquila replied with an ever-so-slight nod. "Tarqk Nahru'tzhri."

Tarqk's sharp eyes shifted to Khusaaq. *"And Sha'ashahn. What a charming picture."* Then his gaze fell to Khusaaq's bandoleer and its empty scabbard and he grinned. *"But I see they've pulled your teeth—a wise move, since you have so ably proven that you will, if given a chance, bite the hand that feeds you."*

Amalfitano, listening to the terse conversation, stared at the transmitted image, but it wasn't the alien vessel's bridge layout that caught his attention. It wasn't even Tarqk's insolent smirk or the haunted glances of his crew.

The Hahtooshan captain's hollow-cheeked face was streaked with rivulets of sweat and his upper lip appeared to be crusted with blood. As Amalfitano looked more closely, he wasn't sure if it was due to the odd lighting of the alien bridge, but Tarqk's dusky skin appeared to be not what he'd come to know as the healthy olive-brown for a Hahtooshan, but rather a pasty gray and his tattoos were a lurid purple instead of bluish-black.

"Nahru'tzhri," Aquila began, "we are running out of time. I ask one more time, abort or we'll open fire."

Tarqk, pointedly ignoring Aquila, kept his fierce eyes on Khusaaq. *"I wished to look upon your deceitful face one last time, Elkanaghalli. I wanted to see for myself just how far the Hero of Cotopaxi had fallen..."*

Amalfitano glanced at Khusaaq. *Hero of Cotopaxi?* Then, as he turned back to the suspended image, he caught the startled, sidelong glances of the rest of the control room crew.

"...and I wanted the crew to know what a traitor looks like," Tarqk added.

"They've been looking at one all along, Nahru'tzhri," Khusaaq fired back. "You're the one who's betrayed the elders of the Q'shaathrah and the Elkanasu—"

"The Elkanasu!" Tarqk sneered as he lurched forward in his chair, startling several control room crew into instinctively pressing back into their seats. *"You and Qharubi, that's all you ever talk about! You... sicken me!"*

Khusaaq opened his mouth, but Tarqk held up his gauntleted hand, cutting him off. *"At least Tu'indai will not suffer your dishonor. She's bonded to me now. But so you may die knowing that your beloved wife is in good hands, I'll show my magnanimity and allow you to speak with her one last time."* He snapped his fingers. *"Quh!"*

Amalfitano cast a quick, sidelong look at Corsali before his attention, and his curiosity, was drawn back on the suspended image just as a tall figure emerged from the gloom of the Hahtooshan back-bridge and stopped beside Tarqk.

Amalfitano was immediately taken aback by the woman's elegantly featured face and understated tattoos. She was, Amalfitano realized, strikingly handsome, despite her ferine expression—even her facial tattoos weren't a distraction or even a detraction. If anything, they enhanced her exotic beauty, but, as with Tarqk, her skin had an oily sheen and an ashen undertone.

"Toq-bhir," Khusaaq began. "Tuh maqh—"

"In Standard, Sha'ashahn," Tarqk interrupted sweetly. *"We would not wish your Rimmer friends to feel... left out, now would we?"* He leaned back in his chair, crossed his arms and smiled. *"Now, you were saying?"*

Khusaaq shifted his uneasy stare back to Tu'indai and began, "I never—"

"You betrayed me, Sha'ashahn," she interrupted heatedly, her strident voice a startling contrast to her delicate appearance. *"You've betrayed us all, all in some foolish, misguided attempt at recapturing our past—"*

"I did what I did to defend the Orthodoxy against this madness that will bring ruin to us all!"

"Defend the Orthodoxy?" She blinked in unabashed astonishment. *"By allying yourself with the Coalition? You of anyone should realize the terrible cost of placing your faith in the hands of..."* her lip curled in a sneer of revulsion as her soul-freezing gaze swept the faces of the Baidarka's command crew, *"Rimmers."*

She turned her full attention back to him and regarded him with a look of utter disgust, then as if by rote, said, *"I no longer remember you; I no longer know your name. You cease to exist, as does your family. Your line's exploits will be removed from all records. You and they never existed, to us and... to your beloved Elkanasu."* She glanced at Tarqk, and, at his curt nod, stepped back, to stand behind him.

An awkward hush fell on the control room, every eye glued on Khusaaq.

He shifted his unblinking stare from Tu'indai to his captain and replied in an unexpectedly composed, quiet voice, "It is you, Tarqk, and you alone who've betrayed all that we once stood for. You've mocked the Elkanasu far too long. You shall know their wrath soon enough, whether it be at the hands of the Coalition, or the Elders of Q'shaathrah. As for the other matter..." He paused, and to everyone's surprise, chuckled, a soft, strange barking laugh and shook his head. "Had you simply asked, I would have happily given Tu'indai to you as she's far more trouble than she's worth. But let's make it official, for what little time you have left. I would not wish even you to face the Elkanasu alone."

He crossed his arms, clearly savoring the look of impotent rage on Tarqk's face and wide-eyed incredulity on Tu'indai's. "She who is Tu'indai, fourth daughter of Jauz'hani Alhstoo'nhe, lower house of the Taqlth-khu, ninth caste of the Shar'ataan is yours, Tarqk—and good riddance... to both of you."

Tarqk, his eyes bulging and his face darkening in rage grabbed the armrests on his chair, but Khusaaq held up his hand and Tarqk, to everyone's surprise, hesitated in mid-rise.

"Rest assured Tarqk, I will make sure the Q'shaathrah is fully apprised of your unauthorized actions as well as Tu'indai's complicity and—"

"You assume you will survive this encounter!"

Khusaaq smiled coldly. "You assume I won't?"

Tarqk's wild eyes bulged in rage and he spat out: *"They won't listen to a traitor!"*

"I *am* the Hero of Cotopaxi, *remember?"* He smiled coldly; his eyes sparkled. "High time I use that honor for *my* benefit, and that means they'll have no choice but to allow me to speak. And once they've heard the facts, I have absolutely no doubt whose families' wealth and standing will be forfeit and whose lineages will be... *expunged."*

"Why you—" Tarqk lurched unsteadily to his feet and just as he lunged forward as if he could actually grab Khusaaq by the throat, the transmission ceased, replaced by the tactical grid.

An awkward silence fell on the control room as the crews' startled stares flicked between Khusaaq, Aquila and Amalfitano.

"The Dabih Negus had a saying, Commander," Khusaaq said, his narrowed eyes fixed on the tactical display. "He whose fists are clenched cannot think." He paused, met Aquila's stare. "Tarqk's insane and now he's very angry. Use it to your advantage."

Aquila stared at him, not sure what to say.

Khusaaq jerked his chin towards the holographic display. "He'll head directly for the planet and use tracer or seeker torpedoes to release the weapon into the atmosphere. He has, no doubt, locked an automatic firing sequence into the tube bay computer. You must destroy *Makhaira* before she gets to within weapons range of Tuli."

Aquila hesitated before replying, "Understood."

Khusaaq fingered the enameled gorget and whispered, *"Elkanasu chah'duu rheeth chtak,"* then favored Aquila with a sidelong look and what was clearly a very forced smile. "May the Elkanasu guide and guard you, Commander."

"Thank you. We'll take all the help we can get."

Khusaaq replied with a slight nod, then turned and strode through the airlock, his guards on his heels.

"She's in range, sir," Zayyad said, watching as Khusaaq vanished into the outer corridor. They've locked on, aft rail guns powering up."

Amalfitano shook himself free of his own paralysis and hurried after Khusaaq, but just as he stepped through the airlock, he overheard Aquila's calmly worded order, "Fire all seekers."

Chapter 21

"A hit?" Aquila asked as the tactical display registered a distant flare.

Zayyad replied with a vigorous nod. "Yessir!"

"I've got weapons lock-on," Lesedi reported.

"Fire seekers!"

"Firing, aye sir!"

"Sir," Stoker twisted in his chair to face Aquila, "I'm receiving a message feed from the Coalition envoy on Tuli—the planet's sensor net's detected the Hahtooshan sh—"

"Reassure him we're on her tail and she'll be stopped before she reaches the planet."

"He sounded real panicky, sir. I'm not sure I can—"

"Tell him to sit tight!" Aquila smacked his fist against the arm of the chair as the grid-lined display recorded a seeker hit, this time against a chunk of Oort debris. Scowling at the suspended holo, he searched it for any sign of the fleeing warship. "Where the hell are they?"

"There!" Zayyad hissed just as the tiny red dot reappeared. "We've got a positive lock-on—"

"Fire seekers!"

— ii —

"Incoming." Qharubi's report was raspy and barely above a whisper.

"Evasive!" Tarqk replied even he knew it was too late.

Qharubi hung on; a moment later the ship shook violently. "Direct hit—we've... lost aft seeker tubes—"

"Then... then fire... aft particle cannon," Tarqk managed before succumbing to a fit of harsh, body-wracking coughing.

The weapons officer managed a nod, no longer able to speak between labored, wheezing breaths.

Qharubi watched the crewman struggle to tap in the correct parameters then shifted his gaze to his own console. The hit had done more than just take out *Makhaira*'s aft seeker tubes. The massive energy burst had caused a critical cascade: systems all over the ship were affected and failing fast and the ship's schematic showed numerous breaches—venting off breathable air. Diffusion screens were down to less than fifteen percent. The environmental board was alive with flashing telltales warning of imminent and catastrophic failure of what few systems were still functioning.

Another alarm began to blatt, joining the strident chorus, his head throbbing in sickening cadence. He hit the mute with his fist, cutting off the alarms, startling nearby crew and momentarily plunging the bridge into an eerie, and to him, delicious quiet before other sounds, sounds that had been drowned out by the alarms, filed in the void: the ominous creak and groan of the dying ship, the hacking coughs of her crew, the undulating whine of the failing air scrubbers...

He clutched his head in both hands and briefly closed his burning eyes, hoping for another reprieve, brief as it might be, from the rhythmic flash of the telltales. And in that self-imposed darkness, Qharubi experienced a sudden lucidity, a level of clear-headedness he hadn't felt in... he couldn't remember.

Something Khusaaq had said that finally gelled: *Rest assured Tarqk, I will make sure the Q'shaathrah is fully apprised of your unauthorized actions...*

At the time, it hadn't registered. The shock of seeing Khusaaq alive and on the bridge of the enemy ship—*standing among Rimmers*—in combination with everything else...

Then he felt something else: intense rage. *Tarqk—this was your plan! Ru'asooli isn't following, there'll be no last minute reprieve, no rescue—no heroes' welcome home for a crew who did the impossible!* The assurances Tarqk had repeatedly voiced to the crew since leaving Rasal Ghul, that this had been the plan all along—a secret plan known only to him and the Q'shaathrah, words that buoyed their flagging spirits—*all lies*. Worse, Qharubi had known they were lies... once. Yet somewhere along the line, he'd begun to believe what Tarqk promised. *You've doomed us all, along with an utterly defenseless planet. And this will just be the start—you'll bring the wrath of entire Rim down on us!* He risked a quick, over the shoulder glance at Tarqk. *Enough!*

He slowly, cautiously slipped his pistol from its holster—nearby crew were too busy just trying to get another breath into their burning lungs, too busy just trying to survive the next few minutes to notice. *There's still time to stop this madness,* he told himself, using that assurance to steady his hand as he carefully adjusted the settings.

He swallowed hard, tightened his hold on the grip, said a silent prayer, rose, turned and fired.

The narrow-angled beam struck Tarqk squarely in the back of the head, exploding his skull and throwing his body forward, into the tactical well.

It landed with a soft *thump* at the feet of the stunned helmsman; he looked down at it, then up at Qharubi, eyes wide as if fully expecting to be the next victim.

For a moment, no one moved, no one spoke, the silence broken only by a scattering of hacking coughs. Then Tu'indai asked hoarsely, "Ta'ahn, what... are your... orders?"

Qharubi flicked a fragment of brain and bone from the command chair before assuming the seat, along with command. "Helm... get us beyond... their weapons range." Out of the corner of his eye he saw Tu'indai quickly take over his abandoned station, and, effectively, his position as second-in-command. "Evacuate... all decks aft of fore vane bulkheads... then shut down systems in those areas. Divert all reserve power... to aft screens."

He turned to the com-op and without missing a beat ordered, "Hail *Baidarka.* Tell them we're breaking off the attack," his eyes briefly flicked to the helmsman, caught the man's acknowledging nod, then he turned back to the com-op, "and request that they stand by for the possible evacuation of our crew." When the officer only stared at him, dumbfounded, he bellowed, *"DO IT!"*

The com-op hurriedly turned back to his console and tapped in a series of commands. Getting no response, he cursed softly and looked up to find Qharubi staring at him. "Ta'ahn, the last hit... it must've damaged the flatspace net—"

A loud *bleat* from Qharubi's usurped console drew everyone's startled gaze to Tu'indai.

"Ta'ahn," she began, her expression confirming his worst fears, "they've... fired another barrage—"

"Taking evasives," the helmsman interrupted.

Qharubi's eyes flicked to the tactical display. This close to the massive planet and its ring system they had little maneuvering room and even fewer choices. He muttered another heartfelt prayer as the helmsman banked *Makhaira* hard, plunging her towards the planet's luminous and thickly seeded belt of tiny moonlets.

"Ta'ahn?"

Qharubi turned to the weapons officer. The man's fingers where hovering over his console. *"Don't fire!"*

"But ta'ahn, we... must defend our—"

"I said hold... hold your fire!" Qharubi held on tight as a strong shudder ran through the ship. Lights dimmed and for a moment the only sound was that of the deck plates chattering loudly. He held his breath, not sure if he would breathe another.

"Explosion to port," Tu'indai reported then added with an audible, albeit wheezy sigh of relief, "No structural damage."

Qharubi spun his chair to face the communications station. "Fix... the damage to... to the net, quickly!"

— iii —

"What the hell're they up to?" Aquila asked no one in particular as he watched the caravel heel over then dive, headlong, into the gas giant's dense halo of moonlets. No one in his right mind would enter a field of potential ship-killers, even to evade a projectile barrage. *But then again, if Khusaaq's to be believed, Tarqk is not exactly in his right mind—*

"Maybe they've lost weapons capabilities, or screens," Izraad suggested.

"Or helm control," Eisele muttered.

Zayyad nodded his agreement, adding, "Maybe they're seeking cover while they attempt repairs—"

"More likely they're trying to draw us into a trap," Lesedi countered heatedly, "by having us think just that."

Aquila looked back at the tactical display as it registered first one, then a whole series of tiny explosions as one projectile after another struck a hapless moonlet.

Something's wrong. His eyes narrowed. *Very wrong.*

Even without Khusaaq's remarks, he'd fully expected Tarqk to head directly towards Tuli, all guns blasting.

Instead the ship had abruptly changed course, making a mad dash from the Oort Cloud to an outer planet's ring system and had yet to fire a single shot.

He dropped his gaze to the com-unit, briefly tempted to recall Khusaaq. Instead he settled back in his chair and motioned angrily at the grid. "Flush 'em out of there."

— iv —

Qharubi nodded his approval as he studied the tactical display. The helmsman had picked a very effective, albeit unusual way of fulfilling his orders. "Power down... the main engines—let her drift. Use... positional thrusters only to avoid collision. Tu'indai, cut all non-essential systems—warn the crew—everyone stop what they're doing unless it's absolutely critical. Everyone's to take hold... stay where they are. I... I want *silence*."

Tu'indai nodded, turned to her board and relayed the orders via the ship's multitude of visual displays—slower and less efficient than relaying them via the overhead, but in keeping with his orders. A moment later, the ever-present background hum abruptly ceased—even the scrubbers rattled to a halt—leaving in its place a gnawing silence punctuated by the muffled but nevertheless disquieting ping and clatter as bits of dust and debris skittered across the hull. It also left Qharubi with the reasonable worry that the failing systems, temporarily deprived of power, might not start again. But at least for now the *Makhaira* was safe from detection, surrounded by an escort that made an effective camouflage, scattering any sensor probes into a multitude of false images.

Qharubi rose unsteadily from the command chair and cautiously stepped into the tactical well. As he made the circuit in complete silence, he was met with nervous smiles and wary, sidelong glances; he acknowledged each crewmember with an encouraging nod or a commiserating smile as they did their best to muffle their harsh, body-jolting coughing with their cupped hands. With the air getting more unbreathable by the second, it was impossible not to cough.

He stepped over Tarqk's body and looked down at the helm console, then gave its harried operator a reassuring pat on the shoulder. "*Excellent, Tuktoh, excellent,*" he said in the man's ear then walked on to the communications console. As he stopped beside it, the officer manning the station turned to him.

"*I'm still attempting repairs, ta'ahn,*" he whispered, clearly anticipating a violent reaction. "*Damage was extensive and—*"

"*I know you're doing the best you can, Bulaan—*"

"Ta'ahn," Tu'indai hissed, drawing every eye on the bridge, *"they've launched another barrage…"*

Qharubi swore under his breath as he looked up at the tactical display.

"…but in a random targeting pattern."

"They don't know exactly where we are. But it won't take long for them to locate us." He resumed his seat, rubbed his burning eyes then stared at the tactical display as tiny explosions continued to pockmark the suspended projection. They were getting closer. He leaned forward in his chair, whispered. *"Helm, could we use the detonations to conceal our escape?"*

"I believe so, ta'ahn. But the detonations would have to be quite close, and at best we would only have a moment or so before they spot us."

"How close?"

"Very close, ta'ahn."

Qharubi's eyes cut to Bulaan. *"Time to completion?"*

"I'm almost finished, ta'ahn."

He turned back to the helmsman. *"Be ready to power up engines on my order."*

"And our heading, once in free space?"

Qharubi looked at his board. Life support had collapsed the moment power had been diverted as had the screens—what if the Coalition vessel refuses my plea for help? These are duplicitous Rimmers after all—the same Rimmers who tricked and murdered Telipinu, Saar'kali and Ichkeul.

That left one viable option—and *Makhaira* had never failed to do what had been asked of her.

"Ta'ahn?" the helmsman prompted in a hushed but strained voice.

Just once more, I beg you. Qharubi took a deep, steadying breath and his fingers curled around the armrests of his chair as he lifted his gaze to the tactical display. *Just once more. "The planet, Tuli, maximum speed—divert all power to the engines. Tu'indai, notify the crew to prepare to abandon ship—have Medical move all injured and non-essential crew to the main forward flickerstage. Bulaan, the instant the net's up, contact the planet, tell them we seek… asylum."*

The order was answered by stunned silence, then, somewhere behind him, he heard a muttered oath, followed by something about Elkanaghalli traitors.

He also overheard murmurs of relief.

"Do it!" he hissed, his raspy voice almost gone.

"Yes, ta'ahn," Bulaan replied and turned to his station.

Qharubi forced himself not to tap out the seconds as he watched the wave of explosions move ever closer to their hiding place.

The ship shuddered. Tu'indai barely had time to report, *"Explosion to starboard,"* before it shook again as more exploded debris impacted against the hull.

"Ta'ahn...?" Tuktoh whispered urgently, glancing over his shoulder, hands hovering above his board.

"Start powering up... but do it slowly, I do not wish them to spot a spike in energy readings," Qharubi murmured calmly as another nearby detonation chattered through the deck plates. In the background, the faint, background hum returned, softly at first, but getting louder by the second.

A moment later the ship was rocked by a massive concussion and the tactical display whited out. "Full power to all engines—*now!*" Qharubi yelped and was immediately thrown back into his chair as *Makhaira* leapt from her rocky blind and tore upwards, through a rapidly narrowing gap in the debris field and towards free space.

An alarm sounded and Tu'indai looked up. "They've spotted us!" Another bleat drew her eyes back to her console. "They've launched another missile volley!"

Bulaan glanced over his shoulder. "Com-net up—"

"Commence broadcasting on all channels—tell them we are not attacking the planet—tell them our engines are going critical, life support has collapsed and we must abandon ship!"

The com-op nodded and tapped in a series of commands.

For a moment—only a moment—Qharubi felt a flush of relief, then the com board came alive with telltales as the hastily repaired net abruptly collapsed.

Bulaan stared down at the blinking warning lights and cursed loudly, *"Chooslah!"*

Qharubi swallowed hard as he slid his gaze back to the tactical display and the pursuing rail volley. The rest of the bridge crew fell silent as they too watched the barrage gain on them.

He abruptly straightened up in his chair. "Haadar. Did you still have rail and targeting capabilities before power was cut?"

The gunner nodded eagerly. "Yes, ta'ahn—"

"Power up those systems!" He held his breath, waiting to see if the rail guns would re-initialize. After several thumping heartbeats he saw what he'd hoped to see. He settled back in his chair. "Fire, point defense mode! It may give us the time we need!"

— v —

"Sir—she's fired!"

Aquila looked up at the holo. *About damned time.*

His relief dissolved immediately as Zayyad added in a bewildered voice, "They're tracking our seekers only, firing rail gun bursts to destroy the missiles—"

"No counter attack?"

"Nossir."

"Ship's heading?"

"Towards Tuli. Speed's increasing." Zayyad paused then added, "Sensors are picking up massive power fluctuations in their fusion generators and they've lost or cut all power to all sections of the ship except engines and weapons—including life support. Screens down…"

Aquila looked back at the tactical display just as it registered a distant explosion. "A hit?"

"Yes… but it hasn't slowed her—"

"ETA to planet?"

"Three minutes, forty seconds, present speed."

Aquila dropped his gaze to Lesedi as she tapped in new firing coordinates. "Make 'em count, Ensign."

"Aye sir," she replied grimly as she hurried to complete her task.

— vi —

Qharubi staggered to his feet and squinted into the smoke-filled chaos. "Damage report!" he bellowed over the moans and hacking coughs of his crew.

When no one answered, he jumped into the tactical well and, stumbling over bodies and debris, managed to reach the helm console. He leaned over the slumped body of Tuktoh and tapped in orders. The board failed to respond.

He smacked his fist against it and the few remaining telltales flickered, briefly then blacked out. He backed up an unsteady step as he wiped the stinging soot from his eyes, then using chair backs and consoles for support, made his way to the communications console.

One look and he realized it too was beyond repair in the time he had left.

He glanced around. Everywhere his burning eyes touched, he saw ruined consoles and dead or dying crew. He gave his eyes another rough wipe and beginning to hack uncontrollably, staggered back to the command chair.

— vii —

"She's losing power," Zayyad reported. "Dropping to point nine six... nine five. Sir, I'm picking up massive power surges in their fusion generators, flatspace engines are reaching critical—"

"We've got lock on," Lesedi interrupted. "Seeker tubes powered up and—"

"Hold your fire! Open a channel to the Hahtooshan ship. *Cyllo,*" Aquila continued urgently, "locate all life sign readings on that ship. Perou...."

The engineer gave him a harried, over-the-shoulder look.

"Have the cargo bay flickerstage standing by." He smacked the chair's com-unit. "Security!"

"Security here," Delatorre's voice replied.

"Prepare for the flick-over of the Hahtooshan crew."

"Sir?"

"We'll flick them into the cargo bay."

"But sir," Lesedi protested, "she has a crew of at least two hundred and fifty—"

"Channel open, sir—"

"Makhaira, this is Commander Aquila. Your engines are about to go critical! Alter your course, turn away from the planet and prepare to abandon ship! We're standing by to assist, but you must turn away from the planet, now!" He squinted at the tactical display, mentally ticking off the seconds.

Answered only by the soft *rasp-rasp-rasp* of interplanetary static, he flicked Izraad a sidelong glance as he tried again, *"Makhaira*, alter your heading! Turn away from the planet, prepare to abandon ship—"

"She's dropped to point eight nine... eight eight... sensors are detecting numerous internal explosions..."

Aquila turned to the com-op, eyebrows raised.

"Nothing sir. I can't tell if they're receiving and just not responding, or their net's down..." His fingers and gaze shifted to another telltale demanding his attention. "Sir, the Coalition envoy's insisting—"

"Corsali—"

She looked up from her console.

"—deal with him!"

She glanced at Stoker, nodded, then turned back to her console and began speaking to the planet in a hushed, but harried voice.

"Makhaira," Aquila began again, "if you do not alter course or respond immediately, we will destroy you!"

Lesedi glanced over her shoulder. "She'll be in weapons range of Tuli in one minute, thirty sec—"

"Zayyad, any way of determining if she's still capable of firing her missiles?"

"One minute, twenty seconds," Lesedi murmured.

"No way of knowing for sure, sir."

"One minute, ten seconds...."

Aquila's hands balled into fists. *"Damn you to hell, Tarqk!"*

Lesedi turned to him. "Sixty seconds."

Aquila took a deep breath; he'd waited as long as he dared. "Fire all seekers." He slumped back into his chair and raised his eyes to the holo as it registered the volley's release.

— viii —

Qharubi pulled his Elkanaghalli dagger from its scabbard and placed it across his lap as another massive explosion, somewhere deep within *Makhaira*, violently rattled the deck plates.

He dropped his stinging eyes to the knife and ran his fingers along its length. *"Tash'mishu...* I have failed, I—"

The sudden, rapid blinking of a telltale on the control pad of his chair drew his preoccupied gaze and he squinted at it for a moment before realizing what it was desperately trying to tell him: the forward tracer bay had powered up, and the two modified tracer missiles were being loaded into their tubes. *Makhaira*, even in her death throes, was managing to fulfill one last command.

He glanced at Tarqk's body, smiled, briefly, and quickly tapped in the code Tarqk thought only he knew, countermanding the preprogrammed firing order.

The telltale obediently darkened just as a *blatt* of an alarm warned of another approaching salvo.

Qharubi lifted his gaze to the suspended tactical display and the swarm of telltales that marked the oncoming missile barrage and settled back into his chair to wait and watch with a sense of detached curiosity.

Then a murmur, barely audible above the snapping and popping of circuits from nearby consoles and the muffled sounds of distant explosions, drew his gaze back to his dagger.

Come...

He blinked. *It... it can't be.* He knew what it meant to hear the voices of the dagger—to hear the voices of the Elkanasu.

He managed a stunned, gasping, *"Tash'mishu?"*

Come, the voices urged.

He took a ragged gulp of the smoky air, coughed explosively then rasped, "Elkanasu toq-bhir, I... I thought—"

You've fulfilled your last duty to us.

"My last duty?" His startled gaze darted back to the now darkened telltale then his stinging eyes widened in sudden comprehension. *You mean—*

We await you. Come.

He looked again at the tactical; the missiles were almost upon *Makhaira*. There was nothing he could do for the crew. Most were already dead. In a matter of minutes, the rest would follow.

He nodded as he wrapped his fingers around the dagger's thick haft. "I'm ready."

Then come, now, before it's too late.

He rose unevenly from the chair as another internal explosion rocked the ship.

Gripping the dagger in both hands, he looked back at the display, took a deep breath, and plunged the blade into his chest.

PART III

Chapter 22

The *Baidarka*'s control room crew watched in silence as the first seeker impacted the *Makhaira* amidships. It was quickly followed by three more direct hits that sheared the caravel cleanly in two.

Another seeker struck the now wildly tumbling forward impeller vane; it was immediately engulfed in a blinding fireball as a massive explosion ripped the remaining superstructure apart and sent large chunks of the warship wildly spinning off in different directions.

"Aft impeller hub located and targeted, sir," Lesedi said matter-of-factly, interrupting everyone's private horror.

Aquila tore his gaze off the tactical display and the rapidly approaching planet. "What?"

"Their impeller hub, sir."

"The location of their aft seeker bays," Zayyad broke in, his voice a hoarse whisper.

"They still pose a threat to Tuli," Lesedi continued, "and at the impeller's rate and angle of approach, it might penetrate the atmosphere intact—"

"And the seekers could release the disease upon impact," Aquila finished for her. He looked back at the tactical display and added flatly, "Destroy it."

A moment later, the tumbling remains of the impeller exploded just short of the outer reaches of the atmosphere and he let loose the breath he'd been holding.

"Sir!" Cyllo gasped. "I'm picking up numerous but very faint life sign readings from what schematics suggest is the bridge and forward flicker—"

"Can you get lock on?" Aquila asked as he turned to Perou.

"Trying sir, but—"

"Too late," Zayyad said quietly. "It's been captured by the atmosphere."

The holo registered a streak of dazzling white light that arched across the planet's upper atmosphere. It quickly dropped into the lower, denser layers, leaving a bright orange trail in its wake, and finally vanished completely as it plunged below the southern hemisphere's heavy cloud cover.

After several tense minutes, Cyllo reported, "Debris has impacted the southern continent."

Aquila hesitated before asking, "Intact?"

"Impossible to tell, sir, the planet's rotation has taken the site beyond sensor range, but the rate of descent and angle of approach would not preclude a relatively soft landing."

He looked at Stoker. "Transfer the information to the planet's High Council. Ask if they have any recovery assets within the zone of impact."

Stoker nodded and after a brief exchange with the planet, turned back to Aquila. "Seismic stations on Tuli have pinpointed the impact site, approximately two hundred and seventy kilometers north, north west of the southern continent's settlement of Cape Bon..." He listened intently to his planetary contact then continued, "They report the area to be dense, rugged and largely uninhabited forest... they have no ground assets that can reach the impact area, and Cape Bon has no atmospheric craft. They ask if the *Baidarka* can assist in securing and decontaminating the debris and the surrounding area."

"Tell them we'll help in any way we can." Aquila thumbed his chair's com-unit. "Sickbay."

Drakin's harried voice responded, *"Sssickbay here—"*

"What's your status, Lieutenant?"

"We're ssstill getting casssualty reportz in from all over da ssship, sssir, but zo far no fatalitiez."

Aquila's eyes flicked to Teague as he said, "A portion of the Hahtooshan ship impacted the planet. I'll need a team from medical to accompany a security detail to assess the situation on the ground and, if needed, establish a quarantine perimeter. Have them ready to flick down in a half an hour—can you spare Amalfitano?"

"I sssuppose zo—"

"Then tell him to report to the flickerstage immediately." He cut the link and rose from his chair. "Lesedi, you have the conn." He motioned to Teague and Corsali. "With me."

They wordlessly followed as he strode through the airlock and into the curved corridor.

Ahead, a breathless Amalfitano stepped out of the stairwell.

As Aquila came abreast of him, he took in the doctor's darkly stained med reds with a raised eyebrow.

"What?" Amalfitano snapped. "Pull me out of triage, what do you expect?"

"I wanted you to accompany us, to answer any medical questions the Tulians might have. But if you're needed here—"

"Jenna's got everything under control, plus if she needs me, she knows how to reach me."

"Right." Aquila started up the corridor, Corsali at his side as Teague and Amalfitano fell in behind. "Tell me about the political situation on Tuli, specifically this High Council."

"The first people to inhabit Tuli after its discovery and the determination that it harbored no indigenous sentient life were granted the right to colonize after they'd successfully proven to Coalition Central Committee that they were a persecuted religious minority who'd been marginalized on other Coalition worlds. The original colonists envisioned an agrarian world—"

"The planet was originally called New Eden and the sun, Uriel," Teague interjected sourly. "Its four major oceans were likewise named Tigris, Pishon, Gihon and Euphrates and its two major continents Kush and Havilah. Most of the colonists were religious zealots and idealistic fools who had no idea what they were getting themselves into—the vast majority had no farming experience, much less experience setting up a viable colony, but... they had damned good lobbyists who convinced the Central Committee that as a persecuted minority, they deserved the right of first colony."

Aquila favored the man with an over the shoulder, arched glance.

"My great, great-uncle was one of them," Teague replied with an audible hint of bother, leaving Aquila to wonder if he meant his relative was a colonist, or a lobbyist. *I'd bet the latter*, he thought to himself. Vildur had once joked that Teague had to have come from a long line of bureaucrats as he had the vocation down pat, a charge Teague did not, at the time, dispute.

When it became obvious Teague had no intention of elaborating, Corsali continued, "Part of the agreement was that these colonists had seventy-five Standard years to establish a self-sufficient settlement. If they failed, a new group would be offered the chance. When most of the Earth crops they'd planted failed to grow, the founders realized it wasn't going to be as easy as they'd first assumed. They began aggressively recruiting colonists with promises of large plots of land on a planet whose major landmasses fall in the temperate zone, with climates and soil conditions ideal for farming—just not Earth crops.

"But because over eighty percent of Tuli's surface is covered by water and dotted with huge archipelagos—"

"And of course the wreckage had to hit land…" Amalfitano grumbled.

"—many who came turned to fishing rather than farming, which was far more lucrative, and this in turn prompted another wave of colonists, many directly from Earth, specifically from the islands of the Pacific who saw in the planet an unspoiled world very reminiscent of that from their own, albeit very distant past. Meanwhile, many of the original colonists gave up and returned to their home planets. Within two decades most of the first-wave colonists were gone. But they did leave behind a thriving, self-sufficient colony—just not the one originally envisioned—with a unique culture based loosely on that of the ancient Terran Pacific islands.

"A few years after that the planet was, by majority vote, remained Tuli and its sun Tangaloa. Ninety percent of today's Tulians claim decent from that last wave so would be designated Pacific islanders by original ethnicity and they make up the six clan-states, four of which are spread over the largest island chains. There are also two non-ethnically based provinces, the populations of which are largely made up of the remnants of the original first-wave colonists."

"So people who came to Tuli as a persecuted minority end up a minority in their colony?" Amalfitano asked.

Corsali shrugged. "Basically, yes, except they aren't being persecuted any more—in fact the seven families who claim direct descent from the first colonists are some of the wealthiest on Tuli—"

Amalfitano and Aquila looked at Teague. He replied with a 'don't-look-at –me' shrug.

"—as they bought up all the best farming land as other colonists gave up and went back home then leased it out to the newcomers. Many consider the two non-ethnically based provinces 'privately owned' and in truth they are."

Aquila snorted, shook his head then said, "What about their current political structure? What or who are we going to be dealing with?"

"The planet is governed by the council," Corsali answered, "whose members are the elected leaders of each of the planet's six clan-states along with the two provinces." She paused as they entered the flickerstage and Aquila gave last-minute orders to the flickerstage tech, then she continued, "There's a president, who's elected by the council and serves two Tulian years—"

"Who's the current president?" Aquila asked as he equipped himself with a tac-pac.

"A man by the name of Seitakap—"

"What about Coalition representation?"

"The Coalition maintains a consulate in the provincial city of Girsu, which also serves as the seat of the High Council."

She stepped close to Aquila as Amalfitano and Teague crowded into the small chamber. "However, the Coalition's ambassador to Tuli retired recently, and until a replacement can be appointed, an individual by the name of John Henson, the representative of a major, off-world aquaculture conglomerate, has been acting as the Coalition's envoy."

"You spoke with him," Aquila said.

Corsali nodded.

"Opinion?"

She hesitated. "Off the record, sir?"

"Off the record."

"He's a self-aggrandizing ass, with a truly amazing repertoire of colorful epithets… sir."

"Wonderful." Aquila blew out his cheeks as he motioned to the tech to activate the flickerstage, then barely had time to murmur,

"Glad to have you along, Ensign—*again,*" before the flicker effect washed over them.

— ii —

Aquila took a deep breath of the hot, cloying air as he gave his alien surroundings a quick glance. The flickerstage had deposited them at the edge of a large, building-dotted plaza that in turn was surrounded by lush, tropical forest.

The plaza at first appeared deserted. Then he caught the murmur of voices and turning, immediately spotted several people standing on the shadowy verandah of a nearby building.

Two detached themselves from the others and quickly descended the building's stairs. At Aquila's signal, the *Baidarka*'s officers started towards them.

"Anything else I need to know?" he asked with a sidelong glance at Corsali.

"I'd say that this whole matter has come as a terrible shock to the Tulians—they've never been attacked by anyone."

"I'll bear that in mind." He turned his full attention on the two men who were approaching them. One was tall and burly with flaming red hair. The other was slightly shorter but just as solidly built, with dark hair and a nut-brown complexion.

Corsali didn't have to point out who was whom. Or, at least who was Henson.

"See anyone familiar?" Aquila whispered innocently out of the corner of his mouth to Teague.

Teague eyed him then replied in kind, *"Lobbyist,"* confirming Aquila's suspicion and putting to bed any further speculation on Teague's connection to the colony.

The taller man, his puffy, sunburned face instant reminding Aquila of an overripe peach, started to open his mouth as they stopped before the four but the other man deftly cut him off.

"Welcome to Tuli..." the Tulian began as he searched their unfamiliar faces, "...Commander Aquila?"

Aquila identified himself with a slight nod and a murmured, "Sir."

"I'm Seitakap, elected leader of the Lamilaroi and current High Council President, and this," he gestured unhappily to his companion, "is John Henson, your Coalition's envoy."

"Mister President, Mister Henson," Aquila replied and turned to his officers. "This is my second in command, Lieutenant Teague, my medical officer, Doctor Amalfitano..."

Seitakap's gaze briefly dropped to Amalfitano's bloodstained jumpsuit before meeting the doctor's stare.

"...and my adjutant, Ensign Corsali."

He smiled at her, then said, "I am honored," as he bowed his head to each.

"We are also honored, Mister President," Aquila said. "I only wish our meeting was due to more fortunate circumstances—"

"Indeed," Henson growled. "And we all know who's to blame—"

"You'll have ample opportunity to speak your mind, John," Seitakap interrupted with just a hint of exasperation. "But at a proper time and place, as we *agreed.*" He turned back to Aquila, smiled and gestured towards the building from which he and Henson had just come. "For now, let us adjourn to the Council Chambers, Commander. We have much to discuss and, I gather, not much time."

Henson grunted, favored Aquila with a contemptuous, head-to-toe look, then spun on his heel and stalked back towards the group of Tulians who had remained under the covered verandah of the building.

Seitakap shook his head then gave Aquila a sidelong glance. "He's a most intense man, Commander. He takes his position here, like everything else, very seriously."

"I respectfully disagree, Mister President," Aquila replied as he eyed the receding back of the envoy. "There's one thing he doesn't take seriously, and that's me. Not that I've given him much evidence of my competence."

Seitakap replied with a tactful, "If you will come with me? The High Council is waiting." With that, he led them up the pathway, up the stairs of the building's broad verandah, then through the wide doorway of the council chambers.

Aquila squinted into the chamber's relative gloom. The large, low-ceilinged room was open on two sides, permitting a sultry breeze to blow through it; beyond, the forest stretched off into the late afternoon haze. The hot, oppressively humid air was full of the soft tinkling sounds of numerous wind chimes, the sweet, heady perfume of flowers and the lilting whispers of the council members and their aides—whispers that stopped the instant the group strode through the doorway.

Seitakap motioned Aquila and the others to woven mats as he knelt on another. Henson and the other councilors were already seated.

Aquila expected open hostility, but as he looked around him, he saw only concern and a sense of bewildered sadness in the eyes of the Tulians who faced him. Their expressions left little doubt that, while they fully understood the true depth of the crisis that now faced them, they could not grasp why they had been the target of such an attack.

"Commander, allow me to introduce you to the High Council," Seitakap said, aware of Aquila's uneasy scrutiny of the surrounding semi-circle of faces. Starting at his left, he began putting names to the councilors: "Iatmool, of Kulamba; Varron of Havilah, Aitutaki, of the Halburi; Taitulu of Kurnai; Pakanga of—"

"Mister President," Henson interrupted irritably, "may I suggest we skip the formalities and get right to—"

"There is always time for courtesy, John," Seitakap replied evenly, then continued, "Pakanga of Jidgantjara, Mele of Wojobaaluk, Tzetzes of Kush and the Hinter Islands, and lastly Tupou, of Ungarinhin."

Aquila acknowledged each with a quick nod. If there were ethnic differences, he was hard pressed to see them; the Tulians all looked very much the same: stocky, shy-faced humans with sun-browned skin, black hair and dark eyes. He nodded again to Seitakap then motioned to his companions. "This is Lieutenant Teague, my second in command, Doctor Amalfitano, my chief medical officer, and Ensign Corsali, my adjutant."

There was a soft murmur of greetings from the council, before Aquila added, "We will attempt to answer any questions you might—"

Henson snorted and started to open his mouth, but Seitakap again cut him off. "Commander," he turned to him, "since the debris impacted in the highlands of the Wojobaaluk homeland, I shall ask their representative to speak first. Mele?"

A middle-aged woman dipped her head to Seitakap then turned her penetrating gaze on Aquila. "I wish to be the first to thank you,

Commander, and your crew," she briefly looked at Teague, Amalfitano and Corsali, "for your valiant attempts at saving our world. I know you did everything you could to prevent this crisis. Full responsibility for this despicable act rests squarely on the shoulders of the Hahtooshan captain, and he has paid for his actions, as have his crew."

Aquila heard murmurs and saw nods of agreement among the other councilors.

"I must add my words of praise also," a wizened old man said.

Seitakap leaned close and whispered in Aquila's ear, "He is Pakanga, our most ancient and respected councilor." In a louder voice he said, "It is Pakanga's clan-state, that of Jidgantjara, which borders Wojobaaluk and whose major population centers lie downwind of the impact zone. We've begun evacuations and had already commenced a mass ring vaccination program against all likely infectious agents," Seitakap added with a nod to Amalfitano, "based on the information supplied by you, Doctor, but both will take time." He then looked back at Pakanga.

"Unlike your Coalition's envoy," Pakanga began with a sharp look at Henson, "who, no doubt, means well, we do not blame you for this unfortunate happening. Mele says she blames the Hahtooshans, but we must accept blame as well. Years ago the Coalition offered us the means to defend ourselves, but we, in our naïveté, in our pride, refused. We have always considered ourselves safe since we were nonaligned, fed anyone who came asking, even if they could not pay and most of all, with no military and no expansionist aspirations, we posed a threat to no one. So, Commander, do not torment your—"

An untimely *bleat* from Aquila's tac-pac interrupted the councilor.

Aquila responded with an apologetic smile, pulled the small machine from its holster, brought it to his mouth and whispered irritably, "Yes?"

"Sir," Lesedi began urgently, *"we may have located a missile—"*

"Where?" he asked with a sidelong glance at Amalfitano as he thumbed the volume control so everyone in the room would hear the exchange.

"Approximately one and a half kilometers west of the primary impact site. Sensors are having trouble seeing through the radioactive cloud—it's real hot down there, so we can't make a positive ID—but a moment ago they detected a trace of the radioactive signature of the propellant used in Hahtooshan missiles. If it's indeed a missile, it must've broken apart on impact and is now leaking propellant."

Along with who knows what else, Aquila added to himself as he looked back at Seitakap.

Seitakap stared back at him, his eyes wide in quiet horror.

Henson, however, was far from silent. He muttered a profanity under his breath, but in the stunned silence of the council chambers, everyone heard him, including Lesedi, who replied, *"Sir?"*

"Why don't you just flick the goddamned thing into space," Henson suggested with an angry wave of his hand, "and blow it up? Seems the simplest thing to do!" He crossed his arms and fixed Aquila with a smug glare. "Or didn't that occur to you, Commander?"

Aquila took a deep breath before answering calmly, "Even if it was possible to make a positive lock-on, sir, which it's not under the present conditions, there's the very substantial risk that the missile, which is obviously damaged—"

"Would release the disease into the atmosphere in the process," Amalfitano finished for him while favoring Henson with an icy look. "Or didn't you think of that… sir?"

Henson, undaunted and pointedly ignoring Amalfitano and his testy remark, scowled at Aquila. "Then what the hell do you plan on doing?"

Aquila broke the staring match and dropped his narrowed gaze to the tac-pac. "What are the conditions like within the zone of impact, Ensign?"

This time it was Cyllo who answered, *"Far from ideal for containment, sir. I've run circulation models and it looks like we have less than five hours before the radioactive cloud rises high enough to be picked up by the prevailing trade winds and blown over populated areas. The risk of radiation fallout will be minimal due to the estimated rate of atmospheric dispersal, but if the biological agent's been aerosolized—"*

"It'll be drawn up into the air column and into the same dispersal pattern," Aquila finished for her.

"Yessir."

"Lesedi, have the landing detail stand by. Aquila out."

"That's it?" Henson snapped. "Mister President, I must protest—"

"Mister President," Aquila interrupted as he too turned to the Tulian, "may I suggest that we postpone further discussion until after the crash site and this missile have been secured and the biological agent identified and, if possible, neutralized?"

"Of course, Commander," Seitakap replied. He rose; everyone followed suit.

Aquila motioned to his companions. "Let's go."

— iii —

"Sha'ashahn?"

Khusaaq recognized the voice. *Pierson.*

The medtech took a cautious step into the dimly lit cubicle. "I'm sorry to bother you, sir, but—"

"What do you want?" The painkiller Amalfitano insisted he take after their return from the control room, in combination with the very last of his uniform's depleted stores had indeed taken the edge off the intense, throbbing pain that had spread from his thigh to his hip and up his spine to his skull. But neither had done anything to dull the venomous sting of Tu'indai's words or the searing knowledge that *Makhaira* and all aboard her were doomed. *All due to my actions—my words, just like... Cotopaxi.*

Left alone in his cubicle with his restive guards, constantly reminded of what was going on outside by the groans and shudders of the alien ship around him, he could think of nothing else.

Even long after the world around him had steadied, his thoughts continued to churn.

Everything she said, his mind began yet again, *everything Tarqk said was true. Perhaps if I'd—*

"Sir, Doctor Amalfitano requests your presence in his office."

Khusaaq squinted at the blurry figure silhouetted in the doorway. *So. It's over.* Then, out of the corner of his eye, he caught the flicker of movement as one of his guards stepped forward.

The marine motioned to the doorway with the muzzle of his shocker. "Go on, get up!"

Too numb to argue, too numb to even muster annoyance at the man's less than respectful tone, he carefully eased himself off his bunk and shuffled slowly after Pierson, into the narrow corridor and into the small airlock.

The guards crowded in behind him, the lock closed and for a moment, he stood sandwiched between three Rimmers with the muzzle of a shocker pressed into the small of his back. He was suddenly struck by the realization that this was the way it was going to be from now on. *Watched. Confined. Mind-stripped....*

The humans' odd smell in the closed space was overwhelming. He squeezed his eyes shut, clenched his teeth and tried not to breathe, but too late. Their pungent scent detonated in his mind, showering him with shards of memory, sharp, painful. *You cease to exist....*

"You okay, sir?"

His eyes snapped open. Pierson was staring up at him with genuine concern, but before he had a chance to reply the exterior lock opened.

"Out!" The marine guard prodded him in the back with the shocker.

Khusaaq lurched forward, on the medtech's heels and out of the airlock.

"This way, sir," Pierson said with an apologetic look and a wave towards Amalfitano's office.

Another sharp prod in the back by the guard prompted Khusaaq to limp after him.

Pierson stopped at the office doorway, said, "In here, sir," and Khusaaq stepped across the threshold.

"Sha'ashahn." Amalfitano rose from his desk, smiled tightly and gestured to a chair. "Please, take a seat."

Khusaaq did as he was told then met Amalfitano's concerned stare. The infinitesimal grain of hope, for his ship, for her crew—for himself, vanished. *"Makhaira* has been destroyed, yes? No survivors."

Amalfitano's carefully thought out, well-rehearsed explanation visibly crumbled on his tongue. "Yes. I'm terribly sorry. Really I am. If there'd been any other way—"

"Is this why you asked for me?" he asked hoarsely.

"Yes—"

"Then you have fulfilled your duty." He grabbed the arms of the chair, forced himself unsteadily back to his feet and turned for the door only to find the guards, shockers drawn, blocking his path.

"I didn't say you could leave," Amalfitano replied firmly. "Please, sit down."

"Do as he says," the surlier of the two marines growled as he motioned with his shocker to the chair. *"Do it!"*

Khusaaq glared at him, then at Amalfitano.

Amalfitano replied with a quiet, calm, "Please. Sit down, son, before you fall down."

After a tense, awkward pause he resumed his seat.

"I also asked to see you because I thought you might want to talk to someone."

"Talk?" he squinted at him. His lips, his tongue felt suddenly thick. "About what?"

Amalfitano studied him intently for a moment; he stared back, intensely uncomfortable with the man's equally intense scrutiny.

"Anything. Whatever's on your mind."

"Meaning the death of my ship."

Amalfitano shrugged. "It's up to you."

Khusaaq dropped his pinched stare to his knees and swallowed convulsively. *Makhaira...* "I would very much like to return to my cubicle." He briefly raised his gaze, squinted at Amalfitano. "Or am I now to be housed in your brig?"

"You can return to your cubicle, if that's what you want, but will you permit me to give you something to help you sleep?"

He shook his head and replied in a tight voice barely above a whisper, "I am A'tuu'shahn." Realizing he had said it more for his own benefit than the doctor's he looked up to find Amalfitano staring at him, clearly unconvinced.

"Uh-huh." Amalfitano pulled open the bottom drawer of his desk, withdrew a fat-bellied bottle and a short, squat glass then filled the glass almost to the brim. "Here. Doctor's orders," he added with an encouraging smile as he pushed the glass towards him.

Khusaaq reluctantly leaned forward, warily picked up the glass and took a sniff of the amber liquid. He slid his gaze back to him. "Alcohol?"

"Best whisky money can buy." Amalfitano paused then at Khusaaq's hesitation, added, "Your species imbibe in ethyl alcohol, right?"

"Yes." *Far too often in fact.*

He motioned to the glass. "Then bottoms up."

Khusaaq scowled at him. "*Tuh maztsaeh.*"

"Drink it. *All* of it."

"Ensign Corsali told me I drink too much."

"But Ensign Corsali isn't here."

Khusaaq nodded, added quietly, "No, she's not," then after a moment's pause, he brought the glass to his lips and took a small sip. He allowed the odd tasting fluid to pool in his dry mouth and surround his gummy tongue. Finally he swallowed, and his eyes narrowed to slits as the potent liquor trickled past the excruciatingly tight muscles of his throat.

Amalfitano grinned at his watery-eyed grimace. "See? Smooth as silk. Now drink up."

Why not. Khusaaq brought the glass back to his lips and downed its contents in one loud, wincing gulp.

Chapter 23

Amalfitano watched as Khusaaq polished off yet another glassful. *That makes three—let's just hope your new gut lining's up to the challenge.* "Now, how about something to sop that up with?"

"*Juu'maz... teh?*"

He smiled at Khusaaq's noticeably slurred response. *About damned time it kicked in.* "Something to eat." Not waiting for a reply, he tapped an order into the desk's servo-panel.

As Amalfitano turned back to Khusaaq, he saw his patient staring rather forlornly at his now empty glass. Amalfitano picked up the bottle. "How 'bout a little more?"

In reply Khusaaq pushed the glass across the desk.

Amalfitano refilled his glass and pushed it back, adding, "Chow'll be up in a jiffy," as Khusaaq brought the glass to his lips.

Amalfitano couldn't help but lick his own lips and swallow reflexively as he watched the mercenary greedily drain it. It was his very best stock, two hundred year old whisky, shipped all the way from Earth and saved for very special occasions. Khusaaq was downing it like water and Amalfitano made a mental note to keep a bottle of far less costly hooch in the bottom of his desk drawer ready for any future matters requiring alcoholic immoderation on the part of someone who wouldn't know the difference.

Then, hearing the chime of the wall dispenser, he returned the almost empty bottle to its drawer.

"Here you go." He withdrew a covered tray from the servo-door and placed it on the desk in front of Khusaaq. "I want you to eat this, all right?" He lifted the cover to reveal a bowl of steaming gruel. "Matoosh told me this is similar to the standard rations on your ships?"

Khusaaq eyed the bowl as his nose twitched and by his less than thrilled reaction Amalfitano wondered if it might be less a close analog to Hahtooshan field cuisine and more an example of what he and his staff had come to recognize as Matoosh's rather perverse sense of humor, this time at the intended expense of Suhjai. The concoction certainly didn't look or smell in the least bit inviting.

Come to think of it, Matoosh always found an excuse not to eat it—and so had the others. Amalfitano had just chalked it up to what he considered typical Hahtooshan mulishness; in fact the mercenaries had quickly developed a fondness for cheeseburgers—with extra dill pickles—pancakes and strangest of all, anything with chocolate—all presumably very alien food to their palates. He'd never gotten around to asking exactly how the Hahtooshans had learned of these gastronomic options, but strongly suspected Izraad had offered them up in hopes of winning over their cooperation. Since the majority were teenagers, and cheeseburgers had become extremely popular among the *Baidarka*'s younger crew after a group had visited a retro diner on Mirfak during a stopover, cheeseburgers seemed a logical place to start—or so he assumed.

If the grumbled remarks he'd overheard from the marines who rotated through sickbay on guard duty was any guide, her ploy hadn't worked. Their prisoners were as disobliging, bad-mannered and ungrateful as ever. Same had been true with Matoosh, who had been plied with the same offerings by Drakin and Pierson in trade for cooperation during his dressing changes and therapy, and with the same sorry results: a stack of empty plates and an untouched foul temper.

Any excuse to be a pain in the butt, but…. Amalfitano lifted his gaze. "Maybe you'd prefer to try one of my favorites?" It wasn't cheeseburgers, it wasn't pancakes and it wasn't chocolate. It was even better.

At Khusaaq's suspicious stare, he muttered, "I'll take that as a 'yes, please'," and quickly tapped in an order.

After a moment's hesitation and a sidelong glance at his sullen companion, Amalfitano grinned, said, "In fact, I'll join you," and placed a second order.

A few minutes later, he heard another *bleat* and turned to the servo-door as it opened. He withdrew two plates, placed one in front of Khusaaq, the other in front of himself and lifted the covers with a flourish. *"Voila!"*

Khusaaq squinted dubiously at the latest offering: a brown-flecked yellowish mound heaped on the plate. "What is... this?"

"Frittata di Fungi Lazzaro," Amalfitano grinned as he eagerly scooped up a forkful from his own plate.

"You... eat this?"

"It's a family specialty. Took the galley awhile to get it right considering it's all artificial, but now... *perfection!"* He slid the forkful into his awaiting mouth and grinning, savored the taste as he chewed.

Khusaaq cautiously poked the rubbery mass with the tip of a tattooed finger.

"It won't bite."

The mercenary jerked his hand away and looked sharply at Amalfitano then sniffed his finger and made a face.

Undeterred, Amalfitano continued, "All right, so it's not made from real eggs, but close enough a chicken would be proud to call them hers. And the mushrooms aren't really mushrooms either..."

"Mush... rooms?"

Amalfitano forked another piece. "A type of fungus, very tasty too."

"Fungus?"

"Mamma used to make this every Sunday for brunch." Amalfitano sighed, "Boy, that woman could cook."

Khusaaq's gaze darted to the bowl of gruel, then back to the other, equally unappealing offering and slowly eased himself back into the chair. "I... I'm not hungry."

Amalfitano swallowed his mouthful, tossed his fork onto his plate then crossed his arms and sighed. "Look, son, you're gonna have to eat sometime."

Khusaaq glowered at him.

"Maybe you'd rather try something—"

"Doctor Amalfitano?" Teague's voice crackled unexpectedly from the desk-com.

He thumbed the desk-com. "What is it, Edwin?"

"The landing party sent to investigate the crash site has returned."

"And...?" His eyes locked with Khusaaq's.

"They located an intact missile..."

Khusaaq's eyes widened, ever so slightly.

"...which will be flicked up momentarily. The commander's requested your presence in the cargo bay—"

"Be right there." Amalfitano cut the link, hastily wiped his mouth on his napkin and rose. He circled the desk. "I want you to stay here," he tapped the back of Khusaaq's chair.

The nearest guard stepped away from the door. "But sir…"

Amalfitano silenced him with a glare then looked back to Khusaaq. "I'll have someone from the galley to come up here, and you tell them exactly what you want to eat, all right? Your men seem particularly taken with the cheeseburgers and chocolate milk—no worries about allergens. Like this," he motioned to his plate, "they're all artificial. Besides, my staff ran sensitivities just to be on the safe side. We weren't about to give your medic—"

"Suhjai," Khusaaq muttered.

"—the opportunity to accuse us of trying to induce anaphylaxis in her and the others, on top of her endless list of complaints. You might give them a try."

At Khusaaq's less than enthusiastic nod, he hurried from the office.

— ii —

Aquila risked a quick, exasperated look at Teague as he, and by default the entire control room crew, sat silent and motionless, listening to Henson's upbraiding.

"And another thing—"

"Sir…?" Stoker broke in before Henson could continue.

Aquila, happy for any interruption and eagerly hoping for news from Amalfitano and the contents of the missile, jerked his chair around to face him. "Yes?"

"I'm receiving a priority message feed from HQ."

He blinked. "HQ?"

"Yessir."

Aquila dropped his gaze back to the chair com-unit. "We'll have to continue this… discussion at a later time, Mister Henson. Aquila out." He cut the link with more force than was needed, then took a deep breath and prepared himself for yet another, and this time official, tongue-lashing. "Let's hear it."

"Message reads: *Baidarka*, situation has been reviewed in emergency session of the Coalition Central Committee. You're hereby granted full discretionary powers to take any and all actions to protect the planet Tuli."

"In other words," he muttered with a sidelong glance at Teague, "we're on our own."

Teague nodded.

"...the *Walafar*'s been dispatched," Stoker continued. "ETA, eighteen hours."

"*Walafar?*" Aquila interrupted as he turned back to Teague, but it was Izraad who answered: "She's a cutter just recently assigned to Intelligence, sir."

"Oh." He looked back at Stoker. "Go on."

"All Hahtooshan prisoners deemed medically stable are to be immediately isolated from further contact with your crew."

Aquila flicked Izraad another look; she stared back, clearly just as baffled.

"You'll be briefed fully upon *Walafar*'s arrival," Stoker added, "by Captain Mladić of Headquarters Intelligence."

Aquila caught Izraad's ever-so-slight widening of the eyes. *Uh-oh.*

"Signed, Admiral Keon, CEF Sector Command. Verify message received. End message."

"Verify. And notify Sergeant Delatorre. Ensign Cyllo, anything more from the planet?"

"The radioactive cloud is beginning to disperse just as models suggested, sir," she replied. "Evacuations are continuing without incident, but coordinators on the ground say it will take a minimum of twelve hours to evacuate everyone from the highest risk areas."

Aquila nodded and turned to the tactical display. As he stared at the computer-generated image of the planet and beyond, the system's massive sun, he began drumming his fingers on the arms of his chair.

It was a waiting game now. Waiting for word from Medical; waiting for word from the planet. *Waiting for the other shoe to drop—*

He jerked his head up as he suddenly recalled Izraad's quickly concealed reaction to the mention of Captain Mladić. "Lieutenant Izraad? With me." He rose from his chair and strode through the airlock.

He waited for her just outside, and once the lock had closed, he turned his questioning stare on her. "Spill."

She raised her brows. "Sir?"

"Mladić. You know him."

"Not personally. Never even met him. All I know is what I've heard second and third hand—"

"But what you've heard isn't good."

"Nossir. Very bad in fact."

He looked around, making sure the corridor was empty, then lowering his voice said, "Is there any way we can protect our Hahtooshans?"

She smiled. "Our?"

He brushed it aside with a gruff, "You know what I mean."

"They risked their lives to save yours, sir, and the lives of Ensign Corsali and Corporal Gianakis. There's nothing to be ashamed of in wanting to return the favor—but back to the matter at hand. Asylum is their only chance, even temporary sanctuary—"

"But I never offered them asylum."

"HQ never told you not to, did they?"

"Likely never occurred to them."

She smiled. "Very likely not."

He exhaled, rubbed his tired eyes with his fingertips then looked back at her. "Normally I'd ask you to be present, but..."

"My presence could, and likely would be construed as an attempt at coercion."

"So, any suggestions on how to approach Khusaaq?"

"Yeah. Have William lay the groundwork. Once that's in place, then sit down, lay out all the facts, his options and hope he makes the smart choice."

He gave her a skeptical look. "Will...? Not Ensign Corsali?"

"If he accepts, it must be of his own free will, with absolutely no taint of compulsion of any sort."

"But Will—"

"Sir, trust me on this one."

He sighed, nodded, then walked over to the nearby wall-com and pressed the activator. "Sickbay?"

Drakin's voice responded, *"Yez, Commander?"*

"Where's Doctor Amalfitano?"

"Ssstill outsssside da cargo bay, sssir, oversssseeing—"

"Have they crackled the missile yet?"

"No, not yet—"

"Then tell him to come to my quarters immediately." He cut the link, flicked Izraad a sidelong look, exhaled and shook his head, then started up the gently rising corridor.

He arrived at his private quarters a few minutes later, and had no sooner circled his desk when Amalfitano's familiar voice said, "What's up? Drakin said it was urgent?"

Aquila nodded and motioned to a chair. "Take a seat."

Amalfitano sat, folded his hands in his lap and, overhearing the door close behind him, fixed his now very apprehensive gaze on Aquila. "What's happened?"

"Is Khusaaq medically stable enough to be transferred to the brig?"

Amalfitano, taken off guard by the question, hesitated. "May I ask why?"

Aquila eased himself down into his own chair. "Just answer the damned question, Will. Yes, or no."

"No. Besides—"

"You're willing to state that in your official log?"

"Of course, already have, each time I've made rounds, now what the hell's going on?"

"I just received orders from HQ. We're to isolate the prisoners immediately. They're to have no further contact with the crew."

"What?" he arched a brow. "But—"

"HQ's dispatched a ship, the *Walafar*. It'll be here in less than eighteen hours."

"Why do I have a bad feeling about this?"

"It gets worse, much worse. She's bringing a Captain Mladić from Intelligence."

"Intelligence? But... *Khusaaq!*"

"Yeah." Aquila exhaled forcefully and rubbed his forehead. "Khusaaq. His only chance—not to mention the other Hahtooshans—is asylum—"

Amalfitano snorted angrily. "Intelligence would just love to get their hands on him—"

"I know.

"He wouldn't survive another mind strip—*wait.*" Amalfitano fixed him with a pointed stare. "Asylum? Who's offering him and the others asylum? Surely not the Tulians."

"Surely not—no, we are."

"We? Meaning the Coalition?"

"No. We meaning, well... *me.*"

"You?"

"Uh-huh. Izraad's idea when she heard about the *Walafar* and Mladić."

Amalfitano chewed on that for a moment, then, "As much as I personally agree with the sentiment, and would normally defer to her far greater expertise in the area, I do have to warn you that simply making this offer, whether he accepts or not, could cost you your career, you do know that."

"I owe him my life, Will—we, the Coalition *all* owe him."

"I fully agree. But... your career, for a merc."

"And yours, too."

"Mine?"

"Yeah."

"Why mine? What the hell did I do?"

"I haven't told you yet. Now, I want it understood that you can refuse what I'm about to ask of you, because if you agree, you'll be putting your career on the line, every bit as much as I am. And just so you know, I'm keeping Izraad out of it, even though it was her idea. No need to scuttle everyone's career."

Amalfitano settled back in his chair and crossed his arms. He fixed his gaze on the wall behind Aquila as he chewed distractedly on his lip, then after a brief silence, nodded and said, "Understood."

"First, I need you to officially log—not just your round reports—that in your medical opinion transferring Khusaaq to the brig would have a detrimental effect on his recovery. I want to keep him away from the others—in particular Suhjai."

Amalfitano raised his brows.

"Asylum's gonna be a hard enough sell, I damn well don't need her interfering—and if given a chance, she will, trust me—screw things up just to screw them up."

"No need to warn me on that account," Amalfitano grumbled.

"And besides, transferring him to the brig might have a damaging effect on his trust of us, and we're gonna need every ounce of trust we can get."

Amalfitano nodded. "You got it."

"Next, we've gotta get him to accept asylum before the *Walafar* gets here—"

"Leave it to me," Amalfitano pushed himself out of the chair and started for the door.

"Will…"

He stopped and looked back at Aquila.

"Your career."

"Yours too," Amalfitano replied.

"And one more thing, I don't want to hand him and the others over, but we can't coerce him."

"I wasn't planning on coercing him. I'm not sure how one would even go about trying to coerce a merc—"

"You can lay out the facts if he asks," Aquila continued, "discuss his options, again, only if he asks—including him *asking* for asylum—but I have to be the one to accept his request—or offer it. Given my purely selfish druthers, I'd prefer the former, but…"

Amalfitano nodded and tapped the release and the door opened. "Less than eighteen hours, huh?"

"Yeah."

"Don't get your hopes up. He's one headstrong son of a bitch."

"You've noticed."

"Let's just say I'm familiar with the type." He managed a smile and took a step, then stopped. *"Mmm… wait."*

"Problem?"

"Maybe. I just remembered that I left him in my office and—"

"Your office?"

"Under guard," Amalfitano added hastily. "I thought he should know about his ship—"

"And…?"

"I hoped I might talk him into taking something, you know," Amalfitano shrugged, "just to take the edge off."

"But you couldn't."

"No."

Aquila hesitated before asking reluctantly, "So, you…?"

"Got him drunk?"

He looked away and blew out his cheeks. "Great. Just… *great!"*

"It seemed like a really brilliant idea at the time."

Aquila squinted sourly at him.

"Don't worry, I'll get him sobered up and—"

"Then you better get to it, hadn't you?" Aquila growled.

— iii —

"Khusaaq…?"

He turned away from the voice. *Go away.*

"Khusaaq?" the voice said again, more insistent.

"I said go away…" he mumbled irritably in his sleep.

"Khusaaq, come on, wake up… ah, *tanhah?"*

Fingers lightly grasped his shoulder and his eyes snapped open.

A face appeared in front of him, a strange, yet at the same time, vaguely familiar face.

A Rimmer face! He recoiled, his nostrils sucking in air. *"Tu-mazneri!"*

"Easy, son, easy!" Surprisingly, the fingers tightened their hold rather than wisely letting go. "It's just me, Amalfitano."

He squinted at the face and repeated slowly, "Amal… feetano?"

Suddenly the name, face and, most importantly, *scent* fit, like keys in a rusty lock and he took a deep, ragged breath as the surge of panic subsided.

He looked around and vaguely recognized his surroundings. He licked his lips, then met Amalfitano's concerned stare.

"You had me scared there for a minute."

"Then we're even," Khusaaq grumbled hoarsely as he slowly, cautiously straightened up in his chair. "What am I doing…" his eyes again searched the cluttered room, "…here?"

Amalfitano's relieved smile faded. "I had Pierson bring you here, to my office, a coupla hours ago… remember?"

He gave his surroundings yet another look as Amalfitano glanced at the uneaten frittata, the bowl of congealed gruel… and a new addition: an untouched cheeseburger.

"The guards told me you sent the cook away—or, should I say, you scared the cook away."

"I told him I wasn't hungry." Khusaaq massaged his pounding temples. "He, like you, would not believe me. He needed a little… persuasion."

"Well, you're going to have to eat sometime, or would you rather I have Drakin shove a feeding tube down your throat?"

Khusaaq dropped his hands away from his face and glared at him, but the icy expression was tempered by a slightly green-about-the-gills hue.

Amalfitano, catching the visual clue, snatched up the plates and bowl, placed them in the dispenser and pressed the discard button. "Just telling you the options." He waited until the food had vanished then he tapped in a new order.

A moment later the servo-panel chimed and he reached in and withdrew a pitcher and two cups. He filled one cup with a steaming black liquid then offered it to him. "Here."

As Khusaaq accepted it, Amalfitano continued, "Coffee. Helps clear the mind. Or if you'd prefer, I could give you something, a mild stimulant..."

Khusaaq looked at him, suspicious anew. "First you get me drunk, and now you want me sober—why?"

Amalfitano lifted his gaze to the marines. "Kipurs, Tanser, I'm gonna have to ask you boys to do your guarding outside."

"But sir," Tanser began, "our orders—"

"I'll take full responsibility. Now go on."

Tanser stood his ground. "I'll have to notify the commander, sir."

"Be my guest. But *outside*. Now go on—and close the door behind you."

"Yessir." Kipurs backed out of the office.

Tanser hesitated, then he too reluctantly stepped across the threshold, but not before flashing Amalfitano a 'be it on your own head' glance.

Khusaaq, aware of the exchange, turned his curious, bordering on worried stare back on Amalfitano to find the man pouring himself a cup from the pitcher.

Amalfitano sat down and took a deep gulp from his mug.

Khusaaq, following his lead, brought his cup to his lips as he heard the door slip shut behind him.

"Now, we need to talk."

Khusaaq took a cautious sip, winced at the coffee's surprisingly sweet taste which was at odds with its rather bitter scent, swallowed then replied cautiously, "About what?"

"Your immediate future."

Khusaaq looked down at the cup he clutched in both hands. "I just lost my ship, my friends—*everything*. I no longer care what happens to me."

"Well I do, so does Commander Aquila. Look, son—"

"I'M NOT YOUR SON!" He smacked the cup down, splashing its scalding contents across the desk as he forced himself to an unsteady stand. Rage, desperation, crushing guilt... all the raw emotions that the alcohol had dulled, suddenly reignited into one excruciatingly tight knot in his gut and he croaked, *"I'm A'tuu'shahn!"*

Amalfitano stared, wide-eyed up at him, utterly taken aback as he managed a hasty if stammering, "It's... it's just... just an expression!"

Khusaaq's baleful stare deepened, unimpressed, and at the same time he was gratified, comforted by the sudden smell of fear in the human. To Amalfitano, though, the mercenary no longer looked as if he was about to leap over the desk and rip out his throat.

"If you've counseled as many young soldiers as I have, it just becomes part of your vocabulary. I'm very sorry it offended you—it was not meant as an insult. Now, please, *Sha'ashahn*, sit down and hear me out, all right?"

Khusaaq remained on his feet while visibly trembling and continued to glare at him, unwilling to give up what little advantage he had.

"Okay, *stand* there and hear me out." Amalfitano leaned back in his chair, took a moment to collect his thoughts sent scattering by Khusaaq's unexpected outburst then began cautiously, "The Coalition's never going to let you go, you're too valuable a source of Intelligence—you know that. You had to have realized that no matter what, you aren't going be returned to your people—at least not right away." He met Khusaaq's baleful scowl and added, "There's a Coalition Intelligence ship on its way here, and—"

"Once I am handed over to them, I'll be mind-stripped again." Just the thought generated a fresh surge of adrenaline. Mixed with the alcohol and caffeine on a very empty stomach, it left him feeling dizzy and intensely nauseous. He unsteadily resumed his seat.

Amalfitano toyed with the handle of his cup, murmured, "Yes," and looked up; his eyes narrowed in sudden concern. "You feeling all right?"

Khusaaq desperately wanted to say no. He wanted to say that he suddenly felt like he was going to vomit, but to say that would require him opening his mouth and if he opened his mouth, telling the doctor he felt like he was going to vomit would be redundant. He settled for a quick shake of his head.

Amalfitano hurriedly rose, snatched up his bio-scanner, circled the desk and held the small machine close to Khusaaq's chest. "Core temp's up, as is your cytokine production. Heart rate's through the roof." He scowled at the scanner as it began chirping rapidly. "That is if I can trust this damned thing." He smacked it against his other palm then met Khusaaq's sidelong, pinched stare with a mildly frustrated one of his own. "Those micro-sensors we implanted in you during surgery are starting to fail."

Khusaaq glanced down at himself, new misgivings piling on to old. *You implanted—*

"Nothing to worry about. They were designed to disintegrate after a hundred hours." Amalfitano gave his pasty-faced patient another once over. "Now, how 'bout I give you something for that headache? It'll settle your stomach, too." He stuffed his hand in his pocket and pulled out a ject-it. "Let's have your arm."

Khusaaq found himself sorely tempted to agree. His head did hurt and his stomach continued to roil. It made thinking very difficult. *But....*

He dropped his gaze to the ject-it and licked his lips as long held suspicions held sway. *Convenient you just happened to have that in your pocket.* Better to be physically sick, ridding himself in the most expeditious manner of both the coffee and the liquor, than risk whatever drug might be in the ject-it. "*Chulh.*"

"Damn, you're predictable!" Amalfitano shoved the ject-it back in his pocket. "You don't have to constantly prove to me you're a tough guy, okay? I'm convinced—*happy?* And I'm just your doctor. Far be it from me to—"

"When... when does this ship arrive?"

"Ship? Oh, yes...ah, in a little over seventeen hours." He resumed his seat. "The commander and I don't want to hand you over—"

"Why? Why do you care what happens to me? I'm A'tuu'shahn."

"Damned difficult to forget with you reminding me every nanosecond, and to be totally honest, a week ago I wouldn't have cared. A week ago I'd have happily—no, *gleefully* turned you over and good riddance. A week ago I'd have dismissed anyone as being space happy for even suggesting that I'd ever be sitting unarmed and alone in a sealed room with a hung-over and not particularly cheerful Hahtooshan. But here I am." He leaned back and crossed his arms. "A lot's changed in a week."

"You still haven't answered my question. Why?"

"I saved your life—I was up to my elbows inside your insides. That gives me a vested interest not to mention a strong desire not to have to pay a return visit."

"I think not."

"All right, smart guy, since you clearly know all the answers, you tell me."

"I've already told you, I *don't* understand," he growled as he eyed the Rimmer who sat across from him at the cluttered desk. *What do you want from me?* "As you yourself said, I'm a valuable source of intelligence. Therefore it would be in the best interest of your Coalition to turn me over." *And get it over with—perhaps that's it. Perhaps you're hoping to break me by just the mere threat of another mind-strip?* His eyes narrowed and he added grimly, "If our situations were reversed, I wouldn't hesitate to hand you over to be interrogated."

"I don't believe you."

"It's the truth," he grumbled as he massaged his temple with his fingers.

"Then why rescue Robert and the others? From what I understand, you put yourself and your men at great risk. In fact, according to Ensign Corsali, you lost two of them in the process?"

Khusaaq dropped his slitted gaze to his knees. *Jabooreh. Vur'taas—good men, loyal Elkanaghalli'i and kinsmen, killed trying to rescue those crewmen Aquila accused me of abandoning... now added to the list of those whose deaths are solely my responsibility. And all for—*

"Why?"

"It wasn't out of any misguided notion of compassion, I assure you." He met Amalfitano's steady gaze with an embittered one of his own. "I rescued Aquila for one reason, and one reason only, to stop Tarqk," he said, his voice suddenly sharp-edged, surly, baiting. "Just like you '*saved*' me in order to mind-strip me—"

"*Let's get something straight right here and now!*" Amalfitano snarled, banging his fist on the desk for emphasis, hard enough to send an untidy stack of flimsies cascading over the edge and onto the floor. "I saved your life for one goddamned reason and one goddamned reason only, I'm a doctor! That's what I do!"

Khusaaq rubbed his painfully throbbing temple as he scowled at him, yet felt strangely pleased that he'd finally managed to goad the man into losing his temper.

Amalfitano exhaled then lowering his voice, said, "You still haven't answered my question. Knowing your people's well-documented penchant for making mischief, to put it mildly, I'd have thought you'd have happily gone along with this captain of yours, but you risked everything..."

And lost everything, Khusaaq added to himself. *Even more than I thought possible—*

"So, I ask again, why?"

"I was not about to stand by and permit Tarqk to hand your Coalition a justifiable pretense for exterminating us, once and for all."

Amalfitano paused, clearly sensing he was not telling all then asked, "Why take Ensign Corsali and Corporal Gianakis, too?"

"You mean you'd have been happier if I'd left them to those creatures as well?"

"Of course not—"

"Had I done so, I would have validated your blind hatred of A'tuu'shahn'i."

Amalfitano sighed, "That's not what I meant and you damned well know it."

Suddenly uneasy with the line of questioning, angry that Amalfitano was no longer angry, that he'd lost what little advantage he'd had, Khusaaq grabbed the arms of the chair. He pushed himself to a stiff-legged stand and replied with equal stiffness, using terms he knew Amalfitano would associate with a mercenary: "It cost me nothing to take them, and they gave me leverage over Aquila."

Amalfitano remained where he was, seated behind his desk and began to surreptitiously mop up the spilled coffee with a napkin before it reached another stack of flimsies while Khusaaq, favoring his right leg, slowly wandered around his office, his eyes briefly touching on each of the room's mismatched and worn furnishings.

How can you tolerate living in such disarray? He thought back to his austere cabin aboard *Makhaira*. *Makhaira... Gone now. All gone—*

"That's it?"

"Yes," Khusaaq replied as he found his attention eagerly drawn to the far wall, a wall covered with awards and certificates—anything to get away from thinking of *Makhaira*, of those aboard her.

"You certainly don't make things easy, do you? All right, let's try this tack: I owe you. The commander owes you. The Coalition owes you, not that this Intelligence officer will see it that way."

"If I were him, I wouldn't," he answered distractedly as he studied the certificates. He found himself impressed, albeit very begrudgingly. *I'd be wise not to underestimate you.*

Amalfitano responded with another loud, exasperated sigh, and then, "The commander is hoping, once you have some time to think about the choices before you, you'll request asylum."

Khusaaq jerked his startled eyes towards him, not sure he'd actually heard what he'd just heard. *"Asylum...?"*

"Yes. Asylum." At Khusaaq's clearly shocked stare, Amalfitano added, "Don't tell me your people don't consider that an option, even one of last resort?"

"I... I don't know—I've never heard of an A'tuu'shahn asking for, or being offered asylum." He looked away, tried to collect his thoughts. This was one possible he'd never considered. "As universally reviled mercenaries, we aren't used to being shown mercy."

"You're honestly telling me you didn't consider this as an option when you rescued Aquila? What did you think was going to happen? That you'd be welcomed with open arms then immediately given back to your own people? You had to have considered the greater likelihood that you'd end up a prisoner, subject to interrogation, and yes, even mind-strip by our Intelligence."

"You assume I had everything planned—every contingency considered."

"You mean you didn't?"

Khusaaq snorted, almost but not quite a harsh laugh. "No. I knew Tarqk had plans to rid himself of me, just as he'd done with Ou'dayaah—*Makhaira*'s senior medical officer who, like me, had become a great frustration for him—but I never expected to be awakened out of a sound sleep, dragged from my bed—told I was to organize and lead a landing party to investigate an abandoned Coalition site on an island our scanners had detected.

"While I knew my selection to lead the party was no coincidence, I had no idea when I flicked down that your ship—any ship for that matter—was going to pick up that distress call, and when I was ordered to reach the wreck before you could and ambush your landing party, I realized I could use this. I could grab some of your crew, hold them hostage, bargain with you—their lives in trade for you disseminating the data, thus making it worthless to Tarqk, to whoever contracted us in the first place."

"So this was all reacting to events, rather than a premade plan on your part?"

"I'd like to believe I'd have done a far better job of it had I had time to plot out every possibility and plan accordingly. As it was, I used what I had."

"And you assumed the Coalition wouldn't just put a lid on this, rather than allow it to be known it ever had a secret base on the fourth planet—something it had clearly worked very hard to conceal for the past one hundred odd years?"

"I felt the least the Coalition would do is stop Tarqk when it realized he planned on testing it—which was the whole point. I assumed I'd reach the island before you could find us; I assumed I'd have a chance to show Aquila the data, convince him the threat was real; I assumed, using the island's shielding, that I could stop you from taking us prisoner."

"You mean you planned on *remaining* on the planet? Shielding or not, you couldn't have survived more than another week or so."

"As I've already told you, my goal was to stop Tarqk, stop him from testing the weapon. What happened after that, well..."

"How very heroic."

"Not at all. Death, any death, even that from radiation poisoning, is a far better fate than being taken captive by your Coalition."

"The very same Coalition you were trying to protect."

"I was trying to protect the Orthodoxy first and foremost."

Amalfitano inhaled slowly then exhaled even slower.

"We were marooned on the planet—I'm sure Ensign Corsali told you that—we were expected to die, *we* expected to die. We'd accepted our fate, had made plans..." Without realizing it, his hand reached unerringly for his missing pistol. He shook his head, quickly clasped his hands in his lap. "No matter."

"Well, it damned well does matter. Because as you know, there's been a huge change of plans. And now you have different options—and a little bit of time to think about the option of asylum."

Khusaaq glanced back at him. *Asylum.* Just the thought brought a fresh taste of bile to his mouth. *I don't want to live among you!*

"All I ask is that you will think on it, okay? Give me your word you'll at least consider it—"

"You're asking me to trust you, to put my faith in you, to turn my back on my beliefs and everything and everyone I've ever known." *To forgive—*

"I know, and I know I can't even begin to imagine what that's like."

"No, you cannot." As Khusaaq turned back for his chair, a small holo caught his eye. It might have easily gone unnoticed among the elaborately framed honors that filled the wall. Might, had he not been A'tuu'shahn, with an A'tuu'shahn's memory for even the most miniscule or mundane detail and eyes that never missed a thing. Had one of his guards not taken obvious delight in informing him of each crew members' personal or familial experience with A'tuu'shahn abuses, real or attributed.

He gave the image of three friendly faces—a woman and two young children—a quick study and smiled. *Yes.* He looked back at Amalfitano. "Your family?"

"Nope." He rose from his chair. "I have no idea who they are, or were, as the case may be."

Khusaaq shifted his now slitted gaze back to the holo, not sure whether to be bitterly disappointed in his answer, or find cold comfort that his deeply held distrust of all things Rimmer had just been validated. *I just gave you a chance to tell me the truth... to prove to me you alone are capable of telling me truth—*

"Here," Amalfitano said as he joined him and handed him his forgotten, replenished cup of coffee, which Khusaaq reluctantly accepted, then Amalfitano motioned to the holo. "I enlisted fresh out of medical school. Thought it'd be good experience. Never planned on making a career out of it, then again I never thought we'd be so damned stupid we'd get ourselves embroiled in another war with the

Matarrans so soon after the first one. Little did I know then that two wars still weren't enough."

He shook his head, said, "Gildun used to say... " then glanced sidelong at Khusaaq and said by way of explanation, "she was a good friend," and at Khusaaq's slight and wary acknowledging tip of the head continued, "anyway, she used to say 'Each time history repeats itself, it gets more expensive.' And boy, was she right. The last war came far too close to fatally crippling the Coalition. Had it gone on another two, maybe three months, well..."

Amalfitano paused, fixed his suddenly bright gaze on the far wall, then after a moment cleared his throat and flicked Khusaaq a glance and at his stone-faced reaction, said, "I spent the first few years being bumped from one ship to another. Then came the war and I was assigned to the *Pharo*, a troop transport." He released the holo from its wall holder and smiled down at the image. "When you're a troop ship's doctor, part of your job, a big part of your job, is listening to frightened, homesick or traumatized soldiers...."

Khusaaq pointedly ignored Amalfitano's pointed, sidelong look.

"...and I quickly discovered that not having a family put me at a distinct disadvantage." He hesitated, then added, "Six months after being assigned to the *Pharo*, I wangled a two day leave on Mirfak Prime. Found this in an old pawnshop. Cost me one whole credit. Best money I ever spent."

Khusaaq slowly turned to face him. "One of the guards told me your family had been butchered... by A'tuu'shahn'i."

Amalfitano winced, muttered, *"Cacchio,"* then added with audible anger, "Which guard?"

"Does it matter?"

"Yes, it does. A great deal. I'll *not* have my patients goaded. Who was it?" He looked accusatively at the door. "I bet it was Tanser. It was Tanser, wasn't it?"

Khusaaq hesitated, suddenly unsure. "Then he was lying in hopes of... provoking me?"

"Provoking you, undoubtedly, but... no, he wasn't lying, damn his hide. Was it Tanser?"

Khusaaq squinted at him, confused. "Then what you just told me is a lie."

"No," Amalfitano replied emphatically.

"It cannot be both—"

"My parents and sister." He looked down at his cup and added softly, "They were on Raumalle."

Khusaaq continued to glower at him. *You're wondering if I was there, aren't you? But you don't dare ask—you're terrified to ask.* Aloud he growled, "Ironic then that you found yourself forced to save an A'tuu'shahn's life, yes?"

"At the time I can't say I was thrilled and if you'd died on the operating table, I wouldn't have shed a tear, but I also wasn't forced. I could have refused."

Khusaaq snorted, "Indeed?" then looked back at the holo, and after an awkward silence, sneered, "So, you lied about having a wife and children."

"No, not exactly. I put this in a prominent spot and just allowed people to assume what they wanted."

Khusaaq eyed him. *And what else do you allow people 'to assume' about you?*

Amalfitano reattached the holo, stepped back and gazed fondly at the image. "I planned on throwing it away when I transferred to the *Baidarka*, but I—"

"Did not."

The doctor turned back to him. "No. Not sure why, to be honest. What about you?"

"What about me?" Khusaaq replied suspiciously. *What do you want from me? What are you trying to trick me into revealing?*

"Your family. Your father and—"

"Ja'andai—my *ta'katleh* was killed when I was very young," he replied stiffly. "I barely knew him."

"I'm sorry to hear that."

Khusaaq replied with an irritable twitch of the shoulders.

"And your mother?"

Instead of answering, Khusaaq pointedly fixed his narrowed gaze on the holo and Amalfitano, sensing he'd touched a sore spot, quickly moved on.

"So, uh… how old were you when you joined up?"

Khusaaq shifted his stare to him, still angry, still suspicious and now genuinely perplexed. "Like all A'tuu'shahn'i, I have never known anything but service. As an Elkanaghalli, I was pledged at birth to serve the Elkanasu and then, when I was old enough, I was given over to the Orthodoxy to be trained in whatever field they determined I, as an Elkanaghalli, was best suited."

"Which was—"

"Killing." Finally seeing the desired response on the man's face, he added harshly, "That's what you think, isn't it? A'tuu'shahn'i are nothing more than cold-blooded butchers—*that's what all Rimmers think!"*

"Commander Aquila told me you're a signals specialist."

He shrugged again. "That too."

Amalfitano shook his head, exhaled forcefully. "You're not making this any easier, you know that."

"For you or for me?"

"I didn't think we were working at cross purposes."

Khusaaq scowled at him and angrily motioned to the holo. "Why tell me this... *story?"*

"It's not a 'story', and... and damn it, you asked—"

"And you thought you'd gain my trust by confiding in me?"

"Did anyone ever tell you you've got a very suspicious mind?"

He started to reply, 'I am A'tuu'shahn'. Instead he growled, "Yes. Many times."

"Well, I wasn't confiding, just so you know. Everyone on board knows—about Raumalle and yes, this holo. And you're going to have to start trusting someone sometime."

"Meaning you."

"Not necessarily. You couldn't go wrong with Robert. He's as honest as they come. Or what about Sirin?"

Khusaaq jerked his gaze back to the holo, then to the awards that covered the wall. After a very awkward moment, he said, "An impressive record of accomplishment."

"Same could be said for you." Amalfitano motioned to his medal encrusted bandoleer, collar and gorget.

He looked down at himself and ran his tattooed fingers over the insignia then replied with curt nod as he looked back at the holo.

"You were at Cotopaxi."

Cotopaxi. Taken off guard, his mind clenched painfully around the memory and the sudden realization—the truly horrendous irony—that he was the last, the sole survivor. *Telipinu, Ichkeul, Saar'kali... all dead, killed by the Coalition. And now... Qharubi. And these Rimmers are asking you to trust them!*

Amalfitano gave him an appraising stare. "That was eleven Standard years ago. Which means you were a highly decorated combat veteran by the age of *fifteen?"* He crossed his arms. "Just how old were you when you—"

"Became a professional murderer-for-hire?" he interrupted coldly. "By your reckoning? Not quite thirteen."

Amalfitano winced and replied softly, *"That young?"*

Khusaaq turned his attention back to the wall of certificates. "We A'tuu'shahn'i mature much faster than you humans."

"Physically, maybe, but psychologically?"

This time Khusaaq refused to look at him.

Amalfitano chewed on his lip for a moment then said, "Why hide the fact that you were awarded a Coalition Battle Commendation? I would've thought—"

"It does not hold the same significance to A'tuu'shahn'i as it does to Rimmers," he grumbled as he pretended to study the numerous awards.

"But it means something to you."

Khusaaq flicked him a sidelong glare as the old hatreds bubbled to the surface unbidden; he couldn't have stopped them even if he'd tried.

"And by the look you're giving me right now, it clearly means a hell of a lot." He instinctively backed up a step but persisted, "And your captain called you the 'Hero of Cotopaxi'—so did you, saying it afforded you special privileges. What did he and you mean by that?"

"He meant it as an insult."

"A rather odd insult coming from—"

"A merc?" he growled.

Amalfitano sighed, "All right, yes. But if that's the case, then why wear the commendation?" He motioned to the hidden medallion.

"I was ordered to always wear it, to remind others..." his tight voice trailed off and he fixed his suddenly narrowed gaze on the far wall. *To never forget.*

Amalfitano waited, watching him, then prompted gently, "Remind others of what?"

Khusaaq dropped his gaze, cleared his throat and said, "I listened to those older and wiser who told me I was a hero. I desperately wanted to believe them, but..." he shrugged, "I quickly learned the truth, that the award was nothing more than a consolation prize."

"A... *what?* You mean... because you didn't die."

Khusaaq chuckled. "No. Because others did—and the Orthodoxy found they desperately needed living heroes, not just dead ones—we've never been lacking with those. Didn't exactly work out as everyone anticipated."

Amalfitano replied with a baffled stare, began, "I don't..." then stopped and started again, "So what really happened—after the awards ceremony I mean?"

"Does it matter?" he replied, unable to keep the bitterness from tainting his voice. "As you said, it was a very long time ago." *A lifetime ago.*

"Yes, it does matter. Tremendously."

"Why?"

"Because whatever happened clearly left a deep imprint on you at a time in your life when you were still very impressionable, and in turn is going to profoundly influence your decision on the matter of asylum."

Khusaaq fixed his narrowed gaze on the holo as his fingers sought out the hidden medallion. *You're right—Tu'indai was right. Why should I trust you? Why should I trust any human? You've done nothing but try to exterminate us ever since—*

"So the rumors were true."

He turned to find Amalfitano back at his desk. "Rumors?"

"About a secret award ceremony that went... shall we say, terribly awry?"

Khusaaq, his right leg beginning to throb to the point he could not control the muscle tremors, shuffled back to his chair.

Amalfitano settled back in his seat and cradled his cup in both hands as Khusaaq slowly eased himself down into his own chair. "Those images... of the ceremony...."

Khusaaq warily met his gaze.

"They were leaked of course—to scare the living beegeebers out of everyone and it worked, perhaps a little too well—threw everyone into a total panic. All you could see was this eerie distortion, like heat ripples. The official media said there'd were five of you, but for all one could tell there could have been a hundred... or just one—many said this proved the prevailing theory that your people were shape-shifters, but then, added to that frightening prospect was the rumor that maybe you weren't even from this dimension, that what the vids showed was you phasing in and out." Amalfitano suppressed a shiver. "Truly frightening…"

"Indeed." He arched a brow, then with a thought, his uniform seemingly vanished, leaving only his head and hands remaining and Amalfitano, who'd just picked up his forgotten cup, came perilously close to dropping it in his open-mouthed shock.

Another thought and his uniform reappeared.

"Holy crap…" Amalfitano breathed. "How'd you… I mean… oh, hell, I don't know what I mean."

"You were saying?" Khusaaq prompted, finding himself intensely pleased, only realizing now that it was too late that he'd just given Amalfitano every reason to separate him from his uniform and as quickly as possible—and all he had left was his uniform.

"I was?" he lifted his unblinking gaze from the ghillie suit to meet Khusaaq's gaze. "I mean… oh, yes, I was… about the vid." He cleared his throat, tugged on his collar, motioned to the ceaselessly morphing surface of the uniform and said, "That's a hell of a thing," then licked his lips and continued, "For months after, you couldn't go into a bar without overhearing whispered stories of either sabotage by some ultra-fanatical group opposed to giving your people anything in recognition for what happened at Cotopaxi, or the explosion was a Matarran plot to stir up hostilities between us—the old divide and conquer theory.

"People were already suffering from a severe case of post-war jitters and were scared, damned scared we were teetering on the brink of yet a third Matarran war, one that everyone knew the Coalition wouldn't survive, so they started seeing Hahtooshans everywhere—any unexplained ship disappearance, any explosion at an outpost was blamed on Hahtooshans—"

Khusaaq took a gulp from his mug to conceal his grimace.

"—one particularly unscrupulous and desperate colonial politician even went so far as to pin a rash of exceptionally brutal street crimes on your people hoping such fear-mongering would get her elected—hit all the major news vids, adding to the mass hysteria. Sad to say, it worked. She was elected—as were a bunch of her cronies. Worse, I'm not sure they ever found the real culprits—don't think anyone really looked once Hahtooshans had been blamed for the thuggery. Other politicians, all over the Rim, realizing how effective her tactics had been, began employing them as well, and with the same results. Of course the official Coalition explanation was that the explosion after the ceremony was nothing more than a case of pilot error—"

Khusaaq snorted, loudly, *Pilot error indeed*, as he fixed his narrowed gaze on the cup he clutched tightly in both hands.

"You have to see it the way we saw it, Sha'ashahn. Everyone was convinced we were about to be set upon by phasing, shape-shifting aliens hell bent on revenge..."

And we would *have retaliated*, Khusaaq thought grimly, *had we not been so spread thin trying to extricate the Ti'finagh collective—*

"....isolated colonies were clamoring for protection the Coalition couldn't provide, extremist politicians were using it to their advantage to recruit even more radical followers and whatever goddamned governmental committee had thought it would be great propaganda to leak that vid was now in full damage-control mode. But you were *there*, at Cotopaxi, at the ceremony... and you survived whatever happened afterwards."

"Yes, I was there," Khusaaq replied softly. "And yet again... I survived."

"Yet again...?" Amalfitano paused, then after a moment of awkward silence, continued, "Something truly terrible happened, didn't it? Something the Coalition paid dearly to cover up."

Khusaaq twitched his shoulders in reply. He'd already given away too much, already exposed a vulnerability, a weakness. *Which was probably what you were after all along*. If he made eye contact now, he'd confirm it. "What happened *happened*. Nothing can change it." He took an angry gulp of his coffee to wash away the bile that again filled his mouth.

"But can you change your mind about us?"

Instead of answering, still refusing to meet the man's gaze, Khusaaq took another, deeper gulp of coffee and realized it tasted even worse cold.

"Look," Amalfitano said with a trace of exasperation, "I'm not going to say that I fully appreciate what you're going through, or what you're facing, because I don't. I can't. I'm not going to claim I understand what we're asking you to give up, because in truth I have no idea. But the choice before you is clear-cut. Ask for asylum and make a new life for yourself, or don't, and... well, no need to belabor the point."

Khusaaq quickly took another sip of coffee to hide his involuntary wince. *And this time you'll finish the job, won't you? But you won't kill me; you won't allow me to die—you'll never give me the opportunity to take my own life. You'll keep me alive, my body alive, in order to learn all of our weaknesses, everything. What I had hoped to stop, I've only made worse, much, much worse—I thought the virus was the ultimate weapon. I was wrong. I am, and against my own kind.*

"We'll need to know your answer, and soon. And speaking of answers, I also want the name of that marine. He'll be reported and reassigned, immediately, I promise you."

Khusaaq set the now empty cup back on the desk and stared at the holo. *Family. I have no family now, except...* "What is going to happen to my escort?" He looked pointedly at Amalfitano.

Amalfitano blinked, clearly taken by surprise. "Escort? Ah... well, I'm not sure. If you were to request asylum, and being that you're their commanding officer, I'd imagine they'd be covered as well, but I'd have to double check with Commander Aquila—"

"And those left behind on Rasal Ghul Seven?"

"Rasal Ghul? Oh, ah... yes... those too," he added a little too quickly.

Khusaaq's eyes narrowed. "You forgot about them, forgot to mention their presence on the island to Aquila, didn't you—even though you gave me your word you would do exactly that?"

"No," Amalfitano began then stopped. "All right, *yes.* I did forget. I started to, then all hell broke loose and... *look,* all I can do is say I'm sorry, terribly sorry, but there's still time—"

"And what if they all wish to return to the Orthodoxy? I'm solely accountable for my actions. The Q'shaathrah would not hold them in any way responsible."

"Then perhaps something could be worked out to repatriate all of them under your request for asylum. To be blunt, it's you Intelligence wants—you know that as well as I do. But if you request asylum, then willingly cooperate, tell them what they want to know—"

"Despite my recent actions, I'm not a traitor by habit, Doctor."

Amalfitano visibly winced. "I didn't mean to suggest—"

"Besides, as we both know, when I've told the truth, I've not been believed. What makes you think anything I said voluntarily would be accepted without question?"

"I don't know, but—"

"Can you guarantee my escort's safe return to the Orthodoxy?"

"Me? No."

"What about Aquila? If I were to request asylum, does he have the authority to guarantee their safe passage?"

"I'm not sure." Amalfitano reached for the com-unit. "But let me call him—"

"No."

"No? But—"

"I would like to return to my cubicle." Khusaaq pushed himself out of his chair and back to his feet. "I'm very tired and, as you said, I have much to think about."

It was an excuse, a stall, but it was also the truth. He was tired, extremely so. And he had more to think about than his brain, in its present sodden state, could hold. It felt like it was about to split at the seams, starting at the base of his skull. "I'll give you my decision before this ship arrives—when?"

Amalfitano glanced sidelong at the desk chronometer. "A little less over seventeen hours. And that's all I can ask—"

A *bleat* from the door startled them.

"Perfect timing...." Amalfitano smacked the door release. "Come... *oh!*"

Khusaaq, warned by Amalfitano's startled stare, glanced over his shoulder. *Sirin!*

Corsali managed a nervous smile as she stepped into the office. "I just got off duty and I was hoping—I'm not interrupting anything, am I?"

Amalfitano cleared his throat and risked a sidelong look at Khusaaq. "Ah well..."

In that brief exchange, Khusaaq read his thoughts. *You're afraid I'll think this is a ploy. Maybe it is.* He looked back at her and realized that it didn't matter. He was pleased—in truth intensely relieved—to see her. "The doctor and I were just discussing my options."

"Options?" she asked, her eyes darting between the two.

"*Cazzo!*" Amalfitano smacked his forehead with his palm. "I was supposed to give the Tulians an update fifteen minutes ago! Totally slipped my mind! But first I must notify Commander Aquila about those left behind on Rasal Ghul Seven." He hurried from the office.

An instant later, the door slipped shut.

Khusaaq squinted at it then dropped his dubious stare to Corsali. "I assume this means it's now your turn?"

"My turn...?"

"To convince me to request *asylum*. That's why you came, yes? The doctor's efforts were not succeeding, so—"

"I came because I just got off shift. I've been worried sick about you all day. I didn't know anyone was talking about asylum."

He took a step closer to her as his earlier anger returned—anger at her, at Amalfitano, at Aquila... at himself most of all for allowing them to think they could manipulate him in such a fashion. *Mind-strip or no, I'm still Elkanaghalli!* "Aquila has ordered you to be my... my *reward* if I do as he clearly wants, and make the request, yes?"

Her eyes widened. "I beg your pardon?"

"Why is your commander so desperate that he would go to these lengths?" He fixed her with his most menacing stare but to his sudden consternation, she didn't cower. He sniffed the air. It was no bluff... she wasn't afraid and that only made him angrier. "It doesn't make sense—so what would my request gain him? A promotion? A new ship? Fame? What?"

"I don't know what you're—"

"Tell me."

"Please, Khusaaq, you've got it all..."

He ran his tattooed finger down her jaw, the unexpected gentleness of the caress startling her into silence. "*He wants something,*" he whispered in her ear. "*What is it?*"

"I don't know what you're talking about!" She started to step back but he grasped the back of her head in one hand, her waist with the other and jerked her tight against him.

She shut her eyes but did not resist as he roughly kissed her.

He immediately let go.

She took a deep, ragged breath and scowled defiantly up at him as she tugged her uniform back into place.

"I am, admittedly, no expert," he replied heatedly, "but I sensed that was not your best effort? While I realize being kissed by a... *yowie* must appall you, for the sake of your beloved commander, you really must try harder."

Keeping her eyes locked with his, she wiped her mouth with the back of her hand then snapped, "Try asking next time!"

His baleful stare crumbled into a startled blink. "Asking...?"

"If I want to be kissed, dammit!"

"But I... I thought—"

"Then you thought *wrong*, buster!"

"But—"

"This act of yours doesn't work on me anymore," she said, emphasizing each word by poking him in the chest with her forefinger.

"I don't—"

She jabbed him again, hard. "The big bad Hahtooshan! Every time you get cornered, every time you get scared, you puff yourself up and pretend to be oh-so threatening, but I see right through you, so drop the damned act!"

"*Tuh maztsaeh*... I... I don't understand." He backed up an unsteady, panicky step and glanced around, desperately looking for an explanation... or a way out. "I thought... I mean—"

"Oh, shut the hell up." She grabbed his bandoleer before he took another step back. "And dammit, hold *still*, will you? Sheesh!" She stood on tiptoes and wrapped one arm around his neck, the other around his waist. "Now, this is how you kiss someone." She tugged him close and gently pressed her lips against his then as he hesitantly responded in kind, she slipped her tongue into his mouth.

Startled, yet instantly aroused by her unanticipated move, he remained stock-still, slightly and uncomfortably stooped, afraid to repeat his earlier mistake, afraid anything he might do would result in her breaking off the embrace.

Finally, she slipped her arm from his neck and stepped back.

He stared down at her, unblinking and mouth agape as his heart hammered madly against his ribs. *And her scent...* No longer the cloyingly sweet stink he associated with Rimmers, this unexpected, potent and incredibly gratifying spoor coated his lips, his mouth and filled his nose, throwing his mind and body into total anarchy.

She looked up at him. "More to your liking?"

Unable to form words in A'tuu, much less Standard, unable to think beyond a frantic need for her to kiss him again, to taste her, smell her again, he replied with a breathless, eager nod.

She grinned smugly. "So much for Drakin telling me I was wasting my time reading those romance novels."

"*Tuh maztsaeh...?*" he managed hoarsely as he gave his collar a tug. His skin suddenly felt as it had fused with his duty uniform in some sort of physiological conflagration.

Before she could answer, the door opened again and she turned to find Kipurs and Tanser standing just outside. Corsali glared at the two. "What the hell do you want?"

The marines looked at Khusaaq then back at her as their faces first registered shock... then comprehension—rapidly followed by intense embarrassment mixed with horror.

Nonplused, Kipurs managed, "Ensign... I mean, ah, well... Doctor Amalfitano—"

"Isn't here."

"Oh."

"Now how about you close the door again?" She started for it, intent on making sure there would be no more interruptions.

"But—"

Kipurs was cut off as the door, as if by itself, snapped shut.

They both heard the telltale *click* of the lock and outside, a heated, albeit muffled conversation, and then, abruptly, silence.

"Now, where were we?" She turned back to him. "Oh, yes, I remember." She crooked a finger at him then pointed to the deck in front of her. "Come here."

The flicker of a nervous smile darted across his mouth as he quickly obeyed.

She grasped his hands and planted them on her hips then she wrapped her arms around his neck. "Now, just *relax* and do what I do." She kissed him again, and this time he responded a little less clumsily.

Suddenly, hungrily, he pressed his lips tightly against hers as his hands desperately shifted position to get a better grip on her body.

She winced and managed a muffled "ouch" as the medallion covered bandoleer and empty scabbard dug into her chest.

He immediately released her and backed up, bewildered, appalled by his body's response, the overwhelming urges, the loss of control. "I… I'm sorry… I—"

"Whoa." She grabbed the bandoleer, stopping him in his tracks. "How about we just get rid of this?" She gave the wide strap a tug.

He stared at her, even more confused. "But… I thought—"

"Ah. There's your problem." She grinned. "Don't think. Just follow my lead, okay? It's supposed to be enjoyable, not a race."

At his hesitation, she lightly brushed his lips with her fingertips, then standing on tiptoe, tugged him down so she could whisper in his ear, *"Take it slow… half the fun is getting there."* To emphasize the point she slipped her hand up under his hauberk.

He gasped involuntarily as she caressed his crotch, every-so-lightly at first.

"See what I mean?" Encouraged by his response, she slipped her hand between his legs, gently wedging them apart. *"Much better…"* She began sliding her fingertip back to front, then back again as her other hand took over fondling him, and not quite as gently as before.

His breathing quickened; his legs suddenly felt like rubber. He grabbed her shoulders and widened his stance to steady himself, which only encouraged her more.

"Do you know how long I've wanted to do this?" she murmured, grinning up at him.

"Nnnn… n-n-no," he managed to stammer, his eyes locked with hers. He was shaking now, his entire body quivering in time to her stroking, her caressing.

"Oh… *my,*" she breathed, her own eyes widening as his hips, without conscious guidance on his part, began to move in cadence as she increased the tempo.

Squeezing his eyes shut he groaned softly and she suddenly stopped.

Gulping for breath, he stared down at her, not sure why she'd stopped, what he'd done, what she wanted, what he was supposed to do. He knew what he wanted. He wanted her to go back to what she was doing and he grabbed her hands, pressed them hard against him again and held them there.

"Take it *slow*, remember? No need to rush things."

"Rather… rather difficult with… with you doing that."

She grinned, clearly extremely pleased and said, "Well, now that I have your undivided attention, let's get rid of this." She again tugged his bandoleer.

You are Elkanaghalli! part of his mind pleaded, but he ignored it in preference for his body, which was urging him on. Years of self-denial, years of Tu'indai's taunts, her unremitting, unabashed attempts at seduction, fueled its demands for release and with Sirin's help he managed to rid himself of the bandoleer and tossed it aside.

"And now this..." She fingered the rapidly morphing hauberk. "It's kind of a distraction—and it's in the way." She gave him another fondle, smiled up at him. "I like to see the results of my handiwork."

He eagerly nodded, started to pull it off, then another voice warned: *And this could just be another Rimmer trick!* That froze him in place as effectively as a barked order.

He stared down at her, his mind awash in conflicting emotions. She didn't look like she was trying to trick him. She looked like she wanted this as much as he did—*Is this possible?* To add to his confusion, he could smell *her* intense arousal, which only added to his. *But if it is a trick...*

Suspicion won out; it was the only instinct he knew he could rely upon.

He licked his lips, too late realizing they tasted of her, then shook his head and whispered huskily, "I... I cannot... do this. I thought I could, but—"

"It's all right," she whispered but her eyes said it was anything but all right. "I *was* rushing you."

He took a deep, steadying breath, then said, "It is not you—I want to." He glanced down at himself and noticed that that was more than apparent; in fact it was *excruciatingly* apparent, even with the thigh-length hauberk. "I just..." He looked up to see that she was staring as well.

He felt his face flush in intense embarrassment. "I'm not ready." Mentally, perhaps, but physically... there was no point in denying the obvious. He wanted to turn away, to run... but where?

She reluctantly lifted her gaze and ran her fingers down his tattooed cheek, following the sinuous pattern of a scar-furrow to his lips. "It's okay, really."

I want to believe you, I want you, but—

"As I said, there's no need to rush things. I just... well, there you were and I couldn't help myself."

He took a deep, rattling breath, managed hoarsely, "But the ship—"

"What ship?"

"An Intelligence ship. It's coming for me... unless I request asylum, first, I'll be handed over to them..."

Sirin couldn't help but visibly wince.

"...It will be here, soon."

"How soon?"

He shook his head again, immediately regretted it as it stirred up his earlier throbbing headache and fingering his temple, mumbled, "I don't remember." He placed a hand on her shoulder again, again to steady himself as he was feeling decidedly wobbly. "Tomorrow?"

"And you thought I was trying to coerce you..." She looked away and muttered, "Well, shit."

He dropped his own gaze to the floor, suddenly and deeply ashamed, but he wasn't sure if it was over his eagerness to cast aside everything he had always claimed he represented... or his lack of follow through. Everything was happening too fast—too many changes, too many choices with little or nothing to go on aside from these humans' assuring him they were telling him the truth when he'd lived his whole life with the hard-won knowledge that humans could never to be trusted.

The whole experience left him feeling shaky, empty and intensely nauseous.

She placed her hand on top of his, pressed it firmly against her shoulder, locking their fingers together. "I wasn't trying to coerce you, truly I wasn't. I didn't know—"

"I don't feel well." He squinted at her as he massaged his forehead with his free hand. "My head and leg... *hurt.*"

"I'll page Doctor—"

"No. *Please.* I... I just need to lie down for a while. I'm really tired."

"Exhausted is closer to the mark, and maybe more than a little hung-over?" she added with a hint of reproach then looked past him to the door of Amalfitano's private quarters. She wrapped her arm around his waist, pulled him close. "Here. Come with me—you can use Doctor Amalfitano's bed."

He hesitated. "Perhaps I should return to my cubicle."

"Think you could make it if I helped you?"

Catching the quickly concealed look of yet more disappointment in her eyes, and realizing she was also right—he'd be lucky if he reached whatever lay within the darkened room, much less his cubicle on the far side of sickbay—he conceded, "Probably not." With that he draped his arm around her shoulder, then leaning heavily against her, limped awkwardly beside her as she led him into the darkened side room.

"Lights—twenty-five percent."

The room abruptly brightened to reveal a bunk, a bedside table, a small fold-down desk that fit into the far corner, and beside it another doorway leading into another darkened room.

"Okay." She let go and pointed to the bunk. "Now get undressed."

He looked down at the bunk then slid his eyes back at her.

"I'm not going to try to take advantage again, if that's what's worrying you."

He only stared at her, not sure whether to take that as a threat or a promise.

"I just thought you'd be more comfortable if you took those off." She motioned to his boots and hauberk.

"Yes." He somehow managed to tug the heavy tunic over his head then with her help, he pulled off his boots. Stripped down to his sleeveless under-tunic and trousers, he just stood there, awaiting her direction. It seemed so much easier that way—no need to think, thinking suddenly was just too much work.

"Now, lie down."

He sat, then supporting his right thigh with both hands, lay back and sprawled out. The mattress was soft, too soft for his liking, but the bedding was deliciously cool and he closed his eyes and tried to focus on that to the exclusion of all else.

Too much was happening too fast—his head felt like it was going to explode, the rapid pulse of blood in his ears ticking down the seconds.

A moment later he felt her sit down beside his hip and he barely caught himself before he visibly flinched.

"Leg still bothering you?"

"Yes."

"How 'bout you let me see what I can do?"

At his uncertain nod, she lightly grasped his thigh and he willed the fabric of his right trouser leg to release its rigid, cast-like embrace.

Slowly, carefully, she kneaded the bunched muscles while he took in every centimeter of her face. *A Rimmer face—a naked, utterly unadorned face. Not at all like... Tu'indai—*

He squeezed his eyes shut and clenched his teeth.

She stopped in mid-stroke. "Did I hurt you?"

He shook his head.

"Want me to stop?"

He shook his head again then reopened his eyes to stare up at her.

She replied with a warm smile, and widened the area of her massage, running the heel of her hand from hip to knee in slow, regular strokes until the taut muscles finally relaxed.

"There," she said, dropping her hands into her lap. "How's that?"

"My head hurts too."

She chuckled, scooted up to his shoulders and taking his head in her hands, began to rub his temples. It felt wonderful and his eyes drifted closed as she moved on to work the corded muscles of his neck.

"Better?"

His eyes snapped open. *Better?* It took him a moment to realize that he'd briefly fallen asleep. He also realized the deep throbbing behind his eyes had faded to a tolerably dull ache. "Yes. Much."

She rose, picked up the blanket that was neatly folded at the foot of the bed and drew it over him. "Now get some sleep, all right?" She tucked the blanket up around his shoulders, kissed him lightly on the forehead and started for the doorway.

"Sirin."

She looked at him, eyebrows raised.

"Don't leave."

"I'm not going far, just out to the office. I have some work—"

"Stay?"

"You're exhausted, you need to get some sleep."

"I will sleep, if you stay." He scooted over and pressed his back up against the cabin wall, making room for her on the narrow bunk. "I give you my word?"

She paused, just long enough for his heart to start pounding again, for him to regret asking.

Then she smiled and lay down beside him.

He hoped his relief was not too obvious as he drew the blanket over both of them.

She smelled wonderful and he nuzzled her ear, savoring the taste of her skin; she responded by lightly kissing the base of his throat.

Asylum, part of his mind murmured as he fingered a lock of her blond hair. A new life. Perhaps it would not be such a terrible thing, if....

He cautiously draped his left leg across her, a slightly possessive move, and awaited her response.

She slowly ran her hand along the length of his thigh, from knee to hip, then over and down, lightly exploring his backside. "Nice," she smiled as she gave his rump a gentle squeeze, *"very* nice indeed."

"By A'tuu'shahn standards I am considered exceedingly handsome," he replied simply, his tone matter of fact.

Corsali stifled a chuckle then met his now uncertain gaze.

"You do not think so?"

"I think you are *exceedingly* handsome—as you might have noticed, if given the chance I find it extremely hard to keep my hands off you."

"You did not think so when we first met. You found me utterly repulsive."

"No, not... utterly repulsive. Frightening. I thought you were a shaper—I had no idea what you really looked like—I had no idea what you wanted, what might happen."

"But you're not afraid of me now."

"No."

He nuzzled her ear again, privately grinned at her satisfied sigh then asked, "So when did you change your mind about me?"

"When I realized I could see through these," she replied as she ran a fingertip over the elaborate tattoo and underlying scarification that snaked its way along his jaw line to his mouth. She gave his lower lip a tug. "And what I saw underneath I found very, *very* attractive." She again ran her other hand over his backside and murmured, "And the rest is just, well, the proverbial icing on the cake."

He wasn't quite sure what she meant by the last comment, but sensing it was intended as a compliment, he drew her even closer and pressed himself against her. *Now I'm ready—*

"Go to sleep," she whispered just as he began fumbling, one handed, with the seal-seam of his trousers.

Now? But I thought you—

"Later, when you're feeling better. I won't have it be said I took advantage of you in a moment of weakness."

"But—"

"Later." She pressed her lips against his, her passionate kiss effectively stifling further protest, then murmured, "Sweet dreams," as she snuggled up against him, tucking her head under his chin.

He wrapped his arm tightly around her, dutifully closed his eyes and exhaled with contented weariness, *Yes....*

Chapter 24

Amalfitano, seated at the main nurse's console and his attention riveted on the read-outs of one of its monitors, didn't hear the sickbay doors open to admit Aquila. He didn't hear the man's subdued, but insistent throat clearing, or the anxious, repetitive tapping of his fingers on the console.

Finally, irritably, Aquila prompted, *"Will?"*

He reluctantly looked up. "Huh...?"

"Well?"

"Well what?" he replied as his distracted gaze immediately returned to the monitor.

"What's his answer?"

Amalfitano knit his brows as his eyes darted back and forth, taking in the monitor's readouts. "You... mean Khusaaq."

"Of course I mean Khusaaq! I've been waiting to hear from you—the *Walafar* will be here in a little less than fourteen hours."

"I know. And...I don't know." He tapped a button, leaned forward and squinted at the screen.

Aquila exhaled as he looked around, arms akimbo. "Okay, where is he?"

"My office."

Aquila started for the door, but took only two steps before Amalfitano added, "Wouldn't do that."

He wheeled around. "And why the hell not?"

"Sirin's with him."

Aquila's glower dissolved into a startled stare. "Oh."

"Wasn't having much luck. Thought I'd give them some time together—" He waved off Aquila's protest as it formed on his lips. "I know, I know—it can't look like he was coerced into requesting asylum. He clearly wanted to see her, and she him. I figured a little alone time couldn't hurt."

Aquila crossed his arms, clearly unconvinced, but not sure what he could do about it now.

"I'll tell you one thing that came out of our conversation, something that might give you a hint as to what he'll decide."

"And that is?"

"He's clearly more concerned about his soldiers' welfare than his own. He's gonna make the retrieval of those left behind part and parcel of any agreement—"

"I did notify Admiral Keon about them."

"And?"

"The best he could offer was to say he'd contact the Orthodoxy through diplomatic back channels, nothing official, alert them and leave it up to them to retrieve them."

"But that could take days or longer, and assuming the Orthodoxy has any ships that could reach them in time. Even under a diffusion screen and with their higher tolerance for radiation exposure, I can't imagine they'd last longer than a couple of weeks, if that."

Aquila shrugged in shared exasperation. "I did everything I could, Will. After all, these are Hahtooshans we're talking about—it would've been a really hard sell at any time, but right after they launch an unprovoked attack on a defenseless planet?"

"Yeah, well, he also asked if you had the power to grant his people safe passage back to the Orthodoxy if he voluntarily cooperated with Intelligence."

"And what did you say?"

"I told him I didn't think you had that kind of authority."

"I don't. That would have to come from HQ, from Admiral Keon himself." He looked back at the office door. "Think it's safe to leave her alone with him? I mean—"

"Yes, I do. We're asking him to trust us, so maybe it's time we start trusting him, too. Besides, she didn't exactly need any arm-twisting. They're quite smitten with each other in case you hadn't noticed."

Aquila made a face and Amalfitano chuckled. "All in the eye of the beholder, Robert."

"Yeah," Aquila replied dubiously, leaned close and asked, "Has Izraad talked to her yet?"

"No—but not to worry, Zarijan told me she has everything all planned out. Besides, to be honest, I don't think it will make a whit of difference to her."

"And him?"

Amalfitano shrugged. "Dunno, guess we'll find out soon enough."

Aquila gestured to the monitor that had had such a grip on Amalfitano's attention. "Anything?"

"Nothing definitive." He tapped the screen with his finger as it rapidly filled with new information. "Right now we're waiting on the codon analysis." He gave the readouts a quick study. *"Humm. This sample looks promising."*

Aquila circled the console and leaned over his shoulder to peer down at the screen. "How long before you—"

"Don't know," he interrupted. "This is the thirty-fourth sample we've run. Most of what Xosé retrieved from the missile's payload bay was so thoroughly cooked we couldn't recognize a single base pair, much less a sequence, certainly nothing worth putting through the amplifier."

Aquila, catching Amalfitano's not so subtle sidelong look, straightened up. "Well, I guess I'll leave you alone, too."

— ii —

Amalfitano smacked his fist against the console as the analyzer registered yet another unusable sample. He gave his tired eyes a vigorous rub as he tried not to let his mounting frustration get the better of him. The answer, the key to the puzzle, was so tantalizingly close he could taste it—*or smell it*, a part of his mind added as his nose wrinkled at a familiar aroma. He looked up.

Fleming held out a cup of coffee as she slipped onto the chair beside him. "How goes it?"

He accepted the cup with a grateful nod. "We're on sample number two hundred and eighty nine."

"Then how 'bout you take a break? You've been at it for hours."

"But if Xosé—"

"If Xosé finds anything, I'll tell you. Now *shoo.*"

"Okay, okay." He rose stiffly, stretched, and by habit turned for his office, but as he spotted a new pair of guards at the door, he stopped. *"Mm,* wait."

"Yes?"

"Sirin and Khusaaq—"

"Are still in there."

"Maybe I should go check to make sure everything's okay?"

"Maybe they'd like to be alone."

"They've *been* alone, for over five hours."

"Maybe he's a *real* slow learner."

He scowled at her.

"Maybe you should make rounds. Corporal Gianakis has been nagging me about being discharged and Drakin's making noises about changing Matoosh's physical therapy schedule." She smiled at his sour look, added, "Just a suggestion," then swiveled her chair around to face the bank of monitors.

Suggestion my ass. He stared at her back for a moment then reminded himself it was pointless to argue with her, especially when she was right. "I think I'll go make rounds." He walked away and into the isolation unit.

Drakin looked up from her monitoring console and grinned a toothy grin. "Afternoon', Chief."

He replied with a nod and a smile of his own. "Pretty quiet in here."

"Yez, wit only one patient left."

"And how is Matoosh?"

"Ssstill up to hiz old trickz. Plus, hez come up wit a few new onez."

Amalfitano turned to the glass-walled bank of cubicles and questioned if he was really up to dealing with the young merc. He looked back at her. "That bad, huh?"

"Dat good," she replied with a sly wink.

"If I didn't know better, I'd say you're quite taken with him." In fact it was no secret several of his staff were smitten with him. *It's the exotic looks*, he told himself. *Or more likely because he's hung like the proverbial—*

"Lez juz sssay I find him a challenge." She dropped her gaze to something hidden from his view.

Intrigued, he stepped closer to the console.

"I'll give da Hattoosssinz credit for one ting." She held up Matoosh's freshly laundered hauberk and he realized it had been draped across her lap.

He wasn't quite sure what to think of that.

"Dey do have lovely uniformz."

He arched a brow; Khusaaq's heart-stopping but thankfully brief demonstration of its abilities was still fresh in his mind—then he recalled what this particular uniform looked like after Meerut's quick rip and strip job in the triage bay, ditto Khusaaq's after Drakin had finished with it. "Anyone ever tell you you're one hell of a seamstress? Sha'ashahn was incredibly pleased when he saw—"

"Wiz I could take credit."

He raised a brow. "Then who...?

"*It.*" She caressed the slowly morphing, coppery hauberk in a way he found very unsettling. "Itz sssself-repairing you sssee. Put da piecez together and it doez da ressst. Very clever."

"Too damned clever if you ask me—"

"Ssshame itz only a uniform and not deir real ssskin."

He smiled uneasily. "Mm, yeah. But... wasn't it black...?"

"Yez, before I wassshed it."

He raised both brows. *In what?*

"It waz filty. Besidez, Sssirin told me itz sssupposssed to change color."

"Right." Among other things.

She draped it over the console and added with a wistful sigh, "Pity hez a monk."

"Yeah... I suppose so," he replied slowly. He glanced at the cubicle, said a silent prayer for Matoosh and his virtue and turned back to her. "Jenna mentioned you wanted to change his therapy schedule?"

"Yez." She handed him a report flimsy, gave him a moment to study the information, then continued, "Az you can sssee, hez resssponding well. I tink hez ready for a more aggresssssive approach."

He put the brakes on his active imagination before it took her suggestive comment and ran with it. "How 'bout we stick with the present regimen for now? No need to rush things, is there?"

She shrugged and sighed, clearly disappointed. "Wat ever you sssay, Chief." Her eyes drifted back to the cubicle as her hands resumed their suggestive fondling of the hauberk.

Amalfitano placed the flimsy on the console, and, leaving Drakin to her less than pure thoughts, wandered out of the unit. He made a quick, obligatory detour into the ward only to find Gianakis fast asleep. Then he left, satisfied he'd fulfilled his duties.

As he walked back towards the main nurses' station, he found his gaze turning to his office.

He glanced at Fleming; she appeared to be totally engrossed in studying the monitor's readouts.

Just a quick peek. He casually walked over to the door, nodded to the guards, and pressed the activator. The door opened with what seemed to him to be an abnormally loud *click* and he cringed.

So much for a quiet peek. But since I'm here....

He peered inside. The outer office was empty. Then he happened to notice Khusaaq's discarded bandoleer on the floor. He grinned. *Good work, Sirin! But...*

His eyes flicked to the open doorway of his darkened private quarters and he took a hesitant step, then another as his curiosity got the best of him.

Halfway to the open doorway, a finger tapped his shoulder; he flinched violently and spun around.

Fleming leaned close. "Ever heard the saying 'Let sleeping Hahtooshans lie'?"

"I wasn't—"

"Shhh." She jerked her chin towards the office's outer door.

He stalked after her. Once outside, he snapped, "I needed something off my desk!"

She looked unimpressed. "What?"

Amalfitano hesitated just a second too long.

"As I thought."

"No, it's not!" he replied heatedly then suddenly noticed she was grinning broadly. He squinted at her. "What's so goddamned funny?"

"Aside from realizing you're a voyeur?"

"I'm not—"

"You'd prefer dirty old man?"

"Voyeur's classier," a new voice said and Amalfitano turned around to find Crewman Xosé Tasende standing nearby. "I'd go with that if I were you, Chief. And not to change the subject, but..." He held up a sampling tube and at Amalfitano's expectant look, wiggled his thick eyebrows. "I know what our bug is!"

— iii —

Amalfitano grabbed Tasende by the arm before the tech followed Aquila and Teague into the Tulian High Council's chambers. "Remember what I said, Xosé—you're to be on your best behavior."

Tasende looked aghast. "Whatever do you mean?"

"You know damned well what I mean. No repeat of the last time—"

"Will? Coming?"

Amalfitano pulled his warning gaze off Tasende and turned to find Aquila waiting for them just inside the chambers. Beside him stood Seitakap. The Tulian was outwardly calm and composed, with a sincere but decidedly apprehensive smile. Behind them paced a puffy-eyed, agitated Henson.

"Coming, sir." Amalfitano let go of Tasende's arm and walked into the brightly lit council room.

With a shrug, Tasende followed.

"Mister President," Aquila began, "you know Doctor Amalfitano and Lieutenant Teague."

Seitakap replied with a slight tip of his head and a murmured, "Doctor, Lieutenant."

"And this is the ship's pathologist, Crewman Xosé Tasende."

"We are honored, Crewman."

"Same goes for me," Tasende replied with a smile. Overhearing a muffled cough, he gave Amalfitano a sidelong questioning glance.

Amalfitano mouthed, *'Mister President.'*

"Uh," Tasende looked back at Seitakap. "I mean I'm honored to meet you too, *Mister President*."

"And this is John Henson, the Coalition's acting envoy," Seitakap said as he motioned to the man who now stood beside him.

"Pleased to meet you too," Tasende held out his hand, "Mister Hen—"

"You said you had news?" Henson asked as he turned his cold gaze on Aquila.

"Yes—"

"I've convened the entire High Council to hear your announcement, Commander," Seitakap interrupted as he motioned to the room. "Gentlemen, please, come with me." He turned and walked into the semicircle of seated councilors.

As the others followed, Tasende leaned close to Amalfitano and jerked his chin towards Henson and whispered, *"What's with him?"*

"He's attained critical ass, that's what's wrong with him," Amalfitano replied in kind. *"Nothing a swift kick up the ego wouldn't cure."*

"Oh." Then Tasende's coal-black eyes brightened. *"Oh!"*

Amalfitano growled, "Whatever you're thinking, Xosé, *no,*" then he walked over to where Aquila and Teague stood.

"Please," Seitakap murmured, "be seated." He gestured to several woven mats and sat down cross-legged on the floor.

Aquila, Teague, Tasende and Amalfitano followed suit.

"Now, Commander?" Seitakap prompted as Henson seated himself beside Seitakap.

"Let me first tell you, Mister President, that we've positively identified the organism brought here from Rasal Ghul by the Hahtooshans, thanks to the hard work of Doctor Amalfitano and Crewman Tasende." He looked around; the faces that stared back bore a mixture of concern and relief.

Aquila favored Amalfitano with a look and at Amalfitano's nod, said, "I now believe it is time that I turn the rest of the meeting over to the one responsible for actually identifying the organism. Crewman Tasende?"

"The organism," Tasende began without preamble, "as we suspected, is indeed a virus. Although of a previously unknown strain, it's closely related to a group of well-known viruses, classified under the general name of orthomyxoviruses."

Amalfitano overheard an almost inaudible gasp and caught the look of understanding in the eyes of the wizened councilor Seitakap had identified as Pakanga.

"Are you sure?" Pakanga asked, his voice cracking with excitement.

"Yessir," Tasende replied. "The nucleoprotein antigen and serologic tests confirm it is, without a doubt, a strain of—"

"Get to the point!" Henson snarled and Tasende blinked then looked at Amalfitano.

"He just did, sir," Amalfitano replied evenly.

"Well I for one failed to see it among all the…" Henson flailed his hand about, "…the mumbo-jumbo, so how about repeating what you just said—*in Standard?*"

"Of course, sir," Amalfitano answered dryly. "We didn't mean to confuse you with precise terminology. Crewman, in Standard if you please."

"Yessir." Tasende met Henson's stare squarely. "What I was trying to say, sir, is that the biological agent is an organism related to a well-known and very prevalent virus—"

"Then you have a cure?" Henson said.

"Ah, actually, no," Tasende replied innocently, then visibly struggled not to laugh at the explosive look on the man's face or Amalfitano's pained wince.

"Aquila!" Henson turned his ominous glare on him. "If this is some sort of snow-job to cover up more gross incompetence on your part, it won't—"

"It's influenza," Amalfitano interrupted.

A stunned silence descended on the conference room a strained moment before Pakanga began to chuckle softly.

"What?" Henson hissed, his eyes darting between Amalfitano and Pakanga.

"Influenza," Amalfitano repeated. "A common and widespread virus responsible for common and widespread illnesses. Granted, a new strain, but—"

"The... *flu?"* Henson spluttered.

"Yes," Amalfitano replied. "The flu. Based on antibody and antigen tests, we've classified it as Type BH forty-seven NA Ten Rasal Ghul Tasende, or B Rasal Ghul for short—"

"But this was supposedly some terrible biological weapon!"

"And had research continued, it probably would have become just that," Amalfitano said. "Keeping it simple, sir, from what we can determine based on analysis of the virus's RNA, the researchers were attempting to fuse two known strains which infect humans, using another species as an intermediary. Influenza viruses do this quite normally. It's a method by which they naturally mutate, and when they do, the end result is often a virus that can infect both species with pandemic results. Crewman?"

"In this case," Tasende began, "each 'parent' virus had a particular trait or traits the researchers were after. One virus had the ability to mutate with incredible rapidity, thus making it unrecognizable to antibodies and impossible to vaccinate against. It also had highly adaptable 'spikes', another mechanism which aides in camouflaging it from antibodies, a combination which made it a very virulent strain. But it was also rather fragile, as viruses go.

"Take it out of its ideal medium and it turns up its toes," Tasende continued, "metaphorically speaking, which didn't make it a very good candidate as a weapon, even though it's an exceedingly lethal organism, with a plus ninety eight percent mortality rate. We suspect this is what wiped out the base back on Rasal Ghul, along with the crew of the base's supply ship.

"But the other parent, while considered to be relatively harmless to an otherwise healthy host, was very hardy. So hardy it could remain viable for extended periods in an aerosolized state and in far from ideal conditions.

"The end result, had the researchers succeeded in their aims, would have been a super-virus, for lack of a better description. One which had the desired traits of both parents: extremely virulent and difficult if not impossible to vaccinate against and with the ability to be held for indefinite periods of time in an aerosolized state, which also happens to be an ideal way of unleashing a biological weapon on its target. But," Tasende added with a shrug, "as it turns out, as an infectious agent, this particular bug is pretty much of a dud, hence no need for a 'cure'."

Henson scowled at Amalfitano. "So, now what?"

"So now we do what we'd do if we were looking at a normal influenza outbreak: we start a planet-wide vaccination program for those in high risk groups. With any luck, we should be able to stop this bug cold, if you'll excuse the pun, without so much as a sneeze or a sniffle to show for all the trouble it's caused."

Seitakap slowly shook his head in stunned relief.

"The crisis is over, Mister President," Aquila added for good measure.

"It doesn't seem enough just to say we thank you, Doctor," Seitakap replied as he tipped his head to Amalfitano and then Tasende. "And especially you, Crewman."

"We were just doing the jobs we were trained to do, sir," Tasende replied as his eyes darted to Henson. "Nothing more."

An aide knelt beside Seitakap, whispered in his ear and they both looked briefly at Pakanga; Pakanga nodded. Seitakap then turned back to Aquila. "Commander, Councilor Pakanga has made a suggestion, and I fully concur. Councilor?"

"Commander," Pakanga began, "I would like to extend to you and your crew the warm appreciation of my people. And the best way to show that appreciation is to offer you unlimited shore leave."

"I second that," Mele said enthusiastically.

"Shore leave anywhere on the planet!" another councilor offered and there was a rush of agreement among the rest.

"It is the least we can do," Pakanga said with wink at Aquila.

Amalfitano looked at Tasende; Tasende grinned and rubbed his hands together. "Now that's what I call—"

"Thank you, all," Aquila replied. "I accept, contingent, of course upon Headquarters' approval."

"Of course," Seitakap replied.

"I knew there'd be a hitch," Tasende muttered, his shoulders slumping.

Amalfitano only nodded as the mental image of sharing a week, or more, with Izraad on some deserted tropical beach dissolved into the more likely scenario of spending a two-day leave at one of Mirfak Prime's tacky hotels that catered to off-world traffic.

"Doctor?"

Amalfitano's mind snapped back into the present.

Henson stood in front of him, hand extended.

Amalfitano scrambled to his feet and reluctantly grasped the man's hand.

Henson replied with a firm, albeit stiff handshake. "Congratulations, Doctor."

"Uh, thank you, sir."

"It would appear that I underestimated you," Henson continued with the awkward gruffness of someone unused to being contrite.

"Well…" Amalfitano began, but before he could finish, Henson turned and briskly walked away. "Fuck you too," he added under his breath. He shook his head and looked around.

Teague and Tasende were nearby, the two engrossed in an animated conversation with Mele and Pakanga—something about which archipelago, Jidgantjara or Wojobaaluk, had the best beaches—while Aquila and Seitakap were nowhere to be seen.

He started for the doorway, suddenly feeling the need to be alone with his thoughts but as he stepped out onto the verandah, he overheard Seitakap's now familiar voice: "…and if I may have access to your ship's foldspace net, Commander, I'll personally speak with your headquarters about shore leave."

Amalfitano squinted into the deepening twilight and quickly spotted the two, not far from the stairs, his planned escape route. *Cacchio!* He scowled at them and then with an irritable shrug, walked towards them. *I'll just make my excuses....*

"My crew's been through hell these past few weeks," Aquila replied, "and I can't think of a better place for R and R—"

"Ah, Doctor, please, join us," Seitakap said as he spotted the man, then, as Amalfitano came abreast of them, continued, "I was just telling the commander—"

"Mister President?"

They turned towards the sound of Henson's familiar voice.

"Sir, if I may have a word?" the man continued, motioning urgently to Seitakap.

Seitakap sighed, "Now what," then added in a louder voice, "If you'll excuse me?"

Aquila nodded, and as Seitakap walked back into the chamber, Amalfitano started down the stairs.

"Where are you going?"

"For a walk."

"Mind if I join you?" Aquila asked, following him.

"Would it matter if I said yes?"

"No." Aquila then had to hurry to catch up with the taller man's long strides. "This is the first chance I've had to say congratulations."

"Yeah."

Aquila eyed him. "You don't sound real happy about the fact that you and Xosé saved an entire planet."

"We didn't, or, should I say I didn't," he replied wearily, stopping in his tracks, "since it was Xosé who identified the virus, not me. So your congratulations should go to him. And the planet never was at risk."

"Okay, technically, you're right, but—"

"No buts," he interrupted, suddenly angry. "Don't you see? All of this was for nothing. All those deaths—Gislasen, Lundgren, Arctoi...." He shook his head, added softly, "Julie Jarvis." *I'd almost forgotten about you.* He looked at Aquila out of the corner of his eye. "As well as our crew killed during those skirmishes and the crews of two Hahtooshan ships—what's that, at least five, maybe six hundred? Not to mention the crew of that Wuotani freighter, and yes, even the bases' staff and who knows how many others." He looked up at the dazzling early evening sky and his dark eyes crinkled into a scowl. "All for... *nothing.*"

"Just be glad it's finally over."

"For us maybe, but not—"

"Khusaaq," Aquila interrupted.

"Or the other Hahtooshans, yeah."

Aquila glanced around him then lowered his voice to a whisper. "I contacted a friend, at HQ."

"What? When?"

"While you were acting as matchmaker."

Amalfitano squinted at him.

"I would have told you earlier, but... well, to be honest, I was concerned it might distract you."

"Meaning it's bad news and you didn't want it to affect my overseeing the work on the virus."

Aquila exhaled forcefully. "Okay, if you want to be blunt about it—"

"So what did this 'friend' say?"

"She confirmed what we both suspected—" Aquila overheard the murmur of conversation and looked back at the building. Several people now stood on the verandah. "It's a beautiful evening. Let's go for that stroll." He started to walk casually towards an ornamental stand of flowering trees. "Coming?"

"How fucking romantic," Amalfitano replied sourly, following.

Aquila waited well beyond earshot, within the dappled shadows of the grove, until Amalfitano joined him. Then he continued, "My source says she's heard a rumor that the Coalition Central Committee and the Orthodoxy have been in high level, very hush-hush negotiations, something to do with the secret base. It was a major breach of every existing treaty, even back then."

"But we've never had any treaties with the Hahtooshans."

"But at the time we did with the Matarrans, Thalamians and Loopers, not to mention a host of non-aligned systems—"

"And if the existence of this base became known, it would generate a major diplomatic incident."

"To put it mildly," Aquila agreed. "And the timing couldn't be worse, with the whole matter of who the Hahtooshans really are just waiting to explode. And then there's the extraterritoriality negotiation over Poonda Five. From what I hear, the talks are reaching the delicate stage with the Thalamians. Plus, if the Matarrans ever got wind of this—"

"Assuming they weren't the ones who contracted the Hahtooshans in the first place," Amalfitano interrupted angrily. "Hell, they might have realized from the get-go that they could work this both ways, the classic win-win scenario."

"My friend thinks the Hahtooshans will agree to keep quiet in trade for getting their people back, along with a sizable pay-off—in other words, the typical Hahtooshan response: blackmail."

"Now wait, let me get this straight," Amalfitano said as he crossed his arms. "The Orthodoxy accepts a contract from god-knows-who to retrieve a biological weapon no one's supposed to have created in the first place, from a base that supposedly never existed, presumably for the purpose of using this weapon against whomever god-knows-who doesn't like."

Aquila knit his brows. "Uh, yeah, I think—"

"Then some lunatic merc takes it upon himself to breach the contract by launching an unprovoked attack on a defenseless, nonaligned planet, using this weapon no one is supposed to know about and when that fails, the Orthodoxy has the moxie to blackmail the Coalition into giving them everything they want?"

"Not everything, at least not right away."

"You mean Khusaaq, right?"

"The way my friend heard it, all those medically fit are to be repatriated immediately—an Orthodoxy ship will be rendezvousing with the *Walafar* in neutral space—"

"And Khusaaq?"

"He's not medically fit—"

"And I wonder where they got that idea," Amalfitano muttered angrily. "We played right into their hands!"

"Looks like. Officially, as the sole surviving officer, he's to be held for questioning—"

"You mean mind-stripped."

"But the Orthodoxy does want him back, eventually."

"So he can be tried as a traitor—after he's allowed, as the Hero of Cotopaxi to speak his peace of course—and presumably executed."

"Most likely."

Amalfitano chewed on his lip for a moment before adding sourly, "But if he were to die from his injuries while in the Coalition's hands, then everyone's pesky little problem would be solved."

"That's one way of looking at it, and a prospect both sides have likely planned for. And knowing mercs, if it were to happen, then they'd demand even more compensation for the loss of their hero—"

"And the Coalition would happily—well, maybe not so happily—pay it."

"Yeah," Aquila muttered.

For a moment neither spoke, then Amalfitano's dark expression suddenly brightened. "But what about asylum? There's still time—"

"But he *hasn't* requested it, and my source raised a possibility that hadn't occurred to me."

"And that is?"

"That his request wouldn't be honored—he might have to prove that returning to the Orthodoxy would be a death sentence—"

"Even though everyone knows it would be."

"—and that could be very problematic and could drag out for months, years... meanwhile, he would have no protection from being 'questioned'."

"Meaning mind stripped."

"And the Hahtooshans would have every reason to stop him from talking, voluntarily or not."

"So we're back to everyone having a damned good reason for wanting him dead."

"Yup. He's become the proverbial political hot potato."

"Cazzo!" Amalfitano scowled at his tranquil surroundings. "I need a stiff drink—no, make that five."

"Gimme some time, Will. Maybe I can think of some way out of this unholy predicament."

Amalfitano fixed him with a dubious stare.

"Yeah, I know, unlikely, but..." Aquila jerked his chin towards the nearby council building. "We'd best get back. Seitakap mentioned something about a get-together in our honor."

"Thanks, I'll pass."

Aquila opened his mouth to protest, but was cut off by the *bleat* of Amalfitano's tac-pac.

"Now what," the doctor grumbled as he yanked it from its holster and brought it to his ear. "Yes?"

"William," Fleming said, *"can you break away?"*

He knew that tone; he adjusted the tac-pac's volume just enough so that Aquila could overhear. "What's wrong?"

"Khusaaq. I think the scanners are trying to tell me he's suffered a pulmonary embolization."

"Be right there."

Aquila favored him with a skeptical stare. "If I didn't know better, I'd say you had this escape planned."

"Make my excuses, will you?"

"Do I have a choice?"

"Nope." Amalfitano started out of the grove, towards the flick down coordinates.

"Will. Wait."

Amalfitano stopped and glanced over his shoulder.

"Is this serious?"

"Doubt it, but—"

"Perhaps this can work in our favor."

"What are you talking about?"

"If his condition were to deteriorate—"

"It won't if you let me and my staff do our jobs." He took two steps, stopped then looked back at Aquila. "Are you suggesting what I think you're suggesting?"

"Depends. What do you think I'm suggesting?"

"I think your suggesting we lie to HQ, lie to Intelligence."

"His prognosis is extremely guarded, you just said that."

"I did?"

"In a manner of speaking, yes."

Amalfitano thought about it then nodded. "Yeah, you're right. I did."

"Then it wouldn't be a lie, would it? It'd be more like... well, augmenting reality."

Amalfitano snorted.

"And it would be a way of delaying his meeting with Intelligence, at least until I can figure some way out of this mess?"

"If we can convince this Intelligence officer that he really is that unstable, maybe."

"Well, I don't think there'll be any problem there."

"I don't follow."

"Can you name me one Coalition doctor who's had more hands-on experience with Hahtooshans than you, in fact any experience at all?"

"Uh," he tapped his forefinger on his chin then added, "Jenna?"

Aquila squinted at him. "Okay, allow me to rephrase: there's no one outside of *Baidarka* medical staff who've had any experience. There's no one who can dispute your claims or Jenna's with any authority—think she'll go along with this?"

"You mean lie to HQ? Yeah," he replied with dead certainty. "She feels the same way I do, so no worries there." He rocked back and forth on the balls of his feet for a moment, thinking about what Aquila had said then added, "You're right." He gave him a sidelong look. "In fact, you're damned right."

Chapter 25

Amalfitano stopped just beyond the doorway of his brightly lit private quarters, his arrival having gone unnoticed by those within, and took the opportunity to assess and absorb the goings on within the tiny cabin.

Khusaaq's uniform, like pieces of a discarded snake's skin, lay scattered across the floor and bunk while Khusaaq, seated on the edge of the bed, shivered uncontrollably and labored for each breath as he stared, glassy-eyed, at the far wall.

Sirin sat to his left, closest to the door, her back to Amalfitano. She was murmuring soothingly to him and stroking his back while Rosen, was seated to his right, ran a hand scanner back and forth across his heaving chest.

Fleming knelt in front of Khusaaq, an open triage kit on the floor beside her, a ject-it in one hand and several vials in the other while Pierson stood behind her, a portable ventilator in his arms.

Amalfitano cleared his throat.

Fleming jerked her eyes off Khusaaq's ashen, sweat-streaked face and rose as Amalfitano stepped into the cabin. "Boy, am I glad to see you!"

"What the hell happened?" he asked as he slipped around Pierson.

"Sirin called me a few minutes ago," Fleming replied, "to say that he was having difficulty breathing."

Amalfitano turned his questioning gaze on Corsali.

"He was sound asleep. So was I, but I woke up when he started getting restless," she answered in a frightened voice. "It first I thought he was dreaming—"

"And?" he prompted calmly as he squatted in front of his patient to get a better look at him; Khusaaq stared back in exhausted anxiety as he continued to labor hungrily for air.

"Then I noticed he was hot, real hot, and suddenly he started shivering and gasping for breath—that's when I called for Doctor Fleming."

"I can't make heads or tails out of these readings," Rosen growled and handed Amalfitano her scanner.

"I was sure he'd thrown an embolism due to the sudden onset," Fleming continued, "but now... clearly acute bilateral pneumonia."

He gave the scanner's erratic read-outs a cursory study, leaned forward and pressed his ear against Khusaaq's heaving chest.

"Cultures were drawn," Fleming added.

Amalfitano nodded, still listening to the cacophony of wheezing, crackles and rubbing squeaks, then he sat back on his haunches while Fleming knelt beside him and held out her hand.

"Another four hundred milligrams of supoxizine."

Rosen had anticipated her order and slapped the loaded ject-it into Fleming's waiting palm.

Fleming pressed the ject-it against Khusaaq's arm, handed the expended ject-it back to her, then sat back as Amalfitano again pressed his ear to his chest.

Satisfied, Amalfitano got to his feet. "I want continuous blood gas sampling, and a complete blood panel every five minutes—"

"Already ordered," Fleming said.

"Start a supoxizine infusion... I want his blood kept well oxygenated."

"Yessir." Rosen began gathering the needed supplies from the triage kit.

"Best get him back into isolation," Amalfitano continued, "so get a stasis board in here. And get Perou and Cyllo down here on the double—"

"They're already on their way," Fleming said. "Paged them right after I called you—"

"—see if they can't find some way of overriding this damned interference." He suddenly stopped, gave Fleming a sidelong look. "Sorry, Jenna, I should've realized you'd have—"

"No offense taken, we're both just trying to cover all the bases."

He exhaled, *"Yeah,"* and turned back to Khusaaq to find him staring up at him with frightened, helpless eyes. "Everything's going to be all right, son." He gave his shoulder a squeeze. "Trust me."

Khusaaq managed a nod and a breathless, *"Paq—"*

"Doctor Amalfitano," Masursky's voice crackled from the bedside com-unit, *"report to C and C immediately."*

Amalfitano, keeping his eyes on Khusaaq, smacked the activator. "Control, Amalfitano here, look, I'm a bit busy right now."

"Sir, Commander Aquila wanted to remind you the Walafar will be here—"

"That's the least of my problems!" He broke the connection and turned for the door. "Where's that goddamned stasis board?"

— ii —

At the sound of approaching voices, Amalfitano gave his desktop terminal's latest read-outs one last glance. He, Izraad and Fleming had spent the entire night and all morning pouring over the truly staggering mass of medical data they'd collected on their Hahtooshan patients, taking full advantage of the *Walafar*'s communications silence until she attained orbit.

They'd judiciously edited here and there, hoping critical omissions wouldn't be noticed—at least not immediately—within the veritable deluge they would dump on the *Walafar* the instant she made contact. Hoping a quick look-over would be enough to convince her MO and Intelligence that Khusaaq was far too unstable, that he was far too valuable to leave to the ministrations of a doctor who knew nothing about Hahtooshans.

It had to be enough—too late now to do anything about it if it wasn't. The *Walafar* now trailed a few hundred kilometers behind *Baidarka*. The data dump was complete and Mladić had flicked aboard a few minutes before.

The matter of asylum was now moot. Time had run out.

"Doctor?"

He lifted his gaze as Aquila entered the small office, followed by Izraad and an average sized, average built man with average brown hair and average brown eyes. "Yes?"

"This is Captain Radomir Mladić, of Headquarters Intelligence," Aquila continued.

Amalfitano rose, leaned across his desk and extended his hand. "Captain."

Mladić replied with a firm handshake and, "I'm very pleased to finally meet you, Doctor."

Amalfitano prided himself on being expert at identifying accents, but this man had none. Like his unremarkable face,

Mladić's voice was just a little too commonplace. It was the bland, uncluttered and immediately forgettable voice of a news vid-announcer, colonial politician... and spook. "Finally?" he repeated as he gestured to the ring of chairs facing his desk.

"I've heard a lot about you over the years," Mladić said as he followed Izraad and Aquila and sat down.

Amalfitano resumed his own seat. "I'm not sure if I should be honored, or worried."

Mladić laughed, an easy, straightforward laugh. "It was meant as a compliment. You've developed quite an impressive reputation back at HQ. I've read all of your monographs—and I found your latest, on the incidence of Asopus-Sastani syndrome among rail gun technicians to be most interesting. From what I hear, and as a direct result of your findings, HQ has requested a full review of all procedures, with an eye to refitting all CEF vessels."

"Oh, well... ah, thank you." Amalfitano felt a flush of pleasure despite himself. He'd worked very hard on that particular monograph and aside from Vildur and Fleming, no one whose opinion he valued had found the time to read it. Mladić was certainly nothing like the bogeyman he'd been warned to expect.

"And I must apologize that Doctor Liebert could not accompany me—she was so engrossed in the medical data you transmitted I couldn't tear her away; said she needed to study up before taking over the Hahtooshans' medical care."

"Completely understandable," Amalfitano replied; he fought the urge to swallow, despite his mouth having suddenly gone dry. "I'd have done the same."

"And speaking of—Hahtooshans are *really* human?"

"They're as human as you or me," Amalfitano answered cryptically.

"That's going to come as a shock to a hell of a lot of people."

"Indeed," Izraad said, speaking for the first time.

Mladić nodded to her, then settled back in his chair and crossed his arms. "Now, Commander Aquila's informed me that the officer's condition's taken an unfortunate and sudden turn for the worse?"

"Yes. Late yesterday afternoon he developed a low-grade fever with an associated rise in across-the-board cytokine production. But we'd just discontinued his dichelazine treatments—"

"And in moderate to advanced radiation poisoning cases," Mladić interrupted, "it's not unheard of for there to be a several degree increase in core temperature and rise in cytokines when the treatment ends."

"Exactly."

"But it's my understanding that this withdrawal reaction lasts only a few hours."

"Usually. But he went on to develop acute respiratory difficulties and his core temperature rose to forty point eight degrees. My staff's initial and very reasonable impression was that he'd thrown an embolism—"

"But you've ruled that out."

"Yes."

"Do you know what is wrong with him?"

"He has influenza."

Mladić blinked. *"Influenza?"*

Amalfitano leaned forward, tapped the face of the active desktop terminal and turned it so that Mladić could see the screen, and the results, for himself. "He's suffering from acute myxoviral pneumonia, no doubt about it."

Mladić, recovered from his own surprise, snorted with laughter and shook his head. "You really had me worried there for a minute, Doctor. I thought he had some sort of life-threatening condition."

"In his case, it is."

Mladić's grin froze on his lips.

"He has absolutely no resistance to the virus."

Mladić replied slowly, almost hopefully, "Are you telling me mercs have no immunity—"

"I said *he* has no resistance."

"And why doesn't he?"

"Right now my best guess is radiation poisoning in combination with liver damage. Doctor Fleming agrees—"

"Best guess?" Mladić repeated softly, but with a look in his eye that belied his outer calm. "Doctor, might I remind you that this prisoner is a priceless source of intelligence? Too valuable to be making guesses about—"

"And might I remind you, Captain, that this individual is an aggressively bio-engineered... human? There's still a helluva lot we don't know about their physiology. Any assumptions we make based on our knowledge of non-Hahtooshan humans might be wrong—*dead wrong*—so right now an educated guess, based on what little we do know about them, is the best we can do."

"Please accept my apologies," Mladić replied with unexpected sincerity, "I meant no slight. Now, you said radiation poisoning in combination with liver damage?"

Mollified, Amalfitano continued, "Doctor Fleming discovered that as part of their bio-engineering, the Hahtooshan liver is a major producer of antibodies, and as I detailed in my report, we were able to salvage only two lobes of the officer's liver. The rest had suffered too much damage, and not surprisingly, we had no compatible donor tissue on hand.

"At the time we felt what was left was adequate until tissue replicated from viable samples could be transplanted. I should have realized something was wrong when he failed to respond as expected, but again, at the time—"

"Doctor," Mladić interrupted, "as you just said, there's a lot we don't know about their altered physiology and I believe I can speak for HQ when I say that no one will hold you, or Doctor Fleming, responsible for this unexpected and unwelcome turn of events. But do you have any theory as to how he came in contact with the virus in the first place?"

"From the crew of the survey craft that visited the base on Rasal Ghul Four—"

"Rasal Ghul Four? But... I thought the disease, along with everything else on the planet, had died out over a century ago, that it existed only as data within the computer banks."

"Unfortunately not. The Hahtooshans didn't have the time to recreate the virus based purely on the data they'd recovered. They must have retrieved viable samples, probably from one of the base's still functioning stasis chambers."

Mladić nodded. "There must've been numerous safeguards and redundancies, to protect against accidental power failures or sabotage which would have destroyed irreplaceable cultures."

"Exactly," Amalfitano said. "And it would have been very simple, once they had even a small sample, to then generate more, enough, at least, to create a viable weapon. Even the most basic of ship-board labs would have the equipment needed."

"And so they contaminated themselves with these samples?" Mladić turned to Izraad and grinned, "Not very bright, but typical of mercs, wouldn't you agree, Lieutenant?"

"The virus recovered from the base," Amalfitano continued before Izraad could even open her mouth, "and loaded into the tracer missile we retrieved from the impact site are one and the same, Captain, but they're not the same virus infecting the officer."

Mladić's suddenly grim gaze snapped back to Amalfitano. "I don't follow."

"Then allow me explain. Most viruses are tenacious little critters, able to survive for long periods without a suitable host and in what might appear to be a totally hostile environment. But one virus the base was working with was exceedingly tenacious. It was hoped its offspring would carry that trait as well, but things didn't exactly work out as planned."

"So, you're saying the merc has this parent virus?" Mladić asked.

"Yes. Somehow it escaped containment, possibly when the base was abandoned or later, when the Coalition attempted to destroy the base from orbit and it's remained viable all these years. The crew of the scout craft became contaminated when they entered the base and then unwittingly contaminated others who came in contact with them.

"The sequencing's conclusive," Amalfitano continued. "The virus we recovered from the missile was the offspring, and what the officer has is one of the parent viruses, Type A HA twenty one, NA fourteen Vetrarbraut Sixteen to be exact."

"Type A... what?" Mladić asked.

"Type A HA twenty one, NA fourteen Vetrarbraut Sixteen, named after the colony where it first appeared and was identified, and hemagglutinin twenty one, neuraminidase fourteen, which identify its surface proteins. In fact variants of this particular strain have been around for well over a century, carried along with humans as we spread out into space—the modern-day equivalent of shipboard rats.

"Every so often it still crops up on some planet or outpost—lucky for us, it's about as harmless a flu bug as you can find. But even as harmless as it is, once we'd terminated the dichelazine, it had no difficulty in overwhelming the officer's already compromised immune system."

"Of course," Mladić murmured. "A precursor to dichelazine was a well-known viral inhibitor, and if I'm not mistaken," he looked back at Amalfitano to see the doctor staring at him in mild surprise, "dichelazine is still used in that capacity when other inhibitors are unavailable."

Amalfitano nodded. "And it's also mildly hepatotoxic, which is why, in the case of the officer, we terminated it as quickly as we thought safe. But, may I ask how you knew that? It's not exactly common knowledge."

"I was married to a virologist for a coupla years and I quickly found if I didn't take an active interest in her bugs, she didn't take an active interest in me, if you follow me." Mladić wiggled his eyebrows.

Amalfitano suddenly realized he was smiling back at Mladić. Then he happened to catch the look Izraad gave him and his smile crumbled into a throat-clearing cough.

Oblivious, Mladić continued, "I read your report on their tattoos and those scars that underlie them and your hypothesis about their likeness to archaic circuitry patterns. I found it most interesting. It would certainly explain a lot, if your conjecture about turns out to be true."

"It's a lot more than just conjecture, Captain," Amalfitano said.

"A poor choice of words," Mladić replied, "my apologies. Now what I'd really like to know is have you isolated the source of this interference they emit?"

Amalfitano felt a cold chill crawl over his skin. Taken off guard by Mladić's unexpected expertise and, yes, his flattery, he'd almost forgotten whom he was dealing with. *Almost.* "In case you didn't notice, Captain, we've all been just a little busy."

Mladić smiled an appeasing smile. "Doctor, I wasn't suggesting otherwise. But this ability of theirs is of crucial importance. Do they use it strictly for camouflaging their exact number? Or is it something by which they can communicate—"

"Ensign Cyllo did say that upon close examination, there appears to be a distinct pore pattern which underlies the tattooing and parallels the scarification perfectly," Amalfitano replied.

"Any idea what this means?"

"Nope. I'm no physiologist, but Ensign Cyllo said these pores reminded her of something she'd heard exists in certain species of cartilaginous fish back on Earth—"

"Fish?"

"Sharks, and their kin."

Mladić repeated, *"Sharks...?"*

"They have small pores called..." Amalfitano knit his brows in concentration as he coaxed his mind to remember what Cyllo had said. At the time they'd been attempting to override the interference and track down what had caused Khusaaq's sudden deterioration and it hadn't seemed terribly important. "Ah... yes." He smiled. "Called the *Ampulae of Lorenzini*. They're electro-receptors, and from what I gather, highly accurate locators, but," he shrugged, "that's for someone who knows more about electro-physiology than I do to determine."

"Interesting—definitely something to look into. And now," Mladić rose unexpectedly from his chair, "Now, I'd like to see the prisoner."

"You doubt what I've just told you?" Amalfitano asked, hoping indignation would camouflage his sudden panic.

"On the contrary, Doctor, your credibility's beyond question."

"But then—"

"Call it," Mladić smiled, "morbid curiosity. I've never seen an unmasked merc."

"You'll be seeing nine in short order, and—"

"I can demand it you know."

"There is no need to demand anything, Captain," Izraad said in an appeasing tone, drawing the man's narrowed gaze, "the prisoner is critically ill and Doctor Amalfitano's just concerned that any unnecessary agitation—"

"I have no intention of agitating the prisoner," Mladić said and turned back to Amalfitano. "Doctor?"

Amalfitano knew Mladić was not telling all; there was something lurking behind the man's bland, saucer eyes, something very ugly. *I'm too goddamned tired to play show and tell, but if it gets you the hell outta my sickbay—* "You up on your immunizations?"

"Of course. In my line of work, you never know, at any given time, where you'll be, or who or what you'll be dealing with."

Takes one to know one. Amalfitano pushed himself to his feet. "Then come with me." He strode out of his office, through the unusually quiet sickbay and over to the isolation unit. He stopped long enough for Mladić, Aquila and Izraad to catch up with him then he tapped the airlock control and the door slipped open to admit the four into the cramped confines of the lock.

He fixed his eyes on the control pad, mentally counted off the seconds as the airlock cycled, then stepped out the instant the inner door snapped open. "This way."

Only the soft, flickering lights of the monitors illuminated the cubicle itself and as Amalfitano entered, he gave the room and its occupants a quick sweep with his eyes. Nothing was amiss; all was as it should be—enough, he hoped, to satisfy whatever 'morbid curiosity' Mladić needed satisfying and make their visit as brief as possible.

"Captain Mladić, this is Doctor Fleming."

Fleming saluted. "Sir."

Mladić replied with a curt nod. "Doctor." He barely gave Corsali and Pierson a glance as Amalfitano introduced them by name and rank only before turning his full attention to the person on the narrow bed. "No restraints?"

"In his present condition, he poses no threat to himself or my staff, Captain, and the restraints are a hindrance."

"You should never underestimate a merc, Doctor."

"And you're questioning my judgment again, Captain. Besides…" He motioned to the ever-present guards who stood nearby.

Mladić responded with a conciliatory nod. "Yes, of course."

Amalfitano busied himself with one of the ventilator pods while keeping a wary eye on Mladić as Mladić gave Khusaaq a *very* thorough head to toe visual inspection.

"I see what you mean about the tattoos similarity to archaic liquid circuitry patterns," Mladić murmured, leaning close to Khusaaq's hollow-cheeked face and nodding. "And you say there's an underlying pore pattern that parallels the tattoos exactly?" He reached out with one finger, but just short of actually touching his cheek, he abruptly straightened up and looked at Amalfitano.

"Yes."

As Mladić's eyes darted back to Khusaaq's slack face, Amalfitano thought he saw the faintest of smiles on the man's lips. He risked a quick glance at Izraad.

She stared back, her own face expressionless.

He knew that face; it was what she called her 'party face'. It did not bode well. *Uh-oh*—

"Forty-one point six degrees?"

Amalfitano jerked his eyes back to Mladić to find him now staring at an over-bed monitor. "As soon as we realized what we were dealing with, we started infusing him with tammanadine."

"Tammanadine? Oh yeah, an antiviral. But that hasn't been used in years—decades."

"I know. We ran sensitivities. He's allergic to most of the modern antivirals and those he's not allergic to are all moderately hepatotoxic. I felt the risks weren't worth the possible benefits. From all the sims we've run, it's pretty clear Hahtooshans can tolerate higher core temperatures than you or I—"

"But how high and for how long?"

"I guess we're gonna find out. Nothing we've tried has managed to bring his core temp down. Eventually the tammanadine will do the trick."

"Eventually may not be soon enough, Doctor."

"I understand that, Captain, but we've run out of options. Our lab's working on a method that will, we hope, induce his remaining Kupffer cells into producing antibodies in great enough numbers to overcome the infection. They're also coming up with an artificial antibody as a backup, but both of those will take time. Until then, the tammanadine is our best and only bet."

"And if these efforts fail, then what?"

"Then your priceless source of intelligence dies," Amalfitano replied flatly.

"Can you give me a rough prognosis?"

"I'd say less than fifty-fifty." That was the raw, albeit slightly stretched truth of it, no need to edit his words here—the redacted data he'd supplied the *Walafar*'s MO would back him up if Mladić had any doubts. "And even if he does survive, there's a substantial risk he'll have suffered measurable brain damage, possibly to the point of complete incapacitation." Another truth but also the absolute worse-case scenario—one he hadn't had a chance to broach to Sirin and he gave her a quick, sidelong look but at least outwardly she showed no reaction.

He dropped his gaze to his patient and realized that Khusaaq's eyes were open. *Cacchio!* He leaned over him, blocking Mladić's view, to make an unnecessary adjustment to an infuser then glanced back at his unwelcome guest. "Now, if your curiosity's been satisfied, perhaps…?"

Mladić said, "Yes, of course," then followed Aquila and Izraad out of the cubicle.

Amalfitano straightened up only to find Khusaaq staring dully after Mladić.

"Hauduut-sseh?" he asked in a thick, hoarse whisper.

Amalfitano patted him on the arm and replied softly, "No one you need worry about." *I'll do it for both of us.* He turned to Fleming, rolled his eyes, to which she replied in kind, he then favored Sirin with another, this time what he hoped looked like a reassuring glance before he pivoted smartly on his heel and strode out of the cubicle, down the short corridor and into the awaiting airlock.

At Mladić's questioning stare, he replied, "Needed to do a little tweaking to the dosage levels."

"Of course." Mladić paused as the lock cycled, then as the outer door opened, he asked, "Is there any chance the other one, the trooper, might go on to develop influenza? Your initial report stated that his liver had also sustained serious damage and a portion had to be removed."

Amalfitano stepped out and replied, "His viral screen confirms that he's been exposed, but so far his immune system seems to be holding its own. And until we've developed an effective antiviral they can tolerate, I'm keeping him on the dichelazine and a prophylactic regimen of tammanadine. I've updated Doctor Liebert on the latest lab results and drug protocols—"

"Doctor Liebert and I spoke before I flicked over. As you know, she'd had time to make only a very cursory study of the material you provided…"

Amalfitano tried not to look as panicky as he felt—were their frantic efforts at subterfuge about to pay off? Or would everything have been for nothing? Khusaaq's life, and possibly his own career and those of Izraad and Fleming hung in the balance. It was all he could do not to steal a glance at Izraad, hoping for some reassurance for himself—

"... and we believe it would be in everyone's best interests to leave both prisoners in your expert care until the *Baidarka* returns to Mirfak Prime. The *Walafar* just isn't set up for this sort of situation I'll be damned if I'm going to hand the Hahtooshans any cause to say these two suffered permanent disability, possibly even death due to deliberate negligence when the very best medical care the Coalition has to offer was available—knowing them, they'd demand even more on top of what they've already demanded and gods know what else—and likely get it—to make the matter, and them, go away."

Amalfitano wasn't sure he'd actually heard what he'd heard. *"Both?"*

"I do hope this will not create an undue burden on you and your staff?"

Realizing he'd said 'Both' aloud and at the same instant realizing their ploy *had* worked and worked better than planned, he tried not to look as intensely relieved as he felt. "No, no of course not... plus it'll give Doctor Fleming and me more time to learn all we can about merc physiology."

"Excellent!"

Thought you'd like that, Amalfitano puckered his lips in distaste the instant Mladić shifted his gaze to Aquila.

"That is if Commander Aquila agrees to this last minute change of plans?"

"I suppose it makes sense," Aquila replied, he even managing to sound rather put out. "As to the remaining prisoners..." He looked expectantly at Amalfitano.

"Doctor Fleming's already gone over the instructions in their release packets with Doctor Liebert," Amalfitano replied.

Mladić smiled. "I do hope we find another time when we can have a proper talk about that monograph, Doctor, and the one I'm sure you'll write on this truly unique experience?"

"Of course."

"Commander Aquila?" Meerut said as she rose from the nurses' console. "You're needed in C and C. A Mister Henson is demanding to speak with you?"

Aquila exhaled, shook his head and said to Mladić, "The Coalition envoy."

"I know," Mladić replied. "He's quite a handful, or so I've been given to understand."

"That's an understatement," Aquila said, then turned to Izraad. "Perhaps…?"

She replied, "I'd be pleased to escort the Captain to the brig—give us a chance to 'talk shop'."

Mladić grinned at that and Aquila, with a curt nod to Izraad, Mladić and Amalfitano, strode from the unit.

"Captain?" Izraad motioned to Mladić as she too started for the main doors.

Mladić turned to follow, then stopped and looked back at Amalfitano.

"Yes?" Amalfitano asked, hoping he didn't sound as apprehensive as he felt.

"You lost your family at Raumalle."

"That's common knowledge, Captain."

"I just wanted you to know that I fully appreciate what I'm asking of you."

"Thank you," Amalfitano replied.

"HQ will be informed of just how valuable your assistance has been, Doctor—and Doctor Fleming of course."

"Just doing our jobs, Captain."

"We all are, Doctor. We all are."

Amalfitano stared after him, but as Mladić and Izraad stepped into the corridor, his rigid smile dissolved and he whispered, *"Only you enjoy it too goddamned much."*

Chapter 26

He smiled, almost smugly, safe in the knowledge that no one could see his expression. *I deserve this—everyone says so.* It was an honor beyond all others: a Coalition Battle Commendation, historically reserved only for those most elite members of the Coalition Expeditionary Forces who had shown bravery far above and beyond the call of duty. *I deserve it. We all do, and then some.*

It had never been awarded to anyone outside of the CEF, and now it was being awarded not just to one A'tuu'shahn'i but one hundred and one, all but five posthumously. And here they were, the five survivors of Cotopaxi—*the sole survivors*—come to collect the honors for themselves and for their fallen comrades and commanding officer.

Cotopaxi had started out as just another routine contract, nothing more than a show of A'tuu'shahn force to frighten off a Matarii raider who'd been harassing ships supplying the Coalition's newest colony.

One hundred crew, not one past his or her mid-teens, most much younger, and a soon to be decommissioned training corvette, *Huui'teh,* under the command of an aging, highly respected officer, Gaalan Tashar'anhi. It was a simple, straightforward job: scare the Matarii raider into fleeing back across the border then stick around long enough to make sure it didn't come back.

By standard, contractual agreement, there was to be no contact between the colony and the crew of *Huui'teh*, except by tac-net.

Simple.

Until the raider returned, this time accompanied by three Matarii heavy destroyers with stated plans to make *Huui'teh* an example of what would befall the colonists if they did not immediately abandon what the Matarii claimed as their planet.

Only forty-three of her crew managed to flick down to the planet before the corvette and her commanding officer were blown to bits. Then the destroyers turned their missile bays on the planet and stated their demands.

The colonists refused.

The orbital siege lasted fifteen days, after which the Matarii landed en masse to capture the colony and mop up what resistance remained. They hadn't counted on the tenacity of the handful of surviving A'tuu'shahn'i, or the grim determination of their newly-minted Ruh'ta'aq to carry out his commanding officer's final orders to hold the colony at all costs until the promised reinforcements arrived.

They did arrive, but not before the last of the colonists had been killed, along with all but five A'tuu'shahn'i.

"Raz... ta'aq," the human hesitated, in the process drawing Khusaaq's thoughts back to the present, "ah... Telapan. I mean Telapnow?" he ended lamely.

Khusaaq flicked Telipinu a sidelong look. He didn't need to see the trooper's face to know his expression. Just like it didn't matter that the presenter couldn't pronounce Telipinu's use name. Even the sizable bonus they were to be paid seemed unimportant.

All that mattered was what the Coalition representative held in his right hand.

A Coalition Battle Commendation! But it was not just a medal, not just an award for extraordinary valor. It was also a symbol of recognition, a tangible validation of A'tuu'shahn worth, of A'tuu'shahn loss. They would no longer be nameless mercenaries—blood currency for the warring hegemonies to be spent with little or no guilt. He'd been dazzled by the prospect, buoyed with the hope this might mean a return to the old ways, or, at the very least, a reexamination of those ways. Of turning back to the heady promises of the Elkanasu so long ignored, ridiculed and relegated to the private thoughts of only the most devout.

No one can ever take this away from us. Or so his superiors had told him, so the Q'shaathrah had assured him and the others. *Never mind the messy details or the terrible costs...*

Telipinu took a step forward; while the Rimmer couldn't actually see him, he could clearly see the odd distortion of Telipinu's battle armor's camouflage shift and enlarge and the presenter responded by swallowing nervously.

Khusaaq knew just how much the Telipinu hated Rimmers. Finding out after the fact that the Matarii were in fact the rightful holders of the planet, that the colony had been a risky gambit on the part of the Coalition to push further into disputed space, to test Matarii resolve while both hegemonies were still licking their wounds had only heaped more bitterness on the whole matter. Yet here he was, not only in the same cargo hold with well over two hundred of the despised, deceitful creatures, but he was being presented with the highest Coalition award for his heroic efforts to save a Rimmer colony. And despite Telipinu's sense of foreboding, the soldier was clearly enjoying the moment. *And why not?* Along with the prestigious medals, they'd all been promised a hefty bonus by the Coalition, plus a rise in rank by the elders of the Q'shaathrah upon their return. The dead had already received a promotion by one rank, and their families were to receive compensation for their losses based on that rank status. But for him, at this moment, none of this mattered; all that mattered was—

"In the name of the Rim Coalition," the presenter said, interrupted Khusaaq's thoughts, "and in the memory of the colonists of Cotopaxi for whom you fought so courageously, I present you with the Rim Coalition's highest military honor, the Battle Commendation." He held out a small, innocuous looking box in a visibly trembling hand then opened it to reveal the medal within.

Over their private channel, Khusaaq overheard Telipinu's soft, throaty chuckle as he snatched the box, prompting a startled yelp from the human as the presenter stumbled back, panic-stricken and pale-faced. It was as if the box had suddenly vanished into thin air—or in this case, very viscous, visibly rippling air, air that as it brushed across the human's bare skin left the sensation of cool scales sliding across his hand. Clearly an unnerving experience for the presenter, not to mention those behind him and Khusaaq couldn't help but chuckle. *Yowies indeed.*

As Telipinu stepped back, clutching his prize, the presenter tugged at his dress uniform in an attempt at collecting himself then he cleared his throat and turned to unhappily accept another box from his aide. As he did so, Khusaaq lifted his slitted gaze and using his visor's scanners surveyed the surrounding sea of grim faces. The presence of so many had been explained as a sign of respect, but to his eyes he saw them for what they were: a motley collection of Rimmers with itchy trigger fingers.

He wouldn't have been surprised to learn that the 'honor' guard ringing the catwalk high above had been given orders, at the first sign of trouble, to open fire on their distinguished guests. As far as he knew, heavy shocker rifles and combat armor were *not* standard Coalition honor guard equipment. But he and his companions had come well-prepared for any contingency as well. No standard duty uniforms this time, no. This meeting required full battle panoply—a matter of survival, Telipinu had groused. A mark of respect for the fallen, he'd been told by his superiors. It was, after all the same body armor they'd worn defending Cotopaxi, the same armor that still vaguely stank from prolonged wear and bore the telltale scars of heavy combat, honors in their own right.

His trained eye had also immediately spotted the poorly concealed but notably pristine body armor of the presenter and his aide, and the telltale bulge of a shocker grip under the aide's jacket each time the man turned to hand the presenter another award box.

Khusaaq's lip curled into a contemptuous sneer.

It was no secret that many within the Coalition had opposed the ceremony. A radical but powerful few had fought against giving the bonuses, much less the prestigious medals, to what most within the Coalition openly considered the galaxy's terrorists-for-hire. But Coalition protocol required it—and the Orthodoxy had demanded it as partial compensation for their losses.

So, here they were, the five survivors, in full battle panoply—not that any of their Coalition hosts could tell; to them they were nothing more than faint, telltale shimmers, flickers of movement caught out of the tail of the eye and then gone, essentially invisible to eye and instrument alike, but very clearly present. To each other and viewed through their helmet visors they appeared as pulsing, slithering coils of light suspended in space, each a slightly different color. *Beautiful...* Khusaaq smiled, staring at his companions then realizing he'd briefly let his mind wander, he turned back to the matter at hand. He needed to keep his wits about him, not be lulled into a false sense of security.

These were Rimmers after all and with Rimmers, nothing was as it appeared to be. They'd lied about Cotopaxi, lied about who had discovered the planet first and therefore who had the right under universal Rim law to colonize it.

As for the hastily arranged ceremony itself, it was taking place on a utilitarian Coalition transport ship, as far from the center of the Coalition as possible, in fact right on the edge of neutral space, with little fanfare and even fewer official attendees, but.... *It doesn't matter—nothing matters but the medals. So get them and then get out.*

"Kon ta'aq Ka... roobee?"

"Kon ta'aq Sahr'qharubi ket Rasharawan'tischinjgra to you, *filth*," Qharubi growled indignantly as he stepped forward.

"Manners, Qharubi, manners," Khusaaq murmured sweetly.

Qharubi made a rude noise as he peered down at the human with a mixture of curiosity and distaste. He'd come to respect the Cotopaxians, for their dogged resolve in the face of certain death if nothing more, but Rimmers as a whole...

At least this one stood his ground this time as Qharubi's oddly shimmering, undulating yet utterly transparent presence approached. Khusaaq grudgingly gave him that much.

"In the name of the Rim Coalition, and in the memory of the colonists of Cotopaxi for whom you fought so courageously, I present you with the Rim Coalition's highest military honor, the Battle Commendation."

Qharubi wrinkled his nose at the human's odd, cloying odor as the man reached out with the box, closed this time, and holding it between thumb and forefinger, clearly hoping to avoid actual contact this time. *"Chiku!* They smell as bad as—"

"Qharubi..." Khusaaq warned.

"Fine." Qharubi irritably plucked the box from the human's fingers, and the human quickly backed away while Qharubi peeked in the box to make sure the medal was inside. Satisfied, he looked up. "That's it?" he asked in a wounded voice. "Not even a kiss on the cheek?"

"If you wanted a kiss on the cheek," Telipinu grumbled, "you should've turned around."

Unprepared, Khusaaq snorted, then realized his spasmodic jerk had caused a ripple effect, startling several of the dignitaries and sent yet another ripple—this one of obvious unease—through the large number of heavily armed Coalition security personnel who ringed the cargo bay, both on the main floor and high above.

"Now you tell me," Qharubi replied as he neatly back-stepped into line.

"Ha'tat ah... Isha kool?"

Ichkeul, with Telipinu's help, broke ranks with his companions and slowly limped forward. Before they could cover the space between their line and the presenter, the human started speaking.

"In the name of the Rim Coalition," the presenter said, this time making little effort to make it sound fresh or meaningful, and offered up the box to what to the Rimmers looked like nothing more than empty air and which in fact was.

Telipinu cursed softly, then reluctantly left Ichkeul and hurried towards the human.

"...and in the memory of the colonists of Cotopaxi for whom you fought so courageously..."

Khusaaq, half-listening to what sounded more like a dirge than a celebration of heroism, found his attention drifting to the aide. There was something hauntingly familiar about the human's otherwise unremarkable face. He shook off the sensation and turned back to the ceremony. *Keep alert!* he chided himself.

"...I present you with the Rim Coalition's highest military honor, the Battle Commendation."

Telipinu angrily grabbed the small presentation box, then turned and stormed back to where he'd left the wheezing, trembling Ichkeul. Ichkeul had gone against the medical officer's advice by attending, and the decision was clearly taking its toll. Khusaaq had been aware of the man's labored breathing from the start, but now, having walked only half way to the presenter before he could go no further, his breath was coming in short, sharp gasps. The body armor with its sensor-distorting camouflage could do only so much; its continuous infusions of painkillers and stimulants could only help so much.

Even some of the audience sensed something wasn't right as Telipinu helped Ichkeul limp slowly backwards into line.

"Perhaps we should speed this up?" someone within the gallery of dignitaries asked pointedly.

"Before he drops dead in front of you," Telipinu growled. "You ungrateful bunch of—"

"Yes, of course." The presenter accepted yet another medal from his aide. "Ha'tat Sara... kay lee?"

Saar'kali eagerly stepped forward and as he was handed his medal, Khusaaq straightened up.

"And lastly," the presenter said with audible relief as he took one more box from the aide, "Ruh'ta'aq, ah... Koosap?"

Khusaaq inwardly flinched and felt himself deflate, if just a bit. He stepped forward, ignoring the snickers of his companions. Even Ichkeul managed a half-hearted chuckle.

"Ruh'ta'aq Koosap, in the name of the Rim Coalition, and in the memory of the colonists of Cotopaxi for whom you fought so courageously, I present you with the Rim Coalition's highest military honor, the Battle Commendation."

Khusaaq watched with a broad, smug smile as the human offered him the box. He accepted it, politely. No snatching, no grabbing, as befitted his rank.

"And the rest," the presenter added, almost dismissively, motioning to a large, open carton the aide now offered up.

Khusaaq accepted the container holding the posthumous medals with the respect it was due and after a quick glance at its contents, closed the lid.

Then it was over. Dignitaries rose as one and quickly and wordlessly filed out of the cargo bay as the presenter hurriedly vanished through another airlock without so much as an over-the-shoulder glance. That left only the fidgety aide and the equally uneasy security escort.

"Well, that was fun," Qharubi muttered.

"What did you expect?" Telipinu replied. "They're like vermin scuttling back to their burrows."

"Please..."

Khusaaq turned towards the polite but insistent voice to find the speaker was none other than the aide.

"...come with me." The human motioned to the massive, heavily guarded airlock through which they had entered the transport's cavernous bay less than a quarter of a Standard hour before then started towards it, widely skirting around the major area of distortion, clearly having no desire to accidentally bump into one of them.

Khusaaq didn't have to be asked twice. There was something not quite right about the situation and it was getting more uncomfortable by the second. He'd felt it from the moment they had arrived, but had, at first, chalked it up to his own deeply entrenched distrust of Rimmers in combination with fatigue—the voyage here had taken over a week, during which time he'd been forced to play parent to the constantly bickering Qharubi and Saar'kali, not to mention he and Telipinu acting as 'round the clock medics to Ichkeul. In fact none had fully recuperated from their injuries, but the Coalition had adamantly refused to delay the ceremony by even an hour from the time they had set as part and parcel of the compensation agreement, due to 'political considerations' or so the Rimmer negotiators had said—*more like political ramifications*, he added sourly to himself.

The return trip to the awaiting assault transport ship *Khargeh* promised to be just as taxing. Telipinu's repeated assertions during the journey, that the ceremony was nothing more than an elaborate ambush, certainly hadn't helped and only fed his own inner voice.

He'd pointedly ignored both, but now that voice was verging on a yell.

He tucked the container under his arm then strode past the guards who stood rigidly on either side of the airlock. The others wordlessly followed.

Saar'kali trotted to catch up with him once they were in the corridor that led back to the docking ring and their foldboat. "Ruh'ta'aq, what about the bonuses, the compensation—"

"They haven't forgotten, Ha'tat." The same thought had occurred to him, but out-manned and out-gunned, there was little he could do if the Coalition had decided to renege on the promised remuneration—but he was not about to admit that to the headstrong and hot-tempered Saar'kali.

Saar'kali murmured dubiously, "Yes, Ruh'ta'aq," then fell back, to help Telipinu and Qharubi with the flagging Ichkeul, whom they'd resorted to half-carrying, half-dragging. The aide kept well ahead of them, never once looking back to see if they followed. Finally he stopped at the only doorway that marred the otherwise smooth-walled corridor. Beyond the four heavily armed and armored marines who stood two abreast on either side of the opening lay the docking ring and their escape from the anxious confines of the transport ship.

"And now…"

Khusaaq jerked his eyes off the sullen-faced sentries and back to the aide to see the man reach into an inner jacket pocket. He stiffened and his hand immediately dropped to his weapons belt and the grip of his maser pistol. Without looking, he knew his companions had done the same.

"…your bonuses and the compensation for your losses," the aide continued, oblivious.

Khusaaq exhaled and dropped his hand to his side as the aide withdrew a small pouch.

"As promised, twenty thousand credits, *each.*"

He reached out, his ghostly fingers carefully lifting the pouch from the aide's outstretched hand, avoiding actual contact.

"Count it if you'd like," the aide added with a nervous, almost sneering smile.

Khusaaq studied the anxious human. Despite the temptation and his overwhelming distrust, he knew to open the packet and count the credits went against Coalition etiquette. He would not play into this smirking minion's hands by doing exactly what he and the sentries expected an A'tuu'shahn—*a merc*—to do.

He tapped his chin on the helmet's tac-net, activating an open link for the first time, then growled in his deep, most menacing 'when-dealing-with-aliens' voice, which was enhanced by the tac-net's metallic rasp, "That will not be necessary, will it?"

The aide visibly paled and Khusaaq grinned, satisfied.

"But ta'ahn—" Saar'kali protest was cut off by Telipinu's throat clearing cough.

"Well… ah," the aide stammered, backing up as his eyes darted between the pay packet that appeared as if suspended in mid-air and the odd, liquid-like shimmer that filled the passageway, wall-to-wall, "if… ah… if that's all?"

"I hope we do business again." With that, Khusaaq stepped through the docking ring and into the short connecting tube then stepped aside, waiting on the others.

Telipinu and Saar'kali body-lifted Ichkeul over the docking seals and into the tube, Qharubi right behind them, and the instant he was through, the docking ring closed with a resounding *clang.*

Qharubi lurched forward in surprise then wheeled on the ring as he felt his rump with both hands. He turned back to Khusaaq. "I sense they're in hurry to have us leave."

Khusaaq chuckled, a very relieved chuckle, then he stepped through the foldboat's airlock and into the tiny craft itself. He waited by the lock until everyone was aboard, then he smacked the release with his gauntleted fist. "Kon ta'aq, get us back into free space."

"With *pleasure,*" Qharubi replied as he slipped into the pilot's chair and began punching in commands.

Khusaaq, drawn to the sound of labored breathing, turned his gaze on Ichkeul.

With Telipinu's help, Ichkeul had managed to remove his helmet and was now leaning heavily against a nearby bulkhead as he struggled to catch his breath. The soldier looked terrible, far worse than when they'd arrived, less than a Standard hour before. His deathly pale face was streaked with sweat, he was shivering and a telltale coating of foamy blood rimmed his ashen mouth and staring at him, Khusaaq was left to wonder if Ichkeul would survive the hour, much less the return trip.

Khusaaq murmured, "See what you can do," over the tac-net as he placed the awards container, along with his personal medal, in a nearby storage locker.

Telipinu nodded then he again wrapped his arm around Ichkeul's waist and together they slowly made their way to the rear of the boat's cramped cabin and their makeshift sleeping quarters.

Khusaaq felt more than heard the familiar hum of the boat's engines and the faint *click* of the docking ring releasing its hold.

"We're free of the dock," Qharubi confirmed. "Course laid in, implementing now."

"Go to fold five as soon as we're clear of their pickets."

"Ta'ahn?" Saar'kali began. "What about the bon—"

"Telipinu needs your assistance, Ha'tat."

Saar'kali grumbled, "Yes, ta'ahn," and started towards the back of the cabin.

"And Saar'kali?"

Saar'kali turned expectantly to Khusaaq.

"Never appear too eager to be paid off."

"Ta'ahn?"

"While it may be customary among the Barkaat," Khusaaq said and almost grinned at Telipinu as the soldier removed his helmet and favored him with a sidelong, offended squint, "it's *most* unbecoming of an Elkanaghalli."

"Yes, Ruh'ta'aq."

Khusaaq tossed him the pouch. "Now, perhaps you'd like to count—" He was cut off by Ichkeul's soft groan.

"We're past their pickets, engaging foldspace engines," Qharubi announced as the background hum subtly changed pitch. "Increasing to fold five—"

"Make that fold nine," Khusaaq murmured.

Qharubi nodded, "Fold nine, aye."

Khusaaq looked back at Ichkeul and again cursed the Coalition for not permitting even a junior medical officer to accompany them on the trip. Only the five who were to receive the award would be permitted through the Coalition's pickets—or no award and no bonus. Not that the Coalition would have known, but the Orthodoxy would, and the Orthodoxy always kept its word.

He also cursed Ichkeul for not agreeing to allow a stand-in to accept his medal. The Coalition would certainly never have been the wiser, but Ichkeul had stubbornly refused, saying if he'd wanted a stand-in, he'd have asked for one before being deployed to Cotopaxi.

Saar'kali gave the packet another look, then walked over to Ichkeul, pulled off his helmet and knelt beside him. He pressed the pouch into the soldier's trembling hands. "Here, Ha'tat, *you* count it."

Khusaaq smiled as he watched Ichkeul fumble eagerly with the pouch's unfamiliar catch. Then suddenly an inner voice screamed, *NO!* an instant before Ichkeul popped the catch and the bomb exploded—

"CHULH!" He awoke with a violent start.

"Shhh," a voice murmured as he felt something cool touch his cheek. "It's all right."

He turned his startled eyes towards the voice.

"Welcome back." Sirin smiled and dabbed his forehead with the wet cloth.

He squinted at her for a moment before rasping, *"Sirin?"*

"Of course." She lightly kissed his forehead as he ran his tongue over his gummy lips.

"Thirsty?" She held up a small glass.

He nodded and she pressed it to his lips. He took a sip, winced as the deliciously cold water trickled down his hot, sore throat, and then took another sip, this time deeper. He eagerly started to take yet another, but she lifted the glass away.

"Not so fast—we don't want it coming right back up."

He stared up at her for a moment, then, suddenly realizing where he was, his eyes darted back to the doorway. Someone stood in the rectangle of light. He'd heard voices. Amalfitano—and someone else. He squinted at the silhouette. "*Hauduut-sseh?*"

"That's Rafe," Corsali answered, following his gaze. "You remember Rafe."

Pierson approached the bed and into the flickering glow of the monitors. "How're you feeling, sir?"

Khusaaq squinted at the medtech. He wasn't the one he remembered standing there, but he did look familiar.

"That bad, huh?" Pierson replied with a commiserating smile.

Khusaaq shifted his gritty gaze back to Sirin as she brought the glass back to his lips.

"Now, take it slow, okay? *Sips.*"

He took a sip, and another, allowing each to pool in his dry mouth before letting the water slide down his parched throat.

— ii —

"Doctor Amalfitano?"

Amalfitano lifted his head from the pillow and squinted, bleary-eyed, at the bedside com-unit and its pleading telltale.

"*William,*" Fleming's insistent voice continued, "*please answer—*"

"Okay, okay, give me a damned minute!"

"William… wake up—"

"I *am* awake," he growled as he lurched to his feet, "and up, thanks to you!" He thumbed the button. "What?"

"I thought you'd want to know that Matoosh's begun to display symptoms of influenza."

"Be right there." He released the activator and hurried from his cabin.

A few moments later he stood beside Fleming in the doorway of Matoosh's cubicle.

"Tell me everything," he said as Meerut positioned a ventilator pod against Matoosh's heaving chest.

"Just like Khusaaq. He became restless, his core temp shot up and he started wheezing—it all happened within the space of a few minutes."

"And he's still on the dichelazine?"

Fleming nodded. "And tammanadine."

"Doesn't make sense." He wandered into the cubicle to get a better look at the bio-comps and their readings. "Remind me to tell Cyllo she came up with a very ingenious solution to override the interference."

Meerut glared at him. "Yeah, but she didn't have to insert it, did she?"

He gave the sensor lead that disappeared under Matoosh's hip a pointed glance. "It was the least invasive…"

"Tell *him* that," she jerked her thumb at Matoosh. "And I ain't gonna remove it."

"You don't have to," Fleming murmured, "Drakin's already volunteered."

Amalfitano privately winced at the thought and turned his critical gaze on his patient.

Matoosh looked up at him with the glazed, panicky stare of someone unable to catch his breath—the same stare Khusaaq had given him hours before.

"You're going to be okay, son, just relax and let my staff do their work—and don't fight them, all right?"

To his surprise, Matoosh managed a slight nod.

"Are you having any pain?" he asked as he pressed his palm against the soldier's incredibly hot, sweat-sticky forehead.

Matoosh fingered his chest, then his throat and for good measure winced as he swallowed.

Amalfitano smiled his best bedside smile. "We'll do something about that, too, all right?" He gave Meerut a sidelong look and she turned to the drug cart.

"I'll be back to check on you in a little while." Amalfitano motioned for Fleming to follow him out of the room.

"Doctor," Matoosh gasped and Amalfitano looked back at him, surprised. It was the first time Matoosh had ever called him anything but 'Rimmer', or, if he was in an especially foul mood, *'Pih-dar'*, which Izraad had happily translated into something loosely akin to 'filth'.

"Yes?"

"Sha… Sha'ashahn…?"

Amalfitano plainly heard the fear in his gravelly voice made even raspier by the virus. He sat down on the edge of the bunk and looked directly into his glassy eyes. "Your brother's very ill, Matoosh. I'm not going to tell you he isn't, but just like you, he's going to pull through, I give you my word."

Matoosh managed a relieved, albeit tired smile and a very hoarse, *"Jaas-nhe."*

Amalfitano patted his arm, rose and followed Fleming out of the cubicle and into Khusaaq's, then stopped just inside and looked around, allowing his eyes to adjust to the subdued lighting.

Pierson and Rosen stood off to one side talking quietly as they stared at a monitor. Sirin sat on the chair beside the bed, dabbing at Khusaaq's face and throat with a wet cloth. Khusaaq's eyes were open and as Amalfitano took a step closer to the bed, he slowly shifted his gaze to him.

Amalfitano smiled. "Thought I'd stop in and see how you're doing."

Khusaaq stared back with an exhausted expression then his eyelids drifted closed as Sirin draped the cloth across his forehead.

Amalfitano's smile faded. He turned to Rosen and whispered, "How is he doing?"

She pointed to a monitor. "I believe the expression is 'a picture is worth a thousand words'?"

"Forty-two point one degrees?"

"It spiked at forty-two point seven about an hour ago," Pierson said.

Amalfitano, his eyes now fully adjusted to the dim light, looked back at Khusaaq and was startled to see that he was packed in ice bags. His eyes darted back to Pierson.

"Don't knock it, Chief, it managed to bring his temp down a half a degree—Doc Fleming's idea."

He turned to the woman beside him as she said, "The antipyretics and the bed's built-in coolers just weren't doing the trick. I figured... what the hell."

Amalfitano shook his head then asked, "Anything from lab?"

"Not yet," Fleming answered.

He let out a sigh and turned to leave when Tasende burst the room.

"Guess what!"

Khusaaq groaned.

"Shhh!" Sirin hissed angrily.

Amalfitano pointed to the corridor and Tasende nodded, but the instant the two were in the corridor, the lab tech blurted out, "The tammanadine's working, Chief! The virus' growth is beginning to slow. And something else—I think I've figured out how this whole thing fits together!" He grinned with nervous excitement. "As you know, I've been trying to develop a more potent, Hahtooshan-specific form of the drug—"

"And?"

"And in doing so, I ran some tests on some of the liver tissue you removed for cloning, to see what kind of cellular response I got to various derivatives." Suddenly he realized that Amalfitano was tapping his foot impatiently. "Get to the point, right?"

"Right."

"Well, I started to get curious as to why the remaining liver, despite our best efforts, refused to start producing Type A Vet-specific antibodies in any great quantity. Like you, I suspected it was due to a combination of trauma and radiation poisoning, as I've been monitoring the virus closely and it hasn't mutated significantly, so I knew that wasn't the problem. Turns out we were right, but one thing we hadn't considered was the effect their radiation exposure had on the virus itself."

"Which was?"

"The Hahtooshans were exposed to more of Rasal Ghul's radiation than our people. A *helluva* lot more."

"So?"

"So they got a healthy, or I should say a very unhealthy dose," Tasende continued, his excited voice rapidly picking up speed. "At the same time, or about the same time they were exposed to the virus. But the virus, removed from the protection of the base, was also exposed to the same radiation and it immediately retarded the virus' growth, giving the Hahtooshans' immune systems time to identify it as a foreign entity and mobilize against it. They probably never knew they'd been inoculated!"

"Whoa! Slow down," Fleming said, stepping out of the cubicle to join them. "If that's the case, why have Khusaaq and Matoosh gone on to develop—"

"Because their livers, hence their immune systems, were damaged, and—"

"And by removing them from the radiation source," Amalfitano interrupted, "we removed the one factor that was effectively keeping the virus in check and replaced it with one that was only marginally effective." He shook his head as he walked back into the cubicle.

"Now what?" Fleming asked softly as she and Tasende followed.

"There's no going back, we can't re-irradiate 'em," Tasende answered. "And there's no point putting them back on the dichelazine. The tammanadine'll work, eventually. But before that, computer simulations suggest there's a risk they'll develop severe swelling in their nasal airways and in those enormous sinus cavities of theirs—"

"He's already suffered two nosebleeds," Fleming offered as she pointedly wiped the stained front of her med reds.

"—and since the bony walls between the sinus cavities and the brain are relatively thin," Tasende continued, "there's a risk of brain damage from hemorrhage. There's also a major risk of the virus spreading to the brain from the sinus cavities."

"I want them tapped," Amalfitano said to Fleming, "just in case," and nodding, she began pulling the needed supplies from the bedside supply locker.

"And we need to get his core temp down," Amalfitano added, "and—"

Khusaaq sneezed then moaned and clutched his forehead.

"Easy, easy," Sirin murmured as she dabbed his nose with the washcloth.

Amalfitano noticed fresh blood on the cloth. *Nosebleeds.* He took a step closer to the bed. *Something about—*

Khusaaq arched his head back and sneezed explosively, liberally splattering himself, Pierson, Amalfitano and Corsali with blood. Then he sank back onto the bed and groaned loudly as his fingers clawed at his forehead.

"Gee, thanks," Pierson grumbled as he wiped his face with the back of his hand.

Sirin ignored her own blood-speckled face and uniform as she pried Khusaaq's fingers away from his forehead and pressed an ice bag to the bridge of his nose.

It worked; he quieted almost immediately.

Amalfitano continued to squint distractedly at his patient. *What is it about nosebleeds? Something important. Something—* His jaw dropped and his eyes widened in horror as his mind unlocked a mnemonic curio box. *Oh... shit!*

"Nosebleeds!" he hissed as he wheeled on Fleming. "The captain of the battleship," he replied unsteadily, "he'd clearly had a recent nosebleed! And I'm not completely positive, but I think at least two other crew had as well."

"So?"

"So what if Khusaaq's lack of response *isn't* due to a compromised immune system?"

Fleming's only response was to stare, open mouthed.

Tasende managed a stammering, "But... but... *uh-oh.*"

"They were exposed, we know that," Amalfitano continued, his hushed voice edged in mounting panic. "But the virus couldn't overwhelm them as long as they were being bombarded with radiation. But as soon as they got out from under the radiation sphere..." He squeezed his eyes shut as the full impact hit him. *"Gods!"*

Tasende whispered, "You're suggesting Hahtooshans have no resistance, *period.*"

"But both of the Hahtooshan ships were destroyed," Fleming interrupted, "and along with them, the virus. As long as we keep those we have isolated while they're infectious—"

"But the rest are scheduled to be turned over to their government in a matter of hours!" He smacked the activator of the wall-com. "C and C—this is Amalfitano! Get Aquila and Izraad down here on the double!"

"But you said they were being taken back to HQ," Fleming began the instant he released the activator.

"That's what everyone was supposed to think!" He gave Khusaaq one last, horrified look, said, "Jenna, get those sinuses tapped! Matoosh's too!" then grabbed Tasende by the arm and started for the doorway. "Come with me!"

"Where're we going?" Tasende managed as he stumbled alongside.

"To stop the goddamned transfer, what the hell do you think!"

— iii —

Amalfitano and Tasende had no sooner stepped out of the isolation airlock than a rather disheveled Aquila dashed through the sickbay's main doorway.

"What the hell's the emergency?" He fixed his sleep-reddened gaze on Amalfitano and quickly took in the doctor's blood smeared face and uniform, but it was what he saw in the doctor's eyes that stopped him in his tracks. "Khusaaq—"

"Have the Hahtooshans been handed over yet?"

Aquila hesitated, his worry dissolving into a perplexed stare. "I have no idea, why?"

"They can't be repatriated!"

"Just a coupla hours ago you didn't seem to mind, in fact—"

"A couple of hours ago I didn't know that they have no resistance to the influenza virus!" Amalfitano hurled himself down into a chair at the nurses' console and began punching up information.

"Wha-what?" Aquila spluttered as his eyes darted back to Tasende; Tasende nodded unhappily.

"Khusaaq's influenza isn't a result of a compromised immune system!" Amalfitano jerked his eyes off Aquila just long enough to acknowledge Izraad's arrival with a curt nod. "He has no immunity—none of them do!"

Aquila walked over to the console. "I thought you'd given the prisoners a clean bill of health—"

"I did, that's the whole fucking point!" Amalfitano glared at an active monitor as he tapped it angrily with his finger. *"See? Here!"*

Aquila peered down at the data-filled screen and barely had a chance to recognize it as Suhjai's medical file before Amalfitano added, "The virus had been so inhibited by the radiation they were exposed to, it acted like a live-killed or attenuated vaccine, allowing their immune systems to recognize then begin to mobilize to the threat by producing antibodies."

He glanced up at Aquila, then Izraad. "We found traces of these antibodies and assumed, incorrectly, that they were proof that they had a prior exposure to at least one strain of orthomyxovirus and had, therefore, at least, minimal immunity."

"It would be reasonable to assume," Tasende added, "based on what we now know, that if they'd remained within the radiation sphere of Rasal Ghul a little longer, the radiation would have kept the virus in check long enough that they would have become completely immune."

"But they left before that occurred," Izraad offered.

"Yeah," Tasende nodded. "And the other prisoners, while not displaying any overt symptoms are, nevertheless, *highly* infectious carriers. Carriers that will, unless stopped, introduce the virus into a highly vulnerable population—"

"Remember the physical appearance of the *Makhaira*'s crew?" Amalfitano prompted, drawing Aquila's stare. "Tarqk—he'd clearly suffered a recent nosebleed and—"

"Nosebleed?" Aquila snorted. "You're telling me you think a nosebleed is convincing evidence that they have no immunity? I'm going to need a hell of a lot more than a bloody nose or two before I try to stop the transfer—"

"If we don't," Amalfitano interrupted, "every last Hahtooshan will die, and god knows how many Coalition citizens once the Hahtooshans realize what's happened! Can't you see that? They'll think this was a deliberate attempt at genocide, seeding their population with a deadly, highly communicable disease. They'll react accordingly. If we don't stop the transfer, we'll have unleashed god knows how many Tarqks on the Coalition with nothing to stop them but the virus!"

Aquila squinted at him. "But—"

"Xosé's determined that the disease affects the Hahtooshans by attacking the large sinus cavities they have in strategic areas of their skulls, part of their Neanderthal heritage augmented by their bio-engineering," Amalfitano interrupted. "These sinus cavities act as a cushion against concussive forces to the brain that would kill a non-Hahtooshan human," he said, emphasizing his point by smacking his balled fist into his other hand. "It was a prominent feature in the original Neanderthals as well—massive browridges overlaying equally massive sinus cavities, which were an adaptation to the cold—not to mention protection against head trauma."

Aquila crossed his arms. "So?"

"So the interior walls of these sinuses are relatively thin and highly vascularized," Amalfitano replied. "Once the virus has been introduced, it quickly localizes in the sinuses and begins to rapidly multiply. The result is massive swelling and hemorrhage—hence the nosebleeds—and later on brain damage due to pressure created by the swelling and by bleeding *into* the brain.

"Also, Hahtooshans can't breathe through their mouths as we can, they can exhale, but not inhale effectively—again a likely early adaptation by Neanderthals to protect their airway against the cold. Once infected, their primary airway slowly closes up, causing oxygen deprivation, which rapidly leads to alterations in blood gases, deprivation-associated psychoses and eventually death.

"Plus, they rely heavily on their highly specialized, highly acute sense of smell, very much like Zarijan does," he nodded to Izraad, "using their vomeronasal organs in their noses to detect emotional states and who knows what else—I suspect a lot of their social dynamics depend on smelling the moods of those around them, in fact I wouldn't be surprised to find that what they all possess a highly specialized form of *synesthesia*, where senses blend—they see sounds and taste colors, for example. Again, a well-established Neanderthal trait and one the Elkanasu kept or perhaps even augmented.

"If they lose that ability," Amalfitano continued, "it would be as effective as putting them into a sensory deprivation chamber, which would rapidly lead to paranoia. And a common result of acute influenza is a diminished sense of smell, so even if some do survive the acute phase of the disease, they'd be unable to rely on their sense of smell to give them the clues they rely upon in order to function."

Aquila glanced at Izraad as she said, "It's true even in non-Hahtooshan or non-specialized humans."

"In the case of the Hahtooshan crews," Amalfitano added, "the initial changes would have been so insidious I doubt their medical personnel ever noticed, especially when you take into account that they were also affected. And if the virus actually invades the brain..." He shook his head, leaving the rest up to Aquila's imagination.

"All of which might explain Tarqk's seemingly insane desire to carry out his plan," Izraad said, "even after it had been found out."

Amalfitano nodded vigorously. "Exactly! It might even explain his decision to unleash the disease against Tuli in the first place, which was clearly going against orders."

Aquila turned to Tasende, "There's no way to vaccinate the Hahtooshans?"

"Sure there is, sir," he answered, "plus antivirals, like tammanadine have shown a marked degree of success in inhibiting the release of the infectious viral nucleic acid into the host cell if monitored very closely. But sir, we're talking about treating an entire population whose true numbers we can only guess, and which has no resistance. Plus there'd be the monumental problem of convincing the Hahtooshans to agree to a Coalition-initiated vaccination program—"

"Robert," Amalfitano grabbed Aquila by his elbow, "we've got to stop the transfer!"

Aquila looked down at the painful grip the man had on his arm then met Amalfitano's frantic stare. "You realize, of course, it may already be too late."

"Not if I have anything to say about it!" Amalfitano turned back to the console and hit the com-unit's activator. "Control."

The swing-shift com-op answered, *"Yessir?"*

"Burnham, I want a secure channel to Doctor Liebert, the MO of the *Walafar*—hurry!"

"Aye sir." A moment later, the com-op said, *"Sir, I've attempted to establish a secure channel with the Walafar, but I can't get a cipher key match—"*

"Then I'll talk to her on a clear channel!"

There was another pause then Burnham replied, *"Sir, they refuse any clear channel—"*

Amalfitano slammed his fist down on the console. "You tell them—"

"Will!" Aquila snapped. "This isn't helping. The *Walafar*'s com-op's just following orders."

Amalfitano squinted up at him. "How many times has that been used to excuse genocide?"

"Let me try something, okay?" Aquila replied, exasperated.

"Sure!" Amalfitano motioned furiously to the com-unit. "Help yourself!"

"Burnham, get me Admiral Keon of Sector Command, highest priority."

"Yessir, immediately."

"And get Teague down here on the double."

"Yessir." Burnham cut the link.

"Now what?" Amalfitano snapped.

"Now we wait," Aquila replied, "in *your* office. We'll take it from here, Crewman." He nodded dismissively to Tasende then stalked out of the unit, through the unusually quiet sickbay and into the office. He seated himself behind the desk just as Izraad and Amalfitano entered.

Amalfitano scowled at him but Aquila refused to budge.

Izraad slipped into another chair and patted the one next to hers. "William, it might take a little while. Why don't you sit down?"

"I don't want to sit down!" he snapped just as a breathless Teague entered.

"I came as quickly—"

"Take a seat, Edwin," Aquila said. "We've got a major crisis on our hands."

"That's a fucking understatement!" Amalfitano snarled.

Teague gave the distraught doctor a glance as he sat down in the chair next to Izraad, then looked at Aquila and raised his brows.

"We've just discovered that the Hahtooshans have no immunity to the influenza virus," Aquila replied.

Teague absorbed the statement without so much as a blink. "Oh."

"The prisoners we turned over to Mladić are going to be repatriated later this morning,' Aquila continued, "and if we don't stop it—"

"Any Hahtooshan they come into contact with will become infected," Teague interrupted calmly.

"Yes," Aquila exhaled as he stared at the silent desk-com. "We've attempted to raise the *Walafar*, but our cipher keys don't match and her com-op's refusing to accept anything that isn't encoded."

Teague replied, "Not unexpected for a spook ship—"

"But pretty goddamned convenient if you ask me! Especially as they were able to communicate perfectly well a few hours ago."

"Will," Aquila murmured as he met Amalfitano's heated stare. He then looked back at Teague. "I've put a top priority call into Admiral Keon."

Teague nodded, leaned back in his chair and crossed his legs; Izraad fixed her gaze on her knees as Aquila toyed with the desk-com activator.

Amalfitano began to pace.

For the next few minutes, time was kept by the rhythmic scuffing sounds of Amalfitano's grip-boots and Aquila's distracted finger tapping.

Then came an unexpected knock at the door.

"Come," Amalfitano and Aquila snapped in unison; they scowled at each other.

The door opened to admit Drakin. She carried a tray, decanter and cups.

"Coffee," she announced as she sat the tray on the desk. She pointed to the data disc that was also on the tray. "And all da data on da virooz." She then hastily withdrew.

Aquila looked back at the silent desk-com; it was taking too long. He pressed the activator. "Burnham, anything?"

"I'm still trying, sir. I'm in contact with the Admiral's office, but—"

"Did you explain to his staff that this is of the utmost importance?"

"Yessir."

Aquila looked back at Amalfitano to see that he'd resumed his caged-lion pacing. "Calm down, Will. We're doing everything we can."

Amalfitano continued to pace.

"Okay, don't calm down." He sagged back into the chair and stared gloomily at the desk-com.

"Sir?"

Aquila lurched forward and Amalfitano stopped in his tracks at the sound of Burnham's urgent voice.

"I've got Admiral Keon on closed channel. Please enter your personal code, sir."

Aquila replied by tapping in the proper sequence of numbers.

There was a pause then Burnham said, *"Coming through, now."*

There was a faint rustle of static then a familiar voice boomed from the com-unit, *"Lieutenant Matho rousted me out of a very important meeting, Commander, so this better be damned important."*

"It is. I have my CMO, IO and exec with me. Sir, you must stop the *Walafar*'s repatriation of the Hahtooshan prisoners."

There was an awkward silence before Keon said, *"What are you talking about, Commander?"*

"Sir, I know about the transfer and it must be stopped."

"And what, exactly, do you know, Commander? Or, should I say, what do you think you know?"

"I know that the *Walafar* and an Orthodoxy ship are to rendezvous within a matter of hours, sir, and all but two of the Hahtooshans my crew took captive are to be repatriated at that time."

"And how, may I ask, did you come by this information?"

Aquila hesitated just long enough for Amalfitano to stalk over to the desk and say, "I have a friend at HQ. He told me, sir."

"Commander, who is this?"

Amalfitano answered for him, "William Amalfitano, CMO of the *Baidarka*."

"Indeed," the admiral replied with the unspoken, 'but not for long' frosting his already notably chilly voice.

"Yes. And he told me all about this transfer."

"Commander," Keon interrupted. *"Is this true?"*

Aquila briefly met Amalfitano's unequivocal gaze, swallowed and replied, "Sir, I—"

"And who is this friend, Doctor?" Keon asked impatiently.

"I don't see that that's important—"

"I do, Doctor. Because whoever this person is, he's committed a very serious crime."

"Then you admit what he told me is true?"

"I said nothing of the kind. Leaking highly sensitive information—accurate or not—is a court-martial offense. Now, tell me who this individual is, and perhaps I can spare you the same fate."

"Not until you stop the transfer."

"Doctor," Keon growled, *"do you have any idea what you're doing?"*

"Yes. I'm trying to stop the Coalition from committing *genocide*, Admiral, while you're sitting on your fat butt doing nothing!"

Aquila visibly winced as Teague's eyes widened; Izraad dropped her head into her hands.

"What did you say?" the admiral replied after a moment of ominous silence.

"I said I'm trying to stop the Coalition from committing genocide, while you're sitting on your fat butt doing nothing! *Are you deaf, too?"*

"Commander, what the hell is he talking about?"

Aquila quickly gathered his thoughts before answering, "Sir, the prisoners are carrying a virus, a virus for which the Hahtooshans have no immunity."

"What...?"

"We didn't discover this until after the prisoners were handed over to Captain Mladić of Intelligence. If they're repatriated, they'll spread the virus—"

"Are you absolutely certain of this?"

"Yessir," Aquila said. "I have all the data encoded and ready for transmission, but Admiral, we don't have time for HQ to do a full analysis. You must countermand the order, sir, now, before it's too late."

"Captain Vildur was a good friend, Commander," Keon said. *"I trusted her opinion, and she had an exceedingly high one of you. And it's because of that I'll overlook the tone of this conversation. But from now on, if you ever permit one of your officers to speak to me, or any superior officer, in such a fashion, you'll be held personally responsible. Do I make myself clear?"*

Aquila glared up at Amalfitano. "Perfectly, sir."

"Now transmit that data on the virus and let me see what I can do. Keon out."

Aquila tapped the activator. "C and C?" He slipped the data disc into the desk-com's slot. "Burnham, I want this information encoded and transmitted to Admiral Keon immediately."

"Yessir."

Aquila cut the link and sagged back into the chair as Amalfitano sat down on the corner of the desk and appeared to deflate.

Teague favored Amalfitano with a sidelong look. "I do hope you haven't set your sights on a second career in the diplomatic service?"

Amalfitano's retort was a half-hearted grunt.

Aquila squinted furiously at him. "Will, what the hell were you thinking?"

"It got his attention, didn't it?"

Aquila threw up his hands in exasperation. "If you'd just let me handle it—"

"Your career would have been destroyed, along with someone else's—someone whose only crime was trying to help. I wasn't about to let that happen."

"And what about your career?"

"Fuck it."

"I think that's just what you did."

"That was always a risk," Amalfitano fired back.

Aquila flicked Teague then Izraad a sidelong glance, then fixed his narrowed glare on Amalfitano.

He took the hint and shrugged angrily. "Fine. Besides," he growled as he shoved himself back to his feet, "it was my fault the prisoners were handed over to Mladić in the first place—"

"Your fault?" Aquila asked. "But—"

"I signed them out, remember?" He smacked the top of the desk with the flat of his hand. "I signed their death warrants and god only knows how many others!"

"William," Izraad began, "Mladić had the authority to take the prisoners whether you agreed or not. Had you refused, he would have taken them anyway, and Khusaaq and Matoosh as well, which would have meant you might never have realized they had no immunity."

"Then I would have stopped him!" Amalfitano snarled.

"How?" Aquila asked. "I know you're upset, we're all upset, but be practical!"

Amalfitano glared at him for a moment, then cursed and turned away.

Aquila took a deep breath, exhaled slowly, then began again, "Will—"

"Need to see how Fleming's doing with that tapping." Amalfitano marched over to the door and hit the release. It opened and he strode out.

— iv —

Aquila poured the last of the now tepid coffee into his cup, then sat down on the corner of Amalfitano's report-strewn desk and took a wincing sip.

It had been over an hour since he'd spoken with the admiral. He knew because he'd counted every passing second. "What's taking so long?"

"Perhaps the admiral doesn't have the correct cipher key," Izraad quipped.

He squinted at her over the lip of his cup.

"Perhaps HQ doesn't want to stop the transfer," Teague murmured as he picked a piece of non-existent lint from his impeccable command blues.

Aquila couldn't pretend to be shocked; Teague had only voiced what they'd all been thinking. Now it was out in the open.

"Some might think this turn of events is an incredible case of ironic justice," Teague continued as he lifted his gaze to Izraad.

She nodded. "And something else. Even if the transfer is stopped, how long do you think it'll be before this information gets out? One leak and it'll be common knowledge within a month, and then what? Every colony ever treated to the Hahtooshans' brand of persuasion will be clamoring for the virus. And how long after that before some enterprising sort supplies it?"

"I'd say a week." Teague looked back at Aquila. *"Tops."*

Izraad shifted in her chair. "Sir, there's something I should have mentioned earlier. At the time it seemed only a curious coincidence, but now—"

"And that is?"

"Captain Mladić. He's very adept at concealing his emotional state from chempathic eavesdropping, as one would expect, in fact just based on my brief encounter with him, I'd say he has some latent chempathic abilities, but there was just an instant, when he was examining Khusaaq and before he realized that he was... leaking... that I sensed that he... well, that he knew Khusaaq—"

"Knew? But how's that possible?"

"I was doing some digging when you paged me here—he was at the Cotopaxi medals ceremony. He's officially listed as being a civilian aide to the diplomatic attaché who was acting as the presenter, but other records I've managed to uncover make it clear that he was already a veteran IO with a rather unsavory reputation, even among his fellow operatives."

"Unsavory?" Teague asked. "You mean where the ends justify the means?"

"Exactly. Now, there's nothing necessarily sinister about an IO using such a cover, in fact, I suspect no official attending that ceremony was who he, she or it claimed to be. But, as we all know, something terrible happened afterwards. The official account of the incident stated that all of the Hahtooshan attendees had been killed shortly afterwards when their foldboat blew up—due to pilot error. We now know the part about all of the Hahtooshans being killed was false. Khusaaq was *there*. It's possible some of the others survived, too."

"So," Teague said, lacing his fingers together, "if the account was wrong about that, maybe it was also wrong about the incident being a tragic accident?"

Izraad shrugged. "There was a lot of speculation at the time that it was actually the result of sabotage by an ultra-fanatical group within the Coalition. Khusaaq might be the key to unlock what really happened… and, even more importantly, if it was a deliberate act, who was behind it."

Aquila thought about what she said, what Teague suggested and found himself shifting uneasily in his chair. "You don't think Mladić was directly involved, do you?"

"An hour ago I would have said, 'No', but now…" she looked at the silent com-unit. "I'm not so—"

"Commander Aquila?" the com-op's disembodied voice interrupted, startling them.

Aquila punched the activator. "Aquila here."

"Sir, I'm receiving a leader for an encoded message from Sector Command."

"About damned time," Aquila muttered as he circled the desk. "Put it through," he added as he sat down. "And notify Doctor Amalfitano to return to his office immediately."

"Yessir. Ah, personal code is required again, sir."

"Fine." Aquila punched in the sequence with more force that was necessary.

"Transmission coming through now, sir."

There was a brief pause punctuated by the soft rustle of interstellar static, then an unfamiliar voice, a woman's voice, said, *"Commander Aquila...?"*

"Yes."

"I'm Lieutenant Matho," the woman replied in a clipped, all-business tone, *"Admiral Keon's adjutant."*

"I was expecting the admiral himself, Lieutenant."

"The Admiral is in emergency conference with the Central Committee, Commander."

As she spoke, the office door opened and Amalfitano hurried in.

Aquila, in no mood for a repeat performance, gave a nearby chair a quick, pointed glance and was relieved when Amalfitano, albeit sullenly, took the hint.

"He asked me to contact you concerning the Hahtooshan prisoners." Matho hesitated. *"Commander, we find ourselves in a very unhappy situation."*

Aquila's stomach lurched as he repeated slowly, "Unhappy situation, Lieutenant?"

"The admiral transmitted the information to the Walafar, *which, at the time, was in direct contact with the Orthodoxy battleship dispatched to make the transfer."*

"And...?" Aquila prompted uneasily, his eyes locking with Amalfitano's.

"The Orthodoxy vessel's commanding officer, despite being informed of the situation, demanded the immediate return of his people—"

"And they happily turned them over," Amalfitano whispered, but in the deathly quiet office, everyone heard him.

"You're..." Aquila paused, wet his suddenly dry lips, and then finished, "you're telling me that they *were* repatriated?"

"Yes."

Amalfitano squeezed his eyes shut.

"If we'd reneged—"

"YOU IDIOTS!" Amalfitano exploded as he shoved himself from his chair. *"YOU STUPID, SHORT SIGHTED BIGOT-BLIND IDIOTS! DON'T YOU SEE WHAT YOU'VE DONE?"*

Aquila only stared up at him; there was no point silencing him.

"Commander," Matho began coldly, *"we had no choice. Besides, the Fleet CMO has reviewed the data on the virus and it's his belief that your medical staff are mistaken about the Hahtooshans' lack of immunity—"*

"MISTAKEN MY ASS!" Amalfitano bellowed. *"Listen, you STUPID—"*

"Sector Command... out."

Amalfitano stared at the com-unit in impotent rage. He punched it with his fist, snarled, *"CAZZO!"* then nursing his bloodied knuckles, launched into a rosary of curses.

Chapter 27

Amalfitano gave the report a quick study, winced and turned his critical gaze on the equally critical Matoosh. *I'm really sorry, son, but I'm not sure I'm going to be able to keep my promise.* He gave the unconscious teenager a comforting pat on the shoulder then realized it wasn't Matoosh he was trying to comfort. "Up the supoxizine infusion by fifty milligrams a minute."

Drakin nodded glumly; there was no point hiding the fact that they were losing the battle.

"Give it ten minutes and if his saturation doesn't rise above ninety percent, up the rate to eighty milligrams a minute, and keep upping it in increments of thirty milligrams every ten minutes until you get a sustained ninety percent."

"Yez, Doctor."

He handed the flimsy back to her then walked out of the cubicle and down the short corridor. He stopped in the doorway of Khusaaq's cubicle, braced his shoulder against the doorjamb and let his weary gaze sweep the small, machine-packed room.

Meerut stood beside the bed, her back to the door. Sirin was curled up, fast asleep in the fold-down chair, her head on Khusaaq's pillow.

Khusaaq, his cheek resting against Sirin's forehead, mumbled restlessly then began to twitch.

"Shhhh, it's all right," Meerut murmured as she stroked his arm, then, catching Amalfitano's silhouette out of the corner of her eye, turned towards him.

He replied to her tired smile with a tired nod.

"Temp's down," she whispered and motioned to a monitor, "to thirty-nine point one."

"Blood gases?" he asked as he stepped into the cubicle.

"Finally within normal." She pointed to a flimsy that lay on top of another monitor. "He's clearly over the worst of it."

"I sure hope so." He picked up the report and scanned its readouts. "I sure as hell don't need both of them suddenly turning sour on me."

"I heard."

He looked back at the young nurse. She looked every bit as exhausted as he felt, and he'd had the benefit, such as it was, of an hour and a half's nap. "Some first tour, huh?"

She chuckled softly. "Must say, I never thought I'd be doing primary care, or any care for that matter, on a yowie."

He chuckled, "You and me both. How 'bout you take a break? I'll stand watch for a while."

"Sure?"

"Go get yourself a cup of coffee."

"I was thinking more along the lines of a shower, clean med reds and a big, hot breakfast?"

He chuckled. "That too."

"Thanks, Chief." She slipped around him, but as she reached the door, she looked back at him. "Can I bring you anything?"

He thought about it for a moment. He wasn't really hungry, but he couldn't remember when he'd last eaten. "Yeah, anything that looks good."

"You got it. Back in a bit."

"Take your time." He sat down on the empty fold-down chair, wrapped his fingers around Khusaaq's wrist and felt for a pulse. It was slower and stronger than it had been only a few hours before. Khusaaq's breathing, too, was less labored.

Amalfitano gave him a pat on the forearm, then exhaled and crossing his arms, studied the bank of monitors as he fought back the urge to yawn.

— ii —

"Commander?"

"Huh?" Aquila stirred and slowly lifted his head out of the crook of his arm. He squinted at his surroundings, not sure what had awakened him, or why he'd apparently fallen asleep at his desk. Then a vague memory surfaced of returning to his quarters, making a log entry and starting on a long neglected stack of reports.

That stack sat within his limited and still rather fuzzy field of view.

Clearly he hadn't gotten very far.

"Commander Aquila?" the voice came again, this time louder and more insistent.

Realizing it was the com-op, Masursky, and not a dream, he tapped the controller and mumbled groggily, "Aquila here."

"I'm receiving a priority message from Admiral Keon, sir."

Aquila sat bolt upright.

"I'll need you to enter your personal code, sir."

He tapped it in, cleared his throat then combing his hair off his forehead said, "Patch him through."

"Yessir."

There was a crackle of static then Keon's voice boomed from the speaker, *"Commander?"*

He winced. "Yessir."

"There have been developments I felt you should be informed about."

"Developments, sir?" he replied, hoping his still sleep-raspy voice didn't sound as apprehensive, or as squeaky, to the admiral as it did to him.

"First, the Tulian High Council President has requested that you and your crew be granted a month's shore leave on Tuli."

He blinked, taken off guard, then realized he'd said, 'a month?' out loud.

"Yes, Commander. A whole month—and considering what you and your crew have been through, I was more than happy to grant it."

Aquila blinked again, not sure if he'd really heard what he heard. "Sir?"

"You and your crew have been granted a full month's, all expenses paid shore leave on Tuli, Commander, compliments of the Tulian government. Enjoy yourself, you're certainly the envy of everyone back here."

He sat back, utterly dumbfounded. *All expenses paid...*

Keon allowed him a moment to absorb what he'd said before he added, *"That was the good news."*

"Sir?"

"I just came from an emergency session of the select commission of Central Committee. There's still some... um, shall we say spirited disagreement among the experts as to whether your CMO's

assertion about the Hahtooshans' lack of immunity is correct, but the commission was united in its response: we must hope for the best, but plan for the worst. For now it shouldn't affect your shore leave, but I want it understood that this is a highly fluid situation that could change at any moment."

"I'll have my exec modify shore leave rotations accordingly."

"Good. Now, what's the status of the Hahtooshan officer?"

"I'm not sure, sir. I haven't had an update in a couple of hours, but if you'd like, I'll have Doctor Amalfitano—"

"That won't be necessary," Keon interrupted just a little too hastily. *"What I meant was, is he going to survive?"*

"When I last spoke with Doctor Amalfitano, he said there was some slight improvement."

"Excellent." Keon paused, then said, *"Commander, I've stuck my neck out here, a very long way by notifying the Central Committee that I've granted the officer—and the soldier who remains on board* Baidarka*—temporary asylum, under the terms of the* Gare de l'Est *charter, section six, subsection eleven, effective immediately."*

"Sir?" Aquila swallowed convulsively.

"Commander, I've read your full report on what happened on Rasal Ghul Seven. This officer saved your life and the lives of two of your crew at great personal risk to himself and his men, losing two of his own in the process. And in Ensign Corsali's report, she stated he told her that he had tried, repeatedly, to contact the Baidarka, *all unsuccessfully of course. While he did not explicitly state so, this, I believe, constitutes an effort on his part to request sanctuary aboard your vessel, hence section six, subsection eleven of the charter. I've been assured by legal that I'm on solid legal ground here, not that the politicos won't have a field day demanding my head..."*

Aquila released the breath he didn't realize he'd been holding in one spasmodic rush of air, too late to worry if the admiral, who was still speaking, had overheard it.

"...and his assistance was vital in intercepting and destroying the Hahtooshan ship and without him, we would not have known of the threat at all until it was too late. So, I'm not trying to trick you, or more importantly, trick him, into anything, but we must find a means to diffuse this current situation, and quickly. Hopefully, he'll

see the merits of accepting asylum as it's unlikely he'd be received as a hero by the Orthodoxy for his actions. Quite the contrary.

"While granting asylum to a Hahtooshan isn't going to be popular within the Coalition—it certainly caused an unholy uproar when I announced it at the Central Committee meeting—I am sure we can find some arrangement that he would find acceptable, up to and including permanent asylum status, if he so chooses."

"Yessir." It was the only thing Aquila could think to say.

"I needn't remind you that the Matarrans have become more and more provocative with a noticeable increase in border violations over the past few months—their ambush of your vessel was just one of many. Clearly they're probing for weaknesses. War is, sadly, looking more and more like a certainty. It's just a matter of when, and the last thing we need is for them to take advantage of this situation, or for us to be forced to fight a war on two fronts. This officer just may be the means we need."

"Yessir, but—"

"Through him we might, perhaps, just perhaps, convince the Orthodoxy that this was not a deliberate attempt at genocide. He might also be of great assistance in developing a Hahtooshan-specific vaccine or at the very least, a therapeutic vaccine to slow the virus down until we can come up with something more effective. So, aside from temporary asylum—which comes with no strings attached—I want you to make that crystal clear to him, as that decision was based purely on his actions to safeguard Tuli and the Coalition, not to mention rescuing you and your crew—I'm also offering him anything he wants in trade for him volunteering his services to help bring about a quick end to this crisis."

"Anything, sir?"

"Anything, Commander, short of the Committee Secretary's job... or mine," he added with a forced laugh.

"And what if he refuses?"

"To help?"

"No sir. Asylum."

"I already have Intelligence breathing down my neck, Commander, and then there's the whole issue of exactly how and when we go public with the news that Hahtooshans are human, a bombshell that will have far-reaching ramifications to say the least—"

You don't know the half of it, Aquila thought as he massaged his suddenly pounding head. Then again, if HQ had had time to look over the data, their specialists had to have put two and two together—

"—and then there's the potential threat of retaliation from the Orthodoxy over the virus release—plus how they'll react to finding out that they're human—not to mention the Matarrans who will, no doubt, use the resulting pandemonium to their advantage. Bottom line, Commander, if he refuses asylum, it won't be long before the Central Committee will demand that he be turned over to be interrogated by the most expeditious means. Once that happens, I won't have any choice but to agree."

"How much can I tell him about what's happened?"

"Tell him only what you need to tell him in order to gain his cooperation—I'd confer with Lieutenant Izraad on this—and heed her advice."

He squinted sourly at the speaker-grille. *Really? Ya think?* Then aloud: "And how much time do I have to gain this cooperation—assuming he hasn't suffered permanent and debilitating brain damage?"

"The most I guarantee you is three days. That should give your CMO time to determine if he's indeed sustained brain damage and if so, just how incapacitating, and time for you and the lieutenant to come up with a plan on how best to approach him, again, assuming he hasn't suffered serious damage. After that...all bets are off."

"I'll do my best—sir, there's a matter that likely will have a direct bearing on his decision."

"And that is?"

"The five Hahtooshans left behind on Rasal Ghul." Aquila paused then added, "Having the Coalition retrieve them might go a long way to demonstrate our good faith to Sha'ashahn."

"Do you think they could still be alive?"

"Doctor Amalfitano believes it's highly likely—"

"Let me look into what assets we have in the area—and I'll have our contact with the Orthodoxy follow up, see if they've already dispatched a ship—we're spread extremely thin, rather not divert a vessel unless I have to, so if he raises the issue, simply tell him we're doing all we can to repatriate them."

"Yessir." Aquila's gaze happened to fall on a nearby flimsy and his heart sank. "Uh…" He picked up the report and stared glumly at it. "What about the *Herrick*, sir? We—"

"I've already assigned the Themistocles *to the task. At this point, Commander, I doubt we'll ever find her—Intelligence is convinced she was the victim of a Matarran attack—but that's now my problem, not yours."*

"Yessir." Aquila hesitated, then: "And… uh, sir?"

"Yes?"

"One more thing—I meant to notify you earlier, but—"

"We've all be a bit busy, Commander, so…?"

"About the Hahtooshans, sir."

"What about them?"

"They aren't just human sir. They're bio-engineered Neanderthals." *There. Done. Out in the open. Simple….*

What followed was a long pause, long enough for Aquila to visualize the admiral clutching his chest and keeling over, stone-cold dead.

"Neanderthals…?"

"Yessir. No doubt about it."

The admiral paused again then said with deadpan delivery, *"That does add a bit of a kink to everything, doesn't it?"*

"Yessir." To put it mildly.

"Well," Keon exhaled, *"we'll just have to deal with that too—but one thing at a time, Commander. Who of your crew knows about this?"*

"My CMO and three of his staff, my exec, Lieutenant Teague, my CWO, Ensign Lesedi and of course Lieutenant Izraad."

"I want you to keep the lid on this—keep it between you, those you just listed and me—at least until we can get a handle on everything else. I've already put a strictly need to know seal on the data here, providing the Central Committee, not to mention the specialists with just enough information—to avoid anyone, um… jumping the gun? Last thing we need, with emotions running as high as they are, is for people to take matters into their own hands like they did with that goddamned award ceremony vid. If this were to become public now, well, I shudder to think what would happen. For now I'm the only one who's had access to all of the data, not that

I've had a chance to fully analyze it. And speaking of... can your people be trusted not to say anything to other crewmembers?"

"I've already sworn them to secrecy, sir. And yessir, I have complete faith in each of them—they fully understand the ramifications."

"Excellent." Keon paused again then added softly and with an audible tone of wonder, *"Neanderthals. How the hell did they—well, not important right now. But, my gods... Could the universe get any stranger?"*

"I'm not sure how to answer that, sir."

"I'm not sure I want you to answer it," he replied, then, *"Good luck, Commander. You're going to need it—we all are. Keon out."*

Aquila stared down at the com-unit and blew out his cheeks, then tapped its activator. "Sickbay?"

"Sickbay here," Fleming answered.

"Doctor, tell Amalfitano I need to speak with him as soon as it's convenient, in my quarters. And doctor?"

"Yessir?"

"What's Khusaaq's condition? Any improvement?"

"Yes sir, dramatic improvement. The tammanadine's working just as we hoped it would."

"Good. Aquila out." He released the button, sagged back into his chair and ran his fingers through his disheveled hair. "Now comes the hard part."

— iii —

Khusaaq twitched and muttered in his sleep as his mind, disoriented by the lingering effects of the virus, replayed bits and pieces of unrelated memories.

Then, out of the muddy swirl of disjointed thoughts, a distant voice called to him. *"Khusaaq...?"*

He slowly turned towards it.

"Khusaaq?" the voice called again, stronger this time. Closer.

He squinted at the fuzzy shape that hovered over him. "Who...?"

"It's me."

He blinked at the all too familiar rich baritone. *"Qharubi?"* He squeezed his eyes shut then opened them again and Qharubi's smiling face came into instant focus. "But... what, I mean how?" He tried to lift his head, to look around. "What are you doing here?"

Qharubi pressed his palm against Khusaaq's shoulder and he winced at the gentle pressure.

"Don't move." Qharubi risked a quick, over-the-shoulder glance before adding in a conspiratorial whisper, *"Or that officious medical officer will order me to leave."*

"Medical officer?" He looked around again; his surroundings looked familiar, and yet at the same time, totally out of place. He turned back to him. "Where am I?"

"Aboard *Khargeh*, Ruh'ta'aq."

Khargeh? The name shook loose a memory of an assault transport, the ship he and the surviving members of his platoon had been assigned to immediately after Cotopaxi, and from which they'd left in order to attend the awards ceremony—

"You don't remember?"

Qharubi's concerned question drew his mind back to the present. "Remember...?"

Qharubi sighed as he carefully eased himself down on the empty bunk next to Khusaaq's. "They said you might not, at first. You took a terrible hit when..." He fixed his suddenly narrowed gaze on the far wall.

Khusaaq stared at him, really stared at him, and noticed the livid bruises that marred the man's face. "What hap—" His eyes widened and he gasped, *"The pay packet! It was booby trapped!"*

Qharubi, still not looking at him, nodded solemnly.

Khusaaq lifted his head and glanced around the empty ward as the horror of that instant rushed back into his mind. "Ichkeul?" He looked back at Qharubi to see that he was now watching him with bright eyes. "Saar'kali?"

Qharubi slowly shook his head.

Khusaaq wet his bruised lips before asking softly, *"Telipinu...?"*

"The medical officer said if Saar'kali and Telipinu had been wearing their helmets as we were, they might have survived. Ichkeul..." He shrugged. "He took the full brunt of the blast." He took a deep, ragged breath before adding tightly, "The explosion was powerful enough to blow the locks, and at such high fold speeds, well, it almost tore the foldboat apart. It took three days for *Khargeh* to get within range and flick us aboard—the medical officer said everyone assumed we'd been killed outright and were amazed that you and I were still alive—albeit barely."

Khusaaq quickly took stock. *Saar'kali. Ichkeul. Telipinu—all dead... no.* His jaw muscles bunched. *Ensnared then murdered in cold blood.* He gave Qharubi a sidelong look. "How badly were you injured?"

Qharubi forced a lopsided and clearly painful smile. "A few bruises, some cracked bones. I was lucky—the pilot chair largely protected me from the blast."

"And me?"

He abruptly rose from the bunk. "I think it best if the medical officer speaks with you about that."

Khusaaq grabbed his wrist before he moved out of reach. "Answer me."

Qharubi only stared down at him as he gently tried to free himself.

"Answer me!"

"Shhh," a new voice soothed and Khusaaq jerked his head towards it as the bright, sterile world of *Khargeh*'s ward dissolved into a dim blur of winking lights and shadowy, moving shapes.

"Do not forget," Qharubi murmured.

"Forget?" He looked back at him. Qharubi was now no more than a shadow himself, a silhouette outlined by blinking telltales.

"What they did," he answered in a voice barely above a whisper as his hand slid from Khusaaq's loosening grasp. *"They murdered us. They murdered us all. It's up to you to avenge us...."*

Then he was gone and Khusaaq felt his fingers clench around air. "Qharubi!" He tried to sit up but found his body unable to respond. *"Qharubi!"* he called out frantically.

"Easy, son. Easy."

A new face swam into view, a chameleon face, blurry and alternately colored red then green then yellow then blue by the flickering glow of the telltales.

"Qharubi?"

The face broke into a friendly smile and he squinted at it; now he was sure. Whoever it was, it wasn't Qharubi. *Who are you?* "Where's Qharubi?"

The smile faded.

"Qharubi guuch-sseh!" he snarled as he looked around.

"Now just calm down—"

"Ithsu baktai!" he hissed as he turned his wild eyes back on him.

"I don't understand, son—"

He felt a hand lightly grasp his shoulder and the face moved closer—*a Rimmer face!*

"—speak in Standard—"

"Tu-mazneri!" He jerked his shoulder out from under the hand's grasp and struggled to sit up and this time succeeded.

"No one's going to hurt you," the voice continued in a calm, measured voice while wisely moving back, almost but not quite disappearing into the surrounding blur of flashing lights. "I'm William Amalfitano, remember? You're aboard the *Baidarka.*"

Khusaaq squinted at him. *Baidarka?* He squeezed his eyes shut and shook his head to clear it but it only made his throbbing headache worse. He clutched his head in his hands and groaned, *"Tuh maztsaeh—"*

"William Amalfitano, your *doctor,*" the voice continued firmly.

Khusaaq reopened his eyes to glare at him. *"Chulh!"*

"Yes. And we're aboard the *Baidarka*—"

"Khusaaq?" a new voice asked and higher pitched; a heartbeat later he felt warm fingers wrap around his wrist and he jerked his eyes towards the source of the voice and saw another strange face—another Rimmer face and female.

He flinched and yanked his arm away. *"CHULH!"*

"Careful, Sirin, he's extremely disoriented—"

"It's me, *Sirin,* remember?" the woman continued, undaunted, both by the warning and Khusaaq's baleful stare.

He watched as her fingers grasped his wrist again, but this time with a much firmer hold, then lifted his slitted eyes back to her.

"Please, Khusaaq, try to remember. It's me. Sirin."

Sirin? The name did sound vaguely familiar. The face, too—but a Rimmer face? *It doesn't make sense.* He glanced around again, desperately. *I don't understand! Where am I? Where's Qharubi?*

"It's okay... you're safe," she soothed. *"Maz-akanj."*

The warm touch of her fingers against his cheek drew his panicky gaze.

"It's Sirin, Khusaaq. *Sirin.*"

He squinted at her, nostrils flaring. *You do look familiar. I can't smell you... help me!* He grabbed her arm, clutching it tightly as he would a lifeline. *I... don't know where I am!*

She visibly winced at his painful hold then, using her free hand, wiped a lock of damp hair from his forehead. "Everything's going to be okay, you're just a little confused. *You're safe*—no one's going to hurt you."

He stared at her, his terrified eyes searching hers.

She lightly stroked his sweat-glossy face, murmured, "You know me. *Think.* Try to remember."

Sirin? His mind latched onto that. *Yes!* Now he was sure. *I do know you!* He rasped, *"Sirin?"*

Her lips parted in a relieved smile. "Yes. Now please, lie back down." She pressed her hand against his shoulder and he collapsed back against the sweat-soaked mattress and closed his eyes, but kept his grip on her other arm.

Sirin. Yes. The other is... Amalfitano? That seemed right. He took several deep breaths then reopened his gritty, burning eyes and slowly turned them towards the man. "Doctor... Amalfitano?"

The doctor grinned, a clearly very relieved grin. "In the flesh."

His eyes drifted back to Sirin. "I... I was talking to... to Qharubi. He... he was trying to tell me something."

"No one's been here but me and Sirin, now I need you to let go," Amalfitano answered as he tried to pry his fingers from Corsali's arm and Khusaaq, realizing he was hurting her, immediately released his hold. "You've been running a high fever since yesterday. It's made you see things that aren't there."

"I'm not aboard *Khargeh?*"

"No," Amalfitano said. *"Baidarka."*

"And Qharubi was not just here?"

Amalfitano shook his head. "No."

Qharubi's dead. That sudden realization hit him like a fist to the stomach. He instinctively tensed and gulped for air. *No! He cannot—Makhaira!* He squeezed his eyes shut and clenched his teeth against the near-suffocating crush of sudden recollection. *Everything, everyone... gone. Dead, murdered, all but me, all because of me—*

"Khusaaq...?"

Prompted by Sirin's worried tone and the comforting touch of her fingers as she stroked his cheek, he licked his gummy lips then replied hoarsely, "Of course he would not be here. He was aboard… *Makhaira.*"

She laced her fingers between his. "He was a close friend."

This time he only nodded, not trusting his voice.

"I'm so, so sorry," she replied as Amalfitano pressed his palm against Khusaaq's forehead.

"How's the head?"

Khusaaq squinted up at him.

Amalfitano tapped his own temple. "Headache?"

He nodded again.

"Not surprising. How about your throat? Still sore?"

Khusaaq's grimace as he swallowed was answer enough.

"Any discomfort breathing?" Amalfitano asked as he ran his hand over Khusaaq's chest, visibly pleased and amazed that the surgical incisions were almost completely healed.

Khusaaq took a deep lung-full of air, exhaled slowly then replied hoarsely, "A little."

"You put your chest muscles through a hell of a workout, not to mention me and my staff."

Khusaaq touched the bridge of his nose. "My… my sense of smell…"

"Is a bit off?"

"Yes," he replied apprehensively.

"That's normal. It's not permanent. It'll come back all on its own but I'll give you something that should give it a kick start along with a mild pain killer, okay?" He turned to the drug cart and withdrew a vial and ject-it.

"What happened?" Khusaaq's eyes darted back to Sirin as Amalfitano pressed the tool against his upper arm. "The last thing I remember was," he knit his brows, "I was lying on a bed… somewhere, with you?"

Sirin nodded. "Yes."

"In my quarters," Amalfitano explained. "Sirin realized you were having problems breathing, and we brought you back here. Seems you picked up a hell of a nasty bug back on Rasal Ghul."

"Rasal Ghul?" He glanced up at Amalfitano then looked back at Corsali. "Have you been here—"

"The entire time?" Amalfitano answered for her. "You bet. Couldn't have dragged her away—"

"*Ah*. There you are."

Amalfitano turned to find Fleming, arms akimbo, in the doorway. "Like you think I'd be somewhere else?"

Fleming ignored the testy comment. "The commander asked to see you. In his cabin."

Amalfitano raised his brows, to which Fleming shrugged. He looked back at Khusaaq and acting as if nothing was amiss, smiled and said, "I'll be back in a little while. Just relax, okay? You're gonna be fine, just fine."

— iv —

Aquila looked up as the cabin's door opened to admit Amalfitano. "You're just in time for a cuppa coffee." He held up an extra mug and the decanter and motioned with his chin to a plate on his desk. "And some fresh-baked anisette cookies?"

Amalfitano surprised him when he waved off the offer as he sat down then, clearly suspecting the cookies were an enticement, asked uneasily, "What's up?"

"Well, for starters, Seitakap was good to his word—we've been granted shore leave on Tuli."

"Not bad for starters, but why do I suddenly feel like I should be looking over my shoulder?"

Aquila squinted over the rim of his cup as he took a sip, then: "Maybe because you're a paranoid old man?"

Amalfitano scowled at him. "Maybe."

Aquila grinned. "A month, Will. Four weeks on Tuli—*all* expenses paid for the *entire* crew."

"Paid? Four weeks?"

"The Tulians' way of thanking us."

"Some thank you."

"Yeah."

"Have you told the crew?"

"Not yet. I wanted you to be the first to know."

Amalfitano glanced over his shoulder.

"What is it?" Aquila asked, following his gaze but seeing nothing but the dull gray door of his quarters.

Amalfitano slowly turned back to him, said, "I was just looking to see what was coming next. It's not good news, is it? The shore leave was just the sweetener, right?"

Aquila paused then asked, "What's Khusaaq's status?"

Amalfitano snarled, *"I knew it!"* as he gave Aquila an angry glance. "He's coming back for him, isn't he?"

"He?"

"Mladić of course!"

"Not if we can get Khusaaq to agree to asylum."

Amalfitano stared at him for a moment, cocked his head to one side. "Haven't I heard this before?"

Aquila grinned. "This time it was Admiral Keon's brilliant idea."

Amalfitano raised his brows. *"Keon's?"*

Aquila chuckled, "Yeah—can you believe it? And along with asylum, the admiral's given me the authority to offer Khusaaq anything he wants in trade for his help."

"Help? What kind of help?"

"Convincing the Orthodoxy this wasn't our attempt at genocide...."

Amalfitano arched a very dubious brow. *"Really."*

"Yes, *really*. Along with assisting in creating a Hahtooshan-specific vaccine."

"In his spare time," Amalfitano added sourly.

Aquila sighed, "I know we're asking a lot, Will, but what other options do we have? This is what we were after, after all—in fact better—"

"Better?" Amalfitano blurted out. "We've just unleashed a disease on a totally vulnerable population and Keon's only making the offer because—"

"Okay!" Aquila threw up his hands. "Better was a poor choice of words."

"Very poor," Amalfitano grumbled.

"What I meant was that this time the matter of asylum was Admiral Keon's idea—we don't have to worry about getting his blessing after the fact—"

"Or not." Amalfitano eyed him, took a deep breath. "Khusaaq has every reason to deeply distrust the Coalition and he does, believe me."

"I know—so does the admiral. So he sweetened the pot, *a lot*."

"How?"

"For starters he's arranging for a Coalition rescue of the Hahtooshans left on Rasal Ghul as we speak—assuming the Orthodoxy hasn't beaten us to it."

Amalfitano grabbed a cookie, took a big bite, muffled warily, "That's a start," and began to chew, slowly. He made a face, muttered, "Too dry," and returned the half-eaten cookie to the plate.

"On top of that, he can ask for anything, Will."

"Anything." Amalfitano borrowed his cup of coffee and took a sip.

"Anything. Keon's word on it."

Amalfitano brushed the cookie crumbs off his medreds, still unconvinced. "Gildun once told me that like Greeks, one should be very wary of Admirals bearing gifts, like a month's shore leave—or promises of *anything* in trade for cooperation."

"In this case we have little choice. Keon's convinced that Khusaaq might be key in resolving a whole host of problems. There's talk back at HQ that the Matarrans are up to something big and the last thing we need is for them to use this to their advantage. So the admiral doesn't have much of a choice either—just as you suggested. Call it trust through mutual self-interest."

Amalfitano stared down at his now clasped hands for a moment, then lifting his gaze back to Aquila said, "And what if Khusaaq refuses to… help? Asylum was going to be a hard enough sell, but once he learns the full extent of the mess—"

"Let's see what he says, all right? Hopefully he'll see there's no other option. So, when can I talk to him?"

"He's awake now, but that bug really knocked the stuffing out of him—"

"Any evidence he's suffered brain damage?"

Amalfitano scowled at him. "He. Just. Woke. *Up.* I was just about to run some tests when Jenna showed up, told me you needed to see—"

"When?" Aquila interrupted impatiently.

"Tomorrow—twenty-four hours, forty-eight would be even better. I should have a good idea as to whether there's any residual damage—"

"Will, if the Hahtooshans decide to retaliate or the Matarrans get involved or gods forbid, *both*, all bets, as the Admiral warned me, are *off* and we'll have no choice but to hand him over to Intelligence. I wish I could give you all the time in the world, but the sooner we get his agreement, the sooner he's untouchable and safe from the likes of Mladić."

Amalfitano squinted at him, replied, "This evening then, contingent on the results of the tests I'll run today. In my medical opinion, that's pushing it."

"But—"

"Take it or leave it," Amalfitano growled and crossed his arms for emphasis.

Aquila blew out his cheeks, replied, *"Fine.* Say… nineteen hundred?"

Amalfitano replied with a curt nod, rose and walked out of the cabin.

Aquila stared after him then shaking his head, thumbed the com-link. "Control?"

"Control here."

"Masursky, have Lieutenant Izraad report to my office."

"Yessir."

As he cut the link, Aquila squinted at the now closed door. "Let's just hope to hell nothing else happens between now and then."

— v —

Amalfitano leaned back in his chair, stared morosely at the untouched glass of whisky in his hand and let out a long, weary sigh.

"William?"

He slowly lifted his head. "Yeah, Jenna?"

Fleming stepped into the office. "I thought you'd like to know that the increase in supoxizine has had a dramatic effect on Matoosh's oxygen saturation. It's maintaining at ninety-two percent."

He smiled, motioned to a nearby chair, said, "Take a load off," and withdrew another glass from a desk drawer.

She sat down, shook her head at his offer of a drink. "Bit early, isn't it?"

He raised his brows.

"It's oh-eight thirty."

"Oh-eight thirty to others. To us it's more like twenty thirty—since neither of us have had more than a catnap here and there over the past thirty-six hours. Which actually makes this a nightcap."

She nodded at the truth of it, then pursed her lips, unimpressed by his logic. "Bad news from the commander?"

He took a sip of the potent alcohol, winced as he swallowed.

"Definitely bad news." She leaned back in the chair. "Okay, let's hear it."

"The entire crew's been granted a four week, all expenses paid shore leave on Tuli."

"Four weeks?"

"Yup."

"All expenses paid...?"

He nodded, took another sip, followed by another wince.

"I don't get it. Why the long face?"

He stared down at the glass he held as he swirled its contents. "Ever feel like something sounds too good to be true?"

"Meaning?"

"I dunno." He took another sip before adding, "Maybe Robert's right."

"About what?"

"About me being a paranoid old man."

"Sometimes a little paranoia can be healthy."

"Maybe. Then again, maybe I've just seen too much, been around too long to take things at face value any longer."

"But Xosé told me the Tulian president was the one to suggest shore leave?"

"I'm not talking about shore leave, I'm talking about Keon's offer."

"Uh, what offer...?"

"The admiral's granted Robert the authority to offer Khusaaq anything in trade for helping us, the Coalition, out of this unholy fix we've gotten ourselves into."

"Oh. *That* offer."

Amalfitano eyed her.

"And if he refuses?"

"Exactly!" He smacked his fist on his desk. "What if he says no? Why should he trust us? I know the hell I wouldn't—"

"Maybe you should ask him, instead of chewing your insides up wondering?"

He scowled at her.

"Maybe he'll realize he has no choice, just like we have no choice."

"That's just what Robert said: trust through mutual self-interest."

"If it averts a Rim-wide war, don't knock it."

"Why do I bother to talk to you?"

"Hell if I know."

He chuckled despite his mood, and, grabbing the decanter in one hand, his glass in the other, carefully poured the remaining whisky back into the bottle. Then, noticing her oblique stare, he replied, "Waste not, want not."

"You put a whole new spin on that saying, you know that?" She rose from her chair. "Now, how about you make rounds, starting with Gianakis? If you don't discharge him, I will—right out an external airlock."

He arched a brow as she pointedly rubbed her rump. "You mean...?"

"Yeah. Claimed he didn't realize it was me—" She grabbed a lock of her flaming red hair. "*Really?* He even pinched Rafe—yet another accident, or so he says."

Amalfitano chuckled at the image of the diminutive medtech being goosed by the burly marine. "I wonder who was more surprised?"

Fleming grinned. "Probably Gianakis. Drakin's always tweaking Rafe's butt to the point I wouldn't be surprised if he's developed calluses."

That image made Amalfitano wince. "Definitely time to be discharged." He draped his arm around her shoulder and together they walked out into the main unit. "Now I know why I talk to you."

— vi —

Amalfitano stopped in the doorway of Khusaaq's cubicle and stared at his patient in open-mouthed astonishment.

Khusaaq was not only sitting up in bed but also making quick work of what looked, to Amalfitano's discriminating eye, like the remains of a frittata. Shaking his head and smiling, he stepped into the room just as Sirin tried to take the plate from Khusaaq's hand. He deftly jerked it out of her reach.

"There's plenty more where that came from," Amalfitano said, drawing both Khusaaq's and Sirin's gaze.

"Don't encourage him," Sirin muttered, "that's his fourth helping."

"Fourth?"

Khusaaq smiled sheepishly at him as he ran his finger around the lip of the plate, then, with a sidelong, defiant look at Sirin, he stuck the finger in his mouth.

"Whatever you gave him to help his sense of smell return," Sirin added sourly, "appears to have worked. Perhaps a wee bit too well."

Amalfitano chuckled.

"I warned him that if he keeps this up, he'll explode," Meerut said as she slipped around Amalfitano and into the cubicle. "And I'm not cleaning up the mess."

Amalfitano turned back to Khusaaq just as Sirin managed to snatch the plate out of his hand while he was busy sucking on his finger.

She flashed him a triumphant grin; he replied by sucking all the harder on his finger.

Amalfitano chuckled then leaned close to Meerut's ear. "How the hell'd you get him to eat?"

"Remember me asking you what you wanted for breakfast?"

"Dimly."

"Well, by the time I got back with one of your favorite frittatas, you were gone. So, I offered it to Sirin. She offered him some and before we knew it, he'd eaten it all and was asking for more. And more, and more, and *more.*"

Amalfitano looked back at Khusaaq to see him still sucking on his finger. "Are you still hungry?"

Khusaaq pulled his finger from his mouth and turned a hopeful smile on Sirin, then, at her less than favorable expression he sighed, looked at Amalfitano and slowly shook his head.

"Tell you what, how 'bout we get you cleaned up, then you can have more to eat, as much as you want, anything you want."

"I'll go get the bed bath set-up," Meerut began, but Amalfitano grabbed her arm before she made good her escape.

He leaned close, whispered in her ear, "Not. So. Fast. I want him *showered*. He *stinks.*"

"*Showered*, sir?"

"Have Sirin help you, and Drakin's in Matoosh's cubicle if you need an extra pair of hands."

She squinted up at him. "I thought you liked him, Chief."

"Get one of the other nurses then, or Rafe. Hell, I don't care how you do it, but I want him scrubbed from stem to stern—and *everywhere* in between, understood?"

"Everywhere, sir?"

"Everywhere."

She swallowed hard as her gaze slid back to their unsuspecting and smiling Hahtooshan patient. "Yessir. *Everywhere*, sir."

Chapter 28

Zarijan Izraad watched Amalfitano out of the corner of her eye as he worriedly fingered a lab report.

His nervous tension had been building all day. While Izraad had spent the time formulating the best way to approach Khusaaq, Fleming had reported to her that Amalfitano had tasked her and Drakin with running the battery of mental, neurological and physiological tests to rule out any damage—all of which, to everyone's relief, had turned up negative. Amalfitano had begged off running the tests himself by claiming he was going to take a well-deserved nap, but shortly thereafter reappeared and began prowling sickbay, the bane of any staff unlucky enough to find themselves in the path of his preoccupied gaze. He'd missed breakfast, skipped lunch and picked at his dinner tray, then spent almost an hour rearranging his prized collection of antique medical texts… then rearranging them again.

Now his distracted attention fell on the hapless flimsies.

Izraad had ordered all of Amalfitano's favorite dishes with the hopes of a pleasant dinner; instead she'd been left to marinate in his worry, leaving her with a throbbing headache and very sour stomach. In truth she'd barely touched her own meal, despite the galley having gone all out. "You're supposed to read those, not feel them."

He glared at her as he carefully placed the flimsy back on top of the pile of unread reports. He then began straightening the disheveled mound.

She exhaled irritably. "Robert said he'd be here as soon as he and Edwin finished dinner. So quit fiddling!"

He stopped his nervous shuffling to slump back into his chair. "What if he says no?"

Here we go again. It was a topic that had already been raised during dinner, and, she had assumed at the time, *settled.* "Then he says no."

"You're a *big* help."

Izraad clasped her hands together on top of the stack of long-neglected memos she'd brought to his office in hopes that she'd finally get a chance to catch up. In truth she hadn't gotten any further than Amalfitano—and for the same reasons. "What do you want me to say? All I can do is *reiterate* what I've already told you," she held up a finger, *"One,* we have to tell him *everything,* but in steps, give him a chance to absorb it piece by piece—it's going to be overwhelming as it is, doubly so if we hit him with everything at once. *Two,* we have to answer all questions he asks completely and with no hesitation. If he senses we're deliberately holding anything back it will only feed into his extreme and, I freely admit, very reasonable mistrust of the Coalition—"

"Easier said than—" He jerked his head up at the sound of Teague and Aquila's voices and echo of approaching footsteps and fixed his apprehensive stare on the doorway.

As the two men entered, Izraad placed the memos on the floor near her feet, rose and turned. "Commander," she murmured, "Lieutenant."

Aquila nodded to her with the same strained expression as Amalfitano then he turned to Amalfitano as the doctor started to get to his feet. "Not quite yet, Will. Let's wait for Ensign Corsali to bring all the paperwork."

Amalfitano dropped back into his chair and began drumming his fingers on the desk.

"Must say, you two don't look real optimistic," Aquila said.

Before either could reply, Corsali arrived with a valise bearing the Coalition standard.

Izraad glanced at the desk chronometer. *Eighteen fifty-six.* Aquila had cut it close.

"I've drawn up the documents agreeing to the terms of temporary asylum under the *Gare de l'Est* charter, section six, subsection eleven, according to Lieutenant Matho's very precise instructions, sir." Corsali walked over to Amalfitano's desk, opened the valise and began pulling out documents. "Sha'ashahn needs to thumb-seal each at the bottom left, and you, sir, and Lieutenant Teague need to thumb-seal each at the bottom right, and this last flimsy…" she set it on the desk, "requires Lieutenant Izraad's and Doctor Amalfitano's seal as well. *Here."* She pointed, looked at

Aquila and at his acknowledging dip of the chin, managed a tight smile then turned for the door.

Aquila's eyes flicked to Izraad; Izraad nodded. She'd finally broached the matter of what Khusaaq was with the ensign earlier and had come away pleased but not entirely surprised that Sirin didn't seem to care one way or another. She'd accepted Khusaaq as a Hahtooshan, then as a human... and now, as a distant descendent of a Neanderthal. She could only hope that Khusaaq would take the startling news with equal aplomb.

"Ensign?"

Corsali stopped just short of the doorway and turned back to Aquila. "Yessir?"

"We'd like you to be present."

"Sir?"

"Unless you'd prefer not to be?"

"No sir, I mean... yes, I'd every much like to be present. Thank you, sir."

Aquila turned his expectant gaze on Amalfitano.

He got to his feet, smoothed out his med reds and said, "I'll go get him," then walked out of the office.

— ii —

Khusaaq stared down at his dinner plate, a cheeseburger this time, with extra pickles—Pierson's helpful and hearty recommendation—with a side of chocolate milk. He gave the strange-looking and untouched offering a prod with his finger then with a sigh, pushed the tray away.

Amalfitano had said Aquila had asked for an after-dinner meeting—no explanation, no suggestion of what the meeting would be about. All he knew was that his ever-present guards had suddenly and inexplicably been reassigned, presumably to a less obtrusive way of keeping an eye on him—he knew he was too valuable to be left completely to his own devices—and Amalfitano was obviously nervous when he briefly stopped by, mid-afternoon, as the doctor said, to "Check up on his star patient," and give him the results of his tests.

He'd been permitted to keep, to wear his duty uniform—at least for now.

He looked at the doorway, wondering when they'd come fetch him, wondering what this meeting was about and trying not to let his imagination, his suspicions, get the better of him. Certainly it was about his immediate, if not permanent disposition. He hadn't thought to ask if asylum was still an option.

Perhaps they're going to tell me they have no choice but to hand me over to their intelligence. Apologies all round, profuse regrets, but in the end...

Suddenly panicky, he lurched to his feet. He happened to catch his reflection in the darkened face of a nearby monitor and was shocked by what he saw. It was the face of a stranger, hollow-cheeked and sunken-eyed. Only the familiar clan-glyphs remained, a stark reminder of who he was and what he had been. Even those were partially obscured by the dry-scabby blisters that still pockmarked his gaunt face.

The Hero of Cotopaxi, he thought to himself and snorted, *Hero indeed. More like coward of Cotopaxi—I'd trade everything to avoid another mind-strip.* And that was the bitter truth of it. Death, collaboration... anything but another mind-strip, to have his very soul cracked open then poked and prodded, rifled through by Rimmers in search of validation of their hatred of all things A'tuu'shahn, teasing out secrets only he knew, exposing every ugly thought, every brutal act, every horror he'd witnessed, ordered or participated in, in the process uncovering all of the awful truths.

The first mind-strip was only a taste of what was to come.

He squeezed his eyes shut, tried to force down his panic, his close to suffocating dread—

"Khusaaq?"

He flinched and wheeled around to find Amalfitano standing in the doorway.

The doctor replied to his startled stare with a tight smile and, "The commander's waiting in my office."

"Yes," he licked his lips, swallowed convulsively, "of course."

Amalfitano's eyes darted to the untouched dinner tray. "Not hungry?"

"I ate too much this morning." It wasn't quite a lie. He'd spent a good portion of the morning, after the exhausting, humiliating ordeal of the shower, trying to sleep off his excesses.

Amalfitano chuckled, but to Khusaaq, the sound was forced, hollow. "Come on then."

Khusaaq shrugged his bandoleer into place and his fingers briefly lingered on the empty scabbard then he glanced at the fold-down chair. *Completely alone.* He shook his head, took a deep breath then limping, followed Amalfitano down the short corridor and into the airlock.

The inner door closed, sealing the two inside.

He kept his eyes fixed on the outer door while painfully aware of Amalfitano's concerned, sidelong stare, not to mention the scent of fear. *No, not fear—mounting dread. You too?*

He cleared his throat and shifted his weight. No point putting this off—likely I won't get a chance later. "Doctor."

"Yes?"

"Now seems as good as any to say something I have should have said much earlier."

Amalfitano tapped the outer door's locking mechanism, activating it just before it would've opened, guaranteeing them complete privacy. "And that is?"

"I wanted to thank you, for saving my life and the lives of my escort. I fully appreciate how difficult it was for you, and I certainly didn't make it any easier—none of us did. I deeply regret that."

"You're welcome." Amalfitano reached for the activator.

"And one more thing."

Amalfitano looked back at him, his fingers hovering millimeters from the activator. "Yes?"

"I wasn't there."

"There...? Where?"

"Raumalle. Neither was Ja'andai, my *ta'katleh*, my... my father, or any of my close kin."

Amalfitano only stared at him.

"I thought you should know."

Amalfitano hesitated before answering softly, "I realized you couldn't have been there of course—that was almost thirty years ago, but... thank you." After an awkward silence, he flashed him another tight smile then tapped the activator.

The outer door snapped open and Amalfitano stepped out.

Khusaaq followed; ahead, he saw the open doorway of Amalfitano's office, saw Aquila inside, his back to the door, heard murmured voices.

Halfway there, Amalfitano stopped, grabbed his arm and said, "Do me one favor?"

"And that is?"

"Just hear us out, all right? Just do that. Please."

"Of course."

Amalfitano let go and motioned to the doorway. "Ready?"

He nodded. *And get this over with.*

"Come on then." Amalfitano led the way then stopped again at the doorway to allow Khusaaq to enter first.

As Khusaaq strode across the threshold, his gaze immediately fell on Corsali and he almost smiled. *Sirin!* He had hoped she would be here, but hadn't dared to ask—and would they be about to deny him sanctuary if she was present? Could they be that cruel? The answer came quickly—too quickly. *Yes, Rimmers could—*

"Sha'ashahn."

He jerked his eyes off Corsali and turned to Aquila. "Commander."

"I believe you remember Lieutenant Izraad," Aquila continued with just a trace of discomfort.

Khusaaq met Izraad's calm eyes with a reflexively hostile stare then quickly shifted his attention to the unfamiliar officer who stood at attention next to Corsali.

"And this is my second in command, Lieutenant Teague.

"I am honored to finally meet you, Sha'ashahn."

To Khusaaq the human didn't look honored, he looked deeply unsettled. He acknowledged Teague with a nod and a murmured, "Lieutenant."

"Please, be seated," Aquila said as he motioned to the ring of chairs.

Khusaaq eased himself down into one, by long habit one with its back to a wall and closest to the door. Sirin seated herself next to him.

"Sha'ashahn," Aquila began as the others seated themselves, "I believe Doctor Amalfitano raised the idea of asylum with you?"

Khusaaq replied with a curt nod, heart suddenly thumping anew.

"You never gave us an answer. And there have been developments," Aquila continued. "Developments which we feel you should first be apprised of as they have a direct bearing on the matter of asylum." His gaze briefly shifted to the documents spread out across the desk.

Just hear us out, all right? Khusaaq's eyes darted back to Amalfitano; the doctor was watching him intently. *Just do that.* He looked back at Aquila as a cold knot gelled in his stomach, his worst fears realized. *Asylum's no longer an option—that is what you're going to tell me.* "What's happened?"

Aquila turned to Amalfitano. "Will?"

Khusaaq fixed his apprehensive stare on the doctor and Amalfitano, by his expression, had clearly been dreading this moment.

"Sha'ashahn…"

Khusaaq raised his eyebrow at the doctor's use of his rank. *Just hear us out…*

"…first things first, and I don't know how to say what I'm about to say but to just say it."

"Then please *do* so," he growled, his mouth dry, his heart pounding madly against his ribs.

"Here goes: you and your people are human, every bit as human as us…"

Khusaaq's stare narrowed to a suspicious squint as he again glanced around at the circle of faces. *What does this have to do—*

"You've been aggressively bio-engineered, but you're still one hundred percent human, just not the same species. We're homo sapiens *sapiens*," Amalfitano continued, "you're homo sapiens *neanderthalensis*, basically the same with the exception of a few chromosomes. Neanderthals became extinct—on Earth—around twenty thousand years ago." He turned to the desktop monitor. "I can show you the evidence—"

"A'tuu'shahn'i were *created* by the Elkanasu—"

"From Neanderthal stock. Analysis is conclusive." Amalfitano studied him intently for a moment, then his eyes began to widen. *"Gods*—you've known it all along, haven't you?"

Khusaaq met his gaze squarely. "I am Elkanaghalli, defender of the true faith, keeper of the past and beloved servant of the Elkanasu. The Elkanasu have *no* secrets from the first caste."

Izraad and Corsali replied with sharp intakes of breath; Aquila just stared at him in open-mouthed shock. Teague reacted with understated surprise.

Amalfitano, still recovering from the shock of startling Khusaaq's revelation, stammered in sudden comprehension, "That's... that's why you... you risked everything. You *knew*—"

"What does this have to do with the matter of asylum?" Khusaaq interrupted, fixing his hard gaze on Aquila.

"Everything, Sha'ashahn. And let me assure you before we continue, asylum is *still* an option."

Khusaaq allowed himself to ease back into his chair, just a bit. But the looks on the faces of those around him did little to allay his fears. Something was very wrong.

"But we feel you need to be fully apprised of the situation so that you can make a wholly informed decision."

He wet his lips, crossed his arms and nodded, "Continue."

"Now it's my turn to say *we* need *your* help."

"Help?" His bewildered gaze moved from Aquila to Amalfitano, then back to Aquila. "But..." His eyes widened in horrible realization. *"The target planet!"*

"Tuli's safe, Sha'ashahn," Izraad said. "Thanks to you, and to Doctor Amalfitano and his staff's quick action in identifying the biological agent."

"You were able to start an inoculation program?" He looked back at Amalfitano.

"Wasn't necessary, at least not on a planet-wide scale. As far as we can tell, the bug never got loose, but even if it has, it's essentially harmless."

"Harmless? But how could that be? The data—"

"Was wrong," Amalfitano interrupted, "or should I say incomplete. The virus your people collected from the base was a benign strain of a well-known virus family we call the *orthomyxoviridae.*"

"Yes. I remember... that name appeared in the data. But the weapon was supposedly exceedingly virulent."

"One of its parents, Type A HA fifteen—"

"NA nine Cnidos-Saak," Khusaaq finished for him.

"Yes, Type A C-S is, or should I say was extremely virulent, until it was finally eradicated about forty years ago, and had the research continued down that path, the resulting virus might have been even deadlier than Type A C-S."

Khusaaq turned warily to Aquila. "Then why do you need my help?"

Aquila gave Amalfitano another sidelong look.

"Doctor?" Khusaaq prompted.

"The other parent virus, Type A HA twenty-one, NA fourteen Vetrarbraut Sixteen, while not a deadly disease, had an ideal trait for a biological weapon: it could remain viable for extremely long periods of time in an otherwise hostile environment. The researchers had clearly hoped the offspring would have the virulence of the one and the hardiness of the other—"

"How long can it survive?"

"Decades, possibly—"

"Over a century?"

"Yes."

"And the base was contaminated with this organism," Khusaaq continued, his eyes locked with Amalfitano's, "yes?"

"Yes."

"And when the scout's crew entered the base, they were exposed to this virus."

"Yes."

He hesitated before adding, "And this is the... 'nasty bug' as you called it, that I had."

"Yes."

"But... but you said it was harmless."

"It is, to just about anyone who's had prior exposure to any of the orthomyxoviruses and whose immune system can then identify it as a foreign invader and generate antibodies to fight it."

Khusaaq dropped his gaze to his knees as his mind rapidly put the pieces together. Suddenly, the cold knot in his stomach cinched tight, catching his breath in his throat. "My people have no immunity." He lifted his gaze to Amalfitano. "That's what you're trying to tell me?"

"Yes. Your people's increasing lack of genetic diversity, in combination with your isolation—"

Khusaaq chuckled softly and shook his head.

Aquila gave an equally perplexed Amalfitano a sidelong glance before asking, "You don't believe us?"

He snorted then said, "Strangely enough, yes, I believe you."

"Then…?"

Khusaaq took a deep, voice-steadying breath before answering, "The scout's crew found some vital areas of the complex still on line and fully powered, including its diffusion screen. In many of the deeper level laboratories, air-tight seals were unbroken. Ou'dayaah—our senior medical officer—repeatedly warned Nahru'tzrhi that we had to be exceedingly careful about contamination, that it was possible that whatever killed the base's staff might still be viable and if it was, we could just as easily succumb to it as its intended targets.

"Qharubi Sha'ashahn and I separately raised the distinct possibility that the base had been booby-trapped—that perhaps the entire matter had been a feint, a baited trap, as it were." He caught the quick exchange of pointed glances between Aquila and Corsali. "At first Nahru'tzhri agreed to proceed with caution, but later, when he learned that viable samples were there for the taking, along with the data, he became impatient… too impatient to order the proper precautions be maintained, in fact quite the opposite.

"When the scout returned, its crew apparently no worse for their collecting, Nahru'tzhri said this was proof that we were being too cautious." He dropped his gaze back to his knees. "That Ou'dayaah, as an overly pedantic Dakkeesh and Qharubi and I as hidebound Elkanaghalli'i... we… we all worried too much. He accused me of endeavoring to undermine his authority, of attempting to contact Ru'asooli Kshira'tzrhi, who was in command of the entire mission—and when those charges came to nothing, of plotting to lead a mutiny against him. But because of my status, unlike Ou'dayaah, he couldn't just have me executed. Too many questions would be asked and Qharubi knew *Makhaira* inside and out. Tarqk needed him—"

"So he marooned you and the others on Rasal Ghul Seven," Amalfitano said, "believing the planet would do his dirty work for him."

Khusaaq nodded, "Using the excuse that we'd been contaminated with the virus and using our warnings about the risks to rationalize the decision to abandon us, not that the crew believed him." After an awkward silence, he lifted his gaze to Aquila. "Now those warnings have been realized and beyond even our worst fears—unfortunately Nahru'tzrhi is no longer alive to hear them."

"Yes. Most unfortunate."

Khusaaq, hearing an odd tone in Aquila's voice, gave him a narrow look. Then he turned to Amalfitano to see him staring at him with the same expression as Aquila. "What's happened?" He straightened up in the chair. "My escort? Matoosh?"

"You and Matoosh suffered severe liver damage," Amalfitano replied, "which in turn compromised your immune systems. That was not the case with the rest of your escort, all of whom escaped serious injury. Like you, they were all suffering from radiation exposure, but that actually worked in their favor, as it did with your scout crew, because the massive dose of radiation each absorbed also inhibited the viruses' growth, allowing their immune systems adequate time to recognize the threat and mobilize against it—"

"And Matoosh?"

"He's suffering from acute myxoviral pneumonia as well, but he *is* finally responding to treatment. He should be over the worst of it by tomorrow."

Khusaaq exhaled, briefly relieved. Then he noticed that Amalfitano's apprehensive expression hadn't changed. Neither had Aquila's... or Corsali's. "Then what's happened?"

Aquila replied, "The Orthodoxy demanded your return and the return of all those Tarqk marooned on Rasal Ghul Seven in partial payment for keeping quiet about the base on Rasal Ghul Four. The Coalition is mounting a rescue to retrieve—"

"But my escort are highly infectious. They cannot be returned until—"

"Those we had aboard have already been repatriated," Aquila replied.

He blinked, blinked again.

"Sha'ashahn, the instant we realized your people had no immunity, we tried to stop the repatriation, but by then it was too late."

Khusaaq continued to stare at Aquila, dumbfounded, then, as the true depth of the horror began to take solid form in his mind, his eyes narrowed to slits. "This is why we never surrender, why we never allow ourselves to be taken prisoner, never leave our dead behind! We knew if you ever captured one of us or even retrieved our dead, you'd cut us open, realize who and what we really are—learn our weaknesses… exploit them…!" He shifted his now hateful gaze to Amalfitano and snarled, *"I trusted you!"*

"Sha'ashahn," Aquila began, drawing his fierce gaze, "you must—"

"I rescued you in hopes that together we would stop this madness—and this is how you repay me? At the first opportunity, you unleash this disease on my people?" He pushed himself out of the chair and turned away from the ring of concerned faces as he struggled to come to grips with the enormity of the situation. *Human faces! How could I have ever thought I could trust any of you? Your kind tried to kill mine millennia ago—the moment our two peoples met, you set about trying to exterminate us, and you would have succeeded—*

"Sha'ashahn," Aquila tried again, "the Coalition's willing to do everything it can to save your people—"

He wheeled around to face him. "You had your chance! And *you* handed them over!"

"Before we knew they—"

"Why should I believe you? Every time A'tuu'shahn'i have trusted Rimmers, every time we've believed you, done your bidding, you've betrayed us—*killed us!* You did the same with my ancestors! You refused to share a planet with us—now you refuse to share the galaxy!"

"All I can do is give you my personal word that I'm telling you the truth—this was all a terrible accident… no one intended to infect your people—"

"And if I were to tell you that your 'word' is no longer good enough?" he sneered.

"Sha'ashahn, if you don't help us, many of your people will die," Aquila answered. "That's a certainty—"

"Isn't that what your Coalition wanted all along? The death of all A'tuu'shahn'i? That's what you humans have wanted all along—to wipe out any evidence of a parallel race superior in every way but sheer numbers! It's always been that way, you've always outnumbered us, overpowered us—drove us from our homes—but relegating us to the shadows was not enough—*you wanted us dead!"*

"I can't speak to what happened tens of thousands of years ago Sha'ashahn, and I won't deny that today many within the Coalition hold those views, albeit for vastly different reasons. But in this case, even the hard-core factions would have to admit that this crisis, if allowed to play out, will only serve Matarran interests. Maybe you were right... maybe this was a baited trap, baited by the Matarrans—"

"Don't try to shift the blame for this onto the Matarii! It's your Coalition who has infected my people, not the Matarii! It's your people who have always hated us, feared us, not the Matarii!"

"But Sha'ashahn, the Orthodoxy isn't just going to sit back and watch its people die—it'll retaliate, attack the Coalition—"

"We have a right to defend ourselves and now we have the means—that's why you're so scared—this time *we* have the means to defeat *you!*"

"And next thing you know, it will be all-out war!" Aquila fired back. "And the Matarrans will just wait until all the shooting's over, then come in and mop up what resistance remains. Then they'll have everything without having risked anything! Do you really want to be party to that?"

Khusaaq began to visibly tremble with rage.

"Sha'ashahn, please," Aquila continued, forcing down his own anger, "*listen* to me. I've been authorized to offer you anything you want, on top of asylum—"

"You think I can be *bought*?" he hissed. "As a mercenary—as a savage, stupid brute—I would sell out my own people?"

"*No!*" Aquila shook his head vehemently. "That's not what I—"

"*Get out!*" he snarled through clenched teeth as a cold fury washed over him, his uniform darkening in response. "*All of you... get out!*"

Amalfitano and Aquila exchanged glances. Then Aquila held up his hands and said, "All right, we'll give you a few minutes—"

"*GET OUT!*" he shrieked as his fever-weakened body began to shake uncontrollably.

"Go on," Aquila motioned to the others and Amalfitano, Izraad and Teague quickly filed out of the office, followed by a very reluctant Sirin and, finally, Aquila.

Khusaaq strode after them, punched the door activator with his fist. The door slipped shut, cutting off Amalfitano's, *"Khusaaq, don't—"* just as he managed to thumb the lock function. He punched the panel again, this time with all his strength, disabling it and bloodying his knuckles in the process then starting to wobble, he staggered back to his chair.

This cannot be happening! He fell heavily to his knees beside it, dropped his head into his hands and began to sob, deep, body-heaving sobs as Amalfitano's warm, fatherly approach, Sirin's unconditional affection—emotional attachments he'd never known and which, he suddenly realized, he'd been seeking all his life—warred with this new reality, of the ultimate betrayal, of taking what he'd so desperately hungered after, exposing these intensely personal desires for all to see then using them against him—against his people.

I knew better than to trust humans! I should've listened to my instincts, I should have listened—

But you did listen... to us.

He flinched violently and glanced over his shoulder, fully expecting to find the Rimmers standing behind him, having somehow managed to override the lock, forcing the door open without him noticing, their deceitful faces masks of compassion. He was alone in the ominously silent office, the door and the blood-smeared activator just as he'd left it.

"Who's there?" he hissed, lurching unsteadily to his feet, his eyes now fixed on the darkened doorway of Amalfitano's sleeping quarters. He angrily wiped his eyes and his nose with the back of his shaky hand. *"Show yourself!"*

Is this how you greet us?

He wheeled around, almost falling before grabbing the chair back to steady himself— *No, it can't be!* "I must be hearing things—"

Yes, you are.

He glanced around, saw only Amalfitano's cluttered desk. *"Siah'ushu...?"*

His fearful hesitancy was greeted with a ripple of soft laughter; his skin prickled in response. *Of course.*

"But... but how? Where?"

In front of you.

He followed the chorus of whispered voices back to the desk. "How do I know it's really you and not another Rimmer—a human trick?"

You know.

He squeezed his eyes shut and rubbed his forehead. *Maybe I've indeed gone mad... who would blame me?* "Yes," he murmured and realized he was actually relieved, "That must be—"

You're not insane, toq-bhir.

"If I'm not insane, then why now? *Why speak to me now?*"

How many times have you called upon us to speak to you, to tell you what to do, guide you? Now that we reveal ourselves to you, you... you question our timing?

"But I've failed! I've betrayed you, betrayed the Orthodoxy—"

No, you haven't. You couldn't.

He took a hesitant, unsteady step closer to the desk as he dug his fingers into his throbbing temple. "I was..." He grimaced before finishing, "I was mind-stripped—"

We know, the voices whispered with shared anguish.

"And you still reveal yourselves to me? I allowed myself, my escort to be taken prisoner—"

You did not allow anything. We allowed it—we... arranged it. The Rimmers picking up that SOS was no fortuitous—

"You...?" He felt a sudden flush of anger at the thought of being manipulated, even if it was by the Elkanasu. Worse, to be betrayed—

You've always been the obedient servant of our will, toq-bhir, the voices gently reminded him. *Your life has been directly guided by us; nothing was by chance—*

"Cotopaxi?"

At the voices' collective silence, he added tightly, "Even... even the mind-stripping?"

This time the answer was a soft, *No. But neither would we have stopped it.*

"But... *why?*"

It was time.

"Time? I don't—"

We were mercenaries once—

"I know—"

Even you do not know all, toq-bhir, the voices chided irritably. *You must first listen before you can learn.*

He dipped his head in acquiescence, murmured, "Apologies."

Mollified, the voices continued, *We were also the Rim's major arms dealers—a very, very lucrative trade then as now. But we eventually grew tired of being the profiteers of death, grew disenchanted with the enormous wealth we'd acquired, wealth of such proportions even we could not imagine it, of the tremendous power and fear we wielded and as our dissatisfaction grew, we began to question what made us who and what we were, at first individually and then collectively.*

To question one's purpose, toq-bhir, to question one's existence, or the existence of one's kind is always a perilous undertaking, as you yourself have discovered, because often as not, the questioner will arrive at an answer that is as startling as it is unflattering.

Which is exactly what happened to us. We came to the terrible realization that we were responsible for the wanton extermination of entire sentient species—not just one or two, but thousands—unique life forms that had taken billions of years to evolve were being wiped out in the veritable blink of the eye and over what in truth amounted to little more than petty squabbles...

He lifted his watery gaze as the voices trailed off.

It took the destruction of one small and insignificant world to bring us to our senses, the voices continued softly and tainted in sorrow, *to make us see that in reality the real treasure in these disputes was never what was being quarreled over, but rather the very species who were doing the quarreling. And strangely, we were not even involved this time, at least not directly. We supplied the weapons only and in our conceit didn't question the stated intentions of the Ufar'a, which was to forcibly evict the inhabitants of an illegal settlement from a planet the Ufar'a claimed as their own.*

The colony, the Ufar'a asserted, had been given numerous opportunities to peaceably abandon their settlement and had refused—they'd even gone so far as to murder an Ufar'an negotiator. In truth we didn't care if what the Ufar'a told us was true or not—they paid our price and we gave them the weapons. It was nothing more than a minor dispute over territory as far as we were concerned, a simple and straightforward matter that did not require our direct involvement.

Only later did we learn that the colonists were not colonists at all, but a sentient species indigenous to the planet. The Ufar'a, upon discovering the planet immediately claimed it, but when they realized it was already populated and that the sentient species was going to take time and valuable materiel to subjugate, neither of which the Ufar'a had in abundance, the Ufar'a, in their frustration, ignited the planet's atmosphere—using our weapons, our technology—hoping to not only eliminate the indigenous species but any evidence it ever existed thus being able to claim and colonize without interference or outside objection. But they wildly miscalculated, didn't know how to control the forces they'd unleashed and ended up incinerating the planet's surface, reducing a world teeming with life to nothing more than a sterile ball of rock unusable even by the Ufar'a.

In our rage at their deceit and that others held us equally culpable in what was, in essence, the murder of an entire planet, we decided to make the Ufar'a an example of what would happen to any sentient species who thought they could deceive us: we destroyed the Ufar'a, hunting down every last one. We left their home world and colonies intact but unpopulated. We foolishly thought by doing so we proved to all that we were wiser and more judicious in our dealings with those who crossed us, but when others immediately rushed in to claim the spoils and wars broke out over who had the right to claim Ufar'a territory, we realized we were no better than the Ufar'a, that we were, in fact worse, far worse. We had set ourselves up as gods—deciding which species lived and matured and which died in infancy.

It was then that we were confronted by the awful realization that directly or not, we were ultimately responsible for the irretrievable loss of unique life forms, so we left behind our terrible vocation and set about with one goal in mind: to make amends. And in doing so become gods of a different kind, to find as many sentient and proto-sentient life forms as we could and protect them from outside harm using the very skills we'd used to such terrible effect. In our travels we searched the entire Rim and far beyond, mapped systems and worlds no one had heretofore known existed, cataloged their myriad of life forms and then placed them under our guardianship.

This is how we first happened across your home world and your ancestors, half a million Standard years ago.

It was always our intention to leave any sentient or proto-sentient species we found to grow and mature on their home worlds, to evolve as they were intended to evolve without outside interference by using our fearsome reputation to shield those we found from the avarice of more advanced species. Once we extended our protection to a world, few dared to challenge it and those who did never repeated their mistake. Of course many grumbled that all we were doing was grabbing worlds to further enrich ourselves—which in many ways was true as we'd come to learn what true wealth was, and more importantly, what it was not.

But when we realized just how truly unique your people were and how precarious your population, we broke the promise we had made to ourselves—not to interfere unless it was to protect the life forms from outsiders—and set about collecting small groups to breed with the hopes of reintroducing your kind in greater numbers. But there weren't enough, there were never enough, not without fatally undermining the populations we left behind, or so we believed—but when we discovered that your species had in fact reached the precipice of extinction through a fateful combination of dramatic climatic change, pressures from your far more populous cousins, and yes, our at times injudicious collecting, we abandoned all efforts to reintroduce your people and along with those we already had in our safekeeping, we took all pure stock that remained—no more than a few hundred or so—to give your kind a new life—a far better life as our beloved A'tuu'shahn'i.

You have served us well, toq-bhir, you and your people; you have far surpassed all of our expectations, although in truth we were deeply saddened by your decision to resume our terrible trade—granted, not entirely by choice, the voices added as he started to open his mouth to protest and he wisely closed his mouth again.

And as mercenaries you've come close to surpassing our accomplishments; you've certainly matched, if not exceeded our fearsome reputation, which, paradoxically, is a point of immense pride for us. But that which has always set your kind apart, made A'tuu'shahn'i so exceptional in our eyes even before we made our enhancements has also made A'tuu'shahn'i vulnerable, defenseless not just against the enemy from without, but the enemy from within—a regrettable oversight on our part that has only one solution: you and your people must rejoin your kind, toq-bhir, mix your genes with theirs, as many of your kind did millennia ago, or die—and if you die, we die, as you are the last of those species we so closely fostered—

"If the flame is ever extinguished..."

Yes... we all perish, vanishing into that greater darkness, forever.

"And what of Qharubi? What of—"

He is with us now, all are with us now.

"Even Tarqk?"

Yes... but not for long.

He hesitated. "And Tu'indai?"

She chose her path, toq-bhir. While we can light the way, even to those who are not Elkanaghalli, ultimately the choice is theirs as to whether to follow or not.

He squeezed his eyes shut. "I did love her."

We know.

"And she loved me too, at least she did at first—so I beg you, do not punish her for Tarqk's actions."

There was a long pause before the voices replied unhappily, *As you wish.*

"What of those left on Rasal Ghul? Are they with you as well?"

No, not yet, but... the voices paused then sighed, *soon.*

He winced then jerked his head towards the doorway as he overheard muffled voices and sounds from just outside. "They're trying to force the door—they've called security—"

Come to us, the voices commanded. *Hurry!*

He made his way around behind the desk then squatted in front of it. "Where?"

Here.

His hand reached unerringly to the top right drawer. He carefully slid it open, wary of a built-in alarm, then pushed aside the untidy pile of reports and crumpled food wrappers.

"Siah'ushu!" His breath caught in his throat as his watery gaze fell on the dagger. He grabbed it.

We are one again, its chorus of voices whispered.

"Yes..." He ran a finger along the blood channel of the blade and the knife responded with a soft, satisfied sigh.

Suddenly the overwhelming guilt, rage and fear were gone. They drained away so sudden it left him light-headed, almost giddy and he fell forward, onto his knees, his shoulder coming to rest against the corner of the desk.

After a moment, the dizziness subsided and he slowly lifted his head.

Now, do exactly as we tell you, toq-bhir, fulfill your destiny, answer the pleas of the dead and we will set you free—

"I don't want to be free—I want to join you!" He turned the blade so that the tip now faced him, faced his chest.

NO!

He squinted at it, bewildered. Then he had a horrible thought. "Because I'm no longer pure, because I almost succumbed to—"

No, toq-bhir. Because your people need you, now more than ever. The voices hesitated, then continued, *We know your life has been particularly hard, harder than even we could have foreseen, that you carry with you so much, but it is because of that, because despite everything, you've served us far beyond our wildest expectations, because you've proven to us that you've always known what took us so long to accept, you've earned a life free from our direction—and, toq-bhir, the one is near.*

He looked around him, even more confused. "The one?"

The one you've sought. The one we've all sought for so, so long.

His eyes widened in sudden comprehension and he looked back at the closed door, horrified. "One of them?"

No, toq-bhir. You will know the one. Now, do exactly as we say and all will be as it should be.

He reluctantly nodded, then, overhearing the sound of the outside door panel being removed, of several people speaking in hushed, angry voices, he slid the dagger under his hauberk and down inside his under-tunic, its bulge well hidden behind the shifting, camouflaging textures of the hauberk and bandoleer.

The knife purred against his bare skin; he felt it vibrate through his chest, flowing along the lines of his tattoos as rainwater fills a dry riverbed, quenching a deep and prolonged thirst. Tears followed, traveling down the matching and equally elaborate pattern of grooves. *Follow your heart, toq-bhir. In doing so, you follow us. This has always been true.*

He shut the drawer and managed to ease himself into the chair nearest the desk. He was shaking violently now, every muscle quivering, overcome with exhaustion, the effects of the virus… and from simple, raw emotion.

Out of the corner of his eye he saw the door suddenly snap open, but only half way, as if forced. He braced himself, expecting to be confronted by an armed security detail.

Instead Amalfitano's familiar voice asked, "Khusaaq…?"

Not Sha'ashahn. Khusaaq. And he found himself craving that. Yearning for that strange familiarity—that visceral connection. He swallowed, hard, wiped his streaming eyes, his nose with the back of a very shaky hand then turned. Amalfitano stood in the partially open doorway, alone. He assumed the rest, including security, were wisely keeping out of his sight. But they were there, just outside—he could smell them, smell their fear. At least ten, maybe more, fully armored no doubt—against a cornered A'tuu'shahn. He didn't like his odds.

"I thought I'd just check on you." Amalfitano took a cautious step closer, then another. "Can I get you anything, son?"

Son. You've called me that a lot. I found it deeply offensive at first, an insult, to have a human call me 'son'. But… then something changed. He stared up at Amalfitano with blood-shot eyes as the doctor took another step closer and as their gazes locked, Amalfitano reacted with a deeply agonized look of his own.

Ja'andai never called me son—I was his Doh'ha, his duplicate, nothing more—you call me 'son' and you sound and look like you mean it—could it be you really do?

Not trusting his voice, he gave his throbbing head a quick, sharp shake.

"Khusaaq… I…" Amalfitano bit his lip then started again, his voice strained, husky, "I should considered the possibility your people had no immunity once I realized who you really were. No wonder your people did everything possible to keep yourself shielded from us. Your ghillie suits, your armor—it wasn't just to protect you from the obvious, was it?"

Khusaaq shook his head again then gave his nose, his eyes another wipe.

Amalfitano cautiously eased himself down in the chair next to him, started to reach out and then clearly thought better of it and instead tightly clasped his hands in his lap. "So if you're going to punish anyone, punish me. Don't punish your people and most of all, son, don't punish yourself, and that's exactly what you'll be doing if you refuse."

Your people need you now, more than ever, the knife whispered.

Khusaaq fixed his pinched stare on the desk, on the documents and swallowed, hard.

Fulfill your destiny...

"Matoosh told me that to a Hahtooshan, to be forgotten was worse than death." Amalfitano paused long enough to draw Khusaaq's wary, sidelong gaze. "Perhaps a legacy of your people's extinction on Earth. Your kind was forgotten about, for tens of thousands of years. And when we finally unearthed some of your skeletons, you were looked upon as something not quite human—no, something *less* than human.

"We no longer believe that, but there remains this lingering question: what really happened to Neanderthals? Did we, meaning homo sapiens sapiens breed homo sapiens neanderthalensis out of existence? Did massive climate change happen so fast your ancestors couldn't adapt? All we knew, up until now, was that suddenly, about twenty thousand years ago, homo sapiens neanderthalensis as a distinct species disappeared, just like that," Amalfitano snapped his fingers, then smiled. "But your people didn't die due to climate change, you weren't bred out of existence, you didn't become extinct. You... *evolved.*"

Khusaaq dropped his gaze to his knees, bit his blistered lip.

"Don't you see, son? This is a way to defeat oblivion, just as your ancestors did with the help of the Elkanasu—"

Khusaaq couldn't help but flick Amalfitano a sidelong glance, wondering if the man could sense the presence of the dagger. What he saw in the man's watery eyes assured him that whatever Amalfitano was feeling, it wasn't the dagger.

"—this is a way to defeat Tu'indai's words," Amalfitano continued, "defeat Tarqk and defeat those who sent you and the others to Rasal Ghul in the first place. If you agree, if you help us stop this *now*, you'll be remembered not only by your own people, but by mine, as the individual who had the courage to defy everyone and everything you've ever known, to risk and lose all and still do what needed to be done to save the very people, on both sides, who would stop you."

Khusaaq closed his eyes and clenched his teeth as fresh tears trickled down his hollow cheeks, along the deep grooves that had been carved into his skin, using the very dagger that now purred against his chest, so long ago he barely remembered the agonizing ritual. This time he made no effort to wipe the tears away.

"Admiral Keon's granted you temporary asylum—you don't have to ask for it, all you have to do is accept. That'll give us some time, give you time to figure out what you want to do, where you want to go." He paused, looked at the documents spread across the desk. "You don't have to agree to help. But please, *I beg you*, accept asylum. Just that. Give yourself some breathing room. You can't go back, you know that, and without accepting asylum we can't protect you..."

Khusaaq took a deep, rattling breath, roughly wiped his cheeks with the back of his hand then exhaled, slowly.

"I understand completely why you believe I betrayed you, and after what's happened, I certainly don't deserve your trust, but the Commander's never lied to you, son, he's telling the truth—"

Follow your heart, toq-bhir.

He took another ragged breath, released it then looked at Amalfitano and asked hoarsely, "These are the papers I'm to sign?"

Amalfitano blinked, taken aback. *"What?"*

He leaned forward and picked up the closest flimsy. "I'm to thumb-seal this, yes?" He twisted in his chair to face Amalfitano and held out the document.

"Ah... yes—"

"Where?" He looked down at the flimsy. "Show me."

Amalfitano glanced back at the door. "Lemme get Robert and the others. They need to witness it." He rose and hurried back to the door then motioned urgently to those who'd remained outside and were now crowded around the partially opened door.

Khusaaq looked down at his hand, at the flimsy and realized his hand was trembling. He quickly set the flimsy on the desk, got to his feet, roughly wiped his eyes, his cheeks then clasped his clammy hands behind his back just as Aquila entered, followed, single-file, by a very worried Sirin, then Teague, and finally, Izraad.

He looked at each, his gaze lingering on Sirin, and then he turned to Aquila and said flatly, "I accept."

Sirin sank down heavily into a chair and daubed her eyes with her sleeve. Teague cracked the faintest of smiles.

Amalfitano grinned broadly and tightly grasped Khusaaq's shoulder, the last of his fears evaporating.

Khusaaq met and held Izraad's suspicious stare for a moment then turned his full attention on Aquila as the man asked, "You do? I... I mean I want to get this straight, you *are* accepting our offer of asylum?"

Khusaaq nodded, reluctantly. "And to... assist you in any way I can to stop this madness, which is what I had hoped to do from the start. As you said, if I do not help you I am party to the..." he paused, flicked Izraad a sidelong, icy glance, then looked back at Aquila and added with a slight sneer, "the second and but this time purely *unintentional* genocide of my people."

"Commander," Izraad prompted, her own narrowed gaze never wavering from Khusaaq, "might I suggest you contact Admiral Keon and inform him of Sha'ashahn's decision?"

"Yes, of course." Aquila strode over to the desk and tapped the desk-com. "C and C?"

"Control here—"

"Get me Admiral Keon of Sector Command. Highest priority." Aquila risked a quick glance back at Khusaaq to see him watching him, his blood-shot, pale eyes glittering. "Perhaps you'd like to read over these papers while we wait." He began to gather them up.

"Trust must start somewhere, yes?" Khusaaq stepped forward despite his knees feeling like they were going to buckle. "So where do I put my mark?"

Aquila quickly spread the papers back across the desk. "Uh... well, right here... here, here and here." He pointed to each thumb-seal.

Khusaaq pressed his thumb against each then stepped unsteadily back, allowing Aquila, Teague and Amalfitano to add their thumbprints to the documents. As they did so, he gave Sirin a sidelong look.

She stared up at him, a faint smile on her lips; he winked at her.

Izraad stepped forward to place her thumbprint on the last of the flimsies and as she did so, she gave him a sidelong, thoroughly appraising look.

"You appear displeased by my decision, Lieutenant."

Izraad turned to face him, crossed her arms. "Not displeased, Sha'ashahn, in fact *very* relieved, but I readily admit I'm fascinated by what can only be described as a truly miraculous transformation on your part."

"That's because A'tuu'shahn'i learned from the mistakes of our long-distant ancestors, Lieutenant."

"I don't—"

"Unlike our ancient forefathers, *we* are highly... *adaptable.*"

"So it would seem," Izraad replied dubiously.

He replied with an impervious and decidedly smug smile. *Wonder all you want, Lieutenant, suspect all you want. You cannot touch me—touch us*, he added as the dagger resumed its soft, reassuring purr. *No one can touch us now.*

"Sir?"

Everyone turned to the doorway. A man Khusaaq did not recognize stood in the doorway.

"Door's fixed," he replied, his uneasy eyes briefly darting to Khusaaq before nodding to Aquila then hastily withdrawing. As if to prove his point, the door immediately slipped closed.

"Sir?" the comp-op's voice boomed from the speaker, drawing everyone's startled gaze, *"I have the admiral. Please enter your personal code."*

Aquila slipped onto Amalfitano's chair and quickly tapped in the sequence.

There was a hiss and snap of static, and then the admiral's voice asked, *"I hope you have good news, Commander?"*

"Yessir." He looked up at Khusaaq. "I have Sha'ashahn here with me. We've fully explained the facts to him. In turn he's accepted asylum, and our offer in trade for his help."

"Most excellent, Commander! And his asking price?"

Out of the corner of his eye, Khusaaq caught Amalfitano's involuntary wince.

Aquila too looked intensely uncomfortable as he looked sidelong at him and asked, "Sha'ashahn, the admiral would like to know what you want in trade? You can ask for anything you want, that was the deal—"

"Yes... I know."

Aquila's face registered a twinge of apprehension at the underlying note of amused delight in Khusaaq's still raspy voice. "Do you need more time to think about it?"

"No." He crossed his arms, in the process pressing the dagger more tightly against his skin. The blade throbbed in response; it made his skin tingle. "I ask for four things."

"And they are?" Keon asked a split second before Aquila could.

"Those left behind on Rasal Ghul—"

"A ship's already been dispatched, Sha'ashahn," Keon interrupted and Khusaaq flicked Amalfitano a sidelong look, to which Amalfitano smiled and nodded. *"They should reach the system in approximately five standard days."*

Khusaaq jerked his eyes back to the speaker grille. "No sooner?"

"The Briseis *was the closest available ship, Sha'ashahn. It was my understanding that your men had managed to power up a radiation diffusion screen?"*

"Yes, but it may not be enough." He looked away, and fixing his narrowed gaze on the wall, took a deep, reflective breath. *And if they truly believe they've been abandoned...* His bleak train of thought was interrupted by the reassuring purr of the knife, but before he could fix his mind on that, to seek solace in its soothing contact, the admiral continued, *"I've notified the* Briseis *that your acceptance of asylum extends to your men as well, and for as long as they remain with the Coalition's sphere of influence, that they are to be provided with all medical care they may require—"*

"I've sent the CMO of *Briseis* all pertinent protocols," Amalfitano whispered to him, to which Khusaaq nodded.

"—and that they are to be delivered directly to you, unless you'd prefer they—"

"To me, Admiral." Khusaaq's eyes darted back to the com-unit. "And my second, Matoosh?"

"The same."

"As far as the actual rescue," Khusaaq continued, "I think it best that I provide the proper guidelines so that the retrieval goes smoothly. I wouldn't want there to be any misunderstandings as to your Coalition's intentions, which could prove very costly to both sides."

"Ah... yes," Keon replied. *"A very wise move, thank you, Sha'ashahn, now, as to your other conditions...?"*

"Yes." He paused, then said, "First, my men and I are to not to be subjected to any form of interrogation," his eyes flicked to Izraad, "including all forms of mind-strip."

"Of course, that goes without saying. It's specifically forbidden under the terms of the Gare de l'Est *charter—"*

"I am asking for *your* personal assurance, Admiral."

"You have it, then. Next?"

"I require a tac-net so I may contact my people on a *secure* channel. I assume at least one was retrieved when we were... *rescued*... from the planet?"

This time Keon didn't answer immediately; seconds stretched into a very awkward pause.

Khusaaq scowled at the silent com-unit. "Given the chance, Admiral, I might be able to stop this, *now,* before it spirals any further out of control."

"Agreed," Keon replied, albeit with a hint of reluctance.

Aquila turned to Teague.

Teague said, "I'll go retrieve one from security," and hurried from the room.

"And your last demand?" Keon asked with an audible mixture of apprehension and relief.

Khusaaq had been waiting for this moment; he was both intensely anxious and eager. He felt the dagger purr, *Follow your heart, toq-bhir.*

"I ask for Ensign Corsali." He turned to her; she stared up at him, wide-eyed.

The stunned silence that followed was finally interrupted by the startled splutter from the admiral, *"But... but..."*

Khusaaq turned back to the com-unit and asked in his most menacing tone, "Is there a problem, Admiral?"

"Well... I can't... I mean, you're asking me to give her—"

"I'm not asking *you.* I'm asking *her.*" He looked at Sirin. "Do you agree?"

She slowly pushed herself out of the chair. "Yes," she managed, then in a stronger voice, added, "I most definitely agree."

He held out his hand. She took a step closer and wrapped her fingers around his.

He drew her against his hip and turned back to the com-unit, suddenly finding he needed her support to steady himself. "Then it's settled, Admiral, yes?"

"Yes... well, I... I mean if the ensign's agreeable... I suppose..."

Khusaaq smiled down at her; she responded by tightening her embrace.

"Commander?"

Aquila turned his full attention to the com-unit. "Yes, Admiral?"

"Mirfak Prime's labs have been tasked to deal with the medical aspects of this situation."

Khusaaq flicked Amalfitano a sidelong, questioning look; Amalfitano nodded his approval.

"I'll dispatch a ship to pick you up, Sha'ashahn—I'll get back to the commander with the details as soon as things are arranged... and Commander?"

"Yessir?"

"I want Sha'ashahn's acceptance of temporary asylum, as well as the terms of our agreement officially logged as quickly as possible."

"I'll transmit them immediately, Admiral." He started to hand them to Corsali, but realized that she, literally, had her hands full. "Oh."

Izraad rose, murmured, "I'll take care of it, Commander."

"Sha'ashahn...?"

Khusaaq reluctantly took his eyes off Corsali and fixed them on the com-unit. "Yes, Admiral?"

"The Coalition owes you, personally, a debt of gratitude we can never repay."

Khusaaq's eyes narrowed to slits and he growled in his most menacing voice, "I've heard those heartfelt words before, Admiral—*after Cotopaxi*. Let's all hope that this time they're backed up by equally sincere actions, otherwise it will not just be A'tuu'shahn'i who suffer the consequences."

There was another uncomfortable pause before the admiral cleared his throat and said, *"Yes... well... good job everyone. And I'll see what I can do about speeding up that rescue. Keon out."*

For a moment, no one spoke then Amalfitano chuckled and clapped Khusaaq on the shoulder, nearly knocking him off his already precarious balance. "You enjoyed that, didn't you?"

He nodded as he caressed Sirin's blond hair. "Yes. Very much."

Amalfitano grinned as his eyes darted to Aquila. "So did I."

"Sort of thought you would," Aquila grumbled, tugging at his collar as Teague reentered the office, tac-net in hand.

"Sha'ashahn?" He offered it to him.

Khusaaq murmured his thanks as he accepted it, then he slipped from Sirin's embrace. "I ask for a few moments *alone*, Commander."

"Uh... oh, yes, of course." Aquila motioned for everyone to leave.

Corsali hesitated, then, at Khusaaq's pointed stare, nodded then turned and wordlessly followed Amalfitano.

Once the five were well away from the door, clearly assuming they were beyond of his very acute earshot, Khusaaq overheard Amalfitano whisper, *"I wonder who he's gonna try to contact?"*

"Who knows," Aquila replied just as the door started to slip shut. "That battleship's long gone and I seriously doubt if that device can reach all the way—"

The door closed, cutting off further casual eavesdropping—on either side.

— iii —

Hearing a soft knock at his door, Aquila lifted his gaze from his desk's active terminal. "Come."

The door opened and in walked Amalfitano, Izraad and Tasende.

Aquila raised his brows at the unexpected company. "What's up?"

"Have you heard anything more from Keon?" Amalfitano asked.

"No. Not yet." Aquila tapped a button on the monitor and the data displayed obediently vanished, replaced by the Coalition's standard. "Why?"

"Well," Amalfitano began as he glanced at Izraad, then Tasende, "we've been talking."

"About what?"

"Sir," Izraad replied, "we think it would be a good idea for us to accompany Sha'ashahn—"

"All of you?" Aquila looked to Amalfitano as the ringleader in this little coup.

"Xosé and I have been on top of this bug from the get-go. It'll take the medical staff on Mirfak days to get up to speed and every minute is critical."

Aquila turned to Izraad. "And you?"

"The decision to grant Sha'ashahn full, albeit temporary asylum is not going to go over well with a lot of people, sir, especially those in Intelligence, and then there's the matter of how best to broach the subject of Hahtooshans being Neanderthals—"

"Robert," Amalfitano interrupted, "it's just for the month the *Baidarka* will be here, that's all we ask—just four weeks. That'll give Khusaaq time to adjust to his new surroundings and—"

"Those working with him time to adjust to working hand in hand with a Hahtooshan?"

"Yeah."

"And what about the medical needs of my crew?"

"Jenna'll be here," Amalfitano replied. "She's the best all-around surgeon and diagnostician I've ever met. She can handle anything that comes up, and there's always the hospitals on Tuli if something totally out of the blue happens—"

"And Matoosh? Is he stable enough to make the trip?"

"I've already spoken with Jenna and Drakin about him. We all agree he should stay aboard and finish up his physical therapy—I'll have to speak to Khusaaq about it, but I'm sure he'll agree. By the time the *Baidarka* returns to Mirfak, he should be up and walking again." Amalfitano, seeing the less than enthusiastic look in Aquila's eye, added quickly, "He's come a long way, physically, and more importantly, in how he interacts with my staff."

Aquila's expression turned down right skeptical.

"Okay, so he can be a real pain when he wants to be—he's a teenager for god sakes, with all the typical teenage angst—but he *won't* cause any problems, Drakin'll see to that."

"Plus I hear he's developed a bit of a crush on Meerut," Izraad slipped in, grinning at Amalfitano, "and is usually willing to do what she asks without too much complaining, and late at night when he can't sleep he's been known to play vid games with Rafe and his guards when no one's looking—or so they think."

Aquila shifted his less than happy stare to Amalfitano as he leaned back in his chair and crossed his arms. "And what about shore leave? If anyone deserves some R and R, it's you three."

"Some things are more important than shore leave, sir," Tasende replied.

"Agreed, but if things turn sour, you might not have another chance for a very long time, and Admiral Keon might not approve your temporary reassignment."

Amalfitano dropped his gaze to his feet and sighed, then met Aquila's stern gaze. "Look, Robert, I know I blew it, but to let that get in the way..." his voice trailed off as he realized Aquila was now grinning. He scowled at him. "You... *bastard.*"

Aquila laughed.

"Why put us through this?"

"And deprive myself of the rare treat of hearing you admit you blew something?"

Amalfitano, pointedly ignoring Tasende's chuckle, replied, "So, I take it by that that you agree?"

"Of course. I was planning on raising the idea to you. Now all we have to do is get the admiral's okay."

"You don't think he'll say no just because I called him a fat ass, do you?"

"No, but I suspect he's gonna want to see you squirm a little first."

"Just like you."

"Yup."

"Well," Tasende said, "since I didn't call anybody any names, I think I'll go get packed. If you'll excuse me, sir?"

Aquila nodded then nodded again to Izraad and Amalfitano. "You two better do the same."

Izraad smiled. "Thank you, sir."

"Don't thank me. I don't envy you your public relations job."

"Yeah." She shrugged, then, with a sidelong look at Amalfitano, hurried after Tasende.

Amalfitano hesitated. "Uh...."

"Yes?"

"What about Sirin? She'll want to come too."

"I assume she'll ask for a permanent transfer." Aquila paused, waiting for the doctor to broach the subject of his own request for permanent transfer.

When Amalfitano only nodded, Aquila looked back at the screen, not sure whether to be angry, hurt or hopeful. "If it hadn't been for her—I owe her my life, Will, every bit as much as I owe Khusaaq—and you." He sighed and shook his head. "You should've seen her down on that planet—up to our eyeballs in Hahtooshans and I never saw her lose her composure, not once." He shifted in his chair. *Unlike me.* "Gildun would've been so proud of her."

"She'd be proud of both of you."

"I'm putting her up for a commendation."

"She certainly earned it. And don't be surprised if you get one too, along with a bump up in rank. Now, get some sleep. You'll need to be well rested to chase those Tulian women." Amalfitano wiggled his eyebrows.

"What about the admiral?"

"Let him catch his own."

"I don't mean that. I'm waiting for his call-back, remember?"

"Oh, right."

"I'll let you know the minute I hear from him."

"I thought you wanted to see me squirm again."

"As tempting as it is, I really think it best if I'm alone when I raise the idea with him."

"Thanks." Amalfitano smiled.

As the doctor walked out of the cabin Aquila's gaze dropped to the screen and its stand-by display of the Coalition's emblem; he tapped a controller and the hidden data obediently reappeared.

He'd happened across Amalfitano's request for permanent transfer purely by accident while preparing the paperwork for Corsali's commendation. At first he wasn't sure what to think. The doctor's request had been filed while he was still on Rasal Ghul. But in the days since it hadn't been deleted.

He tried to chalk it up to Amalfitano forgetting it was there. *But now...* He lifted his gaze to the door. *Now I'm not so—*

A *bleat* from the desk-com drew his distracted attention and he tapped the desk-com activator. "Yes?"

The relief com-op said, *"Sir, I'm receiving a message leader from HQ Sector Command. Personal code required."*

Perfect timing. He tapped in the proper sequence. "Done."

"Coming through, now, sir."

The com-op's voice dissolved into interstellar hash; a moment later, Keon's familiar voice boomed, *"We're in luck, Commander!"*

"Luck, sir?"

"The Walafar *was pulled off Intelligence patrol duties and should be rendezvousing with you in little over thirteen hours."*

"Walafar, sir?"

"She was the closest available ship." Keon paused then asked, *"Is that a problem?"*

He squinted at the com-unit. *Oh, hell yeah there's a problem.* Aloud he said, "Well, sir, I assumed HQ would dispatch another ship."

"It's not like we're spoiled for choice here, Commander, and it seemed more important to get Sha'ashahn back here as quickly as possible."

Aquila pushed aside his unease. "Yessir."

"And please notify Sha'ashahn that Captain Pelenor of the Briseis, *when notified of the supreme medical urgency of his mission, believes he can possibly reach the planet a day sooner than originally projected. A half day at the very least."*

Aquila squinted at the com-unit. *In other words, you gave him a swift kick up the ass.* Aloud he said, "Sha'ashahn will be very pleased to hear that, sir, and sir? My CMO, IO and chief lab tech have all requested that they accompany Sha'ashahn back to Mirfak and to be temporarily assigned to the vaccine project, for the period of time the *Baidarka* will be here. They feel that—"

"They'd be of vital assistance during the first few weeks?"

"Yessir."

There was a long pause, long enough for Aquila to realize that he was beginning to squirm.

Finally Keon replied, *"Agreed, but on one condition, Commander. Tell your CMO to keep that temper of his under control—his reputation can excuse only so much. Just one outburst will result in him being dismissed from the research team."*

"I'll tell him, sir."

"And you might warn him that once this immediate crisis is over, he's going to have some serious explaining to do."

Aquila licked his lips, answered, "Yessir."

"*I'll have Lieutenant Matho notify the* Walafar *to expect three extra passengers. Is there anything else?*"

"Ensign Corsali—"

"*Is expected to accompany Sha'ashahn. I've already had the transfer papers drawn up. She's now Sha'ashahn's official liaison to the Coalition Central Committee.*"

"She'll do a fine job, sir. Thank you."

"*If that's all, Commander?*"

"I believe so, sir."

"*Now go enjoy your shore leave, Commander. You've earned it. Keon out.*"

Aquila smiled. Everything had worked out better than he'd hoped. *Well, almost everything*, he quickly reminded himself, his smile instantly evaporating.

He shook his head, grumbled, "No point putting this off," and tapped the desk-com's activator. "C and C? Have Doctor Amalfitano report to my cabin." He cut the connection and sagged back in his chair. "Why the hell did it have to be the *Walafar?*"

Chapter 29

Amalfitano rose from his desk. He'd spent a sleepless night and an anxious morning awaiting the return of the *Walafar*. Now she was in orbit, trailing only a few hundred kilometers behind the *Baidarka*.

"Chief?"

He turned towards the doorway; Tasende held up a duffel bag and a sampling satchel. "My bugs are packed, I'm ready to go."

Amalfitano grabbed his own travel bag and sighed, *"Yeah."*

"Something wrong, Chief?"

"Huh?" He turned to Tasende.

"You don't look real happy. In fact, I'd say you're having second thoughts about this whole undertaking."

"That's because I am."

"But—"

"Doesn't it seem just too damned convenient that the *Walafar* was sent to get us?"

"Unfortunate, yes, Chief, but I wouldn't see some deep dark plot behind this. She was the closest ship, simple as that. Besides, Khusaaq's untouchable."

"Yeah, you're probably right."

"And don't forget, I'll be there to protect him if anyone gets ugly." To emphasize the point, Tasende dropped his bags and placed his hands on his hips and puffed out his chest.

Amalfitano couldn't help but chuckle at the absurd image of the short and stout Tasende defending the mercenary against... well, anything more dangerous than a fly.

"Now c'mon, get a wiggle on." Tasende scooped up his duffle and satchel.

Amalfitano nodded and picked up the holocube from his desk. He stuffed the cube into his bag and, without looking back, followed Tasende into the abnormally quiet sickbay.

Ahead, bracketing the main airlock stood his entire staff. *I was hoping we could avoid the good-byes. Guess not.* He managed a tight smile as he stopped in front of them. "Now you lot behave yourselves."

"Uz?" Drakin lisped.

"Especially you," he countered, poking her in the chest with his finger.

Fleming stepped away from the rest and wrapped her arms around him. "We're going to miss you."

"Naw, you'll do just fine without me. You won't even notice I'm gone."

She kissed him on the cheek and whispered in his ear, "You take care of yourself, you old buzzard."

"You too," he replied as he gave her a bear hug. Then, as she stepped back, he cleared his throat. "See you all in a little over four weeks."

There was a strained murmur of agreement.

"Bye," he said, then strode into the corridor and started up its gentle rise towards the flicker chamber as Tasende hurried alongside. Ahead, they saw the open airlock, and as they approached they heard Aquila's exasperated voice: *"Captain*, Admiral Keon—"

"Commander, as I've already told you—" Mladić stopped in mid-sentence and turned. "Ah, Doctor."

Amalfitano, immediately sensing something wasn't right, in fact very wrong, looked past Aquila and the grim-faced Mladić. Two crewmen from the *Walafar* stood by the flickerstage. Both were holding heavy-duty shockers.

"Where's the merc officer?" Mladić asked impatiently, drawing Amalfitano's gaze back to him.

"Hello, Captain," Amalfitano replied, outwardly unfazed. "Looks like we are going to have the chance to talk about that monograph after all—"

"We're running under a very tight schedule here, Doctor," Mladić interrupted. "I was told the merc would be ready for transport the minute—"

"Sha'ashahn wanted to spend a few minutes alone with his soldier, presumably to tell him to behave himself."

Mladić blew out his cheeks, then turned to the nearest guard and muttered something to him under his breath. The guard nodded as his sharp eyes darted to Amalfitano, then Tasende.

"Is there a problem?" Amalfitano asked innocently, looking first at Mladić, then Aquila as he fought down a growing sense of foreboding.

"You could say that," Aquila answered angrily. "The Captain here says—"

"I was just explaining to your commander," Mladić interrupted with equal heat, "that the *Walafar* is not a passenger liner. She's been modified for Intelligence work, meaning every square centimeter of extra space is being utilized. We simply have no room for four extra people."

Amalfitano's openly startled gaze shifted back to Aquila. "But I thought—"

"And I was just trying to explain to the Captain that Admiral Keon approved your transfer, and," Aquila replied, "I'm sure the admiral made that decision fully aware of the *Walafar*'s limitations."

"We didn't expect private cabins, Captain," Amalfitano said. "We're perfectly willing to double-up—"

"The *Walafar*'s crew's already *tripled* up. It was difficult enough to make suitable accommodations for the merc—as you can imagine, no one wanted to room with him."

Amalfitano and Tasende exchanged glances as Mladić turned to Aquila and continued, "It's my understanding that the *Briseis* has been tasked to pick up the mercs on Rasal Ghul Seven? Perhaps she could make another detour and pick you and your companions up—"

"I'm sorry," Amalfitano shook his head, "but that's just not acceptable. And neither is this display of force." He gave the two security men and their unholstered shockers a pointed stare. Then he looked down at Mladić's own holstered weapon before meeting the man's stony gaze. "You're not transporting a prisoner, Captain, you're—"

"I know exactly who and what I'm transporting, Doctor, and to be blunt, what's acceptable to you and what isn't *isn't* my problem…"

Amalfitano, out of the corner of his eye, caught Aquila's quick, pointed glance at the flicker tech and the man's slight, acknowledging nod as he surreptitiously pressed the silent security alarm on his console.

"…getting the merc back to Mirfak as quickly as possible so we can resume our patrolling along the Matarran border is. But…" He motioned to the two guards and they reluctantly reholstered their shockers. "Satisfied?"

"No, not by half."

Mladić shrugged and turned back to Aquila. "Now, I must insist that he be handed over immediately." When Aquila didn't react, he added evenly, "Do I have to make that an order, Commander?"

"Perhaps we should contact Admiral Keon before anyone goes anywhere," Amalfitano offered.

"I have my orders, Doctor—directly from Senate president pro tempore Behardien."

"Behardien?" Amalfitano repeated, looking at Aquila, "What the hell…?" but before Aquila could reply, Izraad entered, followed by Corsali.

Then Khusaaq stepped through the hatch as his gaze swept the small room and its occupants. He stopped in his tracks as his eyes locked with Mladić's.

Mladić grinned, "Ah, Sha'ashahn."

Khusaaq's eyes widened and Izraad audibly gasped as his horrified reaction—his instant recognition and comprehension—hit her like a fist to the stomach.

She screamed, *"NO!"* but too late.

Khusaaq lunged forward with lightning speed, seized Mladić by the throat with one hand, his shocker with the other and using Mladić's body as a shield, spun around and fired the weapon, striking both guards before they could react. He briefly released his hold, just long enough to jerk the hidden dagger from under his hauberk then snarled in the wide-eyed Mladić's ear, *"Cotopaxi prahaj!"* He plunged the knife just under the man's ribcage, gave it a vicious twist, then thrust up, briefly lifting him off the deck.

Using the knife as a handle, he then hurled Mladić across the chamber, freeing the dagger in the process.

Then he too was hit, as Delatorre fired his shocker from the hatchway.

Khusaaq stumbled into the still frozen-in-place Izraad. He wrapped his arm around her and brought the gore-covered blade up against her throat as he lurched around to face his attackers just as three marines arrived and joining Delatorre, trained their shockers on him. "No... one m-moves... or s-she dies!" he stuttered as he brought Mladić's shocker to bear on Aquila. He grimaced as his body continued to violently twitch and jerk with the after-effects of the shocker hit as his ghillie suit, discharging most of the weapon's energy, shimmered and sparkled. "Y-y-ou t-too!"

Aquila held up his hands. "Okay... calm down—"

"T-tell them t-t-to... to drop their weapons—*DO IT!*" he barked and Izraad flinched and shut her eyes.

"Okay, okay... just don't hurt her," Aquila said and turned to Delatorre. "Do it."

Delatorre, keeping his eyes on Khusaaq, carefully placed his shocker on the deck and kicked it aside; his men followed suit.

"Khusaaq," Sirin pleaded as she took a step towards him. "Don't—"

"*C-chla-k-k-kaz!*"

Tasende grabbed her arm and jerked her back.

"You d-did... did... did not... think I... I would remember, d-did you?" Khusaaq sneered as he began backing unsteadily towards the flicker chamber, Izraad clumsily back-stepping alongside, the dagger pressed to her neck, just below her ear.

"Remember?" Aquila began. "I don't know what—"

"Do not p-play the f-fool with... with me!" He took another shuffling back-step towards the flickerstage. "Flick us d-d-down to the planet!"

"Sha'ashahn," Aquila tried again, "please, listen to me—"

"Flick us d-d-down, *now,* or I will k-k-kill her!"

"All right... we'll flick you down, but please, let her go."

"So you can flick me... me into a c-c-cage... or into s-space? I think not!"

"I give you my word—"

"*Tah!*" He glanced over his shoulder, assured himself the small chamber was indeed empty and began backing into it, taking Izraad with him.

"If you want a hostage take me," Sirin pleaded. *"Please—"*

"Stay where... where you are!" he snarled, pointing Mladić's shocker at her, and Tasende drew her even closer to himself in the process shielding her.

"Sha'ashahn," Aquila said, drawing his fierce glare as well as the muzzle of the shocker, "don't do this. Please, let's talk this—"

"I listened to you once—*I listened to all of you!*" His wild eyes swept the chamber, the muzzle of the shocker following his gaze. *"Never again!"*

"All right," Aquila replied in a calm voice. "We'll flick you down—"

"No tricks! I... I want to find my... myself in the midst of nowhere... no people, no soldiers... *no nothing*, do... do I make myself clear?"

Aquila's eyes darted to the flicker tech. "Do as he says."

The man didn't react, his terrified, unblinking gaze fixed on Khusaaq.

Aquila strode over to the console, gently pushed the tech aside and began tapping in a series of coordinates. "I'm flicking you down to a site in the eastern continent's tropical lowlands. There aren't any known population centers within a three hundred kilometer radius." He looked up. "Acceptable?"

Khusaaq replied with a curt nod and, "I... I know you will... will follow, so I want... want a ten minute head start."

"You can't escape."

"And you... you underestimate me, Rimmer, underestimate what A'tuu'shahn'i are capable of, and believe... believe me when I tell you, I *will* escape. Ten minutes... or she... she dies."

"Ten minutes," Aquila repeated.

"Khusaaq," Sirin said as Tasende tightened his restraining hold on her. "Don't—"

"Flick us down, *NOW!*" he barked, refusing to even look at her.

Aquila tapped in the final command. The flickerstage door closed and from within came the familiar high-pitched whine.

Amalfitano shook himself free of his own stunned paralysis, knelt beside Mladić and made the token gesture of feeling for a pulse as Aquila smacked the com-unit.

"C and C?"

Teague's voice responded, *"Control—sir, what the hell's going on—"*

"I need a full security detail ready to flick down to the planet in five minutes!"

"Sir?"

"Khusaaq just murdered Mladić! He took Izraad hostage and demanded to be flicked down to the planet. Notify the Tulians... I'm transmitting the flick-down coordinates—tell them we're dealing with the situation, tell them it was unavoidable… tell them, oh hell, Edwin, you know what to say better than me. And notify the *Walafar,* but warn them *not* to interfere—no one's to interfere—we're handling the situation. Out." Aquila blew out his cheeks then said, "What the hell set him off? And where the hell'd he get his hands that goddamned dagger—"

"Cotopaxi… prahaj," Corsali whispered as she stared down at Mladić's disemboweled corpse.

Amalfitano's eyes widened as his mind made the quick translation. "Remember—"

"Remember Cotopaxi," Corsali finished for him.

"Sir!"

Aquila turned to Delatorre to him squatting between the two *Walafar* crewmen.

"They're dead, sir."

"Dead?" Amalfitano and Aquila replied in startled unison.

Amalfitano started towards them as Delatorre rose, one of the guards' shockers in his hand. "This weapon's been modified, sir, with only one setting." He met Aquila's stare. *"Kill.* The captain's must've been as well."

Amalfitano wheeled on Aquila. "Those bastards never planned on taking him back to HQ—"

"And he must've thought we were in on the double-cross when our security…" Aquila shook his head. *"Damn it to hell!"*

The pounding echo of approaching feet drew their attention.

An instant later, six more marines arrived, only to slide to a stop as their eyes fell on Mladić's body and the surrounding pool of blood.

Aquila turned to Delatorre to find him adjusting the setting on his own shocker. "I want him taken alive, Sergeant."

"Sir?"

"Alive," Aquila repeated. "Captain Mladić wanted him dead for a reason. I want him alive to find out why. *Understood?"*

"Understood, sir."

Aquila glanced at the flicker console's chronometer. *Three minutes.*

"Robert," Amalfitano said. "I think I'd better come. If he's cornered—"

"You might be able to talk him into surrendering," Aquila finished for him as he equipped himself with a shocker and weapons belt. "Unlikely."

"But worth a try, yes? Plus I should come along just in case someone gets hurt." He gave the ring of marines a sharp stare.

Aquila gave the chronometer another glance. *Two minutes, five—*

"I request that I come along as well, sir," Sirin said.

Aquila shook his head. "No, absolutely—"

"I think it's a good idea," Amalfitano interrupted, in the process of pulling a triage kit from a locker next to the flickerstage.

"But—"

"Robert, if we can convince him to surrender and no one gets killed, the risk'll be worth it, won't it?"

One minute, ten seconds. Aquila nodded to Delatorre; the sergeant and five of his team crowded into the flickerstage, but the door remained open, awaiting his final command. Aquila then turned to Sirin. "Ensign, I really think you should remain here. In the state of mind he's in, he's capable of doing anything."

"I understand, sir. Completely. I still want to go—please."

"On one condition: you do exactly as I tell you—no arguments. Agreed?"

"Agreed, sir."

Aquila took a deep breath, held it then slowly released it. *Time's up.* He looked at Delatorre. "Go."

The flickerstage door snapped shut.

No sooner had the whine of the mechanism faded, than the door reopened and Aquila stepped into the cramped chamber. Amalfitano, Corsali and the remaining marines followed.

— ii —

Izraad kept her head bowed and her eyes shut as Khusaaq, having picked a direction purely at random, took off at a run. Now, minutes later, he continued his headlong and heedless plunge through the thick underbrush. The flick-down site was on the edge of twilight and the surrounding forest was already thick with shadows, the deep lavender sky above sprinkled with stars. Whether intentionally or not, Aquila had given him a very slight psychological advantage.

But at that moment it was his deteriorating physical and mental state that held Izraad's full attention. She felt his heart thumping wildly, heard his lungs straining in breakneck cadence with the uniform's rapidly morphing texture. His roiling thoughts were scattershot, from Sirin, Amalfitano... Matoosh... to Mladić then back to Sirin in a dizzying intermingling of scents, images and voices, while raw emotions warred with each other, running the gamut from sheer panic to the sharp bitterness of betrayal, from murderous fury to the depths of utter despair. The flood washed over her in non-stop waves to the point she found it hard to catch her own breath, and with each jarring step he took, the re-sheathed dagger's blood-sticky grip rubbed against her.

It didn't take long before the oppressive heat and tangled undergrowth began to take their toll. She measured his body's failing strength by his increasing missteps.

Finally, as he staggered into a small clearing, he caught his dragging right foot in the loop of a vine, tripped and unable to compensate, fell heavily to his knees. His face twisted in an agonized grimace and he sucked in a spasmodic gulp of air, then another as his body shivered violently.

"Sha'ashahn—"

"Be... be quiet!" he hissed through clenched teeth as his wild eyes searched the forest.

Then she heard it too: the distant cry of startled birds.

"Please, surrender, you have my word—"

"You had... had your chance... you were going to hand... hand me over to the one responsible... for the deaths of... of my friends!"

"No! That's not true—"

"And if... if you try any... of your mind tricks on me... I will... I will kill you!" He tightened his hold on her and somehow managed to lurch unsteadily to his feet.

He flicked one last glance over his shoulder, fixing the direction in his mind then favoring his right leg, he hobbled out of the clearing and back into the cover of the jungle.

— iii —

Delatorre stopped and raised his hand. Everyone clustered around him as he knelt beside the smeared imprint of a boot. Nearby was another one, and another.

He followed the trail of prints until they vanished under the heavy, damp leaf litter. "Leg's definitely slowing him down." He rose, then swept the forest with a hand scanner. He stopped and pointed. "That way, sir. Just under nineteen hundred meters."

Aquila murmured grimly, "Let's go," but before he took two steps, his tac-pac beeped softly. He yanked it from its holster, brought it to his lips and whispered, *"What?"*

"Sir," Teague's harried voice replied, *"I've got both the second in command of the* Walafar *and President Seitakap demanding to speak with you. Seitakap says it's vitally important and—"*

"Deal with 'em!" Aquila hissed and shoved the tac-pac back into its holster.

— iv —

Khusaaq staggered to a wobbly stop and heaving noisily for breath, looked around. The surrounding forest was unusually raucous and among the startled cries and calls of birds, they both heard the muffled snap of branches.

There was no need for Izraad to tell him his pursuers were gaining on him. There was no need to tell him he was physically spent. The muscles of his arms were quivering with exhaustion—his lungs were desperately straining for air. He had finally pushed his injury and fever-weakened body beyond its limit.

He loosened his hold and she slipped from his arms as he gently placed her on feet.

"Go." He motioned with his chin. "That... that... way. They... they're not... far."

She glanced back the way they'd just come and silently urged, *Hurry up!*

Hearing a twig snap underfoot, she jerked her attention back to him to see him start to stagger, to limp on, futile as it was.

Stall... just a couple of minutes. "Sha'ashahn. Listen to me... please." She managed to grab his arm and gave it a hard tug, jerking him to a stop. "Damn it! Just listen for once!"

He reluctantly met her gaze as he continued to labor for breath.

"If Captain Mladić was involved in what happened after Cotopaxi—"

"If...?" His eyes flashed. "I... I know he was. I... I was *there*. And you... you know it too."

"I suspected, *yes*, but the Coalition will—"

"Will... will do what?" he managed. "I'll tell... tell you what... your Coalition will... will do. It will do what it's... it's always done, and that's to... to cover up its crimes—"

"Not this time, I promise you."

"Tah! The... the promise of a Rimmer! That gives me... me much comfort." He yanked his arm from her grasp and took an unsteady sidestep away as he slipped his hand under his hauberk and withdrew the tac-net.

Her eyes widened as his parting words to Aquila came back to her: *Believe me when I tell you, I will escape.*

She almost smiled, watching as he stared down at the tac-net. *You had everything planned, every contingency covered, didn't you—*

He suddenly and angrily hurled the tac-net aside and she inhaled sharply as she felt a fresh surge of betrayal wash over him, betrayal now from every corner of his universe as well as the soul-suffocating sense of utter abandonment and total defeat.

Then, to her surprise—her horror—he yanked the bloody dagger from its scabbard.

Gods! She looked back the way they had just come. *Hurry!*

"*This... this was not... not what I thought... you meant,*" he whispered between gasping breaths.

"Me? I—"

"The... the Elkanasu." His slitted gaze briefly shifted to her before returning to the dagger. "They promised me... if... if I avenged Cotopaxi, they... they would set me free. I thought... I thought that meant I would have true free will, not... not *this.*" He chuckled bitterly and shook his head. "It's... it's no longer important what... what I thought, what I believed."

"Please, Khusaaq, come back with me, tell—"

"I'm tired... tired of talking. I'm... so tired of... *everything.*"

"What about the virus? Your people? What—"

"Just... just one more lie."

"*A lie?* But—"

"Another feint... another lie, one... one designed to lull me into dropping my guard, thinking... I was given asylum, promised a new life..." His strained and labored voice trailed off into a deep uncertainty and she could, literally, feel his soul ripping apart at the seams.

Then, at the very edge of her hearing, her ears picked up a faint susurration. For an instant she thought it was the breeze—but there *was* no breeze, the surrounding vegetation was perfectly still, the jungle suddenly and eerily silent.

Khusaaq too had clearly heard the soft, keening sound. He dropped his watery gaze to the dagger and whispered, *"All... lies."*

"No! That's not—"

"You knew I'd never... never agree for my own sake," he continued hoarsely and she was struck with the realization that he was not speaking to her. "So you tell me that... that without my cooperation my people will die?" He rubbed his forehead with his free hand and mumbled, "All lies... even from you, Siah'ushu," as tears rolled down his gaunt cheeks. "Your punishment... for my failures, for not—"

"What about Matoosh?" Izraad took a step closer, hoping he was so preoccupied, so caught up in his roiling thoughts, his soul-deep agony that he wouldn't notice that she'd begun to exude a sedating pheromone, its faint, sweet scent lost within the damp, earthy smells of the forest and the heady perfume of night-blooming flowers. "And what about those left behind on Rasal Ghul? They're all going to need you, now more than ever."

He winced and as he squeezed his eyes shut, forcing out more tears, she caught just a glimpse of a face... not Matoosh's—Khusaaq's... but much, much younger, very angry, yelling and gesturing wildly... a name... *Qar'qaah.* Then the face was gone, swept away, lost to the dizzying whirlpool of anguish and guilt and most of all the crushing sense of abandonment that was about to drown him.

"And what about Sirin?" she asked softly and as he looked sidelong at her, she saw the flicker of hesitation in his pale, watery and torment-filled eyes.

He took several deep, unsteady breaths, unintentionally inhaling more of the pheromone.

She heard his raspy breathing slow, ever so slightly; she sensed his exhausted body quickly succumbing to it. She glanced around her. *Hurry up! I can't—*

Suddenly he began to sway and the dagger slipped from his loosening fingers and fell to the moist earth at his feet with a soft *thud.*

He made no effort to retrieve it and for an instant she thought the battle was won—but it was only an instant—until he somehow managed to yank Mladić's shocker from his belt as he took a stumbling, drunken step away from her—away from the dagger.

"You're in love with her and she's in love with you!"

He took another, ragged breath, and as he raised the shocker's muzzle to his temple the keening sounds turned an undulating wail.

"If you're uncertain about everything else," she pleaded, "be certain of that!"

"It's too... too late—"

"No! It's not too late! You can still choose to come back with me—*please,* Khusaaq. Don't do this! *You don't have to do this!"*

The hand holding the shocker quavered, ever-so-slightly. He squeezed his eyes shut, struggling to keep his grip and whispered, *"Tell Sirin—"*

He never finished; hit with the combined force of ten shocker beams, he was lifted bodily and hurled backwards, into the trunk of a large tree.

His head struck it with a dull *thwack* and the impact sent the shocker flying from his hand. He then slid down the tree to end up in a twisted heap at its base.

Delatorre stepped out from the underbrush, shocker drawn and pointed at Khusaaq's unmoving body. He strode past Izraad and over to him, snatching up the fallen shocker as he went then he cautiously prodded Khusaaq with the toe of his grip-boot.

Getting no response, he then gave the weapon a glance, grumbled disgustedly, "As I thought," and stuffed in his waistband. He then knelt, and despite the ghillie suit still morphing madly and now sparkling with the discharge of energy, he warily but thoroughly patted Khusaaq down for more, hidden weapons.

Finally satisfied that he was unarmed, Delatorre rose and looked around. "All clear."

Aquila, Amalfitano, Sirin, along with the rest of the security detail emerged from the forest.

Amalfitano hurried to Izraad and looked her up and down. Her face, throat and uniform top were smeared with blood. "Did he hurt you—"

"I'm fine," she murmured as she wiped a sweat-damp lock of hair from her face. Noticing the red stains on her sleeve, she murmured, "It's Mladić's."

Amalfitano smiled a relieved smile, gave her elbow a squeeze, then pushed his way through the ring of marines and over to Khusaaq. He knelt beside him and gave him a quick once over with his eyes. Khusaaq looked every bit the rag doll that had been carelessly tossed aside: arms and legs sprawled every which way, head lolling to one side and mouth agape.

With a sigh and a shake of his head, Amalfitano placed the field kit on Khusaaq's stomach, opened it and began sorting through his stock.

"Well?" Aquila asked as he, Izraad and Sirin clustered around him.

Amalfitano looked up from loading a ject-it. "Out cold." He pressed the tool against Khusaaq's neck as Sirin knelt beside Khusaaq's left hip and Izraad next to Amalfitano. "And this'll guarantee he stays that way till we can get him back to the *Baidarka*—"

"Not so fast."

Heads snapped up and eyes turned towards the unfamiliar voice just as a woman wearing Coalition Intelligence grays stepped into the small clearing. Three men, also wearing gray jumpsuits followed and quickly fanned out. All were carrying shocker rifles, their weapons trained on Aquila and the others.

"Who the hell are you?" Aquila snarled.

"I'm Lieutenant Hosatu of the *Walafar*—"

"I gave strict orders that your crew was not to—"

"You haven't the authority to order us to do anything, Commander. Now, hand over the merc—"

"We're not handing anyone over to anyone, Lieutenant. Least of all to you."

"It was not a request, Commander. You're surrounded, outnumbered two to one."

"I only see you and three others. I think that means we outnumber you."

"Are you so sure?" To emphasis the point, she looked around, and in response they all heard movement within the surrounding underbrush.

"Now," Hosatu said, turning back to him, "let's be reasonable. Hand over the prisoner or—"

"You'll kill us too?" Aquila said, placing himself between her and Khusaaq.

"Kill you?" Hosatu feigned surprise. "Of course not! We're all on the same side, Commander."

"Are we?" he replied defiantly as he crossed his arms.

"Well, let's just say I know where my loyalties lie—and it *isn't* with the Orthodoxy."

"It doesn't appear to be with the Coalition, either."

"I'm not the one who aided and abetted the escape of a merc prisoner who'd just murdered three of *our* people in cold blood, Commander, so I'd be very careful with your accusations."

Sirin, keeping her eyes on Hosatu, whispered to Amalfitano, *"You can't let them take him."*

He looked at her then Izraad as he selected a new ject-it and vial from the kit. Izraad replied with a slight, albeit reluctant nod before giving Sirin a sidelong glance. Sirin entwined her fingers with Khusaaq's, then biting her lip, met Amalfitano's covert stare and, like Izraad, nodded.

Amalfitano slipped the vial into the ject-it, double checked the dose then palming the small device, positioned it close to Khusaaq's carotid artery, concealing the movement behind a casual check of his pulse.

"Come, Commander," Hosatu said, oblivious to the exchange. "Don't make it worse for yourself. Hand over the merc, voluntarily, and I'll make sure the proper authorities are made aware of your cooperation—"

"Sir!" Delatorre's startled gasp drew everyone's gaze. "I'm picking up on a lot of low-level interference. Varying from one point three to one point six gigahertz…"

Everyone looked around, weapons turning outward.

"Pinpoint," Aquila snapped.

Delatorre made a slow sweep with the scanner and managed a very sickly smile as he looked back at him. "All around us, sir."

"What kind of trick is this?" Hosatu snarled, wheeling on Aquila, her shocker aimed at his chest.

"I was about to ask you the same thing."

Izraad, still kneeling beside Amalfitano, felt her skin begin to crawl: the darkening forest had taken on a curious shimmer, all too reminiscent, she realized to her growing dismay, of the infamous Cotopaxi vid.

"Gods," Amalfitano whispered as he too made the connection and instinctively placed a protective hand on Khusaaq's barely moving chest while keeping the other pressed to his throat.

"Put down your weapons!" a deep voice boomed, seemingly from their midst.

Izraad squinted into the gloom.

A ghostly figure appeared and started towards Hosatu, faintly visible only by its liquid-like movement.

Behind it, in fact everywhere she looked, more shadowy shapes had begun to emerge from the encircling jungle as if the trees themselves were shape-shifters.

When no one moved, the voice repeated ominously, "Lay down your weapons… *now,* and no harm will come to you."

Aquila jerked his eyes off eerily glimmering forest and turned to Delatorre. "Do it." He tossed his shocker aside. *"All of you!"*

Delatorre nodded to his men and they each squatted and placed their shockers on the ground, then rose, slowly, holding their now empty hands above their heads.

Hosatu and her companions kept their rifles trained on the forest. She risked a sidelong glance at Aquila. "I don't know what the hell kind of game you think you're playing—"

"I'm not playing any kind of game, and I doubt he is, either."

"He?" Hosatu's eyes widened as a massive Hahtooshan in full battle panoply solidified next to Aquila.

Then, one by one, and then rapidly in twos and threes and fours, more Hahtooshans appeared, as if precipitating out of the humid air, their body armor a now all too familiar iridescent black which glittered and shimmered ominously in the waning light of dusk.

Izraad lost count after forty. She flicked Amalfitano a sidelong glance, caught an odd look in his eye and looked down to see that the ject-it was still cupped in his palm and his hand was still pressed to Khusaaq's throat.

"Commander Aquila?" the Hahtooshan asked as he stepped back, and at Aquila's slight nod, the soldier added, "Narbrooi Hahtra'tzrhi, of the Orthodoxy destroyer, *Faridour.*"

"*Faridour...?*" Hosatu hissed. "But... that can't be!"

"You thought we'd all be dead by now, yes?"

She tore her eyes off the expressionless but nevertheless deeply menacing visage of his blast visor and looked past him, to the surrounding jungle.

"Hoping for rescue?" the merc added.

She pulled her tac-pac from its holster and brought it to her lips; he made no move to stop her. "*Walafar*, respond!" Answered only by the pulsing whine of interference, she tried again, this time bellowing into the tac-pac, "*WALAFAR!*"

"I believe they're a little preoccupied right now." The Hahtooshan tilted his helmeted head back, his blast visor facing skyward.

Izraad, like everyone else, couldn't help but follow his lead and look up.

As if on cue, they all saw a faint burst of light that rapidly expanded outwards and quickly faded into the deep lavender and star-dotted evening sky.

"*Walafar,*" the mercenary announced, drawing their astounded, turning to horrified stares. "And now... to finish the job." He raised his pistol and squeezed the trigger, vaporizing Hosatu, then each of her equally stunned companions in quick succession.

He reholstered the weapon and turned to a wide-eyed Aquila. "I suggest you contact your ship, Commander, and order them not to do anything... foolish."

Aquila managed a wordless nod and started to pull his tac-pac from its holster.

The Hahtooshan clicked his tongue and pulled his tac-net from his weapons belt, adjusted the settings, then offered it to him. "Please, Commander, be my guest. I've set it to the correct frequency."

Aquila, after an instant's hesitation, plucked the strange device from the massive soldier's equally massive, gauntleted palm and brought it close to his face. His eyes remained fixed on the Hahtooshan's blast visor which was only slightly less unnerving than the mercenary's eerie, undulating and shimmering ghillie armor. He swallowed, hard, licked his lips then began, *"Baidarka,* this is Aquila. *Baidarka,* respond—"

"Commander!" came Teague's harried but clearly very relieved voice. *"Are you all right?"*

"Yeah. We're all okay—"

"Sir, a Hahtooshan warship just destroyed the Walafar—"

"I know—"

"And sensors have detected Hahtooshan interference patterns all around you—"

"Actually… right in front of me."

There was a pause then Teague replied slowly, *"Right... in... front... of... you?"*

"Yes. I have Narbrooi Hahtra'tzrhi of the Orthodoxy destroyer *Faridour,* standing here in front of me, along with at least fifty Hahtooshan troopers—"

"One hundred and twenty," Narbrooi shrugged, "but who's counting? Now, as long as you and your ship make no hostile moves," he continued, loud enough for Teague to overhear, "you and it are in no danger. Our dispute was with *Walafar.*" At his nod two Hahtooshans separated themselves from the rest and, removing their helmets, walked over to where Khusaaq lay as Delatorre and his marines wisely and hastily gave way.

Izraad slowly got to her feet and also backed a short distance away, but Sirin and Amalfitano stubbornly remained where they were as the Hahtooshan medics squatted on either side of Corsali, then, with the occasional, uneasy sidelong glance at her, began their own exam.

Narbrooi gave them a moment, then stepping closer, asked, "Murh'sooli, kuuthok-sseh?"

One of the medics looked up. "Paq, ta'ahn, tuu'baqh—"

"He was going to kill himself," Amalfitano interrupted, looking first up at the faceless Narbrooi, then at his Hahtooshan counterparts. "He's just been—"

"Wake him up," Narbrooi growled.

The medic who'd spoken briefly dropped his gaze to Amalfitano and in that instant the two shared the simple, universal frustration all military medical personnel have with non-medical superior officers.

Amalfitano knew the medic would not dare to question the order, but he was under no such constraints. "I think it would be best—"

"I was *not* speaking to you, Doctor." Point made, he turned to Aquila. "We've been monitoring your transmissions for several days, Commander. It would seem that we owe you, your crew and in particular, Doctor Amalfitano a debt of gratitude."

Amalfitano's eyes widened. "So it was your ship that was sent to pick up—"

"Yes."

"Then you still have the others onboard..." Amalfitano leapt to his feet, oblivious to the dozens of maser pistols that had suddenly come to bear on him. "You've got to isolate them immediately! They're highly infectious—"

"I know," Narbrooi said calmly. "Or, should I say, I know now."

"You mean your crew is sick."

"Not all, but some, yes. Sha'ashahn managed to warn us, but not quite in time—"

"We know what to do." With that Amalfitano walked over to Aquila, grabbed his hand and spoke into the alien tac-net, "Edwin, tell Xosé to get started replicating tammanadine as fast as he can." He looked up at the visor-faced mercenary. "We can supply you with enough to treat your entire crew—how many?"

"Twenty thousand."

Amalfitano blinked, mouthed, *Twenty thousand?* and by his expression was privately begging his knees not to fail him, then continued a little unsteadily, "Ah... okay, well...uh, that might take a little time, but we can start with those infected—"

The Hahtooshan looked past him. "Murh'sooli, chu-sseh'teh?"

The medic, who, along with his companion was in the process of helping a very unsteady Khusaaq to sit up, replied, "Dschin tan-t'ajis, ta'ahn."

"Four hundred and fifty-seven—at last count," the mercenary officer translated as he turned back to Amalfitano.

"Okay," Amalfitano breathed an audible sigh of relief. "We can supply that amount in a matter of a few hours. And I'll have my staff transmit all of the data we have along with the treatment protocols."

"Most acceptable." The Hahtooshan motioned for another trooper to step away from his companions, said, "Assist the doctor," then he turned his attention back on Khusaaq, who was now on his feet, but only with the help of the medics.

The officer slipped off his helmet, tossed it to a nearby soldier and walked over to Khusaaq. He looked up him and down, then motioned to the medics to let go of him and growled in Standard, "What do you have to say for yourself?"

Khusaaq only stared back at him, clearly having to put his full concentration into keeping on his feet as his support was hastily withdrawn.

"Well?"

"You... you c-c-certainly... t-t-took your time g-g-getting here," he managed in a hoarse, slightly slurred, stuttering voice. "I was b-b-beginning to... to think—"

"Satshah!" Narbrooi grabbed him by the bandoleer and gave him a vicious shake, enough to knock Khusaaq's rubbery legs out from under him, followed by a back-handed slap across the face that sent his head snapping back.

"STOP IT!" Sirin snarled.

To everyone's surprise, the officer immediately let go and Khusaaq sat down, hard.

He groaned, dropped his head into his hands and slowly toppled onto his side.

Sirin rushed to him and knelt, placing herself between Khusaaq and the officer then looked up at the Hahtooshan with a defiant glare as she placed her hand on Khusaaq's shoulder, offering both comfort and a challenge.

"Who *is* this?" the mercenary growled, turning his startled turning to very unhappy gaze on Aquila as if to affix blame as well while accepting Khusaaq's recovered dagger and tac-net from a trooper.

Before Aquila could reply, Khusaaq answered in a husky, albeit stuttering voice, "I'm h-h-honored to say s-s-she's my wife, Hahtra'tzrhi," as he managed, with Sirin's help, to push himself back into a seated position. He worked his jaw, then sniffing, wiped his profusely bleeding nose and lip.

The Hahtooshan stared at the unassuming yet brazenly insolent Sirin for a moment then looked down at the dagger he held and growled, "Then you'll no longer be needing this, will you?"

Khusaaq met the officer's gaze and replied simply, "No, ta'ahn, I... I won't. The... the Elkanasu have released me from... all vows."

The Hahtooshan blinked, repeated, *"Released you...?"* clearly taken aback, then quickly recovering—at least superficially—shoved the dagger into his weapons belt and turned and looked past Aquila and Amalfitano. "You can come out now, Mister President."

There was a rustle of vegetation, and a group of troopers deferentially parted to allow Seitakap to step into the clearing.

"Mister President...!" Aquila gasped. "What—"

"No need for concern, Commander," he said as he came abreast of the Hahtooshan officer; he smiled and nodded to his taller, heavier companion as if the two were age-old friends. "Everything's quite under control."

"Under control...?" Aquila replied, dumbfounded. "But—"

"Yes, Commander," Seitakap added with a slightly reproachful smile. "Had you heeded my call earlier I would have told you that the Tulian High Council had just entered into a contract with Narbrooi Hahtra'tzrhi, and that upon learning of the situation—"

"I offered my assistance in ending this... deeply regrettable hostage matter," Narbrooi ended for him.

"But," Aquila said. "I mean when—"

"We've been in high level discussion with Narbrooi Hahtra'tzrhi for the past day," Seitakap explained. "You see, Commander, we took to heart the lesson learned about our total lack of defense and our naïveté that we were somehow immune to all the troubles that surround us. We all felt that in light of the rapidly deteriorating situation between your Coalition and the Matarrans, not to mention the potential of violence between the Coalition and the Orthodoxy, we should rectify that oversight."

"By aligning yourself with the Orthodoxy," Aquila replied, still flabbergasted and just as clearly appalled, then realized he'd said it out loud and in a tone that left nothing to the imagination.

Fortunately, the Hahtooshan didn't take offense. "In payment for our... protection, Commander," he said evenly and Aquila's eyes slid back to the imposing mercenary, "the Tulian government has offered to put at our disposal their research and medical facilities in order to develop an A'tuu'shahn-specific vaccine—just in case your Coalition is unable to create one in a... *timely fashion."* His gray eyes sparkled maliciously; point made, he turned to Seitakap. "As agreed, Mister President, Sha'ashahn is yours now. And…" He squinted in distaste at Sirin as she helped Khusaaq back to his feet, *"Hers."*

"Yours?" Aquila asked, also turning to Seitakap.

"Part of the contract, Commander," the man replied enthusiastically, "The council felt that, in light of the sacrifices he made for us, the least we could do is offer him sanctuary here, but—"

"A'tuu'shahn'i do not ask for, nor expect sanctuary," Narbrooi growled as his pale eyes flicked to Khusaaq before returning to Aquila, "or asylum—"

"So we bought his services," Seitakap added quickly, "as we're clearly in need of an advanced communications system."

"Of course," Aquila nodded. "As a signals specialist—"

"Sha'ashahn has the knowledge and expertise we desperately need," Seitakap ended for him. "Narbrooi Hahtra'tzrhi agreed, on one condition: that he would personally mete out punishment for disobeying a direct order, but it would not in any way affect Sha'ashahn's abilities to fulfill his service agreement."

"Direct order?" Aquila asked, turning to Narbrooi.

The mercenary smiled, not a pleasant smile, not at all. "Ambushing and killing you."

Aquila's eyes widened and his mouth formed a silent 'O'.

"It does solve our problem, Commander," Izraad said. "And, assuming that our shore leave isn't revoked by the Central Committee, and of course if our continued presence is acceptable to Hahtra'tzrhi…"

The officer nodded and murmured, "Of course, Lieutenant—your presence and assistance is most welcome."

"…we can work here every bit as well as we could work on Mirfak."

"In fact better," Amalfitano added, looking at Narbrooi. "With the willing cooperation of your medical staff and crew."

"You will have it, Doctor." Narbrooi then fixed his now hard stare on Khusaaq. "Let this be a lesson to you, Sha'ashahn… do not be too hasty in assuming the absolute worst of people, be it Rimmer, A'tuu'shahn... or even the flawed Hero of Cotopaxi."

Khusaaq, to Izraad's surprise, looked aptly embarrassed, as he dipped his head and murmured, *"Yes, ta'ahn."* Whether it was over his own rash actions or the public rebuke they garnered, it was hard to tell. Then she realized it didn't matter. *Maybe there's hope for you yet.*

Aquila shifted uncomfortably, cleared his throat then said, "If you will excuse us, Mister President, Hahtra'tzrhi, my crew and I must return to the *Baidarka*. I need to apprise HQ of..." he couldn't help but briefly glance skywards, "...developments."

"Of course, Commander," Narbrooi replied. "I believe your HQ has some developments they need to apprise you of as well."

Aquila gave the mercenary a worried look, to which Narbrooi only smiled, a decidedly sphinx-like smile.

Narbrooi turned to Seitakap, motioned to the ring of soldiers. "I'll be flicking down more troops within the hour, Mister President, as agreed."

"More?" Aquila couldn't help but ask as he eyed the thick wall of armored mercenaries that completely surrounded them.

"Yes, as part of our agreement," Seitakap replied. "To protect the planet's vital infrastructure, as Hahtra'tzrhi felt it only prudent and the High Council heartily agreed."

"Oh," Aquila replied. "Yes, well..."

"And once you've made your report to your headquarters," Seitakap continued, "perhaps I can twist your arm into joining the High Council and myself in a late supper?" He glanced at Narbrooi, then back at Aquila. "Hahtra'tzrhi and his top officers have already accepted, a way to cement the contract. I do hope you and yours can tear yourselves away from official duties as well?"

Aquila nodded, albeit hesitantly. "Of course, we'd be honored, Mister President, thank you."

"Excellent!" Narbrooi said. "It will give us a chance speak further—"

"Not *all* business, Hahtra'tzrhi," Seitakap chided softly. "Commander Aquila and his crew are in dire need of shedding their official duties as soon as possible in preference for shore leave, isn't that right, Commander?"

Before Aquila could answer, Narbrooi replied, unoffended, "Oh, yes, most definitely," then he grinned at Aquila's glancing, uneasy preoccupation with the surrounding ring of soldiers. He gestured to the troopers and as they quickly and silently melted back into the darkness, he added, "Rest assured, Commander, you and your crew won't even know we're here."

Chapter 30

Aquila leaned back into his chair, propped his grip-booted feet on Amalfitano's desk and stared contentedly at the glass of exquisitely aged whisky he cradled in his hands. "This sure has been one hell of a day."

Izraad, curled up in another chair, chuckled. "You could say that again."

Amalfitano, in the process of pouring himself a glass of his very best, smiled. "Must say, as delicious as that dinner was, it's good to be home again. I'm *bushed.*"

Aquila eyed him. "I assume that means you're going to withdraw your request for transfer?"

Amalfitano stopped in mid-pour. "Oh. That."

"Yeah. *That.*"

"Consider it done." Amalfitano shot Izraad a sidelong glance as he stoppered the decanter and set it on his desk, then he swirled the amber contents around in the glass. "So, Mladić and his buddies were indeed in cahoots with some radical colonial faction?"

"That's what Admiral Keon told me," Aquila answered. "Turns out, Hahtooshan skills at eavesdropping on secure channels are a lot more at advanced than we ever thought possible—a *helluva* lot more advanced."

Amalfitano arched a brow.

"Mladić and Hosatu would be facing charges of high treason right now, if—"

"They weren't already dead," Amalfitano finished for him.

"Yeah. But based on the evidence Narbrooi turned over to Admiral Keon, there are still a lot of people out there who're going to have a lot of explaining to do—people in high places."

"How high?" Amalfitano asked, eyes darting between Izraad and Aquila.

"Members of the select commission of the Central Committee itself," Izraad answered. "Mladić was telling the truth when he said Senator Behardien had overridden Keon's orders for the four of us to accompany Khusaaq aboard the *Walafar*—unbeknownst to Keon or his immediate staff by the way."

Amalfitano's eyes widened.

"She's already in custody," Aquila said, "as are a number of others. There are a lot more out there—this was a widespread and well-organized conspiracy, clearly going back years, decades in fact—but now we have a good idea who the rest are, and where to find them."

"Thanks to the Hahtooshans," Amalfitano said.

Aquila nodded, took a gulp of his whisky then grinned. "Gildun used to say 'there is only one thing more useful in politics than having the right friends and that's having the right enemies.' But I doubt even she could have ever foreseen this."

Amalfitano smiled, murmured, "Or meant it that way, but... I get your point."

"Speaking of," Aquila dropped his feet to the floor, straightened up in his chair and looked around, "Where *is* our Hahtooshan? I haven't seen hide nor hair of him since you insisted he be flicked back up—"

"I wanted to make damned sure he hadn't finally succeeded in busting that amazingly rock-hard head of his."

"And...?"

"He's with Sirin... in her cabin." Amalfitano took a measured sip of whisky before adding, "I did warn her to believe him if he said he had a headache."

Aquila chuckled then began to laugh, a full-bellied, soul-clearing laugh.

Amalfitano grinned broadly then suddenly sobering, stared down at his glass. "You know, something's been niggling at me..."

"Just one thing?" Aquila asked as he brought his glass to his lips.

"Okay, a lot of things, but topmost: why was Khusaaq so important to Mladić and the others? It wasn't just because he was the first high-ranking Hahtooshan—the first Hahtooshan period to be taken captive, was it?"

Aquila shook his head. "No."

"Then...?"

"They thought he knew something about Cotopaxi, something Behardien, Mladić and their cronies didn't want to ever get out. They had assumed—hell, we'd all assumed—there were no survivors from Cotopaxi, and yes," he nodded to Izraad, "Mladić was at the awards ceremony, was in fact the one who handed Khusaaq a booby-trapped pay packet, which exploded—"

"So not pilot error," Amalfitano interrupted.

"No. Premeditated murder. But then, when we discovered that there was at least one survivor, they had to—"

"Finish the job," Amalfitano growled, "before Intelligence could mind-strip Khusaaq, or he voluntarily told us and whatever this dark secret of theirs was revealed."

"Yeah."

"But the Hahtooshans had to have known that pay packet was booby-trapped—Khusaaq certainly would have told them. Why didn't they retaliate?"

Aquila took another sip before replying, "You'll have to ask one. In fact Narbrooi's waiting for your call."

Amalfitano's eyes widened and he swallowed convulsively.

Aquila chuckled. "Just joking."

Amalfitano took a hasty sip of his whisky, then said, "Yeah, well, to be honest I'm not sure I want to know the answer. But... well, do we know what it was that Khusaaq knew that was so damaging they wanted him dead?"

"Not yet, but I'm sure that's the first thing Intelligence is gonna be asking Behardien."

"Wouldn't want to be her," Amalfitano muttered.

Izraad nodded, "I agree with you—I wouldn't want to be her, either. No way in hell."

Amalfitano settled back in his chair, chewed on what Aquila said, then asked, "Why didn't Mladić just take Khusaaq with him the first time? We couldn't have stopped him, and if his intention was to silence him once and for all—"

"Why take the risk?" Izraad asked.

"Risk?" Amalfitano replied.

"Of being discovered. You told Mladić the odds were greatly against Khusaaq surviving—"

"I lied... well, not exactly. I exaggerated."

"I know. And it worked. He believed you and weighed the benefits verses the losses and decided it would look a lot less suspicious if Khusaaq died under your care, rather than his—questions would be asked. But when Khusaaq recovered, well… that changed everything. And it wasn't just 'convenient' that *Walafar* was the closest ship, and so the logical one to come collect him, any more than it was coincidence that *Walafar* was dispatched in the first place—"

"Behardien," Amalfitano interrupted.

"Yup," Izraad answered, "She and Mladić and their followers had every possibility, every contingency planned for—well, *almost* every one."

Amalfitano nodded distractedly as he chewed on his lip, then said, "That just leaves one major mystery: who contracted the Hahtooshans' services in the first place, to recover the virus?"

"The Matarrans," Aquila replied, then took a deep, wincing gulp from his glass.

Amalfitano blinked. "How—"

"If you hadn't been so busy chatting up the *Faridour*'s CMO," Izraad interrupted, eyeing him, "you might have learned a few things."

"I wasn't 'chatting her up'—she's a Hahtooshan for gods' sakes. We were talking shop."

"Uh-huh," Izraad replied.

Amalfitano ignored the remark, leaned forward and asked eagerly, "So, what did I miss?"

"A lot," Izraad replied. "For starters, Narbrooi isn't just the captain of a destroyer. He's a Hahtra'tzrhi, a *fleet admiral*." She then turned her pointed stare on Aquila.

"And?" Amalfitano asked, eyebrows raised in begging interest.

"I figured if anyone would know," Aquila replied, "he would. So I asked him."

"You… *asked* him?" Amalfitano replied, staggered. "A Hahtooshan *fleet* admiral."

"Yup."

Amalfitano laughed then added, "Gildun always said you had brass balls."

"I figured what the hell," Aquila shrugged, feigning nonchalance. "And that's not all he told me—told us," he added with a sidelong look at Izraad.

"Like what?" Amalfitano asked, his eyes darting between the two.

"Well, for one thing… those ritual daggers," Izraad began.

"What about 'em?"

"They're *sentient.*"

Amalfitano looked down at his hands as he remembered the odd sensations he'd felt when he'd briefly held Khusaaq's *athamé.* "That's a hell of thing."

"Tell me about it," Izraad grumbled as she absently wiped her palms on her uniform. "According to Narbrooi, they're the embodiment of the Elkanasu—and in case you didn't happen to notice, Narbrooi's Elkanaghalli too, which kinda explains why he was more than a tad ticked off at Khusaaq, even more so when Khusaaq told him Sirin's his wife."

Amalfitano rolled his eyes. "I'm surprised he didn't vaporize them on the spot like he did Hosatu."

Izraad nodded, "I'm sure he wanted to, but you see, Khusaaq is… well, I guess the best description is a cultural, and in particular, an Elkanaghalli icon, the Hero of—"

"Of Cotopaxi, yeah," Amalfitano finished for her. "But Khusaaq told me that the title wasn't an honor by any means, but rather an insult."

"It was an insult from the likes of Tarqk, who was from a rival clan, the Khighalli, and clearly Narbrooi bears some personal antipathy against Khusaaq that far predates this whole matter—what that is, only Narbrooi or Khusaaq can say, but no, to most Hahtooshans, Khusaaq is, well, a celebrity of sorts, just a very reluctant one. According to Narbrooi, Khusaaq always had his choice of plum assignments, and always refused, seeking no special treatment and strenuously rebuffing any recognition when offered. Same was true of the other survivor—there were in fact two survivors of the Cotopaxi award ceremony—an officer by the name of Sahr'qharubi ket Rasharawan'tischinjgra whom I verified was one of the five listed as attending the Cotopaxi ceremony and who, by sad coincidence, happened to be the second in command of *Makhaira.*"

"Not coincidence," Aquila corrected, "According to Narbrooi, the two were not only very close friends, but close kinsman and as such could and usually did choose to serve together—a not uncommon occurrence, especially among certain very old Elkanaghalli families—the Tischinjgra line being one of the very oldest—and this other Hahtooshan, again per Narbrooi, shared

Khusaaq's attitude towards fame. Neither took advantage, in fact both seemed intensely uncomfortable with the whole idea."

"Which could explain the animosity, both by Tarqk and this Narbrooi chap," Amalfitano countered. "People as a rule like their heroes humble but not ungrateful—the military especially so."

"You can bet Narbrooi, if he'd been given these laurels, wouldn't have shied away from them, not at all," Izraad said. "He quite likes the limelight."

"When I asked Khusaaq about it," Amalfitano replied, staring down at his glass, "why he hid the commendation like that, he said something to the effect that he considered it a consolation prize... for *not* dying at Cotopaxi, although there was clearly more to it than that. A hell of a lot more."

Izraad began, "He..." then stopped and started again, "Something terrible happened on Cotopaxi, something he witnessed, perhaps something he took an active part in, maybe even ordered. I sensed it during the mind-strip—"

"Care to enlighten us as to what that was?" Amalfitano, in truth was not really sure he wanted to know. He'd come to look upon Khusaaq as a son, no longer saw him as a Hahtooshan and all that implied, but that didn't mean Khusaaq had suddenly stopped being a Hahtooshan—a merc.

"I wish I could, William, as I think it might be key to why Behardien and Mladić wanted him dead—but it wasn't what I was looking for at the time, and time was of the essence, so I didn't pursue it. But he's clearly still suffering, psychologically, from what happened all those years ago, what he was forced to do, to keep his men, keep the colonists alive. I believe that's part of the reason he's kept a low profile, why he surrounded himself with his kinsmen—especially one who was there with him, providing mutual support for this shared, unresolved psychological trauma. He was, what, only fifteen at the time? Even taking into account Hahtooshans maturing much faster than us, that's still a lot to place on a fifteen year old."

"And now that kinsman is dead," Amalfitano replied then took a sip of whisky.

"And as a direct result of Khusaaq's actions," she said.

He exhaled, shook his head then took another deep gulp from his glass.

"And something else," Aquila said.

Amalfitano raised his brows.

"Hahtooshans know who and what they are—not just Khusaaq."

"You mean that they're descended from Neanderthals," Amalfitano replied.

Aquila nodded. "Yeah. And remember that friend at HQ, and the rumor the Hahtooshans were in discussions with the Coalition Central Committee? Everyone assumed they were negotiating a payoff. Turns out that's what everyone was *supposed* to think, especially the Matarrans…"

Amalfitano took several deep gulps of his whisky, anticipating the need for fortification.

"…in fact they were negotiating a *mutual defense treaty*."

Amalfitano choked on his last mouthful, coughed again, then wiping his lips, managed a hoarse, *"What…?"*

"We're now allies," Izraad said simply, then laughed at his open-mouthed reaction. "Brothers in arms—in more ways than one."

Aquila nodded. "Narbrooi even offered up his flotilla's accompanying space dock and its crew to repair the *Baidarka*. Said it was the least he could do since some of the damage was inflicted by Hahtooshans. I told him I'd have to get the okay from HQ, but… well, all I can say is… *wow.*"

Amalfitano chewed on that for a moment. "That's certainly going to put a crimp in any plans of the Matarrans to start another war."

"You could say that again." Aquila lifted his glass and peered at its contents. "It also might explain why Behardien and Mladić felt it necessary to risk exposing themselves by Behardien overriding Keon—"

"Yeah," Amalfitano said. "Having the Hero of Cotopaxi die at the hands of Coalition Intelligence within days of signing a mutual defense treaty could, and likely would give the Hahtooshans reasons to reconsider."

Aquila smiled a decidedly smug smile. "And that's not all. Turns out Khusaaq and I were right all along. The base? It *was* a baited trap…"

Izraad said, "It now appears that the Matarrans did indeed know ahead of time that the virus posed an even greater threat to the

Hahtooshans than to us—the classic win-win scenario, for the Matarrans."

"Which means they know the Hahtooshans are human, too," Amalfitano replied.

"Yes," Aquila said. "Narbrooi said a Hahtooshan ship on a routine surveying contract disappeared without a trace a little over a year ago—now, for us this isn't exactly unheard of, take the *Herrick*—just the latest in a long line of mysterious disappearances. But to the Hahtooshans it was an unprecedented event. Their ships are... well, they're not exactly sentient like the daggers, but close. He tried to explain to me but to be honest I couldn't follow the combination of technological jargon and religious mumbo-jumbo—to be honest, I'm not sure I believed half what he was telling me—"

"But he does, so do all Hahtooshans," Izraad interjected softly but pointedly. "It is at the very core—*is* the very core—of their culture, their belief system."

He took heed of her subtle warning with a nod then continued, "Suffice it to say, the ship just... *vanished*," he snapped his fingers, "like that, no warning and without a trace, taking with it a crew of fifteen."

"And the Orthodoxy thinks the Matarrans had a hand in it? They somehow got their hands on the crew and discovered what and who they really were?"

Aquila shrugged. "Narbrooi did say Hahtooshans *never* leave their dead behind—by the way, he said their armor self-destructs when it senses the wearer is very close to death and with no Hahtooshan medical care nearby, or dead, leaving no biological residue—"

"Well, that's good to know," Amalfitano muttered.

"—and for good reason. By keeping such tight wraps on who they really are served a lot of purposes. He also said at the time he never would've suspected the Matarrans. The ship's last known location was on the far side of the rim, at the end of the Dubhe arm—about as far from Matarran-held space as you can get—mapping a potentially habitable star systems for a client. And reasonably there was no connection made when about a month ago an unidentified, third-party consortium came to the Orthodoxy with a very lucrative contract offer..."

"Unidentified? You mean they had no idea who they were dealing with?"

"It's not unheard of, according to Narbrooi," Izraad said, "for the Orthodoxy to accept contracts from parties who wish to keep their true identities—and motives—hidden. Their business philosophy is pay them enough and they won't ask any pesky little questions. But then a week or so ago the Hahtooshans started picking up chatter from the Matarrans, chatter that mentioned that missing ship. So, it would appear that the Matarrans took advantage of this 'don't ask any questions' policy to send the Hahtooshans off to recover a virus the Matarrans knew damned well would prove fatal to the Hahtooshans if they, like Pandora, opened the box."

"Cute," Amalfitano muttered before he took another gulp of whisky.

"Clearly the Matarrans didn't want to be fighting on two fronts either," Aquila continued, "they wanted to eliminate the Hahtooshan threat once and for all before launching an attack on the Coalition—"

"And if they could get the Hahtooshans and Coalition to go for each other's throats," Amalfitano interrupted, "all the better—with Behardien and Mladić playing right into their hands."

"Yup. Assuming they weren't in cahoots with the Matarrans from the get go."

Amalfitano whispered, *"You don't think..."*

Aquila shrugged, took a sip from his glass then added, "I guess we'll find out soon enough. But this also could also explain why the Hahtooshans were suddenly willing to agree to a mutual defense treaty—the cat is out of the bag, so to speak."

"Yeah." Amalfitano blew out his cheeks, too a deep swig of whisky, then said, "I've spent my entire adult life hating Hahtooshans, hating everything they represent and blaming them for every terrible thing—"

"So have a lot of other people," Izraad replied, "like the vast majority of the Coalition."

He looked sidelong at her. "So how do you change that? How do you stop hating? You can't just... *stop.*"

"You did," she answered simply, "when you saw them for who and what they really are, not as we all imagined. There's hope, Will. It won't be easy, and both sides have a lot of distrust and yes, hatred to overcome, but... as that old saying goes, "the enemy of my enemy—"

"Is my friend," Amalfitano finished for her.

"Exactly."

For several minutes no one spoke. Aquila nursed his whisky along; Izraad took a small sip, made a face, then set her barely touched glass aside; Amalfitano only stared down at the glass he cradled in his lap.

Finally, he said, "As I see it, the Matarrans' plan had only one flaw."

"And that was?" Aquila asked.

"They didn't count on a Hahtooshan disobeying a direct order." With that, he held up his glass in salute, smiled and said, "To Chercjengh'khusaaq Abhijit'tischinjgra. May he be only one of many, many more." He then swallowed the potent liquor in one loud, wincing gulp.

Books by J. E. Bruce

Hide and Sidhe*
Redoubt of Ghosts
Snakestone and Sword*
Stalking the Apocalypse

*A Centurion in the Land of the Fae